the loop

JACQUES ROUBAUD
the loop

Translated and with an Afterword by Jeff Fort

Dalkey Archive Press ▣ Champaign and London

Originally published in French as *La Boucle* by Éditions du Seuil, 1993
Copyright © Éditions du Seuil, 1993
Translation copyright © Jeff Fort, 2009
Afterword copyright © Jeff Fort, 2009
First English translation, 2009

Library of Congress Cataloging-in-Publication Data

Roubaud, Jacques.
[Boucle. English]
The loop / Jacques Roubaud ; translation and afterword by Jeff Fort.
    p. cm.
Includes index.
ISBN 978-1-56478-546-6 (pbk. : alk. paper)
I. Fort, Jeff, 1966- II. Title.
PQ2678.O77B6813 2009
843'.914--dc22
                              2008048973

Partially funded by a grant from the Illinois Arts Council, a state agency, and by
the University of Illinois at Urbana-Champaign

Ouvrage publié avec le concours du Ministère français chargé de la Culture -
Centre National du Livre

This work has been published, in part, thanks to the French Ministry of Culture -
National Book Center

www.dalkeyarchive.com

Cover: design by Danielle Dutton, illustration by Nicholas Motte

Printed on permanent/durable acid-free paper and bound
in the United States of America

CONTENTS

Branch Two: The Loop

STORY

INSERTIONS

interpolations

bifurcations

"It would be very difficult even for a saint
to dream of his prenatal life."

story

Chapter 1

Inverse Flower

1 During the night, the mist on the window

During the night, the mist on the window had turned to ice. **I see that it was still night, six-thirty, seven o'clock; wintertime then, and dark outside; no details, only darkness; the windowpane covered with the patterns of the frozen mist; on the lowest pane, on the left-hand side of the window, at eye level, in the light; this light from an electric bulb, yellow against the intense darkness outside, opaque and wintry, clouded by the mist; not a uniform mist, as when it rains, but an almost transparent frost, forming patterns; a web of translucent patterns, with a certain thickness, the slight thickness of frost, but with variations in this thickness, and, because of these miniscule variations, forming patterns on the glass, like a vegetal network, an entire system of veins, a surface vegetation, a cluster of flat ferns; or a flower.**

I scratched a fingernail against this snow, this false snow: neither white nor powdery; not melting but fading, the dirty snow of springtime lingering on the sidewalks under the boxwood trees; or crushed snow, rather: worn down, dusty and colorless, ephemeral; with my fingernail I traced a path on the glass, and the crystallized mist accumulated against my finger, turning to water because of the warmth of my finger, quickly disappearing in tiny rivulets and evaporating into a damp coldness on my numb finger; or else I held my palm flat against the glass, and under its pressure the clump of frost became a sheet of glassy ice, so that the night suddenly showed through, almost watchful in its proximity; all the vegetation of the frozen traces erased, with its imaginary petals, stamens, and corollas; now it was smooth, like glass on glass: the map of my hand, the sensitive network of its lines, left no imprint.

→ I § 51*

Still using my fingernail, very carefully, I was able to slide these blades of ice over the surface of the glass, toward the bottom, placing them next to one another in polygonal figures, fractured rectangles; the upper half of

*Such cross-references direct the reader to the interpolations (I) and bifurcations (B) in the second half of the book, beginning on page 199.

**the windowpane then seemed to be bare for a moment, directly adjacent
to the night, contiguous with that still impenetrable mass, blue and somber; but only for a moment, for this space was soon covered in mist: a fine
mist, impartial and isolating, the same mist that floated through the air in
clouds, born from respiration; at every moment this breath-turned-mist
held the nocturnal exterior at bay, and if I rubbed it with my elbow, with
my pajama sleeve, it reappeared immediately.** From this thicket of images
one could deduce that it was cold inside the room as well: not so cold as outside, perhaps, so that the mist could still cling to the window, but cold enough
for the air to condense those frozen vocables (**I see them**) like words escaping
from a silent voice.

But this would mean indulging in a superfluous exercise of deduction, since
at the very moment of my saying what could be deduced, <u>before</u> saying it,
I <u>know</u> it; this memory knows it, and it does not lie. I do not mean that a
memory is, or is not, sincere, but only that, like a dog, it cannot lie (no doubt
a lie is only an act of saying, an act of speech, turned outward). It really does
appear this way, in this <u>image</u>; and every image is undeniable. This memory,
my memory, <u>knows</u> that it was so: **It was nighttime, and it was winter; it was
cold; cold outside and inside the room; I scratched with my fingernail, I let
the *granito* of foggy crystals from the mist accumulate against my nail, I
lay my hand against the pane, I pressed against the pane with my face, with
my breath.** And yet, every line in the story of this memory contains a great
many implicit conclusions. And it is precisely here that error, if there is any
error, lies in wait for me at every turn: because in memories, in my memories
(I am speaking only for myself), there is only seeing. Even touch is "colorless,"
anesthetized. I have no other adjectives to identify this apprehension of material things by thought alone, without form, without sensuous qualities, as they
arise gray and pasty, made of some kind of conceptual clay (according to some
of the first theories of memory from Antiquity). In the process of remembering, I do not feel that my finger is cold, nor do I feel the mild and already
fading sharpness of the frozen dust scraped under my nail. I know—because
it is universal and common knowledge that frost exists and that this mode of
the physical existence of water is cold—I know, then, that the night was cold,
and therefore know everything that follows from this. And I can recall this

knowledge from experience, as one says. But the image that I reconstitute at this moment is numb to this knowledge—it is indifferent.

Writing on glass is like writing on water: regardless of what one tries to inscribe on these surfaces, such writing is always also a metaphor for the ephemeral nature of all things. True, a certain kind of mythifying fiction has sometimes tried to change this metaphor into its opposite, by imagining a message engraved on eternal glaciers, in the deep polar snow, protected on all sides by the uniform whiteness, a kind of immense graffiti—indeed, it would have to be a message of colossal proportions—and preferably in an incomprehensible and therefore immortal language, presenting a truth at once indispensable and indecipherable. And yet, from the moment one first masters the gestures of writing—and probably, for some people, up until their writing hand can move no more—there is a compulsion, a desire mixed with anguish, to write words and signs that can be erased almost immediately: in sand by a wave, in dust by footsteps, in pencil by an eraser; or else by water, rain, time, or tears smudging the ink.

It was winter, most likely a wartime winter: 1938–1939, at the earliest, 1944–1945 at the latest. I couldn't have been in that room before the first date, or after the second. Since the mist had frozen, it must have been towards morning. A very cold night, which was a rare phenomenon. It doesn't freeze much in the Aude region. I try to think of a very cold winter from this period: 1940? 1942? There was at least one very cold winter during the war. It was bad enough to have stuck in everyone's memory for a long time, including my own, and was all the more memorable because people didn't heat their houses then, or at least we didn't. Our bedroom was unheated. If this image is correct, and pure, if it's not distorted or mixed with others through resemblance, confusion, or mere repetition, if it is indeed the lower pane of the window that I see, then it must be the earliest, the first possible winter. But as soon as one breathes on any image, any memory, it too becomes covered with mist, and reveals itself to be thoroughly webbed with imprecision. <u>Around</u> it is the past, which, like the dark night of that winter, is impenetrable.

To the left of the window, I see my bed: is this another image, another moment, or the same one? I don't know. **I feel the cube of the room around me, the bed in the corner, square against two walls, lengthwise in relation**

to me, behind my head; a little farther, the door opens, is open (this sense of what is "around" me is part of a retrospective vision, which, like light, is sometimes able to "turn corners"). Of certain bedrooms, certain beds, I can evoke only a single image that always remains the same, and everything that isn't part of this image remains hermetically sealed to me. But of this old room I have a multiple but unified vision, assembled like a collage, through the superimposition and then the fusion of numerous separate images that have since become inseparable: beginning from a particular point, the one from which "this" is seen—a central point, at the "top" of the bed, almost in the very corner of the room. (Seen from above, the bed has a "top" and a "bottom," as if while lying on it I imagined myself as vertical—the "point" of my vision being at the top left corner of the "page," where one writes the return address on a letter.) No colors, no, there are no colors. To see all the other images I recall from this same place gathered together in the same way—the fingernail on the frost-covered window, the nighttime windowpanes, what the daylight will make visible through the window—all this presupposes a viewer with multiple eyes, innumerable hands. He who remembers is at once Argos, the giant with a hundred eyes, and an octopus, a creature with a hundred arms.

In the cold of the room, my bed was divided into different regions, warm and cold; the intense cold bordered sharply on the warmth; it nipped at my ears, my nose. Here, then, is something truly "inevitable": the banality of temperature. In the evening, one conquered as many territories held by the cold as possible, waging battles analogous to a Russian campaign, which provided a strategic model for this game of conquest, renewed night after night (I am speaking not of the disastrous Napoleonic campaign, but of the one that was unfolding contemporaneously, at the time I am recalling, in the immense bed of the Ukraine, news of which was relayed to us every evening on the London radio broadcasts, filled with details of the "Allied" victories, and then confirmed after a delay when the broadcast from occupied Paris announced new "elastic retreats" on the part of the Germans). **The Siberian regions of the three edges, bounded by the vertical sides of the mattress and the covers that were tucked in well underneath it, always remained impervious to comfort; but in the morning, the diffuse warmth of my sleeping body**

had beaten back these pockets of resistance, this Stalingrad and its armies
of ice.

There were two other beds in that room, I see them; on the other side of
the window, my sister Denise's; and at the far end of the room (still looking
out from that same point), to the left of the door, my brother Pierre's; seen
from the door, however, this layout, which was of parental origin (I mean
it was determined by our parents), organized the space of the bedroom
according to the age of its occupants (that is, if one imagines this space as
unfolding along the natural movement of one's sight, as I am in the habit of
doing, and as if the flat surface of the world, not only that of my bed, had become vertical, like a page: read from left to right, and from top to bottom). It
seems to me that the Spartan light did indeed come from a naked bulb on
the ceiling; everything else has disappeared, more or less.

2 Like the world of the skeptic

Like the world of the skeptic, as conceived by Russell, the universe, already
containing an image of the past, has just come into being; and, containing this
image, it will just as quickly cease to be—that is, almost instantaneously. The
image of the past that we call a memory has no duration (and, in fact, every
image is of the past). It comes into the world, it becomes a world, and without
a caption, without instructions for use, without explanations. It implies a great
deal, but offers no guarantees, no justification of its existence. As soon as one
lingers over it for a moment, rather than accepting it without hesitation—as
though it told the truth about the past, as though it brought with it a knowledge of the past upon which we could found reasonable beliefs—as soon as
one begins to inquire into this curious non-duration of individual memories,
one cannot help but be seized by doubt.

And yet certainty too (which, given the above, I can hardly claim is founded
on any reasonable precepts) is always there: I enter this bedroom, in the present, after almost a half a century of separation, and facing the window, facing
the frozen night, I am enveloped in exactly that way of seeing, exactly this
gaze. I see, intensely see, the glassy path emerge, squeaking under my nail,
and the tiny pellets of colorless ice accumulate on my fingertip. The inten-

sity, the physical proximity of the world are two of the essential features of this memory: this night is so close to my gaze that it can only be real, can only show something real, can only have been so.

But how is it that I can inhabit this same gaze now, in which the window is high, the bed is vast, viewing a piece of the world with a much older scale of vision? It's a miracle that would leave me incredulous if I weren't in the habit of experiencing it every day, without question—like everyone else, no doubt. I inhabit—and I say "**I**" meaning "me, here and now," meaning "me in the present"—I invade the center of sight, that place within a body where images are formed (the "imaginary center of the self," the point in relation to which the one who is seeing situates the world, and his vision: I assert nothing more than this; nothing in particular concerning any physical basis for the images or their possible localization in the brain; I leave these suppositions to the peremptory "cognitivists"), and this body is that of a being who disappeared a half-century ago. One cannot see oneself, says common sense. I would add that not only can one not see oneself outside of oneself now, in the present, but also that one cannot see oneself in the past. It is also said that one cannot both "be and have been," simultaneously. I would say, rather, that at no moment can one not be—that is, one can never have internal proof "of having been." What continues today, in me, of that room, of that night, is not "me," but a world.

From these reflections, which express a skepticism that is after all quite moderate (although perhaps oriented in an unusual direction), I can derive an explanation for the feeling of annoyance that's always taken hold of me when reading "childhood memories," independent of their effectiveness as stories, descriptions, or political or moral convictions; particularly by those who attempt, naively (I believe), and sincerely (I hope), to reduce or even to efface and annul the distance between the present "self" of the narrator and his or

→ I § 52   her hypothetical former "self," his or her childhood "person." I'm repulsed by phrases like "I thought that . . ." or "I believed that . . ." when they are presented as immediate certainties rather than indirect deductions based on other considerations (written documents, letters, a "journal," for example, which constitute physical evidence observable in the present). To be sure, the closer we approach the moment of our birth, going backward in time (and certainly if one goes as far back as the end of our second year, the end of everyone's true "primary school"), these attempts at reconstruction are, at the very least, rather implausible (or so they seem to me). (Most of us, however, aspiring to immortality in both directions, make a touchingly obstinate effort to locate the moment of our "first memory" as close to birth as possible.)

But my incredulity goes much further, and is much more radical. Coleridge's famous "willing suspension of disbelief" asks the reader (I limit myself here to the reader) to interrupt, momentarily and voluntarily, a skepticism that is quite natural given the impossibility of believing that anything recounted in fiction is true. I interpret the formula thus: as a slight twisting and an implicit particularization of the ancient axiom, it too of a skeptical nature, of a "suspension of judgment," and therefore as demanding the "suspension of a judgment (however inevitable) of impossibility." One generally applies it only to the novel, but in fact it seems to me that it must be invoked even more forcefully in the context of an autobiographical narrative; which I would place, on a scale of implausibility, at least at the same level as the historical novel, and almost as high as "science fiction." As for me, it is practically impossible to achieve this degree of willing suspension.

And again I must insist: what I just wrote aspires to no physiological, neurological, psychological, cognitive, or philosophical relevance. Why not? Because what is offered here for you to read is nothing other than a <u>story</u>: the beginning of what I call a <u>branch</u> (the second) of a work of prose (being the second, it naturally follows the first, which like this branch is of a certain length (but at the same time it's not necessary to have read the first in order to approach the second, nor the ones that follow, should there be any)), a prose work that I qualify as a <u>story</u>, since I haven't found a better, more particular generic term that expresses my intentions. The things said in it are said in the present moment of telling a story, as the storytelling itself moves forward, and said in the form in which they've presented themselves to be recounted by me, inscribed line by line now in "12-point New York" on my computer screen. These things can't be detached from the story that contains them, and therefore they can in no way claim any status as truths—not even the truth of a "possible monad on the shelf of essence" (Leibniz).

On an immobile space (a screen, then a piece of paper) I set down an image:

an image of my past, and an image which seems to me to be one of the oldest in my repertoire (I firmly believe in the oldness of this image). The difficulty of describing it comes not only from all the implicit conclusions that I draw (and "force," in a way, into the image itself), from what I know or imagine I know concerning the circumstances in which the image was initially created, nor even from the fact that, in this particular case, it is not likely to be a unique image, but is rather a reiterated, composed, and composite scene. The difficulty has to do with its instantaneousness. As soon as it appears, the image disappears: to describe it, I must repeat it, invoke it, call it forth, according to the various experimental modes of voluntary recollection, which each person constructs for himself. In making it appear again, I weaken it. Even this image, the first of the story, so intense and so "primary" (and intense because "primary"), is weakened at the very moment I call it forth for description. By repeating it, I blur it, deform it, discolor it.

In short, I destroy it. Perhaps not right away, but in the end. I destroy it in the sense that, becoming weaker and paler, it doesn't so much disappear as become something I can no longer evoke, no longer revisit except as a second-order memory, the memory of my remembering it, and of all the moments in which I insistently contemplated it during the time spent on its **description**, under the effect of the words and thoughts that this **description** gives rise to. (Above all, it is the words of the description that bring about this **destruction**, that end up substituting another image for the initial one—an image born, this time, from words. And words irremediably make it what it in fact has become: an externalized memory.) But also because this very description, turning the image into a still image or a "freeze frame," necessarily gives the scene a different status, very similar to that of a <u>photograph</u>. Photography has profoundly changed the perception of childhood memories (of all memories, but especially of childhood memories: Childhood and photography now have an almost consubstantial link—"All photographs," as someone once wrote, "are childhood photographs." I would add: and all childhood memories are seen as photographs (or, in even more contemporary terms, as "video images")). Through it, they have proliferated in the world, like an "album of times long past." But it has also given them a model, to which all memory images henceforth attempt to conform: and this model, so immobile, so "idle," so unique and so fixed, is mistaken and false.

And that's not all: in this specific case (which does not apply to all images), the image in question does not remain isolated, even if it remains brief or passes quickly. It does not rise up as a monument in a polar landscape. I cannot impose limits on it, or a frame. When the image ceases, the frozen windowpane does not leave my field of vision, like some Bérénice speaking in alexandrines as she leaves a Racinian Titus on the stage of the Théâtre-Français. When the image ceases, most often its ending merges into others: It continues to change. It goes elsewhere, very quickly, very far away (in both time and place), and often it doesn't seem to matter where. I said that to look at an image of the past is to be Argos. Certainly: but Argos struggling to capture Proteus.

3 My returning to this image

My returning to this image is itself something that began long ago: when I think of the past, the most distant past (according to the chronological markers available to me), the image seems to be one of my first: first both in terms of the (hypothetical) moment that it marks, and the readiness with which it comes to me. It is one of the most significant visions of my childhood. It is intense, important, charged with emotion. It is an image from the beginning of time. Seeing that nocturnal windowpane covered with its flowers of frost has become habitual for me, very familiar. And sometimes the image appears to me on its own, at random, removed from its natural setting, without any particular thought of this memory preceding it. But I recognize it immediately—I can hardly fail to recognize it, since it resembles nothing so much as itself. That too is one of the "photographic" features of certain memories, memories that have already emerged and become recurrent in one's mind. Indeed, there's more than a family resemblance between the images I retain of two later moments in which I've recalled that initial memory. The temptation to believe in an <u>identical repetition</u> is irresistible.

But one day (a day that I can't date precisely, except to say that it no doubt goes back more than twenty years, and in any case must have come later than the <u>dream</u> that was the distant cause of all this writing, this undertaking that, for four years now, has devoured the first nocturnal hours of every one of my days), one day I managed to associate this image with a spoken word, a word from a poem (if I grant for a moment that poetry is speech, a "music of the mouth proffering speech in meter," as Eustache Deschamps said), a word spoken, then, and put down on paper centuries ago, and now caught on this paper between the blank spaces, the "margins," that define verse:

Er resplan la flors enversa

These words make up the entire first line of a *canso* (a "*chanson*," a music-poem) by the troubadour Raimbaut d'Orange, written more than eight centuries ago in a language that's almost dead today, but which for me is the origin-language of poetry, "Provençal": "Now shines [is resplendent] the inverse flower." I call the language "Provençal" in this narrative, rather than "Occitan" or *Lemozi*, as the Catalans used to call it: these other names open onto different, and for me less moving, ways of imagining this poetry. I have my reasons for choosing the first name. Raimbaut d'Orange wastes no time in revealing the primary sense of this strange grouping: "**quals flors**" he says ("which flower?"). And he answers himself, taking the spontaneous and absolute solipsism of all verse even further: "**neus gels e conglapis**" ("snow, frost, and '*conglapi*'"), introducing, with this last vocable—so rare that it appears only here—who knows what sort of frozen thing. I have decided to understand it, according to the needs of my own composition, as a vitrified conjunction of *neus* (snow) and *gels* (frost): as the condensation of a mist-noise and a cold substance, emblematic of the cold itself; and I hear in it an entire "*glapisse-ment*," a kind of screech, along with the scratching sound made by those transparent pellets of cold as they were scraped up, crying out under my nail:

> *Er resplan la flors enversa*
> *Pels trencans rancx e pels tertres.*
> *Quals flors neus gels e conglapis*
> *Que cotz e destrenh e trenca.*

> (Then shines the inverse flower
> among sharp cliffs and hills.
> Which flower? snow frost and ice
> that cuts and torments and slices.)

Now, every dawn is a new spring, even a dawn covered in frost. And in this paradoxical beginning of a lover's *canso*, Raimbaut d'Orange—instead of following a tradition that would have him echo the sweet and didactic love songs of the teacher-birds, the teachers of the song, *essenhadors del chan*—gives voice instead to abstract nightingales (the expression "teachers of the song" is from another troubadour, Jaufre Rudel: the birds are the ones that "teach the song" in the "sweet gentle season"; and "teach" should be understood here in the Languedocian sense of "showing how to find": "*Je t'enseignerai la lièvre . . .*" **I'll teach you the hare, said one hunter to another, and it still rings in my ears fifty years later**). The poet sees blocks of ice in place of the craggy red mountains, which are now invisible; in place of the orioles or larks, whose throats are now numb; in place of their song now dead from the cold:

> ***Vey mortz quils critz brays siscles***
> (I see dead calls, cries, noises, whistles)

For Raimbaut, invoking the great aviary cold of the hills, now gripped by frost (cold weather seems more absolute in landscapes that aren't used to it), is a way to make the three-in-one flower of song, poetry, and love still more brilliant—the <u>inverse flower</u> absent from every bouquet (and here the absence is double). When I read this image, when I found myself gripped, transfixed, and benumbed by these words, **flors enversa**, I recognized them as my own (this was near the very beginning of my reading of the Troubadours, I still knew virtually nothing about them), and I spontaneously and sentimentally placed myself, implicitly and without at first realizing it, in one of the two camps—each devoted to a certain method, simultaneously antagonistic and interwoven—of the **trobar**, the art of the Troubadours. Raimbaut d'Orange is without doubt the first accomplished representative, if not the inventor, the *trouveur* or "finder," of one of these methods—preceding and surpassing his best-known disciple, Arnaut Daniel, who was chosen and destined by Dante to represent this <u>manner</u> and notion of poetry.

For this is not simply an insolent metamorphosis of the tradition's "springtime" metaphor (the beginning of poetic singing, in the spring, identified with the love songs of the birds), but also the affirmation of a certain way of speak-

ing in poetry, which goes far beyond the privileged moment in which the sing-
ing flowers of the frost are discovered. One could dub this the **Way of Double
Negation** (which has its related and parallel forms in philosophy, theology,
→ I § 58   and even logic): the frost negates both the flower and the song.
But in the desert of frost, a paradoxical flower blooms—in its
silence an insistent disharmony resonates, and from this "hirsute" blossoming,
→ I § 59   as from this polar atonality, are reborn, in the vibratory evocation of the verse, both a happy music and its simultaneous and
hopeless disappearance.

As I said, I immediately recognized this way, this *via negativa*, as my own.
But I also recognized that it wasn't only a matter of poetry: what I saw, felt,
and heard in "snow, frost, and '*conglapi*'" was henceforth, and inseparably, the
childhood image of the windowpane covered with its wintry layer of ice, and
the scraping movement of my fingernail became the inward accompaniment,
hidden beneath the vision, of the fractured unfolding (fractured by conso-
nance and its obstacles) of the verses of the *canso*, that characteristic mark of
Raimbaut's "negative poetics." Beneath the voice, as beneath the frost on the
window, there lies the nocturnal nothingness of things passing and gone.
The poetic method called "obscure" and "closed," according to Raimbaut
d'Orange and Arnaut Daniel, never forgets that beneath love's greatest "joy"—
its "*joi*"—lurks the frost of fulfillment, the ferocity of a reality mingled with
death. This is the inverse side of the flower of love, but also of every childhood:
the childhood of our mortal flesh, of prose, of the "Romance" (the novel). And
of languages.

This is why, even if it wasn't within my power to dissolve this association
between childhood and a fragment of poetry, I did not for a moment refuse it.
As I progressed (slightly) in my knowledge of the *trobar*, as I formed a clearer
idea of it—perhaps an imprecise one, but one in conformity with the demands
of my **Project**, which the Troubadours, and Raimbaut no doubt more than any
other, decisively influenced—this association became deeper and still more
necessary, losing the sudden, fortuitous, and arbitrary character of its origins.
The memory image of the square pane made hazy with frost, the night that
it hid and then revealed, and the bedroom around me all acquired from this
association a greater force of conviction (the conviction of being an authentic

and significant revelation of the past) and a greater legitimacy; it became obvious that this was the place where I had to begin searching for the "earlier" paths laid out for my **Project**, everything that had contributed, initially, to its conception (and it is precisely this **Fore-Project** that will concern me in this branch): A place and a path that, at the same time, contained—like a second seed, like another "inverse flower"—its future failure.

4 The blue darkness of the night

The deep blue darkness of the night was outside the window, not spread onto its surface. Around that time we had been ordered to cover the windows with a painted-on night. Thus it was hoped that no light would escape from the houses of the town and therefore that these houses, and the town with them, would remain invisible, simply withdrawing themselves, via this little bit of color (little but resolute)—like the houses of Calvino's city of *Phyllis*—from the hostile gazes looking down on them from high in the air. It had been decided that the buzzing planes and the whistling bombs would spare the town because of this. This was referred to as Passive Defense. But what airplanes did one really need to fear out there, descending like clouds swept by a *cers* (the mistral of these regions) from the Black Mountain on a windy day? The question still leaves me perplexed.

In fact, all of France, which merely by virtue of this painterly stratagem (a new version of the "camouflage" that, according to Gertrude Stein, Picasso said was inspired by cubism) should have been impenetrably sealed beneath protective layers of night-colored paint—showing nothing in the darkness but dyed, uniform walls, neither breathing nor making even the slightest sound when the air raid sirens went off—this darkened France on the contrary revealed itself, abruptly and most peculiarly, to be quite visible after all, when only a few weeks later, in the spring of 1940 (that "cloudless May"), it was transformed into an immense and perfectly passive "open city" (Passive Defense had thus been merely a prefiguration of this impending national passivity). And in this particular area, so far from the front, the painted windows quickly become even more ridiculous, since they bore witness to an illusory state of safety and to all the hopes that were so sadly crushed by the Defeat—

that event whose capitalized name marked it as a moral rather than a military event. So in most cases the paint was scraped off in order to return the windows to their original transparency. Later, after Al-Alamein and Stalingrad, the paintbrushes should have been brought back into service against the threat of other, different airplanes (and I imagine that this was indeed the case elsewhere, in Le Havre for example). But our town didn't take the trouble to go through the process again, more out of weariness, I think, than insubordination. Perhaps there was quite simply no more paint, after it had been "requisitioned" for use on the far more endangered windows in the Ruhr, or in Dresden. In our house, only a few traces remained here and there, on which I put my fingernails to work—as with the misty frost, but in a different mode. Finally, the only place durably "protected" from external eyes was the one that at the time was still called "the privy." Given its very particular insertion into the "topology" of the house, keeping the passive painting there may well have responded to necessities quite unrelated to any Defense.

(There is another way for houses to keep their visual silence, to remain incognito in the dark of night. In order to avoid giving off any revelatory glow, one can always consider simply not producing any. Then the windows are the blind eyes of an owl: the houses are as though abandoned to the night. The town isn't hidden, but returns to the state of those prehistoric stone huts adopted by the shepherds, the "Bories," which may have preceded the invention of fire. I have no memory of any such real darkness, except during storms, when everything was "on the blink," or the electricity had been cut off (the dark nights of winter 1944–1945 provided many occasion to marvel at its capriciousness: *I remember* a drawing by "jean effel" and the caption: "She appears, she disappears, she's the Electricity Fairy." But I was already in a different house when I saw it, in a different city.) It's true that my brothers and sister and I were usually asleep at night.).

In pursuing the metamorphoses of the image of a mirror frozen onto the tain of night and revealed by my fingernail's inscriptions, I chose to follow one path among many. I did not adopt in this instance (but was it even necessary?) a general, constraining, and perceptible principle of organization. What principle could I have chosen? The chronology of moments, their marked, measured, conventional succession? An internal timeline—if there is such an alternate time—a time that wouldn't be the basis of a strict chronology, but disordered, full of gaps, moving at variable speed toward its own exhaustion? Image-memories aren't easily subjected to either of these structures, even assuming that they could ever be situated in a precise way using these kinds of coordinates. In the perpetual present of memories—site of the Augustinian trinity, "present of the past, present of the present, present of the future" (the future is above all a reminiscence, or even just a memory itself)—there is almost always, I think, an irreducible certainty about the respective positions of "before" and "after." And even if adopting an exterior organizing principle had been possible, that was not how I conceived my story at its origin, from the moment—close to its beginning, but in no way prior to it—when I finally realized, and clearly, what this story would be. By following time, physical (or even internalized) time, I would always have bypassed what I was looking for.

The fact is that the sequences that are significant for memory are never discovered in this way. To begin with, in any given memory there are as many anticipations as derivations. Not only are the very notions of "before" and "after" in such an image unclear, they are necessarily contradictory. I do not mean to say that an external time, one-dimensional and irreversible, doesn't inevitably pull them along (somewhat like a supporting fluid, empty of properties, in which the memories are suspended—an aether of time, associated with an abstract space that is itself empty). But the time that concerns me, and that I'm pursuing here, the time of **memory**, necessarily moves in two directions, or at least two. Every memory, even if precisely situated in space and time, looks back toward the past as much as toward the future (and the future is itself always, ceaselessly, a <u>future anterior</u>). If I scratch the frost on the window, I do it perhaps because I'd previously darkened → I § 60-63 my nails with the night-paint, or vice versa. But this image is above all the indispensable switch that clicks open a door leading into memory, and toward other windows (especially one *before, behind, between, above, below*).

I have always been attracted, as far back as I am able to go in this perception of things, by the pre-morning darkness: I don't like to wake up in the daylight. There are luxuriant nights, traversed by glimmering lights, by the moon, by lamps and stars, by an "obscure clarity" (Corneille), as one reads in an alexandrine as famous as it is banal—having been rendered banal, that is, if not ridiculous, by all the scholastic admiration once lavished on it. There are black and white nights, or black and gray. But above all there are entire nights, compact, impenetrable, opposing the yellow light of lamps with something akin to their own black radiation. This "beauty of black," which renders the world incomprehensible and inexplicable, and which assures me that the world is and will remain incomprehensible and inexplicable, this "blackness unvarying to the eye" (which is the world, the world withdrawing into itself in disdain) attracts me, it keeps me pressed against the window, unmoving, watching.

But I do not want to look blindly. And the black, that particular black, outside, needs some light in order to exist, and to be absolute as I desire it—close, touching my eyes, but not covering them. If the room is unlit, if it's blacker than the night outside, it makes the night lighter, full of vague forms preparing to take on definite shapes in the light of day. Feeble glimmers float about in it. Fortunately, my lamp, when lit, prevents them from approaching. It protects my window from the day, the day of the cold present, of the frozen future. And the window, in its rigid panes, is as though painted—painted black.

Thus, I have gotten used to the night, to its black ways, but not in order to live in it. At night, when I can, I sleep. I need only the precarious night-on-the-wane, the night that belongs to no one (for the end of the night, in the urban world of the last decade of the twentieth century, is more and more empty: the waking life of cities has penetrated more and more deeply into the night, but only by invading it at the other end). I am searching for this form of the night, which—since I'm alone in it—properly belongs to me. In the house where I'm writing these lines, gray now rather than black, no window is lit at the moment. I tap the signs, the keys of the keyboard that composes the words "I write," but in fact the words only appear on the vertical screen facing me, an electronic "writing" of the present moment, even more precarious than that of a pencil or of ink on paper—a fascinating precariousness linked to the intoxication of "writing" words that the "*cut*" command can condemn to annihilation at any moment (a supplementary intoxication transcending that of the simple eraser). Outside (in the building's courtyard) it is dark, as dark as it can ever be in this city always gnawed by lights: Paris.

Thus, at the outset of a multiple passageway through memory—namely, this book—my recollection brought forth a completely dark night, rendered more impenetrably black by physical distance, by the intervening years, by winter, by the war. This recollection directed itself (infallibly, I might believe—without groping and without intent) toward a sort of maximum degree of night, as if something of night-in-itself had been there, waiting for me; as if the child's fingernail had cracked open and scratched the ice only for the sake of this very reconstitution.

5 The passageways of memory are reversible

The passageways of memory have a strange reversibility (at the very heart of their general lack of direction). Having set out on this particular path at an imprecise place in time, with an image that is of "no moment," so to speak, since it could have come from any number of moments, I bring in another image along behind it, an image that it seems to call forth spontaneously as one that is meant to come after it, namely the image of windowpanes painted not by night itself but by an *ersatz*-night: the dark painting of war. But if, on the contrary, I evoked those literally painted windows first, it would only be to depart, just as spontaneously, in the other direction, down the path of a memory already traveled many times, toward the frozen pane in my childhood bedroom. The respective, objective chronological position of the two images escapes me. And yet, even if I managed to date them exactly, I could still easily follow the above route in both directions.

So it is in the tradition of the **Arts of Memory**: in the story of the foundation of these arts (as found, for instance, in Frances Yates), which comes immediately after the **Tale** that functions as a kind of entrance hall, as a preamble to their history, relating the adventure that befell their inventor, their *trouveur*, the poet Simonides of Ceos, who was "inspired" by the celestial twins Castor and Pollux (or was it only by one of them? If by one, I don't know which—though this is an important issue, since one of the two has a divine origin and the other a terrestrial one (that is, before their eternal sidereal union within a single constellation), and depending on whether one or the other was the inspiration, or else both together—given that the twin or twins in question are, in effect, the "patron saint(s)" of memory—one is dealing with radically different conceptions of this faculty), we are told of another poet of Antiquity, who, armed with his training in the arts of memory, was able to recite the entire *Odyssey* both forward and backward (a feat that I can't resist comparing in my mind to the one accomplished by girls jumping rope, or else to certain awe-inspiring exploits in the world of knitting). (I'm not unaware that the texts on the subject refer to this poet reciting the *Iliad*, but I much prefer, and find more satisfying—indeed more fitting—that the story should involve the wanderings of crafty Odysseus. And I can allow myself such a slippage without breaking the unilateral promise to be truthful that I made earlier, in the first branch of my book, since I am doing so without omitting this confession, which signals to my reader the fact that I do not wish to deceive him or her, and further because what I'm in the process of composing here is a story, not an academic "memoir.")

To associate, in the most immediate and restricted manner possible, what one wants to remember—whether it be speeches, arguments, or the verses of a poem—with an arbitrarily chosen path (the **Arts of Memory** insist on this arbitrariness of the memory-sign) situated in an already familiar place in one's memories (and it is indeed in a familiar place that I begin, in a room where I used to sleep, the room of a house that I inhabited for seven years, from my fifth to my twelfth year), is in fact only to mimic, render voluntary, and give order to the spontaneous and universal function of memories. The methods

→ I § 64   and prescriptions invented in the Middle Ages and in the Renaissance on the basis of enigmatic, fragmentary (and exasperatingly imprecise) indications from Cicero or Quintilian are here put to use for my own purposes, in order to imitate, order, and make describable the things I must teach myself to tease out, coherently, from my recollection—since these are the things that first came to mind and were remembered, if chaotically, as I set out to compose this branch. (The unstated objective of my narration brings them up from where they've remained continually subjacent, even if this objective does not predetermine them.)

Here too, in this reversal, I'm putting to work the negative poetics—with its strategy of Double Negation—of which I spoke in reference to Raimbaut d'Orange. Reliving the odyssey (uncapitalized) that is a life, at least in "episodes" or in limited segments of the past (and it can be any life at all, including my own; which, like that of Odysseus, is also the life of "nobody")—this is something we do every day, whether in our sleep (by dreaming) or in a state of wakefulness (by remembering). The direction of these passageways of memory can be apprehended only with recourse to a two-way, reversible <u>movement</u>, for which the *Art of Memory* provides a few rule-governed examples.

Unlike demonstrations in mathematics, which are strictly oriented (although it should be noted that the truth of a proposition can be understood only by going backward to the beginning, returning to the initial premises), the deductions of memory differ remarkably depending on the direction chosen for their presentation. And any understanding of even the most meager memory comes at this price. Therefore, to put it simply, for a person undertaking such a journey, the countryside of his return is not identical to that of his outbound trip. What remains invariable is not the countryside but the site, the space in which it exists—the stuff of memory, which, for someone who hasn't entered it, is made of a substance so indeterminate as to be indistinguishable from emptiness.

One of the principle reasons for this simultaneous non-equivalence and yet non-indifference concerning the direction of travel in memory is that, as soon as one changes direction, what appears to us next will not be the same as what we've just passed, and indeed will never be the same again. (Nor is this specifically related to the general impossibility of a palindrome—so difficult and so "strange" in language, particularly in a spoken sequence—in real time (lived time).) This happens at every moment. At every moment, something arises beyond what we've just seen, and this something necessarily differs on the "way out" or on the "way back." Regardless of the path being followed, a lived moment takes its sense and direction only from what it anticipates. For a moment is not a "now," but rather—according to a theory of time for which I have a certain fondness—it is "what will have been a 'now.'" **Scratching the frost on the window, I see my fingernails turn blue from the paint**, and I enter into the war years; **then, behind the paint that hides what's outside the window, I see the night, this night in the Aude region, pressing heavily against the frosty pane**.

The reverse passage follows the passage forward like its own shadow, its ghost. Just as, when looking through the window of a high-speed train, one can see the movement of fleeting, dissolving slices of landscape—the backward rush of houses, trees, silent figures in the streets, streams, and fields of rapeseed—and then, behind these, seemingly moving in the opposite direction as what we've seen in the foreground, ochre-colored or dark green hills, automobiles on the roads; and then, farther away, trains of clouds moving in the same direction as we are, only more slowly, as though they were being held back, were stuck, weighed down by the earth, gripped by a certain hesitancy or else an inclination to stay put until they disappear entirely. And so on: The successive slices, each physically farther and farther away, trade off the directions of their apparent motion—each layer moving with greater and greater vagueness, heaviness, and slowness.

Every image of the past is therefore a <u>double</u> image, revealed by the movement that pulls it along, a movement that is only arbitrarily forced to stand still when such an image is put into words. The only possible (partial) reconstitution of an image consists then in displacing the vision <u>successively in both directions</u>. Besides, the progression never follows a line, as in the ordinary reading of a book: it is at once densely ramifying and discontinuous, leading one to believe, inwardly, in the existence of atoms of time, indivisible and unmeasurable, since each displacement ceaselessly presents to me the divergent possibilities of what comes <u>after</u>.

A slightly simplified metaphor for this situation came to me one night in America (as we say when we refer to the United States): I was in a car approaching a city (Seattle, on the Pacific coast), coming from the airport. The road from the airport was leading to a larger highway down below, an "expressway" that one had to take in order to reach the city center, which had been visible in the distance for quite some time. It was already nighttime, but the traffic was still heavy (it was October, the beautiful October of the New World, more red than rust-colored), and the two lanes of cars moving in both directions flowed continuously, like luminous rivers. There were also "exits" from which little streams escaped on each side of the two vehicle-rivers, though of course these "streams" were different in each direction: they were streams that "flowed" only "one way." This is how canals and waterways work. It was dark, and all the cars had their lights on. But on the cars that were moving away from me, I could only see the red rear lights, while the cars coming toward me only showed me their yellow headlights.

Red streams, then, fled forward on the right, while parallel yellow streams were moving rearward on my left. My height and distance gave a certain serenity and completeness to this field of vision and allowed me to grasp those two strips simultaneously in thought, to apprehend as continuous those two moving rivers of color.

6 In the cold air, the cloud born from my breath

In the cold air, the cloud of mist born from my breath encountered the window, settled there. Breathing mist onto glass turns the otherwise transparent surface into yet another page, one that can be inscribed with signs, with words that then restore transparency to small, discrete areas. Then the breath, the mist, can again serve as an eraser. This kind of writing leaves no stains: it doesn't have the irreversibility of ink, but is more like those other marks made in childhood, as with elderberry ink (that "friendly" ink—a spy's ink?). It is ephemeral, which is not necessarily a deficiency or defect. I constantly find myself (in the past) writing on windowpane glass—though not always with my breath, which requires cold (too exceptional a circumstance) or else rain outside (also comparatively rare). But one can always count on the dust that snows down from the sloping ceilings of attics, or collecting in sheds, on the stained-glass windows of that strange lexical flower, the "*buanderie*"—the little "steam room" or washhouse behind the house, where the laundry is done (its dusty panes are stained glass for lay people); one can always count on dust and smoke.

During those years, **a thick, heavy, ashen smoke, gray and dirty, would rise from the locomotives in the train stations and along the railways, lingering in the air and inexorably covering the windows of their compartments with a greasy and intractable layer of soot.** The trains were slow, dragging along, stopping inexplicably on rail sidings, sitting and waiting, then departing again in silence, without any warning. **Once again my gaze seeks the night outside, as in the wintertime bedroom, and, much as happened in that room, it distinguishes nothing, or almost nothing; in this memory** (that is, in this family of composite memories, crowding each other out, merging together) **I see the corner of a window in a train compartment** (and "corner window" is also the official name for this seat), level with my finger, **the same finger that scraped the ice, the same finger that is now being covered with grimy, tenacious, leaden soot from the locomotive-smoke** (like graphite from pencil lead, like the thick ink that used to cover the metal plates of a printing press).

Once a month we went to Toulouse by train. It was always on a Sunday, since the other six days of the week were completely taken up with school. My mother brought us—my sister and me—to test our progress in learning to play piano by having us perform for Mme. Vidal, who ran the school headed by Marguerite Long (the "great pianist" inspected me personally one day, with a haughty and largely disapproving expression on her angular and imposing face, setting her immense and immeasurably rapid fingers into motion to perform demonstrations, and in order to correct my own fingering in turn **(a large oblique nose; a hand covered with rings covering my own for a few seconds)**). We would leave very early in the morning (I see nothing but night). We stopped at Bram, at Castelnaudary, at Villefranche-de-Lauragais; we arrived at the Matabiau station. We presented the "pieces" we'd learned at home: by Clementi, by Kühlau—Kühlau especially—and perhaps a little Mozart. Toward the end I also played some mazurkas, some polonaises by Chopin, extravagant tasks for my fingers. We returned after nightfall.

My father would come with us to visit and have a chat with Canguilhem, his old classmate (from the École Normale Supérieure), and to spend the time during our lesson at the Trentin bookstore (we went there to look for him sometimes), but also for other kinds of meetings and other sorts of conversation whose true significance I wouldn't grasp until later (after 1944). We would have lunch at the Canguilhems' house; their two oldest children, Bernard and Francette ("Cécette") were about the same age as my sister and I. The ceremony at lunch was impressive, and the table manners in that house quite strict (completely unlike what we were used to at home): The children didn't speak among themselves, nor did they join in the conversation of the adults; they kept both hands on the table and silently held their utensils in the proper hands. The Anglican maxim ("children should be seen, not heard") was applied to them with an altogether Calvinist rigor.

But they made up for this as soon as the parents disappeared into other regions of their dim apartment (**I see it as dim**): I'd never heard so many "forbidden" words spoken in so short a time (essentially scatological in their inspiration; I think that we were entirely unaware of the sexual register of some of them (or else it's quite possible that an adult's censorship has imposed itself on my memory—I don't know)) as came from the mouths of those two children, given such a scrupulous upbringing by an already eminent philosopher with very black hair and very black, very thick eyebrows as well.

(My sister Denise, who was generally rather shy, caused a sensation when, during Georges Canguilhem's first visit to our garden, she spontaneously climbed up onto his lap: I don't know if she was performing some sort of exorcism, or if she had an intuition of what was in fact the essentially indulgent good nature of this epistemologist, who was so strict when it came to concepts (not to mention the philosophy teachers that he supervised over the years) and so generally bad-tempered. Then again, he couldn't have been excessively intimidating to my cousins and brothers, or even myself, since we habitually greeted his arrival with a battle song, composed, with a rising rhythm, especially for his benefit: "Mean old Can! Mean old Cangui! Mean old Canguilhem!" As I've recently been making preparations—on behalf of an institution I work with: the Collège Internationale de Philosophie—to help stage a tribute to him, I've been feeling a certain belated childish satisfaction (this was almost a half a century ago!) in recalling the casualness with which we then treated the eminent author of the *Essai sur quelques problèmes concernant la frontière entre le normal et le pathologique* (known in English as *The Normal and the Pathological*), which has been (and still is) of considerable importance in French philosophy, and a signed copy of which was in my parents' library. It's true that philosophy, my father's professional occupation, has never ceased to impress me.)

We would return home at night. Arriving at the Matabiau station well in advance, we would colonize a compartment of the darkened train waiting at the platform. The train remained unlit almost until its departure, and then practically throughout its inverse route through Villefranche-de-Lauragais, Castelnaudary, Bram, and finally Carcassonne. The → I § 65 very dim light (as dim as a nightlight: Passive Defense?) gave the journey a vesperal atmosphere that to me was by turns soporific and exalting. A bedtime one hour later than usual, the tension of the piano test now behind me (even

though Mme. Vidal had been calm, maternal, not too strict) gave an adventurous hue to those Sunday returns, the greatest attraction of which was the train
itself. I had already inherited (from my grandfather, no doubt) a great passion
for the railroad.

My preferred occupation on these journeys was (after my writing in soot
on the windows had been discovered and was strictly forbidden to me)—**and
I see myself doing this—to hang from the copper crossbar that divided the
window in two, horizontally, at its midpoint, out in the corridor of the
train car** (the mere possibility of such an exercise is an indication of what my
height must have been at the time). **Climbing up on the window ledge, then
grabbing the bar with my hands while also hanging from it by my feet,
I imitated** (I probably imagined myself being) **the animal referred to as a
sloth** (an animal from the pangolin family, like armadillos, as indicated by the
mnemotechnical saying used by naturalists in French (a gift from my brother):
"*T'as tout l'air d'un pangolin paresseux*" (You look just like a slothful pangolin).
**I tried my best to maintain the dreamy immobility of this animal, but was
unfortunately unable to stuff my mouth with a clump of eucalyptus leaves**
(which I believe are the exclusive diet of the "sloth"—unless I'm confusing
them with koalas).

**Then we walked home from the station, suddenly overcome by an im-
mense fatigue, under the clear or cloudy night, under the dawning stars
of winter, first crossing the canal, then following the narrow side streets,
going across Davila Square, down the Rue Dugommier, and finally down
our own street, Rue d'Assas, along the high wall of the military barracks, to
the tallest pine tree, the front door, the dark house, asleep; and the silence,
and our rest.**

7 In this handful of childhood images

In this handful of childhood images I can see a common feature: the rarity of
the natural (and also non-natural) phenomena that elicited them. I mean rarity in terms of the site of their production, but rarity too in terms of the gaze
taking them in. More precisely: winter coldness and frost are rare in Aude.
The blue paint that camouflaged the windows during the war was an excep-

tional phenomenon. Finally, the night itself was rare, since for a schoolboy in 1940, it was not a habitual feature of life: Children of that time were usually in their beds at night, and were usually asleep. (Children had their lives strictly regulated, and were thus the last (involuntary) throwbacks to their peasant ancestors. There's a definite duality between phylogenesis and ontogenesis in the customs and physiology of the species.) (But perhaps, if I may judge by comparison with Catalonia, or Italy, this was only a familial habit, more Dauphinois or Piedmontese than Mediterranean; reinforced by the "hygienic" beliefs of the school teachers of the Third Republic (of which my maternal grandparents were typical representatives, and in which they had an unshakable faith); as well as a result of the traditional school hours, according to which classes convened every morning, in every season, everywhere, in any weather and any circumstances, at eight A.M., ever since Jules Ferry. All these factors came together to make sunlight the most reliable constant in a child's life; and darkness, its absence, the exception.)

I don't mean to imply that these images are the only ones still remaining to me from my childhood. Only that my memory spontaneously seeks them out and calls them up before any others. Their irruption is proof of a negative insistence, in "historic" times that were themselves exceptional (when virtue, the Machiavellian *virtù* shown by Canguilhem, by my father, and by their mysterious friends, meant being included among those who said <u>no</u>—such people being for a long while rather rare in this country); it is proof of a very old attraction that was first of all aesthetic, but secondarily and inseparably ethical as well, and that for a long time I have seen no reason to deny: an attraction to what is not habitual, proper, or ordinary (or, more precisely, concerning which it is not habitual or ordinary to act in a manner that seems proper). The frozen mist on the window, the electric light frozen by the blue night paint, the train waiting in darkness on the track—these are visions and circumstances that were certainly "original" during the first twelve years of my life. And when my memory finds them again, something of that "originary" exaltation remains with and accompanies them.

They are surrounded by a sort of halo of starkness combined with happiness—something that doesn't come from any sense of well-being but from a joy and light that have been concentrated and assimilated by the images. It's as if, instead of placing myself down below in order to look up at a memory—below where the brightest light reveals many particularities but where it is also the weakest, the dimmest, and the most obscure—I have situated myself on the contrary in the seraphic position of the contemplator, up above where the light is concentrated, simple and universal, where it is most able to retain the unity, the strength, and the brilliance of its source. Thus, the atmosphere of these images is one of <u>contemplation</u>. They are contemplative images. Their insistence, their persistence, make them akin—despite the essentially non-photographic nature of all the things I'm referring to as **images**—to those photographs from significant moments of our past that we find ourselves re-visiting so often with a questioning gaze. They are like images both evoked and reconstructed by the passionate contemplation of photographs. And they hold light, since they have no color (only a photograph "colored in black and white" has, and offers us, light). Once presented to my gaze, these images maintain a hold on it. I go from one to another; I turn in the circle in which their triangle is inscribed, with no desire to exit.

And yet, particularly when I think of the first image, the inverse flower of ice, I note that these memories seem to have an outside, an "**out-there.**" Cu-riously, I can reach this outside quite easily, but only by backing into it, as it were: that is, by moving inward from outside only to find myself, once again, in the wintertime interior of the room, facing the window, via a rapid suc-cession of images that indeed implies a previous exit into the day (or into the night) and then a return, but with the precise moment of this egress missing, as though it had become infinitely separated from me because of its distance from me now, or else because of an excessive number of spatial transitions (much like the hare in the paradox, my gaze is obliged to pass there, and then there, a point hardly any further along, and so on, until it is overwhelmed by a simple but inexhaustible "enumeration" of points).

One of the most elusive properties of memories, and perhaps the origin of some of the rather strange "solutions" that have been put forth in response to the question of time (a question as ancient as thought itself), is in fact <u>speed</u>. To the first paradox of continuous movement through space, in which one must pass through no less than an infinity of (potentially) enumerable points, one is tempted to "respond" by adding a second paradox, one involving not only a completed infinity of moments (which would resolve nothing (nothing is really resolved with this second paradox either, but at least we can create the illusion of having done so)) but also the domination of temporal progression with respect to crossing spatial distances (which in a word are more materially inert) given sufficient speed: a memory absorbs the infinity of visible points by giving itself (by disposing of) a greater infinity—many times greater, one could say—of infinitely short moments.

It follows that, in order to be faithful, the narration of a memory would be in constant need of the resources provided by Hermogenian rhetoric, speed being an important concept—I would even say the central concept— in the Hellenistic treatise on oratory written by this author. It also → I § 66 follows that this is not at all the case in narratives as they actually exist, and that this fact contributes to the feeling such accounts give me of a "betrayal" of the real. It's true that there's no really satisfactory solution to this problem, since it's impossible to apply, in writing, the infinitizing and (probably) contradictory arithmetic I just referred to; one can do no more than imagine analogous strategies, the most natural being that of discontinuity (based, in the end, on the hypothesis of multiple *quanta* of time, already envisaged by ancient philosophy). To my knowledge, no one has ever really attempted to use such a strategy.

(Another strategy would be to increase speed through contrast: to attempt to give an utterly exhaustive description of the paths traversed in memory would demonstrate, indirectly, the irreducible excess of what has happened and is being remembered in relation to all the potential utterances that could recount it. (The birth of Tristram Shandy, in short, interpreted as a metaphor for the "conception" of autobiographical writing.) The scrupulous accumulation of details would reveal its own inability to give an account of the simultaneous emergence into view of these same details.)

Be that as it may, the shifting movement of memory, its speed as it takes hold of individual memories one by one, is a fact—and it's not at all clear to me that the organizational structure that we tend to choose for telling a recollected story betrays memory only because it moves too slowly. The rapidity of memory is that of an illumination. In the fractured territories of the past, in its inhomogeneous milieus, memory proceeds, through reflections and refractions, by rummaging around with the end of its stick, which is at once rigid and broken (perceptually broken).

(Whereas the habitual modes we have of narrating the past seem to depend on imposing an artificial order, one originating in ideas that remain external to the brute fact of a given memory: these modes offer up reconstructions by deriving them from immobile, artificial *snapshots*.)

8 In the winter of this memory, every time I leave the room

In the winter of this memory, every time I leave the room with its ice of inverse flowers on the window, every time I leave, in the present, in the present of the past (since the present is the essential mode of poetry—the mode I have adopted as my own—since one must be able to say of every poem: it takes place "now"), **I then find and see snow; outside it is white; outside there's a garden covered in snow, or discovered in snow, a snow freshly fallen in the silence of the night, like a surprise left by the night, and nothing, not a single footstep, has disturbed it yet, cleared any of it away, or made it seem old; the outside is asleep under a white overcoat, under thick down covers; white; white with a white that is nothing else but white: no idea of cold is connected to this whiteness, nothing harsh: all the ice is inside, in my room, on the window; but the white outside is the white of a calm and gentle sweetness, a sweetness given substance; pure white.**

The white of the snow gives off light. The light radiates outward and is present; that is, it has reached me through all the quasi-infinite light-years of the past. But unlike the light from the stars that comes from their own quasi-infinite distances (the speech of stars bearing witness to their singular pasts as stars, to its unsurpassable constant speed, unsurpassable too in terms of the monotony of universal constants: a tremendous speed, but miniscule despite everything, given such distances), the light from the snow in this image, outside, is present, is reiterated ceaselessly, emerges ceaselessly from the cushions of snow, the shapes in the snow covering the shapes of the ground, the trees, the walls. It's a snowlight, at the place where I go out (but who ever goes out?), where I find that I'm a seer, a seer who is not dazzled, not blinded, not bedazzled.

And if the snow is a light-substance, ceaselessly present, and always re-iterating and repeating itself, something like Olbers's paradox is at work in this memory: given a presumed infinity of time, that is, infinite in duration before the present moment, and a presumably infinite →I § 67 number of stars filling a likewise infinite space—constant, homogeneous, and immobile (that is, until their recessive movement, as a result of the expansion of the universe, was theorized by Hubble)—the night sky would be completely swollen with light: a sphere surrounding us with an endless number of infi-nitely intense lights, making it completely impossible for the night to be dark; and the same holds for the whiteness and light of this snow from the past, of the past outside the windowpane—filling it, the rest of the window, the gar-den outside the window, and my own eyes with its omnipresent daylight. **This snow is a luminous density through and through; it is entirely present, in a full and gentle whiteness without any night.**

Whenever I venture outside the nocturnal room of the primary memory, I find snow. I pass from black to white. There are no other colors in any of this. And it's not only that there's no color in this memory (except black and white, any colors in my memories are colors in name only: language colors): more intrinsically, the moment of the world that I am reconstituting shifts the color to a secondary plane, in order to retain only the light, and the non-light, of the night. Or else, if you like, we may say that it's a question of a time-memory restricted to a lexicon of colors that only contains (as happens in certain lan-guages) the options "black" and "white." Everything that happens, therefore, in this image, everything that can be deduced from what happens, is defined by light or by its absence: from the light, or non-light, of one thing, it is pos-sible to deduce the light or non-light of some other thing. **This** world is the totality of its light.

In my memories, I always go out into the snow. And this is true regardless of whether I'm revisiting the memory of the ice flower on the windowpane or reconstituting the memory of the window painted with blue-black night: **in the shadows I scratch the colorless fern of ice, or the dark blue paint of Pas-sive Defense, and outside is the snow on the garden; the snow that fell dur-ing the night, thick with silence, imbued with this peaceful silence as well as a total absence of all the primary qualities of physical substances, with** the exception of its luminosity, and its contours, also luminously defined; these contours are those of the garden, the garden of the house where I am, where I lived during those years, Rue d'Assas, in Carcassonne, in the *département* of Aude; there are high walls along the street, a small and narrow street, another house, other gardens that lead down, garden after garden, toward the river.

The light comes out of the snow, rises from the snow, rather than falling from the sun, which, however, is still present in the sky: a white sun. I like this final paradox of white and black: I don't see the "Black Sun," the one that hides its light, enigmatically withholding it, keeping it inside itself out of disdain, or else raining down the dark light of the night, the dark night of the soul (the Black Sun is the dark night of the World Soul: the sign of starry melancholy, of the entire macrocosm's despair at its discovery that it has been deprived of its God); instead, I see a **white sun** (without the capital letter of a proper name and likewise without the definite article): luminous without light, which it receives rather than gives—figure of another mode of the Double Negation that constitutes my memory of childhood. I pass from white to black, then once again to white, but to a white that has the properties of a fall, a privation: **I see a snow sun.**

Everything happens as through the transition from inside to outside, the crossing of the transparent space of the windowpane by my vision, were accompanied by a similar, temporal refraction: **the moment when I am looking from inside the room, up against the frost, is a night moment; it's night outside, a very dark night, without moonlight or starlight (the stars have been interrupted),** but the next moment of this memory is **in the full snowy daylight: the sun is there, a winter sun, certainly, but already high in the sky, itself white, a less intense white than that of the ground given over to snow, thus a secondary white; the trajectory of time has been broken, and the slow passage of night to day, the winter dawn, the emergence of the heavy, lethargic sun, have all been erased; and yet the sun itself is present, though having abdicated its role as the star-father of days.**

The sun rose and disappeared, not into the night but into the luminous white of the snow; **it is an empty sun.** For its own part, however, the papery whiteness of the snow is full: full of light, the way a white on white painting might be (but a white on white that wouldn't be inspired, as in Lars Fredrikson, by the immensity of those wintry regions where snow is the rule, where snow dictates the lay of the land: that kind of snow repulses me, makes me anxious, irritable. It's Jack London snow, or snow that belongs in stories about the conquest of the Himalayas—"yeti" snow. To me, this can only ever be the snow of fiction). The full snow of this memory, outside, reconstitutes a light that belongs to it, that is its own, that is moved and inspired by whiteness, by its consistency, its thickness, its breath.

Moreover, this vision has nothing nostalgic about it. This snow isn't deadly (as it is in the novels of Jack London), nor is this light indifferent or neutral. It represents a true exit into the day, an honest wonderment. The truth of the garden is revealed in it: its nature is separated from its use value as well as from the "Austenian" or "Reptonian" value of the moralized garden—all to the advantage of an axiomatic clarity: the precision of the trees, the sentimental geometry of the walkways, the box trees, the beds of dahlias and tomatoes (but without any tomatoes or any real flowers: it's winter). **I see the movements of magpies (black and white), of crows (black and black);** the crows are a continuation of the bedroom, of the night, by other (aviary) means: **I do not hear them (I don't hear anything), but I know that they are squawking.**

9 There is no sadness in this memory

There is, then, no sadness in this memory, no desolation in this wintertime garden. The mental climate into which it plunges me is one of pure illumination. But neither is there any joy in it: wonder, perhaps, but hardly any surprise. The image generates a profusion of snowy light, clouds invade the sky and dampen the white sun. **From farther and farther away** (in the separate moments of the memory, reiterating the image) **come the crows, the black movements of the crows with their inaudible cries, circling over the snow, then disappearing in sequential patterns, in Morse codes, over the garden wall, farther still, over the wall of the barracks that runs along the other side of the Rue d'Assas; they go toward the *Cité* (the walled fortress of Carcassonne) to attend their perpetual conference, to engage in their ferocious**

theological colloquies; birds of Medieval prose, mysterious signs; the magpies, for their part, remaining perched in the tall pines.

Memory's selection of a winter landscape and, within that winter, of a moment of snow, in order to designate—via the metonymy of a reflection extended in space (the snow is a part of the light)—that most ancient of lights, the light that contains all of childhood: all of this is still inscribed within the same paradox that I've been pursuing since the beginning of this second **branch** of my story (condensed in the title of its first chapter, which has not yet been entirely explained): what has been chosen, without any deliberate decision on my part, is not the profuse, incessant, inevitable light shining almost every day in that Mediterranean city. The light that fascinates me isn't the light that tourists and vacationers from the north find so inspiring, but rather, on the contrary, is the light that underscores sadness, a feeling of the irremediable, of what's long past, desolate. The usual light of a climate that's almost entirely cloudless and can go without rain for weeks on end during the summer months—that abusive light from that ostensible sun holds no attraction for me whatsoever (I'm not a Frank, and neither am I a Helvetian, a Viking, or a Teuton). My recollection foregoes this common light without hesitation, in order to bring back that rarer light, rare as the commodity with which I've identified it—the gentle, supple, unusual, surprising snow of the garden.

I believe that I have retained every single moment of snow from those years, since each one was so exceptional and memorable. One day, while reading the poems of Guido Cavalcanti for the first time, I was "transpierced" (like some Saint Sebastian in a garden of poetic delights (delights, of course, and tortures as well: "exquisite," in the English sense of the word, which fits so comfortably into the expression *"exquisite pain"*)) by two particular lines (and they'll be followed by two more, which a kind of deductive landscape links together for me):

> ***aria serena quand' apar l'albore***
> ***e bianca neve scender senza venti***

> [calm air when the dawn appears
> and white snow descending without wind]

The sudden tranquility, the "serenity" of the air when the dawn comes, the "white snow descending without wind": these verses are luminously clothed in thirteenth-century Italian hendecasyllables, with all the self-evidence and abrupt novelty of a truth, as displayed by the world appearing in its natural aspect at the (metaphorical) dawn of vernacular lyric poetry in the West; I see in those two lines a first explanation of my memory-snow, of its "aura," its dazzling not-not-cold, since it is this snow that, in falling, softens the great nocturnal cold, stills the wind, becomes a protective covering for the ground, for the air, for living beings, for **memory**.

Such moments are infinitely rare in poetry, in any kind of poetry: striking a miraculous balance between the sharp detail of poetic particularities (in which being itself is manifest as singular, revealing itself in its *haecceity*, which Hopkins calls the *inscape* of a thing, of each thing) and the usual vagueness of most descriptive propositions ("it snowed"; "the wind dies down"). Such moments, it would seem, can be spoken only once. And the poems in which they occur thus occupy a place in the poetry of a language (or even of a family of languages) from which they can never be dislodged.

Additionally, in my ear, I also heard a linguistic fusing of two antonyms: dawn and dusk. The dawn is represented here by its proper noun, *albore*—close to the Provençal word *alba*, which designates a variant of the love song, one concerned with the separation of lovers at dawn (found in every poetic tradition); while the dusk casts its shadow in the word *serena*, which evokes for me the Medieval Spanish figure of the *sereno*, watchman and protector of urban nights.

Cavalcanti's snow does not fall, it "descends" with an infinite slowness, whiteness without air, without wind. Translating the second line, the one with the snow (or, rather, appropriating it for a poem of my own), evoking the atmosphere of my remembered image, that of the winter garden at dawn, covered over by snow, I turned it into the following: *La neige blanche descendue sans vent* ("The white snow descended without wind"). Having thus arranged for the snow to emerge with the slowness of a long decasyllable (plus, in order to mark its linguistic origins, it seemed necessary to use what, in the terminology of the versification manuals (the "second rhetoric"), is referred to as an "Italian caesura,"—a device seldom seen in French poetry), I also saw **the**

perfect whiteness of the ground, its silent and muted repose; there is light within this snow, and it illuminates the entire verse; snow and light come together.

Chi è questa che vèn, ch'ogn'om la mira,
e fa tremar di claritate l'âre

go the second pair of Cavalcanti lines that I've combined, in my "conception" of them, into a single, piercing arrow ("who is this one coming, whom everyone looks at / who makes the air tremble with clarity").

It's this couplet in particular that made Ezra Pound tremble. In the sonnet (it's from a sonnet), the answer to the question is obvious: the one who's coming is the "lady," the *donna*. But the arrow that I received from these four lines of verse, poetically speaking (in the mathematical discourse I'm accustomed to, one speaks of an arrow's "source" as well as its "target"), also had its source in that dawn snow, at the heart of the white snow fallen without wind onto the garden, in <u>that</u> snow.

The vibrating clarity that it carried with it was contained in its name: **Memory**.

→ Bif A § 132

Chapter 2

The Fig Tree

10 At Christmas in 1942, my father took me to visit his Uncle Roubaud in Toulon.

At Christmas in 1942, my father took me to visit his Uncle Roubaud in Toulon. He lived at 7 Impasse des Mûriers, in Saint-Jean-du-Var (at the time this was a lively small town on the road to Hyères, but it's been completely absorbed by the city now). This was the home of the only three surviving members of the family: an uncle, an aunt, and a cousin (Cousin Laure). My father eventually inherited and still owns this house (but probably not for much longer). I write **"Saint-Jean-du-Var" and "Impasse des Mûriers," and before my eyes I see a flurry of gray plumage with white spots, guinea-fowl in motion; at the same moment I hear their agitated cry, similar to a pulley's rusty chain; a confused and frantic scattering of gray fowl, their rusty screeches stretching across the distance of half a century, inseparably tied to these words, liberated by them: "Saint-Jean-du-Var; 7 Impasse des Mûriers"; I also see a henhouse, laurel trees, a small narrow street.**
whispering silkworms in a white mulberry tree, surrounded by fruit; and then other mulberry trees, with their red fruit lying exploded on the ground around them, like wine, or blood. But I know → I § 68

they don't belong there. I don't refuse them, that's impossible for me, I can't just "cut" them from this image and "paste" them in somewhere else, into another mental "file" where it would be more reasonable to put them (the "*Orangerie*" file (for the white mulberry trees) or the "Delphi" file (for the red ones)), as in a "word processing" program; nor can I retain or immobilize the movement-cry of this image, infinitely more rapid than the original scrambling of the guinea-fowl over the narrow street. **They surge forth, chaotic, and disappear; and then surge forth, and screech, and disappear again**, from the well of ten thousand days, from my heap of rusty time.

Uncle Roubaud, my great uncle, had a very pointed chin, a white scratchy beard; his name was Denis. Denis is my middle name. I've forgotten the name of my great aunt. I used to know it, but I've forgotten. The things that we're told but that aren't really a part of us are forgotten more quickly than the rest. It becomes necessary to find a documentary trace in order to remember. Moreover, since I first began to erode my memories by interrogating them for use in this book, it seems to me that my memory has been affected by the process even more extensively, and more profoundly, than I had foreseen. The act of putting moments of the past into words, however rarified, however careful and restrained, deforms and erases them, as I've said—but this process also acts upon adjacent moments, moments that haven't been under direct scrutiny, but which, without one having realized it, were an integral part of the initial moment, the moment being written. I liked my aunt in Toulon very much, but now I've forgotten her first name.

My father was orphaned at a very young age. Here's an expression that's practically never used anymore, a "pulp-novel" phrase from the time of Gambetta, or Clemenceau: "*orphelin de père et de mère*" ("orphaned of father and mother"). My grandfather died when my father was two weeks old. He obviously can't remember him. His father was a postal worker & was often out running around. These two things seem connected, and in a way that's not entirely causal (but almost), to the primordial fact of this death in the stories my father told me. His mother was a school teacher, born with the name of Garnier. She died when he was five years old. He was living with her at the time, and with his grandmother Ciamponcin; or Chiamponcin, we're not sure. For my father, this uncertainty about names was always emblematic of his status as an orphan. He was always telling us about these figures from his early life, figures that had become purely nominal, and uncertain even in their nomination. When they were all gone, my father went to live with his grandfather Auguste or Gustave Roubaud, the older brother of Uncle Denis Roubaud, already in Saint-Jean-du-Var, not far from La Farlède.

In the case of this older brother, the onomastic uncertainty reigning in the family had found a very peculiar solution, one that stands as the characteristic signature (literally) of this original personage, my great-grandfather Roubaud: he was given a portmanteau name. According to my father, when his grandfather's father (who was thus in the direct paternal line) went to declare the birth of his son at the public records office in Soliès (by which I mean the real village of cherries and hills, not the flat Soliès-ville or the Soliès-pont out in the valley), he suddenly realized that he'd forgotten to think of a name for the child. It was said that, after scratching his head for a moment, he responded to the functionary's question with, "Oh, Gustave!", which, in the record-keeper's administrative script, was interpreted in the "literal" form of an oral pronouncement as "<u>Augustave</u>." Thus, my great-grandfather was named neither Auguste nor Gustave but Augustave Roubaud.

The genealogy passed directly to me on this side of the family goes back no further. And concerning my great-great-grandfather, that distracted and nonconformist winegrower from the Provençal hills, all I "know" in addition to the above story is that he was the only one in his village to vote against the imperial ambitions of Prince Louis-Napoléon in 1852, thus inaugurating a republican lineage, which I've inherited, marked by a certain propensity for unpopular positions. That my father remembered and chose to tell us these two "facts," and these two facts alone (and that I've re- → I § 71 tained them in turn, in place of so many other things), that he used them as the basis for a "brief life" of his own great-grandfather and thus located him as the stubborn point of origin for his own branch of the family—all of this provides a model illustration, in abbreviated form, of the "didactic relationship" between the generations. Such stories determine our moral vision at least as decisively and with as much influence as genetic patrimony, and if I judge by my own experience, they also influence our speech, which is itself transmitted in turn (becoming, for example, a part of the <u>ethos</u> of → I § 72 the **"great fire of London"**).

Given such a casual birth, and with a moral heredity so little inclined to obedience, Augustave Roubaud went on to carve out a rather rough life for himself: he joined the navy and served as a quartermaster mechanic under Admiral Courbet. He received a medal for heroic service when, after his ship was struck by canon-fire and was ready to explode, he stubbornly continued to man the engine, alone, in water up to his chest, and to everyone's astonishment was able to bring the vessel back into port. This was at once the most glorious and most bitter moment of his life: lauded and decorated for his courage, but also reprimanded for his disobedience (his refusal to obey the order to evacuate), he maintained an absolute contempt for the military hierarchy after this incident, which he didn't fail to transmit to his descendents, with innumerable ramifications and extensions.

My father spent the years of World War I with him. At the time he was the only adult presence in my father's life: his other companions were the schoolchildren in his gang of friends, his *raille*, as one said (in the sense of the word *raille* as used in the counting rhyme: "*cent dix-huit, cent dix-neuf / la raille, la raille, la raille / cent dix-huit, cent dix-neuf / la raille du cul du boeuf*" ("a hundred eighteen, a hundred nineteen / the gang, the gang, the gang / a hundred eighteen, a hundred nineteen / the Ox-Rump Gang")). And Saint-Jean-du-Var was not—and I mean not at all—a place full of desirable company. My father's grandfather was retired. His savings were dwindled away in government funds used to build canons to fight the "Krauts." His retirement too was becoming less viable as trenches were dug into the chalky ground of the squalid Champagne region, where he owned land. He lit his pipe with leftover Russian bonds and Panama stocks, while working in the garden on his melons and tomatoes. He wasn't much for conversation, he minded his own business, sometimes he brandished his cane in anger at some enormous insolence on the part of his grandson. But my father was quick on his feet. These years were a time of absolute, anarchic freedom for him. There was little to wear, little to read, little to eat, and precious little affection, but there was the sea.

From the harbor to Mount Faron stretched a rocky zone, full of scree, sand, rocks, customs paths, crevasses, boats, foam. The area is so suffocated now by highways and vacation homes that it's quite impossible to imagine what it looked like then. Step by step, during those days before the beginning of 1943, on our visit, I followed these same traces, I saw, heard, or dreamt the tales of the mussels, the fishermen's nets, the octopuses, the crabs, and the mollusks called "limpets." I heard the legend of the conger eels, the moray eels, the *loups de mer* (or sea bass), the jellyfish, the sea breams, the anchovies, the sardines, the oysters. And above all I tasted—bitten from the diamond of a seashell, from the concentrate of the iodine soul of the seas—the unlikely, tormented, misshapen sea violet, whose flesh is a more or less soft yellow but whose flavor strikes me as blue, violent. It's something that no one or almost no one eats, since its taste is so strange, but it's my father's favorite (the Catalonians call it *bugnols*, as in "*beignet*"). With the coming of the war, the second one, and with the poverty, famine, and silence brought on by the war, the Provençal countryside had regressed thirty years, and—it was a perfect lesson—I saw the sites of my father's childhood in states that were almost identical to those in which he'd first known them.

11 I was not familiar with the sea.

I was not familiar with the sea. I know that I had already seen it, four years earlier, but I had almost forgotten it by this time. **It was** → § 73 **sunny, quite cold; during the days of the Provençal winter; a mild blue sky, not too much wind from the mistral; a very small white cloud sometimes peeking out over the left side of Mount Faron, timid, quickly disappearing; the sea was calm; that was it, that was the sea; I didn't touch it, not really; only with my hand, with my foot; cold.** On an "excursion" to the "Sablettes" with my uncle and aunt & cousin Laure, **I lay down for a long while, I lie on my side, a hand between one cheek and the cold stone (a pier?), lying parallel to the water, eyes closed under the weight of a Sunday's gentle winter sun; eyes open, seeing; at the junction of sea and air I see the leaping light of the barely moving water; farther and farther the still-luminous water, its sheer luminosity speckled with flashes, nothing but a dazzling surface, reiterated, as though spontaneously, beneath eyelids now closed once again.** ("The Sun," as was written twenty-five centuries ago, is "an intelligent fire lit by the sea.")

From the top of Mount Faron, the immensely calm, flat sea, joyously, sumptuously reflective. Later, in Catalonia, in Roda de Barra, in Italy, in Ponza, I had similar quasi-immobile Mediterranean visions, as though the sea were emitting light toward a sun that had no connection to this shimmering light, reduced to being a mere secondary source of illumination, less universal, less exuberant. I have not preserved a clear sketch from that time, from Toulon, from that moment, of the sea's incandescent flatness. But the image was there, without a doubt. And it always gave me the intense desire for a reciprocal exchange, a desire to reverse the light's course, to be lying flat in the sea, sheltered, and to see, in turn, the beaches, the mountain, the hills in the distance.

This kind of familiarity with the sea, which comes from swimming far out into the open water, is now an intimate part of me. I acquired it much later, and I owe it to no one. But the **idea of the sea**, a nostalgia for the sea, came to me from my father. He left the sea behind at the age of twenty, when he moved to Paris to study at the École Normale Supérieure on the Rue d'Ulm. He almost never went back. (Which might be for the best, considering what's happened to Toulon.) The valorization of the sea, and hierarchically of the Mediterranean above every other sea, above the oceans themselves, is for me one of those ethical chromosomes inherited from the paternal genealogical branch of my family, this "acquired trait" having been fixed by my great-grandfather Augustave, since it was he who came down from the hills, leaving the elevation of Soliès not in order to set himself up on a mediocre little plain (Soliès-pont!), but to conquer the only truly "pontic" plain, La Farlède unfurling its name— the Sea. Here one says "*la Mar*" (instead of "*la Mer*,") and in the Toulon accent it becomes "*Marrr*," with multiple rolling *R*s projected out of the throat's shadowy cavern—and saying it this way seems inevitable, since the Côte des Maures is so rocky.

On my father's scale of culinary values, the "bounty of the sea" rates the highest by far. If he learned to appreciate nearly all kinds of food, extending his knowledge and his appetites whenever he had occasion to do so, particularly into the domain of wines and cheeses, if he resolutely adopted red and even raw meat (generally a nonnegotiable effort for someone from the Mediterranean), if he consistently evidenced a curiosity for strange and foreign flavors, this was all, as with philosophy and literature, an intellectual and cultural conquest on his part, as well as a result of the influence of his friends from the ENS (his best friend from the École was from Normandy, and this man's wife was my agnostic godmother). But the supreme trinity of fish, crustaceans, and shellfish remained sovereign for him. And among these one could still isolate and draw an emblem of sorts in the form of a hexagram, composed of the very first edible sea creatures (first, that is, in terms of childhood discoveries, at the beginning of World War I), the ones he had learned to catch and prepare himself, by hand, with a knife, over the fire: the oyster, the mussel, and the violet, the octopus, the anchovy, and the sardine.

All these foods were "of the people," in the days when this distinction was a sharp one ("people" as opposed to aristocrats: though admittedly food is a domain in which, quite often, it was possible for the tastes of the social extremes to converge). His uncle, his aunt, and his cousin had little taste for sardines, whose olfactory imperialism is intolerable to any well-organized housekeeper. In their manners as in their habits and convictions, they were quite poor and inflexible petits bourgeois from Toulon, but at the same time they were infinitely generous and kind, in perpetual contradiction with their modes of life and thought. They adored and admired my father; and I liked them. But when it came to the sardine and the octopus (whose movements terrified them), they remained intransigent.

When he became part of my mother's family (this was much later, though he was still the quasi-hoodlum from Saint-Jean-du-Var, always quite unpresentable: but he was a friend of her brother Frantz, which removed a great many obstacles), my father once again had to wage, at least verbally, the "culinary class struggle" that had begun with his aunt, this time against his in-laws. The Molino family wasn't much acquainted with seafood, except in the form of dab and hake, rendered bland (moreover) by long and conscientious treatment in a pot of boiling water. These fish can certainly have a decent enough taste, but prepared in this fashion they reach new heights of blandness and are to the sardine what the endive is to salad greens (in terms of coloration). As for shellfish, they were totally unknown, or else had been banished; while crustaceans were beyond the means of teachers, and crabs were simply unspeakable.

Thus, two series of causes converged to form a well-established refusal in this regard:

—the modesty of the family's financial resources in relation to the cost of the food (there has been, as we know, a considerable reallocation of household expenditures in France, as one says sociologically: my grandparents certainly would never have been able to pay for a lobster without great sacrifices—not even on special occasions; on the other hand, no one today in public service, even at the highest level, would be able to afford the rent for a house like the one they lived in at the time);

—the ideology of hygiene and its dietetic "arguments": to my grandparents, all maritime food products (with the exception of hake and dab, already mentioned (as well as sole, which was a luxury)) were dangerous. And, to tell the truth, they were not entirely wrong. In the absence of effective refrigeration, fish still didn't travel well, and the family lived in Lyon. (For similar reasons, the meat served in Provence at the time was always very well-done.) Still, the phobia against mussels, for example, according to which one could catch typhoid merely by touching them (or nearly), went well beyond any merely precautionary considerations.

Mussels and sardines were excessive foods, impudent & impolite. They elicited a displaced vestige of the nineteenth-century fear of the "dangerous classes," a fear that in other respects my maternal grandparents, with their "progressive" ideas, sincerely and vigorously rejected. But their political views were not what one would call revolutionary—and clearly sardines belong to the far left-wing of the fish world. So to justify their distaste, they hid behind hygienic reasons alone. Besides, fried sardines—a Provençal culinary tradition—were cooked in oil, olive oil. But olive oil was classed by Raspail, one of my maternal grandfather's *maîtres à penser*, in the category of "heavy" foods, thus strictly opposing it to butter, the "lightness" of which had an almost medical sanctity. This was a supplementary reason for abstaining.

And then, to these two universal and somewhat anonymous reasons, two other, personal ones could be added:

—for my grandmother, the imperious commands of her "liver" (an organ invented by the French);

—for my grandfather, the imperatives of an early upbringing by his mother in Savoy that had definitively oriented his preferences toward "the" supreme dish: *gratin dauphinois.*

My father succeeded in almost entirely converting my mother, but without ever obtaining from her a truly unreserved attachment to mussels → I § 74   and sardines. And yet this is still a remarkable accomplishment if one takes into account how difficult it is to change any culinary tastes after childhood, particularly when it comes to aversions based on fear. I believe in fact that at the age of twenty my mother had never even <u>seen</u> an oyster lying open on a plate.

12 In any case, he had not converted his own family.

In any case, he hadn't managed to convert his own family. He treated them with a slightly ironic affection, a trace of the intense and ancient disagreements that remained visible beneath the cheerful polemics concerning those dangerous "fruits of the sea." There can be no doubt that things hadn't gone smoothly when, after the death of my great-grandfather Roubaud, they first took in this violent boy, used to doing exactly as he pleased, whether it was pulling on doorbells and running away or putting eels, frogs, or even crabs in the mailboxes of the good pious ladies of Saint-Jean-du-Var (he was twelve years old); in short, a real "hoodlum," or a *voyou*, to use the vocabulary of the time. And the sudden irruption of this perturbing element into their very ordered lives must have seemed all the more troubling to them since Cousin Laure was there, a girl who had been raised according to the best principles, and on whose behalf a certain contagion might be feared.

It was by chance alone, as my father described it, that he did not opt for the other path that presented itself, the one that was chosen by all the most energetic, boldest, and most resourceful of his school- or playmates: the path of outright delinquency (a third option was that of the navy: one of his *lycée* classmates "ended up" an admiral). It wasn't fear that stopped him, he told me, nor any newly acquired submissiveness to the rules of society. But the example as well as the sarcastic comments of his grandfather had been complicated by the influence of a teacher who'd decided to enter my father in a scholarship competition, which would, if he won, allow him to pursue secondary studies without excessive cost to a family that didn't have much money. It was a clever calculation. Besides, my father didn't like to lose. He got the scholarship, and he went to the *lycée*.

Cousin Laure didn't fulfill the (poetically inspired) expectations that her name might have aroused. When I knew her, aside from no longer being very young, she was somewhat disillusioned and resigned, and slightly musta-chioed as well (she was never very beautiful). She didn't get past the eighth grade, never went to the *lycée* (for girls it was impossible to imagine even set-ting foot in the place), learned no trade. On the other hand, she did receive a serious education in sewing and Provençal cuisine from her mother (accord-ing to the precepts of the great Reboul). And her father, my great uncle, paid for piano lessons, which were considered indispensable. Then she grew up and waited, always living with her parents, rarely going out, without any great yearning for independence. She read novels by Georges Ohnet, & *La Petite Illustration*. Time passed.

Time passed, but her one way out, marriage, never came. Her parents grew old, then died. Their savings had lost value. She had to look for work. She found a position in a daycare for children. All told, she was quite happy there: the kids loved her, since she was gentle, calm, and loved them in return. She rented the upper floors of the house at 7 Impasse des Mûriers to middle-aged women, colleagues who were unmarried like herself, then she retired, still staying in that house; she acquired a television. Her old renters are still there (Laure too eventually died), and today they pay my father a rent that's hardly changed since 1960.

At the death of Cousin Laure, my father took over my grandfather's few remaining "effects"—his legacy, in sum: this included some papers that he gave me last year, especially the "military booklet" detailing all the "campaigns" of the old sailor Augustave (it really was his name after all! I read it myself!), and some volumes of *L'Histoire Socialiste* by Jean Jaurès—he was a "red," like his father before him. I liked my father's cousin Laure very much, as I did my aunt and uncle, even if I didn't go see them very often in Toulon: I liked them less than my maternal grandfather, no doubt, but certainly more than my grandmother. At Christmas in 1942, I was happy and curious to meet them. I was enchanted by the house, **the squawking and scattering guinea fowl, Mount Faron, the rocks, the distant shimmering of the sun over the open sea, and everywhere the sea itself, its immense waters, luminous and green; blue, green.**

The next phase of my father's story seems to me to include a large dose of the inevitable. Once he'd set out on the path of his studies, the only real way out for him, this time, was to see them through. The same providential and republican opportunity as had allowed him into school in the first place occurred once again after he received his baccalaureate. Prepared to enter the "active life" of civil service, in the footsteps of his own father, he took a "placement examination" and obtained, as he had the first time, a scholarship: This one took him to Marseille, into what was called a "primary superior" class, or, more familiarly, the "*hypokhâgne*"—the first year of a two-year, high-level preparatory course for entrance to the École Normale Supérieure. Three years later, in 1927, after an initial failure, he entered the École on the Rue d'Ulm. My mother, who came from the same "*hypokhâgne*" in Marseille (she went to her "*khâgne*," as the second year is called, in Lyon, at the Lycée du Parc), was accepted after taking the same round of exams as my father. (There were three young ladies at the École Normale that year—an exceptional phenomenon at the time.)

→ I § 75

Although since the death of his grandfather he had made great progress in his studies, having learned Latin, math, even philosophy, my father's character didn't seem to change very much. He stayed more or less the same throughout his life: violent, independent, difficult, audacious, intransigent, ironic, obstinate, argumentative, only able to tolerate being contradicted with great difficulty, not very susceptible to influence, recognizing no authority other than intellectual authority. As he got off the train at the Gare de Lyon, on his way to take the oral exam for entry into the École, his accent was so thick that he found it impossible to make himself understood by the locals he asked for directions. He had a small-town accent from Toulon—the Toulon of the nineteen teens—which was as rough, "hirsute" and guttural as the pure Provençal accent from Arles (spoken by his friend Paul Geniet, for example) is, on the contrary, clear and "combed." And my father claims that when it came time to respond to the oral questions on the entrance exam, he had recourse to an almost desperate tactic: He imitated the voice of a classmate from Lyon, who, during the school year, had seemed to him to have the most ridiculous and "punctilious" northern accent imaginable—but one that was no doubt more accessible to the Parisian barbarians.

Still, if he did compromise, little by little, when it came to the violence of his accent (it always came back, later, when he got angry), he didn't abandon any of his other violent characteristics. The authorities of the École Normale Supérieure, and later the military authorities and the academic committees for the *agrégation* exam, came into conflict with him about as often, I think, as the professors, censors, and proctors at his lycée in Toulon, and then at the one in Marseille. The struggle against the Germans who'd dressed themselves up as Nazis was, in a sense, simply the most extreme form of this spirit of contradiction. The stakes were higher—and less strictly personal no doubt—but the mental disposition was the same.

My father did not, however, play the part of the solitary rebel. Beginning when he was very young, he was a committed supporter of the Toulon rugby

team (he still is). Rugby was for him <u>the</u> game par excellence, and he continued to play it wherever he lived, even in an environment so little favorable to
the sport as the Rue d'Ulm (during the war he played with his students from
the Carcassonne lycée). He managed to form a team at the École, which he
coached for several years, sometimes constructing his scrums according to
constraints that I would describe as pre-Oulipian: one day his third line was
composed entirely of bald players, for example, or else he chose as "props" two
players named, respectively, Bélier and Taureau (Ram and Bull). His esteem
for Samuel Beckett long preceded the fame of *Waiting for Godot*, based as it
was on the remarkable qualities shown by the young Irishman —this "reader"
at the ENS, who'd been recruited to the École's team by my father—when he
played as a scrum-half during a difficult match with the *AS Police de Paris*.
This match was so terrible (the police were both better trained and seriously
brutal) that S.B. walked off the field slightly "dazed," shaking his head and repeating with vehemence: "Never again! Never again!" "What a shame!" added
my father when he told us the story of this match: "He had *la vista!*" (I am very
happy to be able, with this story, to add my little stone (a veritable cornerstone,
if you ask me) to the majestic edifice of Beckett criticism.)

13 In back of the house, the fig tree

**In back of the house, there was a small yard, where I see nothing but the
very blue sky (so blue it seems black to me) and a fig tree; the small yard
looking into the house through a low window** (very low, no doubt, since I
saw it as low even then) **that gave light to the kitchen, and on the floor were
octagonal tiles, in irregular positions, cracked and broken apart; because
the fig tree, leaning against the wall of the house, had embraced it with
such passion that it had <u>dislodged</u> the stones of the wall, its roots working
their way inside and pushing up beneath the colored tiles of the floor; a
very particular atmosphere pervades this image: fascination, incredulity,
almost fear; that a tree could have such strength, such stubbornness, such
power to destroy even something as solid as the wall of a house, as its floor,
covered with the beautiful ordered geometry of hexagonal tiles, shiny
and red.**

This was a particularly beautiful fig tree; I see its large thick leaves, their deep flat green, the network of veins. For fig trees are beautiful trees. I like them very much. Very often in Provence, in the Aude region, they are planted this way, right up against a wall, very close (at the Tuilerie (as we call the farmhouse where my parents now live), a fig tree was planted to the right of the front door, the one that opened onto the street, and thus both door and tree were doomed by the eventual explosion of automobile traffic on the Minervois road—the tree itself died from it). **I've kept the idea of its smell in me, the smell of its large leaves: neither pleasant (its aroma), nor unpleasant, in no way repulsive; but a very conspicuous, tenacious, corporeal smell.** The fig tree is a living body. The invisible movement with which it forced its way into the kitchen, from beneath the earth, gave it—in my view—a vital animation, a veritable animal soul. It was from this that it derived its disjunctive power.

This is true also in that the place that the tree occupies (that was chosen for it) is almost that of a familiar animal—a dog's or a cat's: close to where the food is kept, in the kitchen, near the fireplace, and in those days close to the well too: thus, between fire and water. As something familiar, it acts as a protector; but is also threatening at the same time: It threatens the wall with destruction, with cracks (the walls, too, are fissured by long cracks), it threatens to make the floor cave in, it introduces disorder (ants advance as a "fifth column" along the furrows of the fractured floor tiles). Its intentions are unclear: at times beneficent, at others—as on a stormy afternoon, for example—rather sinister, premonitory: in short, it has an ambiguity that could almost be called divine: Where does this force come from, this fibrous wooden impetus, this irresistible pressure being exerted as though consciously on the stones, on their cohesion, on the bond holding the masonry of the house together? What's the meaning of this disturbing impulsion, and why is it manifesting here, under these particular circumstances? What demon is inhabiting this tree, disguised as a household God?

Between fire (the sun, the sky) and water (the well, the sea), between the flame and the wave, through the glass (of the low window at the back of the kitchen), the image-smell-threat of the fig tree thus forced its way too into the anguished and beguiling "deduction" that began with a dream I once had, a dream that characterized one of the ten styles into which my words are divided, specifically the "style for taming demons," or *rakki tai*. The **fig tree** showed me, then, in this style, a house, the house on the Impasse des Mûriers, the house that had been my father's home (but which did not belong to him at the time). (It does belong to him now, however, after he inherited it from Cousin Laure. And all this may be why I can't make myself act on the decision we made to sell it, a decision made necessary by the threat of ruin now weighing on the unoccupied buildings of the Tuilerie property.)

The fig tree (image) is interwoven with the image of the **dream** in the fictive deduction that organizes my narration as a whole. The fig tree (the real fig tree, in the past) was itself entangled with the wall of the kitchen. The childhood image of this fig tree gives rise to several other images, and in the chain that I am now unlinking into distinct moments, it is connected to the nodal image that gives a meaning and a name to one of the **image-centers** of the present branch: this nodal image involves an act of naming, the ancient childhood invention of a word, "**oranjello**," that is not part of the language, that I force on the language, that I forced on it long ago (for it is contemporary with this chain of memories). In the deduction itself, the tree appears explicitly only one other time, following an advance in the deduction, in its forward movement, linked with a decision, the decision, one of the deduction's three primary **nodes** (the two others being the dream and the **Project**). It appears there because the decision itself is presented in the "*rakki tai* style," and thus is destined to be used in a struggle with demons. But I cannot as yet disentangle this image further.

The beneficent side of the fig tree, its ordinary and reassuring aspect, is also embodied in its fruit. In those days of general hunger, the fig, which escaped the sinister regime of the "ration cards," was a wonderful source of sugar, and it also contained in itself a quality likewise essential to the prestige of sugar at the time: scarcity, which is something it had in common with "fat"; nowadays, the labels on containers of cheese or *petits suisses* advertising *20%* or *40% fat* are designed to place greater emphasis, and greater value, on lower numbers (the "fat content" thus acting as a marketing strategy aimed at "dieters," for whom the supreme number is *0%*), but when they initally appeared at the end of the war, during those first few years before the return to abundance, the commercial advantage lay, on the contrary, in higher numbers. Our parents' tales of the "pre-war period," which we were always eager to hear, included descriptions (often demanded and often repeated) of the foods that had completely disappeared from urban France beginning in the winter of 1940. Butter and desserts were particular favorites. But our figs, like all fruit, held out the promise of sugar, delicious sugar.

→ I § 76

And unlike the strictly mythological fruits such as oranges or bananas, or others that were occasionally glimpsed, but still almost completely absent from the Aude region, like apples or raspberries (the dark blueberries of the Pyrenees, so blue, as though covered with a mist of blue, also had this quality of being exotic, of being sugar), fig trees, like grape vines, represented a source of sugar in a free state, unfettered by any administrative constraints and without the intervention of any "Occupation Authorities." Moreover, figs, which usually reach maturity a few weeks before the grape harvests, can be preserved and consumed well into other times of year, for instance as "attic figs," dried on "racks" and straw (or, even more attractively, when figs are preserved on the tree itself, through an invention of the benevolent side of the fig tree's nature, often mistakenly called a "fig-flower"). Since the fig tree is a poor tree, without distinction, growing on the low walls around terraced fields, called *restanques*, and along the sides of the roads, black and green figs weren't as closely watched as cherries, and were quite accessible to resourceful children.

We might also have thought of making jam. During the first years we spent living in the Minervois, when "pure sugar" or "100% fat" remained the culinary ideal of our generation, we indulged in veritable orgies of jam. For reasons that are at once intrinsic (I like the taste) and external, oblique—and also because of everything implied in the idea of the fig tree, which I am presently explaining—the reigning queen of jams was for me the one made with whole preserved figs. Each fruit was transformed into a crystal of jam, and was devoured whole (a property shared by its rival, green tomato jam, which for its part had the novelty of not being a redundancy (an insistence on the sugariness of a fruit that's already sweet), but a paradox, since the living tomato is not eaten as a sweet). Alas, however, fig jam wasn't possible during the war, because one needs sugar to make jam. And our attempts to use substitutes, such as grape sugar, never met with any success.

But I don't think I was familiar yet with the ultimate expression of the fig's excellence. This version of the fig that had a prominent place among the many wonders of my father's childhood on the rocky slopes of Mount Faron, and as such he had described it countless times (his figs were usually stolen from neighbors, of course, but there were a few in his grandfather's "garden" in La Farlède, products of some since-lost family land): I called these figs (or rather, I will call them: this awkward expression, anticipating the act of nomination, is bizarre), I called them "*penneque* figs." "Preserved" right on the tree in the heat of late August or early September, these figs offer at once the living flavor of the fruit and the extreme concentration of sweetness found in jam: they are the fig itself, its ideal, angelic form, its gustatory holiness. When I first had a *penneque* fig, in Les Corbières in the fall of 1943, I was not disappointed.

14 At dinner one evening in the 1950s

At dinner one evening in the 1950s, my father told us the story of a rather unexpected encounter; here is the gist of it, more or less: He used to frequent the Secrétan market in the XIXth arrondissement in Paris (the one closest to the Rue Jean-Menans, where we lived at the time), and the privileged anchoring point (if I can put it that way) of his visits to the market was determined by his unfailing love for the things of the sea: the fish stall. His favorite fish stall was run by a couple from Brittany, and my father was generally served by the wife, Mme. La Baïs (I can't vouch for the spelling), who was still quite young and strong (though thin), a lively light-haired woman, quite reserved and above all very precise in her vocabulary. She showed a certain respect for my father, both because of the frequency, the abundance, and the variety of his purchases, spanning all three types of seafood (fish, shellfish, and crustaceans), but also, for less mercantile reasons, because of his general competence in all matters relating to the sea. They had interesting exchanges concerning onomastics; including, of course, frequent digressions on cooking. (The names of marine species vary a great deal, almost with every bend in the coastline; my father thought it very important to give every fish its true name, almost a proper name, which is to say the one by which it was known in its native waters. He would ask about the names used in Brittany and, having clarified this to his satisfaction, would counter with the ones from Toulon, which he had never forgotten.)

Mme. La Baïs had another customer, a woman well into her fifties, who sometimes found herself at the stall at the same time as my father, and whom he had identified as Toulonnaise because of her accent and the way she addressed the fish merchant, whom she called "*MaBelle*." And that, in return, was the nickname given to her in my family, following the memorable incident that I, following my father's outline, am about to relate. "MaBelle" had only one leg. She leaned heavily on her wooden leg, picking up sea breams and comparing their weight in her hands, with the air of a woman who'd learned long ago to live with her infirmity, and who in spite of it had maintained a robust attitude towards life. That day, a stubborn rain was falling, and "MaBelle" felt it necessary to indicate the effect this was having on the border region between her own flesh and that of the wood, which she confirmed with a "monstration" for the benefit of my father, Mme. La Baïs, and the other customers who happened to be present, by lifting her black dress up to her thigh, which was cut off a little above the knee.

At that moment, a kind of light—this is how he presented it to us—dawned in my father's mind. Without even stopping to think, he said to "MaBelle": "It happened in 1918. You were trying to catch the tram in Toulon when you had your accident." This was correct. At that moment, with her skirt lifted, my father had **seen** the scene in question, seen it precisely, how the pretty young girl of the time had turned completely red, but had not said a word, had not let out a cry, while people gathered around her trying to stop the blood that was pouring out of her. The unlikely identification had been made via an obscure and winding path of recollection, more than thirty years long—but what astounded us all was the fact that it had occurred at just this precise moment (it's true that if he had been wrong, no one would have thought twice about the incident, and my father might not have even mentioned it to us. Such is the paradox of coincidences).

What had astonished him even more than his "illumination" was the way in which MaBelle had received his surprising identification, an unorthodox version of what popular novels of the past called "the voice of blood": that is, with a complete absence of surprise. She behaved as if nothing could have been more natural, as if it was inevitable that this gentleman, whom she did not know, would have so clear a memory of this episode of her life. The moment of her accident, which had without any doubt been an essential, tragic, overwhelming, and unforgettable moment of her existence, was so integrally a part of her that it excluded the possibility of any external curiosity. At least, this was one of the hypotheses that we considered in trying to explain her behavior, which was after all only an extreme form of what is in reality a fairly widespread psychological disposition: There are people, and we all know someone like this, who carry their worlds around in such a solipsistic way, who are so intimately and unconsciously convinced that what they see and how they see it is the only "possible world," that the first time they ever set eyes on you, despite your having only just entered their field of vision, they speak to you as though you yourself had always been present for them, had been there for their entire lives—*ipso facto*, simply by becoming a proximate object—and consequently that you already ought to know, and in detail, the circumstances surrounding the events of which they happen to be speaking, the names of the people mentioned in their stories, and indeed their entire genealogies. This is what I propose to call "provincialism of the self."

In the discussion that followed my father's story, there was no need to re-iterate (since we were all aware of it) that the intensity of his memory of the accident—which became evident when my father, stimulated by the vision of the scar, was suddenly able to "recognize" in the truculent and nearly sixty-year-old MaBelle the young, pretty, and courageous Toulonnaise of the past—was due not only to the fact that the initial scene had taken place in front of the eyes of an eleven-year-old child, but to another fact as well, namely that he too had been the victim of an accident at around the same time: less seri-ous, to be sure, but whose result had likewise been an amputation. To tell the truth, given the near total autonomy of the life my father led while in the care of his grandfather, it's almost a miracle that this accident was the only one of its kind:

As he was trying to dig the dirt out from beneath a heavy rock, the rock fell over and crushed the index finger of his right hand: the top two sections have been missing ever since. **I see what remains of the finger, short, round, and smooth**; this is certainly a very old image, and very persistent in its original form, which I know because I always get a slight shock when I see it again—the real one, that is—in the present day, in its actual dimensions, since these are much smaller than the ones in my mind. (I'll speak about my own accident, also involving my right hand, elsewhere.) As for the culprit rock, it was, I'm quite sure, an earthbound, inland rock. I imagine it as enormous, resting in a deceptive disequilibrium on the slopes of the Faron, that mountain which is a Toulonian deity at once tutelary and malignant, like the divine fig tree, like all divinities: capable of harboring lizards, grass snakes, vine peaches, and cherries, but capable also of setting traps, like the one that closed on my father's finger.

One might have expected maritime accident instead. The rocky coves in the area were inhabited by all kinds of dreadful wildlife (or so it seemed to me, since I was only familiar with the underwater world of a river, the Aude itself): conger eels, moray eels, crabs, octopi (magnified enormously in my imagination after a reading of Victor Hugo's *Toilers of the Sea*, in which, as a sort of "remake" of the Anglo-Saxon poem *Beowulf*, there's an epic battle between the hero and an octopus-demon); or else the stinging embrace of the jellyfish, its sinister gliding across the calm surface of the water, its rainbow-color like a film of gasoline; not to mention the risk of diving, the perfidious "bends," or the treachery of a storm-driven wave suddenly crashing into the cave into which an unwitting swimmer has ventured. But, then, might it not be possible that the falling stone was the ineluctable revenge of the ancestral mountain (Soliès) on the tribe that had abandoned it?

I don't remember what my father expected to find under that rock (crabs maybe), or if he himself even remembers. In any event, the effects of the accident weren't limited to the simple loss of a finger—at least not in the story that goes with it. For my father the accident was also the undeniable cause of an allergy that appeared, he said, a short time later: He could no longer eat honey. The manifestation of this punitive intolerance was not a phobia or an insurmountable dislike; every attempt to violate the injunction, "Thou shalt eat no more honey!" from then on was accompanied almost instantaneously by a terrible burning pain in the stomach; as if the road to hell had been under that rock, and my father had discovered it was paved with honey.

After the war, I heard him joking with his friend Albert Picolo, who had returned from Buchenwald. Albert Picolo had always suffered from a certain food phobia, one that used to be rather widespread: He couldn't stand cheese. It disgusted him—the mere sight of cheese nearly sent him into a frenzy.

"What would you have done," my father said to him, "if in the camp the Nazis had forced you to eat a Camembert, or a tangy Brie?" They both had a good laugh.

15 The fall of the Berlin Wall precipitated me into this chapter

It was the fall of the Berlin Wall that precipitated me into this chapter, that provided the urgency for it to be written—written at this point in my story, and according to the following modalities: the Maison des Écrivains decided to send a dozen writers into those countries where socialism was collapsing (the socialism that was once referred to as "actually existing" (how far away all that seems now!)), so that they could have a look around and then report back on what they'd seen; when they asked me to participate, I said yes, and without even thinking about it I chose that semi-country formerly called the GDR. So I went to East Berlin. This was during the last days of February, 1990; it was cold, gray, and snowy. I quickly fled the breakfast room of the Hotel Metropol, since, beginning at seven o'clock in the morning, it had been invaded by impatient West German and Japanese businessmen, anxious not to lose a second of their busy days, so hungry were they—for land, for factories, for a workforce that would be grateful, poor, modest, German-speaking, and highly skilled.

Out where I was walking, by the Spree, I ended up on a little island in the middle of the river. I walked around it, to get a better look at it, to see. Since that was why I was there: to see. The sun was already out. It becomes daylight much earlier there, at the far eastern edge of the same time zone as Paris. The East Berliners (some still existed; contrary to what I was led to believe by reading the Parisian newspapers, they hadn't all rushed into the embassies or from the other side of the Wall) were walking their dogs in a hideous Chirac-style playground. The sky was filled with virulent-looking clouds pressed onward by a coming storm in a dark and tumultuous *Drang nach Osten* (rush to the East): Them too, I thought to myself.

A violent wind silenced the gulls and the timid black ducks with white beaks that congregated under the bridges—unless it was only that censorship hadn't yet been abolished in the animal kingdom. I walked freely along the

Spree in the gray morning, as in the past—at the beginning of the 1960s—I had walked along the Canal de l'Ourcq, before the demands of modernization had rendered that particular private activity impossible (in Toulon today, like nearly everywhere along the Mediterranean, it's even worse: the freedom to carry out private construction, like the freedom given to automobiles, makes the freedom of pedestrians so precarious that it's no longer possible to exercise it). A caravan of freight barges stretched along the quay, all loaded to the top with coal: brown lignite.

→ I § 77

And I could read the traces of the old war on all the façades that had been spattered with bullets: the telltale signs of a history of walls. On the official buildings, for instance, the stonework had been replaced with clean new pieces, perfectly rectangular replicas. On some of the more modest façades, the holes had simply been filled with mortar, leaving large daubs of gray cement overflowing onto the surface, like the lumpy excretions of enormous pigeons. But almost everywhere else the holes remained as they were at the moment of impact, and in one of the houses on the island I saw sparrows ensconced by the dozen in some of these holes, like the bursts of an aviary machine gun. In April and May of 1945, each one of these holes was no doubt the marker—unadorned by any flowers—of a dead Nazi, a dead Soviet.

It was at this moment that an image was projected into my recollection, an abrupt image abruptly reborn after forty-five years of oblivion. **I saw**, superimposed on the pockmarked façade on that Berlin island, **the wall riddled with** similar **holes on the Luxembourg Palace, one extremely cold day in January 1945 (even the fountains in the garden had frozen). I was with my father,** who was going to the Senate building, where the first post-war assembly was located then, the Consultative Assembly put together by de Gaulle to prepare France for its return to a republican normality. **I can situate this façade with great precision, together with the gesture that, in this image, my father made when he pointed to the wall, pockmarked as though riddled with the nests of sinister black birds, like those in the prints of Charles Méryon: it's across from the arcades, which, on the right, near the entrance to the Rue Garancière, still shelter that little known Parisian personality, a horizontal copy of Mr. Standard Meter,** whose prototype resides at a prestigious address in the "Pavillon de Breteuil" that schoolchildren had once been taught to revere (before his decline in favor of the use of a simple and immaterial wavelength to determine the length of a meter).

These are the circumstances. But it is clear that there's more than a mere superimposition evoked by a resemblance behind the return of this buried image. The wounds on those walls are directly related: they resulted from the same war, and it is of this war that my father's gesture toward the façade speaks, inviting me to remember. I've passed in front them countless times since that day, going down the Rue de Vaugirard. For a long time the holes were still visible, when the patches dressing the stone were still identifiable for what they were (not so today, when I look at the spot corresponding to my inner image: it's been camouflaged by the "stripping" and "resurfacing" our senators indulged in: a kind of "face-lift," the emblem of all the efforts undertaken to rejuvenate that "chamber of old-timers" and make it suit the not-so-brilliant image of our limited democracy). But the sight of those semi-ruins in East Berlin all but annulled my gentle observations, made in passing, on the

→ I § 78
façade in the days since the war, restoring to me all the violence of my initial vision (violent, that is, to me, as someone who never had any direct knowledge of the war's language of bullets and explosions). There had been fighting on the island in the Spree, and there had been fighting in Paris a few months earlier, right next to the Luxembourg Gardens. The machine guns had "sprayed" the houses, riddled the windows, killed. In Paris, in 1945, there were still fresh flowers lying on the streets, the same streets, the same places where someone had fallen.

It was as though the "regressive error"—of Ulbricht's and Honecker's Stalinist "socialism"—had, in disappearing, restored the German landscape, and thereby the French landscape, to the states in which they'd found themselves on May 8, 1945, when the weapons fell silent: much as one can find, after some abrupt seismic catastrophe, the imprint left deep in a riverbed, beneath the dark layers of geological sediment, by a prehistoric animal belonging to a species that has vanished entirely and forever. But this particular image was only able to return to me with such force because it was of direct and particular importance to my political childhood.

Still more precisely: The impulse that had led me, without any reflection, to say yes to the proposal from Martine Segonds-Bauer—as communicated to me by Michèle Ignazi—immediately upon being asked, and also to choose, without a moment's thought, to come here, to Berlin, where the last savage battles of the war had taken place—all this didn't result simply from the desire no doubt unconsciously deep, for an opportunity to reflect again on a period that was so decisive for me; surely it also came from an even less conscious need that was ready nonetheless to seize on this indirect justification—in the hopes, perhaps, of mastering the sequence of childhood images that I had already set out to elucidate (still following my initial vision of an enormous single "page" being darkened line by line with prose): namely, a need to speak of my father.

→ I § 79

And it was a unique moment in Germany: a sort of historical no-man's-land in which the reign of the defeated had come to an end, yet that of the victors—whose avant-garde I had seen rushing avidly and frenetically through the lobby of my hotel—had not yet been established. It was a moment of suspension, almost a moment of the future anterior. Enlightened by this understanding, it was possible—and only possible then, for the first time—for me to find my way back to another image, also indelible, located two years prior to that of the bullet-riddled walls: the image I've been working toward since the first lines of this chapter. The filiation between the two is quite evident, as we will see. I understood this, then, and on my way back to my hotel I followed Planckstrasse, proud of honoring, with this nominative gesture—and in the guise of the inventor of quantum theory—a much less troubling Germany.

16 On Christmas day we crossed the port on the little boat from the promenades

On Christmas day we crossed the port on the little boat from the promenades, which, in a praiseworthy effort to imitate normal times, was still taking lovers and children on excursions to "Les Sablettes": a tradition of the Toulonnais, the same now as it had been before 1940. But one had to cross the port and leave the harbor. **The boat was nearly empty, we were almost alone; it was a clear quiet morning (that's how I see it, full of a slightly solemn clarity, with no sound but the one made by our gliding over the water); all around the water was green in the sunlight; the little boat floated along next to the**

large broken-down ships that lay overturned, tilting, limp and misshapen in the harbor; they barely protruded from the surface, some were completely submerged, the largest were leaning on their sides, empty: a squadron of phantom vessels.

A majority of the French navy's ships were there. This was shortly after the "scuttling" of the naval fleet, which was unable to decide whether it should surrender to the Germans or to join up with the FFF, the Free French Forces of General de Gaulle, on the other side of the Mediterranean. **My father's face was tense, severe, full of that silent fury that I recognized so well in him.** I don't think he said a single word. Not out of prudence, nor in order to hide his thoughts from me, for our parents never bothered to conceal the fact from us that they were wishing (to paraphrase and reverse the terrible words of Pierre Laval) for England's victory (and more recently that of the Soviet Union and the United States: Pearl Harbor had happened, the battle of Stalingrad had been the previous winter)—but because there was in fact nothing to say.

I understand very clearly today that the visit we were paying then to the Impasse des Mûriers was not only for the sake of a meeting between what remained of my father's family and his own oldest child, me, but also for the sake of a silent observation, a verification of the disaster that had overcome those large and impeccably new ships, not even completely submerged but sagging here and there in the magnificent harbor, without the slightest dignity, without having taken part in even one battle. My father was reconnecting, at least mentally, with his grandfather, who had once stayed on alone in the engine room of his damaged and abandoned ship, and his inwardly pronounced judgment was certainly the same as Augustave's had been: a condemnation of all cowardice, without appeal.

That Christmas, my father was two days away from his thirty-sixth birthday. He was, therefore, the same age I was at the time of the "events" of 1968 (I often indulge in such numerical comparisons). I don't believe that he had "joined" the active Resistance yet (an opportunity to do so, in the form of a call from London, led him to take that step a short time later), but I deduce that our journey also represented an opportunity for him to verify the necessity of a serious decision that was soon to be made. In taking me with him—and I'm certain that he was perfectly aware of some of the possible consequences of this decision (he confided to me later that he had spoken of this at length in private with my mother. It's clear that these consequences implicitly concerned us as well, my brothers, my sister, and myself, but it was impossible to speak of them openly)—he wanted to give me, in the event of a possibly tragic future (in which his children might, for example, have ended up as orphans, just as he had), a political lesson.

I am not a nationalist. But I learned something from my father that I would designate with a word that today is not held in very high esteem: patriotism. And to a certain extent, I've remained a patriot, in a manner I would describe as "latent": my profound disgust with racism, xenophobia, and "Le Penism," and my shame at certain aspects of the present state of France, are certainly based on this, at least in part. I propose this distinction-opposition as a transposition of the one proposed by Sloterdijk in his *Critique of Cynical Reason* between cynicism properly speaking and what he calls "kynicism," that is, briefly stated, between what is imposed from the top down and what, on the contrary, looks up from below. I regard patriotism as a necessity in a nation that is oppressed by another; and it was blindingly obvious that this was indeed the case, at that time, for my father and his friends as well as for General de Gaulle (but the marine officers in Toulon had clearly not seen this), in a France that had just been totally occupied. But I find nationalism insufferable when it's practiced in the other direction. And, sadly, with regard to their own minorities, small- or medium-sized nations often find themselves inhabiting these two mental dispositions simultaneously, and without even realizing it.

More than any other consideration (anti-fascism or anti-racism, for example), it was patriotism that pushed my father to get involved with the Resistance. And he didn't do it halfway, either. A disciple of Alain, a pacifist student, an antimilitarist in the 1920s who had refused (as did his friends at the time) to enter the Officer's Training Program and so voluntarily did his military service as a simple soldier, he nonetheless placed himself in 1943 at the service of a general whose political and religious convictions he hardly shared (and he went his own way when the war was over, precisely for this reason: Their only point in common was a refusal to accept the national degradation represented by the armistice, by the reign of the Germans and their French disciples, the "collaborators").

The decisive political event of his life took place on May 10, 1940. In the months that followed the defeat (I'm using this designation quite deliberately, this "dated" expression for the military collapse of the lamentable French army in the face of the Nazi offensive—the ultimate outcome of the 1930s, a time referred to by the English poet Auden, in his poem written after the invasion of Poland, as "a low dishonest decade," the decade of "appeasement," of nonintervention, and of Munich), as my father reestablished contact with the people he had known, in visits or through letters—as he did the rounds, so to speak—he reviewed all his friendships. The rift was definitive. He never revised the judgments that he made then, in that light, or the decisions he reached concerning certain of the people who had been close to him.

He didn't see Guy Harnois, his best friend, again until after the Liberation. Harnois had been in the Resistance. My father had never doubted this. He often told the story of running into Paul Geniet on a train platform—a friend who had been at the Marseille lycée at the same time as him (my father was in the "*khâgne*" course and Geniet was in the "*taupe*," the preparatory course for the school of civil engineering. They didn't know each other well at the time); they recognized each other, with a few phrases, as being "on the same side." And from then on they always remained connected. Within this camp, however, my father also recognized a second, less grave, but no less distinct division: between those who were favorable to the Allies, but who never acted on this conviction, and those who actually took the risk of engaging in the struggle.

The Resistance was his great moment of freedom. Everything that followed was not only a disappointment but, even more decisively, an "anticlimax" (Paul Bénichou, my first father-in-law, whose own political evolution and destiny were very different, said to me one day (and this made a real impression on me) that at heart my father was what one used to call a "man of action" who had somehow wandered into philosophy, and that it was a true historical misfortune (for which he essentially blamed Stalin (though I don't entirely follow him in this regard)) that after World War II political practice was made more or less impossible for people like him. It's true that his participation in the Resistance is what I, his son, am most proud of in his life. But I never had the slightest sense of rivalry with him, or the desire to emulate his actions, which, in very different historical circumstances, would inspire (sometimes tragically) other sons (a few years younger) of a different generation of "resistance."

17 For a child, the family circle is a pre-Copernican planetary system

For a child, the family circle is a pre-Copernican planetary system; and the result of the Copernican revolution, for the adult melancholic, is often that one leaves, at the now-vacant center of the universe, an absent sun, which is death. This is especially true of families like ours, which were called "numerous" (after I'd studied "grammar," the construction of this idiom, "*a numerous family*," left me momentarily dumbfounded). It would be useless to specify the relative roles of each figure in this representation; the sky is filled with all sorts of "celestial" objects, up to and including the parents' friends and acquaintances, whose identities and points of relation long remain obscure. (In the work of the memorialist Marcel Proust, his identification of the respective links between the two nominally distinct "ways" through his microcosm is akin to the famous identification connecting two stars, cosmologically indistinct and yet nominally separate: Hesperus and Phosphorus, whose apparent distinction and actual indistinction fascinated the astronomers and philosophers of antiquity, and have continued to give logicians a great deal of trouble since the beginning of the century.) The respective positions of these fixed stars, the relative ancientness of each one's light, require the formation of cosmogonic hypotheses that may never be subject to verification in later life.

Over the years, I came to recognize several such configurations in the paternal sky. Canguilhem (I hope I'll be excused for this curt use of his surname, which, in designating not the scholar but the man, might seem excessively familiar, but it's difficult for me to act, without hypocrisy, as though this weren't the way I regularly heard him referred to during my childhood. And I've already related how we children gave him an even more familiar name) belonged to a first circle, the oldest, made up of those school friends from the École Normale with whom my parents had maintained relationships—a circle that gradually decreased with the passage of time, as is inevitable (but what is no doubt remarkable, on the contrary, is that today, more than eighty years later, my father is still close to at least two or three of them).

Death came first for my uncle Frantz, in 1938; and death's decision in this regard had enormous consequences for our family, which I won't confront directly in these pages. But I will mention one other death at this point: that of Simone Weil, who died after moving to London during the Occupation. Not long before leaving France for England, passing through Spain, she visited us in Carcassonne. I remember: she gave me a skittles set.

If I try to identify the unifying factors holding together my parents' band of ENS friends—in what does indeed seem to have been a sort of group or "gang"—notwithstanding their common and contemporary connection to the "Rue d'Ulm," or even the imponderable and indecipherable ramifications of affection (though the common elements that I'm going to mention—intellectual, ethical, and political in nature—could as easily have been found among other people who were not, for whatever reason, their friends), I come up with the following: They were all "literaries" (which simply means "students in the Letters Section of the École Normale Supérieure"); they were all pacifists and antimilitarists; and, more or less directly (indirectly in the case of my father, who was never anyone's "disciple"), they were all students of the "philosopher" Alain.

→ I § 80

Their "Alainist" antimilitaristic pacifism left a few written traces that have recently found their way into a book (which my sister and I rushed to get our hands on as soon as it appeared: *Génération intellectuelle*, by Jean-François Sirinelli): I copy these phrases from a 1928 petition in support of the philosopher Alain, who had been attacked by the future collaborationist Right: "Judging that thought is betrayed when it accepts a law other than that of the object toward which it is directed; approval is expressed by those who are seeking out in good faith the causes of the Great War; and blame by those who would like to suffocate and even to 'dishonor' the free examination of this matter, with the sole purpose of preserving ideas that are accepted only for their utility, which is in fact merely local and provisional." And on the list of signatories that follows, I find most of the names that make up the first "circle" I referred to above.

The troubles between the pacifist Normalians and the administration of the school, as well as the military authorities, on the occasion of the institution of the Officer's Training Program (known in France as the *Préparation Militaire Supérieure*, or PMS) are described at length in Sirinelli's book. My father often spoke of a successful feat carried out by Canguilhem when he knocked over a heavy machine gun during an inspection, and as though by accident, right onto some colonel's foot. And I can't resist the pleasure of relating an incident here that's characteristic of my father's own insolent "style," which he never really abandoned, since it was only a continuation—refined by his studies—of the same audacity demonstrated by the small-town hoodlum from Saint-Jean-du-Var: "Consider for example," writes Sirinelli, "[. . .] Frantz Molino (1904–1938), son of a grade-school inspector, a graduate of the *khâgne* at the Lycée du Parc, a Normalian in 1926, *agrégé* in literature in 1930; or his future brother-in-law, Lucien Roubaud, who was a year behind him and who, like Camille Marcoux, would be brought before the disciplinary council in July 1929.

"Whereas Frantz Molino was exempt from military service and did not have to confront the problem of military preparation, Lucien Roubaud [. . .] showed himself to be far from regular in his attendance of the meetings of the PMS: in 1928–1929, for example, he was [. . .] absent twelve times, and when the director of the École Normale Supérieure demanded an explanation, he justified himself in the following terms:

" 'Monsieur,

" 'I have concluded that it would be utterly useless for me, and for others, if I were to participate in the intensive preparation for an examination, the result of which, as far as I am concerned, is already decided. I will add that I was prevented from taking part in the meetings in Romainville, which I had in fact planned to attend, only by the thought of the *disruptions that my lack of experience could not fail to introduce into the maneuvers.* Respectfully yours.' " (J.-F. S. adds a note: "Arch. Nat. 61 AJ 198." The passage in italics was underlined by its recipient, who wrote the following assessment in the margin: "Reason inadmissible.")

In any event, the gradual narrowing of this first circle (by which I mean the weakening of the bonds of friendship by causes other than the accidental intervention, direct or indirect—though always radical—of death) originated essentially in History (I believe this to be a feature of that terrible "first twentieth century," which lasted from August 1914 up to the death of Joseph Stalin in 1953). For the certainties shared by everyone around 1930 were shaken by two successive traumas, which, like everyone else, I will call, firstly, the Occupation, and then, secondly, the Cold War. I must tell you, and I don't intend this as a value judgment, that my father only maintained confident and close relations with people who took, in the first case, the same side as him, and then, in the second, a position at least not antagonistic to his own.

But perhaps, without undertaking too political a "reading" of his itinerary, I should quite simply have mentioned a supplementary particularity, a hidden parameter—namely, his love of rugby? In the last years of his life as a philosophy professor at the Lycée Voltaire in Paris, impatiently awaiting his retirement in order to devote himself at last to his passion for gardening and his experiments with melons, tomatoes, and strawberries, my father gathered no less than three of his friends from the ENS days around his television set on the occasion of the games played in the Five Nations Tournament: Marcoux (the "Camille Marcoux" mentioned by Sirinelli), Rolland, and Harnois, thus forming a quartet of "old boys" (as my sister called them) whose expert passion and high level of technical knowledge concerning the game greatly impressed me, when it happened by chance that I watched one half of a "France-Wales" match in their company.

As for the teachings of Alain, they contained another ingredient that could also be found among those who continued to be my father's friends: a disdain for money, for honors, for careers. The École, through the competition for the *agrégation* certificate, led to teaching; and it was not a question then of a position in the higher level Teaching Establishment, but rather in a *lycée*. And they took up their places in front of a classroom not as a stopgap, in the expectation of working their way to something nobler (intellectually) and more lucrative. It was a deliberate choice, the mark of a real vocation. Until he went into hiding, my father was a passionate teacher of great conviction (my mother remained so all her life). The rupture of the war, prolonged by his brief time in de Gaulle's Consultative Assembly, and then by numerous and ever more disappointing years as General Inspector of Athletics, into which position he'd been dragged, in a post-Liberation spirit of reformist euphoria, by the rector Sarrailh (while Georges Canguilhem became a General Inspector, both beloved and dreaded, of philosophy teachers), resulted in his losing all pleasure in *lycée* teaching, once the evolving political situation returned him to it.

His patriotic refusal in 1940 was transformed, after the downfall of Hitler, into another kind of rejection: He wanted no part in the world of political racketeering that he saw emerging, even in the very first days of the new era, and that was soon to vanquish the hopes (which it is now considered good form to dismiss as "utopian") of the generation of resisters—that is, his own. But, at least for my father, nothing more or less than this refusal would have been possible.

18 Among a few rare papers that had survived the disorder and the disasters

Among a few rare family papers that had survived the disorder and the disasters of decades, one day my father was struck by a name: Catherine Argentin. He couldn't locate this name in his direct genealogical memory. And this blind spot in his memories was like the insistent trace of an irremediable amputation: the premature death of his parents. This unknown feminine name occupied such a primary place all the more readily in that it was (and still is in 1990) constantly recalled by a homonymy: His interest in sports had led him to follow, on television and in the sports pages of the newspaper, the career of an Italian racing cyclist likewise named Argentin.

I can understand this insistence. Upon reflection, I find that it goes very far back in time for me. It marks, in its way, an essential parental dissymmetry: My maternal family (named "Molino") was omnipresent in our life (and the losses that had so seriously affected this family remained proximate for us, before actually becoming contemporary). But on the other "side" (along the other "way") there were only absences, enumerated, like so many tombstones, by names alone. → I § 81

I have no genealogical curiosity. These days, a recent vogue has sent hundreds of family members scrambling for the more or less deeply buried traces of their ancestors. City halls are flooded with demands for birth records, churches for baptismal certificates. One can even buy guidebooks written for this new type of gold prospector. Some of them have thrown themselves into the search in hopes of discovering some famous or simply notable name from the past among their predecessors (and it matters little what reasons they discover, whether worthy or vile, behind this survival in the halls of posterity), allowing them to share—if only within the circle of the people they know— some apparent resemblance with the true modern princes, TV stars.

Still others (stimulated by some such story appearing in one of the newspapers) hope to track down a great-great American uncle whose fabulous estate is still unclaimed (because, foreseeing what would happen, the great-great uncle would never allow himself to marry a foreigner, and thus he died "intestate," as the notaries in crime novels say), and would naturally be poised to fall, at last, into their (legitimate) hands. Most of them, of course, do it out of simple sheeplike curiosity (it's "something one does," as Françoise Rosay says to Michel Simon in *Drôle de drame*).

And, so, not long ago, I received a letter from a Roubaud in Nice, who had seen my name on *Télérama* (not because I'm a TV star, but because of a program on Raymond Queneau, my respected master), and who sent me his "tree," asking if we might not, by chance, be "cousins." If I had responded, I would have said no, not to my knowledge. I would have added that Roubaud is not such a rare name in Provence. There are thirty-three in the 1987 edition of the Paris telephone book. There's even a wine from the Gard region called Château-Roubaud, which from time to time makes admirable efforts at publicity, but has not yet managed to hoist itself up very far in the viticultural hierarchy. And, perhaps most notably, there are, between the coast and the Porquerolles Islands, among the Hyères Islands, two rather dangerous little islets called Big (resp. Small) Roubaud Island (which the maps persist in calling "Ribaud," as Pierre Oster has pointed out to me). I will gladly abandon the wine to my Niçois "colleague," if he consents to leave me these two reefs as cousins. I find them to be excellent candidates for the role of eponymous ancestors of my father.

It seems to me that this sudden surge of interest in uncovering one's ancestors is in fact one sign, among others, of a general disinterest for the living past, the past as it's woven together by the direct transmission, from generation to generation, out of gestures, memories, and stories. Paper genealogy, essentially archival in nature, leads one to do no more than imitate at the individual level the representation of history as presented in mass-marketed journals and books, a history that's already replacing the unanimously scorned "knowledge" one is taught at school (just as participation, whether active or passive (in front of the television screen), in the "spelling championships of France" allows one to dispense with actually knowing the language, from speaking it differently than the anchors on the "primetime news," from reading its literatures with a recognition of the difference between those that elevate the language and those that degrade it).

And, at the same time, actual individual memory has become infinitely dull and short. Memories and curiosities are shoved aside more and more rapidly as obsolete, in a "stock rotation" that affects not only books in bookstores, films in theaters, and the music on "Walkmans," but also, and at least as rapidly, yogurt brands, ideas, opinions and convictions, scientific theories, animal species, friendships, loves. Most of these genealogical trees will end up in the overstuffed city dumps, along with the telltale signs of other equally fleeting fads, when the people who began to assemble them (almost all of them now in the "third age," and thus more or less confusedly aware of the less-than-uplifting effects of this acceleration of "social change") lose their ardor (as they pass to the "fourth age," and then to the fifth and last, that of the grave). Thus, twenty-five years ago, it was discovered that minor languages, particularly Occitan (which for me is always Provençal), would soon disappear. There followed a sort of belated flourishing, which, alas, passed rather quickly.

Which is why, wishing in no way to abandon myself to this general inclination, I am nonetheless concerned by the uncertainty I find in myself, in the process of bringing forth (and thus destroying, burning) the central image of the fig tree in Toulon, which inspired this "sketch of a portrait of my father," an uncertainty concerning all the names he tried to preserve from oblivion, and to transmit to us. This is all the more true when I find that my sister and my brother have in fact retained even fewer of them than I have; as if, implicitly, I were the one in charge of this transmission, and have shown myself unworthy of the task. Perhaps it's not too late.

When the **Project** that I had conceived, along with its double, **The Great Fire of London** (not the one that I'm pursuing now, line by line and day after day, but the ambitious novel that was abandoned), encountered the fig tree-image, it would have done so doubly, at once metaphorically and directly, in a way that was narratively as well as rhythmically abstracted, transformed. And in thus encountering this image, they (the **Project** and its double, the novel) would have subjected it to a formal mutation that dispersed it and then interwove it into their own specific architectures, such that they too came to be determined—without my recognizing what I now find so evident in this image (but no doubt both **Project** and novel had to collapse in order for me to understand it)—by the dark, fragrant, beneficent-malevolent shade of the **fig tree** in which my fore-life moved and was enclosed.   → Bif B § 146

Chapter 3

Rue d'Assas

19 The garden was enclosed by walls.

The garden was enclosed by walls. In each part of this place, this territory, this possession, **at almost each and every point within it,** for more than six years, more than two thousand days, **I was there**: from sky to earth, from sun to rain, from day to night, from winter to autumn, in the fullness of its space, its closed volume, crossed and re-crossed by the movements of my body, by my gaze, my gaze moving ceaselessly, displaced or shifting or fixed, attentive or distracted; atoms of this gaze, in its Brownian motion, in its thermic agitation, knocking against the walls, the barriers that encompass this space: a world within the world. A little world. **I go toward it, from a nocturnal bed-room to a garden; a sunny garden, but a closed garden,** *hortus*

→ I § 82   *conclusus,* **following a path through memory leading out from a center; a path, but a labyrinthine path.** I tug at my thread, but the thread **is** the labyrinth.

How can I reach this place, setting out from the cold windowpane left behind in the last lines of my <u>first chapter</u>? from where shall I plunge in, in order to speak about it?

There are <u>two routes</u>:

—The first: I slip through the window, leaving the room on the third floor of the house: it's an ordinary day, under an ordinary sun. Describe it? But from up there one couldn't see the whole garden; and one saw more than just the garden, too. **I saw far beyond it, over the walls, toward other gardens; a slope, which soon became steeper, all the way to the Aude River.** By descending through the air, then; down to the ground, through the sky, changing direction in midair and turning the corner of the wall, looking all around me; an impossible trajectory for an impossible being? I do in fact have a memory of such a levitating movement, a memory of those imagined and repeated miracles: a multiplication of my points of view, as I swam through air that was suddenly able to support me: a sea of air.

—Or else (the second) turning my back to the window, leaving the room, going down the stairs. And here I encounter something emblematic of my story: the site of a hesitation, and therefore of a choice. I can follow "myself" down one route, or down the other. But I want to follow both of them. I chose to begin this chapter with the first way; but I also intend to follow the other one, and I will offer it, in this branch, as an alternative path of reading, in the form of an insertion into the story: not a brief, momentary insertion, an interpolation, but a second kind of insertion that I call a bifurcation. The two routes differ radically: the first, the one I am choosing here, is not only imaginary but virtually instantaneous: I would go out through the window, I would leap into the air, I would float, I would turn the corner of the building, I would land, I've landed. Taking the second route, I opened the door at the end of the room, I went out, I went down the stairs, I passed through the house, from top to bottom. I was enclosed in time, I took the time needed for this. I opened the doors to each room, one by one, I entered: **I was there**.

→ I § 83

Once in the garden, how would I move around? By following its limits, along the inside boundaries of the territory (the walls, the house, the gate), by touching them, verifying the reality of my confinement in the place, the reality of the stones, real because solid, and of the protonic persistence of matter, as durable as the universe: by advancing in a circular motion in one direction, or in the other, going all the way around, coming back to the center—but what center? There was a center; I remember now. I can begin from there. Because I identify myself as located at this center, spontaneously, at the very moment when I ask myself where to begin, in order to describe the garden; that is, at the moment when I make the lines of this ongoing interrogation appear on my screen, contemporary with the interrogation itself. (And I proceed according to an explicit rule of the composition of my story, which I've respected from its very first moments: to include the circumstances of its composition.)

This center was a point in space located in the past, occupied by an immobile body; the position of the body (my own) was as follows: knees on the ground, where the little rocks, mixed with the rough dirt, dug in; elbows on the horizontal surface of the bench, hands over eyes; and the hands were pressing down on the eyes; with the palm of each hand I pressed on my eyes, which filled with light, a sort of *piezo*-light crossed by flashes and colors within that deliberate and momentary darkness. A center, then, but a <u>blind center</u>. In order to see, I had to take my hands off of my eyes, after an interval of time determined by a count, a counting out loud. (This was the primary rule of a game. It was the center of the game.) (But now I hear nothing: the voice, my voice has evaporated from this image.)

<u>The simple rules of this game</u>: The seeker would be in the position I've described (the seeker was me, me or someone else: one of my brothers, or my sister, one of my cousins, one of our respective classmates, one of the Picolo children, visitors . . .). During the duration of the count, in which the seeker's eyes had to remain covered by his hands, and closed as well (if he wasn't cheating), the other players went off to find a place to hide, at a greater or lesser distance: being close was advantageous, as the next rule will make clear, but rife with danger. Far away, one could be invisible—but then one was far away. This was the player's dilemma. The name of this game (what would it be if it hadn't been given a name?) was, is:

Go-Creeping.

The rules <u>(continued)</u>: When the count was finished (at 33, for example), the seeker removed his hand or hands from his eyes, opened them, and tried to see the players: either they were hiding, or they were moving. The players usually moved. They had the option of staying hidden, invisible; but in that case, while they couldn't lose, they also couldn't win. It followed that they were losing. The seeker had to find, to **see** the players, his opponents, and he had to say so. This **saying** was a ritual, it was part of the game. One said: "<u>X at such and such a place</u>"—"behind the pine tree!", or "in the washbasin!", or "behind the apricot tree!". . . If the declaration was correct, the designated player was immediately **out of the game**, and had lost. The others kept playing.

The seeker could be wrong in two ways:

—There was no one in the designated place, only a shadow, a branch moving in the wind. In that case, no one came out of hiding.

—Or else, whoever was hiding there wasn't actually X but Y. Y wouldn't budge. And the seeker, even if he now understood that it was Y, was not allowed to repeat his announcement with a different name. Being able to simply enumerate the players in such instances would have made the game unplayable. (Despite the fact that the seeker was sure that there really was someone there.)

The rules (concluded): In any case, the seeker didn't have time for that: the goal of the game was to reach the seeker's bench without being seen, but especially without being seen and denounced. Thus everyone attempted to move forward while eluding the seeker's gaze. They crept over the pebbles, over pine needles, they jumped up, ran from one hiding place to another, through bushes and around trees. They crossed the distances within the garden. And sometimes the seeker didn't even have to say where X was, because X had been caught in motion, out in the open, without any obstacle between him and the seeker, and this incontestable meeting of gazes, via the law of the "inverse return of looks" was, by common agreement, proof of its own exactitude: The seeker and X saw each other, therefore, X had been seen. But even if X had been seen and knew it, if he had been seen seeing and running toward the bench from a nearby hiding place, that alone did not suffice to send him out among the losers. For the seeker had to say not only that he saw, but whom he saw. And if he perceived X running toward him, he might be surprised (he had expected to see Y, not X; he had, through deduction or intuition, guessed that Y was behind the box tree, the big washbasin), and he might hesitate, and hesitate too long. Then X would have the time to reach the bench and touch it. And if he touched the bench, it was too late for the seeker. It was he who had lost, and who had to give up his place. (The moment of this touch, of the hand on the wood of the bench, its anteriority with respect to the calling of the name, was the source of numerous challenges and disputes. And yet the game on the whole managed to overcome these obstacles.)

The other players then came out of their last hiding places: so that's where they were! The seeker had definitely seen something moving on the left, but he didn't think it was . . . , he thought it was . . . ! Each hider had his favorite itineraries. But he had to vary them, and to disguise any revealing particularities of his clothes, constantly change his habits. The rules discouraged the players from forming coalitions. But it was hard to prove it if they had. (And anyway it hardly mattered, since any such collusion was useless in the end: there could only be one winner.) For example (and this came about quite naturally, without premeditated plans, without alliances), one could reach the point where two or three players were close enough to jump out, to run together, to over-whelm the seeker who would be unable to respond quickly enough to call out everyone's names. But what to do if two players touched the bench at the same time? who was the winner then? I've forgotten. But this must have happened, without a doubt.

20 If I place myself, mentally, in an attitude of voluntary recollection

If I place myself, mentally, in an attitude of voluntary looking, and if I think of myself in this garden, **I find myself again almost invariably at this same spot: on my knees in the dirty gravel, positioned at the center of the bench, elbows leaning on the bench, eyes closed, in the position of seeker in the game; among all the possible locations of my body in play, my recollection chooses this one in preference to all the others (I know that there is noth-ing I could be doing there except this: playing "Go-Creeping"); I do not spontaneously seize on any of the ordinary hiding places of a player in mo-tion** (which were often, however, my own); a sort of automatic pilot of vision begins to operate, directing me toward the bench.

Now, I feel and I describe this as an **image**, an internalized image of what I see when my eyes are open (but they're closed), an image therefore of a scene I do not see, of something that the player I was did not see, wasn't supposed to see, except internally, concentrating on the moment that would begin after the count was over, and internally seeing the bench and the ground next to it with perfect clarity, having seen them so many times before in identical cir-cumstances. (Circumstances which no doubt engendered the clarity and in-sistence of my present image. This clarity and intensity are indisputable, since,

→ I § 88 according to the hierarchy of a **meditation on the five senses** (one that conforms with my own experience), the image goes so far as to restore a certain impression of touch to me as well: the roughness of the dry earth.)

I kneel blindly in front of the bench, and yet **I see; I see and feel the ground against my knees, the wood of the bench against my elbows, and the pres-sure of my hands on my eyes; I see, if I want, at the same time, the focal points of the game, the players' possible hiding places, their itineraries,**

their faces (I recognize them all, these places and these faces). If seeing is always an immediate knowledge based on memory, if a particular memory always restores me to a position of seeing-as-remembering, here I am simultaneously capable of seeing before seeing again and of seeing what was about to be seen. I'm not surprised, exactly, by this doubling of the seer (paradoxical only for a "naturalistic" conception of memories), but rather by what emerges upon further reflection.

For the initial image of the story of this branch presents a substantial analogy with the situation of the seeker in the game: in that image I am facing the windowpane covered with the breath of the frost, I am facing the night, blind to what is there on the other side of the windowpane, which however I can see, outside, up above, in the wintry air, above the snowy garden. The image of the game is not however a **primary image**. The primary image is that of the windowpane, and not simply because I have posited it as such in the story. Even if it isn't necessarily located before the others (the image of the painted windowpane of the Passive Defense, for example, or the image of the train window covered with black soot (and these images themselves also present this quality of a "blind view")), even if I can move toward it by setting out from other images, in a path through memory that would in fact be indifferent to chronology, it is the one that arises first when I think of *this* past, was indeed the one that arose first when I began to write about this past, which arose **so that** I would begin to write.

Relating all these examples to one another, by means of a certain abstraction (and thus establishing a set of relations—determined by resemblance—not between things seen, but between some of the significant elements in the respective situations of the seer), I cannot fail to detect a resemblance of even greater proportions: despite all my efforts to move forward in this "treatise on memory" (which is how I've designated "**the great fire of London**" elsewhere, and that's what it is, at least in part), it's practically impossible for me to do so without returning over and again to material conditions that are precisely and strangely similar (from the point of view of the abstraction I just referred to) to the ones that accompany all the images in question: I must situate myself, physically, within a "fore-night," with darkness reigning beyond the windows (at this moment, in the present that surrounds these words, it is nighttime to my right. The only lights that reach me are those produced by the minimal glow of the lamp close to the bed (it has two settings, and I've left it on the nightlight setting, the weakest), and by the screen of the Macintosh Plus on which I bring forth my narration).

It is not complete and total darkness (that would be stupid), but as deep a darkness as possible nonetheless, and above all one that is a metaphor, perhaps even an allegory of my enterprise as a whole (at least in this aspect). Which also means, inversely, that the pre-morning darkness in which I work on this prose has perhaps produced, as a sort of reverberation, the narrative selection of these particular images before all others (images contemporary with a dream and with the pseudo-axiomatic sequence that follows the dream's articulation in prose: the singularized fragments in the "**bold**" type of the Macintosh are descriptions of **pure images**, or of short sequences of images, first written contemporaneously with the chain of fictive deductions presented as an <u>elucidation</u> of the dream in <u>branch one, chapter 5</u>).

As I advance with great difficulty—desperately slowly, in this chapter— during these first days of July 1990, on the Rue d'Amsterdam, I have tried to persuade myself that, rather than the fatigue and saturation of an academic year reaching its end, and its gradual dispersal into all sorts of other tasks, the very simple reason for my recent virtual standstill was a difficulty having more to do with matters of climate than anything else: it's becoming light too early, nothing more, and since the untimely irruption of daylight into the room (I don't say the bedroom, since I now live in a single room in which I do other things besides sleep), and even more the certainty of this irruption, leaves me only a short time after waking up, it constitutes in itself an excellent cause for all my hesitations, a justification, therefore, of my "delay."

But the analogical situation that I've just discovered leads to a more satisfying hypothesis (if not a more plausible one), narratively speaking: namely that there is a deep resistance to unveiling (by establishing relations between the image-memories) a deeper, more generalized function beneath something I had previously considered to be no more than an utterly contingent preference for certain bizarre working conditions. (This is evidenced in chapter 1, where in order to note this peculiarity in the composition of my book, I use the vocabulary of desire and preference (in words which themselves almost repeat similar words in branch one): "<u>I don't like</u> to wake up in the daylight . . ." "<u>I need</u> only the precarious night-on-the-wane, the night that belongs to no one . . .")

It would be a matter, in this case, of an <u>obliged repetition</u>. In other words (according to this hypothesis), I did not simply choose these arrangements; they did not strike me as appropriate based on a whim; they did not become reinforced and indispensable because of a longstanding practice, out of habit. They were necessary. They were part of the → I § 89–90 <u>initial conditions</u> of my memory, at its origin. The hypothesis thus contains another circumstantial element, which I likewise find hovering around each of the images involved: a feeling of protection. (Branch one, chapter 1, § 1: "I need my night to be fading yet still dark in order to find the courage to go on, even pointlessly, with my work at hand.") The darkness outside guards against an imprecise and indecipherable threat. Like the ostrich of "popular wisdom," I bury my head in the sand of night, be it real or invented (I find a word among all words, I choose and display it—*sand*—because the word "sand," as used in the poetic genre of the *blason*, designates the color of night). I enclose myself in the night (like a prudent Empedocles: a legend in which he, rather than Simonides of Ceos, was the inventor of the Arts of Memory, claims that he put out his eyes so as not to be blinded by the images of the present). I enclose myself in the night: in order to **see**.

21 The main problem for the seeker

The main problem for the seeker in the game was that the spot where the search had to take place, the bench, the center of the game, was a center: which means that around it, all around it, there was a space the size of a garden. One had to survey an entire horizon in all its 360 degrees. But it's impossible to see everywhere at once: one would not only have to have a hundred eyes, like Argos, but also eyes in the back of one's head (a property considered completely natural, however, by the "seekers of memories"). I feel, at this moment, behind me (at this moment of "diction"), uncomfortably, the threat of a sudden and unforeseen "attack" by a child player—I anticipate the unpleasant start in response to a hand suddenly placed on my shoulder.

But in the real conditions of the game such a possibility was very unlikely. For the bench, parallel to the main façade of the house, was separated from it by a terrace that was slightly lower down (some sixty centimeters, down a small set of steps, three I think). And the low wall of brick (?) (of faux marble? of cement?) along the edge of this terrace, covered with red tiles (?) and topped by flowerpots, was itself separated from the terrace by a narrow path. Unless one slipped by without being seen entering it, or took a position there during the seeker's blind count—a ploy that could be noticed from the sound of footsteps moving off only a short distance and then heading down the steps—it was practically impossible to get from there to the bench by climbing over between the flowerpots, and even in this case the assault could not be directly from behind the watchful head, since that's where the **well** was. Therefore, one would have to run at top speed up the little steps at one of the two entry points, to the right or to the left of the bench; and in that case one would not arrive from behind, but from the side, fully within the seeker's field of (non-paradoxical) vision, as in the majority of other, ordinary cases.

Moreover, this way out (behind the bench and to the left) was the farthest away and was very much out in the open. As for the entrance to the terrace on the right side of the bench, it involved a third system of steps going down from the "vegetable" and "ornamental" section of the garden (the one beneath the bedroom from which I fictively launched myself in a spinning levitation at the beginning of this chapter). It was a very unfavorable hiding place. The seeker could thus be almost certain that there was no reason to fear a surprise attack from these regions. And yet, the apprehension remains, even after so many years (I just felt it). Perhaps it's from the house, dark and silent, that this vague threat emanates, a superstitious fear of shadows? or from the well, mythic dwelling place of truth? a shadow, but of what truth?

Having chosen the bench as a center (or having been placed, without really choosing it, in this center of memory), I see the garden. **I see the garden** in a way that is, I know, more complete than I was actually able to see it: multiple visual rays "turn the corners" of the trees, the walls, the foliage (my gaze "passes through" the foliage as though it were transparent. And in fact it was, with the absence of leaves in winter.) But this vision varies even more from the real view I must have had—the one made possible by optics and by reason. For in this vision the garden is not that amorphous and immobile slice of Euclidian space, populated by objects that are themselves stable and calm, as (or as a group of) exact **"piction(s)"** (water color(s), photograph(s)) would "present" it to the eye today, such that one would then be easily persuaded, faced with such evidence, that one is seeing the area again, that one is recognizing it, whereas one is in fact lazily falsifying the much stranger, and much more "distorted," emergence of actual memories.

Seen with the eye of the game, the **points of intensity** in the landscape were very different: they were the ones where something significant, ludically speaking, happened, could happen, or might have happened. These stressed points, in the sense of a Theory of Rhythm "extended" by imagination into space, into these spaces (hiding places, surprise bursts of movement carved into images, sudden discoveries), like stars of high and variable magnitude in the telescopic view of a nocturnal sky—these were the points that turned out to be both more likely and more rapidly sought by the gaze than others (there are even zones on this "map" of the garden that are almost completely deserted, and therefore at a virtually infinite distance (as though at an infinite distance, one might say, whenever my return to the past does not find them again: each one a "well" or a pit with unknown contents, from which the memory-light cannot escape)).

The result of this was that the gaze's trajectory in reaching these points was mentally shorter than the ones that led it to indifferent points, to points of less ludic weight but much closer in terms of the ordinary physical conception of distances. I would say (though it may sound a little pretentious) that the metrics of the garden, from the point of view of the game, were not the usual metrics described as Euclidean; and that a map of the garden drawn according to this new system of metrics would appear rather deformed when compared with that of a topographical survey. (But I imagine that the principles of these metrics are perhaps not so esoteric after all.

Indeed, a morning newspaper recently published a map of Europe based on a similar principle (although its inspiration was apparently less subjective): the large cities of this geographic entity were represented in such a way that their respective distances on the paper were not the good old atlas-like kilometric distances given by the earth's surface—those provided to us by the approximations of geology—but rather the distances determined by the "access time" from a central point, in this case Paris, when traveling on the High Speed Trains, such as they will no doubt exist at the dawn of the third millennium (if millennia have dawns). One was thus provided the peculiar "vision" of a continent recognizable according to our usual sense of a map, but deformed, as though we were being invited to plunge into a past epoch of the Earth (in this case, on the contrary, a future one), before or after much shifting of tectonic plates; or (an even closer resemblance) as though we were looking at one of those medieval maps constructed perhaps implicitly from similar topological constraints (distances associated with the durations of journeys). (If they had taken into account other cities absent from the network, where the High Speed Trains would not stop, the "shape" of Europe construed in this way would have been even stranger, and unrepresentable on a flat surface—but closer to the one I encounter in the garden.))

But distance to the eye is not the only parameter affected in my vision of the garden (what I'm saying here, of course, is in fact largely generalizable. I'm using this example not only because it's very clear, but also because the game and the place I'm speaking of have a metaphorical-allegorical role in my pseudo-novel, which you are reading now: "**the great fire of London**"). There's a sort of reversal of the zones of light and shadow (which my "Macintosh" manual would call an inverse video mode): the places marked by the game were above all the hidden ones that concealed the players. And the sunny, visible places were on the contrary almost without importance. The seeker's gaze did not perceive them, as it were.

Thus, there are "blank" regions on the map (regions that are shadowy in being remembered), regions that, in the past, in the Vidal-Labache atlas, were marked as unexplored, *terra incognita*. And there are, even more exceptionally (and here the comparison must once again refer to maps of the stars), veritable "black holes." A third parameter present in the game, but far exceeding it, comes from the central "game" of life. This is an emotional parameter that renders some of the places on the map "forbidden," as it were, to contemplation. There is one in particular, a place that is occupied by an intense summer light but that has become a "black hole" to my memory. It is located on the left, a few paces from the bench and behind it. I will not look toward it now (and in any case not in this branch).

22 On my knees in front of the green bench, my bare knees

On my knees in front of the green bench (I don't see the green, I don't see any color, but I know (?) it's green, so I call it green), **on my bare knees** (since I feel the ground, the dirt and pebbles on the ground), **between the wooden slats of the bench I saw the green leaves, greener and darker than the scratched and flaking paint covering the wood, I saw the boxwood leaves curled up like shells, the glossy leaves of the spindle trees, which had fallen from the massive heights of the spindle trees rising up before the bench, parallel to the terrace, rising in parallels right next to the bench, between the two walkways.** (I write "heights," but the actual dimensions were certainly much more modest than the ones in this vision, which has remained lodged in a child's body. Moreover, I do not, strictly speaking, see the bench—I am unable to back up far enough to see it in its entirety. The <u>generic moment</u> of seeking, concentrated with innumerable actual moments in this position, attracts and absorbs my vision. And just as the physical color eludes the image, the word "green" added to "bench" nonetheless appears stuck to it, like a label.)

During the game, the dense mass of the spindle trees blocked the seeker's view: a wall full of holes, not really opaque, not opaque enough to conceal the movements behind it, but enough to impede the identification of outlines, silhouettes, and faces, and so it was perfect for the game. With the exception of the territories on the right side of the garden, occupied by vegetables, fruit, flowers, or animals (rabbits, a pig), territories that were (in principle) strictly forbidden, and (on the left side), with the exception of the terrace, the large washbasin, and the "garage" (no car) partly shared with the adults (who had more limited, and more utilitarian, ideas concerning the use of these spaces), the entire territory between the walls (everything was between the walls), from the ground all the way up to the highest accessible branches of the pines, was **in play.** The game or games determine the paths of my recognition, of what I recognize today.

When it was time for the game to begin, I automatically **looked to the left first; I took my hands away from my eyes, I opened my eyes and looked up from the bench, I scanned the circular space in one glance, rapid but continuous**, in a movement I would call "temporal," clockwise (in the direction opposite to that referred to as "trigonometric," which, however, I see as more "natural," because of longstanding mathematical habits. I understand very well that in the past, mechanical restrictions "forced" one to translate the time measured by clocks into a spatial movement, a circular and endlessly repeated sweeping motion that absorbs/effaces minutes and hours, and I understand too that the model selected for the measurement of time was based on the apparent motion of a shadow on a sundial; and

→ I § 91 yet I believe that I could easily have been converted to the idea of aligning the movement of the needles with that of a vector turning in the direction considered mathematically "positive," that is, counterclockwise).

On the left, a walkway; on the other side of the walkway, another clump of plants and trees; like the dense row of spindle trees facing the bench (but the bench, in fact, has its back turned to them: it's only in the game that the spindle trees and the bench faced each other), **it did not reach, it did not go down to the terrace (all the regions planted with bushes and trees were (modest) hills); on its lower left edge** (think of it as drawn on a map), **at the end of the wall, against which the tallest trees stood, higher than the wall, it went as far as the fig tree (this fig tree, thanks to which we were able to leave the house without using the door, stood just outside of it); its eastern edge (the central walkway) was punctuated by some *pulumuse* bushes** (vegetable beings in the form of hemispherical bushes belonging to a plant species important enough for us to have given them a name other than the common name in the language, which in fact I'm unable to recall)**.**

The central walkway went around this latter clump, separating it at its northern limit from the other "hill," at the latitude of the central roundabout. There were several steps by which one could climb up to a first lookout "station": the basin of a fountain attached to the wall, surrounded by its own thin wall in the shape of a slightly flattened Ω. (One reached it, alternatively, through the leafy jungle, **darkened by the trees and the wall; darkened by the glossy leaves, green with white marks on them, as though marbled with white; darkened especially by the walnut tree whose shade was humid, and black, and bitter,** through a path that certainly had not been part of the original layout (one had to stoop down when walking on it)); **the bottom of the round fountain on the wall was covered with dead leaves; I can make water squirt from it, from the flat wall, splashing down on the leaves.**

If my gaze shifts suddenly from the bench to this fountain (by one of two paths: by moving around the clump of trees just mentioned, or by passing through it, bending down below the branches of the large trees), this is, of course, because the memory of the game favors a spot where one could easily be concealed (today my gaze readily follows this imagined displacement,

**sees the fountain, sees the bottom of the fountain, wet and reddish brown
with dead leaves, pine needles**). This is a fixed point, a living point on the
map of the garden, as defined by the game. But there are other games, which
bring other points to life, or the same ones, but differently. And this point is
the unique place for another game, a game involving a fixed point, a game of
immobility.

**The edge of the fountain was very narrow, but with a minimal amount of
skill one could climb up onto it and stand there; I had invented the practice of standing there in the following way: upright and immobile, with an
absolute immobility, as if I had become a stone, a statue, like one of those
statues adorning the fountains of ornamental gardens, placed along the
edges of their basins; I stood on the narrow edge of stone, and I exerted tremendous effort to attain the inner rectitude of the nonliving, the sectarian
fixity of mineral forms; I gave myself over, fanatically, to this immobility.**
One soon sinks (I remember this) into an empty intoxication, into a desert-
like exaltation, a jubilatory catatonia.

My first statue experience, certainly the one that marked the invention of
this game (I don't see this experience as such, but I deduce it from its consequences) in its extreme prolongation (an extended duration is its essential
constraint) had such an effect on those who witnessed it (my brothers and
my sister, all younger than me) that they went to inform our parents of the
anxiety caused by this sudden apparent privation of locomotive faculties (this
event later became a story: "thus," as it is said in the *Prose Lancelot*, "do we
know it still"). Certainly what was most unsettling about this petrifaction had
to do with the uncomfortable strangeness of the position. This is not how one
sleeps, and sleep is the only natural state of immobility (one closes the eyes of
the dead so that they can sleep—one naturalizes them through a simile-sleep).
In any case, the statue-player had to keep his or her eyes open.

This imitation of immobility is one aspect of the art of the mime. On the
corners of very busy streets, on market squares, mimes in makeup looking
like wax figures or personalities from the Musée Grévin or "Mme. Tussauds"
(in the London flea markets), reappear from time to time, though more and
more infrequently, to fascinate credulous passersby. But that wasn't my game:
it wasn't a game of disguise or of "aping," but rather a profession of faith, the

affirmation of a momentary hermit's vocation. Later, when I read the description of the "stylites," those ornamental hermits of the Alexandrian desert who immobilized themselves into salt statues of <u>contemplation</u>, I recognized a vaguely similar intention. But if they presented themselves in this way as a spectacle, it was for a single but simultaneously internal and external spectator: God. As for us, we played only for ourselves.

23 "Never the dawn with great shouts blueing the washrooms"

"Never dawn with great shouts blueing the washrooms / Dawn, lost soap in the water of black rivers . . ." With these two alexandrines by Robert Desnos, a dense crowd of images comes to me. These lines are supreme <u>effectors of memory</u>; (and I've already quoted them, in fact, precisely in connection with this same family of images, in branch 1, § 142, in a commentary on the "knowledge of the dream" (an interpolation from § 60 of that same branch, of which this is therefore a "variant") (a new "theoretical" variety of prose is here revealed!) (but perhaps this is more an "expansion" than a variant) (elsewhere I will develop the "theory," or more exactly what I call the "<u>theoretical fiction</u>," behind these entities)). Why is this? (and why, at a remove of several years, in almost the same way?) Perhaps because I learned them by heart, and retained them, because I learned them very early, because they are by Desnos, one of the poets I've loved for so long a time, and still prefer to the other surrealists; perhaps also because, among the numerous alexandrines by Desnos that I know, they have a particular rapidity (truly "Hermogenian") that stirs up the whirlwind of irresistible images all the more effectively, because their explicit meaning appeals to them so directly; perhaps, finally, because they begin this proliferation of images without really completing it, because the two other lines of the quatrain weaken, for me, its beginning, particularly the final one ("Dawn will never whiten upon this livid night / Nor on our trembling fingers, nor on our empty glasses" (I never have trembling fingers at the end of a night, and I certainly never see the dawn turning white on an empty glass)). They leave (in my inner vision of the quatrain) the first two in suspense, on the crest of a rising voice, announcing other mysterious continuations that will be poetically more sound, but that will never be written.

Among these images there is, extricable, identifiable, the image of the large washbasin itself: the washbasin of this garden on the Rue d'Assas where I "am" at that moment, as I now remember it. On the clock dial of my mental representation of the garden, which I pass over in thought in the temporal or "clockwise" direction, it is noon at the washbasin (it could be midnight, since, absurdly, clocks identify in a single apogee the two extreme and antithetical moments of the solar revolution, the light and the dark. But I'm thinking of noon). (So, on the fictive dial, it would have been six o'clock in the morning for the seeker, in the dust at the foot of the bench, and nine o'clock for the "stylite" standing precariously on the narrow edge of the fountain, petrified in the past in his game of immobility.)

The light, inwardly reflected and poured into this place by recollection (a very strange light indeed!), **an unceasing light, dissolves in the moving water like a piece of black soap** (this simile is very nearly absurd, I know, but I'm not trying to produce a particular stylistic effect here, and certainly not a "poetic" effect); **I see the cloud of light invading the water, a murky illumination; I see it as a sort of materially embodied light, coagulated into the substance of a piece of soap, a black-brown and translucid piece of soap, which, dissolving and disintegrating, turned the water blue in the first of the two separate sinks that made up the large washbasin.**

The washbasin was made of a gray substance, a dull pseudo-marble rendered shiny and smooth by the water and the soap, on the slightly inclined surface of its edges, worn down by the washing, by the blows (the "shouts" of the poem?) **of the wooden beaters on the cloth; the overflowing water, perpetually streaming, picked up the light and absorbed it into itself, then dissolved, as though born from the soap, from the dawn, cool rather than cold; the cold roiling water, on the surface of the washbasin's edges, slick with soap, I know that I feel it on my hand when I dip it in, my numb fingers, next to the sound of the cloth submerged, twisted, pulled back out, struck, submerged again, rinsed, dripping; these are the "great shouts" of the laundry, the sheets white in the daylight emerging from the dark soapy night; the water turns blue from it.**

The washbasin was at the end and to the left of the central walkway, which separated the useful half of the garden on the right (with the vegetables, the fruit, and the animals bound for the table) from the other half on the left—it was once a "pleasure garden" and was later abandoned more or less without reserve to our childish barbarisms (the former occupied the half-plane of "positive" abscissae, in a "Cartesian" representation, while the latter contained the first "negative" coordinates, according to the same division). The ludic side was itself divided into four by walkways intersecting in the form of a cross. The washbasin was built at the edge of a small "hill," similar to the one, even lower down, that stood in front of the bench, similar also to the one that separated the fig tree from the fountain (above the fountain ("higher up" or "farther north," according to the chosen representation), one could see the fourth hill, the most pronounced). Behind the washbasin was the wall, and behind the wall, the street, the Rue d'Assas.

In the water I see the sky, despite the roof; a sky sprinkled with small flakes of cloud; in the water too the purple buds, slightly sweet, that fall from the Judas tree; I see the fragile squadron of paper boats: sheets of paper torn from a notebook, pages of old homework (English exercises, philosophical compositions, already graded, annotated, obsolete); half sheets, quarter sheets folded according to an immutable principle (whether one is making a paper ship or the pseudo-motor of an airplane, the first folding gestures are the same); **newspapers requisitioned for the construction of large heavy "battleships," quickly soaked with water, absorbing the water, sunk in soft pasty masses, formless, made from paper with the awful smell of awful paper from an awful wartime printer; when the identification marks, in capital letters, of the "vessels" in the battle fleet soon disappeared, became blurry, seeping into the paper, ruined by the water from the wash, by the splashing water falling violently in the sinks, by the allegorical bombardments of the imaginary canons arrayed on their soapy edges.**

The presence of a roof, the certainty of the existence of a roof over the washbasin casts doubt on my vision of clouds in the water, but this vision is no less certain for that. In fact, the respective position of both of them escapes me. In any case, it wasn't a washroom-building, as one finds in Mediterranean village squares, but a simple shelter against the rain used for drying laundry. I don't know exactly "where to place it." It seems to me that one of its sides rested against the wall by the street. And perhaps it did not in fact entirely cover the washbasin itself.

My resuscitating vision is not only composite, it's also selective. Even though

I imagine, as I said (counter to all physical probability), that I have an "aerial" view of the garden as a whole (and in this case a reconstruction by geometrical deduction places the center of this view in the air, above the "vegetable garden," somewhere between the window of our bedroom and the ground, and still more bizarrely obliges the eye that "sees" to place itself in front of a surface that would be almost "upright," as in one of those moments during an airplane flight when the plane tilts downward and turns, before descending onto the runway), the "photographic" completeness of such a view is largely fallacious, since focusing the slightest attention on any "detail" brings out gaps, blurry spots, actual "holes" filled only by the mental application of gray sutures: a gray "philosophical" matter, without the slightest "accident" or precise particularity. (I leave aside, to keep the story simple (but, of course, if it were a matter of a "serious" exercise in introspection, I could hardly eliminate this hypothesis), the suspicion that the vision of my, of our paper ships in the water turning blue comes from somewhere else, from another place in space-time, and was introduced here under a false memory-pretext.)

The water disappeared down the drain, sinking in a whirlpool sinking into itself, finally leaving the boats in a wreck on the bottom; I watched and waited for the moment when this miniature "maelström" would appear (the contemplation of which, by projecting an enormous change of scale, was capable of provoking, "sympathetically," a shivering identification with the hero of Poe's story, *A Descent into the Maelström*), **I waited for the moment when the water hollowed into a vertiginous sphincter** (which could be effaced at will), **and for the suspension of the "ships" along the side, together with sticks, hollow vegetable hulls planted with twig-flags** (catalpas), **insects, scattered dismembered flowers; the clouds themselves, white in the gauzy sky, seemed likely to disappear in this way; I followed them up to the final second of the mirage of their disappearance, only to find them again the next moment: immediate, intact, and trembling in the deepest depths of an inflexible, inassimilable image of the sky.**

24 some flowers, fruit, leaves, and branches

"Here are some flowers, fruit, leaves, and branches" (said the poet (as one used to write in school, parenthetically, when citing verses)), and especially vegetables (including those fruits that can be considered vegetables because of their mode of production, like strawberries or melons), within the utilitarian rectangle largely "re-served" (that is to say, forbidden to childish incursions) and making up the right half of the clock dial (the garden to the right of the bench), a large rect-angle divided into smaller ones (as though for a didactic drawing, explaining a "sum" for the calculation of a "Riemann integral"). These are the vegetable "beds," them-selves drawn out, furrowed with straight lines into which the water we poured would run with a gentle hiss, darkening a soil that was never quenched (the ground in the Aude is dry. It doesn't rain much, or often, in the border zones of this landscape, close to the Mediterranean).

I can easily revive a vision of peas, green or white beans (akin to peas in terms of their pods), tomatoes, melons, enormous squash, strawberries: their maturation, their survival, their abundance were, if not vital, at least of great importance in the ordinary life of a family who, like so many others then, truly needed them. Those years were years of hunger, and the winters were all the more dreadful since the land was unproductive. Every vegetable species from those days can generate an intense and well-preserved focus of vision, → I § 92–93   accompanied by colors and almost by smells; I can almost fol-low, with my (inner) eye, the ripening of a tomato on the vine, from green to a voluminous red, passing through pink and sometimes yellow, in a progressive display of the colors of the spectrum in which each tint has its own (increasing) size and weight. The very dimensions of the plants and the fruit (excessive in comparison with current perceptions), the variable but identifiable environment framing my visions of them (the washbasin on the left, or a walkway; the apricot tree, or the vine arbor) both situate and date this sort of accelerated and discontinuous "film." I can even carry the basket, place it on the table, pick up a tomato, take a bite . . .

Symmetrically, the relatively few memories that I have of flowers (which were nonetheless very much present) perhaps have their origin in the same cause (albeit inversely): roses *are*, but one does not eat them. In particular, I do not see any roses. Worse: I have a specific intuition of the nonexistence of roses. And since the rose is a French commodity (I mean to say that the word "rose"—in the French language, and therefore in the poetry of this lan-guage—is a specifically French export, as Dominique Fourcade has shown; and therefore that this isn't, here, a question of "*rose*," a syllable also taken into the English language, and which, for its part, is likewise a commodity of poetic English, as Gertrude Stein definitively declared). I am, I was, a child without roses—that is, a bad little Frenchman, poetically speaking. It will be necessary for me to speak more of this. (The flowers of the Judas tree, however, still follow me—edible and sweet during their infancy as flower buds.) No, I see only dahlias (and I see them as all being the same, with their feather-duster heads, their "O-Cedar broom" heads, as on certain "punk" girls). And, what's more, it seems to me that I see dahlias only because of a "parasitic" association based on my encounter with one of the most characteristic and singular lines in French verse. The word "dahlia" is in effect, for me, an eponym of diaeresis. I will explain: there are two sorts of "dahlias"; one is the name for those flowers I see in the garden, around 1940, while the other occupies the first half of a verse by Max Jacob: "*Dahlias, dahlias, que Dalila lia*" (Dahlias, dahlias, that Delilah bound together). This second type of "dahlia" is trisyllabic ("dah-li-a") and the first is only disyllabic. It is only in a verse as convincing as this one that Delilah (a specialist in bouquets, as we know, and as attested to by the famous one she arranged with Samson's hair) can bind together, subliminally, the two syllables of "*li-a*" (bound) and thus turn them into flowers: the only ones that I haven't forgotten.

"Vegetable garden": this was what we called the rectangular territory that was a bit longer than the other one (almost a square) where we played our game. It ran along the front of the house where our bedroom was, past the "greenhouse" (enclosed in glass, like the "veranda" at my grandparents' house in Lyon). On that side (one of the short sides of the rectangle) a wall separated our plot from the neighbors' gardens; it wasn't very high, but high enough to block the view. Behind the other wall was the street. There was a main walkway cutting through the middle (running lengthwise); there were two other walkways beginning at the base of the wall, and then a third wider one, parallel to these two, that went down some steps (three steps?) to the terrace below, in front of the main facade of the house. Along that walkway hung two curtains of vines, weighed down at the end of August and in September with their infinitely precious cargo of heavy ripe clusters of grapes.

A final wall remains to be raised—so that the garden will then be entirely enclosed by words, as it was, in fact, by a page's margin made of stone. (I'm

thinking here (which is to say, at this point in the prose and at this moment of composition) that it would be good to end this chapter—if I manage to bring it
"*extra muros*," which I hope to do—with a <u>map</u> of the garden's layout; this
would allow the reader to find his or her way through what is, after all, only a
very long <u>description</u> (a description that is in no way a photograph but a topological
<u>narration</u>), and allow me to verify whether the omissions, be they voluntary or
involuntary (the "blanks" in the description, in relation to a reality that is past,
but full), are indeed adequate to the <u>mysteries</u> that memory has suffused them
with. (Such a "map" for the reader is akin, on the one hand, to the maps of various "uto-
pias," the imaginary lands of fiction; and, on the other hand, to those (in fact related) maps
that used to be included in some whodunits from the interwar period in England.))

Along this wall there was the "henhouse." It was generically and pragmati-
cally designed for our hens, an unsavory crew we didn't find very appealing at
all (and that I still don't find very appealing), despite their obvious utility. But
in my opinion this construction's principal virtue was that it also contained

→ I § 95   the hutches, little dwellings for our peaceful and sympathetic rab-
                bits. Our childish and spontaneous anthropomorphism made us
see all animals, more or less (both the animal "parents" and their children) as
individuals of about our own age (they too being dependent on human adults,
and the most indisputable difference between them and us being that the parental power exercised over them included the power of life and death). By
the same token, we subjected them without any hesitation to value judgments
that were no less intellectual than moral. Hens were stupid and mean. Rabbits
were nice, perhaps (apparently) even gifted at math. (This predisposition towards
believing in the goodness of rabbits, resistant to all education and strongly encouraged
even today by various publications and television programs, persists well into adulthood,
sometimes becoming so distorted (generally with the first steps into the "third age") as
to reach dreadful extremes. It's rife among the female Parisian voters who supported M.
Chirac, for example: those who've been stricken by that malady of the soul one might call
the "Brigitte Bardot syndrome," after the ex-sex-symbol of the cinema for the males of
my generation ("Mademoiselle Bardot," as Jean-Claude Milner says), who, having once

→ I § 96   been the very erotic "BB," retired from the silver screen and became a senile
                soft-hearted "Mother Teresa" protecting baby seals.)
We had an excessive and sentimental attachment to the rabbits. Their beige

fur, or gray, or reddish-gray, thick, warm, and trembling under their whiskers, had a lot to do with this. **We pressed our faces against the wire grate of the hutch** (I say "we" because, in the image that comes to me, I can see, peripherally, that I am not alone) **until we felt the familiar snouts on our noses, the gentle and perpetual movement of their incessant innocent twitching; impossible, despite all our efforts, to move our own as quickly; or else one of us held out a green stem from a bush or a spindle tree** (those spindle trees with very dark leaves that were planted just in front of the game-bench), **until the moment when their biting teeth almost took hold of one's finger; the rabbits' teeth quickly stripped the stems of their green outer layer, moist and fresh, leaving only the white wood, also moist, shiny with sap.** (But the wet shiny surface of the white stems didn't last: they turned dull and yellow very quickly when they dried out, just as white translucent pebbles taken from seawater become dull with a salty film.) Just for a moment, they were fascinating lepine sculptures in wood. (My father transposed Baudelaire's "Invitation to the Voyage" (as I later discovered) into a family poem composed with us in mind, from which I have retained the following lines; they bring back to me, instantaneously and with perfect accuracy, this tactile, sensual vision:

> Shining furniture
> Polished by teeth
> Would decorate our room.)

I mentioned the "power of life and death" that parents have over animals. This was by no means simply a figure of speech. Those nice rabbits were raised—in contrast with the hens—precisely to be eaten. Not only did the stews that sometimes appeared on the dining room table leave no doubt about this, my father did nothing at all to encourage, at least as far as I was concerned (I, the eldest), a sentimental and ambiguous amnesia regarding the circumstances by which this transformation was brought about. He was the rabbit executioner. He killed them with a quick blow to the back of the neck, while I held their paws until the convulsions were over. (I was the one who had to help him with this task because both my mother and Marie were physiologically incapable of withstanding the sight of blood.)

Then he bled them (the blood flowed into a shallow plate, and was cooked the same evening, fried into a "*sanguette*," to be eaten with parsley and salt). First he cut the head along the fine silky ears, snipped the skin just above the paws, pulled the fur off in one swipe, and opened up the corpse. Now the belly was naked, swollen, marked with veins (like a beautiful woman's calf lightly laced with blue), steaming slightly, letting off its heat. My father pulled out the entrails, carefully isolated the bitter green gallbladder, separated the liver, the heart, and the kidneys, and cut the rest into pieces, which were then placed in a wide metal bowl: the last stage before being cooked Provençal style (a recipe for which thyme, and other herbs, were certainly not lacking). Today I can't help associating, in a visual deduction-comparison, the spindle trees stripped of their moist and living skin by rabbit teeth, and then these dead rabbits, still warm, steaming and pale on the kitchen table, in 1942 or '43.

25 The semi-fraternity between children and familiar animals inspires a fictive interpretation of the fascination exerted by certain legends like that of Saint Nicholas

The semi-fraternity that one finds in the daily interactions between children and familiar animals inspires a fictive interpretation (which I find seductive) of the delicious fear, the fascination, exerted by certain cruel tales, certain legends like that of Saint Nicholas or the Ogre and Tom Thumb. Somewhere between the companionable but edible animals and children—on the scale of living beings—there are those creatures, like dogs and cats, which are not naturally destined to be eaten. I say "not naturally" because, at least when it comes to cats, it seems to me that their presence had become suspiciously rare in the urban landscape during this period. In any case, we didn't have any cats at our house. (We didn't have any dogs either, not even a hunting dog.) But the ultimate fate of the rabbits, tragic and necessary, could only feed (as it were) (along with the rumors concerning the all-too-explicable disappearances of certain cats) into a latent and unarticulated anxiety—never brought to the surface except in a very emotional identification with the children in the legend—about being victims ourselves of a cannibalism necessitated by the harsh Law of Survival (and by the sheer wickedness of the world).

In the "Song of Saint Nicholas" (you recall: "They were three little children / who went to glean in the fields . . ."; my grandmother liked to sing this song), I recall in particular the face (shown in a sinister illustration) of the ". . . mean butcher / with the sharp knife in his hand." Before the happy ending, with the intervention of the *sanctus ex machina* who revives the dear blond-headed children, the cathartic adventure necessitates their passage (transitory, to be sure, but still!) through the salting-tub, in the form of ham (and the hams there are pink, fresh and fragrant, like the flesh of little children). (We never, in fact, saw any ham.)

One episode from those years, one with an ending that was both happy (though not for all its protagonists) and culinary, occurred around this time. It was set in a structure located next to the henhouse, an *appentis* or lean-to (I believe this is the first time I've ever used this word, which came to me quite naturally, but whose spelling and definition I had to check, to be sure that it corresponds to what I have in mind. And it does, in fact, in its second meaning, which is the following (according to the *Petit Robert*): a small building that leans against a larger one, serving as a shed or a small shelter (I was about to write that this definition is only "almost" correct, for the structure I have in mind, as it was only "leaning" against the wall of the garden. But now in fact I think (indeed, now I'm sure) that this wall was a wall of the neighboring house)). This is where the saga of the pig unfolded.

The constantly recurring threat of family starvation incited my parents, one fine day, to overstep the law (a Vichy law that was morally rejected but all the more feared for that) in order to carry out a clandestine action: buying and raising a pig. (In principle this wasn't very dangerous (they weren't the only ones in the neighborhood to be doing so), but it was more risky in their case, albeit indirectly, since at the time they were engaged in other, much more serious, clandestine activities). And so a skinny young pig (a female pig, in fact, with the lovely name of Gagnoune: but this feminized name was decided purely by chance, and was in no way the sign of any ironic "anti-sow" sentiment) secretly took up residence in the lean-to, filling it → I § 97 with its acidic odor, its splashing slop, and its characteristic grunts and snorts (though all this was relatively sheltered from indiscreet eyes, noses, and ears). We then had to take measures to increase its girth, and, within a reasonable amount of time, to bring it up to a reasonable "competitive weight" that would allow us to convert it (her) profitably into various pork products, as the butcher does with the three children in the song of Saint Nicholas.

This project was easier to conceive than to carry out. If there was very little for humans to eat in those days, there was hardly anything for animals to eat either. The pig was granted a diet consisting largely of leaves and grass, with—as a main course—a bucket full of peelings and scraps (potato skins, carrot tops, cabbage stalks . . .) left over from the vegetable garden. She gulped down everything. But one may suppose this diet did little to sate her hunger, since when my mother took a "serving" out to her, she was greeted with a formidable and aggressive impetuousness. We remained at a safe distance while my mother, after entering the gate to the wire-fence enclosure surrounding the lean-to (a sort of "airlock" providing security against any attempts to flee), prepared herself like a bullfighter in the arena, and holding the bucket of food as far away from her body as possible, she braced herself for the grunting charge of this pink beast. Indeed, it seems to me that this pig had above her snout the most porcine and the least amiable pair of sunken eyes that ever looked out of a pig; and my mother always claimed that the creature had it in for her, for her personally, and that on the contrary when my father went out to feed her she was all sweetness and light; likewise when he sprayed her down with the watering hose in order to strip off the crusty slop with which she piggishly soiled herself, in great abundance and with great delight, and with which she constantly soiled her litter bed and her trough. Only then, after extreme immersion, was the pig-pink color of her hide visible in all its baby-like innocence.

Gagnoune, the female pig, despite her ferocious appetite (she was very conscientiously a pig, it must be said) never reached anything like an enormous weight (I've retained the figure of 80 kilos. With a normal amount of food, she certainly would have done a lot better). She nonetheless prospered reasonably well, and the day of her execution—awaited with such great salivary expectations—finally arrived. I say the day arrived, but it was in fact a night—the clandestine nature of her life in our garden necessarily implied the same conditions for her death as well. We needed a real professional for the task. One was therefore summoned, brought to us by some neighborhood ladies who were themselves enlisted to carry out all the tasks that would immediately follow the slaughter, skilled as they were in the traditional treatment of the animal's various parts. The executioner went to work around midnight, after detailed negotiations concerning the payment of his "honorarium" (payment in kind, of course). Gagnoune's death squeal could be heard as far away as Limoux.

The first "preparation" of the different pig products lasted until morning. Soon enough, from the bustling activity and all the animated conversations coming out of our loquacious laboratory—from the cauldrons, the roasting pans, and the broad bowls—came the ritual emergence of blood and meat sausages, *cansalades* (salted pork breast), *fritons* and *gratons*, the fat sealed in glass jars, the ribs and cutlets, the pure white slabs of bacon. Next came the hams, heavily salted and peppered to resist the humid attacks of what was called the "marine" wind. Almost fifty years later, the mere immaterial resurgence of these words on my screen makes me hungry. Not with a hunger that can be satisfied, but with a hunger of pure evocation, a hunger of reminiscence. For a very long time after the end of the war, in spite of all gustatory evidence, I continued to throw myself voraciously on pork in all its forms, and only with reticence and very slowly did I finally recognize the ineluctable disappearance of its former taste, a disastrous consequence of industrial production. Pork-rib purée—this was the item (of choice?) that I invariably offered to my daughter Laurence, in her first years, when we dined together.

I emerged from childhood with the conviction that the pig possesses an absolute perfection, being an animal that can be entirely transformed into products useful to humanity: I learned not only that it was in large part edible (down to the bones gnawed by dogs), but also that brushes can be fashioned from its bristly hair, and purses and luggage and supple bags made from its tough hide; in short, I realized that my alimentary passion could be backed up by a good humanist conscience. Only much later did I learn of the religious taboos placed upon it. And then I felt (in order to give my preference its own "theological" justification) a considerable pagan affinity with the Celts who, it is said, held the pig in very high esteem. Had not the legendary founder of the Glastonbury Abbey chosen that place in honor of his victory over a fabled pig (a sow!)? And how could I forget to salute in these pages the great mystical boar Twrch Trwyth, hero of the Welsh *Mabinogion*?

It was perhaps a distant echo of this memorable event from our childhood that inspired my sister Denise with a desire to possess a pig, which she satisfied for a year or two: she'd always dreamed of having "her own" pig. It was really only a half a pig, though, since she didn't live in the Minervois region and had to share ownership of the animal with Gérard and Marie-Cécile. But she certainly made sure to show up in person at the decisive moment of its transformation into sausages and hams, carried out in accordance with the best local traditions, at Moussoulens.

26 "My grandfather was in the habit of saying:

"My grandfather was in the habit of saying: 'One must arrive at a train station in time to miss the previous train.'" With this quotation, admittedly apocryphal, I began a "moment of repose in prose" (the first) in a book of poems entitled *Autobiographie, chapitre dix*, and in so doing was in fact rendering a double homage to my grandfather by invoking two characteristic features of his view of the world, which I have since inherited: a difficulty with being late, and a passion for the railway. The maxim coined above unites them both, and I often apply it literally (especially at the Gare Saint-Lazare, where I catch the train that takes me to work, via the "Nanterre-Université" station).

Now, our garden on the Rue d'Assas contained a number of palm trees of moderate height (but, alas, they didn't produce any dates), divided up more or less equally on the four "hills" planted with shrubs and trees and separated by the two walkways in the form of a cross. But even joined together by the word "now" (used in its logical sense), the two immediately consecutive "instants" of prose that you're in the process of reading don't seem to be related to one another in any very obvious way. And they aren't, it's true. But allow me to take a little time to establish such a relation. "Now," I say, the green leafy parts of the little palm trees in the garden were in fact palms (an object which for once corresponds to what one might deduce from its name) spreading out in a fan shape made up of long leaves at the end of a solid flexible stalk (a property that

→ I § 98   will prove to be of some interest to us here). Each enormous leaf, dark green in color, was itself composed of two long thin blades partially folded back around an individual stalk: a subdivision of the main stalk, but thinner.

Now, it wasn't difficult to pull the lowest palms from the tree's fuzzy reddish brown ochre trunk, to cut or tear off the double leaves one by one, to separate each half from its stalk, and thus to obtain a considerable number of fairly long strips (between thirty centimeters and a meter in length) that could be tied together easily with tight, durable knots, thus producing some very adequate stalky ropes, punctuated by knots. By suspending these pieces of rope from various hook-like protuberances on the pine trees, or from the poles holding up the strings running along the walkways of the vegetable gardens, or from the poles holding up the clotheslines, I was able (with the help of some skillful labor on the part of my brother and sister) to create a network that divided the polygonal space of the garden into a regular grid.

It is here that I return to the apparently arbitrary introductory segment of this prose-moment. On a notebook page symbolizing the surface of the garden, I drew out a map of the palm lines and their connections between certain points, each designated by names invented for this purpose; thus developing a perfectly respectable approximation of those other maps, fascinating for any train-lover, appearing in the first pages of the "Railway Timetables" published by "Chaix"—which, during our weekly journeys to Toulouse, I also saw located on the wall opposite the WC at the far end of each car. There, one read the names of cities "served" by the SNCF, with the main routes appearing as solid lines and the secondary routes in thinner lines, together with their route numbers, which then allowed one to identify them in the pages of the appropriate Timetable.

The geography of this railway having been created (thanks to the palms) and transposed onto paper, to my general satisfaction, I was able to undertake the second phase of the operation with the highest chances of success. This phase consisted in establishing the fictive train schedules (whose materialization followed lines that were essentially mental, since I never tried to imitate actual trains) that would pass through my likewise fictive network as high speed, express, or local "omnibus" trains—each one assigned a number indicating its place in line. Armed with my grandfather's old "Chaix" (he always carried one in his bags, and I had an old one on hand that he had given to me), having attributed sufficient kilometric distances to the meters of terrain in which my "company" operated, I worked out the departure and arrival times, and especially the innumerable "connections" (whose vital importance in the organization of a good rail network cannot be overestimated).

I thus made up, for the convenience of my various passengers (not very numerous, to be sure, but of "high quality"), a veritable *"Garden Chaix"*: a high speed train departing, say, at 6:53 in the morning from "Lavoiro Salo" (this was the name, I remember (it's the only one I can still recall) given to the station located at the fountain where the "game of immobility" took place) in the direction of the laundry house, could, for example, by means of a leisurely transfer at "Umbrella Pine," and a second, more acrobatic one in the central walkway, allow one to reach—on a local with an itinerary indicated by smaller characters—"Apricot Tree" station at 2:19 P.M. ("High-speed train 101 from Lavoiro Salo in the direction of the Laundry House is now arriving on platform 6. Please step away from the edge of the platform. A train connecting to Apricot Tree will arrive at 11:14 A.M. on platform 9; this train makes stops at . . .")

The bench used in our primary game, "**Go-Creeping**," was of course an important "railway hub" in this new organization of the space of the garden. But, according to the Theory of Rhythm (in fact, since we're dealing with a surface rather than a sequence, one must imagine an extension of this theory into a "multilinear" space, by means of the "wavelet theory," for example (itself appropriately generalized)), this created a very different imaginary representation of the space, despite everything. For the points of greatest interest, the points of intensity, were not necessarily the same here as in our other games. The time it took to move from one point to another also changed, determined not by one's gaze, but by bodily movements (much slower, even if they were greatly accelerated by the irresistible megalomania of identifying with a locomotive; but, above all, these movements were not discontinuous).

The relevance of my timetable didn't last long. This was because, within the confines of the game, there was always the fact that the schedule itself needed constant revision (winter and summer hours, for example, each necessitated the concoction of a new "Chaix"). But also, outside the game, there was the no less important fact that the palm ropes embodying the rail-lines quickly deteriorated: they turned yellow, came apart, or got broken due to accidents . . . And the game, like all games, quickly grew tiresome. It was abruptly forgotten, though some stalky vestiges of palm rope remained hanging here and there, pitiful and forlorn. Until the moment, that is, when there was a new resurgence of interest (following a vacation, for example, which put trains back on the agenda).

There you have, I hope, the fully justified link between railroads and palm trees from which I began. True, this link is rather abstract. (Children's games are indeed abstract, and more often than one might think—all the more so when they're strictly imaginary.) But the network of hanging ropes was eventually able to serve our purposes in a much more direct and concrete way— quite simply by becoming the material support for the transmission of messages according to a code. Toward the very end of our time in that house, the telephone appeared, lending itself to a very simple interpretation in palm ropes, while also providing a pretext for compiling a book of imaginary listings (symmetrical to the train timetable). But I didn't really have the time to master this new concept before we moved to Paris. In fact, I was never really able to do so. And that's why I still do not like the telephone.

27 **I was not alone in this garden.**

I was not alone in this garden. And yet my description in this chapter has remained confined to the mineral, vegetable, and animal kingdoms. What about humans, human children? Those player-shadows who are there, next to me, at every moment, more or less—in front of the bench, the washbasin, the wire mesh of the rabbit cages? I speak of them only very indirectly. My semi-silence, however, is not a form of solipsism. But any attempt to say more about them runs up against some basic difficulties: the first is that this shared territory of the past is obviously something we all no longer experience in common today. Some of our memories differ, and necessarily more and more, from others'. I am trying to work as far as possible outside of those other visions, as much for the sake of discretion as from simple incapacity. The second difficulty, the second reason is much more powerful; it acts upon the totality of everything I write here: an absence—someone who is absent. (I wrote "reason," but these aren't reasons: they are observations at most. The difficulties are real enough, however—though the first is no doubt only a mask for the second.) I will therefore remain with the animals for a while longer.

The hens and chickens, the rabbits, and the pig were kept within closed quarters. They didn't have the freedom to circulate in the garden. But the family of ducks that suddenly came to be a part of our lives was not, for its part (though I don't really know why) subject to this same restriction. From this one fact it followed with immediate clarity that ducks occupied a higher place in the scale of being—that they were superior, as a species, to hens and pigs, and even to rabbits. So it was that I acquired this intimate conviction. And I've preserved it, internally, at least in a ludic form: I like ducks, and I have great respect for them. I miss no occasion to praise them, whether orally, poetically, or in fiction.

We came, as I said, into possession of a family of ducks: fatherless ducks. In the beginning, in fact, it was only a potential family: a female duck arrived in a basket accompanied by her future children, seven eggs to incubate and hatch. The nutritive purpose of this acquisition was, like that of the rabbits and the pig, completely unambiguous. The mother duck would bring seven little ducks into the world, would raise them with care (ducks raise their young with the greatest care), until they reached a weight suitable for consumption. The mother would then lay more eggs, until she too met her foreordained end in a pot on the stove. But it didn't quite turn out that way.

Let us remark to begin with that **Bacadette**—the mother duck, and the central hero of this adventure—belonged to one of the two species of duck that inhabit the Carcassès (principally the region of Castelnaudary, the land of one of the three competing versions of "cassoulet"): "*mulards*" and "*musqués*." The *mulards* are fatter, the fattest, and their plumage is dull. Their taste is not very refined. Their voice is shrill, their movements heavy and clumsy, even on the water. The *musqués*, on the contrary, are thinner, have a narrower beak, are more elegant in their movements and in their plumage and colors (green and black), speak little but with a gentle voice ("*musqué*" means, according to an old memory that I have not verified, "mute"), show great virtuosity in the water, and are intellectually far more sharp (in my admittedly partial judgment). A female *mularde* would certainly have given us reason to hope for a more substantial quantity of meat. Yet, as one might guess, Bacadette was a "*musquette*."

We set up the future mother in the "greenhouse," where we would go to see her, already admiring her manners, her discretion, her plumage, her beak: to

feel a duck's beak nibbling a grain of corn or a breadcrumb from one's palm—
what a delightful sensation! How warm and soft the feathers on her belly were,
when one lifted her up to check the progress of her brood. The babies were
born: tiny, hesitant, cheeping, yellow and black—very touching. The question
of names arose immediately; my father (whose prerogative this was: the power
of nomination) settled it on the spot: there were seven, but they would not
remain dwarves. Thus, they were to be called, respectively, **Monday, Tuesday,
Wednesday, Thursday, Friday, Saturday**, and **Sunday**.

Respectively, to be sure, but which one would have which name? And how
would we be able tell them apart? (Nothing resembles a baby duck more than
another baby duck.) After a period of shifting indecision and observation,
during which we scrutinized the little troop wobbling on their little webbed
feet, trying to identify their distinctive physical features and (playing the role
of local Lavaters) the physiognomic indices of their future personalities, the
little baby ducks finally received their names, and then undertook to resemble
them as much as possible. And thus it was that the most beautiful, the most
ambitious, and the most brilliant were (in conformity with the preferences of
schoolchildren) **Thursday** (at that time a day off from classes, as Wednesday
is today) and **Sunday** (our family was secular, and for us Sunday was not a
dreary day, in the English manner, nor was it exaggeratedly familial or theological. It was the ludic day par excellence).

But, as happens with ducks no less than with humans, childhood illnesses
threatened. Despite all our attentions, a couple of them died: **Wednesday** and
Saturday, I think, when they were quite young. Bacadette took their death
with stoicism (according to our interpretation, in which the accusation of indifference was rejected with indignation). The others survived, although not
with equal vigor: **Tuesday** was always out of sorts, and had a bit of a limp. As
for **Monday**, he stayed tiny despite all our efforts, and presented us with the
mystery of a veritable bonsai duck (since he ate with as much gusto as his
brothers). I haven't retained any very clear memory of **Friday**. **Thursday** and
Sunday, as I said, were the phoenixes of this splendid family—with perhaps a
slight superiority, overall, in **Sunday**, as was to be expected.

Throughout their childhood and adolescence, the question of their ultimate
fate never explicitly came out into the open, making it possible for the little

"*musqués*" to become marvelous playmates (much more so than Bacadette, who remained rather reserved when faced with the exuberant affection shown by her horde of children); running around beak-first on the terrace, jumping up and down the stairs, swimming masterfully in the large washbasin in train behind their mother, then coming out, in a strict and maternally controlled line, to shake their feathers and dry themselves on the sunny walkways, chattering through their beaks. What progress this was compared to our paper boats: these living vessels with webbed feet that could stroke more powerfully than any oar, with their fine clever heads that dove and reemerged streaming with water but never wet, with beaks that moved and clacked when they drank, with their prismatic colors in the bright light (dark green, a little purple: a little sun on their feathers).

We each (there were four of us) had our "own," our brother duck among the survivors (I won't say which). We argued vehemently about their exploits, their respective merits, their physical and sentimental development. We couldn't tear ourselves away from them. We offered them little delicacies (earthworms we'd caught in upturned clods of earth, for example, or slugs straggling along after a bout of rain). We kissed them on the beak, on their tiny eyes, on their feathers. We imitated their comical rush toward their food or toward the washbasin. We set them on our knees. They were cheerful, restless, familiar, waterproof. Time passed.

28 After some time had passed, the inevitable could no longer be avoided

After some time had passed, the inevitable could no longer be avoided or delayed. The ducks were there to be eaten, and so eaten they were (this story is not a fairytale). I remember the dishes that contained **Thursday** (the separated and roasted pieces of **Thursday**. Why him in particular? Perhaps because his "day" is also the day whose "death" schoolchildren mourn (mourned) most), and I remember the tears shed over them by Jean-René, our youngest brother. Perhaps we too wept. We wept and ate. New and diminutive Gargantuas, we wept while eating and we ate while weeping. Such was the end of the **Week of Ducks**.

Thereafter, Bacadette remained our sole representative of the duck people. A sort of compunction, a slightly melancholic note of noble sadness as she swayed along on her webbed feet, a distinct propensity to avoid mixing in our high-pitched and chaotic games, all this quickly made her a respectable figure but one who was somewhat distant from the family (a bit like the cousin of our parents who'd hidden herself away after some bereavement and always dressed in the same colors). **I see her (I see her clearly), during the day, often immobile on the terrace, on one of the walkways, her feet tucked beneath her, her plumage deep green and smooth, her calm little eyes, as she sat like a boat on the dusty ground**.

She had developed a taste for the dark interior of the ground floor of the house, for the dining room, especially at mealtimes, entering the room silently and without hesitation and hoisting herself up onto the armchair, where she settled in peaceably, benevolently enjoying our turbulent company, and the softness of the cushions. She seemed to be listening attentively to the radio (we called it the "wireless") and to be weighing the pros and cons (there was Radio Paris, but there was also "London," the clandestine broadcast), without giving any hint of her preferences. But one day, as the senile and sinister voice of Marshal Pétain resounded in the room, she descended with dignity from her chair and went toward the door, and just as she made her exit she let drop from beneath her tail—which she suddenly bristled into a fan—a large liquid mess, brown and slimy, by way of commentary.

Bacadette's essential task, which absorbed a great deal of her inner energy (and, as we will see, was also the focus of her preoccupations) was to lay eggs. Every day she laid one and sometimes two of those heavy, precious, rich, flavorful eggs. They were infinitely more flavorful to us—because of their color, shape, size, the density of their darker and more intense yolk and of their more compact whites—than the entirely utilitarian eggs of the imbecile hens. Each of Bacadette's eggs was a trophy, therefore, set aside to be eaten under exceptional circumstances only (a party, an illness, a reward, a birthday).

But Bacadette didn't stupidly and monotonously lay all her eggs in one place or even at the same time of day. She didn't put them all in one basket. On the contrary, she made a constant effort to leave them in different places and even, in fact, to conceal them. I don't know if her desire to hide her productions from our scrutiny was the rule from the beginning or if she was responding to our persistent indiscretion (wishing to lay her eggs in peace, and in her own time, and considering the laying of eggs a serious and private matter that in no way required our observation). Whatever the case, she got into the habit of laying her eggs earlier and earlier in the morning, and of changing her hiding place as often as possible. And here we have, as you can imagine, all the necessary ingredients for a game.

The goal of the game was, of course, to find Bacadette's egg and to place it on the kitchen table before breakfast time. The game was thus divided into two sub-games. In the first, there were two teams: Bacadette vs. all the children. Bacadette hid, the children sought. The second sub-game divided each of us against all the other human players: to be the first to bring back the buried treasure, the gold that was the egg—not to say the golden egg. I had a certain advantage: on the one hand, I was the oldest. Moreover, I had no difficulty getting up very early in the morning (unlike my sister Denise). One particularly annoying situation, however, was when I not only didn't find the egg, but, later in the day, or even on another day, my father or my mother would come across it as one of them worked in the garden and happened to see it under a squash, for example, or at the foot of a dahlia. The real triumph, however, was to catch Bacadette in the act, and to pick up the egg while it was still warm, directly out of the oven (so to speak). Once, at the very crack of dawn, she was so taken by surprise that, as she fled, she began immediately to lay a second egg that was not really ready, as its shell was still very soft.

But most often a very long quest was necessary to find the hidden egg. Bacadette was extraordinarily ingenious (there can be no doubt that when, in the afternoon, she would take up a position in the middle of one of the walkways, her beak on her chest, motionless even when we came speeding by on our

→ I § 99 bicycles or tricycles, she was absorbed with intense concentration in concocting new strategies of concealment). The greenhouse, the vegetable garden, the shrubs, the laundry house, the tomato plants, the roof above the washbasin all allowed for a wide range of variations, and she never repeated the same choice in close succession. In a tiny shed, an ancient and unused cabinet for garden tools set behind a pine tree in the left corner of the wall enclosing our space (the corner of the Rue d'Assas and the "Enclos du Luxembourg," at about ten to noon on the spatial clock that I imagined for this chapter), she thus "invented" no less than a dozen distinct hiding places (which implied on her part a large reservoir of "sites of memory" in order to avoid repeating herself at too brief an interval).

But her most spectacular feat was tremendously simple: one summer dawn, slipping into the house through a door that I had left opened when I quietly snuck out into the garden to look for her, she ended up laying her egg on the armchair in the dining room, where Marie didn't find it until midmorning (we had all left for school and our parents were at the lycée). I remain convinced that she had read, that day, and seriously meditated upon, the lesson of "The Purloined Letter," as found in the gray-green boxed translation by Charles Baudelaire.

Was Bacadette finally eaten, as she would have to be, and as her children were? I will respond at the proper time to this distressing question.

29 I exit the garden and go out into the street, toward the Aude

I exit the garden and go out into the street, to the right, toward the Aude River; I do not leave through the gate at the end of the main walkway in the "ludic" section of the territory; this is always closed, beneath the great umbrella pine where the magpies lurk and jeer; I go out into the street through the open door of the "garage" of the laundry house, shadowy and filled with wood and coal (the anthracite in oval chunks that feeds the stove in winter. It isn't winter, but my path is constructed, in an absolute simultaneity, of images from several seasons); **I go out under the bright flat sun, into the dazzling sunlit surface of the always-silent empty street; a little tar on the blacktop has melted; I touch it with one toe (I am barefoot, the bottom of my feet are like hard shoe-soles, I don't feel the pricking of the gravel); the light is intense; how intense the light is! and how real!**

This light comes from a distance more remote than any galaxy. Yes, the light that reaches us, the light that so impassions astronomers and comes to us from the most distant galaxies, was emitted an infinitely long time ago compared to the light in question, it's true. But I never saw that other light being emitted— from a star, a sun, or a nova. No one saw it, no one will ever see it being emitted. The light of childhood, on the other hand, continues to be emitted, it is emitted and re-emitted, always and again: back then, yesterday, now. When I think of it, it is emitted: it dazzles the street, the Rue d'Assas going down to the Aude River, **my naked foot touching the burning blacktop, the gravel scattered onto the freshly tarred surface, the cement gutter, the sidewalk. It comes, then stops.** When I think it, I see it. Then it stops.

The light, the sun in the sky, do not deceive. It is hot. The street descends steeply on the right (when one comes out from the laundry house). On the other side of the street there's a high blind wall, continuous all the way down, the wall of the barracks. On the right a few houses, but I am situated in such a way that I do not look at them, I do not see them. There is no one out in the heat of the early afternoon, the heat of summertime siestas. (While writing this, I suddenly "hear" a radio on the right, but its voice is merely juxtaposed with the silence, with the insistent light, in which I am alone.) It's in the nature of the story that I go out this way into an empty, idle, solar street. Being "extra muros" means being in a well of solitude. At the bottom of the street, a bifurcation. On one side, to the left, the Rue d'Assas (perhaps under another name, I don't recall) climbs back up as steeply as it went down. On the right, some stairs invaded by weeds, nettles, and grasses continue down to a small footpath heading toward the river. I will not go that way now.

This solitude, in the palpable light, under the stark and imposing sun, is not threatening (neither in terms of its duration, nor because of my departure from home); neither joyous nor sad; no mystery or melancholy in this street; the only shadow to come will be that of the evening, not the shadow or the shadow's shadow falling on the steps of the stairway, not the black shadow divided into square panes of darkness in the window, nor the Shadow that hovers over everything, cast by the state of the world; simply a first shadow, as the evening comes creeping; when the sun turns ochre, and the sky turns green along the broad sides of the houses, when the dust turns white, when the blacktop hardens; when the air grows cooler.

Behind the green bench, at the edge of the terrace, between the two entrances to the two walkways, the condemned **well** offered up its mysterious coping, the invisible surface of its water, its damp smell of shadow, cool and dangerous. In a well that's not too deep one can, by leaning over the side, perceive one's own face in the distance, as though cut out against the sky, and when the water moves—from a pebble breaking its cavernous silence with an echo—one can see oneself suddenly rocking with the pendular recurrence of small surges, wavelets slowly subsiding (**there was a similar well, uncovered, in Antoine's "garden" in Villegly; and another beneath a scrubland vine, in "*Carrière Blanche*" (White Quarry); there, as well as outside the kitchen of my uncle's house in Saint-Jean-du-Var, a fig tree grew, tree of my memory,**

tree of my truth; but there wasn't one near this well in our garden, near the bench).

In a medieval poem with the mysterious title "Lay of the Shadow" (in French, "*Lai de l'Ombre*," which I can't repeat without also hearing it written another way, "*Lait de l'ombre*," milk of the shadow, a combination of words that only increases the title's strangeness), the watery image of the ring held by a lover seated on a well's coping suddenly takes its place, as though on its own, on the reflected finger of his lady, thus announcing that the world of love, impossible here, is on the contrary quite real in there, <u>through-the-looking-glass</u> of the water. And whenever I open the book that contains this poem (a well known edition by Joseph Bédier, entitled *La Tradition manuscrite du Lai de l'Ombre*, whose ultimate purpose is not to restore the text, but to interrogate the very principles of any such restoration), I have always found myself, despite myself, facing the image of the open well invented by my memory, looking in. (And sometimes I wonder if perhaps, in the first days of our arrival in Carcassonne, the well was not in fact open, and only later closed by my father as a precaution, to eliminate any danger it might pose.)

I look into the well and there I see the entire shadow of the house before me (in the position that I would have taken up at that moment, I would now have my back turned to the bench, which would be right behind me, as if, abandoning the game, I had made a 180-degree turn, still on my knees, and were leaning my elbows on the edge of the well, which was very low); **I see the roof and the windows; I see the long balcony on the right and, leaning over onto my shoulder, I see the pine trees, moving in some warm gust of wind and filling the water with their green needles, and I see the very dark spindle trees as well.**

This is an image without anxiety, very peaceful. Is it because I believe it was invented (reworked by other glances into the water of a well whose location I can no longer identify?) that I feel detached from it, unconcerned, like a "third party" in this vision—not really "behind" my then-face or implicated in its reflection? Regardless, if I place myself at the center of the game, but out of the game, out of play, as I face the bench, at the center of a very great multiplicity of real memories, I still, by contrast, feel the ir- → I § 100 rational apprehension of a vague threat, of "something" that might suddenly leap out at me.

But why? → Bif E § 182

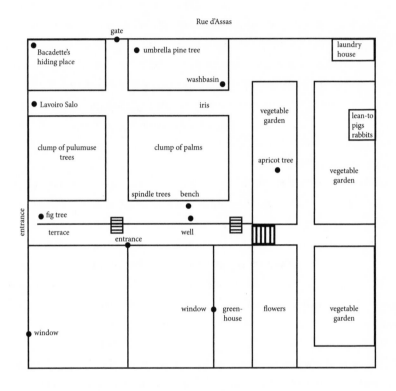

a <u>map</u>, which will allow the reader to find his or her way around in this chapter which is, after all, only a very long <u>description</u>

Chapter 4

Wild Park

30 The Wild Park was right outside, in front of this house

The **Wild Park** was right outside, just a little ways from the farmhouse. I capitalize "Wild Park," in the style of a proper noun, like a person's name (surname + given name: i.e., surname: "Park," given name: "Wild"), or else as though these words designated a well-known locale with an established reputation, located in this part of Les Corbières—a place called "Wild Park." And in the latter case this linguistic form would simply indicate a particular distinction granted to a common noun (or a common grouping: adjective + noun), thus transposing it into a proper name. But this is only a private, individual nomination, absent from every map; in the private, domestic sphere of nominations, this segment of a property in Les Corbières—whose public name was Sainte-Lucie—would have received the following name: the **wild park** (*had* received: the conditional only applies to the status of the name as such, not the materiality of the designation. I'm not just inventing this pairing of words now, to be the proper name of a landscape of memories. My memory has inherited it).

I just wrote "wild park" in lowercase. What's specific, then, to my personal appropriation of the site in question might be defined as this "promotion" of its name. (And first of all, of the adjective "wild": does this mean, then, that I'd actually created an as-yet-unknown grammatical category, that of the "proper adjective," in imitation of the "proper name"?) The usual (lowercase) nomination, "wild park," was originally purely descriptive, a designation shared and recognized among the few people who belonged, then, to the private sphere of the inhabitants of Sainte-Lucie, in Les Corbières; I had received it (orally) because I often used to visit the place. I adopted and transformed this designation for myself, also privately, but this time in an absolutely private and purely individual space. First as part of my games, then in my memories, and finally for the sake of memory itself, I transmuted the purely descriptive term into a

Name: **Wild Park**. Such designations usually leave momentary traces among a small number of people: they thread through the stories they tell, appear in their correspondence, then disappear. It might be said that I'm offering this nomination here as the proper name of these recollections, and against oblivion. Such an interpretation would not be false.

And yet I feel that this name is something more and other than just a proper name. Or perhaps I would like to give it a particular (fictive) linguistic status, and to suppose that it constitutes an essential element in the construction of an impossible language, an absolutely private language (which a single individual would have within him—most often a solipsistic language, but sometimes, in the ideal utopian situation in which a possible world of lovers is created, a "bi-ipsistic" language (these are the sorts of "words" that one would like to give to the person one loves)). In this case, despite the temptation, it wouldn't be correct to designate this new status as a "surname" (in the old sense of an *added* or *extra* name (and the neologism "sur-name" can't be used here either, not only because of its proximity to the undivided word "surname," which is unavailable because it's already been invented, and which, in its common usage in French (where *surnom* means "nickname"), has slid down a pejorative slope (referring to what ought rather to be designated a "sub-name"), but also because the affective and semantic overload or "sur-charge" that I am trying to point to here is more relevant to the first word in the term "proper name" than to the second)), and so not a "sur-name" either, but a "sur-proper name." And this is the reason why I've assigned the name a narrative role that goes far beyond what's required just to preserve a happy memory that left an impression.

One approached the house via the **wide path lined on both sides with majestic cypresses and pines; very tall, immense pines; though the umbrella pines were even more immense, and taller still (pines with "pine cones" and therefore with pine nuts); a path strewn with pine needles and pine cones; the brown, rust-colored carpet of pine needles beneath our bicycle wheels; I hear a great whispering of wheels.** The path opened out at one end onto the road, a road leading through Les Corbières, toward a village called Saint-André-de-Roquelongue (on the left as one leaves the village, about a kilometer away, on a downhill road); at the other end was the courtyard, a large courtyard in front of the main entrance, the entrance of the house there that faced outward, toward the road: Sainte-Lucie.

On the side of the main entrance to the house, in the courtyard, there was generally all the animation of a "farm" or an "estate" with its grape vines, fruit trees, and domestic animals (hens, ducks, guinea-fowl . . . dogs and cats). There was a fountain in the courtyard, around which there was a constant bustle of chickens and buckets. And a slope went very far down (vast were the fields of Sainte-Lucie) toward **a "border" stream, often dry, like all Mediterranean streams: a stream bordered by planted tomatoes, eggplants, peppers (fat tomatoes, extremely red, and small oval tomatoes, red or yellow: "plum" tomatoes).** We didn't go into the courtyard often. There were always too many people, known or unknown, for us to indulge in our own wildness there. But there was never anyone at all in the **Wild Park.**

A wide sandy path, lined with yew trees: very dark yew trees as though in evocation of English mourning; yew trees, with their miniscule elliptical leaves, very dense, very upright; the severe, Calvinist, funereal rectitude of the yew trees; and the red balls of their candle fruit, like candles in a birthday tree; those little fruits which aren't spheres, but insubstantial cylindrical muffs around a hard pit; tempting fruit, but forbidden ("poison!" was the word used for the fruit on those deadly trees); the fruit of the yew tree, not very hard, and so leaving its thick translucent substance on one's fingers if crushed; the fruit of the yew tree, with its dark red color; bright on the tree with a deep, dark brilliance, but $\rightarrow$ I § 101 **quickly losing its color once picked, impossible to keep fresh and bright, shriveling almost immediately, becoming puckered and dull.**

The wide path lined with yew trees was farthest to the left, perpendicular to the private façade of the house, the side that didn't face the courtyard; the path was therefore parallel to the ornamental driveway that served as the majestic entrance from the road; and the dense yew trees, on its left side (against a fence? a wall? the wide path just down below?) isolated the <u>**Wild Park**</u>**; it began there, thickly grown, dense, only a few meters from the house; between the park and the house, I see a stretch of gravel; I see another wide path on the right, parallel to the first and next to a wall, a rather high wall.** (Behind this wall there was a vine, for grapes but not for wine.) (By presenting a successive enumeration almost entirely without verbs, and by maintaining a particular punctuation, I "sustain" (and sometimes replace) the repeated occurrences of "I see," which is the "sign" that I have chosen (accompanied on my screen by a particular formatting of the characters) for the manifestation of a given family of memory-images.)

Along the broad path, in the sunlit sand, at the foot of the yew tree with the deepest shade, a column of black ants; with a little bucket of water, a sand-bucket for the beach, and some water from the courtyard, from the fountain, a puddle formed an obstacle, interrupting the military trans-port-lines of the ants; I, we, disturbed the bustling ants transporting seeds, the regimented ants with their "ant engineering," the ant-pontoneers with their twigs; perpetual movement of ant circulation in both directions; en-counters, passwords, recognition by antenna; dense gatherings, black co-agulations around an enormous dead wasp (like Lilliputians around the bound giant Gulliver). This image has a name: **Yew Tree with Ants.** It gener-ated enough ant-images for an entire lifetime.

Now, back when I was making a first attempt at writing **The Great Fire of London** (the novel), this was the image I had chosen for the beginning. But in keeping with what I took to be one of the strictest principles for transpos-ing events from an author's biographical reality into a novel, I had given this particular vision not to the character who would have represented the novel-ist's "fictive ego" (a conceit that weighed heavily on this version (and which, after abandoning it, I considered "naive")), but to a different one. There was a very conscious strategic "reason" for this displacement. But the ever more numerous and far-reaching repercussions of this decision, all the concentric circles reverberating outward from this huge stone falling into the waters of my mind, revealed their numerous and disturbing effects rather quickly. Little by little, they rocked my "fictional self" to the point of toppling it.

31 I don't know which tree, which trees, near the far end of the park

I don't know which tree, which trees, near the far end of the park (a species of conifer, certainly, but certainly not pine: perhaps fir, larch, or spruce? I no lon-ger "see" them. I've searched for them, but I've never found them again, never recognized them anywhere else: either it was a rare species of some sort, or, more likely, my mind has undergone such a complete translation, such an irre-versible metamorphosis of vision and taste, that I have in fact lost all effective ability to reproduce the experience of this image, whose essential attribute was associated with a single—and in my case, not very trustworthy—sense: the sense of taste) had the needles with a certain enchanting, unexpected flavor— but I made this discovery at the far end of the **Wild Park**, and I gave it a name, a proper name: **Oranjello**.

This was the name that I chose for these needles, and it was above all the name of their flavor. The entire needle was not, in fact, **Oranjello**, nor were all the other needles of this, of these trees; only **the most recently budding needles, the youngest ones, pulled from their resinous sheath and nibbled; only the deep hidden part was important, only their color, a pale light yellow, and their taste, a taste of orange; oranjello; Oranjello**. I must admit that I don't really know if their taste was, in reality, anything like that of an orange. My skull has not preserved an image of this flavor. But there can be no doubt that I imagined such a kinship and that this was the source of my linguistic "invention." The soft and secret seed of those needles had the taste of orange, but not the color. Thus, I invented a portmanteau word, a collision of flavor (orange) and color (yellow).

But if I never again managed to find the least trace of this revelation of mine on any extant conifer, is it simply because my memory has been so shaken by this revelation that it now refuses to allow me to recognize it? Not necessarily: it's clear that if my identification of the flavor of the needles led to their name, on one of the many occasions when we set about tasting all sorts of plant species, with the exception of a few rare ones identified as dangerous after warnings from parents or teachers (rightly or wrongly: was this the case with the berries on the yew tree? was it the case with the **Oranjello** itself, my personal poison and imprudent secret? I didn't know for sure, but I kept this possibility, this threat, always in play), this identification had to be based on a memory-imagination of what an orange tasted like. But the orange was a fruit that had completely disappeared from my experience of taste, at that point—and at least since the fall of 1940. Thus, the stability of such a flavor-memory might well be called into doubt.

More precisely, even if the kinship I had identified between the taste of the needle's root and citrus was in some way legitimate, it is not at all certain that this internal kinship has itself been preserved after so many years. This is true for at least two reasons. First, all the tasting of pine-needle tips that I've attempted since, quite systematically, in the hopes of finding the **Oranjello** (especially in the first moments of the **Project** and the **novel**, since I wanted to give it a major role), took place long after the war; but in all these experiments it would have been necessary for me to distinguish, irrefutably, this partial affinity (per-haps quite fragile and remote in the first place) between the taste of "orange" and this crumbly plant matter (whose consistency was in any case quite unlike that of a fruit), and to identify it in the midst of another, much greater and more obvious affinity—the one that unites all conifer needles in the bitterness of their taste. What's more, I wasn't really prepared to undertake this kind of experiment, since I had never been trained in any way to use my sense of taste, as wine tasters do, for example.

The second reason is that when I took it into my head to try to find the **Oranjello** tree, as an aid to writing my novel and simultaneously as a stimu-lus for poetic compositions, I quite naturally "took along" my accumulated experiences of the orange-fruit as a guide—which had again, and long since, become abundant, even banal (Taking no notice here of their decline in quality due to quasi-industrial commercialization, the extent of which I was able to observe, by way of contrast, when Alix and I visited her parents in Tunisia at Christmas in 1981, where the administrative whims of Canadian diplomacy had taken them). But the **orange** that worked its way into the **Oranjello** was itself only an orange of memory, and, even more importantly, when it was presented to us in my grandmother's stories, it was a symbol. Capitalized, it became the **Orange**, the symbol of a lost pre-war abundance, but also of a future abundance that would return along with freedom, and that was embodied by America (although this was an America that we knew only from hearing stories about it): a future abundance in which oranges would be offered to us once again, a fruit dripping with peace, an intense luxury for the thirsty.

In each needle, carefully pulled from its resinous base, I isolated the soft pale part at the very tip, I found it, the "oranjello," and I chewed it, tak-ing good care not to encroach on the green and properly coniferian part whose bitterness would have entirely obliterated the subtle, shifting es-sence, the orangey "spirit" on my tongue; the slightest error was fatal, for then I would only be able to find the Oranjello taste again after getting rid

of another flavor that, while not unpleasant, was very different: the over-powering and persistent taste of the fir tree (I use the word "fir" abusively, since it was doubtless not actually a fir tree; but within this plant family, the flavor of the ordinary needle is always more or less the same).

At the other extreme from the **Oranjello** (as a physical reality), from its immersion in the body of the tree, there was another substance to avoid, namely sap. The total absence of all sap was just as imperative to the **Oranjello** as the avoidance of any vegetal green: the sap was no more "orange" than the green of the needle, and its taste was no less overbearing. But I felt a violent attraction to sap nonetheless. To the same degree as its odor was captivating, as its oozing from the tree was transparent and lucid—born from a wound in the branches or the trunk—and as its hardening and darkening into a solidified stream, then into brown gum-like drops (which I scratched with my fingernail beneath the bark) was strange, I wished that among all these qualities it could be edible as well. Why? Because tree-sap was so similar in consistency, in luminosity, and in its slow, reticent flow to another precious commodity that had also disappeared since the time of abundance: honey. Behind the **orange-Oranjello** kinship, there was another emotionally similar convergence, an equation in which **sap = honey**, and this only increased the metaphoric intensity of the first one. (I'm not saying that any of this played into my linguistic invention in any conscious way. I'm only thinking of this correspondence now, as I write.) (If there was no experience of an orange contemporaneous with my investigations into the **Oranjello,** I nevertheless *did* have an encounter with honey: an encounter that I would call extreme, in the space-time refuge surrounded and symbolized by the **Wild Park.**)

Later, during the years that seemed to me like a period of exile, in Paris in 1945, in Saint-Germain-en-Laye, and then in Paris again, in the XIXth arrondissement—that is, before the very idea of exile lost its relevance and it became clear that for me there would never be any other condition, that there would be no "return from exile"—the **Wild Park** became, metonymically, the site of childhood. The **Oranjello,** then, while it was first of all a hidden treasure, also became the name of childhood—its proper name, or its title. At the beginning of the **Project,** I had thought of using this name as the title for a book of poems I later completed and published under another (the "*book* *whose title is the sign for belonging to a set"* ($\in$)). But I hesitated, and began instead to lean toward using the word in a part of the novel, **The Great Fire of London**: I would never have directly elucidated the word in the novel. It would have been a part of the novel's mysteries, arising from the "solution" of what was supposed to be the constitutive enigma of the **Project** as a whole. The image of the **Oranjello**, and the image of the <u>ants</u> on the tree-lined path leading to the dark mass of a door (images that were to be associated in the constitutive structure of these mysteries)—each of these would have occupied the respective <u>foci</u> of a narrative ellipse with an absent <u>center</u>.

More recently, after I had renounced the **Project** and the novel and undertook what became the beginning of this interminable forest of pages that I'm in the process of writing, I was again tempted to call a <u>branch</u> of my book **Oranjello**—and then, after abandoning this idea as well, I thought of using it as the heading for a single chapter: this one. But I was just as incapable of following through with this intention as the others. (I won't give any explanation here for this "incapacity." However, I have promised myself, as usual, that I will remedy this omission later (I'm hardly stingy with narrative promises).)

32 My vision shifts without any explanation or transition

My vision shifts, then, without any explanation or transition, from the **Oranjello** to the **Old Basin**. In doing so, it crosses a gulf of pure oblivion, though only with great difficulty (and only with the help of these designations: it is a deductive shift from one term to another). It's also a kind of evasion. The sap and substance of this period elude me. I know (but how?) that the **Old Basin** was located past the far end of the **Wild Park**, and I also know that the natural geometry of the world, presumed to be Euclidean, must locate it, therefore, on the near side of the road leading down to Saint-André-de-Roquelongue. But I see it as entirely isolated—none of the modes of access to it appear to have left even the most minute point of entry in me. I can't manage to reconstruct the least shred of a transition. The **Old Basin** is a world within the world of the **Wild Park**, but an autonomous one, as though even more remote in time than the park itself. Moreover, I see it from within. I am at the bottom of the **Old Basin**—long, empty, and dry, since it's been invaded by thriving vegetation, and its masonry has collapsed into ruins.

Now, it seems to me that the responsibility for this destruction falls entirely on the fig trees. **Tall fig trees growing on the edge of the basin; in one corner, a fig tree has even grown up through the bottom of the Basin itself** (if my vision is correct, this means that the **Old Basin** has been abandoned for a very long time). It's here that the long enduring instant of this image meets another one, no less fixed in its illusory and eternal identity: that of the fig tree from Saint-Jean-du-Var. **The figs, darkened by the sun, fall from the tall trees around the burning-hot basin, figs condensed into themselves, closing around their own sugar and sunlight, the self-preserved _penneque_ figs of September.**

And the _penneque_ fig is the perfect fulfillment of this fruit. This is a truth that was passed on to me by my father in Toulon in 1942—a family truth, then, to which my taste conformed without reticence, entirely and definitively (I've abandoned many beliefs that I once thought were reasonable, but never this one). The _penneque_ figs at the bottom of the basin of Sainte-Lucie, in Les Corbières, in September of 1943, constituted the experimental verification of this truth. The fig is a preeminently untransportable fruit, almost inseparable from the tree. Most of the time you can only eat them immediately after they've been picked. Nothing is further from the real fruit, nothing more pitiful, than those little "crates" of figs offered to the naive shopper in a Parisian market. Apparently people still see fit (as is readily corroborated) to offer those bland things for sale (and they even find unfortunate buyers, who suspect nothing). But I've never seen _penneque_ figs sold anywhere. We are in fact dealing here with an irreducible singularity (one that's even more inviolable than that of the blackberry, which, like the _penneque_ fig, is incapable of being transported and then sold on the market (mass-cultivated blackberries are raised and sold, of course, and they have the bland taste to show for it; but even more importantly, they're grown on (wonderfully symbolic) "thornless" briars!)). To my mind this singularity makes the _penneque_ fig a fruit-symbol of the untransmittable flavor of the past. (The only other possible parallel to this form of the fig is that of the dried fig, which (like the date, in its familiar form) constitutes a "herborization" of its flavor, rather than a fulfillment: brown like the date, equally remote from the living fruit itself, with a gray-brown tint like a black poppy or a dried cornflower pressed between the pages of a notebook: just the opposite of a real "white" or black fig. But _pennequization_ is superior by far to drying, because it preserves moistness and maintains the living consistency of the fruit—always fragile, but even more so as it approaches a state of dissolution.)

As though escaping from the broad dark green leaves of the fig trees, or as though arising by spontaneous generation from the cracks in the ground and along the walls of the Old Basin, large violent-green lizards, stunned by the heat and the light, reigned supreme; they weren't even frightened by my presence, which admittedly was kept at a safe distance because of the lizard's reputation (perhaps undeserved) as fighters with a fearsome bite; one of them looked at me, he looked at me, looks at me, shakes himself slightly out of his torpor, and slips into the shadow of the stonework, or disappears, climbing up toward the jungle of briars, of graminaceae and fennel that frame the Old Basin's outer edges; in each of the smaller fissures, thin lips in the stone, a regiment of impish little gray lizards and a cohort of grass snakes; on the edges of the patterns of cracks, the quick little gray lizards looked at me, look at me, with palpitating throats, pale and curious. The grass snakes slip hissing away.

Wild Park, **Oranjello**, **Old Basin**: thus I trace out an onomastic triangle in which each capitalized word has a symbolic, almost allegorical function (the "Old" in Old Basin is probably not an antonym of "new," for example. In the bygone world of the Wild Park, I can't identify any "new basin" that would have replaced the other one, for water storage and irrigation): an allegory of childhood, of childhood within childhood, absolute childhood. Everything there is more rare, more perfect, and more perfectly and completely *past* than anywhere else: the "country place" around the **Wild Park** (as we called a "farm" in the Aude); the time we spent there (just a few weeks if you add up our occasional visits during vacations, which for the sake of my story (but not only) I've here condensed into a single summer, the end of one summer, the beginning of one autumn); the intoxicating superabundance of freedom, of sunshine (in Les Corbières, back when it was still almost uninhabited: a contrast with the city); the great mysterious adventure of the place.

I had populated the **Old Basin**, the most secret territory of the **Wild Park**, not with the luxuriance of Kipling's *Jungle Book* (which I never found convincing, with its oversized boas and panthers, its chattering "Bandar-logs," and its ridiculous and inept wild child, Mowgli), a luxuriance that was totally un-imaginable in the harsh surroundings of Les Corbières, but rather with the imaginary danger of cobras (whose role could easily have been filled by the in fact harmless and very timid grass snakes) and their mortal enemy, the hero of one of my favorite novellas: *Rikki-Tikki-Tavi* (for this role I had chosen a large green lizard with a decisive manner, whom I baptized, in an even greater distortion, *Mangouste* (mongoose)). I stayed there, giving life to this drama, at least until the excess of sun and figs chased me away, into the shade of the yew trees, or toward the grapes.

It was clear that Sainte-Lucie had previously been a much larger property, richer and better maintained. The **Wild Park** and the **Old Basin** were no doubt the vestiges of a "pleasure garden," and the basin had probably once been filled using a clever system that drew water from nearby springs or collected rain, coaxing the run-off along trenches and inclined paths made of drystone bricks (such as existed more or less everywhere, in Provence, in Catalonia, in Languedoc, before the successive and cumulative disasters of rural depopula-tion, tourism, and "second homes"—that cancer infecting the *ars memoria* of landscapes). There was another vine there too, separated from the others by its topography (between the area behind the house, the Park, and a little stand of pines): a vine of modest dimensions producing grapes with "noble rot," used not for wine, but—as the expression goes—for the table. For us, this was **The Vine** ("The," an adjective-article, or better, a proper-article, the third term of my linguis-tic invention, necessary for the "reading" of language in poetry).

Together with the fig trees, this vine produced almost enough to feed us on its own. Aside from tomatoes and a few other fruits, what food other than grapes could we have found in such abundance then? They were our sugar, our vitamins. They satisfied the insistent hunger left by our insufficient "ra-tions," the too infrequent poultry, the almost absolute absence of red meat, the unappetizing bread. **Like sparrows, like thrushes, we would thrust our faces under the leaves, picking or biting right from the clusters, stretching out our bare earth-colored legs along the dry burnt ground marked with furrows between the vines, and we would eat, we would eat the hot, sugary liquor of the heavy grapes until our thirst was quenched, to the point of drunkenness;**

colors of the triangular grape clusters: muscats; muscats, both black and white; dark red Aramon grapes; white "olivettes," which are almost green and have an irritating, penetrating flavor; new <u>games</u>: pluck off an entire cluster; take all the grapes from a heavy cluster in your hands, rub off the dust, make them as shiny and polished as marbles; carefully peel the grapes one by one with your teeth and take the seeds out without destroying the consistency of the grape itself, spit out the seeds, let the juice flow on your tongue, with a febrile slowness, the slowness of a desert animal, a jerboa; eat the flesh, but keep the skin of each grape in the corner of your mouth, in your cheek, the way hamsters do; keep ten, twenty, fifty grape skins; resist the urge, the need to eat them; then eat them all at once. Finally.

33 Throughout this description I have remained entirely <u>outside</u>.

Throughout this description I have remained exclusively restricted to a few places, and I have remained entirely **outside**. For example, I haven't gone into the house. The fact is that I can only see the house itself in the context of the relative cold of winter, because in winter I had to stay shut up inside—because then I could hardly do otherwise—by default, in short. I only remember the inside as being part of another world, no longer the space of the **Wild Park.** As though, in going back through the years, I were spontaneously establishing a partition between inside and outside (parallel to the one that exists in memory) that would also serve to separate the different realms of the seasons, which only rarely communicate with each other.

→ I § 103–104

But still more decisively, this partition exists because my memories of this place are almost entirely enclosed within the few images I've described (along with a very few others of which I will speak in the coming "moments" of this chapter). They are intense but fixed, almost isolated; each one of them is strictly autonomous, linked to the others only by a present, voluntary effort to make narrative connections, and not by the usual leaps of a spontaneous passage through the labyrinth of memories.

→ I § 102

The contrast between these images and the frosty flower that begins my first chapter is absolute: in the latter case, the image doesn't "remain in place"; it gives rise to a profuse arborescence of other visions (of which I've therefore chosen to describe only a very small part).

Even sharper is the contrast with a territory that is at least superficially comparable, that of the garden which is the sole setting of chapter 3. That garden has no "proper" name, but I can "see" it as a whole (even if this view is necessarily fictive, a physical impossibility). On the contrary, I have no general view of the **Wild Park**; but only of its edge, of the yew trees . . .

Is it because the totality of these memories has remained buried beneath their names: **Wild Park**, **Oranjello** . . . ? is it simply because they were given names? because the attribution of names fixed them, but at the same time isolated them from one another? interrupting the continuous movement that, in the garden on the Rue d'Assas or in my bedroom in winter, for example, ceaselessly sent me "elsewhere"?

One objection I can immediately raise to this suggestion is that, in the garden chapter, I was also dealing with <u>names</u>, and especially with the name of a game, **Go-Creeping**, which itself calls up my vision of the bench (a vision at once "blind" and lucid!). But no, that situation is different. The name of a game isn't the name of a place. On the contrary, it even presumes a multiplicity of places, and a multiplicity of displacements between them. The singularity of the **Wild Park** remains.

Then again, it's not impossible—and this would fit my "hypothesis" on the fading and then destruction-reconstruction of memories by means of their evocation and, even more, through the process of fixing them on paper—that I had already almost obliterated the Wild Park in my memory when I attempted, several times over, to use its images in the novel and in the poems of the **Project**. This too would have had the effect of effacing other, related images (or of rendering them momentarily inaccessible, without any "open sesame") by breaking the associative links between them (perhaps these other images weren't as numerous as those related to the garden, because of the unequal lengths of time I spent in each one, but they were certainly present, and varied, in the beginning).

Be that as it may, it's nonetheless true (and in sharp contradiction to my hypothesis about the fading away of images once written) that these particular images remain very strong. One could assume (taking a spontaneous skeptical position), that this intensity is illusory, that it has more to do with the intensity of other moments—the moments of poetic composition in which the **Oranjello**, for example, must have appeared in the past as magnified, symbolic, iconic—than with any intrinsic power. Anyway, I can't exclude this possibility.

I prefer another interpretation, however, to this last—one that suits the general direction of this chapter much better: namely, that the initial force of these visions was very great; and that to this day they have, therefore, remained intense. And I find in them a certain "proof" of this: namely, the important role played by senses that I am rarely able to re-evoke intact from the past: touch and taste. And the vivid presence of colors: proper colors.

34 **From the Rue d'Assas (Carcassonne) to Sainte-Lucie**

From the Rue d'Assas (Carcassonne) to Sainte-Lucie (the "public" name of what was to me, above all, the **Wild Park**), the distance on the road, by bike, was about fifty kilometers. Taking the same trip by the same route today would be outright torture, and a dangerous experiment to boot, at least during the very first part of the journey, which passes through Trèbes, Capendu, Barbaira, and Moux on the "National" highway (which then heads off toward Lézignan-Corbières, and further still, Narbonne). Then, one used to turn to the right at a fork in the road before passing through Fabrezan (the native village of Charles Cros: the Aude is a *département* of poets: Reverdy (Narbonne), Anne-Marie Albiach (Moux)). At this point one was still in the flood plain. But soon the road entered Les Corbières proper, with immediate and perceptible consequences for the cyclist, who faced an uphill climb.

The years from '40 to '45 were a blessed time for bicycles. The roads were al-
→ I § 105   most entirely free of cars. Our first visit to Sainte-Lucie took place
                          during the school vacation of 1940 or '41. I was just eight (or
nine) years old, but I thought it perfectly natural at the time to travel those few dozen kilometers along the roads by moving forward on a rather rudimentary machine ("gear changes," for example, were completely unknown. Not to mention the difference in weight! Today anyone can command a bicycle no heavier than a pack of cigarettes, setting it into motion, or so it seems, with a simple push of the finger, and rolling along almost without any muscular intervention whatever). The trip was hardly any longer than the one I sometimes traveled myself, riding up and down the walkways, again and again, in the garden of the house on the Rue d'Assas.

Nonetheless, after one had entered Les Corbières, there were some formidable climbs. Certain moments when I stopped, perhaps to rest after an intense effort, have preserved <u>three visions</u> of these climbs for me, and in each case perhaps these visions were also retained because of some abrupt contrast between them and the usual and expected surroundings along the road. In the first vision it was certainly the strangeness, the wildness of the place that caused it to be preserved. A wildness too that made it possible for this image to be annexed to that other set of images—several kilometers away, according to the real topography—which what I've called **Wild Park** has been configured in my memory. The "proper adjective," the sur-adjective, "**Wild**," unifies (oblivion having almost entirely engulfed the intervening landscapes of vines, which were too familiar to be retained) and therefore "telescopes" distant places; it eliminates all discontinuity and imposes an interconnected space of memories, unifying disparate continuities, other topologies (just as our games acted on the topology of the garden).

Firstly, then, **a village, the name of a village: Villerouge-la-Crémade; a late-morning stop beneath an overcast sky (low skies are a rarity in Les Corbières), almost cold; a few houses; clay everywhere; red clay; proper red, red itself, a true color; a few houses along the side of the road, on a steep slope; the bike leaning against a low wall, at the top of a hill; a pause, the natural prolongation of a suspended moment, at zero speed,** → I §
before the intoxicating descent in the abandoned, ruined air: harsh, in no way restful; silence without relief; Villerouge-the-"burned"; devoid of its ordinary violent desert light, this moment of the past seems like a moment after a fire; and it will never be repopulated.

For a long time I situated this vision at the center of a series of fictive imaginings that I would call "Stevensonian" (referring to the harsh Stevenson who wrote *The Master of Ballantrae*, not the more seductive one of *Treasure Island*), inspired by the story of the great bandits, Mandrin, Cartouche, and Rocambole. In my mind, Balzac's *The Red Inn* was set there (for this I beg to be forgiven by its honorable and peaceful vine-growing inhabitants, both past and present—if any such remain). The red of Villerouge was a dark bloody red, like spilled blood, old, drying into brown; like clay coming from a bleeding wound in the earth, during a storm, kneaded and calcified in order to make those walls, virtually devoid of any openings, and without any blue eyes.

I move still farther away and **I see**, in my <u>second vision</u>, **the sea (The Sea)** (with an adjective-article, which is its "proper article," and a true one this time, too), **I do not know when it is or what path I'm on, but I see from a great distance, and from above; its distant shimmering in the immaterial sun, like "blue foam," discovered once again, unceasing**. The inaccessible sea, but hoped for, to be reached only later, "after the war"; **I see only a thin drop of sea, a drop in motion: small, foamy and blue; it's barely a shimmering discontinuity in the ocean of the horizon, the sky-ocean, almost imperceptible between the rocks, the hills falling away one after another into the imprecise outlines blurred by the air, the too-clear air, the sun-mist**. So that, then, was what the future would be like, and peace.

Peace, finally, the absolute peace of the <u>third of these moments</u>, in the **Fontfroide Abbey,** which I can still see today: these three visions are linked by a common approach, by the movement of a bicycle whose speed is neither the speed of walking—which gives one more than enough time to get used to the landscape, and thus attenuates surprise—nor the excess speed of the automobile, instrument of blind touristic bulimia, tearing holes in the fabric of landscapes and ripping places out of their immediate surroundings (hence a feeling I once had, not exactly of disappointment, but of a violent transition, when, for the first time after the war, I stopped at Fontfroide on my way to Agde with my friends the Harnoises; it was the summer Stalin died; as we drove down the highway we learned about the arrest of the sinister Beria.)

A truly cool oasis, but one evoked at least as much by its name, by the watery image called up by "Font-", which is "fountain," and by the promise of being rescued from the oppressive heat held out by "*-froide*" (cold)—not a portmanteau, but a fusion-word, **Fontfroide; fountain of silence amid the deafening cicadas, the locusts, the bicycle wheels squeaking their brakes along the curving, dusty, downhill road, in the dusty and noisy light of August; invisible medieval shade with a rectangular ambulatory; silent shadows protected by stone, by the treasure of water, nurse of peace, by the virtuous stone, protector of silent contemplations.**

And the intact walls of the interior quadrangle, the geometric space reserved for a slow and ancient meditative circulation, were covered with wisteria; an intense and improbable fragrance radiated from their large

blue clusters; not the blue of the sea, as in my second vision, **but a lighter blue; nor the slightly purple blue of irises, but a looping blue, light and cold like a stream of water emerging in a froth from the mouth of a fountain (a fragrance that seemed heavy with the sugar held within the shifting name of the plant that clung to the walls, like a rippling dress covering the walls, with clusters of grape-like flowers,** outside of the dull patina of the past, **wisteria (*glycine*)).**

I've held on to these three visions because they were obviously a part of the **Wild Park**: because they became attached to it by a terrible, desolate threat—or else by a hope, an enchantment—to the secret discovery of the **Oranjello** (and each one was like a plane of possibilities associated with my invention—was a specific deployment of these possibilities). I see now that they made up a part of the world, of my own world, but I would say that they were more world than the world itself. Even if I did not know it then, they presented me with all the marvelous, rare, and (inextricably) disquieting things that the world held in store for me.

35 Sainte-Lucie belonged to Camille Boer.

Sainte-Lucie belonged to Camille Boer. The use of Camille as a masculine name (it's also my father's second name) is, I believe, a rather "southern" characteristic in France, and a dated one at that. In its "Roman-ness" I see one of the border-posts between the *oc* and the *oïl* regions—not because the name tends to be given more often to girls, these days, in the lands north of the Loire (I've never encountered it among my students at Nanterre, and have always taken an interest in the generational evolution of given names, over the years, as I've graded my "midterm" exams), but because of a delightful song from the eighteenth century that I learned as a child (and I have a sense of the eighteenth century as being emblematic, who knows why, of the irreducible strangeness of what is "French" in me): "Camille one day granted / a gallant rendezvous to her lover / Whom she madly adored / to fulfill his desires . . ."

In fact, Camille Boer was Catalan. Before the war (the Spanish Civil War), he'd owned a small business that made orthopedic instruments (had he inherited it?) and possessed what we might call a fortune. As an anarchist—and one likes to believe that all Catalans are anarchists, even when they're not—he had devoted every bit of his Catalan resources to financing the purchase of war planes for the Republic, which turned out to be a complete loss because of the infamous "nonintervention" that blocked them at the border. He recounted his conversation with Léon Blum, who obstinately refused to let the planes take off in secret, saying (as Boer told it), "I can't! I can't!" almost in tears (and Boer the Republican narrated this scene with indignation and contempt, as proof of the unexpected cowardice and spinelessness of a Prime Minister of the Popular Front. The impression this story made on me was all the greater because Camille Boer was really and truly not the sort of person who made a habit of pronouncing such judgments against human beings (and in saying this I'm thinking even of Francoists and Nazis, for he believed in the humanity of humans, in general)). In 1939, he took refuge on the other side of the border, in this "country place" that came to him through his wife, Laurentine, who was from Narbonne. He had thick white hair framing a very round brown face, and he was a grandfather, a young and enthusiastic grandfather. And like his grandchildren, like everyone close to him, we called him Camillou.

As I sort out my memories (the very existence of the **Wild Park**, the **Basin**, and **The Vine**, the scale of the buildings, the size of the fields planted with vines, the dimensions of the central courtyard, the number of people who worked and lived there), I realize that Sainte-Lucie had been, and still was, a "large estate." Camillou had taken in and employed a number of field workers, for the most part Catalans and anarchists like himself (short, wild, sunburned men and their wives and girlfriends who were likewise short, sunburned, and wild, with hoarse voices and extraordinary names that often had a distinctly un-anarchistic ring: Concepción, Esperanza, Incarnación!), though it has to be said that the position of "boss" didn't suit him at all, neither ideologically nor on a human level, neither morally nor practically. But in the precarious conditions of the war, this arrangement, autarchic and scraggly, "worked," more or less. (And for us city kids turned loose in this blessed atmosphere, everything went surprisingly well.)

Sainte-Lucie didn't survive long after the Liberation. Camillou had to sell it, and he went on to try his luck in other "businesses." In the process, his belief in the intrinsic goodness of human nature brought him innumerable and ceaselessly renewed disillusionments—this "Rousseauist" belief, in the banal sense of the word, which he never abandoned and which was all-inclusive (something even more difficult to maintain), with very rare exceptions (always the Francoists and the Nazis, but never individually), and always incarnated in actually existing human beings (just as one used to say, only a few years ago, "actually existing socialism"). He put his hopes in the sulfur mines (for too long), and then in the development of Languedoc (too soon)—which later brought glory to his "friend" Philippe Lamour. He lived at the time in Toulouse, and occasionally came to visit us in Saint-Germain-en-Laye, where we went out into the garden to meet him with genuine cries of joy: "Camillou! Camillou!" How can I put it? If his belief in the goodness of the world might appear indefensible and naive, when seen in the harsh light of reason, there was at least one being in the world who managed to justify it by example: himself. He was good.

And his goodness wasn't solely based on a theoretical foundation that brought his life into harmony with his thought. It came quite naturally to him. Goodness was in his being, in even the least of his attitudes and actions. And this was particularly visible in his relationship with children. (Today, of course, I wonder whether the essentially beneficent aspect of such a moral unity was not in part limited to his exchanges with children.) Children adored him: his grandchildren, first of all, the sons of his daughter Noëlle, "little Jean" and "the twins." As did we, of course, my brothers, my sister, and me, from the moment we met him. His indulgence was so free of demagoguery that no one ever took advantage of it. He was naturally and without hesitation on an equal footing with children, as he was with everyone. And children approached him with an immediate, instinctive, and animal trust.

Whenever he came to see us, arriving in his gasogene car (the unlikely *ersatz* of our "requisitioned" gasoline), it was immediately a joyous and festive occasion. He came with gifts, or without gifts, but the joy was always the same, expressed in shouts, laughter, hugs, dances. During one of my last visits to Sainte-Lucie, most likely in '44, he took me to Narbonne one day. We came back with oysters, incomparable oysters, like the ones at Saint-Jean-du-Var. We opened the oysters in the enormous cold dining room, in the white light of winter.

When the question finally arose of the ultimate fate of our duck, Bacadette, and when it became clear to everyone that it would be impossible, hunger or no hunger, to sacrifice her (and when, in addition, our departure from Carcassonne began to loom, it also appeared inconceivable (though we children conceived of it very clearly!) to take her with the whole family to Paris), the solution was obvious: Sainte-Lucie. My father took his bicycle, put Bacadette in a basket attached to the rack—after we'd fervently and with great emotion kissed her beak, her neck, her webbed feet, the soft feathers on her back, the down on her belly, the large feathers of her hind rudder—and then this dear old friend set off for her place of retirement, among the other ducks, ducklings, hens, chickens, turkeys and turkey-cocks, and guinea fowl who shared this refuge. We let her go without a worry, since we knew she would find herself under the protection of our friend, someone we trusted completely, Camillou. One year later, in fact, my father paid a visit to his friends Laurentine and Camille (during the last part of their time on the estate), again arriving by bicycle; he got down off his machine in the courtyard just in front of the house, undid the clasps on the cuffs of his pants, leaned his bicycle against the wall, and felt a beak grab hold of his shin like a little pincer: and there was Bacadette, having run off from the troop of ducks to greet him.

And so I arrive at the final image of this chapter, the last image connected to and merging with the territory, at once real and utopian, of the **Wild Park** (which is both in itself and through itself a concrete image, unified and unique; but also the multiplicity of the other images called up by its name, which can be understood and justified through it alone. I enumerate them again, all seven I've mentioned so far (so eight all together): The **Yew Tree with Ants**, the **Oranjello**, the **Basin**, **The Vine**, **Villerouge-la-Crémade**, **The Sea at Leucate**, **Fontfroide**). I've also given a name to this last and final image. I call it: **Cingle**. And there you have an entire world in a state of completion, constructed from nine images in all, and for good. I hereby take my leave of it.

The **Cingle** was another "country place" in Les Corbières, in an even more distant locale, and wilder if possible, located at a higher elevation. It was the property of a woman friend of the Boers, land that Camillou helped cultivate. I wouldn't be able to find it on a map today (it was perhaps from there, from those heights that I saw, far away, that drop of foamy blue water that I called

The Sea, no doubt from the direction of Leucate). Before entering the **Cingle,** we—Camille, my father, and I—had traveled along **a field sown with rough bristly plants topped by blue flowers, but a liquid blue, already a mountain blue**; what was the name of this plant? Borage. It was borage that I had before my eyes; **I saw a slope overtaken by alfalfa and borage; a tough, stiff plant; tough and blue.**

We went in. On a wooden table, I was served honey on a plate, honey like I had never seen, like I would never see again, **the honey of the** <u>Cingle</u>**, flowing and transparent, intensely flavorful, oozing evenly over the disk of the tilted plate without the slightest ripple, without the slightest hurry.**

There was also a little blonde girl there. → Bif C § 151

Chapter 5

Davila Square

36 The form of a city

". . . The form of a city / Changes faster, alas, than the human heart . . ." While the garden on the Rue d'Assas remains protected for me, internally, maintaining a profound relation of identity with itself between its walls—since I will never again have access to it (I will never again enter the space that it nonetheless continues to occupy in the present (because the house, and, as far as I could tell, the garden, both still existed the last time I passed by there, three years ago))—the same cannot be said of most of the other public places I knew in Carcassonne. **Davila Square** is still called Davila Square, but I refuse to recognize it under this name. I've tried, but I cannot. This is not only because of the horizontal and vertical upheavals that have been inflicted upon it. The sonorous individuality it possessed through this name—its local "genius"—has been destroyed. The four winds (especially the *cers*, which is the local "*maïstre*"—what the mistral is among the Provençal winds (the name means "master")) may well penetrate it from every side, just as they used to do—from the canal, from the broad "avenues," from the orthonormal grid of the central streets—they may crumple the air like an enormous piece of paper, but their outmoded voice, a pagan voice from the past, has been smothered and mocked by the gross hysterical preaching of the automobiles. One can no longer hear their breath. And only a millenarian hope that I don't really possess could ever lead me to believe that "Time will bring back the order of ancient days," or that "The earth shook with a prophetic breath" (Nerval). I pass by on the sidewalk, I stop up my eyes and ears, and I restore for a moment, over and against the "metaphor" of the trucks, the oracles of my ancient gods.

It was there, at the edge of the square, that they reigned. There was a man who sold potatoes (and other things? But **today I see only brown burlap sacks, blackish brown, rough, lying on the well-trodden ground**. Twenty-five years ago my memory stashed some spices there as well, but a tramontana wind of oblivion has since blown over the cinnamon, the saffron). Here was the "house" of Gleize (it disappeared some time after the war. In 1967 it was recalled by the poet of the cypresses, Jean Lebrau, from Moux). I turned it into a Hades reserved entirely for my personal use; behind its doors I projected a dark cavern inhabited by Spirits, Forms, Ideas, Angels, and Archons (as I would say today), but which were then, more simply and more purely, Names. An underground space beneath the "house" was connected, by various paths established in a purely prescriptive manner, to the establishment of my friend M. Dupuis, the cooper on the Rue d'Assas. Only later did I identify the inhabitants of these spaces as Gods (after discovering Mount Olympus in a book). But Gods they were, without any doubt: nominal gods, however, deprived of everything except being, except singularity and residence, their being entirely a "being-there," unconnected with any benevolent or malevolent intentions, without any powers, without visible forms, without ontology, phylogeny, transcendence, essence. Except that they were. They were, that was all. If there is a God, or many Gods, I would be tempted to demand from him, from them, nothing more than that.

Some of their Names were secret. As such, they could not be spoken, with the result that I've now forgotten them. I still knew them ten years ago. I know that I still knew them ten years ago. I could say them then. I remember that. But today, their Names—no, I don't know them anymore. According to Eleazar of Worms, when a newborn comes into the world, his guardian angel gives him a good whack across the nose, and he forgets everything: everything that his eternal soul could have known, and that he will later find out during his stay on earth, by *anamnesis*, but only in snatches, fragments, glimmers. And why does the angel do this? Because without this "compassionate" gesture, the child would see what awaits him here below, and he would refuse to breathe his first breath, to let out his first cry. But perhaps it must be supposed as well that at every moment of birth over the course of our lives (of re-birth after some kind of death, in ourselves: the death of a hope, or of someone close to us), our guardian angel intervenes once again, to make us forget the prescient knowledge we've obtained that would render the future too unbearable.

There were about twenty of these gods, but only a half-dozen or so have survived. And only one has maintained any stability. He was the greatest of all (there was a certain hierarchy among my divine Names). And he may have been a hunter god: His Name was <u>Garenne</u>. I was allowed to say his name (it seems I didn't deprive myself of this privilege). And he himself possessed a few words, which in order to simplify (and under the "Fenimorian" influence of *The Last of the Mohicans*) I often turned into war cries, but these were always really just a summons, an injunction to the lower gods. Thus: "**Trou**goudou! **Ma**nana! Aganu! Agana!" (in that order). (I emphasize the first syllables of what was thus a dactylic tetrameter, but which also formed an alexandrine with an internal rhyme, or two rhyming hexasyllables: a spontaneous and harmonious conjunction of French meter and Greek paganism.)

For my entry into the dwelling place of the gods (whose nectar must have been the "sweet potato," so rare at the time), I gave them (through telepathy) a password: "Glèzundown" (I'm trying to transcribe the sound of the "image" as I remember it, and this implies a distinct phonic "anglicism," thus providing a glimpse of the likely geographical location of these "Elysian Fields": the isle of England, mother of the Resistance to Hitler. But at the time I had not yet recognized it as such, much less deliberately created this association).

At the end of the epoch related in their tales, their mythical age, I gave my
→ I § 106   gods a language called Peruviac. It was a language whose mor-
phology suffered from a formal hypertrophy in the inflection of substantives and adjectives. Its "cases" proliferated like mushrooms, and there were at least nine declensions! On the other hand, the system of verbs was not very imaginative, suffering no doubt from the fact that, in the systematic explication of "Peruviac grammar" that I began shortly before leaving Carcassonne, and which remained pitifully incomplete, these came after the noun and the adjective in the systematic order of "subjects" (moreover, this explication was missing an indispensable counterpart, announced as such in my notebook: the *epitome* of the fundamental texts of divinely inspired literature, consisting of both poems and mythical stories (nothing has survived of this except one fragment of a "Genesis" that's really much more cosmogonic, Hesiodic, and enumerative than biblical, and is now largely incomprehensible, since its corresponding lexicon has disappeared)).

On the other side of the square lived a man, a young man when I was a child, whom I did not encounter very often, but who was related in some way (which has completely vanished from my mind) to someone close to us (I don't recall who), and whom I have forgotten and would not recognize today. But I remember his name. He was called Prudent Padieu. It seems difficult to imagine that this name that I've retained didn't play a decisive role in the revelation of the divine presences in the other realm, in the temple of potatoes, located there where the <u>Padieu</u> family did <u>not</u> live (Padieu, as in *Pas-dieu*, "not-god"). Since <u>no Padieu</u> (no not-god) was found along "Gleize's Way," I cannot avoid deducing from this, immediately, with all the irresponsibility I grant myself in constructing proofs within this narrative (here closer to a tall tale than a novel), that I'd had a childish presentiment of intuitionist logic: I would not have sought the Way of Double Negation here if I had not already found it long ago.

I see Davila Square. I see no vehicles on the square. Only the winds, the sun, the wind, the sun, the wind. I am standing in the sun, surrounded by wind, taken up into the envelope of the wind. The doors of the "house" of Gleize are open. From this mouth of shadow wafts the odor of the gods' dwelling place, an odor of earth and of potatoes; the color of shadows emerges from there, and the speech of the gods, who always speak of shadow, of shades, of oblivion.

"<u>Trougoudou</u>! <u>Ma</u>nana! Aganu! Agana!"

I eventually (1963) made a poem out of all this (what else could I do?):

> On the square lived
> where? Prudent carried away
> to the potatoes (?) by his gods
> but me I was free
>
> the great drums lay broken
> (pounded by twenty winds)
> plume! a wartime winter
> where? absent from roll call
>
> I wandered dreaming
> more of brambles than of schedules
> less of benches than of berries!

the vellum sky flew
toward your cinnamon walls
oh Davila Square!

(I've gathered together in this "prose moment" all the material that might "elucidate" the above sonnet, from my first book (∈) (or else definitively obscure it).)

37 Davila Square was the central station along a route I followed countless times

Now Davila Square was the central station along a route I followed countless times when walking through the city, punctuated by certain sites of memory, sources of the mnemonic waves I'm trying to capture for this description. (The expression "mnemonic wave" was used by Aby Warburg to characterize the iconological nodes he discovered (in which such waves are concentrated), protectors of the afterlife of the ancient gods. He assembled them in a "thousand and three" radiant images on a large black screen, the keys to that forever incomplete library of memory, at once personal and collective, that he called **Mnemosyne.**)

At one end of this route was the door to our house, at the other the Breithaupt bookstore, on the Rue de la Gare, a temple of reading and a sanctuary offering me books to take home (I read them on the way back). Leaving our house and turning right along the garden wall, then left onto the Rue d'Assas (along the wall of the barracks), I arrived at my first station, the palace of barrels. M. Dupuis, the cooper, was my friend. About his name I would say first of all that I never knew exactly how to spell it, since I only ever encountered it orally and never had any occasion to write it down, until now. Perhaps it was Dupuy, or some other variation. But my most immediate association with these two syllables is: *du puits*, "from the well" or "from the pit." Like the well in the garden, like the house of potatoes on the square, Dupuis's workshop opened a door into the dark and bacchic territory of the gods, in which Dupuis himself was something like the friendly Vulcan, the harmless Hephaestus.

He was rather short, not very talkative, good humored, rotund from a certain natural resemblance, out of an unconscious imitation and absorption (or so it seemed to me); likewise his face had turned red, both internally and externally, from the wine-soaked atmosphere. We never exchanged more than a few words. But he was my friend, because he let me watch, in silence, his barrel-making work—the importance of which did not escape me (the Aude is a wine growing region). All the children from our street and from neighboring streets enjoyed this same privilege, and there were always a half-dozen onlookers gathered before his altar. In his hands the very shapes of the barrels were broken down, reconstituted, and constructed, revealing and enriching ever anew the Idea of the Barrel—which is never embodied in any concrete barrel, but transcends them all.

What I liked the most was the extreme care and attention he brought to a living but ailing barrel. Once the plug was out, still visibly wet, the barrel's dark odor, a dark red odor (an adult and autobiographical odor), spread out in the half-light, a wine spirit, a soul. With infinite precaution but with great authority, M. Dupuis slowly loosened the iron bands, the great equatorial circle and then the lesser tropical circles, inspected them in search of rust, cracks, or some congenital imperfection. The wooden slats making up the body of the barrel then came apart, fell away from their conjuncture—as compressed and constrained as the chest of a corseted "beauty" from 1900—and they lay scattered on the earthen ground drenched with wine (a divine libation), like the slices of an orange freshly peeled and then taken apart on a plate.

For a moment, before he separated the various members of this body for inspection and evaluation, the shape remained implicitly legible in its constituent parts, with its system of curvilinear coordinates, since the mental eye projected the reversible topological transformation onto it that, with these clothes fallen away (like those at the feet of a pink-tinted beauty in the erotic postcards of 1900), would cover the nudity of the absent mass of wine. An ugly stain came to light beneath the metal, revealing the corrosion of a fungal decay. He nodded his head, Hippocratically. The internal curvature of the wooden meridians showed a wine-soaked color, a trace of the intimate swelling caused by the liquid, keeping the barrel watertight (a Celtic invention).

The street was on an incline and the gutter-stream was almost never dry, on rainy days bringing an overflow of reddened water from Dupuis's workshop to the sandy and muddy rivers that gushed in a torrent onto the intersection, contributing finally, much farther on, to the flow of the real river, the Aude.

I was particularly attentive to the stream's powers of resistance and assimilation, made visible by the "marker" of the wine. Forced by the combination of gravity and the gutter system to mingle, eventually, with the dominant waters of a mightier street (an avenue in fact), it refused to abandon its identity for as long as it could, holding on for a while to its autonomy as a red vein before finally dissolving completely into the larger flow. I sympathized with its efforts, and sometimes I laid down obstacles (sticks, rocks, even my shoe) at the point where the two branches merged, inflecting their courses, and thus prolonging the colorful memory of the vein for a few more meters. Then I turned around and went in other direction, since the stream wasn't going my way.

I turned right at the bottom of the street, onto a larger uphill street, and then, across from the iron gate of the barracks, or close to it, to the left again, just past the Agrifoul grocery, into the Rue Dugommier. After the Occupation of the so-called "free" zone at the end of 1942, the greenish companies of German soldiers would emerge from the barracks on a regular basis, doing their exercises and chanting "Ah! ee! ah! oh!" They would set off down the hill, like water during the rains, toward some practice grounds beyond the city. They were Germans, and therefore enemies, as I knew, but I also knew that one day they would be gone. I hardly paid any attention to them.

Our three cousins lived with their mother, my aunt Jeanne, on the Rue Dugommier: Jean Molino ("Jeannot," a year older than me), Juliette, my near-contemporary, and Pierre, who was about the same age as my sister Denise (we called him "Pierrot Molino" to distinguish him from my brother, whose first name was also Pierre). We often took this short route, in both directions.

I mentally move along this entire itinerary, from one stopping point to another: the entrance to the house, the barrel maker, the corner at the bottom of the Rue d'Assas (the streams), the grocery store, then number 20 on the Rue Dugommier, and I recognize it continually, particularly along its terrain, on the ground, as though I was always walking with my eyes lowered, looking to find a piece of paper, a twig, a coin. It's true that I went barefoot as often as possible (taking my shoes off along the way, if need be, and putting them back on whenever I entered regions that were more supervised and more civilized (same thing), like my school or the lycée). The "texture" of the ground was therefore of great importance to me. I had to recognize and avoid:

—regions recently strewn with small pieces of gravel,

—stretches of soft, burning blacktop,

—mud puddles.

On the contrary, seeking out and preferring patches of soft ground, of sand, the long patches of clean artificial surfaces, flagstones cooled by the shade, carpets of soft needles beneath the pines, thick tufts of grass that wiped my feet clean, fountains. I carried away my childhood homeland on my soles—not the soles of my shoes, but the solid crust that hardened the bottoms of my feet.

38 This beyond was a dwelling place of gods without shadows

I have now described two entryways into the beyond (and in doing so I identified a third one: the well behind the bench in the garden), but this beyond was a dwelling place of gods without shadows, of divinities without thunder, without miracles, without worshippers. And without human forms. I did not invent or discover them in my own image, in the image of any person, of anyone. They had no icons, no specific territory in the governing of natural forces (when I learned about Olympus, I was incapable of carrying out any transposition of their various functions into my team of Gods. Mine were "all-terrain" deities, by contrast—or, more precisely, they had no proper terrain at all). These gods and goddesses possessed only names, a language, a repertory of shouts and cries. They had no dealings with death, seeing as I myself had no personal dealings with death—though death, nonetheless, was ubiquitous: in human conversation, in the voices coming from across the Channel, shut up behind our shutters and doors so that no one would hear them outside ("Passive defense" against German propaganda), between the lines of the newspapers with their shrunken pages and their dead and lying language, in the hands of the soldiers I passed, singing, on my way to school. And yet it was there, on the square, that I finally encountered it: a civil death, not a war death but a death like the ordinary deaths before the war, or after:

At the end of the Rue Dugommier I turned right again, went past the Picolo drugstore, and down at the end of the street was the square, where winds and avenues converged from every side. It curved a little to let them in, and sloped down a bit, and at the lower end it opened onto the Rue Verdun, a narrow street where my school was located. It was a very cold day during the coldest winter of the war, an extremely harsh winter. It was early morning, before classes had begun, and **the square was virtually empty in the cold hazy daylight, only just beginning to shine, the street lamps still lit; the square was almost empty, since I was early, as I've always been throughout my life, and even earlier than usual because of the freezing cold; I proceeded carefully over the slippery ground; a recent rain had frozen over, and the deceptive patches of ice were covered with dust and gravel, streaked with footsteps; they were blue and solid, but false.**

Against the bare wall to the right of the first house on the street there was a ladder, and on the ladder there were two men, two roofers, climbing up; then I saw the ladder slowly shift, I saw the top part of the ladder slide sideways along the wall, and they fell; the one who was lower down on the ladder, about halfway, raised himself up, then suddenly fell back, he sat holding his right leg; but the one who had been higher fell backwards, landed four or five meters in front of me; he fell back onto the frozen ground (<u>he is falling back onto the frozen ground: I see him</u>), he made a movement, trembled, and I saw, I see, his eyes going blank, cloudy, frozen; a man passing by on a bicycle had entered the square almost at the same time as me, he ran toward them, he shouted at me to stay there, to wait, and he went running down the street; the injured man was still sitting up, repeating "oh la la, oh la la"; then other passersby stopped, other people came, and I left.

I saw death, if seeing a living being die is to see death, but I only said this to myself later, and elsewhere, when I recognized it. No one at the time, on that glacial Davila Square—neither the first man passing on a bicycle, nor the dead man's injured companion, nor the people who came to help, who brought a stretcher—no one said it, no one said to me, "He died," "Death came, and it looked out from those eyes." But I knew. And I did not forget.

And this is why, because of a "geographical" coincidence that memory also makes temporal, I associate this silent, mortal fall (they fell, **they are falling again in my head, in silence, onto the frozen ground**) with a vision: a vision from a later time (1944), which I would have to call "notorious," since I no doubt shared it with hundreds of thousands of other people, perhaps millions. Aragon wrote a poem about it, and this poem was made into a song. On a wall of the square, that infamous poster, the *Affiche rouge*, had been pasted up, for the purposes of intimidation. It showed the garish faces of "terrorists" with unusual names (unusual in the provinces), assaulting passersby with hatred and violence. I saw this poster, like everyone else, and if I had any notion of its meaning, it was the meaning my father gave it for me when we stopped to look at it. I don't recall the exact terms he used, but I have never forgotten the expression on his face.

Not so many years ago (in 1987, I think), I went to Milan on behalf of Oulipo, for an event honoring one of its members, Italo Calvino. The occasion was the (sadly posthumous) publication of the Italian translation of Raymond Queneau's "*Le Chant du styrène*" ("The Styrene's Song"), a poem written to the glory of chemistry; Calvino had translated it as a *canzone*, in accordance with the text's "Renaissance" inspiration. That day, for the first and only time, I met Primo Levi.

I speak of Primo Levi here because the "moment" of this encounter, and the strong impression it left on me, quite naturally entered my mind when my memory, and then my obedient fingers on the keyboard, abruptly joined these two irreducible visions of death together: one of them concrete and "apolitical"—the roofer hurled onto the frozen ground by the inculpable coincidence of his fall—and the other, abstract and political to the highest degree, of the "stateless" and "foreign" anti-Nazi resisters depicted on the poster stuck to the walls of Davila Square. The name of Primo Levi arose spontaneously, establishing another link besides the temporal and spatial quasi-coincidence of the above two visions. It wasn't difficult for me to discover what this link was.

Primo Levi, the chemist, is not only one of the writers who—along with Robert Antelme and François Le Lionnais—gave me whatever slight comprehension I was able to acquire, since my twelfth year, of the incomprehensible horror of the Nazi "camps," and of the sort of collective hope, limited and fragile but real nonetheless, that each in his own way attempted to transmit in their stories; he's also the author of a completely different book (at least in appearance), a kind of book that is at least as rare, and from which that other, inexorably singular death—the death of the roofer—began, despite everything, to take on a certain meaning for me. The title is *The Monkey's Wrench*, and it tells the story of a man's labor, by which I mean manual labor (infinitely more "taboo" in literature than any other activity).

And finally, of course, Primo Levi's own voluntary death—which it's difficult not to see now as a sign, a commentary, and a premonition—acts as a further incitement to mix together, once again, inextricably and "wrongly," these old deaths, these dead moments of my life, in that place devoted to my perishable gods, in the blue air, the ice, and the wind. I read in an interview published not long before his death that Primo Levi, when speaking to a group of schoolchildren about his experience of the war—the old war of his generation—unexpectedly found himself confronted with complete disbelief. It wasn't that his listeners doubted the existence of the camps or the wickedness of the Nazis. What they did not, could not understand was how, in the face of such evil, he—he and those close to him—hadn't been able to pick up a handy televisual machine gun and fire into the mass of those subhumans, those monsters: in short, to follow the example of some Rambo.

39 Saint John's Day Nineteen Hundred and Thirty-nine

Saint John's Day Nineteen Hundred and Thirty-Nine

Saint John verbena through the red crown
none will ever leap again none will see
neither the ring of smoke nor the boxwood ring
will hear in any year the flames of the longest day

what lived back behind the circle of flames
with the order of flames moving in darkness
what trembled each year (a sign? hope?)
this, which was what was possible, stopped the

least distant closest night when all the fires
flickered and the somber circle of songs says
said: yesterday oh yesterday on the hot crest of days

(lyre of charcoal and crumbling embers)
and the long nail of the sky touching us in the street
covered us with stars in the brown and white courtyard

This poem (a sonnet composed in 1962) originated in a memory-image and remains associated with that image: but I can't quite manage to "extract" the moment of this image (at least not to my satisfaction, while also respecting the demands of a story) and set it into prose. I see this image, I can identify its point of view (the window open onto the Enclos du Luxembourg), but I can't speak of it again by itself, independently of the other images in other words that are interwoven with it in the poem. At best, I can isolate a sequence, like this:

> Saint-John
> through the red crown leap
> will see (do see) ring of smoke
>   the flames of the longest day
> back behind the circle of flames
>   flames moving in the dark
> the fires flickered (flicker)
>   somber circle of songs hot
> crest of the games
> charcoal of crumbling embers
> fingernail of the sky covering with stars
>   the white and brown courtyard

(result: an almost telegraphic prosification, as in the first Mesopotamian inscriptions)

The summer of 1939 was beginning. Soon after that (two months later) came the war. The "moment" of the war was the joint declaration of the "Allied" governments (France and England) in response to Hitler's invasion of Poland (I write this and suddenly it's Hitler in person invading. **I see him coming out of a movie theater in Warsaw, a Hitler "composed" of Charlie Chaplin (in *The Great Dictator*) and one of the stars of Lubitsch's *To Be or Not to Be*).** The war also begins for me that day, sitting in front of our radio, the wireless. It is evening; **I see both the radio and Hitler entering Warsaw very distinctly** (this memory is as happily anachronistic as a historian's reconstruction). If I retained the importance of this moment, it's because it was clearly pointed out to us (to me). My father commented on it for us (that is to say, in fact, for himself, for Marie, and for me, almost seven years old). He said that it was a good thing. Hitler had to be stopped (I don't think he could have suspected what was to come). I retained this. This and, especially, the intervention of England. In other words, after the fact, and on occasions such as this present moment, I have marked, I mark in my recollection, England's entry into the war. My "Anglomania" colors this memory, which itself very likely contributed to this Anglomania. If I had not learned (for the sake of truthfulness) to mistrust such roundtrip passages of the past into the present, those pilings up of future moments as they gather around a given moment of the past, defining it as "something changing" (this is what I would call "autobiographical comfort."

→ I § 107   It asserts itself unchecked in the novelist), I believe that I could have allowed myself to write, sincerely: "On that day I heard the voice of Winston Churchill, and it changed my life forever."

No doubt the most difficult year of the war was the '41–'42 school year (for schoolchildren, for students, and for teachers too, calendar time is always syncopated: the civic year and the pedagogical year do not coincide), weighed upon as it was by a triple burden:

—it was my first year at the lycée; in other words, the year when I was torn away (perhaps prematurely: I wasn't even nine years old!) from the almost "Arcadian" comfort of the school where I'd spent the previous four years;

—it was, apparently, the most favorable year for Hitler (but only apparently, for Moscow had not been taken, and England, "my" England, had not been invaded). All hope seemed vain (I was hardly in a position to comprehend this, but the general atmosphere was certainly gloomy);

—it was the year when hunger was most palpably present.

The wartime hunger reached a sort of maximum that year. First there had been the scarcity of supplies, the rationing—then, slowly but surely, the pillaging and theft perpetrated by the Germans (which really accelerated only later, with the difficulties encountered by Hitler's army) had begun to make themselves felt, as had the diminished food production and the lack of exchange between regions. The "provincialist" theory favored by Vichy, which provided the matrix for decentralization (today called "delocalization"), as well as for the regionalist, "anti-Jacobin" claptrap of the '80s, held that each of those venerable historical entities, the noble old French provinces as delineated before 1789—before the twin horrors of republicanism and revolution—would have

to fend for themselves (and this was a sort of expiation for France's sins, punishment for its "hedonism," its flabbiness, its laziness, its lack of respect, its
irreligion, its abandonment of "true values" under the deleterious influence
of secular education, regarded as responsible (I'm not making this up) for the
Defeat). But there is very little that grows naturally in the Aude.
The result being that in the cities, particularly in Carcassonne,   → I § 108
people were very hungry.

Under the simultaneous influence of all these causes, and especially this last
one, which had direct psychological consequences for me (as I would probably say in a novel, a novel in which I would be included as a character; or, in
what would amount to the same thing, an autobiography, a genre that is one
of the last refuges of mechanistic determinism), I devoted myself to my poetic
vocation with more constancy, concentration, and conviction
than to my studies: This madness of poetry (is it not madness?)   → I § 109
is a "sweet" madness, and rather harmless (in my case), but how can we avoid
surmising that it might arise from a derangement of the brain, an anemia of
the "reality principle" caused by a deficiency in the organism, a lack of certain
essential mineral nourishments, certain animal proteins or enzymes?

In any case, my father was very sensitive to the risks that undernourish-
ment might pose to the development of our physiques. Guided by the analogy
between children and plants (not to say vegetables, which might seem pejorative), traces of which are found in ordinary speech (one speaks of children
growing "like a stalk" or "shooting straight up," or else of a child's growth being
"stunted"), he did everything he could to make up for the empty butcher shops
and markets by tending our vegetable garden, for example, or by secretly raising animals. In addition, he undertook what he called "restocking" expeditions, riding off on his bicycle to areas that were better supplied with dried
beans, potatoes, and eggs, over on the Pyrenees side of the Aude and even in
Ariège (and then, beginning in 1943, he also used these trips as a "cover" for
certain other activities).

In this structural homomorphism between plant and child, he was particularly attentive to the "transform" (in the mathematical sense) of the stems and
the branches—that is, the skeleton (and this same figurative language is in
fact found in the medical tradition, when for instance it speaks of a "green-

stick fracture"). Unfortunately, the element considered most essential to the constitution of a child's bones, namely milk, was virtually impossible to find. It was also impossible to keep a cow incognito in our henhouse, as we did the pig. Our parents' palpable anxiety about the supposedly inevitable fragility of our arm and leg bones (confirmed by the two fractured wrists which I literally stumbled over myself to achieve, out of filial respect, and which were duly attributed to a deficient intake of dairy and cheese), gave an almost mystical virtue to the idea of fresh whole fatty milk. When, after returning from Massachusetts, our grandmother described American ice cream as totally devoid of the slightest molecule of water, this robbed sorbet of all its prestige, and since then I have never been able to take it the least bit seriously.

And yet, being the physiologically optimistic animals that we were, we grew up in spite of all the obstacles arising from scarcity and deprivation. On the frame of the door in our dining room on the ground floor of the house, a series of horizontal pencil marks, accompanied with dates and initials, measured our vegetative progress. Heels together, back straight, a dictionary horizontally reducing the deceptive elevation of the hair, we solemnly → I § 110 performed the tri-monthly ceremony of measurement. Dumbfounded (and quite proud), we contemplated the cumulative effects of our bodies' imperceptible daily modifications (at least along that axis), and found it almost incredible, so profound was the intimate and spontaneous conviction of our (of my) persistent, absolute, and unchanging identity.

40 Since a sufficient intake of dairy was impossible

Since a sufficient intake of dairy was impossible, my father fell back on the second pillar of the Scandinavian model. In those last years before World War II, the Scandinavian model, whether Swedish or Finnish, was not, as one might anachronistically believe, a "model of society"—a version of capitalism tempered by trade-unionism that for a long time was the reference point (or the alibi) of the social-democrat parties of Europe in their long quarrel with the communists and with the different varieties of the far Left. Rather, it was a "hygienic" model. It extended, in its own (more modern) way, the no less hygienic model of my grandparents, lifelong schoolteachers.

But it differed on one point, which my father judged to be essential. He believed that primary school (and then the lycée), in their republican and secular forms, had been much too neglectful of physical education and sport. Altogether too preoccupied on the one hand with food that was healthy but not "energizing," and with grammar and math on the other, it had neglected the tracks and the fields, as it were. But according to the Swedish model—and this was the whole "crux" of the matter—milk and sport were brought together within a single physico-aesthetico-moral conjunction, dazzling in its snowy blondness (but non-Nazi, which didn't hurt). We had no milk; what remained for us was sport.

For my father, who was interested in all sports, the ultimate team sport was rugby, while the summit of individual sports was track and field (followed closely by swimming). Rugby (if one can judge by the diet of the great rugby players of the Toulon and Toulouse teams) had little to do with hygiene or childhood growth. But it happened that the Swedish model, based on dairy and long-distance running, had had two spectacular effects that my father did not fail to bring together, didactically, as a means of encouragement. The first was that the young Swedes (like the Dutch, the Danish, and the Norwegians (these latter being infinitely likable, in 1941, for reasons having little to do with hygiene (the Finns of the pro-German Marshall Mannerheim were rather more dubious))), after being subjected to this diet, had increased their average size spectacularly within one generation. And my father, patriot that he was, obviously wanted to see liberated France make the same kind of progress (and despite the apparently insurmountable barriers placed in our physiological path by the war, on this point (concerning size) we gave him complete satisfaction; my nephews and nieces (especially the children of my brother Pierre) have surpassed everyone else in the family, reaching hyper-Scandinavian heights, to the point that my mother actually began to worry).

But above all, as had been proven in the last peacetime Olympics (the ones that were held, shamefully, in Berlin), this regimen had enabled those small countries to achieve a spectacular "breakthrough" in the foot races, and particularly in the most light-footed of all competitions, the middle-distance races (800 and 1500 meters) and the long distance races (5000 and 10,000) (and the javelin throw). As for us, my father had, I won't say Olympic ambi-

→ I § 111 tions, but at least the hope of seeing us honorably succeed in the track and field disciplines. He took us to rugby matches, but also to "track meets" (track only, for the general absence of swimming pools before the 1950s prevented swimming from making the slightest progress, collectively speaking. It was in the Aude River that we learned to swim).

I remember the sumptuous commemorative volume of the Berlin Games, with those photographs of the most significant moments of the competition (and especially the results expressed in numbers, which offered me innumerable speculative occasions for my own imaginary games, complete with eliminating heats, quarter- and semi-finals, and finals with medals awarded at the end) (it was in this book that we saw the admirable Jesse Owens, winner of three events, the 100- and 200-meter and the long jump (with a jump of more than eight meters), but whose hand Hitler refused to shake because he was black).

My father recounted the exploits of Jules Ladoumègue, of Paavo Nurmi. No "discipline" left him indifferent: not the triple long jump, not the hammer throw, not the steeple. He expressed his support for the still-hesitant beginnings of women's track. The vox populi in the Aude region was distinctly more reserved on the question. When one of the first women running champions, "Claire" Bressolles (who had been in my mother's English class) revealed, rather late, that she was a boy, the housewives in the public market, in the Agrifoul grocery, in the Safon butcher shop, all nodded their heads with a knowing air. It was a warning to all mothers: look what will happen to their → I § 112 daughters if they keep acting like they can run these foot races.

Since milk was practically under a ban, we had to redouble our athletic efforts in order to compensate. It was hardly necessary for anyone to recommend that we run. And run we did, constantly. We ran on our way to school, we ran and jumped in the garden, in the street, in the courtyard of the primary school, then of the lycée, in the grape fields, in the ditches of the Cité, in the woods. The intoxication known as a "second wind" was not unknown to us. Laps in the stadium were like candy to us. Running, in this country that war had given over to pedestrians and cyclists, was a natural way to express our childhood freedom. We ran everywhere, and nothing held us back.

Guided by the example of children and animals, certain theoreticians of athleticism have given a particular value to the activities they consider to be "phylogenetically" pure (that is, inscribed in the history of the species, whose lessons, they claim, children spontaneously discover): the standing jump, without a running start, as the measure of an absolute springing motion (both in height and length) without the aid of speed: an intrinsic quality of the young body that it shares with cats and dogs. And, more novel still, these same theoreticians make a case for running on all fours. My father very much favored these innovations (which never caught on, it must be said). We were excellent performers on all fours.

Still in the hopes of a harmonious physical development that would compensate for our privations, my father gave the decathlon, with its "motley mixture" of running, jumping and throwing, and its subtle tables of equivalence between apparently incommensurable dimensions (ten seconds in the hundred meters was "equal," for example, to eight meters in the long jump) pride of place on the list of athletic accomplishments. This ranking necessarily made clear his belief that to the intrinsic, natural qualities of the athlete (a mixture of heredity and predilection) one had to add the rigors of training, the acquisition of techniques that enabled one not only to surpass oneself (to jump higher, to throw farther, to run faster) (and technique is indispensable, since, as Brassens correctly sings: "Without technique, a talent is nothing but a dirty little obsession"), but also, and especially, to acquire a greater mastery over one's movements, a greater endurance (which might well be something useful as human history "progresses"), a deeper har- → I § 113 mony with one's body and with oneself.

41 On the wall of the classroom

On the wall of the classroom, toward the back, a little behind me to my left (it was a mathematics class held in a second-floor room, and I had turned partly toward the wall, no longer listening), **a pale sun** (it was winter) **lit the tortured surface of the wall where week after week, in the hot torpor rising from the radiator beside me, I scanned the map of the Soviet Union, always the same, but enlivened by the rumbling murmur of battles that filled the air.**

Then the hot air, the professorial voice droning out its algebraic and geometric arguments, the heroic reveries born from imaginary configurations

on the wall and from the Slavic syllables of distant earthly battles, syllables straining to reach us through the radio interference, from Germany, Italy, or France, from the BBC, all this plunged me into a heavy optical numbness; then I saw a kind of inverse fountain of air flowing along the wall, but from the bottom up, in fluid veins, in liquid whirls; I was blessed with a vision (a vision of what Japanese poetry calls *kagero*, the effect caused by differences in temperature on the inside of a window, setting the air in motion, a visible motion, a reflection of itself); **the hot air climbed up the classroom wall and the didactic voice now reached me only from a great distance, like a thin murmur from the other side of a deafening waterfall.**

This was a heroic age, but perhaps it was purely and simply heroic only for children who, like myself, took in the murmurs of war through the impalpable fountain of hot air arising from our imaginations, behind the looking-glass of air flowing up against the gravity of a reality that was in fact very dangerous, irreversibly mortal. I knew and did not know what the adults around me were doing, those who were somehow involved with the distant news of the war, with Stalingrad, with the famine, with the bombing of London, → I § 114   with Rommel's tanks in the Libyan desert, with the German soldiers coming out of the barracks chanting "Ah! ee! ah! oh!" I knew, although without knowing, and today I can't remember <u>how</u> I knew, that the people whom the Vichy radio and newspapers were calling "terrorists" were, by a mysterious alchemy, our friends. But up to that point, the models of my heroic representation of history had come from Walter Scott (*Quentin Durward*) or Fenimore Cooper (*The Last of the Mohicans*).

And yet this vaguely felt identification of my family with the Resistance (which was confirmed, without much surprise, a few weeks before the Liberation) did not prevent me (did not prevent us, though the credulity of my much younger brothers and sister is perfectly understandable) from accepting, without the slightest difficulty, the farfetched and improbable explanations given to us (I've completely forgotten them, now) concerning incidents that were perfectly inexplicable outside a context of clandestine activity. For the sake of this story, I will choose two "scenes"—significant images (which, moreover, feature my grandfather and grandmother, but in very different roles), but removed from the **sequence of image-memories** constitutive of my **memory** that I am commenting on in this **branch** (which is the raison d'etre of this branch, itself inscribed within a much broader movement), since their dependence on the "post facto," on their (narrated) <u>future anterior</u>, is entirely explicit (it is always present, and always moving, but in the other image-memories it has remained veiled, allowing for a narrative deduction).

One day we were having lunch in our dining room on the Rue d'Assas. My parents were there, along with Marie, the four of us children, and two guests who were so familiar that, like Bacadette, they were fully a part of the family configuration: Georges (Morguleff) and Nina, his sister. Georges and Nina were in hiding (and were doubly hidden from the police, since they were being sought both as Jews and as resisters). This is of course something about which neither I, nor my brothers, nor my sister, nor the ducks, had any idea. They were there, eating lunch, talking with my parents, sharing our almost nonexistent meal, playing with us; they were part of the family. Then someone rang at the door.

At that moment we saw these two young people from a good family, distinguished people, exquisitely polite in the manner of the Russian *ancien régime*, never agitated, always cheerful, always calm—we saw them jump up from their chairs, run into the garden and leap over the wall with an admirable but for us totally incomprehensible agility. However, the imperious doorbell that had sounded was in no way an announcement of the always-dreaded catastrophe of a police invasion; it was, more banally, my grandfather's doing, who had returned from a visit to our cousins on the Rue Dugommier and who, caught up in his customary distraction (generally associated with an inventor's inspiration), had forgotten to make his presence known by using the agreed-upon code.

Some time previously (it had to be earlier, since Nina's presence at our house would necessarily have been after her departure from Lyon, following the arrest of Marc Bloch), coming out of the lycée and going downhill on the Rue Verdun, I had unexpectedly run into my grandmother: an encounter, banal to be sure, but which would have been truly banal indeed if I hadn't been absolutely ignorant (up to the moment when we met) of my grandmother's presence in our town. She had not come to our house, nor had she been at my Aunt Jeanne's, where I had visited the previous evening. In short, I was quite surprised to see her there. But I immediately concluded (and she was eager to confirm this) that she had just arrived by train from Lyon. This was the most likely hypothesis. No doubt (but I didn't pay any attention to this) it was curious that she should be there, in the middle of the morning, on the Rue de Verdun, without so much as a suitcase, without my mother, and that, therefore, no one (and in particular none of us, her grandchildren from either house) had gone to wait for her at the train station. I offered to accompany her to our house, to surprise everyone. But she said no, she wasn't going to be staying at our house, nor even with our cousins, but with a friend of hers, because she needed to rest. She would come by later. And according to the story that was told about this incident later, after the war, all this seemed—had the immediate appearance of being—perfectly natural to me.

My mother, of course, was perfectly aware of her own mother's presence *intra muros*. The arrest of Marc Bloch in Caluire had led the Gestapo directly to 21 Rue de l'Orangerie, where my grandparents lived. They had not been expecting this. My great aunt Jeanne, my grandmother's sister, had immediately sent word by way of a rather sibylline telegram, in which my grandparents' names were barely disguised: "Friends came looking for Albert and Angeline—stop—Promised to catch up to them soon—stop." My mother arranged for her mother to stay at the house of an old anglophile friend, Mlle Miailhe. It was from there that, disregarding all necessary caution, she had gone out on the day I saw her. (But then where was my grandfather during all this time? I've forgotten—I don't know. It hardly matters.)

As I inscribe the name Mlle Miailhe into this story, I'm suddenly reminded that she was related to the young man who lived on the square, Prudent Padieu: a final gift to the memory of my god of war, Garenne, before I forever close the door opened for him on the square that showed such hospitality to my divinities.

→ Bif D § 165

Chapter 6

Hôtel Lutetia

42 "The sun rises in the west on Sundays"

"The sun rises in the west on Sundays." "I repeat: The sun rises in the west on Sundays." During the first days of June '44, the "personal messages" on the radio that often followed the more and more triumphant "news" from London multiplied like a series of meteor showers. With their enigmatic words and enumerations, aphoristic pronouncements devoid of reference but charged with a meaning that was impenetrable to almost everyone, these messages were a perfect example of that "poetry in action" dreamed of by the surrealists, who were thus its "plagiarists by anticipation" (just as the cubists had inspired camouflage, according to Picasso). And this particular message, which my father had chosen and transmitted to London, was now repeated back to him, two or three evenings in a row leading up to June 6: it announced the much-awaited opening of the "second front," the Allied landing on the Normandy coast. The festive atmosphere was palpable (though we children were unaware of the reasons for it). My father set off down the road (on a bicycle) the very next day, and as a measure of caution we → I § 115
were sent to Marie's, in Villegly, in the Minervois. Besides, I had broken my arm doing the high jump in the courtyard of the lycée, and the school year was practically over in any case.

Two months later, the surrounding plain, as well as the main road to the Minervois and all the passages used by the retreating German army, became just as dangerous as the city. So we set out on the road, all of us—grandparents, mother, and children (my father had disappeared without any explanation: this was one of those strange facts, so common in those days, whose meaning—strongly sensed but still vague—was now about to be revealed). Here I'll let my grandfather write the story (external memory):

Departure for the Aveyron department Numerous suitcases and boxes because our stay which depends on military events may be quite long.

Journey from Thursday August 10 to Saturday 12

From Carcassonne to Laissac.

A veritable little Odyssey! first a 7h wait at the train station (a new record). Arrival at Beziers at 8:30 P.M. Stayed overnight at the Hôtel du Midi.

The next day at 6 A.M. departure in a small van. Arrival in Ceilhes (train station) at 9 A.M.—many people there with their luggage, waiting like us. The Bezier line is cut off 10 km south of Ceilhes. Also between Millau and Séverac (*tunnel blocked by a line of train cars that had been derailed by the FFI.*) [*Forces Françaises de l'Intérieur*] [I admire the change of handwriting that my grandfather introduces in his parenthesis. The main text is written in cursive, but what I just typed in and set in italics above was written in miniscule block letters. The legibility of my grandfather's handwriting—inversely proportionate to that of his wife, in her missives—was always perfect.]

It was necessary therefore to climb up and over the tunnel (riding a donkey over a rocky path). Fortunately, some benevolent porters took some of our boxes off our hands (5 out of 9) ["5 out of 9"! I have no doubt that there were exactly nine boxes and that charitable hands helped with exactly five of them. Grandpa, I adore you!].

I see them climbing up over the tunnel, the travelers, the locomotive waiting down below, on the other side.

Nevertheless, the 800 m trip was hard. Slept in Séverac. Pierrot stl sick, soils his sheets—Small miseries. 8 A.M. departure; arrival in Laissac at 9 A.M.—torrid heat. Finally, relaxation and rest—The Odyssey, it turns out, comes at the price of a lost suitcase containing clothes and toiletries, most of them belonging to Suzette. She accepts this minor misfortune with her usual courage. I blame myself for not having watched our bags more closely.

In Laissac.

Suzette and the 4 children occupy 3 rooms on the third floor of a villa located 500 m from the hotel where we are taking our meals. Almost at the opposite end of the village, *Maman* and myself each have a more comfortable room than the one Suz has. Impossible to exchange: our proprietor doesn't want any children.

The Hôtel Salignac is run by a widow and her two daughters. They just lost their only boy (FFI, 20 years old), killed by the Germans while he was negotiating a prisoner exchange with them. We admire their courage as they the carry out their professional obligations.

A large part of the region is controlled by the FFI and there have already been some bloody skirmishes between them and the invaders. [Contrary to what had been expected, some of the German troops chose to pass precisely through these FFI-controlled regions in an attempt to reach the valley of the Rhone. They were SS. They didn't neglect to burn and kill along the way, but they chose a route that was three kilometers farther south. One day, however, we all went into the woods and spent the entire day there, waiting for the danger to pass.]

The hotel's food is quite good but there's too much meat. Mother and I will soon be obliged to forego the evening beef.

Water is rare. Yesterday, sudden shutoff of the pipes at 7 P.M. Nothing to drink with supper. we had to search in all the cafés and, after much effort, found beer and lemonade.

The days are torrid. The Aveyron River is in fact 2 km from the village. But its water is muddy, reedy. We miss the Aude.

August 17 a storm during the night which did much to lower the temp—

I experienced some of my old insomnia, very unpleasant (from 2:30 to 5:00 day before yesterday)—

The road climbed into the hills, winding upward between the chestnut trees, and we made our way just beneath it, in the woods just below; we heard the sound of motors and three open trucks came around a bend in the road, FFI with tricolor armbands and machine guns; they were singing; we went running toward the village in a state of great exaltation.

The next day, **on the square, the FFI were there; among them, in full uniform, a captain of the RAF; and next to him, my father.** This was a revelation: a sudden and luminous (and, in our eyes, glorious) explanation for the mysterious disappearances and absences of the people close to us, the nocturnal comings and goings, the whispering and the evasive answers to perfectly innocent questions: a moment of pure ravishment and pride, now at a safe remove from any danger. Finally, we knew. And knowing was also part of being free.

Now, when I recalled this moment later on, one day with my father, he pointed out to me that the dashing English captain at whom we'd marveled that day on the public square in Laissac had been parachuted in by "London" (as one said) to serve as a liaison with this group of *maquis* whom my father happened to be visiting. And if he was wearing his fine uniform, it was strictly in order to give himself a chance (minimal no doubt) of not being immediately massacred by the Germans in case he was taken prisoner, in accordance with the so-called "Geneva" conventions (it's not that he was afraid—a lack of courage could hardly have led him this far: he had his orders, that was all).

But even as this Englishman dazzled us and stirred up our enthusiasm (suddenly bolstering our family's prestige in the eyes of our playmates, more or less "ordinary" summertime companions), the presence of this captain made it indisputable for everyone there in the public square of Laissac that the people standing with him belonged to the Resistance, some of whom (including my father) would be leaving that very day for regions from which the occupiers had not yet been driven out (and if one is familiar with the denunciatory enthusiasm shown at this time by a far from negligible part of the French population, there were grounds for being unpleasantly surprised by this highly visible British initiative). Consequently, this encounter between men who had very different conceptions of the war went relatively badly.

I understand very well that this was the case, and that there was mistrust (to stick with this rather prudent word) on the part of the "Allies" toward the internal Resistance, a mistrust that was in part responsible for the massacre of the Vercors *maquis* (in which another former École Normale student was killed, a student of Alain, the writer Jean Prévost). But for me, ardent eleven-year-old "Churchillian" that I was, this was a moment of pure, unadulterated joy, and, much more than the chaotic and at times murky effervescence that followed the definitive departure of the Nazis, it was the unambiguous sign of a new era: the Liberation. That's still the feeling I have.

43 **Two documents:**

Two documents:

a) From my grandfather's notebook (continuation), under the general title:

The Life of Our Family
Very irregular notes taken during
the years 1942 to 1952

(September 1944)

Mother and I want to return to Lyon. But the trains don't go any farther than Beaucaire and Pont-St-Esprit.

Thanks to Lucien, we will have a way to return by road.

15 September, departure by auto from Carc. to Montp. where we are staying the night.

Here we found M. Bellon who runs the newspaper *Midi libre*, the organ of the Committees for Liberation, located in the building of the react. newsp. *L'Eclair*. He is leading a feverish and exhausting life (lost his voice).

Assigned a mission, and with one of the newspaper's autos at his disposal, he is taking us, Mother, Jacqui, and me, as well as two lady friends of his who are returning to the Doubs region. We are very crowded together, but no one complains.

16 September The weather is splendid. The journey will not be uneventful. We were advised not to follow the Rhône Valley, but to pass by way of le Puy and St-Etienne. This itinerary should allow us to avoid the blocked roads. Not all of them, however, because south of Ruoms, we see that an arch on the bridge over the Ardèche River has been blown up. Back the way we came over rough ground and the gasogene auto handles it magnificently.

Rather a good lunch in a small inn past Aubenas.

Passed through le Puy around 6:30 in the evening. We decide to have supper in Ys-singeaux. We find a restaurant there, but we also find suspicious FFI whose lieut't picks our papers apart (they received a report of some collabos in an auto similar to ours).

We finally succeed in convincing them, and we sit down to supper with a good appetite. A copious prix fixe menu: soup, trout, potatoes in fat, roast veal, omelet, fruit.

We leave around 22h—three more quick checks by the FFI. Finally, arrived in Lyon by way of the Pont de la Feuillée. We get home at 1:30 A.M.

We are exhausted, and so is the auto.

b) Letter from the author to his parents, dated September 18, 1944:

[page 1] Dear Papa, Dear Maman, It has already been three days since I arrived in Lyon—after an extremely hectic journey. We left Montpellier at 6 Thursday morning; The night before I didn't go to bed until 11:30, after having dinner in the prefecture at the prefect's house. We therefore left in [*with* marked out here] an intense fog on the road to Alès. There were seven of us. Monsieur Bellon, Grandpa, Grandma, two ladies who left us to go look for their family in the Besançon region, the driver, and me. We did not follow the Rhône Valley because we were uncertain whether we would be able to cross the river and so we preferred to go up through le Puy and St Etienne. We were sure that we'd be able to get there since m. Bellon had seen someone who had arrived in Lyon by this route. This didn't prevent us from having many adventures along the way.

[page 2] We arrived in Alés around 9 o'clock. We ate and then we left. Earlier we had been warned that we would encounter serious difficulties. Many bridges have been damaged and we will have to make some detours. Finally, we left again before we had even cooled off. The trip began very well. The sun danced along the road and we had some serious discussions. Occasionally a destroyed vehicle sat by the side of the road. in each village that we came to I jumped over to the door and waved at everything I saw, men, women children, horses, hens, ducks, etc. I was often met with startled expressions. for the moment everything had gone off without a hitch. It's really too beautiful here is an intersection. M. bellon looks at the map. this way. the car will go over a bridge. We head toward St Jean de Maruejols. Suddenly, an intersection. One of the two roads is blocked. the car stops. In one direction

[page 3] Uzès, in the other, St jean. The driver takes the downhill road. Soon there is a bridge, the St. jean bridge. It's been cut off. The car turns around. We pass through the same villages again, and here we are this time on the right road. The car is now heading toward Vallon, on the Ardèche River. Before entering the village there is a bridge. It appears that this one is intact. An officer passed over it this morning. the car approaches. Barbed wire blocks the road. there it is the bridge is cut off. No point in making a fuss. What are we going to do. Vallons is only six or seven kilometers from Ruoms, at the next stop where we're hoping to eat and it is ten ~~two~~ thirty. We consult the map ~~We~~ A new disappointment. The ~~new~~ second bridge on the ardèche is three kilometers from there, as the crow flies. But it is 40 kilometers if we take the road. We turn around again. To top off our troubles the route that we

[page 4] have to take is horribly bad. It is terribly steep. And we don't know whether the other bridge is still in one piece. After the climb there is the descent, which is even less smooth than the climb. A good peasant fellow whom we very nearly crunched to pieces confirmed that the bridge was standing. Reassured, we set off again. Finally we found the right road. but what anguish when we had to pass another bridge by. But it's actualy quite impressive to see a bridge lying crumbled on the ground. Usually the bridge has not completely fallen down but still it's a spectacle that I wouldn't have wanted to miss. We stopped a few minutes in front of that lousy Vallon bridge and I had time to contemplate the wreckage. with this one the break was clean. Down below, in the ardèche there is an inextricable chaos of stones all mixed up whole blocks of earth were torn out and plunged into the river [the writing becomes a little hurried here]. A fine scene, I must say! Before arriving in Ruoms around one

[page 5] o'clock we contemplatedd the traces left by a bombardment. the target was supposed to be an electric power station and a coal depot. At the center of the target area, A pile of stones and a section of wall that must have been a house. Next to that an entanglement of wires and a small truck overturned, then around some enormous craters. There was charred iron debris everywhere. At 1:10, we entered Ruoms. On the public square were two hotels. Nothing to eat in either of them. We are nonetheless directed to a little restaurant on the edge of the village. the car continues. At a turn in the road m. Bellon makes a sign to stop the car. He noticed a tobacco shop. He gets out and disappears inside. two minutes. Three minutes. Five minutes. still no m. Bellon. Finally he comes out with a pile of newspapers in his arms. We pass them around. the news is good. During this time, the car leaves the village. Here is the restaurant. There's nothing to eat.

[page 6] Discouraged, we continue on our way. But we are really very hungry. The car approaches a bridge that leads to Aubenas. Suddenly, a man comes out of a nearby house and shouts at us. Don't go that way the bridges are cut off. take the road to the right instead. We warmly thanked the good fellow and continue on. The landscape is very beautiful. the ardèche flows down below us we passed beneath an arch cut out of the stone above the road, it's the Ruoms gorge. A few minutes later we end up on the square of a small village. It was a quarter after two. On our right there was an inn. the car stopped and monsieur Bellon got out. He returned a short time later. Now we could eat. After having eaten our fill ~~the car~~ we got into the car and embarked again. We hadn't gone twenty meters yet when pow! the car stopped. Flat tire. it would ~~not~~ take a good twenty minutes. Since it was so hot, everyone immediately jumped out

[page 7] of the car. M. Bellon who was still hungry and still thirsty decided to look for a café in the village. And so off he went, accompanied by one of the two *dâmes* who were traveling with us. Grandma and the other lady were talking in the shade of a tree. As for me, I walked one way then another, without any particular goal. As I walked I counted up the number of destroyed German vehicles that I had seen since Beziers. 127. Finally, the tire was repaired and we got back into the car. We thought of looking for M. Bellon and his companion by slowly driving around. The car went along in front of the houses. No trace of a café. We left the village and went a kilometer down the road. Still nothing. We retraced our path, and suddenly there they are, calmly talking together. Righ away a lively discussion began. And the car took off again. I hadn't slept much the night before, so I began to nod off, on Grandpa's lap. Aubenas. I opened my eyes

[8th and final page] the car headed down a large street that was very animated, more than carcassonne. now and then I wave at the soldiers. The crowd became less numerous, the houses too and there we were on the road to le Puy. We passed slowly through the Ardèche Valley. The car was filled with lively conversation. M. Bellon consulted the map. The car began to climb up and up. The same road winding upward which from one turn to another seems [not] to go much higher . . . when one is below. At the foot of the twisted rock, the car stopped. the driver got out to add some coal. Then we started again. The climb was endless. but finally we arrived at the end a glacial wind greeted us then the car began a rapid descent.

Le Puy, 17 km. the numbered marker on the side of the road passed rapidly before my eyes. I followed attentively, intoxicated by the speed the car's descent toward le Puy. 16 km, 15 km; 14 km. We go on and on The road curves along .... [The end of the letter is missing.]

44 I notice in this letter, with a certain satisfaction

I notice in this letter, with a little satisfaction, a few orthographic particularities that have never left me: a certain lack of interest in capital letters at the beginnings of sentences (no doubt a preparation for the practice of modern poetry), a slight disdain for the established rules of academic punctuation (established, that is, after the sixteenth century), a distinct tendency to distribute circumflex accents with a generosity born of an uncertainty about where they actually belong. It was the omission of one of these beautiful signs, so threatened now by spelling reformers, that cost me the one (and only) quarter point I lost (out of 10) taking dictation for the "6th Grade Entrance Examination" in 1941. I hasten to add that I deserved no special praise for this (otherwise) high score: the examiner was a charming man who clearly enunciated all the endings of his words ("*les faucheur-s fauchai-eu-n-t*" (the reapers reaped)) (this was merely an extreme exaggeration of a peculiarity of Carcassonne French, which, using a pseudo-linguistic argument, I like to attribute to its proximity with Catalonia: one does not say "*la nui*" there, but "*la nui-t*" (night)), thus eliminating most of the difficulty of the test for us poor little creatures. Alas, there was nothing he could do to warn me about that wicked circumflex, about whose usage I hadn't the slightest idea. Can there be any doubt that it was after this traumatic experience (losing a quarter point on the 6th grade entrance exam, I mean) that, to compensate, I got into the habit of putting circumflexes in some rather unexpected places (as on page 7 above in my letter, on "*dâmes*")? This stability of my habits over the course of a half a century has, I don't know why, something reassuring about it: this persistence of the "floating circumflex" provides an assurance of relative identity. Here is the proof that I am not Lichtenberg's knife.

I notice too in this little piece of writing that I already have a marked interest in numbers, and more generally in all the numerical indications that the world places before our eyes, in this case spread out along the edge of the road, on the kilometric distance markers. In an earlier sketch towards a self-portrait, I attributed to myself the characteristic quality of being a "numerical man," a "counter" (as a sign of relative progress on the scale of hominization—although nonetheless archaic, perhaps, untouched as it is by the progress of mechanization and computerization, which has rendered the mental handling of numbers *obsolete*), and I even identified there (a little farther on in my linear text), the site of what I imagine to be my initial discovery of numbers. I had, therefore, an inner certainty of my "numerological constancy," but I'm not at all displeased to see it confirmed → I § 116–118 by a "historical" document as well—an object in the present that speaks only of the past, and that hasn't in any way been colored by the future that awaits or awaited it; and, therefore, not a feature I've attributed to myself retroactively, by reconstructing the past with the aid of the present, but yet another particle of certainty: miniscule but undeniable.

I see in this, though it may seem peculiar—a mere confirmation of old saying about "sour grapes" ("They are too green, and fit only for swine," says the fox in La Fontaine, at the foot of the inaccessible trellis of ripe Muscat grapes)—yes, I see in the above, from the perspective of this branch of my treatise, one more reason not to regret the absence in my compositional process of those childhood "journals" that I never kept (I'm sure I tried a few times, but I never got further than in that eighty-page "daybook" I acquired and gloriously inaugurated, around 1947, with the following word—which was and remained the only word in the book, written on its first undated page—"Today").

My letter, and the pages from my grandfather's notebook: are they effectors of memory? Not really. Before reading the letter and the notebook, I took care to gather my thoughts and memories of this trip to Lyon (and, before that, the one to Laissac). They were neither augmented nor modified by my reading of these documents, as I might have hoped (or feared).

I see a river with charred tanks along its banks; I see a collapsed bridge.

I see Grandma standing motionless by the side of a road, between two plane trees, in a long black dress, her black scarf on her shoulders, other silhouettes in the distance, indistinct; and, to my great surprise, I see that she is standing there "going peepee" (this is the expression I would have used then, and it is the one that spontaneously accompanies the memory).

Somewhere I still have the chronological "framework" of these images, which would provide a "continuous" transmission from that period (but in a continuity that's been more and more "eroded" over time, since it isn't supported by any actual thoughts still connected to that past (and so errors do creep in, but on the whole, before finding those documents again and reading them, I situated the images quite well)). Since these were times that marked everyone collectively, "placing" the images wasn't too difficult. And yet it's as though the two "sources" I've drawn on in this partial restoration of the past, placing them side by side, belonged to two separate worlds, irreducible to one another, and yet neither of them standing in isolation from the other.

→ I § 119

Another "moment" of the trip did reappear later on, confusedly, but of course I don't know now whether or not it's a reconstruction that only came to me after reading: it's the moment of our momentary "arrest" by those suspicious FFI soldiers (it's true that our friend, "M. Bellon" (this wasn't his real name) had an accent that could pass for "foreign"). We were thus subjected to an "identity check" by the Resistance, exactly as we would have been checked by the Vichy Militia, or by the Germans, just two months earlier. The fact is that this sudden transformation of one official France, Vichyist and Petainist, into another one, no less official but now Gaullist, entailed, for certain people (not very many: those who actually took the risk of definitively joining one camp or the other in the struggle were never more than a minority), an almost immediate change of roles: those in hiding came out of the shadows, while the most compromised (or the least protected) among their adversaries attempted, in turn, to disappear into them.

Three or four days before the Liberation of Montpellier, my father was obliged to make a "liaison" trip in a direction that went against the flow of retreating German troops, and for this purpose he managed to find a volunteer driver with a streak of boldness that pleased him. Somewhere along the way, between Pézenas and Béziers, without warning, they came across a German infantry column straggling along a good ten-kilometer stretch of the road. No doubt lost and weary, the soldiers—in order to improve their ability to flee—were in the habit of trying to requisition whatever infrequent vehicles they encountered in their path. They would signal for the car to stop, and each time the driver—as in those American "gangster" films that were soon to be the symbol of another kind of invasion—slowed down as though in compliance, then suddenly accelerated again a few meters away from the soldiers, miraculously escaping the hail of bullets that, in a fit of bad conscience, they always felt obliged to send his way.

But this heroic driver of my father's, it was discovered soon after, was a "*collabo*," and the worst kind, too: he was a killer, a member of the "militia," and in volunteering for this mission, he was making a daring last-minute attempt to escape the fate that awaited him. And everything, at that time, had become a question of identity. The Occupation had led to a proliferation of "papers" of all sorts, and to incessant verifications: ration cards, "priority" cards, laissez-passers, and especially identity cards. False papers proliferated as well. Every resister, every person in hiding, had, successively and sometimes simultaneously, one, two, or even more than two false identities authenticated by more or less "true" false cards (the "true-false" cards were the ones that the police in the Resistance had issued, in complete conformity with the law). Now that they were out in the open, it was imperative to carry out an emergency reduction of this anti-Ockhamist proliferation of "nominals"—in other words, of names, nicknames, and pseudonyms: to make it known that Monsieur X, alias Y, was in reality Monsieur Z, even if the papers in his possession called him T. Looking through my "external memory drawer," among my allotment of papers and photos of every sort, I found an example, in caricatured form, of this particular version of the old philosophical problem of the permanence of identities:

IV FRENCH REPUBLIC

LIBERTY----------EQUALITY----------FRATERNITY

POLICE COMMISSIONER OF LANGUEDOC-ROUSSILLON

Monsieur ASTIER carrying identity card no. 14606 in the name of BLANC Louis as well as the French identity card BR 56651 in the name of ROUBAUD Lucien, is President of the Regional Liberation Committee of Languedoc-Roussillon. The civil and military authorities of the FFI are obliged to provide him aid and protection.

Montpellier, August 26, 1944.

Beneath which, at the bottom of the page, next to the stamp of the "Regional Liberation Committee of Languedoc," one finds written out by hand (I recognize the writing and the signature of my father), these words:

President of the Regional Liberation Committee
Astier.

! ! !

45 Lyon extraordinarily beautiful in September '44

(continuation of my grandfather's notebook)

from September 17 to 23. We move through Lyon with its new physiognomy: all the bridges over the Rhône have an arch that has been demolished by the explosion of Kraut mines.

30,000 sq. m. of broken windows, 15 km of demolished shop windows and storefronts.

As compensation, an atmosphere of détente, of freedom, of hope in expectation of the imminent end of the war and the return to a normal life.

One reads the newspapers; one listens to the Radio; the rapid successes of the Allies bring great joy, almost all of France liberated, the Russians are on the Vistula, and in the Balkans.

Every day long lists of the martyrs of the Occupation are published, hatred grows against the Germans and their treacherous helpers, the militiamen and collabos.

Lyon was extraordinarily beautiful in September 1944. For me, the beauty of this city will always be closely tied to these weeks just after the Liberation. No doubt the water that came out of the taps smelled and tasted like oil, no doubt there were ruins, the Rhône, the Saône were almost uncrossable. But the ruins themselves were beautiful, and their beauty derived from the exceptional and exhilarating circumstances in which they appeared. No doubt one ate even worse than before. My grandparents gradually learned about the deaths, shootings, disappearances, betrayals, deportations (the sinister extremity of which could not yet have been imagined)—all the upheavals that had occurred in their relationships since they first fled from the Gestapo in '43.

But all this reached me in a form that was refracted, muffled, transfigured. I heard only the heroic song, and experienced only the feeling of freedom associated with an extended vacation, in the emptiness of the still-warm streets— but without threats, without curfews, without the tension of the vaguely possible catastrophes (vague to a child's consciousness, anyway) that before had been a matter of constant dread (arrests, bombings).

Now, one of the very first victories of the Liberation was . . . the arrival of the Western. Lyon hadn't been free of its Panzers for more than three weeks before the cinemas around the Place Bellecour reopened, already announcing "ongoing" programs reviving some of those legendary films (films full of legends), with their distinctly "prewar" flavor, and their fabulous cast of stars.

Of course, in September '44, the choice was still limited, and the prints (probably on loan from the American army) were often halted due to malfunctioning projectors or blackouts. But who cared? I'd never seen a more dazzling spectacle. I've retained only one film in particular, however, remembering it as the first of all, my first Western: *Union Pacific* (by Cecil B. DeMille, 1939, according to the old *Dictionnaire des films* by Georges Sadoul; starring Barbara Stanwyck, Joel McCrea, and Akim Tamiroff). Here one did indeed find the Good, the Bad, and the Ugly.

But it wasn't just for the stars that I became so passionate: above all, giving its name to the film (and now the title is about all I can see), there was a magnificent locomotive. (Today, on the white wall to the right of the lamp, between the lamp and the hanging plastic dish rack, above my metallic kitchen sink, also white and slightly covered with black dust (I'm looking at all this right now, so you can believe me), is a portrait-poster of the beauty who, around 1870, was the "star," the "Barbara Stanwyck" of the locomotives of the British Southern Railway: the Bournemouth Belle.)

My grandfather and I would go down toward the Rhône, heading to the riverbank and the tramway along the Montée de la Boucle by way of the "*traboules*," those labyrinthine tunnels and corridors leading deep through the bellies of houses, which turned all the children of Lyon into squirrels. Grandpa went armed with the newspaper *Le Progrès*. We consulted the short list of "programs," and we made our choice.

And sometimes, gripped by a veritable intoxication, when we came out of a movie theater on the Rue de la République, he promptly led me off to another, whose schedule he'd also noted (a sign of premeditation?).

→ I § 120

His return that summer to the Rue de l'Orangerie was a true relief for my grandfather: he was a calm man, and peaceful, a man whom the errors and horrors of the world never ceased to astonish and fill with indignation, and he always dreamed of seeing them eliminated by the reasonable efforts of men of good will (in France, for example, by the "Union of the Left without Exclusion" (that is, including the Communists). He continually reflects upon this in his "notebooks.") In his house, finally regained, he again took possession of his woodworking shop, where, among other inventions destined for the Lépine inventors' competition, he devoted himself once again to his quest for an unattainable perfection—always hoped for, vaguely glimpsed, but vanishing like a *boojum*: the "grail" of the chaise longue that wouldn't tip over. (For the Reverend Milton, maternal grandfather of one of my favorite novelists, Anthony Trollope, the grail was also a dream of stability: that of a dirigible that wouldn't tip over.)

46 Questionnaire:

Questionnaire:

Yad Vashem, Institute for Commemoration
of Martyrs and Heroes

P.O.B. 84—JERUSALEM

PRINCIPAL DETAILS TO BE INCLUDED IN THE TESTIMONY

A. *Information on the witness, the rescuer and the person rescued*

    1. Last name and all given names (in Latin characters)

    2. Age

    3. Current address

    4. Current occupation

    5. Place of residence during the war

    6. *Curriculum vitae* during the war (occupation, economic situation, ghettoes, camps, exodus, resistance, etc.)

B. *Circumstances of the rescue*

    1. How a connection was formed between the rescuer and the rescued.

    2. Description of the rescuer's actions—general character of these actions and details of what was done.

    3. Motives of the rescuer (material reward, friendship, love of one's neighbor, etc.).

    4. Dangers incurred by the rescuer.

    5. Conduct of the rescuer's family members (give their names)

    6. Special conditions and characteristic aspects

The witness can choose to write this testimony in the language he or she knows best. It is important always to indicate exact dates and places. We ask also that the witness communicate the names and addresses of other witnesses who are able to certify or add to this testimony. Likewise we ask that, if possible, documents or photographs be included that bear on the testimony, or else that the witness indicate where such can be located.

Department for the "Righteous."

For my grandmother, however, the return to Lyon was the end of an adventure, the end of what was the most intensely "public" period of her life. More precisely, this period had been filled with a sense of carrying out just and honorable duties within the collective enterprise of the Resistance. This is the meaning I attach to the presence of the above "questionnaire" in my papers. And it is clarified by the following, which I take from the same "file"—a

Certificate (in French and in Hebrew, French on the left, Hebrew on the right.
I reproduce only the French text):

The present diploma certifies that in /
its session of February 28, 1967 /
pending approval by the Commission of the Righteous at /
    the Commemorative /
Institute of Martyrs and Heroes Yad Va- /
    shem has decided, based on testim- /
onies it has collected, to render /
homage to the late / BLANCHE MOLINO /
who, risking her life, rescued /
Jews during the period of ex- /
termination, to award Her the /
Medal of the Righteous and /
to authorize the members of her family (named above) to plant a tree in her name on the Path /
of the Righteous on the Mount of /
Memory in Jerusalem. /
Jerusalem, Israel, /
December 1, 1967 /

This document represents the end result of what was certainly a long procedure, initiated (quite late it seems, despite everything) by my uncle Walter (at
the bottom of a copy of the confirmation letter from Jerusalem, sent to him
and transmitted to my mother, I read the following: "chère Suzette,
just to let you know that our efforts for Bonne Maman were successful"), but which
was no doubt out of the question while my grandmother was still alive. I am
pleased by this recognition (which I had nothing to do with, of course, but
it did please me and even, why not, made me proud. I'm all the more eager
to say this because my affection for my grandmother has remained relatively
moderate.)

I view this initiative on Walter's part as being a gift from him to his wife,
my aunt Renée, and at the same time an homage rendered to the woman who

probably saved his life in 1940. But it was also (I think the date shows this) an act not wholly independent of my uncle's Zionist convictions, convictions which are obviously not my own. For my grandmother, in any case, the way she behaved during the war seemed completely natural to her, and there was nothing more to say about it, once the danger was past and that sinister period was definitively over (so one thought)—except perhaps for the pleasure of telling stories, and the necessary transmission of a few strong moral ideas to her descendants.

At the moment, in the present day, writing these sentences about her, it seems unfortunately to have become necessary once again to reaffirm the value of the principles she observed, and to do so with some insistence. I'm sorry to say that recalling these ethical imperatives is anything but outdated, and will likely remain so for a long time to come, particularly in France. (In the "long term" of collective behavior, one thing is clear: the fact that a majority of the French (spectacularly unlike the Danish, for example) were pro-Pétain (though certainly not all the French: I find the widespread "theory" expressed by the aphorism "*tous des lâches, tous des salauds*" ("all cowards, all bastards") to be not only false, but repugnant), and that this was the case for quite a long time after Stalingrad and Pearl Harbor (implying their willingness, therefore, in a somewhat smaller majority (but not much smaller), to accept the zealous anti-Semitism of the Vichy authorities as natural)—this fact has not ceased "reverberating" in our country.

My grandmother was not directly a combatant. But if she chose to act primarily to rob the Nazis of their designated victims, I would remark, however, that for her (as for my grandfather, who, without being directly associated with all of her actions, approved them (my parents were also entirely and fully in agreement (though the problem of knowing who should or should not say what to whom never had an easy solution))), it wasn't a question essentially of friendship or of charity (even secular). The "Questionnaire" that I reproduced above, in listing the many possible motivations presumed to have inspired the actions of their candidates for "righteousness," maintains a significant silence on one in particular: resistance. Thus, it "twists" the truth.

In the back of the garden on the Rue de l'Orangerie, among other "testimonies," Grandma had hidden the identity card of the resister Marc Bloch (she said sometimes that if on the fatal morning of his arrest he had chosen to go down through the *"traboules"* instead of following the ordinary path of the Montée de la Boucle, he would certainly have escaped from the Gestapo). I'll complete and clarify this whole affair with one such testimony (contained in the same file as the above documents, put together by my uncle).

Information on the Witness

MORGULEFF, Nina
born March 14, 1915 at Leningrad
Currently resides at 77 Rue des Pyrénées Paris 20ᵉ France
Profession: Engineer
Resided during the war primarily at 21 Rue de l'Orangerie Lyon France.

Information on the Rescuer

Mme MOLINO, Blanche, retired public school principal
born April 25, 1880
died September 22, 1964
resided during the war at 21 Rue de l'Orangerie in Lyon
or with her daughter and son-in-law M. and Mme Roubaud Lucien
7 Rue d'Assas Carcassonne Aude France.
aided by her husband M. MOLINO René, retired inspector of primary schools
born June 7 1877
same address

I the undersigned Morguleff Nina certify as correct the following facts that show Mme Molino's devotion to my brother and myself

Testimony:

My brother Georges and I were living in a suburb of Lyon (Champagne) at the beginning of the war. In August 1942, when Jews began to be arrested in the Lyon area, the French gendarmes of the neighborhood warned us that we were in immediate danger, and we went to seek refuge with Mme Molino, who took us into her home.

Mme Molino attempted to secure passage to Switzerland for us. In the course of this attempt, a letter opened by the censor led to a search of 21 Rue de l'Orangerie, carried out by the French police. Thanks to Mme Molino's courage and presence of mind, we were able to escape from certain arrest.

The search brought to light no conclusive proof against Mme Molino, who continued in her efforts to secure lodgings for us, at her sister's house in Marseille and with a friend in Carpentras, among other places. We returned frequently to the Rue de l'Orangerie when there was no immediate danger and when we did not know where else to go, and Mme Molino never ceased providing every kind of support for us.

With the assistance of Mme Mallen and her husband M. Mallen, attorney-at-law, she regularly provided false papers (with all the risks this involved for her), papers that saved the lives of many Jews. Of course I cannot recall all of their names, and some were complete strangers to me, but among the most notable I can cite M. René Mayer, former president of the Council, Dr. Caroli, currently a physician at the Hôpital Saint-Antoine, in Paris, and Professor Lévy-Bruhl. In our case, she provided the first false papers that made it possible for us to survive in September 1942.

During all our stays at Mme Molino's, we witnessed examples of the aid she gave to a large number of Jews: help in the search for work and for lodgings, and monetary aid as well (thanks to funds she collected in the United States during a visit to university circles in Cambridge, Massachusetts, and to New York, during the winter of 1941). I can cite only the names of those whom we knew directly: J.-Cl. Weill, C. Hagenauer, J.-G. Cahen—shot by the Germans at Montluc in the spring of 1944—and M. and Mme Pavlovsky of Nancy.

Some false papers she provided to a person in danger led to a second visit to her home by the French police, who would most certainly have had her arrested if, miraculously, a friendly complicity with one of the policemen hadn't saved her, and M. Molino as well.

When in 1943 I became the secretary of Prof. Marc Bloch, then the regional head of the Resistance movement "Franc-Tireur," I witnessed on a daily basis (since I was living in her home) the constant support she gave him up to the day of his arrest in March 1944 (by mediating a correspondence with his family living in La Creuse, procuring lodgings in the house next door to 21 Rue de l'Orangerie, serving meals to all of us together, letting us listen to the radio, giving friendly comfort, etc.).

It was the arrest of Marc Bloch that triggered a third police search, this time by the Gestapo who were searching for Mme Molino in person. Fortunately she had just left town to visit her daughter in Carcassonne.

I also testify that, during the nights that followed the burning of the Synagogue in which some Jews were assembled, several of the people who had managed to escape found refuge in Mme Molino's home.

47 Appointed as part of the National Liberation Movement

Appointed as part of the MLN (the National Liberation Movement) to the Provisional Consultative Assembly set up by General de Gaulle, my father had to move to Paris (as did we, his family, on the same occasion). The Assembly convened in the Luxembourg Palace (where the Senate, as dusty as the Third Republic that preceded it, still meets today: the rough heavy black overcoat, already old, which my father bought on this occasion, was immediately baptized "the senator's coat." Later I wore it myself, during my student winters at the Sorbonne and then at the Institut Henri-Poincaré). His political disappointment was immediate and intense, especially when he found himself in the presence of the General, with his authoritarian haughtiness and his open contempt for the internal Resistance (which had been led for the most part by civilians)—and even, to a certain extent, for the republican form of his country's government. It hadn't been easy for a pre-'38 (pre-"Munich") antimilitarist pacifist to join the struggle (which was legitimately life-threatening) beneath such a banner (that is, the banner of a superior officer whose "right-wing" ideas were well known). But then to discover, on the occasion of the General's first speech in front of his "consultant" deputies, that the man had

→ I § 121   apparently managed to remain exactly as he'd been "before"— this seemed intolerable and unforgivable to my father. (Though I believe he did forgive him, eventually—but not until much later, after de Gaulle's death.)

We set up house on a street that was homonymous with our previous one: Rue d'Assas, in the 6th arrondissement, not far from the senate building. As you came out of the house and crossed the street, there was a park, the Luxembourg Gardens. This was about all the two houses had in common: the name of the street, and the presence of a garden. But this "house" was only an apartment this time, on an upper floor, and the garden was a public garden— behind gates, locked-up at night—that we had to share with strangers, where we were forbidden to pick up or touch pretty much anything, and where entire regions were off limits. There was no question of walking around with bare feet (besides, it was often cold and wet). It was a big fine beautiful garden, I don't dispute that—but it represented an idea of gardens that we weren't used to and didn't much care for. I've never really forgiven this kind of "garden in the French style" for giving me such an unpleasant surprise at first, and for causing such grief and distress.

And the trees weren't the same either. The only ones I also found in Paris in any abundance were the catalpas (?) which later (in the spring) left those light little shells scattered along the walkways (as were also found in Canguilhem's garden in Castelnaudary) that had provided so many tiny boats for our squadrons in our outdoor washbasin. But how to resuscitate those rough and ready flotillas, essentially private, in the Luxembourg fountain, among the toy ships of such well-groomed, well-behaved, and disdainful children? The only new riches to be found were the horse chestnuts in the fall, especially the ones freshly extracted from their husks, prickly as malcontent hedgehogs, and briefly enjoyed for their brilliant shiny surfaces, similar to the polished wood of the Rue de l'Orangerie, but infinitely precarious, dulled by the air before we'd even returned to the apartment.

Turning left off this new, mediocre Rue d'Assas, a few paces farther along, you find the beginning of a small street, Rue Duguay-Trouin (which still begins there). An extraordinary street, it starts out going straight ahead, like every street, then abruptly changes its mind, turning to the right almost ninety degrees—without however changing its identity, its being, without ceasing to be the same street—and leading back to the Rue d'Assas, whence it came. It was in relation to this street and its quasi-Londonian caprice (the streets of London provide many such examples), as much as in the incredible length, revealed in the heights attained by its address-numbers, of a street like the Rue de Vaugirard (which was located nearby), that we measured the essential difference between Carcassonne (where the streets, at least in the central area, are laid out in well-ordered rectangles, along a rectilinear, rectangular grid) and Paris, the Big City.

To be sure, there was the Metro too (the first subway system in my internal collection, which now includes almost fifty), and there's no point trying to hide the fact that this was an element that made a particularly favorable impression on us. In those days—with so few operational lines, and such hesitant cars, all overstuffed with travelers—it was having enormous difficulty just getting itself from station to station. Our "train conductor"—majestic, responsible, sovereign, weary, and bored beneath his cap—would step out from his command post in the first car, approach whatever doors further down might have arms, legs, bags, hems of skirts, or umbrellas sticking out of them, and jovially push these overflowing traveler-limbs back inside their cars. Then and only then would we set out. And there, in front of me, above the door, between adult heads, I perceived the famous Metro distich, an alexandrine followed by an octosyllable (a noble construction, since it is found in the most emotional "stanzas" of classical tragedy), whose relevance was experimentally verified by the delays preceding each new departure:

> *Le train ne peut partir que les portes fermées.*
> *Ne pas gêner leur fermeture.*

> The train cannot leave if the doors are not closed.
> Do not impede their closure.

It was also the case then that many of the stations closed during the Occupation hadn't reopened yet (and some never would be!): during the slow passage of the train along these abandoned platforms, I gazed in wonder at those desert islands with names promising so much mystery "*à la* Fantômas" (the perpetrator, as I hope you're aware, of a spectacular Metro robbery): Cluny, Rennes, Croix-Rouge . . . We gladly "took" the Metro alone, for pleasure (and often, I'm afraid, without a ticket). It seems there wasn't the slightest notion that this could be unsafe, at that time (as though the liberation of our national territories had inaugurated a time of general tranquility, a peaceful and absolute harmony: "Oh fatherland, oh harmony among citizens" (Victor Hugo)). My youngest brother, Jean-René, "Nanet," was particularly taken with it. And he wasn't even six years old.

Our apartment, unoccupied like countless others (which, by the way, remain so: a large proportion of "noble" Paris is empty), had been "requisitioned" in the name of the higher interests of the republican state then in the process of being reborn (the famous and interminable "housing crisis" was beginning). My parents might well have stayed there until their retirement. But, in keeping with principles they considered to be equally republican in spirit (here there's a very clear resemblance, despite the different generations, between my father and my grandfather; and Pagnol could have said of them both, as in *Topaze*: "Where are you coming from?" "From the university." "I should have guessed."), they told the owner, a rather well-dressed lady, and very pious— a type that's not hard to find around those parts—that naturally whenever her son, a prisoner in Germany, returned and wanted to use the apartment, they would give it back to him, after a reasonable delay (the time needed to find something else). (And equally natural was the fact that the son never did reclaim the apartment, despite my parents being told that this was his intention, and that the landlady immediately rented the apartment to a third party, skimming what was a considerable sum for the time off the finances of the new renter in the process—what used to be called "key money.")

Our definitive departure from Carcassonne took place around New Year's 1945. With all the effervescent novelty that we experienced in this departure (the discovery of the Metro, for example, and our first reading of the satirical newspaper *Le Canard enchaîné*, a commodity then almost as mythical as those prewar oranges (don't worry: I'm not working my way up to the play on words you might be dreading: "*Canard enchaîné . . . à l'orange*")), I don't believe that we were immediately aware of what we were losing in this exchange. (Later, in the confused and muddled years of adolescence, Rue d'Assas (Carcassonne) became the figure of a lost paradise, the green paradise of childhood, and Rue d'Assas (Paris) that of a Purgatory (it would have been difficult to describe it as Hell).)

France was free, but as for us, we had lost a great part of the immense freedom we'd enjoyed in the last months of the Occupation. We found ourselves civilized by force, wearing shoes, following a disciplined and studious schedule (much more anonymous and constraining than in our school in Carcassonne). And it was cold. Always. We left the enclosure of our classrooms only to find ourselves enclosed in the rooms of our apartment (from which it was no longer possible for anyone to flee, as we had in Carcassonne, simply by climbing down from a balcony, or from the edge of a window, slipping down the fig tree, toward the vegetal comfort of our protected family garden—or, farther still, to get lost among the partridges in the fields of grape vines and thyme out in the scrub). We felt lost. And as animals do in the same situation, we of course started grunting, pouting, and gnawing (metaphorically, I should say). I have rediscovered, and will cite it in an interpolation, some

→ I § 122–124   fragments from a "Treatise on Disputes" that I wrote during a few weeks in February '46, before our merciful departure for Saint-Germain-en-Laye. Its auto-therapeutic inspiration is evident. But at the same time it shows that this memory I've preserved from an unpleasant period corresponded to an actual and contemporary reality.

48 The truth of this law of the soul

But there was another more particular and more personal reason for my disenchantment (and it was indeed a disenchantment: exile from a garden which was later imagined as an Eden). Some weeks before the events related above, I was avidly reading Rocambole, especially the section about the love letter received by the antihero; and in describing this reading I wrote (or will write, depending on the perspective one chooses: in the "real" chronology of the times being recounted, the event of the reading in question comes earlier; additionally, at the moment I'm writing this, I've already finished writing my description of the event in question. And yet, if one were to read this book in a strictly linear fashion, my written description comes later, many pages from "now." Then again, in yet another sense, we would once more have to consider it as being earlier, since the first Bifurcation, in which this description figures, is meant to be inserted into my narrative composition between chapters 1 and 2 of the "story." Or else, finally, it is earlier or later because read in this order according to another reading, yours, depending on how you've chosen to proceed through the book),

I wrote, that is (to take up the perspective of that Bifurcation): "I also avidly absorbed the truth of this basic law of the soul: 'Six densely-written pages! She loves me!' For although I was in love myself, I was hardly in a position to receive such a confirmation in return.

In 1943, Marie (Noilhac), who had taken care of us children beginning in Tulle, got married and went to live in the Minervois, thus becoming Mme

Bonafous (while still remaining "Marie" to us). She was replaced by Antoinette (Hernandez). It was with Antoinette that I was, or dreamed of being (which bears a close resemblance), in love. She was a little less than twenty years old. She came to Paris with us, but wouldn't stay long. We knew that she would be leaving, since she was engaged. Such was the fatal knot of my private drama.

But there was something even worse: the severe reduction of our living space, forced upon us by our move from one Rue d'Assas to another, had made it impossible for me to leave my bed at night to go and get into hers, which I had done in perfect tranquility in Carcassonne, where all I had to do was open the door of our bedroom and step out across the hall. Antoinette had never had a room of her own when she lived with her family, and so the shadows beneath the roof, the magpies or squirrels that sometimes crawled around above her head, not to mention the onrushing storms, all left her a little perturbed, alone in her room. She and I thus derived certain advantages from sharing her sleeping quarters, although each of us did so in a very different frame of mind.

I never concealed the incandescent intensity of my feelings from Antoinette, drawing the requisite modes of expression from Walter Scott, Hugo, or Théophile Gautier, always in search of a stylistic register that was—naturally—both the most elevated and the most vague (not at all surprising, given the models I had at my disposal). She laughed at me. This hurt me quite a bit. But I was eleven years old, and she laughed. I was not unaware (after some in-depth discussions at my school or at the lycée with kids who were all older than me) that there were other, very different aspects of love. But my very young age, and the pre-matrimonial state of the object of my sentimental passions, forbade me to aspire to most of these.

I don't seem to have been jealous of her fiancé. To be sure, he was a rather shy and uncommunicative Spaniard. And since the three of us went to the cinema together, on Saturday or Sunday afternoons, I served merely as a tag-along little brother and a chaperone, which couldn't have inspired any warm feelings on his part. Antoinette would sit between us. She chose the films. These were the first cinematic experiences of my life. Her choices invariably favored sentimental movies, and in this register her preferences tended no less unfailingly toward the triumphs of the day, the great "photo-novels" that revolved around songs—the big Tino Rossi hits: I saw *Marinella* three times, and

The Kiss of Fire at least four. To this day I can still hear that invincible syrupy voice very clearly, gurgling in my ear: "Marinella, / stay a while in my arms / with you I want to dance / this rumba of love until daylight . . ." Oh Tino, the voice of Tino! his eyes like fried whiting fish! his voice the color of Argentine hair cream!

I won't hide the fact that such an assiduous and in my view excessive frequentation of Tino Rossi's adventures presented me with a number of aesthetic problems (the fiancé, for his part, was downright exasperated, expressing judgments on the singer that, though communicated in Spanish, seemed to fall within the register of outright crudeness—for which Antoinette punished him by pouting and taking me away by the hand into the narrow streets where we then continued to walk). There was a distinct difference between the flute in the *Suite in B Minor*, on the one hand, and "She is only sixteen but / you have to see how / she already drives them mad / all the men / oh beautiful Catarinetta / *chi chi* . . ." on the other. I couldn't avoid (adorable Antoinette! *sed magis amica veritas*!) placing the voice of the great charmer Tino in the musical category that my parents designated with the word "*dégueulando*." (Which nonetheless didn't prevent me from maintaining a certain tender indulgence for the "marshmallow" murmuring of the "Whispering Barytones." But it's true that they sang in English, and for me, at that time, everything British was sacred.)

(My disdain soon went much further, in fact, extending to all the "*chansons d'amour*" in the French repertory (including Charles Trenet, therefore, and thus I was very surprised later to discover that the surrealists had expressed some admiration for him.) This judgment on my part didn't owe everything to direct paternal influence. I've been told (an external memory, then) that at four or five years old, when my aunt Renée (then going through a rather adolescent and sentimental period) sang, in the unsteady intervals between her dieting and her chocolates, accurately, but more to the point with conviction, a tune that could pass for something from the eighteenth century, which began: "By the side of a fountain / Tirsis bur-urned with love / And told of his pai-ain / It echoed far and wi-i-ide / There Félicité passed by-yi-yi / She could not retur-urn / Torment of my though-ough-ough-ought / if o-only in losing you-ou / I'd lost your memory too-oo!"—I punctuated her infinitely heartfelt and languorous performance with two high-pitched meows, one at the end of the second line, "burning with *meow*," and the other, a double meow this time, at the very end of the verse "lost your mem-*meow-meow*," which had the effect, no doubt intended, of instantly draining away her momentum (fortunately so, since there were many other verses in the song).

But in 1944, I didn't miss a second of the long kisses "on the mouth" between Tino and the volcanic, tumultuous Viviane Romance in *The Kiss of Fire*. Indeed, the lava of these kisses continually set fire to my imagi-nation. And then it happened that, in the dense cold of our in-

→ I § 125

hospitable apartment, beneath the cold heavy skies, under the rainy coffin-lid always descending over the Parisian streets, I had to say goodbye to the sun, to Tino, and to Antoinette, all at once. I had the Paris spleen.

49 The year was renewing itself

I still remember a sonnet by Ronsard that I learned a long time ago. I recited it to myself during the winter of '45-'46, as I crossed the Luxembourg Gardens. I was cold, and even the fountains were frozen. I hadn't discovered the poem by myself: we were studying Ronsard in my next-to-last year at the Lycée Henri-IV, where Guy Harnois, my father's best friend, was professor of the senior class. He had given me this poem to read, and then recited some lines from another one—but they weren't the first lines of this other poem, which meant that it took me a very long time to find them again, and to understand why they were so irresistibly attached to the image of the large fountain in the Luxembourg Gardens. Here they are:

> And tearing their hair, struck their chests
> On the heights of Helicon languishing with emotion
> And mourned the day they became divine
> For being unable to die of pain like you.

(This is how he recited them, or this is how I believe I recall him reciting them.) They are found in the epitaph of a lady named Artuse, a name that Ronsard associates with the nymph Arethusa, and the poem begins thus:

"Here lies, who would believe it, a dead fountain . . ." That, most likely, is the reason for my association, faced with the dead water of the frozen fountain.

Le Sonnet

Lían se rajeunissait en sa verte jouvence
Quand je m'épris de vous ma Sinope cruelle
Seize ans étaient la fleur de votre âge nouvelle
Et votre teint sentait encore son enfance.

Vous aviez d'une infante encor la contenance
La parole et le pas votre bouche était belle
Votre front et vos mains dignes d'une immortelle
Et votre, oeil, qui me fait trépasser quand j'y pense.

Amour qui ce jour-là si grandes beautés vit
Dans un marbre en mon coeur d'une trait les écrivit
Et si pour le jour d'hui vos beautés si parfaites

Ne sont comme autrefois je n'en suis moins ravi
Car je n'ai pas égard a cela que vous êtes
Mais au seul souvenir des beautés que je vis.

The Sonnet

The year was renewing itself in its green youth
When I fell for you my cruel Sinope
At sixteen and in the bloom of your age
Your skin still showed its childhood days.

You had still the countenance of a princess child
Her speech and her carriage your mouth was beautiful
Your forehead and hands worthy of an immortal
And your, eye, the mere thought makes me faint away.

Love which did such great beauties that day show
Engraved them as in marble on my heart in one blow
And if today all your perfect beauties

Are no more as they once were I am no less in awe
For I linger not on what you are now
But on the memory alone of the beauties I once saw.

I have copied it out exactly as it is written in the notebook where I recently found it. And this is the form in which I retained it in my memory. Today I wouldn't present it this way. I would respect the original spelling, I would restore the punctuation (in my "version" I only used periods, or almost only, in agreement with the habits of so-called "modern" poetry (with the exception of the two commas in line 8)), I would eliminate the (nineteenth-century) spaces between the stanzas and their vertical alignment. I have in front of me volume X of the monumental chronological "Laumonier" edition, where the sonnet appears in the second book of the $\rightarrow$ I § 126–127 *Meslanges* with the date 1559. Lines 4 ("*Et vostre teint . . .*") and 8 ("*Et vostre oeil . . .*") are innovations introduced into the 1560 version. They're also the ones that excited me the most at the time, perhaps because it's possible to give them that anachronistic Hugolian pause that I always adopted for my inner recitation: "And your skin / smelled still / of its childhood . . ." "And your eye / the mere thought / makes me faint away" (hence the notation of the two commas, which, in their rhythmic interpretation, constitute an infraction (also modernist) of the strict law of the caesurae). Hugo was very nearly my only reference at the time.

The route I took most often from Rue d'Assas to the lycée, so nobly situated on the Montagne Sainte-Geneviève behind the Pantheon, involved a walk across the Luxembourg Gardens. Immediately to the right on the walkway, just after the gate, there was a little vendor's hut that sold postcards, miniscule toys, trinkets and trifles for the children who populated the garden, but most importantly of all, there was candy. This was a blessed place for calming an irrepressible hunger for sugar that for more than four years had remained unsatisfied. **I see the hard fruit candy, translucent, square-shaped, which I kept like a treasure in my pockets, sometimes encrusted with pieces of lint,**

**and whose hardened crystallized outer shell melted away on the tongue,
which then was soaked with the soft internal mass, a fruity, syrupy globule.**
It was a sort of childish protection against the rough atmosphere of the lycée.

In those years, and in that environment, where I knew no one and was no
longer sheltered by the kind of extended family that the École Annexe had
been for me, or even the small classes of the Carcassonne lycée, my "excessive" youth (I was two or three years younger than most of my classmates)
suddenly became very unpleasant. I felt distant, pushed aside, left behind, no
doubt less intellectually than socially (I'm speaking of the society of the lycée).
I was isolated, and I remained so; thus, I began to dream of an elsewhere, took
refuge in reading, convinced myself of the necessarily isolating character of
poetry, which I had chosen as an activity, a discipline, an ambition, a world. I
contented myself with an average academic performance, involving no effort
and therefore without brilliant results. I became incapable of any effective,
sustained, focused work (before that, up until my second year in the lycée, I
had not felt any need for this). I wasn't a bad student (that would have made
me too dependent on the institution itself, generating numerous conflicts and
absorbing too much time and energy): just an indifferent one.

I'll indicate one notable exception here to this rule of least effort (which was
my rule, alas, for a very long time—much too long). For a few months during
the school year '45–'46 (my first penultimate year, which my parents made me
do over in Saint-Germain-en-Laye, after reflecting too late on the disadvan-
tages of my academic "advance" and wishing to rectify them; but this didn't
do much good, for then I was even more bored with school), I had a truly
extraordinary experience with a French-Latin-Greek professor whose personality was quite exceptional (and almost pathological). His name was Chau-
velon. His spectacular originality had to do with his maniacal attachment,
his overflowing passion for his task, the exigencies of which he took far more
seriously than the most fanatical of the educational directors or inspectors-
general could possibly have demanded of him. But here it will be best simply
to describe the mechanisms of his method, based on one example.

He would give us, say, a Latin translation assignment (either in class, or to
translate at home). We translated, we turned in our work (we had to turn in
our work: if we didn't manage to finish it on the day it was due, no need to
worry, we could turn it in next time. But he expected to have it—he demanded

it). He corrected our assignments, gave them back to us graded, orally proposed solutions to the various problems posed by the texts of Caesar, Titus
Livius, even Tacitus. Nothing in any of this, so far, departs from the common
methodology (except perhaps the impressive frequency of the tests). We then,
however, had to take our papers home, and (here's where things really begin),
a week later, say, bring back a new attempt at the same translation, corrected
as best we could based on our own understanding of our mistakes, and his
explanations. He took *this* paper, corrected it, returned it to us with his observations. If he judged its present state to be satisfactory, meaning perfect, then
the assignment was finished. If not, well, it was time to try again, and then
again. He never relaxed his attention. He didn't spare us a single stage, not one
step in this constant progression towards perfection. Since we had to do not
only translations from Latin and Greek, but also *into* Latin and Greek, and not
only translations from and into Latin and Greek, but short compositions in
French (in which the "grail" of perfection was even more unreachable), one
can imagine the sum total of effort all this required of us.

He called these our "little labors." No delaying tactics (turning in the same
paper twice, excuses, not showing up) could distract him from his goal, which
was to oblige us to achieve—to the extent deemed by him to be sufficient—the
proper completion of every last one of the "little labors" assigned. He came to
class with suitcases in which each attempt, and each individual state of each
attempt, were organized. He never forgot a single page, and knew at every moment exactly where each one of us was in our work. He reread our miserable
handwriting slowly, with minute attention. He was quite mad. (I discovered,
through our friend Harnois, his colleague, that he was eventually found, in the
middle of the night, lost among his "little labors," bewildered and weeping.
Thus did he meet his end.)

I don't know what sort of influence he had on my manner of writing French
prose (I think that it was negligible, and that I managed to remain recalcitrant
before the imposition of his somewhat brutal stylistic ideal). But in Latin I
made tremendous progress. I lived henceforth in Latin alone. And one day,
gripped with a passionate frenzy for the most compulsive
stylistic turns in Titus Livius, I undertook to compose my → I § 128–129
own "History," in Latin, which I still have today.

50 One, two, three, or four times a year I set my suitcase down

One, two, three, or four times a year I set my suitcase down in a narrow up-stairs room of this London hotel on Cartwright Gardens—always the same one—and I look out the window at the semi-circular street where, beginning the next morning, and for one, two, or three weeks, I'll be passing by with the *Times*, one, two, or three stories below, at the empty hour when the milk crates have just been set out in front of the doors of the houses, of the hotels, of this hotel, always the same one, where I stay when I come to London. On Marchmont Street, the last street I take coming back from the British Library, there's a pub, the Lord John Russell. It has wooden tables on the sidewalk: one, two, or three glasses of tepid beer, not completely empty, abandoned on the tables a few minutes before *closing time*, low-slung armchairs, or very low bro-ken-down benches on which one sits among the old gentlemen locals, almost inaudible and virtually unable to speak, and two or three of their girlfriends dressed in unimaginable greens and pinks, chatting with the waitress in the same style. I look at the gray and brown foam of the Guinness that's flowed across the low table, with wood the same color as the *best bitter*, unless it's the *best bitter* that's given the wood its beer color, similar to that of the two or three pennies left on the table. I walk to the door of my hotel in the indistinct August night, beneath the dark leafy trees.

On the narrow bed in my narrow upstairs room I put down the plastic sacks full of books that I've just bought at Dillon's, or at Waterstone's, or at Books Etc., or at Murder One, or at Foyle's; I take the books out one by one as I lounge on the bed, my head on its one narrow pillow propped vertically against the wallpaper, the books laid out on the ground at the foot of the low bed right in front of the door. I put out the light and look at the ceiling in the glimmer of the room's semi-circle of night, and in the peaceful vacancy and vacuity of the night I hear the distant and for me lonely voice of Big Ben, once or twice, or three or four times, its four notes, sounding only once in a downward progres-sion. This, at least, is my usual routine.

But yesterday evening I turned on the television, a new presence and a re-cent innovation resulting from the dangerously modernizing ambitions of the young Mrs. Cockle, who, in collaboration with the longtime owner, Mrs.

Bessolo, now manages the destinies of the Crescent Hotel. I turned on the television, and on the tiny rectangular screen, in the August night, I saw a long series of memory-images, *ersatz* cinematic images, almost all in black and white, and silent: fragments of amateur films made by six soldiers of the Wehrmacht during the Russian campaign, between 1941 and 1944, which they had kept in their souvenir boxes for forty-odd years, and were now being shown, accompanied by their commentary, for the discreet cameras of the BBC. I saw the heavy old faces of today watching the young and indelible faces of both the vanquished and the victors, looking over the ruins, the wheat fields, the snow, the rivers, the canons, the clouds, the prisoners, the trains full of soldiers on leave, the regiments marching over bridges, the blasted tanks, the dead bodies, the black earth, and the mud, and the mud, and the mud. I saw a Russian plane fall from the sky into a resplendent field, sunny and still. I saw blond young men splash each other laughing in the sea (Crimea, 1942). I saw women old and young throwing corpse after corpse into a ditch, heaping shovelfuls of earth onto the bodies of Russian, Ukrainian, and Soviet soldiers, onto the bodies of men who were their husbands, their brothers, their neighbors, their lovers, without once raising their eyes, without looking up at us, to stare out of the color screen of the future. I saw the old man sitting calmly in his toy store, in an armchair, today—the man who had calmly filmed all this.

One of the films presented was in color: the strange colors of a German film stock from 1938 as recorded by English cameras in 1987 filming a film of the Russian winter of '41–'42, and now reconstituted on a television screen in a London hotel in August 1991. And yet nothing could have appeared to me as being more truthfully painted with the colors of the past. From both sides of a deserted road one saw, stretching into the invisible horizon, an endless snow: dazzling, cottony, hazy, and yellow.

From this image, from this snow, out of the depths of the war, at once unreal and irrefutable, I return to another snow, no less irrefutable, no less unreal, and contemporaneous with the first: enclosed in my head, radiant, shining with its incessant light, its uninterrupted illumination, on the beginning of this book. I place these snows in parallel. The essentially random event engendered by Mrs. Cockle and Mrs. Bessolo in Room 37 of the Crescent Hotel places these two images in parallel. Is the peaceful snow of the wartime garden in Carcassonne, like the soldier's yellow snow, a screen-snow, a mask for other memories? I don't think so. But what is there, ceaselessly, in the snowy light of my recollection—when I descend by levitation in the pure, cold air of the garden, from the bedroom with the window covered by flowers of frost—is indeed this other snow, the snow of war, mortal and drenched with blood: the snow of Leningrad, Stalingrad, Orel, Kursk, Velikiye Luki, Bryansk.

→ I § 130

And so it's not only the departure from Carcassonne, the abandonment of our garden, that defines, for me, the limits and walls of the theater enclosing my memory of childhood, the various sites of which I've laid out here. When from this arrangement of places and images I constructed, long ago, the architecture of the **Project**, I didn't stop (chronologically) with what was the direct cause of my departure, of my exile—namely, the Liberation—nor indeed with the moment of this departure itself, with its final glance back at the closed gate, the gate that closed upon the tall pine tree, but went, instead—as I'm going to do here, in this story—a little further, into the first days of May, 1945. (May 8, 1945, is the date conventionally used to mark the end of the war. But I didn't stop there, either.)

On May 1st of that year I participated in my first street demonstration. It wasn't a protest, but a march carried out by an immense crowd, joyous and unselfconscious, from the Place de la Concorde to the Place de la Nation: no doubt the one time in our country's history when this day meant to commemorate the struggles of another century's workers was given a much larger, universally celebrated meaning (though some people in the crowd probably thought, however illusorily, that it was the same meaning). This too was the ultimate blossoming of the idea of "May 1st" (despite the unusual cold: there were even a few snowflakes), before the metastases of the Stalinist cancer slowly but surely managed to deprive it, perhaps forever, of any meaning at all. (Which is also why I'm stopping around this particular time, and am not continuing on to the terrible flash, the "thousand suns" of Hiroshima, the last act in the war against the Axis and the first act of the "Cold War," nor to the famous "Fulton Speech" in which Winston Churchill, in a stroke of strategic genius, invented the metaphor of the "Iron Curtain.")

It was, as I said, my first demonstration in a public place, and many people had brought their children along. Everyone accepted this. It was actually the second demonstration I witnessed, but I'd only seen the first one, on the Place Davila, from a distance, from some nearby streets. I had admired the anti-Pétain demonstrators in 1942, gathered around the monument to the dead—in much fewer numbers, of course, than those on → I § 131 that 1st of May after the Liberation (and no one had brought any children to the earlier ceremony): a demonstration organized by our friend Albert Picolo, for which he was arrested by the Vichy police, exiled, and placed under house arrest (at that point, such resistance—still taking its first steps—hadn't seemed too dangerous). But he continued along the same path. And the next time, it was the Germans who arrested him, and sent him to Buchenwald.

In April '45, the first surviving deportees began to return from the Nazi camps. And those who were more or less able to stand upright were taken in at the Hôtel Lutetia, where their families, or their close friends, came to identify them (because it was necessary, sometimes, to identify them, just as when one goes to the morgue to identify a body from the river, a suicide: yes, that's him), to bring them back among the living. And so it was that one day (let's say that it was in the lovely month of May) my father learned that Albert Picolo was among them. He went to the Hôtel Lutetia. → Bif F § 183 He took me with him. He wanted me to see. **I saw.**

Insertions

interpolations

(from chapter 1)

51 (§ 1) **a vegetal network, an entire system of veins, a surface vegetation, a cluster of flat ferns . . . The map of my hand, the sensitive network of its lines, left no imprint.**

The image evoked this comparison, image upon image, and I did not refuse it. Because the comparison itself evokes a passage from another <u>branch</u> of this work, whose general title is **"the great fire of London"** (you're reading the <u>second branch</u>): **"a roadmap of a country . . . the hydrographic network . . . the skeleton . . . the veins in green leaves."** In that context, the above is both a series of images & a way of imagining the work that I envisioned as a whole, and thus the "great fire of London" as a segment of the overarching **Project** (this **Project,** whose **destruction** I attempted to recount in <u>branch one</u>, and did recount (in part)). It was necessary for me to admit this correspondence here, by virtue of the pact of sorts that I signed (unilaterally, I admit) with my reader. But how to make this admission?

<u>Branch one</u> of my book separated two types of **insertion** from the main body of its **story**: **interpolations** and **bifurcations** ("every time I come upon divergent paths (in the story)—after choosing the main road, which, simply expressed, means the one I'll lead you down uninterruptedly . . . I . . . prepare <u>insertions</u>") (I settled on this procedure only after some hesitation about giving them that particular name) (they were isolated both typographically and geographically from the story itself).

But can what I am writing now be considered an interpolation? and, if so, where should it be inserted? If it is indeed a proper interpolation, it should appear here, of course (and it would be an "upward" thread on the very large sheet of mural paper on which I once invited you to imagine **"the great fire of London"** written out in its totality (the **insertions** were indicated there by colored lines and arrows); but by virtue of its connection to this volume's predecessor, it should also appear in branch one itself (it would be a <u>reversible</u> insertion, a two-way arrow), which statement implies (and this implication will no doubt become more and more prevalent as this story progresses) that <u>additions</u> can indeed be made after the fact to branch one (and, later on, to the other branches as well), contrary to the (repeated) assertion that it was written entirely in the present (without preparation and without revisions), & therefore that it is finished, since by now it's not only complete but published (and the same contradiction would be true of the other branches as well, at the moment of their completion and publication)).

It's true that this is a minimal addition (a new interpolation into a completed branch). It's also true that the potential for the contradiction this raises was already present in branch one, during its composition and eventual publication, since I announce many more insertions than actually appear in the volume. I could of course declare, somewhat speciously, that minimal additions of this kind (provided with a numbered reference indicating an "address" somewhere within an as yet imaginary edition of the entire work, in which all the branches would be included under one cover) do not call into question the veracity of my basic affirmation (allow me to state for my new readers and restate for my old the claim that my narration and the process of its being written are always exactly contemporaneous) (yes, I could resign myself even to this). But, finally, it seems to me that—despite everything—in this particular case (the first of its kind), I must renounce giving this interpolation the combined status of **an interpolation into both branch one and branch two** (naturally it's an **interpolation** into the present branch—that is, in the present of its composition—since I happened upon it here, at this point in the text: decided it needed saying, but that it wasn't the primary thing I had to say) because at that moment of the story, at that point in branch one, and in the absence of precisely the sort of explanatory development that I refuse to include in this work (nothing is "foreshadowed" in my book, but neither is anything *après coup* or "after the fact"): it was and remains something extra that has been added on later.

This means that it will be necessary for me to introduce a third (or fourth) type of insertion: **notes** (I don't really like using this word—they would still be insertions, strictly speaking, and therefore still a part of the text, not exterior to it. "Notes" is strictly a provisional designation). Besides, even though I didn't have recourse to using notes in the first branch, I sometimes felt, if not a need for notes in the ordinary sense—which do not recount but inform, explain, specify (and thus are outside the story, outside the timeframe of the story)—at least the likelihood that they would be useful. I can verify (at this moment) that I did not, then, exclude the future use of other species of insertion aside from interpolations and bifurcations (branch one, § 14: "These continual leaps in my book, potentially represented by the *bifurcations*, *interpolations*, and every category along the lines of an *insertion*, correspond to one of reading's absolute privileges: namely, the ability upon opening a book to be anywhere at once inside it . . ."). At that point, without thinking too much about it, I had renounced the use of notes, partly so as not to add to the complexity of the book's composition (since that branch was meant to become a book), but also to avoid the risk of erasing the peculiar character of the first two types of insertions by using such a traditional procedure (the insertions aren't notes. Nor are they glosses, fragments, variants, remnants, or ruins; they aren't some kind of *pan perdut* in prose).

Perhaps, someday, in the complete book, the present development could be made into a note for **branch one,** and could appear as such in the text, modified and discreetly furnished with the appropriate reference marker; if, that is, any branches other than branch one ever come to completion, and if they ever go into print once finished (this remains as uncertain as the response to the same question regarding branch one was, back when I was still writing it) (in saying this, I'm speaking of a deeper uncertainty than the trivial one which always reminds us that a book isn't finished until you actually reach the end, and that until it's published, it hasn't actually entered the world: I mean that I hadn't decided whether I would ever finish it, much less whether I would ever publish it, quite simply because I didn't know and couldn't anticipate (not until the very moment this decision was finally made, after it became clear to me at a certain moment in the story (and this was a necessary consequence of the "axioms" of composition) what the conditions of its completion had to be)).

52 (§ 2) I'm repulsed by phrases like, "I thought that . . ." or "I believed that . . ." when they are presented as immediate certainties

It's even more difficult for me to comprehend how someone can write, "the child thought that . . ." or "the child thinks that . . ." (in the present) (to me this almost seems worse). Far from consolidating the truth effect indispensable for the reader's absorption (which seems to be the intention of the authors who write such things), it seems to me that these expressions brutally confront the reader with one of the most hackneyed procedures of novelistic fiction: the invitation to slip "into the character's skin." And the younger the child is supposed to be, the more manifest the impossibility is of doing any such thing. (I would insist that it's impossible in any case. But the fictional pact between author and reader consists precisely in playing tricks with impossibilities: rendering them acceptable for a moment, during the time of reading. Though the effectiveness of these tricks changes remarkably over time.) A fifty-year-old narrator, and a reader of indeterminate age and sex, are installed in the body, "behind" the eyes of a five-year-old boy or girl—are superimposed onto them: what an impossibly crowded space! As soon as I'm given such an invitation I think of the panic that overcomes a young child of this age when an adult,

→ I § 53 just before going out into the street for a walk, plays a joke by pretending to put on the child's coat by mistake, instead of his own.

What I am describing here is no doubt simply the "naive" version of the "memoir" writer; that is, someone who is essentially a novelist but who is all the more a beginner in that he imagines himself unburdened of the "expertise" required for fiction. But many strategies that seem to be more "sophisticated" than the above are no less unsatisfactory: for example, intelligently reconstructing a line of thought once followed by a child (and especially by oneself, as a child) (I'm thinking of Sartre, in *The Words*, and of Leiris) involves another type of impossibility that for me is no less troubling.

If I actually interrogate my memories, I can't see at all how any line of thought is in any way capable of exiting the moment, the present tense, in which it took place. Every sequence of deductions made represents a line of thought, and is always, always thought in the present: precisely because it is, essentially, identically repeatable at any given moment. One cannot ever truly think through an old line of thought. This impossibility is concealed when it's a question of a memory from one's adulthood, because one may well believe that the modes of one's deduction have remained stable between that time and this. And in that case there is at least some "plausibility" (but no more than that, I would insist) in saying: my reasoning was as follows (a month ago, a year ago)—I thought in such-and-such a way. But a child's thoughts (supposedly) regained—what a fantastical illusion!

As I've said, stories of childhood memories are in some ways akin to the historical novel; and, I would say, particularly to the historical novel in its own early, historical form—a form that was naturally very loose, as in *Quentin Durward*, *The Three Musketeers* or *Captain Fracasse* (I'm not questioning the charm—the great charm, even—of these books; indeed, I cite them with this in mind). If these works are considered to be within the category of "childhood" literature, this is in fact merely an invitation—and no doubt a reasonable one—to raise the threshold of our incredulity. But their implausibility (with regard to the reality of history) has much less to do with the "adventures" they recount than with the blatant anachronism of the language in which they were written.

The present of a language is inexorable. Efforts to introduce into it the idea of a more or less distant past (for instance, in these first examples of the historical novel, the fifteenth century for Walter Scott and the seventeenth for Dumas and Gautier), like the almost contemporary efforts of Viollet-le-Duc in restoring the medieval fortress, the *Cité*, of Carcassonne (or of the Pre-Raphaelites, with respect to Dante's Beatrice and Cavalcanti's *Monna Vanna*), are essentially "lexical" in nature: one draws on a dictionary of old objects (or words). But the past in a language is no less a matter of sentences, paragraphs, and sequential linkages than of words. It follows that the historical novel is a kind of museum-literature (hence, perhaps, the extraordinary favor it enjoys at the present time, which parallels those crowded sites for the touristic gaze that museums have become).

In a form that is less immediately apparent but no less real, "memories" come up against an obstacle of the same order in language. One does not speak or inhabit a language today as one did fifty, twenty, or even ten years ago. The least phrase, the least thought (and thoughts are nothing if they never pass through the windowpane of a sentence), the least line of reasoning is immediately betrayed as originating in the present, and if it asserts itself as being "of the past," it is pure anachronism. (I won't even mention "childhood speech," which most often resembles the truncated babbling of Tarzan or of the Indians in old Hollywood Westerns.)

53 (§ 52) **when an adult . . . plays a joke by pretending to put on the child's coat by mistake, instead of his own**

For an adult, there is something of this same violation in the game of remembering, a kind of revenge against the vanishing of time. It hardly escapes me that the terror of the child confronted with this joke, as well as the symmetrical impulse of the adult, can be interpreted in a different way, very obvious and very banal (a narrative, that is, of violence, a rape). But I prefer to see it as yet another sign of the irreducible difference between two states of the same person: between "me (now)" and "me (then)."

The fear of the adult's penetration into the sleeves of the tiny coat, formulated for example as, "No! You're too big!" or else "No! I'm too small!" (and not "it's too small") might reveal less an identification of the self with an external object (an analogy) (which is the usual line of thought) than a different conception of what is inside and outside oneself: not "the coat is like me," or even "the coat, that's me," but "the coat is not only mine, it is me, it is a part of me" (but here (you might say to me) you're doing exactly what you've reproached others for, presenting a line of thought as though you were a child. No: I do not claim that this is how things are. I am recounting. I only reproach childhood narratives for not admitting, or for ingeniously hiding, their fictive qualities. Since I'm working here in the mode of a novelist, I prefer to call immediate and direct attention to my role as a fabulist).

For the "ego" that I am as a child, then (and the fear for the too small coat threatened with invasion will be an index of this), I imagine a different perception of what a body is, of its limits and its surfaces, a perception that's closer to the Epicurean conception of the body (in the sense this has in the philosophical tradition, not in the Christian polemic that passed into common speech) than to the one that I eventually learned and experienced and is now my own. Within this perception, there is a limit toward which I tend, from within myself (I situate myself at the moment of the invention of an ancient "ego," ancient in both senses of the word: in the early part of my life, and in the early part of humanity (Epicurus)), a limit that, once it's been crossed, leads me to the outside of my body. But this "border of the ego," this surface made up of invisible lines with no thickness that surrounds my body, should not be localized in a precise and stable manner (and in any case not where it is at the present moment).

What's more, it tends to encompass all my "possessions": my clothes, but also my thoughts, my emotions, my dreams, my memories (which, like all things, are inscribed in space). Far from being (or from only being) a sign of narcissism (to have the objects that are part of my body torn away from me—like the coat, like my totemic stuffed "double"—would be to suffer an amputation, to have a part of myself cut off), this internal idea of the body testifies to a much more central ego, much more stable and assured than it in fact remains after all these years (and after the adoption of a conscious theory of what and where the limits of my person are): in the most inward part of my being, there is a fourth substance, the soul of the soul, the *akatonomaston*. To grow up is to lose it, and thus to become enclosed in a body that is henceforth more strictly bounded.

→ § 54–57

A "saying" attributed to my niece Marianne has been preserved in the history of my family, in its oral tradition. When she was very small, on being welcomed to the table of her paternal grandparents (my father and my mother), she rebelled one day when someone else (one of her brother, perhaps) was offered her seat, calling out, "Not there! that's **myyourplace**!" The story is always told with an (oral) capital letter put on "my": Myyourplace; and occasionally the affectionate variation "**My**yourplace" (emphasis and raising of the voice on "my") is, with an admiring but at the same time slightly moralizing tenderness (an omnipresent family trait), attributed to Marianne.

But it is necessary (in the context of the preceding, and with a shift of emphasis) to "hear" "my '**Yourplace**' "; which means, "This place is mine, since it is a part of my body.

When my body is not in it, however, it is 'yours' (and why wouldn't it be). It is 'Yourplace,' that is, something like 'Paris' or 'the cabinet.' " It is therefore not a question here of an annexation, of a negation of the rights of other bodies, or of an incapacity to recognize the Other who, on the contrary, is perfectly recognized and seen to be armed with the same rights as the Self: in Marianne's mouth, "yourplace"—that little piece of what Lacan calls *lalangue*—should not have been interpreted, as it was in the family story, as a simple quotation of another's discourse (fraternal or grandparental), but as the observation of a similitude and the vindication of a particular right, held by all bodies and justified by physical reality: they cannot coincide "at the same time in the same place."

54 (§ 53) the objects that are part of my body . . . like the coat, like my totemic stuffed "double"

The discontinuous body, the child's body, which gathers itself together at the moment of sleep and must achieve some unity in order to cross this incomprehensible frontier, finds its representative in the different incarnations of the traditional "teddy bear": during the day, this piece of the self, this **stand-in-for-my-self**, continues to sleep, and so ensures my own temporal continuity—Because the limits of "now" are as uncertain as those of the flesh. The night, with its complement of sleep, appears as a scandalous hole in the fabric of the world, which really ought to coincide uninterruptedly with itself. There is no time, since there is only "me," and, all around me, an uncertain "non-me," still indistinctly separated from me in space. My momentary "absence" from the world can no longer terrify me, then, since it will thereby become illusory, with a piece of myself, the "bear-piece," remaining behind, allowing the rest of me to be forgotten, like my left hand is forgotten when I'm doing something with my right. When I'm awake, it sleeps. When I sleep, it stays awake. Thus my unity is preserved. I inhabit alternative regions of what is, always, my body.

This is no doubt the place to work out a "theory" (which is what for the past few moments I have been looking for, along the edges of my consciousness, my consciousness of this prose: an "insertion point" for something I knew I wanted to say. Is this a vacillation in my strict observance of my book's "method"? a new variation in its function? I don't know). This "theory" is the **Theory of the Nyanya**.

In 1968, after a series of events on which we need not linger here, I was living in Dijon, the capital of Burgundy, in a tiny one-room apartment. Furnished with nothing but a bed and a yellow plastic chair, it was located at number 11, Rue de Fontaine. This street is not far from the train station, and it climbs up toward the adjacent principality of Fontaine-lès-Dijon. On the same floor as me, in a reasonably large apartment, lived the Lusson family. This family, already complete (I mean by comparison with the moment of my current narration, the fall of 1989) consisted of five people: the parents, Claire and Pierre, and three children: Mathieu, the oldest, Cécile, and Juliette, the youngest. Juliette, if I'm not mistaken, was not quite three years old at the end of 1968. At the time, then, she was not yet—and was in no foreseeable way destined to become—the student in biochemistry that she later became, to the profound but involuntary indignation of my memory, which adapts only with great difficulty to the absence of stability and rigidity in the image it has formed of this young woman, once a baby I knew well (the "same" person as today!), still designated by the same name.

(Not so long ago, I phoned a little after eight in the morning and, surprised to hear her voice on the line, I asked, "What are you doing up so early?" ("Not-getting-up-early" being part of my definition, one of the familiar characteristics, of the Juliette whom I have always known—hence my astonishment, hence my question.) "I've been up for a long time," she told me, "since six in the morning. I just came home from Blanc-Mesnil." "Really?" I asked, and then, imprudently and without thinking: "What were you doing in Blanc-Mesnil at that hour?" "That's none of your business, Jacques Roubaud," she said. And indeed, it was not in the least any of my business. But my stupefaction, expressed in this thoughtless manner, was merely the expression of a disconcerted "ego," an "ego" standing guard over itself, attempting to preserve and keep intact this immobile being, both identical to itself and paradoxical, who, fifteen or twenty years earlier, would indeed and quite rightly have been astonished to see a little girl of three, four, or six coming home in the morning, all the way from a distant suburb, to her parents' house.

At first sight, Juliette's reaction seems perfectly contemporary with the moment: it's altogether normal for a girl of her age to react energetically to what cannot fail to appear as inappropriate curiosity concerning her actions, gestures, and movements, especially on the part of an old friend of her father's. I was, as one used to say, "put in my place," and I never again made the same mistake. But it still seems to me that Juliette, the Juliette of today—who, to be sure, expresses her thoughts to just about anyone with remarkable forthrightness and "without mincing words"—is not in the habit of speaking in that particular tone. On the contrary, that tone is precisely the one she would have been likely to use with my old "self," the "Jacques Roubaud" of 1968 or 1969 who suddenly and inopportunely sounded in her ear over the phone, and whom the Juliette of twenty years ago, buried in her depths just as that old "I" is in mine, recognized immediately. All this constitutes, in short, an excellent "thought experiment" (a notion that is invaluable to philosophers and physicists) (even though in this case it would be better to call it an unthought experiment)).

But now I must come back to the **nyanya**. In 1968–1969, Juliette the baby had in her possession a precious pink object, an extraordinarily pink piece of fabric that she called her **NyaNya** (with a capital on each "nya"). It was her treasure, the apple of her eye. She loved it "like another self" (as Cicero said of the friend). She would not go to sleep without it, was consoled by its presence, let no one else hold it, and lived in fear that some bandit (brother-and-sister, visitors, friends, even father-and-mother), might try to take it away from her (father rather than mother, though, since the latter, I believe, was the one exception, acting both as its protector and its caretaker and guardian). In other words, she invested it in the clearest, most flagrant and absolute way with the function of "self-representation" which I initially and provisionally accorded to the "teddy bear." In fact, when a child invents it and names it (not all children do this), it is the nyanya, much more than the "teddy bear," that becomes a part of his body, the object that—according to the modalities I began to speak of earlier in this series of insertions—provides protection from the spatio-temporal paradoxes by which the world threatens the child's (very Leibnizian) sense of his own identity (which requires being indiscernible from oneself, without interruption, being oneself in all possible worlds, that is to say in a single world, one's own).

55 (continuation of § 54) **I will give the generic name of "nyanya"**

I will give the generic name of "nyanya" to this same type of object as it is found among many children (the difference from the original designation, namely the suppression of the two capitals, indicates a shift from the particular to the general); its properties have been revealed to me through the attentive observation—I might even go so far as to say experimental observation—of Juliette and her NyaNya during some months spent in each other's vicinity on the Rue de Fontaine, and then one summer spent at my parents' house in Saint-Félix, in the Minervois, and again later in Bourg-la-Reine, after Pierre Lusson—thanks to the "events" of May '68 and their repercussions in the university system—had managed, only a short time before me, to secure his "return from exile," and was once again living near Paris.

I first discovered the existence of the "genus **nyanya**" at my parents' house, by observing my nephew François and his "**Keture**." (As far as I know, Laurence, my daughter,
never had a similar object in her possession.) François's **Keture** (the word is most likely
an abbreviation of *couverture* (blanket) and thus indicates the distant, original form of
this particular object, which rapidly took on an undefinable appearance) was not uni-
formly important to him—it had an "active part," a spot that was especially precious: it
was the silky remnant of a ribbon, a band around the edges of the fabric. In the manipulation of and communion with his Keture, François (who was not yet 1.98 meters tall
(nowhere near it), as he is now, and did not yet do field work on "the invisible economy"
of the third world with the help of his portable Toshiba computer with full-page screen)
would caress the ribbon with one hand, while at the same time rubbing one or two fingers
of the same hand along his eyelashes. (Juliette, for her part, would hold her NyaNya in
her left hand, suck her thumb, and curl a meditative finger over her nose. She is perfectly
capable even today—as she confirmed to me over the telephone not long ago—of repro-
ducing these gestures precisely.)

It was an immutable ritual, a preparation for sleep or a reflexive turning back toward
the self after a walk, a meal, a game. Every **nyanya** (I am now referring to the species)
generates such ceremonies. In these particular cases it is the sense of touch (the hand,
the finger) that assures the corporeal transition between two extreme and sensitive regions of being, that allows messages to pass from one to the other, in what I would call
the current of identity: for it is indeed between the most distinctly peripheral peninsulas
of the body—eyelashes, eyebrows, hair, and nails, on the one hand (the nose too)—and
those manmade artifacts of the world that are the least distant from the body (because
they cover it) on the other—swaddling clothes, sheets, blankets (later a shroud), even
clothing—that there seems to be the widest possible conjunction of inside and outside;
for while the former are detachable like inert debris, the latter double, and redouble,
touch, and even envelope the skin. And this conjunction is even invoked after the fact,
meant to outlive its own dissolution: parents, for instance, in their darkest years, will keep
a sweet-smelling lock of hair from a child they have lost; and a lover might keep the most
intimately perfumed silks of someone he will never touch again.

Switching to a lighter register, I would like to bypass here a first likely dead end of
interpretation: to be sure, the child's relation to the **nyanya** is deeply marked by sensuality (to use a word whose innocent usage has almost disappeared from contemporary
speech). The ritual of the Keture that I just described (like many others) likewise leaves

no doubt in this regard. But despite this, I don't believe that this relationship serves a primarily erotic function. Like animals, most children are, as we know, intrepid explorers of eros, resolute and without dissimulation. Anyone who has never noticed, at the end of a winter's Sunday afternoon, somewhere in the family room, "convivial" and warm—full of friends, relatives, children, cats and dogs, among the clink of glasses, the sound of conversation, games and arguments—a little girl who is calmly, with great concentration, invention and subtlety (dogs, for their part, decidedly lack all subtlety in this case) masturbating in an armchair, on the rug, at the foot of a chair, between two cushions on a sofa or on a welcoming knee—such a person, I say, like the vast majority of adults, singularly lacks any spirit of observation. But the nyanya plays no part in these games.

Another error would be to render the nyanya banal by presenting it as a protective mechanism: but protection against what? against the vague threats of life, which, as we all know, is *full of a number of things*? But then, how could it be a protection? or else, is it meant to be a purely symbolic protection? but symbolic of what? The genial author of *Peanuts*, to whom, it seems to me, we owe the first artistic identification of the phenomenon of the **nyanya,** falls into this particularly American "behaviorist" error by calling the exemplar carried by one of his heroes, Linus, a *security blanket* (this name has a visibly "external," parental origin—or, even worse, has been provided by a child psychologist!).

No, that is not what the **nyanya** is. It is the materialized invention of a primary and spontaneous theory of the body and the world, & perhaps even a specific trait of hominization, as important and universal as the *factum loquendi*, the use of tools, life in society, laughter, rational thought, the unconscious, and the prohibition of incest!

56 (second continuation of § 54) **I flirted for a long time with the idea of a study**

I flirted for a while with the idea of a study on the nyanya: its modes, its genesis, its deep significance in human history (the singular light that it casts on ontogenesis and phylogenesis, the myth of its invention by a "Cro-Magnon" girl (whom I suppose we could call a "*Cro-Mignonne*")). I would have collected extensive data on certain cases, then I would have obtained grants to conduct a scientific investigation complete with a precise questionnaire—a draconian experimental protocol allowing one to distinguish, in a Popperian proliferation of "crucial cases," between certain sub-hypotheses, initially uncertain, but progressively more precise, & of course falsifiable. Then I would have established a typology, according to the nature of the representative objects, the associated rituals, the various names. I would have distinguished the nyanya from other related or contiguous phenomena: from the teddy bear, from thumbsucking, from the apparent absence of all three of these functions in certain children. From all this I would then have deduced an invaluable classification of childhood characteristics, and of their persistence into adult life. I would have become a new Lavater. I would have rivaled Galen and the theory of the humors. I would have opened new perspectives in child psychology, revolutionized many theories . . . It goes without saying that I didn't actually accomplish any of this.

But I will nonetheless relate to you some of my observations. Aside from its primary use, foundational in a way, which is to eliminate the conceptual and existential gulf between waking and sleep (without the nyanya it is strictly impossible for the child to go to sleep), I discovered that there is another privileged moment for nyanya-usage, and I will call this the "**moment of inspiration**":

It is evening, the hour between day and night, the hour of gray cats and twilight melancholy. The little girl (let's say that it's a girl (I have a "Carrollian" preference for little girls)) has taken her bath. She has kissed her father, now back from his indispensable adventures "outside." Her mother is busy in the kitchen. The dog is getting tangled in her legs. Her "brother-and-sister" are busy with their homework. The cat is splayed on the wooden plank covering the radiator. Everyone is waiting to be called to dinner. This little girl, amid the curtained windows, the armchairs, and the stools, is talking. She talks for herself, the talks to her nyanya—that is, to herself; she tells stories, she invents, she reprimands, she comments, she questions, she improvises: one of the major sources of narrative oral poetry, epic or lyric, is found here.

Several times in my life I was able to witness, discreetly—ignored, invisible, silent, and amazed—such inspired "sessions." I remember Jacinta, the daughter of Merche, spinning around in circles on an armchair, like a whirling dervish, and, like the poet-radio transmitting Martian messages described by Jack Spicer, or like Michèle Métail "performing" one of the most rapidly moving sections of her immense poem "Compléments de noms," or else like Tom Raworth reading in Cambridge, she emitted a stupefying and uninterrupted flow of poetry about mothers, painted windows, and flowers, in a deep recitative, an Andalusian-style *Sprechgesang*, while in the room the evening air darkened around her Miróesque silhouette.

This was much more a dance than a meditation in dialogue with the nyanya, but the principle is essentially the same: the nyanya is a catalyst for inspiration, and the time for this inspiration is the moment of the day's disappearance, the dimming of the light, as the dangers of night and sleep approach. The oral shamanistic poem that the nyanya brings out and approves of is the result of a hallucination without hallucinogenics—Jacinta found an equivalent for these in the intoxication of a spinning top, flailing her arms and legs around her.

The few story-poems that I heard from Juliette were, for their part, unburdened by the slightest verbal extravagance. They were precise, clear, repetitive, and emphatically moral. It is at this point, of course, that I could retroactively predict and deduce the future scientific vocation of the author of those compositions, but I will spare you this ordeal.

57 (final continuation of § 54) Juliette, like every inventor of a nyanya

Juliette, like every inventor of a nyanya, was very much attached to it. To put it mildly. It was literally impossible to separate it from her (except by a violent coup that would have felt like a veritable amputation). To measure the intensity of her attachment (still within the (prospective) context of my GTN (Grand Treatise on the Nyanya)) I tried, many times over, to coax Juliette into a momentary loan of her NyaNya. In vain. Despite our amicable and trusting relationship, on this point she proved intractable: no nyanya for Jacques Roubaud.

I tried trickery, promises of candy, rational argument, emotional blackmail (what one won't do for science!), but she remained intractable, firm, and calm—not even anxious, much less uncertain: the answer was simply no! But one day (during a vacation at my parents' house in Saint-Félix), with a flash of inspiration, she put an end to all my efforts. I had explained to my mother, and to everyone who was in the large front room (which I have already described in branch one of the present work) the current state of my investigations into the nyanya (I had as yet no theory providing an explanation of the facts, so I contented myself with collecting examples). And I tried once again, in support of my demonstration, to persuade Juliette, who was present at this discussion of her dear NyaNya, to entrust the object to me.

As usual, she refused. But suddenly, with a blonde and angelic smile, drawing her thumb from her mouth, she held out her NyaNya and gave it to my mother.

That was the shameful end of my Grand Treatise. I still blush to think of it.

(Data gathered on the telephone on the 12th of December, 1989: Whatever happened to the NyaNya? I decided to destroy it, said Pierre L. "I burned it—I was unnerved by the persistence of this childish thing." "No you didn't!" said Juliette, intervening with indignation. "He put it in the garbage one day when we were on vacation in Foix (this was the same vacation when I learned how to tie my shoes), but I screamed so much that he had to take it back out again. They washed it (which it badly needed anyway), and then I voluntarily gave it up a year later. But no one ever dared throw it away. It was still there, in Bourg-la-Reine, when we moved out, but it disappeared during the Plessis-Robinson episode."

Then, later on in the call, while I was discussing the uncertainties of memories with P.L., I heard Juliette say: "He mustn't forget that NyaNya is written as one word, without a hyphen, I insist on that." **That's the secret, I thought—the nyanya is the primal organ of *lalangue*.** And I was proud of this discovery, for about thirty seconds.

58 (§ 3) The Way of Double Negation (which has its related and parallel forms in philosophy, theology, and even logic)

The logical form, known as intuitionism, is a recent development. But I had the pleasure of discovering one of its distant precursors: Nicholas of Cusa, in his *De Li non Aliud*. We can think of his invention,which I am calling the "Way of Double Negation," as a "radical" variant of the *via negativa*, itself originating with Pseudo-Denys.

How to translate the title? "**On Not-Other**" or "**On Not-Other Itself.**" "*Li*" is a Neo-Latin article endowed with a very special charm by which, in its original simplicity, it provides a courteous introduction to whatever word follows. But through its ennobling contact with the mysterious "Not-Other," it becomes an "itself" that doubles back onto itself, it becomes "the being itself" (or "the very being") of **"Not-Other,"** its Idea, the Angel of its definition, an invisible black angel, but one that is infinitely close, affixed to the face of the definite.

> "*Nikolaus: Ab te igitur in primis quaero: quid est quod nos apprime facit scire?*
> *Ferdinand: Definitio.*
> (I ask you, first of all, what is it that best gives us knowledge? —A definition.)
> *Nikolaus:* That is correct, for a definition gives us the essence of an idea. But why is a definition called a definition?
> *Ferdinand:* Because it defines, and there is a definition for all things.
> *Nikolaus:* Perfectly correct. Then if a definition exists, which defines all things, is there not a definition of all things and of definition itself?

<u>Ferdinand</u>: Without a doubt.

<u>Nikolaus</u>: Do you not see, then, that the definition that defines all things is "not other" than what it defines?

<u>Ferdinand</u>: I don't understand.

<u>Nikolaus</u>: Turn the acuity of your gaze toward "*Li Non Aliud*," the "Not-Other," and you will see.

In this way, the Cusan moves toward the idea of God himself. He shows that he is more than not-not-*P* for every *P* (where "*P*" designates a given property: being beautiful, being good, large, perfect . . .), not-not-*P* being, according to his logic, different from (superior to) *P* alone.

Is he the sky? Is he the Good? He isn't the sky, or the Good, he is more; above all, he is "other" than what is not the sky, or not the Good (and that's why he is "the sky itself," "the Good itself"). And so on. One could say that Nikolaus places himself within a Heyting algebra of properties with God as its upper limit, the "uppermost" of all the not-not-*P*s associated with all *P*s, where each one of these not-not-*P*s is not itself *P*. The God of *De Li non Aliud* is the first intuitionist god (I'm extrapolating quite a bit: not only can't it be anything more than a kind of pre-intuitionism, for obvious reasons, it can also only be a quasi-intuitionism. For "Nikolaus-the-Cusan" doesn't say "not-not," but rather "*non-aliud*." However, if there is a "logic of double negation," it is indeed a question of intuitionist negation, for the "not-other" than the "not-other" is implicitly assumed to be identical to the "not-other" itself). This is, in short, a **Categorical** God (in the mathematical sense of the term: located within the Theory of Categories, or "toposist"), a <u>God of Proofs</u> (according to the most recent Bénabouist construction); or, to remain closer to Nikolaus's own point of departure, a <u>God of Definitions</u>.

For if we return to the dialogue's point of departure, we see that the "**Not-Other**," the "**Not-Not**"—in other words, God (a "**not-not God**")—is defined as that which defines, by essence and par excellence. But the movement of every (Cusan) definition of a thing, *d*, is to place itself within that which is not defined as *d* and then to step back out of it by a second movement of negation: *d* is not this, which is not *d*. But, if it's a matter of an actual, given thing, one can never reach *d* in this way, at least in the intuitionist space of proofs by definition. One arrives at *almost-d*, at *quasi-d* perhaps, but not at *d* itself. Except, that is, in the unique case in which *d* is definition itself, *D*. **D, Deus,** or **God,** is the **proof itself** of everything, absent from every definition, from every proof: the inverse flower.

59 (§ 3) **from this "hirsute" blossoming . . . in the vibratory evocation of the verse**

The adjective "hirsute" comes from Dante's *De Vulgari Eloquentia*:

> *Pexa et irsuta sunt ille que vocamus grandiosa . . . et pexa vocamus ille que.*

> The **combed** and the **hirsute** are those words that we properly call sublime . . . And I call "**combed**" those words that, having three syllables (or very close to that number), and neither aspiration, nor acute or circumflex accent, nor doubled *Z* or *X*, nor twinned liquid consonants, nor consonants immediately following a mute, instead seem, as it were, polished, leaving the lips with a certain smoothness, like *amore, donna, disio, letitia, salute, securitate, difesa.*

> Further, I call "hirsute" those words that, in addition to the ones mentioned above, appear necessary to the Illustrious Vernacular, if only as ornamentation. And I call necessary those which we truly cannot avoid, like certain monosyllables such as *si, no, me, te, sé, e, i, o, ù*, & interjections, & many others besides.

> I call "ornamental words" all those syllables that when mixed with the combed words, produce a beautiful harmony in the whole, even though they may have some harshness of aspiration or accent, or doubled consonants, or liquid ones . . . as in *terra, speranza, impossibilità, sovramagnificentissimamente*, this last being a hendecasyllable.

In every story, and particularly in a prose of memory, the smooth and noble flow of the combed words sometimes needs to be interrupted in its flat but majestic procession: toothing-stones must be placed in the river rapids in order to restore some of the flow's impetuosity and velocity, to stir up some foam. An excess of continuity and fluidity tends in fact to immobilize. The sharp shards of ice must interrupt the smooth course of the stream.

The poetry of the **trobar clus** made this one of its primary formal principles, transposing into the rhyme-sounds the opposition of these two states of water, liquid and ice. The famous *canso*, *"L'Aura amara"* ("The Bitter Wind") by Arnaut Daniel, a double antonym, in anticipation of Petrarch's combed canzone and his sonnets to Laura (*L'Aura*), thus accumulates hirsutes in its pattern of rhyme and rhythm:

> **L'aura amara / fa-ls bruoills brancutz / clarzir / que-l doussa espe-
> issa ab fuoills / e-ls letz / becs / dels auzels ramencs / ten balps e
> mutz / pars / e non pars.**

> (The bitter air / makes the branchy woods / light up / its gentleness
> thickens in the leaves / and the joyous / beaks / of ramifying birds /
> become stuttering mute / in couples / and non-couples.)

The first real torrent I ever saw was a large stream in the Pyrenees, in the upper valley of the Aude river, near the village of Camurac. I stayed there for a few days in 1942, when I was nine years old, living in a tent in a "summer camp" where I fell madly in love with the beautiful Marie-Thérèse, called "Rê," our "leader" (she was at least eighteen years old; she was beautiful, her hair was brown; her eyes were black). From the high, jagged (hirsute) peaks in the near distance, the water flowed noisily down into the meadow, limpid, glacial, dense, and viscous with cold. When I stuck my feet in, they turned scarlet, as did my forearms, up to the elbow. My fingers went numb.

I remember the blueberries in the dark underbrush, black, like black eyes: blueberries, *myrtilles*: Marie-Thérèse.

That summer, in all my childish ignorance, I encountered a <u>melancholic eros</u>, face to face. A short time after the Liberation, Marie-Thérèse got married in Switzerland. She came to see us (to see my parents) once, with her husband. She had become Swiss, with a Swiss passport: a "burgher," through marriage, of her canton in the Alps. She was even more beautiful then, with glacier-smooth skin of deep caramel. Her husband looked like a crook. I was told, on another occasion, that he was a smuggler. They both killed themselves, not long after, on a country road, in a car.

60 (§ 4) **The future, which is ceaselessly the future anterior**

This parenthesis, amplified by the following interpolation, contains not a theory of time, which would simply be ridiculous, but what I would call a <u>deduction concerning the nature time</u>, & it will be a deduction (as my narrative "protocol" gives me license to do) that accepts no responsibility for being the truth, and is thus a <u>fictive deduction</u>: an entirely "linguistic" and individual way to resolve the paradoxes of the present instant, the "now," as they have appeared to so many excellent minds since the very beginnings of philosophy, and whose confused and tangled train of solutions, like the shining bundle of seaweed trailing a boat down a river, have thus accompanied the discipline throughout its history.

The "generic" paradox (in which all the others find their "germ") is that the instant is not, for it continually differs from itself, and it follows that one cannot say when it ceases to exist: this cessation can't logically occur while the instant still *is*, for this would risk a contradiction. It cannot already have taken place, but neither can it take place in the following instant, for two punctual instants are never strictly contiguous. It must therefore be necessary for it to cease at some designated point in the future, which is no less impossible, for it would then have to perdure for an infinity of instants (no doubt impossible to count). This paradox is "pure Zeno." Aristotle said all this in his *Physics* much better than I ever could.

My "solution" has its own history, which I will relate in a few "moments."

At the beginning of this history, however, one finds another paradox, a more recent one, known as the "new riddle of induction," or **Goodman's paradox**, named after its inventor, or *trouveur*, the logician Nelson Goodman. Time is essential to this paradox, but as an unexamined given, and it was only after many detours that I extracted from its "fictive solution" my own deduction concerning time.

In Manchester, in December 1982, in the John Rylands Library (which is not the "John Ryland's Library," as I wrote by mistake—and to my shame!—somewhere in branch one), Alix told me that she knew the solution, at least in speech, & she sketched for me, in a few sentences, the imaginary trajectory of this solution, using the favored example of the empiricists: the repeated and daily rising of the sun.

I saw it then as an oblique way to speak about something else: it's impossible, sometimes, to pass over in silence that of which we cannot speak, & when one can't demonstrate it either, one can at least try to speak about it in a roundabout way: to speak, that is, about something else. Someone who, generally stricken with melancholic insomnia, and who never wakes, as it were, after sunrise, still sees the sun there, present, upon opening his or her eyes—if and insofar as he or she does wake. Two years later, I included a version of the above case in a short story, and just as the founding paradox took on the name of its inventor, I decided to give this same name to a character in my little fable, a character who has accompanied me ever since; a character in prose, and a temporal character.

61 (continuation of § 60) **"The Color of Goodman's Wife's Eyes"**

That's the title of my little story. There's also a subtitle:

"On Being Grue"

Goodman had a young wife, whom he loved very much. Every morning on waking (he woke up early) he would watch her as she slept, and, later, when she woke up in turn, he would say to her: "What I love more than anything are your eyes, your beautiful brown eyes." She would smile then, and say nothing.

One morning, however, Goodman felt troubled. His young wife was sleeping, and so her eyes weren't visible, being hidden by her eyelids, and Goodman said to himself: "If she woke up and it so happened that her eyes were green or blue, I couldn't bear it." Eventually she woke up and smiled at him, and her eyes were as brown as on every other morning—but he was not reassured.

"What's wrong?" she asked him a short time later; for Goodman's anxiety still hadn't left him: it had become a torment that left him no peace.

"I love you," he said. "I especially love your eyes in the morning when you wake up and I look at them for the first time that day. I love your eyes because they're brown. But how can I be sure that they *are* brown? I wouldn't like it if I found out that they were blue, or green.

"I was sure," Goodman continued, "that your eyes were brown, because every morning since we've been sharing a bed, I've looked at them and seen that they were brown. But what if they were **grue**?"

"Grue?" his wife asked.

"I posit that they are the color **grue** in the following case: one morning in the past I saw your eyes, at which point the color was brown; but tomorrow they could be green, or blue. Every day, including today, and more than a thousand times, your eyes have been brown; but this in no way prevents them from being "grue" tomorrow; that is, green, or blue. As such, I can't be sure of their color. That's what's been troubling me."

Mrs. Goodman didn't say anything in response, but that night, watching secretly from her place in the bed, she saw that he was crying.

"My eyes," she said to him the following morning, "have always been brown every time that you've looked at them; all that's necessary, then, all you need in order to be certain, is to know that tomorrow, when you <u>will have looked</u> at them, they will have been brown, as before. Let us call this quality of my eyes **bbrown**, if you like. and call the other quality, the one you so dread, **ggrue**: meaning that my eyes *have* been brown, but that tomorrow, when you will have looked at them, they will have been green, or blue. My eyes, you will admit, have always been "bbrown." And they will be again, tomorrow. They've also always been "ggrue"—and they will be again, tomorrow. But what, for you, is the difference? Even if they're still ggrue tomorrow, that means that tomorrow, when you will have looked at them, they will have been brown, as always; while only the following day, the day after tomorrow, will they have been green, or blue. So what does it matter?

"Perhaps my eyes, when I'm sleeping, are blue, or green, or some other color, or none at all, like objects which have no native home. But you can be sure, always, that when I wake up, when you will have looked at my eyes, they will have been brown."

Thus spoke Goodman's wife, née Hume.

And so it was: every morning, for as long as she lived, he looked in her eyes at the moment of her waking—and they were brown.

62 (second continuation of § 60) **Goodman's paradox is a skeptic's paradox**

Goodman's paradox is a skeptic's paradox. He exploits the certainty inherent in his language in a way that sets it in contradiction with itself. The "solution," also linguistic, eliminates the doubt only a posteriori: up to the moment when his wife's eyes are open, they can still be "grue" (and therefore, in this case, blue) or brown, or else "bbrown," or even "ggrue." Once the moment has passed, however, grue is no longer possible. Bbrown and ggrue remain, but they are always in the future. The refutation too, therefore, is in fact a skeptic's refutation. In no way does it reestablish the primary certainty of induction— rather, it provides only the same sort of certainty as was granted by **Merlin**: the truth of these "obscure words" will be known only when the predicted things have "come to pass."

It must be pointed out that it's only because this solution introduces a dissymmetry between a series of adjectives that it can accomplish its goal. The paradox constructs grue in parallel with brown. **Bbrown** is constructed in the same way: those eyes are bbrown that, tomorrow, verified by Goodman's gaze, will have been **brown**. But how can **ggrue** be defined? Certainly not as the eye color that, once seen, will have been **green**, for that color has never appeared here, and the induction cannot confirm it. Then, those eyes are only <u>ggrue</u> that, tomorrow, will have been <u>ggrue</u>. And the inductive certainty of this color is always projected into the future. Her eyes, later, will also have been <u>grue</u>.

If they open again.

It was in a Goodmanian flash that Saul Kripke received the illumination that led to his very personal interpretation of the famous and difficult § 243 of Ludwig Wittgenstein's *Philosophical Investigations*, known as the passage introducing "the private language argument" (that is, the claim that a private language is impossible). According to Kripke, Wittgenstein is forced into this thesis by colliding with a "skeptical puzzle."

And this "puzzle" consists of a doubt that arises at the heart of certainty itself—that is, one that undermines the foundational mathematical operation par excellence: addition. When I produce the result of the sum 53 + 20, Kripke says, why do I write 73? Why not 37, where 37 is the result of the operation of "quaddition," which coincides with the operation of addition as we understand it for every addition that I've carried out in the past, but gives, precisely in the present case (never before encountered), the palindromic result of 37? (For numerological reasons, I have modified the example used by Kripke.) Instead of a "plus," I have in fact used a "quus." The skeptic that slumbers within every philosopher expresses himself in Goodmanian language (and Goodmanian language is strongly Carrollian, with its constant use of portmanteau words (and here Kripke too implicitly uses a portmanteau word, with some help from—and in discreet homage to— the patronym Quine)).

It didn't take me long to establish, in my reading of Kripke, an emotional bond between Wittgenstein and Goodman that was much stronger, for me, than the intellectual one based on an interpretation of the strategy at work in the *Investigations*: for Wittgenstein was a central reference point for Alix, and her reading of Wittgenstein, even more than her own deliberately clear speech, profoundly influenced her strategy of "photographic monstrations." Which is why, despite the refutatory furor of the guardians of the Temple of Wittgenstein—the Tweedledum and Tweedledee of Oxford, Misters Hacker and Baker—I have maintained my spontaneous adherence to Kripke's hypothesis—a hypothesis that appears to me, in the end, to be a sort of implicit plagiarism of Alix: a way for her speech to live on in something like "a possible world of thought."

63 (third continuation of § 60) **For a long time, during the first phase of mourning—during those years of paralysis**

For a long time, during the first phase of mourning—during those years of paralysis—I went no further in my thinking on the subject than the fabulistic formulation of the text that relates "Mr. Goodman's adventure," above. I didn't think of using the same type of **fictive deduction** elsewhere. Nor, oddly, did I think of the *Investigations* themselves. The primary cause of this omission is that I had no aspirations to do any philosophical thinking whatsoever at the time.

I admit that at first, and despite everything, I was impressed by the intense passion of Misters Hacker and Baker, and by the voluptuous avalanche of quotations they provide from the texts of the Master, drawn from his unpublished works, the *Nachlass*, and from published texts alike. This battery couldn't fail to take some of the luster (dazzling, but no doubt oversimplified, I thought) from Kripke's interpretation. Their tone of indignant conviction, while not completely persuasive, shook me just the same. And yet I finally told myself that despite all this, the hypothesis claiming that Wittgenstein was troubled by skepticism remained seductive, and a philosophical interloper like myself could still hold on to it because of its charm, if not because of its veracity.

And this is where I remained, even though, in the meantime, my confidence in Hacker & Baker (already reticent and relative) was severely damaged by other troubling developments in the microcosm of Wittgensteinianism, to which my attention was drawn (as in many other circumstances) by an attentive reading of the *TLS*. So, one day, at Blackwell's in Oxford (that is, at the very source), I bought a book by S. Stephen Hilmy (that initial "S"—"unresolved," as one says in the critical editions of medieval manuscripts—is mysterious to me, and I am tempted, after reading the book, to read it as standing for "Saint"), entitled *The Later Wittgenstein*.

Thus I discovered that the dogmas of the Wittgensteinian Church had been called into question by an Erasmus of its New Testament (the *Investigations*; the *Tractatus* would represent the Old Testament, and the Carnapians its Kabbalists), who at times even took on a tone reminiscent of Luther. According to Saint Hilmy, a return to "the Big Typescript," which the Apostles (Saint Anscombe, Saint Von Wright, and Saint Rees) had "concealed," if not completely, then at least in its decisive theoretical stature (and which, moreover, they had neglected to publish), drastically altered the meaning of the exegesis. Even today (due to laziness) I don't actually know how Cardinals Hacker & Baker responded, nor what position was taken on the topic by the Gallican wing of the Wittgensteinian Church (whose Primate is Bouveresse), but, having read Hilmy, I felt, in short, more at ease in my divagations. Which brings me back, after laying "quaddition" to rest, to the matter of the <u>future anterior</u>.

The use of this very strange tense in a verb's "conjugation" allows one to enclose both past and future, at one stroke, in a present moment of discourse. And it is precisely there that one finds a very simple means for defining what thus ends up being contained within it—that is to say, the **present**. This is the altogether modest secret of my "discovery." To tell the truth, I find myself gliding over a few inherent difficulties, for example concerning the necessary and difficult distinction between <u>instant</u> and <u>present</u>; but for the moment I do not wish to pointlessly complicate my demonstration. I began with the "paradox of the present instant," and I'm going stick to it.

The present instant is the one that *will have been* a given past instant at a given future instant. It is an event (though I don't mean to imply that it is "punctual") whose memory will have been preserved by a strictly distinct future event.

(Thus did I settle—to my own satisfaction, if not to yours—the thorny problem of the paradox of the present instant.)

64 (§ 5) The prescriptions from the arts of memory invented in the Middle Ages and in the Renaissance

The tradition of the arts of memory continued well beyond Giordano Bruno's death at the stake. We know (from the scholarly works by Mr. Paolo Rossi & Dame Frances Yates) that as an adolescent Leibniz played around with these same ideas. Later, considered suspect by men of letters because of the triumph of various Ramist innovations (which were those of schoolmen: imposing rigor, systemization, and method on the links between memory and knowledge—before Pedagogy destroyed these in turn, in the name of spontaneity, in order to preach the freedom of remembrance, with results that we're familiar with now), they retreated into a sort of clandestine, subterranean existence, not far from "magic," "card tricks," and "clairvoyance," in those zones of petty twilight commerce in which craftiness feeds off credulity (although it certainly doesn't hurt when the crafty are credulous as well, which was often the case).

When he was almost eighty years old, my grandfather, always eager to learn (or in any event to struggle with himself against the slight but unpleasant fading of his powers of memorization), became greatly intrigued by an advertisement appearing in a number of newspapers at the time. It began with a story worthy of Simonides of Ceos: In a train compartment (a terribly effective though involuntary *captatio benevolentiae* for my grandfather, a great lover of trains), an encounter had taken place between the story's narrator and a noble and mysterious personage, a man with a radiant, fascinated gaze modestly hidden behind a beard. Borrowing the newspaper of the passenger opposite him (this as a means of entering into the matter at hand), the enigmatic and benevolent Scandinavian (a man whose rigorous knowledge had apparently been inspired by the rigors of cold weather) cast a quick glance at it, both piercing and casual, and after handing it back to him, immediately recited the editorial he'd just read there both forward and backward (especially backward: it's more impressive).

For there was a Secret, you see: and it could be procured by sending, as quickly as possible, a modest sum to Editions Aubanel, in Avignon. My grandfather wasted no time in doing so. (He didn't want this secret only for himself, but also in order to share it with us, his grandchildren, who were all caught up in various respective lycée and university exams). A short time later he received a brochure in which he became passionately absorbed. But his disappointment was bitter: the Secret Method, the Path leading directly to the Grail of Memory—once it was reduced to its basic (and very meager) instructions—was in fact only a bastardized variation on the one I have designated as the "method of passage."

It works, as is well known, according to a very simple principle: with each <u>station</u>, each <u>site</u>, along a familiar path (a walk in the garden, a route through one's own house from the basement to the attic), one associates fragments of the things that are to be retained (texts, arguments, narratives—in the form of <u>visual images</u>), which are thus placed as it were on these coat hangers for memories. It then suffices, when in need of one of these memorized elements, to retrace one's steps and to take down the appropriate idea-overcoats, verse-umbrellas, geographical map-scarves, Roman-emperor or bones-of-the-hand list-hats from their pegs, where they'd been fixed in thought—quietly waiting in the mind of the walker. (And if you've climbed the stairs with "Boaz Asleep" (Hugo), it's not much more difficult, at least in principle, to climb back down again by reciting it in reverse.)

I'm not saying that the method is stupid, or ineffective. But, like any apprenticeship in memorization "by heart," it demands a great deal of training in the use of its particular techniques (to ensure that the things to be retained will indeed remain, unaltered, in the place chosen for them—that they won't just fly off into oblivion), as well as a mastery of progressively difficult exercises, etc.—exercises which the virtuosos of the sixteenth century no doubt still had at their disposal (Giordano Bruno certainly did), but whose secrets have been lost (like that of those marvelous confections called *bouffettes* from Mens (in Isère)—those royal delicacies of old that Jean Rolland used to bring us. The last pastry chef to possess their secret wouldn't relinquish it, and he refused to pass it on before he died).

That mysterious magus who was able to seduce knowledge-hungry grandfathers, that tempter with the name of a Swedish tennis player—no doubt he knew no more than what I've just written about his "art" (and surely must have been manifestly ignorant of its origins). My grandfather's disappointment was bitter, but brief. We made fun of him (gentle fun, I think) and of ourselves as well (his enthusiasm proved to be contagious). He gave up his hopes of making late but decisive progress in the fields of Theoretical Physics or Foreign Languages, and finally absorbed himself in the quest—much older and more fundamental for him—for a different Grail entirely: the construction of a perfect proto-type for **a chaise longue that would never tip over.**

65 (§ 6) The inverse route of the train through Castelnaudary

Sometimes we stopped in this small town. Canguilhem's parents lived there. Canguilhem the Elder (as my own father said) was, I believe, a tailor. Or perhaps it was his younger brother who was a tailor—or both, I don't recall. Be that as it may, **there was a garden, and in this garden I see a tree that I loved immensely** (a catalpa? you can find them in the Luxembourg Gardens); **after this tree had displayed its flowers and shed its fruit, there remained at spring's end a kind of empty half shell hanging from its branches: very light brown, divided in two by a stem, and ending in a pointed rudder; very, very light; and this mode of description ought to indicate clearly enough how I intended to use these shell-boats as I stuffed them into my pockets for the trip home: as ships in the washbasin of our garden, as squadrons in the gutter on rainy days, raising anchor for imaginary, exotic, Arcadian tropics.**

The Canguilhems had a farm in the Ariège region (an infinitely precious possession in those times of extreme hunger). And one day my father took me there to help "do the threshing." Once the wheat was harvested, the ears were "threshed," and the grain that fell out was taken away by the sackful to the attic of the barn. This was the main idea behind an operation that, for me, meant rather a long succession of games in the haystacks, in the straw, and in the piles of wheat—; it meant watching in fascination as the streams of grain flowed under my hand; it meant horses, carriage wheels, and naps in the grass. Months later, in autumn, "whiskers" from the wheat ears and hay would still be sticking out of the wool of my sweaters; suddenly and without warning I would feel them scratching my neck when I was at school, like the involuntary and belated return of a memory.

But the most memorable part of this "threshing" visit is that they fed us. Never did the country people of those regions feed themselves so abundantly, ardently, demonstratively, and ostentatiously, as in those years when the inhabitants of the cities were dying, sometimes literally, of starvation. Even today I salivate over the menu of these sensual words: "white bread," "pork," "dried beans," "goose fat" (an image of thick and very dense strips, very white, supremely delicious): a large table in a low room, all the "threshing people" there together, and the exclamation of the farmer at the end of the meal, rolled out in heavy Occitan—and yet, even in those parts, non-Mediterranean—syllables, remembered by my father for years to come and often repeated by him later, so that I myself would be able to recall hearing it: "If it keeps up like this, we'll all starve to death!"

My childhood instilled in me a terrifying fascination with philosophy. At that time, I probably didn't consider Canguilhem and my father to be philosophers (which my father always denied being) (after all, philosophers belonged to another era—they were Greek and had been dead for more than two thousand years: my reasoning here follows a line of thought analogous to that of a letter I recently received from a little boy, in which I found the following:

"Hello Jacques Roubaud,

My name is Étienne and I'm lerning some of your poems at school. With the teacher we've already learned: the poem about the cat, the rhinoceros, the dinosaurs, the snail [with an "e" crossed out], the marmot, and then I think that's all.

Last week my dad told me that he went somewhere one time when you read some poems with your friend Pierre l'artigue [sic] (he's his friend too). Well I thought you lived in the time of Victor Hugo and I didn't believe him.").

Not philosophers, then, but something very honorable and continually verifiable: professors of philosophy.

In any event, the moment of this fragment of prose coincides, in external time, with plans that are currently being made at the Collège International de Philosophie (where this fascination with philosophy finally led me, this autumn of 1989, with a more or less clear conscience (I don't feel that I'm any more of a philosopher now than I did when I was seven (and I know I didn't feel it then, since that's when I decided to be a poet)))—plans for an event paying tribute to Canguilhem. It amused me to see his most respectable former students anxiously wondering how "he" would react, and who was going to take it upon themselves to broach the subject to the man himself.

66 (§ 7) The narration of a memory would be in constant need of the resources provided by Hermogenian rhetoric (speed being a central concept in the Hellenistic treatise on oratory written by this author)

The conditional is deceptive: the writing of "**the great fire of London**" is strongly influenced by the Rhetor Hermogenes's treatise *Peri Ideon* ("On Style"). Or it might be more correct to say that I chose the Hermogenian "Idea" of speed (also referred to as "velocity," "rapidity," "*celeritas*," "vivacity," or "*prestezza*" by his various commentators during the Renaissance), in order to give it a central role in my own rhetorical strategy. I admit that at first I did this out of curiosity, since this idea is itself most likely an innovation introduced by Hermogenes—one of his most decisive contributions to the tradition, which gives it the undeniable attraction of rarity. But also, and most especially, because during the Renaissance it was held in particularly high esteem—especially in English and Italian poetry, where (in my shameful ignorance of Greco-Latin Antiquity) I first discovered its existence (initially via the work of Giulio Camillo Delminio, author of a treatise (*The Idea of the Theater*) on an ideal and actual Theater of Memory he wanted to see constructed). This Idea also has a central place in the geometry of rhetorical exposition, since, as the fourth of Hermogenes's seven Ideas, it is flanked on either side by three others: Clarity, Grandeur and Beauty before—Character, Truth, and Gravity after.

A fabulous "brief life" of Hermogenes (one of the supreme genres in the style of velocity) was written by Philostratus (and here I'll accelerate it even more and make it even more compact, without however overlooking the fact that it may actually refer to a different Hermogenes, called the Sophist, whom the translator M. Patillon wants to distinguish from the Rhetor). It constitutes an illustration of my interpretation of the rhetorical qualities of speed, & is full of "sweetness" (or "*dolcezza*," or "flavor": a beautiful sub-idea from the *Peri Ideon*, which I've borrowed from the treatise in order to make it serve the ethos of my work, as a "component" of its truthfulness): "Hermogenes, born in Tarsus, had such a great reputation as a sophist at fifteen years of age that the emperor

Marcus Aurelius traveled far in order to hear him. But at twenty years of age, he suddenly lost his gift, apparently due to natural causes. 'Now where are all your winged speeches?' he was asked. 'Have they not flown away from you with the speed of a bird?' He died at an old age, poor and unknown—no one thought of him after his art had deserted him. When his corpse was examined, it was discovered that his heart was larger than normal, and covered with hair."

Sturm, in his 1571 translation of Hermogenes into Latin, speaks of the idea of speed in terms that evoke the impetuous current of a river, and its "rigid" waters (as the "Prose Lancelot" puts it). Speed is a quality that brings the waters of speech to life, as it were— waters that, in its absence, would become a stagnant pool. But since it sometimes suffices to stare intently at a river in order to make it seem as though it has stopped flowing; and since any current—even the most rapid one—that flows too smoothly seems slow and almost immobile after a time, the river of speech must still be interrupted by the occasional interjection of "hirsutes": those words and sounds of *velocitas* par excellence.

The sixteenth century saw speed as the defining style of its time. Minturno, in his *L'Arte Poetica*, cites a verse from Petrarch's "Triumph of Time" as his emblem; a verse, he argues, that describes the irrepressible precipitousness that it itself speaks of with extreme rapidity: "*per la mirabil sua velocitate*." And Andrew Marvell, addressing "his coy mistress"— his fleeing, reticent, and phobic mistress—warns of "Time's winged chariot hurrying near." And more intimately still, the apostrophe of Marlowe's Faust to the horses of the night—itself taken from Ovid—accords entirely with the spirit of the Hermogenian Idea: "*Lente, lente, currite noctis equi*" (a verse to which I give here, typographically, the stress and insistence that I hear in it). Every word in this verse is a word of speed, for in the Hermogenian classification the preeminent meter of this Idea is the trochee, is trochaic succession (particularly trochaic dipodia), which ceaselessly falls from its heights (here, from a height defined by stress and accent: a Latin verse pronounced in English), sending the voice precipitously downward. But the intensification of the effect, its acceleration, results from the semantic precipice in the first two feet, in which the adverb is repeated, as though deliberately invented to embody a "Grelling's paradox" in time: "*lente*," "*lente*." (All this has a very clear sense in Marlowe's English text, where it's a matter of creating, as the verse unfolds, an imbalance in relation to the surrounding iambic rhythmic environment. In the same way, "international free verse"—the contemporary "ifv," based on English-language poetry—obtains its desired effects through perpetual enjambment (consider this a hypothesis as to the origin of the "ifv": the importance of metric instability).)

In fact, everything in the description of this "speedy style" (the description given by Hermogenes's French translator M. Patillon, who dissects the Rhetor and all his examples from Demosthenes) makes it clear to me, after the fact, what it was about this Idea that so immediately seduced me: with speed, there's no time for thought! Brief words chosen quickly, figures of speech with no room for platitudes: instead—interpolations, embeddings; & "the incursive," a marvel that brings with it a cascade of other "ideas," hurling them into an unequal distribution of crag-conjunctions (the *hirsuta* of syntax): commata in the form of asyndetons (but of course!); variants accumulated and brought together; proximate apodoses (fear not, dear reader: this term simply promises the immediate arrival of "the idea that must follow"); the figures of a concise discourse which, however, disguises its own concision (via oblique constructions, enclaves), the figures of a discourse that seems to be concise but isn't (via associations), and even the figures of a discourse that is both concise and appears to be so (imagine!); brief *côla*, pauses without hiatus (no breaks in the voice) ending in instability; & *last but not least!* trochaic dipodia, of course. The brevity of elements and the rapidity of transitions are able to generate various movements (*kinei*) and multiple passages (*metabasis*). Their necessity results from the fact that "the discourse divided into pieces, in becoming flat, needs a corrective (*épanortosis*) in the form of a logical placement in perspective (incursive figure) or a metalogical one (incidental remark). That is what Hermogenes calls raising up (*orthoun*) platitude and awakening (*diégeirein*) discourse." Indeed.

But it is the equivalence made in the sixteenth century between the Hermogenian Idea and the topos of Time that makes it so necessary for my undertaking: in deciding to write within the present moment of my narration, never stopping and never going back, in a constant "now" whose nocturnal composition is enclosed within so narrow a time frame, I condemned myself to the anxiety of the vanishing instant—an instant whose end I will always see coming, and recognize as it comes. Salvation (however illusory) lay in speed alone.

67 (§ 8) something like Olbers's paradox

Olbers is the astronomer who (in the golden years of Newtonian cosmology (this was around 1820)), "discovered" that the night sky shouldn't be black. Quite the contrary: every point in the universe, if considered as the origin of a gaze, ought to be dazzled by infinite light.

I picture Olbers on the basis of the brief descriptions scholars have given of him: the entire upper part of his house had been converted into an observatory, and he devoted the greater part of his nights to astronomy; he was particularly interested in comets and minor planets. I see him as something like a Danish Mr. Pickwick (the hero of my grandfather's favorite book, which he reread every two years or so), & a perfect example of what the English used to call a *natural philosopher*. He certainly must have had a passion, like Goethe, for the classification of clouds (as well as for comparing the merits of Lamarck's system with the one that's still in use today, coming to us from the Quaker pharmacist Luke Howard). But above all he was preoccupied with this difficult question: Why is the night sky black?

Let us admit the cosmological principle: to wit, that the universe—with the exception of purely local irregularities like galaxies—presents the same aspect everywhere. Next, let us consider a very large spherical shell, with an arbitrary center, of radius r and thickness dr (infinitely thin, practically speaking, in relation to the radius). The volume of the sphere (4 pi multiplied by r squared, multiplied again by dr) will be presumed large enough for the light emitted by all the stars that this sphere contains to be equal to the product of its volume (which I just expressed) times U, where U is the product of the average number of stars in a unit of volume multiplied by the average luminosity of one star (and where "average" means average in relation to the cosmological principle, provided that everything is considered on a sufficiently large scale). Do you follow me?

The Reader (*himself a natural philosopher*): I'm ahead of you: the intensity of light from the stars, at the center of the shell of the universe that you imagine—this balcony, for example—is consequently Udr, and is therefore practically independent of the radius of the sphere.

Another Reader: Further, you are therefore assuming the following verified condition: *condition i*: The average density of the stars does not vary with time.

First Reader: And then *condition ii*: The average luminosity does not vary with time.

Me: Olbers was also assuming (and this goes without saying, since neither Lobatchevsky nor Bolyai had as yet published their ferocious hypotheses on geometry, and Gauss was keeping his in a drawer):

condition iii: Space is Euclidean.

But even if one assumes a Lobatchevskian space, our results won't be affected, right?

Second Reader: If you say so . . .

First Reader: I concur. However

condition iv is also necessary:

The same laws of physics apply in all regions of space, and not only on our terraqueous globe. God has willed it so.

Second Reader: But let us also add

condition v, which is likewise indispensable to your hero's argument:

There is no all-inclusive movement of the stars.

Me: Quite so. That much is crucial.

Thus, one can complete the argument, arriving at the same troubling conclusion that so greatly preoccupied Olbers: Since the intensity of light at the center of the sphere is constant, radiating from the stars on the inside crust of our hypothetical shell, let us surround this shell, like an onion, with other shells of equal thickness, concentric to the first and with the external border of one being the internal surface of the next. Then each shell will contribute in the same way as the first to the radiation reaching the center. Since one can add an endless number of shells to the first sphere we posited, it follows that the density of radiation must be infinite precisely at that central point. The Heavens would therefore be filled with infinite light.

First Reader: May we not simply assume that the light *is* in fact infinite as it reaches our eyes, but that we are nonetheless almost entirely blind to it?

Jacques Roubaud: ?

Second Reader The glory illuminating all regions

> within the spirit of the divine
>
> stops at the edge of our vision
>
> and turns in vain
>
> toward the interior
>
> of the self.

Jacques Roubaud (that is, me): ? ? ? ?

First Reader: Is this not proof of a supernatural intervention?

A Third Reader: Infinite light is, precisely, black.

Me: Olbers postulated, a little more prosaically, a rarified gas absorbing the excess radiation—angels' hair floating in the jelly of the ether.

First Reader: Let's be serious!

Me: As a matter of fact, if I understand modern astronomy correctly, one can indeed still maintain the universality of the laws of physics, and the cosmological principle. Nor is it possible to posit that the universe is simply very young, and that most of that infinite light just hasn't reached us yet. What remains is Hubble's hypothesis, which has since been confirmed in many other ways: *condition v* does not hold. The universe is expanding.

And so the notion came to me of a paradoxical infinitude of light radiating from the snow in my old wintertime garden; and then, by association, recalling a biologist who had compared memories to an endlessly falling snow accumulating in crystalline layers somewhere in our brain, I then posited an expanding universe of memory, preventing us from being blinded by the infinite, radiant multiplicity of the atoms of our pasts that we carry within us, an outward movement that would be called, in the temporarily expanding universe of our existence, **Forgetting**.

68 (§ 10) **I also see mulberry trees, with their red fruit lying exploded on the ground around them, like wine, or blood**

This passage, like many similar ones in the first chapter of this branch (others will come later: in other chapters, interpolations, bifurcations, in other branches, & in that no-man's-land of prose articulations that I've named "inter-branches"), is typographically isolated from the rest of the text on the page, a peculiarity that will be found again, in one form or another, in the eventual, hypothetical published version (for the moment I mark this peculiarity by "selecting" the fragment (to use the Macintoshian jargon), which then appears in black on my screen. Then in the "format" column I "click" on the word "bold," which, by virtue of the helpful redundancies of my "word processor," appears endowed with the very "stylistic" quality in question, namely **bold type**. The fragment thus isolated immediately takes on the desired quality: that is, the very one named). (The jargon of these machines, with their infantilizing Franglais, is enough to fill any lover of beautiful prose with absolute horror.)

The first common feature of the fragments thus singled out is that they are <u>descriptions</u> based, as scrupulously as possible, on <u>pure images</u> or <u>brief sequences of images</u>, characterized by a minimal use of <u>deductive recomposition</u>, and <u>which I am able to identify and locate as moments of my childhood</u> (prior to the first months of 1945, at least, where the last of these images is situated—though I can't give it a precise date, chronologically speaking). I introduce them into the text most often with the words "**I see**" (using these words more or less exactly, though they aren't necessarily the first words of the fragment), words that, according to my interpretation of this idea of the image, may be considered substitutes for an impossible "**I see myself**" (Therefore, I'm always "present" in these fragments attributed to the past).

Their second common feature is the <u>moment</u> when these images were first set down on paper (in a form slightly different from the one they have now). It was quite a long time ago. I wrote them all at the same time as I was writing the chain of fictive deductions reproduced (in their palindromic "<u>double</u>") in chapter 5 of branch one, composed of ninety-nine assertions presented as an <u>elucidation</u> of the dream story that "began" my **Project**: in the fall of 1980, nine years ago. The <u>assertions</u>, as I

→ I § 69

wrote there, were initially conceived as "<u>maxims</u>." Likewise, these <u>images</u> were <u>memories</u>. <u>Assertions</u> and <u>images</u> (maxims and memories) are <u>interwoven</u>, and this interweaving is not only a result of their having been written down contemporaneously. Some of these images are "cited," in fact, without commentary, in the assertions. Thus, their reconstitution in this branch will fill certain "holes" in the "deduction."

The third common feature of these images, a consequence of the other two, is that even if I attempt somehow to connect them to one another in this story, I can't actually add anything to them. This is how they were. And my central hypothesis about memory implies that, since they've been written, they are no longer, or no longer purely, present in my memories. They are "told images," and thus are above all what I call "**pictions**."

→ I § 70

There's a certain initial order to this induction of images, namely the order in which they were extracted from the memories they're based on. The order of their appearance is hardly a matter of indifference to me: It was the intense experience of writing from memory—an experience these written images attempt to present—that allowed me to develop my reflections. But I didn't preserve their initial order here, despite having done so for the assertions. The difference is not so much that the original list of these images appears to be strung together in such a haphazard way (creating the impression, in certain concatenations, of a word game like "*marabout-bout de ficelle*" (in which the last syllable of a word or expression is used as the first syllable in the next)). You'll have noticed that I used (deliberately) the expression "induction of images." What I mean is that the linear form in which the descriptions were first set down masks the combinatory character of memory, which is not only not simply "successive" (since any succession would be "in both directions"), but is above all essentially an <u>intrication at a distance</u>, rather than a <u>juxtaposition</u> (a feature that provided the foundation for a <u>mathematical theory of memory</u> that would have "accompanied" **The Great Fire of London**. It was supposed to be a part of the **Project**). Here one will recognize the hypotheses underlying my "fictive solution" of Goodman's paradox, a logical paradox of induction.

By contrast, the assertions in branch one, despite their elliptical discontinuity, do in fact bear the recognizable signs of a necessary term-by-term sequence. This is inherent in every "deduction." But the "correspondences" that link them together do not strictly follow the respective orders of their terms. One result of all this is a possible parallelism (partial, but possible) between the first two **branches** of my story: <u>**branch one** is a (the?) branch that "elucidates," introduces, comments on a deductive chain (the dream, the decision, the **Project**, and their consequence, the unwritten novel, **The Great Fire of**</u>

London). **Branch two, on the other hand,** is constructed as the elucidation of, the commentary on, an inductive sequence of **memory-images**.

69 (§ 68) I wrote them all at the same time as I wrote the chain of fictive deductions that "began" my Project: in the fall of 1980, nine years ago.

In 1980, in the autumn, I wrote the following: "In the autumn of my marriage, I was convinced that I at last had found satisfactory conditions, had struck a reasonable balance between the infinitely more modest tasks of daily life and a prose without obligations" (branch one, § 16). This is not false. But these conditions were obviously not enough to lead me from the very peculiar form of my attempts at that time to the way in which "The great fire of London" is now being written.

The "beginning" of my **Project**, after the Preface (§ 0 of the whole, preceding the beginning of branch one), would have been the story of the dream (branch one, chapter 5). After that would come the placement of the "maxims" (that is, all this would have been the preparatory material; I won't say, I don't have to say, what the real prose would have been—the prose written and destroyed), followed by a record of the "memories." Their "suture points," as it were.

Today I see quite clearly that the "twofold" aspect of this version of the work— which was initially destined for a single, privileged reader (Alix, my wife) in advance of any other, potential ones—was itself a response to its twofold nature (& that this double aspect was the "motor" of Alix's own "project"): as both philosophy and photography.

This assemblage of "maxims," to be read by a "Wittgensteinian," was a displacement into philosophical territory, but in a fictive form. This analogy is both distinct and simple. Its clarity grows out of a Hermogenian distinctness. And, at the time, it was completely explicit: an encounter, conjugal and ludic, between mathematics and philosophy, beneath the gaze of logic.

But it was also, simultaneously, a translation of photography into the description of memories in prose (according to the Steinian aesthetics and ethics of description (*An Acquaintance with Description* is the title of one of Gertrude Stein's books) which also accords with certain maxims in Wittgenstein: Do not explain, describe. Do not say, show). I didn't see all this until much later.

When I wrote in chapter 1 of this branch that "childhood and photography have an almost consubstantial link—'All photographs,' as someone once wrote, 'are childhood photographs,'" I didn't say that this "someone" was Alix (at that moment it was beside the point). But it was natural that I offer the "photographic" writing of these memories to my wife, a photographer.

I'm quoting Alix, now: "The only true photographs are childhood photographs.

"The photographs that we have of our childhood are all fascinating. Even when they're blurry, badly composed, barely visible. Almost all of us have photographs of ourselves as children—not paintings, unless we've grown up with painters. But a photograph of our childhood fascinates us; it shows us a scene in which we were present; we see that we were there; we recognize ourselves in it; but we don't remember the scene first-hand; we never saw it at all. I was there, without a doubt; but I saw nothing— all I can see of it is a photograph. Yet I must have seen: I had two eyes; in the best of cases, I do remember; but I've forgotten. What photography shows me is **the first form of the invisible: oblivion**."

70 (§ 68) **They are images that have already been spoken . . . "pictions"**

In **"the great fire of London,"** I took up a Wittgensteinian distinction (between <u>Bild</u> and <u>Abbild</u>, in German; translated into *image* and *picture* in English). But I made this distinction my own by deforming it (inevitably, by deforming it). It is therefore a distinction that must be attributed not to Wittgenstein himself, but to a "<u>pseudo-Wittgenstein</u>" (just as, when referring to a certain medieval work of prose, one speaks of the "Chronicle of 'Pseudo-Turpin'"), who's been given a much wider "spectrum" of illumination. I don't think it's necessary to justify this appropriation (in any case, I'll give the same "excuse" for it as ever, the one used by any inventor of stories), but I will specify its modalities to some extent in the following "fictive deduction" (which could find a place, among others, in a book with that very title), which is, if you will, a "deduction by pseudo-Wittgenstein." Its "sources" will be easily recognized.

i. An **image** is not a **piction**.

ii. The **image** of pain is not a **piction**, and it cannot be replaced in a language game by anything that could be called a **piction**.
The **image** of pain certainly enters in a sense into the language game, but not as a **piction**.

iii. I name a stone, I name the sun, when these things are not themselves present to my senses. Undoubtedly, I have an **image** of them available to me in my memory.

I name a physical pain, though I am not suffering. This pain is thus also not present. Yet if an **image** of it were not in my memory, I would not know what I am referring to.

I name numbers, and there they are in my memory: not their **image**, but they themselves. I name the **image** of the sun, and it is not the **image** of an **image** that I evoke, but the **image** itself. It is the **image** that comes when I call.

iv. The **image** is the change induced in me by an object, by something in the world.

v. An **image** has no place.

vi. An **image** has no place; no place, no duration.

vii. It is clear that the act of forming **images** cannot be compared to that of moving a body. Indeed, in the latter case, someone other than myself can judge whether a movement has taken place, whereas in the movement of my **images**, it must necessarily be a matter of what I myself have seen.

viii. If someone said to me: My **images** are internal **pictions**, resembling my visual impressions, but subject to my will, I would say that this has no meaning.

ix. Yet, it would be erroneous to say that seeing and forming **images** are essentially different activities. This would be comparable to someone saying that, in chess, playing and losing are different activities.

x. Try to compare the **image** of L. W.'s toothache with his toothache. In other words, we have the **image** of a pain, but we cannot compare it to the pain as we compare the **piction** of a black eye with its model.

xi. **Pictions** are not **images** because they are idle.

xii. A mental **piction** is the **piction** described when someone describes what he imagines.

xiii. **Memory-images** are distinguished from other **images** by some special characteristic.

xiv. An **image** is more similar to its object than any **piction**. Whatever the degree of similitude achieved by a **piction**, it can always be the **piction** of something else. But it is essential for the **image** to be an **image** of that and only that. Which means that one could imagine that the **image** is a kind of super-resemblance.

xv. I would like to be able to say: What the **piction** says to me is "itself," not its object: something that exists in and as its own structure, line, color, form . . .

xvi. The memory of an **image** cannot be represented as "picturing" a **piction** of this image with less vivid colors. The lack of vividness of a memory is something entirely different from the paleness of a seen color, and its absence of visual clarity is by nature entirely different from the vagueness of an imprecise drawing.

xvii. Let us imagine a story composed of **pictions**. It is not necessary for us to translate these **pictions** into realistic representations in order to understand them. In the same way, we do not need to translate photographs into colored paintings. And yet, men and plants appearing in black and white in reality would seem implausibly strange and terrifying. Is it necessary then to say that something is a **piction** only within a **piction game**?

xviii. A sentence in a story gives us the same satisfaction as a **piction**.

xix. If one looks at a photograph that shows people, houses, and trees, one does not feel the absence of a third dimension. It would not be easy to describe a photograph as being no more than a collection of spots on a flat surface.

xx. We see a photograph or a painting on our wall as if it were the object itself (the man, the landscape, etc.). But this doesn't have to be the case. One could for example imagine a tribe that would not have this type of relation with **pictions**, in which people would be repulsed by photographs, would consider the colorless faces or even the faces reduced in scale as inhuman things.

xxi. I just took some apples out of a paper bag, where they had been for quite a while. I had to cut most of them in two and throw the other halves away. A little later, I was copying out a sentence from my notebook, and the end of the phrase was no good. Suddenly I saw this sentence as a half-rotten apple. It always happens that way. Everything I encounter soon becomes a mental **piction** of what I happen to be thinking about at the moment.

xxii. "The style makes the man." "The style makes the man into himself." The first expression is a short and mediocre epigram. The second version opens a very different perspective. It says that the style of a man is a **piction** of that man.

xxiii. The **piction** of an apple tree, even a faithful one, is in a sense much farther from the tree than a daisy.

xxiv. Can one deny a **piction**? The answer is no.

xxv. What I look at is present. What I foresee is in the future. The sun is not in the future, since it already is, but its rising is in the future, since it has not yet taken place. But I could not predict its rising if I did not have an **image** of it in me. No **piction** can lead to a prediction.

xxvi. The **piction** is there. I do not question its accuracy. But what does it apply to? Must one think of a **piction** of blindness as an obscurity of the soul, or perhaps as a darkness in the blind man's head?

xxvii. Whatever is an **image** is not in the same space as what is seen.

xxviii. One cannot attentively follow an **image**.

xxix. Attention does not produce **images**.

xxx. At this moment, I had the following thought before my eyes: . . .
"How so?"
"I mean, I had this **piction**."
Was the **piction** the thought? No. If I describe the **piction** to someone, the thought will not be transmitted to him.

xxxi. The idea of a leaf is not an **image** of the leaf. It is not even an **image** that would contain nothing but what is common to all leaves. The meaning of a word is not an **im-**

age. We have a tendency to regard words as though they were proper names. And then we confuse the bearer of the name with the meaning of the noun.

xxxii. A shadow is a sort of **piction**. But it is absolutely essential that a **piction** we present as the shadow of a thing not be what I would call a "**piction** by resemblance." This doesn't mean that the shadow-**piction** is one that resembles what it represents, but rather only that this **piction** is correct when one recognizes its similarity to the thing itself. One could say that the **piction** is a copy. *Grosso modo*, one can say that copies are **pictions** that can be taken for what they represent.

xxxiii. There is no portrait of red.

xxxiv. **Pictions** are always idle.

xxxv Let us think of a **piction** of a **landscape**. It is an imaginary landscape with a house. Someone asks, "Whose house is this?" The answer could be: it belongs to the farmer sitting on the bench in front of the house. But this is a farmer who cannot go inside his house.

xxxvi. Two **pictions** of a rose in the dark. In one of the two **pictions**, there is only darkness—the rose is invisible. In the other **piction**, the rose is represented in detail, but surrounded by darkness. Is one of these **pictions** correct and the other false? Can one speak of a pink rose in the dark? Of a red rose in the dark? Can one say, at the same time, that one cannot tell them apart in the dark?

Beware of black roses.

xxxvii. If we compare a proposition to a **piction**, we would have to know if we are comparing it to a portrait or to a genre painting.

Each has its merits.

71 (§ 10) a republican lineage marked by a certain propensity for unpopular positions

The reconstruction of such a "moral genealogy" depends without a doubt on the perspective adopted by my father in telling the story of our family origins, and he himself had been influenced on this point by his own grandfather, the sailor. But in recognizing it as my own, I make a choice. I choose to behave as though I were able, as a free and autonomous adult subject, to dispose of my judgments and civic behaviors as I wish, while also realizing that the adoption of these judgments and behaviors was not initially a matter of free choice, as though they included a hereditary component; and, further, that these same qualities resulted from a kind of instruction that I received during the most malleable period of my life, namely childhood, and in a form most difficult to avoid, since its lessons were not presented to me as such, but were hidden insidiously within a story. (Of course, the transmission of a "republican gene" (or even a "radical" one, in this sense) would inevitably be favored by these conditions.)

It goes without saying that I believe in the heredity of acquired political characteristics only in a very limited way—hardly any more, in fact, than I believe (as far as I'm concerned, at least) in the complete determination of these characteristics by some form of "teaching," whether directly or indirectly delivered. Of course, political vision is not vision *tout court*. When it comes to the latter, neurophysiology does indeed seem to have settled the question (at least with regard to kittens, as I recall (but I'd be happy to share these properties with felines)): Without the inherited nervous and cerebral apparatuses on the one hand, and then the learning process that occurs in the very first months of life on the other, blindness is certain.

And in order to arrive at this conclusion regarding people, there was no need to subject human beings to the thought experiment once proposed (during the "Enlightenment," of course) by Jean-Bernard Mérian: take a few human children, raise them in the best material, intellectual, and moral conditions possible, but in total darkness, in the absence of any natural or artificial ray of light, and then, at the age of twenty, expose them all at once to daylight. It would be quite difficult today to imagine a transposition of this experiment into the register of ideas and opinions. (Though the hypothesis of the "noble savage" implicitly assumes such a transposition, even as it decides the results in advance.)

I am certainly not saying that I imagine myself to have escaped entirely from these two determinants (heredity and instruction)and am beholden to nothing more than my own conscious decisions as an adult. And finally, too, I don't mean to imply that the genealogical fiction that I'm constructing here, by recalling my own memories, is itself only important to me because it may or may not contain the truth. I'm incorporating it into my story strictly for the sake of another transposition, at once analogical and differential (the interrogation of certain family resemblances and divergences), within the constitutive system that was once my **Project**.

This **Project** assumed, in effect, the exercise of two faculties: the faculty of mathematization, and the faculty of poetry. And if the **Project** was to be, as it claimed to be, both a **Project of Mathematics and** a **Project of Poetry**, to what extent did its very possibility (and its eventual failure) originate in its prehistory, in the history and prehistory of my family in particular?

I'm not asking whether I was capable or incapable of these faculties: I hold as axiomatic, in this narrative at least, that being capable of language (which is indispensable for my reader) implies being capable of mathematics and poetry. I am simply attempting to untangle their origins.

72 (§ 10) **they also decisively determine our *ethos***

Here too I am taking Hermogenes's rhetoric and turning it to my own ends. I have read—and I'm all the more willing to believe it, since it fits perfectly with what I'm doing here—that Hermogenes's rhetorical Idea of *ethos*, more "<u>rhe-theoretical</u>" in fact than strictly pragmatic, was also not really an ethical injunction, but rather a "technical proof," "inherent in discourse," intended to "evoke an opinion of the author that would make him worthy of one's faith." This is indeed how I want to understand it. This portrait of the Hermogenian *ethos* presents it as one side of a double Idea: "*ethos-aletheia*" (*aletheia*: *veritas, veritate*, verity).

Now, I envisage *aletheia* exclusively (narratively) in terms of truthfulness, in the sense of telling the truth (my own strategy of truth-telling results not from the discovery, but more trivially from the choice of a protective apparatus, and it remains a condition of possibility for this prose). It follows that the *ethos* of my prose, too, is an *ethos* of truthfulness: I recount things that have happened, or are happening, in their nakedness, without any appearance of polishing or preparation. My *aletheia*, in its self-proclaimed state of nature, does not need to be snuck up on, or ferreted out. But it comes with (or would like to come with) all the component qualities that spontaneously belong to it: *glukutes* (flavor, *sweetness; suavitas, soave, dolcezza*)—*drimutes* (subtlety (which is sometimes only an *acutum*: the sharpness of a point, a sting))—*epieikeia* (moderation and modesty).

The relation between fiction and nonfiction in this *ethos* is a difficult one, contrary to what one might think at first glance. At first glance, nothing could be more simple: it makes fiction impossible, since it is strictly impossible to believe in fiction, except by a momentary and voluntary blindness. The <u>*aletheia* of truthfulness</u> (like that of truth itself) is allergic to fiction, to the novel. **"The great fire of London"** is anything but a novel.

But the truthfulness it proclaims is exactly that, proclaimed: a rhetorical affirmation of truthfulness (as Hermogenian as possible, rhetorical despite everything), which in no way guarantees that there's any truth to the things that are said beyond the bounds of the statement itself. I offer no more than a few "technical proofs" of truthfulness—that is to say, a few modes by which this discourse in prose may proceed such that the reader can have faith in what I say, can find him- or herself persuaded by my *ethos*.

However, it could be that all this is only a ruse of fiction, taking advantage of a possible confusion between truth and demonstrability (which must obviously be kept separate in this context, in which the illusion of a logical "completeness" has no meaning: a true story is not necessarily verifiable (one can even say that a verifiable story is not necessarily true; for who would carry out the verification? and who will verify the verifiers (a Carrollian paradox)?)). The affirmation of truthfulness would then merely put into play another Hermogenian idea, that of <u>complication</u>.

I was struck, however, by some of the reactions readers had to the publication of the first part of my work: readers who not only didn't doubt the truth of what I'd set down there, but who seemed moreover to be persuaded of its permanence—quite contrary to my affirmation that I was writing in the present of things as they are recounted; the implication being that, once the book had been printed, they were things of the past, and therefore very likely to be descriptions of past states. I appeared thus in those pages, and thus I had been—and thus, they assumed, I must continue to be. For these readers, my strategy of *aletheia* had succeeded beyond all my hopes!

73 (§ 11) I know that I'd already seen it, four years earlier, but I had forgotten it

It's impossible for me to retrieve even the slightest image related to the sea from this first visit. I can go as far as the sand (it's probably sand I'm seeing), but no farther. The summer of 1938 was the last uninterrupted summer of the "interwar" period, and History made it, for my parents—for the rest of their lives—their one and only summer with a real vacation: that is, spent on the Mediterranean coast. They rented a "villa" close to Hyères from two very bourgeois sisters who were terrified by the progressive invasion of the coast by "those paid vacationers," and for whom academic families, despite their numerous children and predictably "leftist" ideas, seemed to be a lesser evil. They had fled, and the rent wasn't expensive.

My parents, my uncle Frantz Molino (my mother's brother), and his young wife,

Jeanne, all stayed at the villa, as well as six children, including myself: my sister Denise and my brother Pierre, my cousin Jean (a year older than me), my cousin Juliette, and then the other Pierre (who for us, his cousins, is always "Pierre Molino").

It is an immense villa that I perceive above me (I see one end of the façade, some windows), at an angle, over or between the spaces in the banister of a staircase that could be marble, or fake marble; this image is steeped in a violent light, violently opposed to the vegetal darkness, proximate and intense; it is isolated, does not move around me, does not lead me anywhere else (a sure sign of how old it is).

I've learned to recognize this intense isolation of an **image's** circumstances as an indication that it is may be very old. (I speak of an "image's circumstances," because what I see is not detached from me and laid out on the wall of my vision. I am a part of it. In all the images that I narrate, I *am*). Another "archaic" particularity of this memory is the villa's immensity, and its properly "Palladian" architecture. But in the family photographs that have "placed" this image for me, its dimensions are modest, ordinary.

The sea is very close. There is nothing exceptional in the intensity of its light. But the image itself has preserved its initial scale. It has not been adjusted by any (unconscious) revisions according to geometric verisimilitude, perhaps because I never saw the villa again. And beyond the edge of the image, unseen, impenetrable to me now, it continues, into the the surrounding darkness, a darkness just as violent as the light illuminating the villa, the stairs. The following appears to me (but these are things that I can say, not see; perhaps the remnant of some other larger or disjointed image, an image that I once retained, but have since lost):

on the right, beneath the steps, large aloe plants, sharp; a warm smell of Mediterranean vegetation, in the absolute summer dryness.

74 (§ 11) My father succeeded in almost entirely converting my mother, but without ever obtaining from her a truly unreserved attachment to mussels and sardines

And yet traces of a certain ongoing (ludic) "class struggle between my parents" in terms of culinary theory are evident even today. The standard reference book, Reboul's *La cuisinière provençale* (The Provençal Cook)—familiarity with which was all but obligatory for the housewives of Toulon or Marseille at the beginning of the century, and which later conquered a new generation (as proven by countless reprintings), thanks to the invasion of the Mediterranean coast by vacation homes—itself stokes a constantly renewed polemic between my parents.

My father claims to see the book as a perfect illustration of the "bourgeois" point of view in cooking, with its unconcealed contempt for popular practices, its preference for "noble" and costly types of food (accompanied by a suspicious admiration for butter and Normandy cream), and its condescension regarding the recipes of poor and simple people, expressly described in its pages as simplistic and unrefined. My mother defends Reboul in the name of family fidelity (respecting the memory of her aunt Jeanne Thabot from Marseille, who was a tremendous cook), and in the name of the independence of genius—as it transcends such petty distinctions, which in the end are secondary.

My father "proves" the irrefutability of his argument with two examples: the snail (called *limaçon* in Provence rather than *escargot*), which is treated "offhandedly" by Reboul, he says; and the sardine, ever and always the sardine. The lot assigned to the sardine (along with that of its cousin, the anchovy) is, according to my father, the touchstone of a correct attitude in matters of gastronomy. My mother points out to him that the relevant recipes are there. My father retorts that "he" could not decently exclude them, but that his disdain for them is glaringly obvious in every line.

A secondary polemic is then introduced into this central divergence, based around the fact that Reboul is from Marseille. And my father has an instinctive and ancient mistrust of this falsely Provençal city, which overshadows Toulon (the old Toulon), and even plays soccer instead of rugby—well, what more need one say. My mother isn't particularly attached to Marseille, but, having spent her first two years as a *lycée* student at the Lycée Thiers (doing the preparatory courses of the "*hypokhâgne*" and "*khâgne*"), living with my Uncle Pierre and Aunt Jeanne, natives of Marseille, she finds herself—because of her defense of Reboul, and despite her vigorous protests—automatically placed on the Phocian side of the divide.

This double language game, in its repetitive, almost ritual nature, today serves primarily as an <u>effector of memory</u>, since it allows me to reconstitute, if only for a moment, the setting—long past in reality, obliterated by the years—of the preparation of aïolis, broiled sardines, and marinades for anchovies (on my father's behalf). My Aunt Jeanne's "*pieds et paquets*," her "stews," her "*alouettes sans têtes*," and her "cannelloni" are invoked by my mother, and my father pays grudging homage to them.

I have occasionally tried to introduce some conciliatory diversions into these discussions by pointing out the curious conjunction of anchovies and poetry in the work of

César Pellenc, the cook from Aix, in his considerably pre-Reboulian collection, *Les Plaisirs de la Vie* ("The Pleasures of Life"), from 1655. This tactic was meant to show how far back the commingling of the "scholarly" and the "popular" registers actually goes. Such efforts met with only moderate success, I must admit:

<u>The Anchovy</u>

Dauphin, we know that you boast
Of being King of the vast Element,
But surely you must
Be dreaming, or lying:

How now! crowned though you be,
Can this high rank be given
Despite the Anchovy, who merits it most?
Prince Fish, you have nothing:
For there is no jar and no kettle
That is not his subject—but none are yours.

75 (§ 12) (There were three young ladies at the École Normale that year— an exceptional phenomenon at the time)

Taken by surprise, the administration had to accept the fact, in 1926, that nothing really prevented "girls" (*jeune filles*), as they said, from taking part in the same examinations given to boys, or even, if they passed, from becoming students at the prestigious École Normale. The first young lady to achieve this, after having verified (not without some difficulty) that she would indeed be accorded a ranking in the competitive exam, was a scientist, Marie-Louise Jacotin (she ended her career as a mathematician at the Institut Henri-Poincaré, where I took a course or two with her).

The following year, 1927, was the year of the "Glorious Three," as they were called, not without a thinly veiled irony: Clémence Ramnoux was ranked 9th, Simone Pétrement 12th, and my mother, then Suzanne Molino, 17th. (In 1928, only one woman was accepted: Simone Weil) The sheer scandal of these developments was only slightly attenuated by forcing these disturbing female presences to reside elsewhere (my mother spent her years at the École living in student housing at the Cité Universitaire, since her parents lived in Lyon), so as not to trouble the presumably studious and monastic atmosphere of the place; and "fortunately" this scandal only lasted until the war. A "reorganization" of the *École de Jeunes Filles* in Sèvres provided the opportunity to reestablish the necessary separation of the sexes. This arrangement lasted a long time and didn't change until fairly recently.

Thus, the title of <u>alumna</u> of the École Normale Supérieure (Rue d'Ulm) was something extremely rare. If my mother was proud of it, she never let on (she never let it be known that she was proud of anything, I'm afraid). Not all the "*normaliennes*" in this bizarre cohort demonstrated a comparable modesty.

For instance, I read, not long ago, at first with indignation (based on family pride), but then with a certain amusement (once I had regained my composure), an interview with Mme. de Romilly (who entered the Rue d'Ulm in 1933) when she was elected to the Académie Française. The interviewer, no doubt out of ignorance (I hope), mentions, among his interlocutor's countless titles of glory (*agrégation*, thesis, Collège de France, etc., etc.), that she was the first woman "elected" to be at the Rue d'Ulm; and I was stupefied to see that she let this comment go and refrained from correcting him (nor did she do so in the days following the interview's publication. A reader had to write in. Perhaps Mme. de Romilly was suffering from the fact that she hadn't been the first woman in the Académie Française?).

For a very short time (just before her retirement), I was a colleague of the first of the "Glorious Three" (let us respect the order of the rankings!) at the Université de Paris-X Nanterre: Clémence Ramnoux, of whom I could summon only a vague and distant silhouette from childhood, an aural association with the sound of my mother's voice singing, "Her name is Clémence, Clémence, Clémence Ramnoux, menou, menou, menou . . ."

In my recollection, the gentle beauty of this name (one of my favorites) was marvelously suited to such a song. So, hearing her name, it was with no small curiosity that I confronted the eminent specialist on the Presocratics with her ghost from another time. Much as I expected, she was the very same "menou, menou, menou." I was amused and enchanted by her. She asked for news of my parents, and it was then, as she spoke to me (this was in the course of an extremely boring curriculum committee meeting at our common university), I saw in those philosophical eyes that, for her, I had hardly grown up at all. I was still, for her, about four years old.

76 (§ 13) The "prewar" stories my parents told included descriptions (often demanded and often repeated) of the foods that had completely disappeared from urban France beginning in the winter of 1940

Actually, I'm thinking primarily of my grandmother's stories. With her characteristic fearlessness, she had undertaken, in 1941 I believe, an unlikely and dangerous journey across Spain and Portugal, and then braving the oceanic perils of a world at war, in order to see her youngest daughter (Renée, my mother's sister) who had since moved to Massachusetts. The USA hadn't yet "declared war" and had an ambiguous and rather unsavory relationship with the Vichy regime, which had allowed her to wrangle an authorization for the departure, and also for the return.

She was an extraordinary storyteller. She had come back to us across a raging ocean patrolled by submarines, bearing not those inaccessible commodities themselves, unknown, lost, or even forgotten—wondrous and perishable—but their descriptions. And for the children listening around the dining room table, these descriptions were accompanied by the pictures of food that, like so many images of El Dorado, adorned the "magazines" of peaceful America, and that she had brought back in her suitcase: more beautiful than the child's palace of Dame Tartine, filled with more art than the Louvre— "banana splits," "strawberry sundaes," "milkshakes, frappes, & floats," those "ice cream sodas" with their hyperrealist colors—way ahead of their time—and all brought to life by her voice, promising us miraculous and fattening flavors.

If the "pre-war period" represented a paradise lost for us (as were the metro and the erotic aroma of the "premieres" floating around Mireille Balin for Jean Gabin in *Pépé le Moko*), America became—through the voice of my grandmother—the incarnation of a mythical "golden age," essentially culinary, a promised land that would be established in the "postwar period" of freedom and abundance that was still almost impossible to imagine then. But, like all our relatives, she firmly believed in it, against the very convincing evidence of 1941, to the point of taking action (a little later and not without risk) to bring it about. Her hero was Franklin Delano Roosevelt. For us children, it was he who would come to liberate us, "ice cream" in hand.

The most effective image from her stories, one that wasn't accompanied by any "illustrated" support—since the fruit it evoked was too commonplace and banal for wealthy America to accumulate photos of it, but which for this very reason acquired an even greater power over our imaginations—was that of the **orange**. My grandmother told us, and **I saw, how from the globes of six whole squeezed fruits the juice flowed, foamy and fragrant, filling all the glasses of the blessed in turn; I saw those silent spheres quenching desires and thirsts, emerging from the cavern of cold, the fabulous *refrigerator*.**

I have difficulty associating the industrial orange of today's supermarkets, enveloped in that thin paper from Spain or Morocco (Marie collects them), sold two kilos at a time in mesh sacks made of fake red thread (their very color seems artificial, chemical; it stays on your fingers as you break your nails trying to open one of the fruits without just pulling off little shreds of peel, without tearing them to pieces), with that other thing, the **orange itself**, which I heard and dreamed about and awaited throughout those years of deprivation. It cannot be possible that these are the same fruit. The two appear to me in the same relationship of humiliating disjunction—in terms of an identity of nomination accompanied by a degradation of reference—that I perceive in the present-day use of the word "surrealist" in politics, advertising, or journalism. From the "mad love" of the orange to that, it's a long way down!

The initial segment (phonically speaking) of the word that is the hidden subtitle of this branch of my book, "oranjello," refers to, evokes that orange, that first orange "absent from all baskets," the orange of a beautiful story, and not to its modern counterfeits. I should add that my grandparents lived in Caluire, Rue de l'Orangerie. I was born on that street.

77 (§ 15) **A caravan of freight barges stretched along the quay, all loaded to the top with coal: brown lignite.**

Everything about this trip sent me back to my own past, to my own family history, to the war. And not only because of the lingering traces of the old battles but also because the small number of cars, the slow rhythms, the silence of passersby, the poor and dimly lit houses, the bare apartments where the locals welcomed you, spoke to you, still had so much free time to spend on you—because all this also spoke to me of the forties and fifties in France: in Carcassonne, then in Saint-Germain-en-Laye, then in Paris. For me, it all bore a resemblance.

I felt it, and then I suddenly knew it, by seeing snowflakes falling on piles of coal on the sidewalk of a street in Prenzlauerberg. These were not the same anthracite lumps of my memories, but fragments, lighter in color, formless: the brown outer layer of the coal that

I'd seen weighing down the barges on the Spree the day before. However, the kinship in memory was undeniable. In the first days of 1990, the people of East Berlin were warming themselves the same way as my own people did in 1945, in 1950.

Then I suddenly saw again (this is the link between the two moments, the condition of reconstitution, closely dependent on the rapidity of vision), at the back of the garden on the Rue d'Assas in Carcassonne,

the pile of coal under a little snow;

the layer of snowflakes draped lazily over the upper half of the lumps;

you had to shake off the snow before dropping them into the black bucket.

78 (§ 15) **the sight of those semi-ruins in East Berlin restored to me all the violence of my initial vision of the war**

A little later during this same trip, in Dresden, with nightfall well upon us, my next appointment for that evening—an informational visit listed in my program—turned out to be on a street called Papritzerstrasse. So we set off into the night in search of Papritzerstrasse. And there was indeed a Papitzerstrasse on the map, in the village of Papritz, at the edge of town, on a hill overlooking the Elbe. But there were virtually no houses on this street: nothing but countryside, and no number 13. Every now and then, I got out of the car, map in hand, trying to decipher some sibylline indication in the very dim light. And that, no doubt, is how I lost my cap, which I'd bought for myself in Oxford back in 1985.

But why had I come to Dresden in the first place? I understood why all at once when I first reached the outlying houses of the city, at which point my memory had become accustomed to the kinship of ruins that I'd seen re-emerge from the past on the island in the Spree: it was in Dresden, of course, that the largest terrorist bombing of World War II occurred (aside from Hiroshima and Nagasaki, naturally, which are in a class apart), carried out without any military justification—a sore spot in my old childhood admiration for Winston Churchill. Thus, I concluded that the loss of my cap was, in short, an unconscious gesture of "reparation."

Be that as it may, the Papritzerstrasse in Papritz came to an end, continuing directly into another country road with a different name. When I asked an old man on the front step of his house for directions, he said he didn't even think there was any such thing as Papritzerstrasse (even though it was less than a hundred meters from his house!): No, he said, there is no Papritzerstrasse near here. The car continued on its way, went down toward the river. And the road down to the Elbe was like the road down to the Saône in Lyon, with sharp turns curving between sleepy houses, and, down below, at the edge of the water, taking me back forty, fifty years, the familiar-forgotten song of a streetcar. (Papritzerstrasse, the right one, was very close to the false one, but <u>in</u> Dresden, not in Papritz.)

The next day, toward the end of the afternoon, our car was searching for the Elbe amid a howling blizzard, the final eastward effects of a storm that had been shaking Europe since the beginning of the week. Sudden clouds, gray and black, like jets of dirty coal smoke, dumped white snow down to cover the streets, the car windows, the trees. At the end of the now darkened day, the lights went on, and suddenly they were no longer electric lights but actual gas lamps, as though, at every moment, reality was seeking to offer me a world exactly parallel to the world of my memories.

When you're in Dresden, Elke Erb had told me in Berlin, go see Thomas Rosenlöcher. "His poetry," she said, "is . . . it's like an 'ironic chirping of birds.'" Rosenlöcher's house was a splendid and dilapidated building, a beautiful eighteenth-century ruin: wood paneling, balustrades, painted ceiling, a wooden stairway, bicycles in the foyer, a proper laundry, old cribs, children. Thomas Rosenlöcher, however, was in Leipzig. His wife offered me tea and cakes. It was raining in the next room over. The house was very close to the Elbe, just across from the residence of Duke Auguste le Fort, the *Schloss*, which this man obsessed with eighteenth-century Venice left only to go to his ducal palace—by gondola, of course. In that area, one crosses the Elbe by ferry. The ferry cost twenty East German pfennigs (about three cents in March 1990) and, if one was feeling generous on a moonlit night (the ferry runs all night), one gave an ostmark (fifteen cents), and the ferryman would trace looping circles for you in the water with his boat. Near the river's edge, there was a cabin-bar that sold beer, even in the depths of winter, even in a snowstorm. And the title of one of Thomas Rosenlöcher's books of poems was *Schneebier*, <u>Snowbeer</u>.

On the way back, the snow was already melting on the streets, on the banks of the Elbe, a circumstantial snow interceding on behalf of the reconstitution of other moments, other winters. And I heard the ironical chirping of birds from years past on other, older snows, they too ephemeral—as though all snowfalls were from a single war, and from childhood.

79 (§ 15) mastering the sequence of childhood images that I had already set out to elucidate (still following my initial vision of an enormous single "page" being darkened line by line with prose)

Near the beginning of the composition of <u>branch one</u> of this story, I imagined myself as a scribe carefully writing the calligraphic signs of my prose on a large—a very large—sheet of paper, on which each chapter would have taken up a long and individual line: a single black line, written in a small but legible hand, the paragraphs composing the chapters being separated by visible blanks. The likely origin of this moving "piction" (moving insofar as I see the white invaded by black) lies in the particular mode of writing I had chosen: by hand, in a notebook, in densely written black lines, with miniscule and almost illegible characters, advancing regularly with my autonomous morning prose-moments, without regrets, without hesitation, without looking back, in horizontal strips, each topped with a bit of red and green underlined in white.

The great white imaginary mural, that site of memory where mental ink was gradually gnawing away at the desert (a Mental, or Model, Sheet (MS)), as though projected from my notebook by some optic apparatus, gave a certain scale to the task at hand. It's still with me today, here in <u>branch two</u>, even though I've abandoned writing by hand in a notebook (which has now been demoted to the rank of a preparatory notepad), in favor of the Macintosh screen. When, in the nocturnal early morning, I sit down at my desk and the screen lights up, I actually feel much closer to my initial Model than I did before.

In my imagination, however, the scenario of the Mental Sheet, in which I play the role of hermit-scribe, has been enriched, has become more complicated: I see it now as the wall of a circular room of prose, as in a dungeon (where I am a prisoner, perhaps involuntarily—it depends). The writing of each branch, chapter by chapter, takes the form of a descending spiral; which is to say that the <u>story</u> properly speaking (the ninety-eight moments in six chapters of branch one, for example) comes to an end, topologically, on the same vertical line of the cylinder (which is also the sheet), but <u>farther down</u>. The <u>bifurcations</u> are situated in their respective places in the circular succession, also in a descending progression. The <u>interpolations</u>, finally, are below that.

A space at least as long as that taken up by the writing which constitutes the totality of every paragraph of every kind in branch one separates these <u>interpolations </u>from branch two, which is written according to the same principle; the same then holds true for the space left between branch two and the subsequent one, and for the totality of potential succeeding branches (in the outline I've thus far envisioned, programmatically, for "**the great fire of London**," which I will prudently refrain from elaborating upon).

Now, it will be in the first of these empty spaces that I intend to place the initial example of what I've decided to call "inter-branches"—a second set of <u>interpolations</u> (not to be confused with those already published) meant to be appended to the paragraphs of branch one, but also joining up with branch two, and perhaps taking off again on its own thereafter (according to the rather constraining chart prepared for me by Mathieu Lusson (which satisfies certain numerological obligations that will be revealed later)). One part of these new interpolations has already been written (they constituted the essential element of my "mural" work since the publication of branch one, a year ago). I "see" them as invisible, present on the sheet as a "hidden text." (I am using the terminology of my "word processor.") This will be "**inter-branch 1–2**."

In other words, I anticipate that other "**inter-branches**" will follow, since I anticipate there being other branches. The obligation to <u>connect</u> two branches, each of which unfolds, in its own way, according to the rule of strict narrative progression "in the present," to which I still adhere, determines (as an ineluctable effect of writing under a constraint) new <u>moments of prose</u>, and the sometimes difficult "clearing" of new paths (which occasionally brings up (as it did a little earlier in the paragraph from which this interpolation originates) childhood (and other) images that might otherwise have remained buried).

80 (§ 17) **my father was never anyone's "disciple"**

Here is yet another character trait that was transmitted to me through heredity. I have spoken elsewhere of my "master" Raymond Queneau. And yet if Queneau was my master, it is necessarily the case that I was his disciple. How, then, can one be a disciple without being one? But there's no real contradiction here. For one thing, I would most likely never have been recognized as an Oulipian disciple of Queneau's if he hadn't himself recognized me as already being Oulipian without my knowing it, when I sent him my first book of poems (that is, I wouldn't have sought out Oulipo if I hadn't already found it!). Otherwise, it never would have occurred to me to choose Oulipo as a model, even if I had recognized its existence and value.

In any case, throughout the years, I've maintained deep reservations (and a partial incomprehension, as a consequence) about the goals and strategies of Oulipo, fearing for my poetic independence, which I have always wanted to be absolute. (And it's likely for this reason, at least in part, that I haven't been as consistent, or as attentive (I do not say inventive) an Oulipian as Georges Perec, who for his part deliberately chose the position of disciple as a veritable path to salvation, making it the motor of a *sorpasso* of genius.) It was really only after Queneau's death that I claimed the title of Oulipian without reticence. Raymond Queneau is my master, but I am the only one who knows and decides how, in what sense, and to what extent.

I will add, since this touches on an essential feature of the conception of my **Project**, that in this general refusal of obedience, I adopted a particular strategy, which was not to imitate a revolutionary gesture but to seek and to choose a multiplicity of master figures (the fatal illusion par excellence, in politics as in art, is that of the "tabula rasa"): hence Queneau; but also Raimbaut d'Orange, Cavalcanti, and Mallarmé; but also Gertrude Stein and Trollope and Kamo no Chōmei. So much (and this list is hardly exhaustive) for poetry and literature. But there are other things besides poetry and literature. I had masters in mathematics (Claude Chevalley, Jean-Paul Benzécri), and elsewhere, in each of the disciplines taken up as part of the **Project**'s implementation.

In each case, the choice was as much that of a "counter-mastery" as of an example to follow without reservation. It was Queneau against surrealism, Raimbaut d'Orange and Mallarmé against the sing-song conception of poetry, Cavalcanti against Dante, Gertrude Stein against Joyce, Benzécri against Bourbaki, and even Chevalley the Bourbakist against Bourbaki "himself." In at least one case (Trollope), the choice constituted a paradox, a provocation (it was not taken seriously). I took on certain masters in order to refuse others that everyone accepted.

I just said that I chose Queneau against surrealism, but in fact, in place of "surrealism," I should give particular names—Aragon and Breton for example (and before Queneau, the same liberating role was played for me by Tzara, Desnos, and Bonnefoy). The battles waged are as much battles over tutelary figures as ideas or theories. Bourbaki is a name, an Author (a non-anonymous collective pseudonym, as is Oulipo, in imitation of it). This is a battle of names, and I enter it in the presence of antagonistic armies, under the banner of those generals who appear to be losing the day. But I know (or I imagine, it hardly matters) that the future is theirs. Nevertheless, and in any case, I myself remain fundamentally a civilian.

And I don't want my own disciples in turn. I will not place myself among the ranks of possible masters. If I don't like to obey, this implies, as it happens, that I also don't like to command.

81 (§ 18) **absences enumerated, like so many tombstones, by names**

But what kind of identity are we looking for when we read a tombstone? one that could survive death? The dead, according to some, "are" their tomb (and its interior), topped by a tombstone with a name. But that amounts to saying that when they were alive, they "were" their body, clothed and unclothed, that body which contained their thoughts (or their soul). And this body also bore a name, their name. Their identity only persists in the world by way of this analogy.

Others say, however, that the dead are whatever can be reconstituted in the memories (assuming they remember) of people who knew them, if only for a moment. Thus, they still "are," but their reality is divided up, shifting, contradictory, dependent, intermittent, placeless. And when all the people who remember them have died, they are no more. Or, they then only exist at the second, third, then the nth degree of memory, along a rapidly intransitive chain of transmission from being to being, from generation to generation. In this interpretation as well, one can't help but notice that the idea of an afterlife borrows its characteristics precisely from those of life in the world.

Such are the dead: our singular, private, and provisional dead, who haven't been immortalized in the register of official monuments, notary publics, or histories, nor in any archives, nor by works of art. In the contrary case, however, it's a different story entirely—something like a third kind of dead people (if we can agree that the preceding definitions—the merely entombed and the merely remembered—designate two distinct families of beings among the people now absent from this world), to which at times one might be tempted to give preeminence, if only because they seem so much more durable, more stable, more assured (as in the dream of an "enduring bronze"): this is not only the stability of the concrete supports, the stones and documents, the languages and systems of representation in which they've been inscribed, the civilizations that shelter them (here too transmitting themselves to others, in another kind of transitivity, in which the hazards of a physical afterlife and of subsequent decipherment still play a role), but more the simple fact that they belong to a collectivity and to its memory—not only to those with whom they were "close"—who have now been virtually dispossessed of them. Indeed, the "Illustrious Dead" in particular are the most visible but likewise least differentiated of the dead: everyone can recognize them, without any need for a connection with their being-as-having-been, its attributes of flesh, speech, movement, presence; and they "exist" in an absolute passivity imposed by the absence of any previous relationship with the living who still define them as "beings," as "being-dead." Their existence is terribly impersonal.

It maintains no relation of reciprocity with the living. And it tends to invade the name that designates it, to the detriment of those other, private dead people who lived under the same name—those in the cemeteries no less than the ones who have been buried, who have been entombed, in the living minds that remember them.

And if this process of invasion is taking place at a time when that other dead person, the private and precarious version, has not yet disappeared, this event seems strange, even scandalous, to those who keep the latter sheltered inside themselves. Many who were close and even not so close to Georges Perec had just such a troubled reaction when he died. As if the (legitimate) glory of the writer Perec deprived the dead man of his natural death, which ought to speak to each person singly.

A family, in the times and places where these distinctions are preserved, is a particular space offered to death, as a way to circumscribe it, complete it, and not as a way to deny, reject, or dissolve it. The living, those momentary non-dead, trace out in this space the full and opaque aspect of a configuration whose visibility, harmony, and equilibrium are assured by the dead, between limits that go back no more than three generations and can't see much farther than one or two generations ahead. It is in this space that we orient ourselves, and find a place. But this also gives rise to an idea of premature absence, of incompleteness, and the invisible amputations that come with it.

I won't conceal the fact that the image of the **fig tree** in Toulon is akin in my mind to the metaphor of the genealogical family tree. I will spare my reader the banality of commenting on such a discovery. But I would like to pursue my parallelism a little further: the disruption of the kitchen tiles by the roots of the fig tree (archaeologically familial for me) would, in this "fictive translation," be linked to an awareness of a dissymmetrical ascendancy, contingent but rife with consequences, caused by the gaps in the Toulon "branch" of my family. I mean that the dead are like roots, and they grow into a life and shatter it. Their melancholic nothingness hesitates between two forms:

—The nothingness of being no more than a nomination, of never having been anything but a nomination, of no longer being anything but a nomination.

—And then the other possible face of the dead: not to be namable at all (or to be namable only in a different way for each and every person who retains a memory of them), to be an "I know not what," a "*no sai que s'es*" (Raimbaut d'Orange), much more than a "*non sai qui s'es*" ("I know not whom": Guirault de Borneil), or even a "*no sai on*" ("I know not where": Bernart de Ventadorn).

The first two chapters of this branch of my story join together here, and **loop** into a "conjuncture," as Chrétien de Troyes said: that <u>inverse flower</u> of nothingness, in a memory.

(from chapter 3)

82 (§ 19) a path through memory, but a labyrinthine path

I first wrote, then crossed out, "a metaphorical path," and then, "an allegorical path." I hesitated. (I "wrote" "wrote," I "wrote" "crossed out," but in reality I did nothing more than make the words momentarily visible, in immaterial letters, on my screen. And they disappeared on command, without a trace, leaving my path of prose smooth, flat, and right-justified, in "10-point New York": clean, without the sutures that previously, in my notebook, indicated a hesitation at the moment of an <u>interpolation</u>, or—leaving a heavier mark—a <u>bifurcation</u>. Thus, my hesitations themselves are now more easily erased. Too easily, perhaps.) I hesitated to write down the words "metaphor" or "allegory" without any explanation. I hesitated, even more, concerning their relevance at this point.

Because it appeared to me, simultaneously, that the **image** of the garden with its center (a center for my vision, whose movements, whose "disenchantment," I will be describing in the paragraphs into which this interpolation is inserted), was at once a <u>metaphor</u> for the putting to work of **memory**—a <u>mainspring</u> for my <u>story</u> (since it counts/recounts it, while also establishing a certain order)—and an <u>allegory</u> of the **Project**. (But I instantaneously began to doubt the grounds for my "placement" of one or the other of these "revelations" (hence the "erasure"): that's how things happen in my book, which leaves me little room for reflection after I begin a paragraph (these continuities of prose that I call "moments"), one line following another—since I have forbidden myself any revisions.) (And besides, allegories and metaphors seem more like <u>pictions</u> to me than **images**.)

I have not yet advanced far enough in my work to <u>elucidate</u> more precisely in what sense this is the case. But I can say that the irruption of images with an (additional) allegorical function has already taken place, and that it will continue to take place, in a recurrent fashion. This has to do in large part with the fact that my prose writing is essentially medieval in spirit: the model guiding it is that of the *childhoods of prose*, which is to say, above all, since I write in French, the prose of the Grail romances. In the *Prose Lancelot*, there is the dream of Galehaut, the "son of the beautiful giantess." It is a dream deciphered as an allegory of the hero's destiny, a hero mortally stricken with the "malady of heroes," *amor (h)ero(t)icus,* **melancholic eros**. The **dream** of "**the great fire of London**" (and the entirety of "**the great fire of London**" itself, perhaps) is inscribed in this same rhetorical tradition, in the same lineage of <u>rhetorical fiction</u>.

There is nonetheless a distinct difference: namely that the allegorical decipherment of this dream is not presented explicitly (as in the Ciceronian *exemplum* of "Scipio's Dream"): rather, it remains implicit. The initial dream, initiator of "**the great fire of London**," is also an announcement, a vision, a prediction, but it doesn't speak entirely openly. It doesn't have the literary, constructed rationality of the Ciceronian dream (though it too is a written dream). Neither does it have the apparent incoherence of other dreams, as captured "naturalistically" in the "dark shop" of sleep. The dream announces the **Project** and the **novel**, but at the same time it also announces the **destruction** of what it thus announces. For this dream contains its own duplicity, having passed as much through the gate of horn (the true) as through the gate of ivory (the false). And there have been other such allegorical moments in the book: allegories that are more or less densely concealed; slippage from a discussion of the preparation of azarole jelly to the composition of prose, for example (though there the slide into allegory is stated: → branch one, chapter 3, § 27–29). But this is also the case with the entirety of the section concerning the <u>laws of butter croissants</u> (which might, for instance, seem to lay out the laws of fiction itself (I wouldn't deny it)) →(branch one, interpolations of chapter 1, § 103.)

I therefore chose, in a corrective movement of the fingertips, the adjective "labyrinthine" to indicate being enclosed in childhood, in the childhood garden, being placed blindly at the center of the garden, the center of the game. This is the real, this is the time that **goes creeping** toward me-as-seeker. I again become the seeker, a melancholic seeker. The thread now grasped, followed by the gaze, disenchants the labyrinth.

But since this gaze was present at every point in that place, in its moments of living, its innumerable moments of being, the curve of memory cannot be followed as a single straight line—it fills everything, and each point is a border: a sweeping, all-inclusive passage, saturated like the Cantorian ink-black page in *Tristram Shandy* (a metaphor, certainly, for the only "complete story" possible); the only conceivable escape, with an unreal, non-finite duration.

83 (§ 19) **I open the doors to each room, one by one, I enter: <u>I was there</u>.**

To divide up the particular paths of memory in this way, between the **story** and its **bifurcations**, is a violent imposition of prose: for it's clear that my memories, whether summoned intentionally or not, jump perpetually from one scene to the other (and this happens even apart from my hesitations as to direction). With the multiplicity of choices, however, my hesitation grows. Confronted with this problem (which isn't limited to the trajectory of my childhood, but applies to every moment of this prose), I momentarily set it aside by <u>finding</u> (which is to say, by inventing) a new type of fragment for "**the great fire of London**," which I have called an **inter-branch**. But the

function of these fragments shouldn't merely be graphic, limited to   → I § 84–87

a harmonious filling in, within the given constraints, of the imaginary space between branches on the <u>great sheet of memory</u>. (→ § 79, again.)

As a result of my recent reflections on these matters (carried out over the last week, an interruption of my **story**), I have come to envision them in a way that is less dependent on images, but more "strategic." Which means that what I called the "**first inter-branch**," and then "**inter-branch 1–2**," would no longer necessarily have to be the first of these fragments (even while keeping the second designation). This led me to undertake (still in the course of this same "fracture" of the story: in order to occupy this fracture, to bridge this "fault" (a difficulty that should be pursued in a direction that is, I admit, no doubt sentimentally difficult and dangerous, rather than bracketed as a voluntary and deliberate stopping point)) a kind of systematic description, preliminary and anticipatory, of what these **inter-branches** will be (or would be).

This has happened to me quite often, since I began "**the great fire of London**" and especially since I managed to get this far without abandoning it (which in any case would not, as I've said, result in its disappearance). Often, as I continue—with difficulty, even painfully—it happens that I decide on new developments to come, whether formal or otherwise, which are thus, necessarily, nonexistent at the time of their conception; I imagine them in the future. And up till now, I seem to have avoided giving these irresponsible pseudo-predictions the benefit of transcription, preferring to let only what gets written along the way actually appear in my book. But it's become clear that these effervescences and fantasies of a mind (my own) perpetually in the process of proliferating plans for works that will always remain in the future—slightly delirious, and perpetually belied as the future slips into the past—are as much a part of the present of this prose as all the rest. Or at least I can decide that this is so.

Hence the following, on the occasion of a sudden expansion of the role proposed for the **inter-branch**, which had come to "be" for essentially pragmatic and geometrical reasons. But this decision results from still other considerations as well. For I have not abandoned my first intention (first in the published version), implicit in my book's **Preface**, namely the intention not only to give an account of what the **Project** and the <u>novel</u>

"might have been," under the title **The Great Fire of London**, and not only to recount the dream that made them appear initially—not only to elaborate the formal and conceptual reasons for their failure, but also to describe the particular modalities of this failure (of the repetition of provisional failures leading up to the final failure), which appear to be partly contingent.

And these modalities, with the help of a simple transposition of circumstances, are perfectly legible within the sort of intellectual incoherence that, in some irresponsible moment of euphoria, has always thrown me—and still does (although with less grievous consequences, rendered almost irrelevant by my general renunciation)—into excessive adventures of composition or research, completely beyond my capabilities. Merely adding up the time and effort necessary for their implementation is generally the first difficulty the world throws at me, and is enough to bring ruin. Unfortunately, this hardly prevents me from doing the same thing all over again. And such ambitions, definitively relinquished (according to my firm and definitive resolutions), retain troubling powers of resurrection. How many times, encountering by chance some stray piece of paper bearing the pencil marks of some old "program" (mathematical, poetic, Oulipic, or theoretical (in metrics or poetics), or all of these together; with titles and dated phases, and an evaluation of the time needed for completion!), one, two, five, or ten years old, only partly eliminated (this scrap having somehow been left behind when I dumped all the evidence of my exponential follies—a salutary sweeping away that I decide to implement, always in a rage, during my crises of lucidity), I grasp my head (metaphorically) with my hands, and swear: *"Never again! Never again!"* (only to start the whole thing over again almost immediately).

Even more embarrassing (and this is what's been happening to me during this month of August) is when, following such transports of exertion, I find I've accepted tasks with inexorable external verifications: articles, seminar presentations, even books. As soon as I find myself overwhelmed and in a state that makes it almost impossible to respond to all these demands (which I have accepted), I am gripped by an insurmountable torpor, a paralysis at once ridiculous, artificial (I know that its cause is nothing honorable), and perfectly insurmountable. I seek to escape from this *heautontimoroumenossian* trap of self-torment, I persuade myself that my incapacity results from the urgency of more important tasks, nobler and of course completely different. I renounce fulfilling my obligations, I renege on all my commitments, I send letters of apology, I repay advances. *And so on.*

84 (§ 83) This (this new adventure) would have to appear (but much later in the <u>book</u>), thus:

Inter-branch

Part One

Epistemo-Critical Prologue

(alternatively: Strategic and Technical)

(§ 1) **At the beginning of this first <u>inter-branch</u> of my book**

At the beginning of this first **inter-branch** of my book in several parts, or **branches**, "**the great fire of London**," entitled **inter-branch: Epistemo-Critical Prologue**, I consider, in prefacing the text of its first paragraph (or moment) with a new ordering number, xxxx, the following hypothesis to be satisfied:

> the xxxx sections that are presumed to precede it are already written.

At this moment, composing these lines, the initial **point** of its inaugural **moment** (I maintain the terminology that has gradually imposed itself in the course of composing the preceding **branches**), this is not the case. But by the time these lines are published (if they are), the preceding sections will necessarily have been written. I am writing therefore as though they already were.

I place myself, with respect to the linear succession of the different parts of this work, in a situation of <u>anticipation</u>: according to my work <u>program</u> as it stands on this date (August 11, 1990—the date of composition), this **moment** will follow six **branches** of a "**story with interpolations and bifurcations**"; each of which, like the first (**Branch One: Destruction**), the only one now published as a book (the second, **Branch Two: The Loop**, is half finished), is (would be) made up of 196 numbered **moments of prose** (always (?) presented to the reader in the same order: a **story**, then **insertions**: first **interpolations**, then **bifurcations**). I thus anticipate that this **moment** will be read after the **six branches**, the <u>main body</u> of the book. (Which at that point will (would) be almost entirely finished, with the exception of a **final moment**, a moment of <u>revelation</u>, symmetrical to the **initial moment**, prior (chronologically and typographically) to **Branch One**, which constitutes the **Preface** (and, like the Preface, not given a number). The <u>body</u> of "**the great fire of London**" will (would) therefore include xxxx + 2 sections (**moments**).)

I've already been thinking about this **moment** for quite a long time. It was in fact during the rather long interval of time that passed between my decision to publish **branch one**, under the general title of the entire work, "**the great fire of London**" (in the fall of 1987), and the beginning of the **story** of **branch two**, which occupies me now (fall '89, a few months after the publication of branch one), that the idea of this anticipation came to me, at the same time as I was formulating the new "strategic" hypothesis of the **interbranches** (which I am inaugurating here), concerning their number, their role, how they'll be linked together. (Since these latter conjectures (like all the others I come up with for this text, until such time as they're actually fixed in a <u>place</u> in the book), are subject to revision, I'll say nothing more about it.)

Why?

—Because, even if I had not yet begun a new branch, properly speaking, I had never ceased composing these **moments of prose,** which make up "**the great fire of London**" as a whole (the decision to submit **branch one** to a reading literally prevented me from beginning the next branch, but I couldn't remain absent from the prose: it was <u>absolutely</u> necessary for me to continue. It was necessary that the setting down of black lines, morning after morning, remain uninterrupted).

—Because these pages were accumulating anarchically, month after month, when I still hadn't managed to begin the direct composition of **Branch Two.**

—And finally, because it was evident that some of these pages might never find a natural place in the **branches** to come, according to my plans (or even according to any of the changing states of my various anticipations and plans). It was indispensable to invent something else. But if a number of these moments in suspension seemed to remain independent, others, no less numerous, appeared more and more like connections, markers, phases, between **Branch One**, already completed, and the lines (still imaginary, but more and more distinct in my imagination) of the branches that would follow it.

I sketched out, therefore, mentally, moving from branch to branch, these linking, approaching, <u>interwoven</u> paths—always keeping in mind the <u>programmatic image</u> of the large circular sheet of prose in my dungeon of memory, on which "**the great fire of London**" would be inscribed—postulating these **inter-branches**. It became clear almost immediately that no division of the fragments already composed (and continuing to be composed even after initiating the second branch, and then the following ones) into branches-to-come and inter-branches, also to come, could be determined in advance in any fixed way (which would have been an absolute contradiction of one of my extremely rigid principles of composition), and that therefore the "inter-branches" could only appear <u>after</u> the branches themselves. (The choice of the **branch** that will serve (?), for example, as a point of departure for the last of these new kinds of section, **Branch Six**, and thus its "reconnection" to **Branch One**, belongs to another order of considerations entirely.)

But it was important for other reasons to begin writing the **inter-branches** <u>before</u> completing the writing of the branches, since otherwise the strategy of dividing between the two kinds of **moment** being composed would have abusively privileged the branches, and thereby rigidified their unfolding, which I wanted to avoid at all cost (and this too is a principle that was explicitly established from the beginning). While the **inter-branches**, for their part, would have found themselves inheriting the "disjecta" of the branches, making their organization difficult, unnatural, and largely arbitrary in the end (or else I would have been led to inflate them disproportionately in order to remedy the difficulties encountered in linking them together, particularly those arising from very different periods of composition, since the oldest belong to a time "when I was other than I am today" (Petrarch)). It remains for me, then, before going on to define their general characteristics a little more precisely, and entering more directly into the body of this prologue, to say why I am beginning now.

85 (§ 84 continued)

(§ 2 of the prologue) **I have been obliged to wait quite a long time before beginning this "presentation" that will serve as a "prologue" (or "proem")**

Yet even if I've become persuaded of the necessity of the **inter-branches**, I have been obliged to wait quite a long time before beginning this "presentation" that will serve as their "prologue"—a prologue that, if it is published, will be definitively separated by a very long interval of time from the development properly speaking of the last **inter-branch**, since I cannot begin to place the **moments** that will constitute the latter (not to mention the others) until all six branches are completely finished (in the most "optimistic" case I will content myself with having arrived at the end of the story of **Branch Six**). The reason is the same as the one that I gave in the early sections of **branch one**: "I have a relatively crude but in fact stable idea of the sum of scripted material necessary to achieve 'critical mass,' thus bringing **'the great fire of London'** into the world."

To bring **Branch One** to an end, thus ensuring as a corollary of its existence (whatever happens later) the existence of **"the great fire of London"** in its entirety, it was necessary for me to reach a "quantitative threshold." For once this quantitative threshold had been reached, the <u>axioms</u> of the book are such that it will necessarily be finished even if, for one reason or another, I have to interrupt my work. In the case of the **inter-branches** (which I am obliged to set into motion all at once), the quantitative threshold, the critical mass that I have now imposed on myself, is roughly equal to that of **Branch One** in its finished and published form. And this threshold was reached two months ago, on June 11. But beware: if this mass is sufficient for me to decisively pursue the composition of the **inter-branches** as a whole, it does not in any way ensure that they will be finished, for in their case the conditions for completion are very different from those that governed the <u>story</u>.

Since **Branch Six** (and those preceding it) isn't done, I don't know for certain which of the moments already composed will be attributable to this or that **inter-branch** (even if I know more or less which of the moments that were composed in the temporal *no man's land* of my effort between the first and the second branch—and since then as well—will be considered inter-branch moments). Moreover, even if I did know, I still wouldn't know in what order they will be presented, since that depends on the constitution of the <u>interwoven</u> connections uniting the branches in question (in both directions, as the name of **inter-branch** indicates). This implies that, even while I've set out to write this **prologue**, I don't really know if it will remain in a state of pure anticipation (the anticipation of an absence)—which is rather awkward. If this turns out to be the case, it would (will) be better to consider it as <u>not being a part</u>

of the finished "**great fire of London**." (And then I might even eliminate it, or leave it unfinished, for other reasons I can't foresee today.)

This being the case, I have to deal with a question that seems even more detrimental to the initiation, at this point, of these considerations. I said at the beginning, and I have insisted on this (with variations) on several occasions, that I move the prose forward without a pre-established plan, that I forbid myself "the protective measure of a well-thought-out structure, of an organization" prior to the book itself, that the time of composition is the time in which everything is completed, the "proper time" of the work, without plans, without a matrix, without a blueprint. Isn't there a contradiction here? I don't think so. The state of the book, at each moment, its <u>present</u>, is what it would be at its end, its termination (its tomb), if it happened to be interrupted here. Everything in it that has been written and put in place is its <u>past</u>, counted from its origin in the <u>Preface</u>. It <u>is</u>, today, nothing else.

To the extent that it doesn't end with the last of the lines of **Branch Two,** which I wrote the day before yesterday (and I don't include these in this consideration, nor those of the <u>moment</u> that precedes them, for the reasons I just gave above), the present instant of "**the great fire of London**" is not yet defined. It exists only insofar as it has a future. For it is, like every instant, defined as a future anterior, necessarily unstable (as with every future), partly determinate, partly contingent, and above all unforeseeable. But this fact does not in any way forbid me from engaging in speculative foresight—that is, in a mixture of imaginings, intentions (and, in the case of these inter-branches, fragments "in waiting," ready to <u>become</u> prose, if ever they find their place in the sequence that I anticipate), and formal preparations (constraints, or, better and more flexibly, <u>instructions</u> that I give myself and that I make every effort to follow, but without rigidly fixing them).

The **inter-branch 1–2 & 2–1**, for example, will be, like its eventual successors and predecessors, exactly what the name says. But this will only be the case if there are in fact six completed branches before them, and therefore if I manage to write every branch and do not in the process change their number, their nature, or their order. I've already modified these announcements of future developments, addressed to myself, several times. I am in no way obliged to respect them, so long as I haven't inscribed them in what I've already written, in what is already an unchangeable part of the book (and, after all, even then

. . .). It is necessary for me to create a possible world of prose and, in this sense, to avoid crude contradictions. I hold to this as well as I can. It's true that this requirement limits my freedom of movement, as I advance, physical being that I am, toward my end, but isn't it the same with everything I do, in everything I live through?

86 (§ 84, second continuation)

(§ 3 of the prologue) **According to this conception, the relative positions of the two main time lines of prose are reversed**

According to this conception of the inter-branches (as a whole), the relative positions of the two main time lines of prose, which together make up the **twofold time** of " **the great fire of London**"—the time line of the narration, and the time line of the things related in the narration—are reversed. In the six branches, in fact, the narration itself (and by this I mean not only the part entitled story, but also the bifurcations) appears in the sequential order of composition: it is the time of the narration that is supposed to be reflected continuously by what is written. The time of the narrated things, however, ends up being split up by the narration, which must on occasion point to markers identifying this time. The first of these two times is continuous, a concatenation of moments; the second is discontinuous, intricated. But in the inter-branches, properly speaking, this will not be so. They will be ordered largely after the fact, and what will be imposed on me then, so as to respect the same principles as in the composition of the branches, is the necessity of leaving more or less visible traces of the very "moment" of their being placed on my screen. For example, on August 11, 1990 (the day before yesterday: I have thus dated the present fragment as well), I dated the first of the paragraphs of this **prologue**, which is § xxxx + 1 in the overall series (this is the most elementary form of "chronological trace." I will use less obvious ones as well).

But, under these conditions, what kind of **twofold time** will pertain to this preliminary section? It will resemble both of those I just described. As in the branches that precede it, it will ceaselessly and gradually move forward, without ever going back: § no. x will not be placed before no. y, if "y" was written before "x." But since it will not be recounting events from my life, its second mode of time will not be inscribed within a biographical chronology. It will have a proper order, like each of its parts, the specific **inter-branches** that will follow it. However, the principle of this order will not be the same as in each of the inter-branches, where it will be rather to establish the interweaving of the two branches <u>between</u> which they're to be placed. And the succession of its individual moments will not be that of a line-by-line engenderment of narration, as in the **branches**, but a pure sequentiality. This double resemblance depends on a relation-ship of abstraction.

Abstraction: this is something that might give my reader cause for concern. The path I've taken in these pages risks appearing rather arduous, even more so than in certain passages (for which I have often been reproached) in chapter 5 of **Branch One**. That is quite possible. But if this is so, it must be without apologies. For a secondary and adventitious purpose of this section is to establish an even greater distance than before from autobiography. The interpretation and reception of "**the great fire of London**" as an autobiography did occur (and **Branch Two** will without any doubt reinforce this interpretation). It was quite inevitable, and I do not refuse it, even though I assert that the autobiographical aspect is entirely subordinate to another, which in fact governs every page and line and letter of the book, is inscribed in each of its volumes as the figure in the carpet, choosing every word, placing every comma, dotting every *i*, and which results from a principle of conformity to a definition announced but still unstated: "**The great fire of London**" is .. ..

One could also say that, if there is indeed any autobiography here, it's an (auto)biography of the **Project** and of its **double**, **The Great Fire of London**, and consequently, in large measure, an <u>autobiography of no one</u> (or: <u>nobody's autobiography</u>). (One result of this is that, at the same time, the moments that are the most strictly, precisely, and concretely biographical are placed in a light that draws them toward an attempt at writing <u>everybody's autobiography</u>.) But in any case, this present section will not, it seems to me, appear as autobiographical, except very indirectly, and then in a sense so vague as to be irrelevant. As you can see, I am trying to maintain what I imagine to be a certain originality for my book—at least a classificatory one. It is quite obviously not a novel, a tale, or an essay. Setting aside the hypothesis of autobiographical aspirations seems more difficult.

If this section remains at a distance both from the <u>branches</u> and from the other <u>inter-branches</u>, why then incorporate it into this latter division of the whole? Wouldn't it be more reasonable, if it really must appear in the work, to locate it independently, to isolate it? The main reason, I admit with some slight shame, is <u>numerological</u>. And since for obvious reasons I don't as yet have everything that will follow in the book in front of me, nor even, at the moment when I'm writing, the totality of what comes before (only the total number of the <u>moments</u> of the six branches has been decided (and not necessarily finished, if you're reading this, since I'm now only "interpolating" into **Branch Two!**)), I can hardly launch into any convincing or (above all) stable explanation—that is, an explanation not liable to be contradicted by writing to come. The numerological reason belongs, therefore, to the family of revisable formal decisions that never cease to accompany me in my task (and that hardly make it any easier, believe me).

But the very fact of this numerical reason, however arbitrary and fanciful it may be, will have an influence on the content of this section. Indeed, the **prologue** to the division called the **inter-branches** can't be an epilogue added to the division of the six main branches, nor a transitional prose situated between the two. Moreover (since I'm saying something (even if it's only implicitly said for you) about the overall number of parts of this work, as I envisage it here at the beginning, which will in turn oblige me to try to respect the constraints that follow from this statement (they are explicit for me)), this placement into specific numerical structures will orient the book toward another reading, in which the **inter-branches** would precede the **branches**, and would not only be materially prior to them, but would announce them, would foresee them.

87 (§ 84, third continuation)

(§ 4 of the prologue) **By putting off the hypothetical visibility of this section until a future time that is necessarily very distant**

By putting off the hypothetical visibility of this section until a future time that is necessarily very distant, I give myself a degree of supplementary freedom. Everywhere else I feel the weight of a possible and imminent reading, especially after first allowing a branch of this work to cross the border between an unpublished and a published text—albeit not without a long hesitation—some eighteen months ago (this wasn't a private-public border: there was never any kind of solipsistic intent behind **"the great fire of London"**). Since I have succeeded in beginning a new branch, its completion is imaginable in the near future, very near in any case compared to the interval that protects not only the entire inter-branch "prologue"—I'm just placing its beginning here—but its completed totality, along with the inter-branches themselves.

I now have myself and myself alone as a real reader, and for years to come (and perhaps indefinitely). Hence my feeling of freedom. I do not however see this freedom as an authorization to put down revelations of a private nature here. I have no revelations to make that could hold any interest whatever for this book. And what could I reveal to myself that I do not already know, and that would be worth the trouble of saying? Nothing, no doubt (nor will I embark on an attempt at self-analysis). Rather, I find that I am free in a completely different sense: I can continue here with these abstract and formal investigations (in relation to my "subject") as long as I find it useful, without risking incomprehension, and without having to "negotiate" anyone's resistance to the effort of understanding.

In a work presented to readers for reasons other than the transmission of knowledge—the communication of a discovery in the scientific, philosophical, historical or some other domain—any ordered sequence of hypotheses, arguments, and conclusions is a veritable obscenity. The moral condemnation it receives wears the mask of boredom. To be sure, I've never considered boredom to be an aesthetic criterion. The force of dissuasion it wields in the marketplace (particularly in the contemporary age) is considerable, this I do not dispute. Some of the <u>ten styles</u> distributed throughout the pages of this very long prose are particularly apt to provoke it. I have had recourse to their virtues in a completely deliberate way in at least two circumstances (I'm speaking only of the one volume published so far):

—In chapter 5 of branch one, obviously, with its palindromic pseudo-deduction (a supplementary scandal) (and, in a slightly provocative gesture, with a warning to the reader that it would be desirable to skip them).

—But also at the very beginning, with the interminable description of the photographic double, *Fez*, liable to discourage from the outset (since it occurs so close to the opening of the struggle, inevitable in any book, between author and reader) the rapid glances of impatient and unprepared readers. However, some hundreds of pages in this register, like the ones now being planned, are another matter. And I would not be able to embark on them if I weren't certain that I won't have to confront the discontent of a reader (translated, automatically, into the perhaps much more dangerous discontent of an editor) for a very, very long time.

And I don't even have the excuse of being able to vindicate this boredom in some other way, by explaining that it's only the inevitable accompaniment of <u>revelations other</u> than biographical ones: for neither science nor philosophy— to mention only these two—will be called upon in their familiar severity and dryness. What then remains? Not much, it would seem (if one eliminates also the digressive & incantatory virtues of some kind of Shandian preparation). Let us keep for the moment to the three words of the title (two and a half words, if I take account of the hyphen, which I still allow myself, in this age of orthographic simplification (this is an illuminating indication of the compositional chronology of this page)): **Epistemo-Critical Prologue**. With no further explanations.

I am speaking of my new freedom as an author, but it is in the end a rather illusory freedom: no stylistic effervescence, no imaginative fancy. It will instead be a question of a formal extravagance, for I can see no other way out, having almost sealed up the other paths. Didactic boredom is rarely forgivable; but formal boredom is even more unforgivable. Therefore . . .

Here I interrupt, for an indeterminate period of time, this "prologue" (the continuation of a further paragraph-moment soon (?) to come).

88 (§ 20) **according to the hierarchy of a <u>meditation on the five senses</u>**

In the "Ignatian" meditative tradition of the Renaissance (inspired by Loyola's *Spiritual Exercises*), an important place is given to a "meditation on the five senses." I will choose one example (which is in fact the textual outline or summary of a meditation rather than a meditation properly speaking, since meditation is an internal, private matter, not spoken aloud or written), a Spanish sonnet composed around 1570 by "Captain" Francisco de Aldana. Its theme is apparently profane, but it does indeed concern a meditation with a religious essence and purpose, in complete conformity with the "Ignatian line," even if in other respects it testifies to what I would describe here, anachronistically, as its author's "pacifism." This choice of example seems especially appropriate to my story, which, after all, however idyllic it may appear to be (in the Arcadia of childhood), is nonetheless situated during the years of a terrible war.

Aldana:

> *Otro aquí no se ve que, frente a frente,*
> *animoso escuadrón moverse guerra,*
> *sangriento humor teñir la verde tierra*
> *y, tras honroso fin, correr la gente;*
> > *este es el dulce son que acá se siente:*
> *"España, Santiago, cierra, cierra,"*
> *y por suave olor, que el aire atierra,*
> *humo que azufre dar con llama ardiente.*
>
> > *el gusto envuelto va tras corrompida*
> *agua, y el tacto sólo palpa y halla*
> *duro trofeo de acero ensangrentado,*
> > *hueso en astilla, en él carne molida,*
> *despedazado arnés, rasgada malla:*
> *oh, sólo de hombres digno y noble estado!*

(a translated version, purely for purposes of reference:

> *Here one sees nothing other than, face to face,*
> *valiant squadrons setting off for war,*
> *the bloody humors staining the green earth*
> *and to a bloody end the people go running;*
> > *here is the sweet sound that one hears:*
> *"Spain, Santiago! Attack! Attack!"*
> *and as a sweet aroma, to terrify the air,*
> *sulfur smoke ignites in ardent flame;*
> > *a perverted taste seeks after corrupted*
> *water, and touch can only find and grasp*
> *a hard trophy of bloodied steel,*
> > *only splintered bones, surrounded by ground flesh,*
> *harnesses ripped apart, armor burst open:*
> *oh, sole worthy and noble state of man!)*

This kind of meditation is a "descent," a descent into the hell of death by five "degrees," which are the five senses placed in a hierarchy from the noblest to the basest: sight, hearing, smell, taste, and touch. From the color and the nobility of the clashing squadrons, one continues to sink downward: from vision to shouting, from shouting to sulfur . . . all the way down to the final horror of the "ground beef" of the inert corpses. For sight alone among the senses assures the unity of man and the world, a unity that arises from the soul. The body, however, involves rupture, and above all scattering and dispersal. And touch is the preeminent sense of the body, of its mortal nature, its inevitable fall into what Jean de Sponde calls "the chasm of plurality."

Now, I would be very tempted to attribute a "homologous" hierarchy to the respective roles of the senses in memory (or to be safe: in my memory). It's quite natural, from my general perspective, to treat **meditation** as a universal operation of thought, and consequently to treat the <u>meditation on the five senses</u>, with its descending order, as an inevitable particular case, precisely reflecting an ordinary function of the mind. So that a conscious memory, deliberately sought, would be a <u>meditation on memory</u> (which in Ignatian meditation is the memory of the divine), it too subordinated to the same scale of the senses. (Symmetrically, involuntary memories, reveries, and dreams are in this case to be considered spontaneous meditations.)

This is why in memories, in my memories (I stress once again that I can only speak for myself), there is seeing above all. The other senses, if they are present, are phantoms. I remarked (in chapter 1, § 1) that the image of my finger scratching the frozen mist on the window was not accompanied by any sound, that my finger (my finger of today, which would have to be the physical support of the finger in this memory (but is this so certain?)) did not feel the cold, however evident, of that moment. I wrote that I knew it was cold in the room, "because it is commonly and universally understood that frost exists, and that this mode of the physical existence of water is cold," but the image that I reconstituted from that moment was numb to this knowledge, is indifferent. In the image, touch was "colorless."

It is this "argument" that led me to deduce that my memory of being a seeker in the game of Go-Creeping really does have a particular intensity; for in this memory I again find the sensation, almost immediate, of the ground under the bench, of sharp little pebbles sticking into my bare knees. (Even though no **image** in me—this one no more than any other—ever gives me the impression of the "real" sensorial presence of anything other than a vision. It's a vision that shows me that touch is necessarily implicated in the circumstances of the image.)

89 (§ 20) These arrangements did not strike me as appropriate based on a whim, they were necessary. They were a part of the <u>initial conditions</u> of memory, at its origin.

As soon as I discovered this phenomenon of my memory, I proceeded, like a *natural philosopher* of the seventeenth or eighteenth century—son of Bacon, Hume, Locke, Descartes, or Newton (let us resolutely ignore their doctrinal differences: the *natural philosophers* are personages of whom I am very fond, and whom I represent to myself partly with the features of my grandfather, and partly as Mr. Pickwick (for whom, in fact, my grandfather had a secret sympathy—*The Pickwick Papers* was a book that he constantly reread, in an old large format NRF edition))—I proceeded, then, to imagine a thought experiment designed to verify or invalidate the hypothesis suggested in the title of this <u>insertion</u> (taken, as always, from the context of the story, but with an important modification, the rewriting of "**<u>my</u> memory**" as simply "**memory**"):

—that, when we remember an old and very well-known place (a childhood home, especially, where we lived for a long time, of which we have a very precise memory, or at least a very intense one), which we have passed through via multiple paths and moments (infinite, for all practical purposes)—that each time we think of it and thus enter it again in order to inhabit the gaze set in motion by memory, we automatically situate ourselves in one and the same position, or else, failing that,

—in any one among a family of given positions having in common a certain topological situation in relation to the overall volume of the space, and, therefore,

—that (if I extrapolate a little more on the basis of my fictive deduction), this position (or family of positions) illuminates a stable disposition of our "ego" in its relations with the world, from which one could (shrinking from no audacity, like an intrepid *natural philosopher* of the good old days)

—deduce a psychological portrait;

—and a classification of human beings according to a "physiognomy of memory," of which this would be the nodal point.

Of course I immediately undertook this experiment, utilizing the people closest to me. It was a Sunday on the Rue des Francs-Bourgeois, in the apartment where I still lived until 1985, before going back to the Rue d'Amsterdam, and which is now inhabited by Marie, Charlotte, and Ophelia. It was a Sunday, and we (Marie, Charlotte, Ophelia, and I) were finishing a slab of pink Sunday salmon surrounded by herbs, having first removed it from an aluminum-foil contraption meant to protect its natural juices.

Ophelia, steadying herself on the back of Marie's armchair, jumped from there to the top of the refrigerator, from the refrigerator to the upper edge of the kitchen door, and from there finally to the very top of the cabinet (the one that contains the "cat food cans," and which makes her salivate when its doors are opened). She then chose one of the "cat positions" she adopts in this spot (there are several dozen, and she is constantly inventing new ones) and half closed her eyes with a satisfaction tempered by vigilance (having situated herself so that she can see everything that happens down below and, in particular, can survey any new arrivals, if any should present themselves in the doorway).

Under these circumstances, the kitchen table, set against the wall, leaves three reasonable places for lunch. Marie is sitting in the ugly gray armchair, her back to the refrigerator, looking toward the window that opens onto the Rue Vieille-du-Temple. Charlotte is facing her, and I'm on the third side, between the table and the sink, flanked by the dishwasher (the sink, that is, not me). The round clock, very "nineteen forties," elegant but erratic (it has to be wound with a key, and gains ten minutes every hour, at the very least) is to the left of the doorway, which is itself topped by the sign from a pub, brought back from London by Marie, from the market on Portobello Road.

I told them not about my discovery (in order not to influence their testimony), but about my perplexity concerning the memories that one can have of a childhood home (again, without mentioning my hypothesis, of course), wondering, more or less, how, if one lived in it long enough—since one would have found oneself there in countless & constantly changing "geographical" situations—by what miracle do we manage to develop a coherent, total, and complete view of this home (knowing, for example, that one is rarely physically on the roof of one's own house) . . . assuming, of course, one ever had one, which is in no way certain.

90 (continuation of § 89) **And then I asked Charlotte**

And then I asked Charlotte (with all the skill (?) I was able to muster as a *natural philosopher*) to tell me how and from what perspective she saw, for example, her house in Nantes, or her grandmother's house in Lyon. She immediately and quite gladly entered into this game with both energy and indulgence. And to my great satisfaction, her response largely confirmed my hypotheses.

For there was in fact a common feature in all her descriptions. The family of positions reported was, *unmistakably*, of an "Ophelian" nature (named after the cat Ophelia, whose movements I followed in the previous paragraph-moment): in describing herself in the process of seeing, Charlotte always placed herself up high, with nothing behind her but walls, or even ceilings, thereby making it possible to survey the movements in the rooms below—the entries and exits, the opening and closing of doors. Then the presumed common feature appeared: the identical repetition of an abstract localization, suitable to a maximum of curiosity, and showing an obvious childlike animality (which one could associate, along the lines of a typological interpretation of character based on this criterion, with a certain animal "totem" that in fact suits her perfectly. And this animal is indeed the one that immediately came to mind for me, in Cogolin, when I first saw her).

(A "totemization" that functions (here is a new example) according to a two-way double negation: one attributes certain "humanizing" properties and characteristics to a particular animal (the first negation: negation of animality); then one deduces, for a certain human being, the model thus constructed of his or her animality (negation of the negation).)

(The same back-and-forth movement plays a symmetrical role, in fact, as much in our anthropomorphic notions of familiar animals as in the animalization of humans. Thus, the latter is as ethical as the first, and inevitably so. For our bestiary is always a "moral bestiary.")

I don't have many other examples at the moment on which to base my "theory of the central sites of personality" (at least one of these examples came to me before this theory itself: I now draw it from its original context in order to reinterpret the extremely precise descriptions Alix gave me, when we met, of houses from her childhood and adolescent years: Egypt, South Africa, Greece, Ottawa, finally Aix).

I do however have, according to this mode of questioning, a new element I could add to my self-portrait—presented in branch one, chapter 4.

91 (§ 22 & § 23) I believe that I could easily have been converted to the idea of aligning the movement of the needles with that of a vector turning in the direction considered mathematically "positive"

The spatialization of clock time, in imitation of the sundial, conforms also to the cosmic hypotheses of the Ptolemaic conception, and therefore privileges the circle, the sun's path in the sky, and the shadows cast in its light. So much for geometry. The direction of this path, however, never underwent a Copernican revolution. I find this shocking.

(But if clocks had been invented by Kepler, would it have been necessary to choose the ellipse? It would have been far from a simple problem for watchmakers—even the Swiss.)

This question about the measurement of time does not by any means exhaust the list of my various naive astonishments in matters of "natural philosophy," which today are confined to certain columns in the newspaper. For example: **clocks identify, absurdly, in a single apogee, the two extreme and antithetical moments of the solar revolution.** In other words, why is it necessary for noon to be midnight (and vice versa)?

And then, why twelve?

On the clock dial of my mental representation of the garden, which I pass through in thought in the temporal direction, that of the "hands of a watch," it is noon at the washbasin. The representation of time on the clock dial is in fact the projection of a helix. As if time was a moving body, animated and animal, like a ferret: it passed by over here, it will pass by again over there.

We follow only one line of time. But since time is inscribed on a surface, I imagine that I could give a temporal sense to the other points, that I could invent a two-dimensional time, a topology of time with a second imaginary component made up of all the innumerable abandoned times that were never followed.

92 (§ 24) I can almost follow with my (inner) eye the ripening of a tomato on the vine

I can also "place" their smell. But the outsized dimensions of the fruit robbed it of that extra measure of interest indispensable to me when it came to collecting crops from our garden: namely the opportunity to count. From this point of view, peas had a much greater value. Not only could the pods themselves be counted, rapidly rising to several hundred for even the smallest harvest, but then, as I opened them with two fingers and sent them sliding and rolling with my nail into the palm of my hand, there was also the constant riddle of how many peas each pod might contain and, as a corollary, the attempt to find a record-breaker (they all went from three to twelve, as I recall).

(In cases where there's some doubt as to the total, when a few peas are misshapen, unripe, or too small, it is always possible to decide which are "countable" in a simple way: by eating them. The youngest peas are the softest (in consistency and color) and the sweetest: not yet threatened with the great malady of this species, deadly for taste, which is the syndrome of mealiness, a first step toward their final ruination and decline into the hardness of a gray-green pebble, which in the pot becomes the child's irreducible enemy: the split pea.) It goes without saying that, under these conditions, the dish called *pois gourmand* could only appear to me as something hypocritical, just as *mange-tout* peas—from which one can expect nothing, and which are thrown unshelled into boiling water—reeked of pure treachery.

The green bean, even the high-quality "barraquet" bean from the Aude, offers no arithmetical prospects, obviously (the white bean might do in a pinch (or especially the nobler red bean), though it's still unable to really compete with the green pea). Thus, one avoided the work of stringing the beans on the kitchen table for as long as possible; except in one particular case, which, while favorable from one perspective, was unfortunately rather regrettable from another. I will explain. Long and slightly overripe green beans of uncertain quality risk having strings sufficiently hard and tough to make it necessary to remove them with care. The important thing then (this was the game) was to be able to pull the string off in one go, from one end to the other, without breaking it.

But, and this is the other side of the coin, whatever was gained in stringing them, we risked paying for very dearly when it came time to eat: for these beans, even when carefully strung, were extremely likely to be fibrous, stringy through and through, and therefore inedible. For all these reasons, the pea, for me, remained superior to the bean. By the same criterion, the pumpkin, generally present as a single enormous exemplar in the preparation of a meal, was even lower on my scale of values (I leave aside the dried bean, elevated by the honor accorded to the cassoulet, and lettuce, which I appreciated only much later, when olive oil saved it from blandness. As for the tomato, it must be considered a fruit, and, axiomatically, all fruits are good).

Today I still only have an intimate knowledge of a vegetable if its species was among those that my father cultivated in the garden. I also saw & sometimes ate crosnes, black radishes, chard . . . but I'm not familiar with those as they appear in the ground, nor after being picked. Certain vegetables were worse than unknown: one knew them only too well. They were nearly the only thing available in the markets during the months of extreme wintertime scarcity; in short, they were "collaborator" vegetables. For many long years, they remained imprinted in the collective memory with an almost insurmountable negative charge—almost with infamy (it was only recently, for instance, that I saw a crate of topinamburs, or Jerusalem artichokes, on sale again (and I must say that I had no interest in trying them. One doesn't forgive such insults, once tasted). As for rutabagas, they seem to have totally disappeared). (Inexorably, topinamburs, like rutabagas, are also associated for me, via a slippage of unknown origin, with an illness: tuberculosis. If I hear "topinambur" or "rutabaga," I immediately hear, quadrasyllabically, "*tuberculose.*" I don't know why or how, but so it is.)

For a long time, in fact, the turnip, the good old turnip, so unjustly decried because of its pejorative association with bad films (as in the French expression, "*Quel navet!*" (what a crappy movie!)), seemed too closely related to the topinambur to be respectable. Only my love for duck was able to reconcile me with it. And I even adopted its very rare cousin, the "*boule d'or.*" As for the fresh fava bean, which is delicious when young and tender, taken with "just a bit of salt," I had to make a considerable effort to dissociate it from the unspeakable hash called *févettes,* which was ordinary fare for us during one of the most anxious periods of the Occupation. We had virtually nothing else to eat besides these dry mediocre vegetables—into which many insects, especially weevils, had found their way. We had to eat them just the same. But separating the miniscule intruders from their hosts was impossible. So my mother put everything, *févettes* and weevils together, in the vegetable grinder, in accordance with the Epicurean principle "nothing is lost, nothing is created." "Matter remains and form is lost." The result was nutritionally equivalent more or less to the same quantity of *févettes* presumed free of weevils. And we ate this gray mush, which was downright nauseating. Yes, after reconquering the fresh fava bean, I was then able to recognize the fava as a worthy cousin and even an ancestor of the green bean—when Florence initiated me to the *habada* in Madrid, an ancient and venerable "Basque (?) cassoulet." (Here I bring to an end my exploration of this "moralized vegetable garden," and I will spare you for the moment my praise of the chickpea (its time will come, but must be formally justified).)

93 (continuation of § 92) **The garden was planted with the greatest possible variety of edible vegetable species compatible with the climate.**

The garden was planted with the greatest possible variety of edible vegetable species compatible with the climate. It was not at all some kind of gardener's version of "art for art's sake." My father was worried about the dangerous nutritional deficiencies faced by "developing" children who had to live on the pitiless diet imposed by the "restrictions," and he was trying to find a practical way to remedy this problem, at least during the periods favorable to the growth of vegetables. He reasoned that the selection effected over generations by gardening practices had ensured that vegetables (and fruits) (as long as one supplemented them occasionally with some rabbit (he wasn't a vegetarian)) contained very nearly everything the human organism might need—including, most importantly of all, the holy vitamins.

A vitamin chart occupied a place of honor on the dining room wall. A color was attributed to every vitamin known at the time, and each type of food represented on the chart was accompanied by a circular "spectrum" of vitamins, divided into properly proportioned angular sections for each color. A reticence on our part regarding cabbage, for example (I forgot cabbage!), was beaten back, on the battlefield of the soup bowl and then the plate, not only with arguments invoking parental authority, but also with dietetic reasoning. The garden contained everything necessary, sorrel and salad greens, chard, carrots, and radishes . . . But during the many months when it produced nothing, there was a risk of serious deficiencies developing in our organisms, which (like unwatered vegetables) had not "absorbed" a sufficient amount of the various types of food (not to mention the lack of carbohydrates, lipids or proteins, as well as the minerals indispensable to the fabrication and proper development of our bones: scoliosis, scoliosis! lordosis!).

Now this (prewar) chart reserved a special place for citrus, which, according to famous anecdotes from school lessons, was indispensable in the fight against a lack of vitamin C, and its corollary, scurvy. In moments of nocturnal pessimism, my father saw us all as poor little ship's boys (and girl) trapped on the lost vessel of Vichyized and Nazified France, a prey to this terrible malady. No doubt he reassured himself, in the light of day, by considering that the Languedoc populations of the past had been able to live very well both without oranges and without scurvy. Indeed, we too escaped its clutches.

But I remember that, shortly after the Liberation, he managed to get hold of one of those enormous containers that were part of the so-called "American surplus," and thereafter at each meal he would hand out to us some of those brown and rubbery pills—similar in size, color, and almost in shape to a coffee bean—that were inside, among other treasures. Cut open with a sudden sharp bite, these pills spread a dose of cod-liver oil over the tongue, densely concentrated into a precious anti-scurvy vitamin. Then one chewed on the envelope of this liquid: a sort of dissolving rubber. I found the taste of these pills extremely bizarre, but delicious (though I must have been the only one).

As for oranges and lemons, we long awaited their return, and our desire was intensified by my grandmother's stories when, after her last trip to the USA before Pearl Harbor, she recounted the marvel of foamy fresh-squeezed morning orange juice. I had held on to this memory from the "prewar" days (since I was the oldest). And we had a full-color representation of this phenomenon in the American "magazines" that she had brought back from New England. But as late as 1945, Jean-René, who was the youngest, when questioned as to the color of lemons, answered that they were pink.

In the vegetable garden carefully divided into a grid, each row marked off by a string, **"I hear" the regular hissing of the water hose, sometimes flowing silently into the walkway from the end of the row, I see the light dry earth grow darker, penetrated by water that is immediately absorbed by the avid ground beneath the tiny** → I § 94   **tomato plants, the beans curling around their "stakes," the puddle of water disappearing and leaving a thick foam, a milky spume, and the smooth bottom of the hollowed-out row, between the lumpy dirt of the mounds. It is evening.**

94 (§ 93) **The water immediately absorbed by the avid ground beneath the tomato plants**

The "truth" of my images of the garden is solar. There, the sun was "almost everywhere." My gaze has fewer chances of finding the night and the rain, for various reasons, while searching among the more indefinable memory sites: in the washbasin, the walkways, the rows of tomatoes (I don't know in what "possible world" a "modal realist" might place them). My visions of the nights in this site are not only more vague, more fragmentary, they almost appear to be from another place. The same is true for my visions of the garden in the rain. And, unlike the image of snow, the extreme rarity of which ensured, on the contrary, that it would be preserved along with a certain emotion, the image, the images of rain are dull, and their atmosphere is one of boredom—even desolation. (**The soaking wet apricot tree dripping leafless beneath a November downpour, the sad wet smell, the clogs on our feet, the tight squeeze of a raincoat, the slippery clay beneath the sad branches**; in a poem I wrote before I was ten, there is this: *The apricot trees are calm. / It rained.*)

The very clear separation that exists between a vision of the garden in the daytime—a solar vision in every season—and other more fragmentary views at night or in the rain, reveals a pragmatic component to me in the difficulty I have of placing any living beings in the garden other than those (the animals) that never left it (—§ 27—: What about humans, human children? Those player-shadows who are there, next to me, at every moment, more or less—in front of the bench, the washbasin, the wire mesh of the rabbit cages? I speak of them only very indirectly): quite simply, the ever-changing continuity of these beings (particularly children, particularly the ones I've continually seen and been able to identify as themselves) makes it impossible for me to reconstitute their appearance at that time. I can try to see my brothers, in a moment from those years, but what I "see" then is only the immobile <u>piction</u> of a photograph, like the ones I found again in the albums and in the metal boxes I've kept stored in my bedroom, in Saint-Félix. They can't be placed in an animated vegetal context, but only juxtaposed arbitrarily with the bench, the pines, the well—like a color projected onto a wall.

The <u>snails</u> reconciled us with the rain. Like the multiple threads of my memory, of my **Project**, of this prose, which all have their origin here, it's also here that my long common history with snails begins (which will also constitute, inevitably, a thread in my narration, thanks to the metaphor of the trace, the track of silvery slime). I convinced myself early on that, like me, they never actually chose to go out into the rain but were obliged to do so by circumstances (in their case, the imperious need for food, and a physiological fatality). If it were true that they really loved water so much, as people like to say, why would they choose to live in such a dry climate? Why wouldn't they go off, like their cousins—the so-called "Burgundy" snails, those gigantic calves—to slog through water-soaked meadows and saturated groves, oozing with various drizzles and downpours? I say "their cousins the 'Burgundy' snails" since, for me, the only snail worthy of the name is the "*petit-gris*," elegant and alert, with its tiger-stripe shell, and then its companion, with the flatter spiral form—white, beige, or even yellow—found especially in the paths between grape vines or hanging from fennel plants (and which the Provençals, scorning the exact data of natural history, take for its companion, calling it the "female").

I had therefore imagined that the sun was the inaccessible dream of the snail (its daydream. Its night dream? The stars), which it could only perceive during those very brief moments when that great star came out from behind the clouds after the rain, or appeared on the pink horizon at dawn; and that the snail did not linger outside its dwellings of stones or vine-stocks—at the risk of being caught in the paralyzing hygrometric drop caused by the return of the hot dry air—except in the hope of turning its moist, sensitive, peduncular eyes toward the sun, and to receive for a brief moment its dangerous blessing.

We collected snails and put them together on the wet terrace. We put lettuce leaves and sprigs of <u>fennel</u> in their paths, and we watched them "run" (these races are a childhood tradition, thousands of years old perhaps, and it would be at least as interesting to know their history as that of horse or greyhound racing). The extreme and proverbial slowness of snails is an illusion. They are like great ships gliding their way across the sea. With their shells oscillating slightly at the moment they decide on a direction, their antennae well-adjusted to their movements, the most agile on the contrary give a distinct impression of rapidity, or more intrinsically perhaps—to avoid any comparison of absolute speeds—of a perfect mastery of the relation between distances and durations.

I saved the best part of the rain for last: the direct, and extraordinarily voluptuous, relation with snails in their awakened state, trembling and enthusiastic: placing them on a hand, on a knee, and, keeping completely still, feeling the gentle sliding of their living moistness on one's skin.

95 (§ 24) The hutches, little dwellings for our peaceful and sympathetic rabbits

Sympathetic and harmless. I feel very little sympathy, in fact, with dangerous animals. The great wild beasts do not attract me. I do not dream of communicating deep thoughts to crocodiles or scorpions. It's true that this notion of "dangerous" is relative. The cat is certainly not, intrinsically, a harmless animal (as the snail is, for example, or the hedge-hog—two of my favorite animals). But it is somehow "saved" by its size. It's enough for me to carry out a homothetic transformation in thought on the spatial volume occupied by Ophelia, increasing it by a ratio of five or six, to understand that the super-innocent blue of her gaze resting on me would then be of an entirely different nature. But the horror film Alix and I saw one time on some random nocturnal English television station (an American film that could only be classified as a "sub-B" genre picture), entitled something like *Night of the Monster Rabbits*, could, and did, only provoke outrageous laughter.

A reading of the marvelous *Watership Down*, for example, which I owe to Marie, offers a socio-anthropomorphic vision of the rabbit species less agreeable than my own, which has at root remained the same since childhood. I also remember seeing a reproduction of a German drawing from the seventeenth century on the cover of a book in a shop window on the Rue Jacob: it shows a very fat rabbit in its prime, exuding a state of extreme self-content—visibly sexual in origin—from every inch of its luxurious fur: a rabbit who enjoys his share of females. That one surprised me. Nor is it the prototype rabbit, the Platonic Idea of rabbit that presents itself to me when I think of them. (I've even known a rather disturbing example of this species, even more remote from my ideal rabbit, whose owner named it "Stalin.")

A recent advertisement features the *"lapin Cassegrain,"* a large white rabbit with the black sunglasses of a Hollywood mafioso. In his paws he holds a knife and fork and is preparing to lay into some *"petits légumes."* When I saw it on television one day in the apartment on the Rue des Francs-Bourgeois, I was enthralled by his expression. I saw the scene several times over, after it was recorded by Charlotte, who was also kind enough to give me a postcard with a picture of it, which I put on my bookshelf. A vegetarian ferocity suits this species well. It is in such amusements that my **"sentimental and immoderate passion for rabbits"** survives from childhood.

Thus my persistent anthropomorphism remains purely ludic. It carefully avoids sliding into any realistic identification, and sidesteps entirely the tragic fancies epitomized in the stories of London (I mean Jack London). My animals are not merely masks for human figures. The game (a language game, and a story game) has no charm unless the animal preserves the essential features of its own nature, in a more or less comic coexistence with human properties (behaviors, thoughts, feelings), which naturally are entirely invented.

My constant models in these games are the books by Milne (*Winnie the Pooh*) and Kenneth Graham (*The Wind in the Willows*), and above all, of course, those of the "Carrollian" world (I am thinking, of course, of the scene from *Sylvie and Bruno*, in the chapter "A Visit to Dogland"—which was the source of a little text by my master Raymond Queneau ("On the Dog Language in *Sylvie and Bruno* . . .")—in which the King of the Dogs, leaving his Court for a moment walk a bit with the travelers, asks Sylvie to throw him a stick to fetch, and thus reveals his irrepressible canine nature: "His Majesty calmly wagged the Royal tail. 'It's quite a relief, he said, getting away from that Palace now and then! Royal Dogs have a dull life of it, I can tell you! Would you mind' (this to Sylvie, in a low voice, and looking a little shy and embarrassed) 'would you mind the trouble of just throwing that stick for me to fetch?' "

In the days of which I'm speaking, I dreamed more than anything else of meeting other rabbits, free rabbits, from the scrub, the "wild rabbits" whose traces were visible in the grape vines, around the medieval Cité (piles of little droppings in the ditches, between the tufts of thyme); but always running away, unapproachable despite the offer of fennel sprigs, little treats, and caresses, impossible to catch when running, unapproachable unless dead and bloody, brought home by hunters.

96 (§ 24) **Brigitte Bardot, that ex-sex-symbol of the cinema for the males of my generation, who became a senile soft-hearted protector of baby seals**

Objective chance has given this interpolation the peculiarity of being doubly digressive. As I was about to transfer it (along with its neighbors) from the quasi-immaterial state of "screenic virtuality" to the "concrete" and "binding" state of typographical signs laid out on paper by my modest ImageWriter II printer (aside from whatever charms it may have in itself, this work will bear witness to the evolving historical state of "writing" technology as used by a writer with middling resources and a middling passion for innovations in this domain), I noticed (this was yesterday, March 10, 1992) that it had disappeared.

It had disappeared from the "document" that was supposed to contain it on the hard drive of my Macintosh LC (to which I gave, as I did its predecessor, a Macintosh Plus, & just as affectionately, the same generic name: "Miss Macintosh"), entitled **int.3b**. This document, when it was "opened" for printing, revealed itself in fact to begin, at the very top of the page, with § 92 (which you may have just read a few moments ago), and the preceding document, which I just printed, **int.3a**, ended without any possible doubt with § 91 which, if you are reading these interpolations numerically, you may have just read.

And then the "backup disk," labeled LOOP-INT, which I inserted immediately thereafter (without much hope) turned out to be precisely identical to its model, and consequently presented the same fatal defect: the absence of § 92, the interpolation on the subject of the link between baby seals and BB, by way of considerations that were themselves meta-digressive since they led me beyond the chronological boundaries (generally respected in these pages) that I set for myself in this branch (I believe I recall fairly precisely what I'd had written there (telegraphically summarized below, in six points)):

—a memory from my days of military service

—an analogical slippage into eroticism, from baby to BB

—the evocation of a rightly famous scene in *Contempt* by M. Jean-Luc Godard, adding a third term to the "baby-to-BB" sequence: "behind"

—an interpolation internal to the present interpolation concerning a sweater worn by M. Fritz Lang, who in the same film makes an appearance no less famous than the not-so-obscure Bardotian object of desire just referred to

—a protest (a digression imposed by the context) against the pedophilia (or rather infantophilia) of certain television advertisements of which I happened to catch a glimpse in the Minervois (a protest not in the name of common morality, but on the basis of an unpleasant coincidence: when praise for toilet paper coincided with a departure from the dinner table by an already reticent television viewer like myself)

—finally, the memory of watching a movie screened outdoors in an Athens suburb during the summer of 1959, culminating, if I may put it this way, in the concomitant agitation (a light wind was rippling the rudimentary cloth screen) of the same posterior object mentioned above (but in another, more universally famous, earlier film) and the stupefied physiognomies of the Greek spectators, all male (with the exception of Sylvia, in whose company I had come to see the film *starring MPIRIZIT MPARDO*, which we wouldn't have gone to see in Paris if it was the last film on earth).

I soon realized what had happened, by an immediate deduction from the simple fact that, in the organization of my hard drive, the interpolations belonging to chapter 3—to which § 92 belongs—had been divided (in parallel to the division of chapter 3 itself into "**chap.3a**" and "**chap.3b**") into two "documents" (to make the text easier to work with on the screen): § 92, which, in this division, should have been at the beginning of the second part, had accidentally been cut.

At first, I was overcome with discouragement. The prospect of having to reconstruct lines that were already old, of miming a prose-mood already long past, was a rather grim one. I turned off Miss Macintosh and tried to think about something else. But this morning when I woke up (it's now five o'clock) the solution came to me on its own: regardless of what happened, according to the instructions I've given myself, I could not, in any case, rewrite the missing moment as if it hadn't disappeared. I can only write what I am writing in the present, and the present is one in which this moment has disappeared. I merely marked the unforeseen circumstance by changing the typeface. This interpolation, at least on my screen, is now written in Times.

§ 97 (§ 25) **A skinny young pig secretly took up residence in the lean-to**

The porcine model dreamt of by our parents was in all likelihood based on the pigs found in the Corrèze region, which they had discovered before they came to Carcassonne, when they lived in Tulle, where Marie was originally from (or almost: she was from Souillac). The privations of the war had turned a still recent memory—namely the fair in Tulle—into something like an inaccessible pig's paradise lost, an El Dorado of ham, almost as marvelous—and now, unfortunately, almost as remote—as the quasi-mythical Yorkshire pig (with which the Corrèze pigs could be compared, it was said, in flavor and bulk).

Our parents insistently enumerated, using the vocabulary of a Corrèze pig farmer, the technical terms used in describing the evolution of these admirable beasts: first as children, the stammering "piglets" fed by their sow mothers, then the "dogs" frolicking in the barnyard, then the adolescent "wolves" rooting and feeding on chestnuts in the undergrowth, and then they underwent still other onomastic mutations that I haven't retained, before reaching the first serious and strictly hierarchized weight gradations of the adult pig, achieved through immobility and the adoption of a vast, concentrated diet of grainy mush, nutritious and appetizing, to which our poor and meager feedings, alas, could never aspire. (And yet, this was indeed the model that was held out for our own specimen, for "gagnou" is the affectionate name given to Corrèze pigs, and our pig had been named, in a gesture of propitiation, "Gagnoune.")

Thus, she could never truly compete with the performances of the Tullist champions, or reach the weights we dreamt up for her—two hundred, three hundred, or even four hundred kilos: figures which, it seems, were common currency among those fabled animals. Such weights, converted into sausage, lard, ham, or blood sausage, were enough to overwhelm the gustative imagination. Our unfortunate pig fell far short.

This was in no way out of ill will on her part. If we had given her the time, and especially if we had provided her with adequate food, she would certainly have produced marvels when placed on the scale. She had in her an undeniable ambition in this noble direction. And it certainly wasn't her fault if destiny had decreed that she be was born in 1942 in Aude, right in the middle of a world war, and not in the peaceful hamlet of Yorkshire or in the area around the town of Uzerche. Like the Empress of Blandings, beloved pig of Clarence, Earl of Emsworth, in the novels of P.G. Wodehouse, she could then have triumphed in an agricultural competition instead of perishing prematurely, still more or less skinny, and in secret.

Our family's incessant speculations on the evolution of Gagnoune's weight never took away her appetite, which was almost as ravenous as our own, and which, it must be said, was rarely satisfied—any more than ours was. In short, she suspected nothing. I have since discovered, in an English detective novel whose title (and author) I've forgotten, a pig character who represents Gagnoune's perfect antonym, for this one remains perpetually on the verge but just short of the minimal weight that would earn him a one-way trip from the farm to the butcher. He eats, certainly, but does not "take full advantage." The author reports the lady farmer's astonishment at this phenomenon, so unusual in the porcine species, and her voluntarist psychological interpretation of this behavior: it is a *non-doing pig*. And the author of the novel finds this to be a clever attitude on the pig's part, something like a passive resistance to destiny and oppression. The author makes him almost a "Good Soldier Svejk" sort of pig: not skinny to the point of definitively discouraging every effort to fatten him up, since that would have been suicidal on his part, but constantly appearing to make an effort, to be full of good will, and failing only involuntarily to succeed.

I will be harsher still. The pig of the *Contes du chat perché* (known in English as *The Wonderful Farm*) who dreams of being as beautiful as a peacock, also becomes, for a moment, a *non-doing pig*, when he fanatically follows his dangerous daily regime, repeating with fervor: "One seed of a pippin, and a mouthful of cool water." As for myself, I have always found his attitude to be even more disgraceful than it is ridiculous.

98 (§ 26) the green leafy parts of the little palm trees in the garden were palms made up of long leaves at the end of a solid flexible stalk (a property that will prove to be of some interest to us here)

Detached from the trunk of the tree, these stalks—at least the strongest, longest, most rigid, and thickest of them, the green ones with lightly serrated edges (or so I see them before me now, as though they were in my hands again, and I can almost feel their rough edges)—**virtually cried out to be used as bows: notches at each end, a string stretched tight, and then white arrows made from spindle tree or elder (?) branches;**

to shoot; to shoot up into the blue-black sky, half devoured by the pines, the great umbrella pine in the very rear, the sky flat and vertical like a target directly overhead, throwing one's head back to aim, that's how I see it; the arrow climbing toward the high branches; the gravity of the highest branches, hurtling the arrows back down to the ground; arrows caught in the branches, taken prisoner. I still see them. There.

We continually made new bows, stockpiled them in secret places, our hidden store of arrows. Spurred by a reading of Walter Scott's *Quentin Durward* (a very likely source for my love of Scotland), we enacted complex battles scenes, liberations, chivalrous contests, Olympic feats. From what I've been told (I have no memory of this), I almost lost an eye from the accidental arrow sent flying by a boy who was visiting us, a Spanish boy about whom I can recall nothing but his name: Luis Bardagil.

My love for archery didn't extend past those years. Even at the height of my passion for old Japanese poetry, at the time of my frequent visits to the East Asian prints section of the Bibliothèque Nationale, during the years 1965-1970, I never dove ecstatically into the "Zen" or "pseudo-Zen" aesthetics-ethics of that art. And yet, as a result of one of those series of coincidences that would certainly scare off any novelist (and that I find myself incapable of excluding from my story, which is continually invaded by them), it is precisely from archery that I am currently drawing inspiration (no doubt indirectly, but nonetheless on the basis of the same vision of childhood that I've just reconstituted above) for the composition of the 200 poems (the title will be "200 Arrows") that will make up my contribution to a large book conceived by Micaëla Henich (five sets of 200 poems, or fragments, each by a different author, in two languages, English and French (Jacques Derrida, Dominique Fourcade, Michael Palmer, Tom Raworth, and myself), accompanying the vertical rectangles of her 1003 ("*mille e tre*") drawings.

Indeed, as the formal matrix of this composition (made up of "pseudo-*tankas*" of five lines, each divided into three + two), I chose a number of didactic poems from sixteenth-century Japan, which state the principles (at once technical (abstract) and moral) of this art. However, I didn't specifically seek out these poems with this purpose in mind. They came to me entirely by chance, following an unexpected phone call from the beautiful Odile H., who was once my neighbor here on the Rue d'Amsterdam. She wanted my help in putting together these texts (to which she provided me a word-by-word commentary) for a book to be published by her friend, who had become a French master of archery after long years of study and practice in Japan.

Ne pas prononcer
l'air transpercé des palissades
atlantides

C'est à la flèche de décider
de son trop-plein de silence

de ma toile de flèches
couvre-toi silence ainsi
l'arc

me parla et parlant
vint se reposer sur mon bras

Vibres criaient-ils
vibre
gravité de très hautes branches

très loin pesait la terre
vibre criaient-ils dans le bas

[Do not pronounce
the air cut by the long stakes
of Atlantis

It's up to the arrow to decide
on its too-full silence

on my canvas of arrows
silence cover yourself thus
the bow

spoke to me and speaking
fell gently into my arms

Quiver they cried
quiver
gravity of the highest branches

far away weighed the earth
quiver they cried down below]

99 (§ 28) **We came speeding by on our bicycles or tricycles**

In the first, spontaneous version of this sentence I only wrote "bicycles," but then almost immediately added "tricycles," after suddenly recalling one of the rare photographs still to be found among the vestiges of what was once a much more extensive documentary collection (almost all of these are now in the third drawer of the dresser in my bedroom in Saint-Félix, in the Minervois (the "bedroom with the copper bed")); it's one of the photos, the rarest of all, in which one can actually see something of the location where they were taken (for a long time I cursed this almost total absence, particularly of an overall view of the house and the garden on the Rue d'Assas, where I narratively placed myself in the very first chapter of this branch; but today I'm almost happy about it, in fact, because it has obliged me to interrogate my memories without cheating). In one of those photographs, then, one sees my sister Denise on her tricycle, in the middle of one of the walkways in the section containing the vegetable garden, which served as the track and terrain for our cycling competitions.

There are in fact three such shots, very similar, contained in a professional photographer's envelope ("A. Gamonnet Photography, 86 Avenue de Saxe, LYON"), among a dozen negatives, most of which were never printed. In my father's hand, I read: "Carcassonne, winter 1937-38: Denise tricycle" (for once, the minimal contextual information is there). It is in fact winter, judging by the sparse bare vegetation, and the empty flowerpots in the background. The physical background visible in the photo adds virtually no information to my description (in one, I see laundry hanging on a line behind us)—nor does it take any away. All I can draw from it is "tricycle" (the date is a little earlier than that of the memories I am recounting, but I assume that the tricycle survived to be used by my younger brothers).

Denise is perfectly recognizable to me in these pictions (especially the one in which she's looking directly at the camera), albeit with a more amiable expression, less sullen than the one ascribed to her in such circumstances by "tradition" (I deliberately use the "pseudo-Wittgensteinian" word <u>piction</u> because, in accordance with my "theory" (dare I say) of images, these views don't give rise to any actual images from my memories: they remain external, immobile). At the time she was a little more than two years old.

I have not forbidden myself the use of photographs and their description (as attested by the first chapter of branch one). But little by little I have made it a rule for myself to use them only in strictly limited contexts in which they don't run the risk of falsifying the truthfulness (which is however strictly unverifiable, I know) of my memories. Put somewhat differently, they intervene only in certain "styles" of my narration, among the ten that I set myself as a goal (branch one, § 84). And in any case not in the numerous moments of this present branch that are dominated almost exclusively by only one of these styles ("Kamo no Chōmei style"), style III: "old words in new times."

When I took these three photographs from their envelope, I also looked at the unprinted negatives in the nocturnal light of my screen (it is five o'clock). There are other figures (my brother Pierre and myself, no doubt), and there is that mysterious crisscrossing of the naked tree branches created by the inversion of light and dark on the negatives. I don't know why, but the "feeling of the past" seems more "authentic" to me here.

With boundless energy and ardor, we ceaselessly rode on our tricycles and bicycles through the network of walkways—rectangular on one side, curved on the other—hurling ourselves with enthusiasm (and often disastrously) down the three steps leading to the terrace, at the end of a lap on the imaginary "circuit" of our velodrome. For a long time I had an elliptical scar on my upper calf from the scrape of a pedal that had no doubt been bent by a fall, and was twisted into a quite unlikely position—but the furious and anesthetic heat of the race had prevented me from feeling it, even as it gnawed into my flesh, with each turn of the wheel, eventually drawing blood.

100 (§ 29) Out of play, as I face the bench, at the center of a very great multiplicity of real memories

But what does it mean, in these circumstances, to be "out of play"? All the games imagined in this garden were language games. And the only "out of play" in language is, certainly, a silence. All these games, like all games, like all language games, were modes of revelation, the putting into language of a form of life, and therefore they necessitated movement. Thus, being "out of play" was also a suspension of movement (as it is in rugby, where the referee's whistle kills the surge of movement in a three-quarters attack, penalizing it). Being "out of play" is an attack of immobility. Silence, immobility. But wasn't there precisely such a game among all my others, a fixed-point game, a game of immobility—a game of statuary silence, a game without movement (§ 22)?

This was, in fact, only a matter of miming the state of being "out of play," in order to bring "out of play" into the space of the game itself. The identification with statues, with the mute paralysis of statues, had meaning only if everyone else, all around, the mobile and loquacious spectators, brothers, and friends—before they became imitators themselves —made comments and grew worried, even terrified (as was the case when, later, in Saint-Germain-en-Laye, we repeated the same game of mute immobility, frightening our dog, Coqui, with the sudden and abnormal attitude of pseudo-corpses. He immediately came up to us, implored each of us in turn, sniffed at us, pressed his nose against our faces, pushed us with his paw, grew impatient, became frightened, began to bark).

Nor was this in any way an "out of play" born from solitude, a reinvention of the character of the hermit. Quite the contrary: it was something far closer to that paradoxical, eighteenth-century negation of the solitary figure of the hermit, the English "ornamental hermit" (a sinister example of which is the green pseudo-statue in Peter Greenaway's film, *The Draughtsman's Contract*). An ornamental hermit can only play the game of being "out of play," of solitude, because he has an audience. (I find an ultimate, extreme, and sarcastic version of this in the purely fictional hero of a short fable-novel by David

Garnett: *The Man in the Zoo*, who offers himself up, like some voluntary chimpanzee, to live in a cage at the London Zoo, as a representative of the species *Homo sapiens*.)

It would seem, then, that placing someone "out of play" in the game of Go-Creeping would have meant sending the player into the camp of the onlookers, the game's "audience." But that's not how it was. If a player called out by the seeker was immediately "out of play," and so had lost, he did not for all that enter into the neutral state of an onlooker (as an adult sometimes was). For he had lost.

Being "out of play," and thus being out of the game, was therefore a loss, a defeat. Hitting a player by calling his name was like shooting an arrow that pierces its target, like the fencing lunge that eliminates its victim, like the KO that floors an opponent, like the hand that pulls one, now a prisoner, behind the line in the game of *jeu de barres* (prisoner's base).

But if in the end I return to the bench, if I place myself, as I've done at length in this chapter, in the position of the seeker in the game, in the "out of play" (or simply "before-play") position, if today I sense the well as a dangerous presence behind me, if I feel, now, truly "out of the game," it's because of a much more radical exclusion—the exclusion of time. I, too, have lost.

(from chapter 4)

101 (§ 30) **the fruit of the yew tree, with its dark red color; bright on the tree with a deep, dark brilliance**

In rediscovering this vision, and in noting it down, I noted too that I found myself thinking: **child in the tree**. The image of the child in the tree occurs in the Grail romances on several occasions, in several different guises. Thus:

He encountered no adventure, nothing that merits telling, until he found himself about to enter a wood. In a tree that seemed very tall, he saw a child on a branch, sitting so high that no lance could reach him. This is the pure truth that I am telling you. In his hand the child held an apple. You could have gone all the way to Rome before finding a creature more finely formed. He was richly dressed and seemed hardly more than five years old.

Perceval looked at him a moment and then, stopping his horse under the tree, greeted him. The child returned his greeting.

"Come down from there," Perceval said to him.

"No," said the child, "I am not a knight. I hold no land of yours. Many words have I heard fly up to my ears that did not go down again, and those you speak will do no more."

"Tell me, at least, I pray you, if I am on the right path."

And the child responded: "It is quite possible. I am not wise enough at my age to tell you so, if I do not know where you are going." Then he stood up on the branch and took hold of the one above, and he continued to climb higher and higher, so that he became smaller and smaller, ascending into the heights, until he disappeared, and Perceval saw nothing other than the tree, which seemed to go on forever. Nor did he hear anything more.

Later, when the moon had risen, the night remained so pure, so sweet, so sweet and serene, that each one of the stars appeared separately between the trees. Perceval sat astride his horse thinking of the Bleeding Lance, of the Grail, and of the question he would ask. As he went on his way thinking of these, he saw in the distance a tree with many branches, and on the tree more than a thousand candles, which seemed to be lit up like stars on the branches of a candelabra. The tree was all alight with flames but, as he approached, the great brightness decreased and continued to diminish. When he arrived, he faced an unlit tree.

Child in the tree, yews, berries of the yew, candles, dark illumination, red: dwarf stars, extinguished tree.

102 (§ 33 and continuation of § 101) **Images that are intense but fixed; almost isolated**

I'm in no way claiming that this isolation is possible in reality, nor that the perpetual motion of memories can really be stopped. Choosing a title for a memory is an attempt to immobilize it: necessarily futile, in absolute terms, but it can have a certain relative success—it can serve as an <u>effector of memory</u>, and can aid the voluntary evocation of this memory. It can also, however, end up "cutting" the memory off from its environment (as is the case with the examples I'm evoking here).

The always-present, irrepressible proliferation of <u>memories</u> occurs, then, in a very different way—as illustrated by the previous example, "the child in the tree." The "leap" of memory leads into totally unexpected regions. (This also happens, of course, in "ordinary" cases, but there the strange elements in a given association attract less attention.)

In order to interpret the sudden shift (by way of language, in an image deriving from a title) from the candle-fruits of the yew tree to the "candlesticks" of the Grail story, I reproduced a fragment of my book, *Graal-fiction*, in which I presented several examples of this vision given to Perceval during his wanderings in search of the castle of the Fisher King (or the Sinner King: *le Roi Pêcheur/Pécheur*). There are reasons for suspecting that the "child" of the tale is a disguise taken on by Merlin (one of his countless disguises). It is thus a premonitory vision, an announcement, one of those "dark things" that can never be deciphered in time, which the enchanter scatters across the paths of lost people (like all lessons from the past, they can be deciphered only in the future anterior: this is what will have been revealed!).

But if, like the reader of the Grail story, I am trying to decipher the meaning of this leap from the **Yew Tree with Ants** to Merlin's tree (which doesn't appear to be a yew) (and I engage in this deductive effort without making any claim to an effective interpretation of this "shift," which one naturally has the right to attribute to mere chance), I bring to light a certain parallelism between my situation and that of Perceval at this moment of his adventure.

(He is searching, he has set out on his "quest," because he did not ask <u>the question</u> that would have provided him with the meaning of the vision offered to him at the castle of the Fisher King: that of the Grail—a vision which, as I recall it, is flooded with light. The light of the Grail eclipses that of the candles carried by the King's servants. When it appears, carried by the Maiden, "such a great light came from it / that the candles lost / their brightness, as do the stars / when the sun rises, and the moon" (Chrétien de Troyes).) I too remained silent.

In the scene at the foot of the yew trees, I left another image mute, unspoken. And yet another one, called up by that scene, in which ants crawl beneath an immense wooden door, enormously heavy. An entire mental circulation, a whole scaffolding of internal explanations rises up around this silence: the red candles of the fruit, the tree of mourning, the black ants (also the color of mourning), the child, the child in the tree.

103 (§ 33 & § 34) **I haven't gone into the house. I see it only in the context of the relative cold of winter, I only remember it as being in another world**

Looking out at the Wild Park, which began only a short distance away (a transition area of gravel and sand lay across the open space outside, a flat border zone that likewise gives me a sense of complete emotional flatness and neutrality), there was an enormous and very grand living room with a fireplace and a piano. I heard someone playing on this piano. The music, pages and pages of Chopin's *Nocturnes*, came from a long head of disordered hair falling down as far as the player's fingers. It was played with much more technical virtuosity than I could ever have summoned myself (I'm not sure it was really as remarkable as all that, though no doubt I'm mistaken in this), but above all with infinitely more emotion.

I like Chopin, but the hyper-romantic interpretation that flowed from that pale forehead, that hair and those fingers, into a wretched and very badly tuned piano, wasn't at all in aesthetic harmony with the kind of training I received from Marguerite Long, whose lessons (inflected by Mme. Vidal, in Toulouse, and by my mother's own preferences) placed a distinct emphasis on sobriety (I hope that I'm not going to shock the pianist's admirers, justly numerous, in saying so—although, to be sure, not all of these admirers came to their admiration by way of a love of music, as we will see in a moment (of prose) or two), and this drastically heightened my sense of the comic aspect of this scene, which I began to share, alas! with my playmates (brothers and sister, the "twins," and "little Jean").

(One sense of this comic aspect—which, it must be said, was encouraged by what I was reading during this public recital—was this: the pianist was playing for himself alone, in the cold and empty morning, and was paying no attention to my presence. I would add, in order to be more honest still, and to lessen the real weight of my remarks, that I liked being left alone to read in this immense room, and that Chopin, therefore, was disturbing the peace I found there.)

The pianist was named Vladimir Jankélévitch. If I speak of him here in such an irreverent manner, this is for the sake of my story's necessities, and in accordance with what I remember (the same remark applies to Georges Canguilhem). I know (but I did not know it then, and for good reason) that the work of this philosopher includes some studies of Chopin. And I know especially (but I did not know it then, even if I vaguely suspected it) that he was only present because historical circumstances had forced him to seek refuge in order to escape from some highly un-romantic enemies.

Sainte-Lucie was one such refuge. Our friend Nina (who was in Lyon, in the Resistance, as a secretary of Marc Bloch) was spending some time there too, but now with brown hair (which, when I first saw her again, touched up in this way, I thought was a rather mediocre innovation, almost in bad taste. I've always been very sensitive to the naturalness of hair). It was cold in the winter (one feels really cold in the Mediterranean, when it gets cold—much more so than in Norway), and felt even colder since there was almost nothing to eat.

In an attempt to remedy these two difficulties, at least partially, and at one stroke, my father one day asked "Camillou," the man in charge of the place, if he didn't have some alcohol in a cabinet somewhere. Camillou did not drink (all this, of course, should be appended to the portrait of Camillou, as I sketched it in § 34, although there I privileged the child's point of view). He finally managed to dig up a dusty bottle from which he poured two large glasses for his guests. My father (it was he who told this story) took his glass, wet his lips, and immediately set it back down. It was pure alcohol. But Nina swallowed hers in one gulp without batting an eye: proof, my father added, of her fearlessness. But she claimed, for her part, that it was merely a result of her excellent upbringing.

104 (continuation of § 103) The enormous dining room was usually empty when I went there, early in the morning

The enormous dining room was usually empty when I went there, early in the morning, right after waking up. There I found a vast, comfortable, and peaceful space for reading.

I love to read. Even then I loved to read. There were books, a lot of books in the house. It was a house of books. A house without books is nothing but a ruin, or a prison, a barracks, a monument, a museum.

I took a seat in an armchair near the fire, what remained of the fire from the night before, smelling of smoke, vine shoots and logs, sap and embers (embers have their own smell, which comes from the velvet smoothness of their color). I climbed into the armchair, folded my legs up beneath me on the cushion, and read.

The books in Camillou's library were mostly in Spanish. But there were also some French books, among which I could choose without restriction. It was there that I first encountered the grand *Quixote* illustrated by Gustave Doré (and it occurred to me later that this hero, both Dickensian and Dostoyevskian, had a certain kinship with Camille Boer, or indeed that Camille Boer had a "Quixotic" element in his make-up, not so much because he was unable to "make it" in the so-called *struggle for life* after the Liberation, as I sometimes heard said of him with a slightly irritated affection, but because he never ceased confronting the giants and the windmills of this world, for the love of the human species, for the love of our rather dubious "Toboso" (the giant-windmills confronted by the hero are perfectly real, contrary to what the usual hasty reading of *Don Quixote* might lead one to believe: "The joke," as one says in English, "is on us")).

A reading of the *Quixote* in this context became, in short, almost an obligation. And yet, I see two other books being read in the same place, as different from each other as they could be, but both perfectly suited to that solitary space of reading. I am referring, first, to the *Tales* of Edgar Allen Poe, in Baudelaire's translation. (I can only remember the physical appearance of the book, or more precisely I no longer see anything but the gray-green hardcover of the copy that was in my parents' library in the Rue d'Assas.)

The circumstances in which we read are an integral part of reading itself: not only the concrete book in its appearance, its format, its weight, and typography, but also the volume of real space in which we read it: a train, a bed, a patch of grass. The book, the work, is <u>that</u> for us. A book is what we've retained of it (the "circumstances" of our reading are a part of this) no less than the strict letter of the text, which can at least be verified by opening it again (but which isn't always compatible with our memory of it!). No less, that is, than the stable immobility of the words on its pages, the movement of our eyes over its lines, the variable intensity of our gaze.

But the books that we've read "color" in return—in a manner that's at least as intense— the places and the circumstances in which we've opened them. This is why neither winter, nor the winter wind beneath the doors, nor my solitude, were able to connect with the macabre fantasies of "The Fall of the House of Usher," for example, in order to transform the large open room of Sainte-Lucie into a "gothic" space. The main impression that remains with me today is comic: for it was there that I read *Trois Hommes dans un bateau* by Jerome K. Jerome for the first time (and my impression of it at the time was so strong that, contrary to my habit, I do not "feel" this story in English, but in French. I don't think of *Three Men in a Boat* (which, though I've read and appreciated it, just can't replace its translation), but, indeed, of *Trois Hommes dans un bateau*). I read: "*Je n'ai jamais vu deux hommes faire tant de choses avec une livre de beurre*" ("I never saw two men do more with one-and-twopence worth of butter than they did"), or: "*Je n'avais pas 'l'épanchement de synovie.' Pourquoi n'avais-je pas l'épanchement de synovie?*" ("I had not got . . . housemaid's knee . . . Why hadn't I got housemaid's knee?"), and I laughed. I laughed all alone in the large room in the morning, warm, protected, and empty. I pronounce these sentences today, and immediately I am there.

105 (§ 34) **The years from '40 to '45 were a blessed time for bicycles**

Even in the absence of the *Tour de France* (whose last pre-war "edition," in 1939, left no impression on me (the one in 1947 was very exciting. I thrilled at Vietto, who, during that last "Tour" before the catastrophe, finished second behind a Belgian (Sylvère Maës?), but seemed now to have a great future ahead of him; and yet this time he fell behind in the last stage, and lost his chance for a stunning revenge on fate)), bicycling held a considerable prestige for us. It was on a bicycle that my father traveled up and down the roads of the Aude, for the (ostensible but not exclusive) purpose of finding us provisions.

Following his example and encouragement, we too became passionate cyclists: brakes, inner tubes, rubber patches, air bubbles rising in a bowl filled with water (for the detection of wounds in a flat tire), the straight lines of roads running between plane trees, virtuosic descents with "no hands," the characteristic "peppering" of small pebbles on a bloody leg after a skid on a turn, zigzags on a "back road" to climb a "rise," a steep hill, a narrow road (marked respectively with a "<" or even a "<<" on the Michelin map (hills with one or two chevrons, like the first-class soldiers or corporals of our network of roads))—I experienced all this on and off the many roads of the Aude.

But in an inversion of our reaction to the lack of certain foods (pork, jams and pastries, butter, oranges), on which we gorged ourselves later, this child's bicycle gluttony provoked such a saturation, almost a disgust, with the vehicle that after twenty-five years

I've almost never had recourse to this means of locomotion again (not since the first years of our summers and vacations in the Minervois). (It took me a long time to realize, and to accept, that I simply did not like riding bicycles anymore. I blamed the mechanistic element, or the length of my legs, or the heat, or my fatigue.)

(§ 34) The bike leaning against a low wall, at the top of a hill; a pause, the natural prolongation of a suspended moment, at zero speed, before the intoxicating descent

The state of equilibrium of these *maxima* of relief engenders an entire family of bicycle visions that have only this circumstance in common, and a similar setting: the road, the blacktop, the white hectometric markers, the larger kilometric markers, yellow or red.

From the desolate and wintry dark red of Villerouge-la-Crémade, I thus pass into another wild place, in Le Carcassès this time, near the village of Aragon. **It is the height of summer, we have stopped, my father and I, at the summit, and lower down, on the road, in the soft tar of the blacktop, scorching hot, my mother and Canguilhem have gotten off their bicycles, they are there, fifty meters below, at a bend in the road: the incline is too steep, and above all it's too hot; a heat without wind, beneath an unimpeded sun;**

the sky pours down heat; nothing moves; except the grasshoppers; innumerable grasshoppers with their brown bodies and red wings, or blue wings; in the palm of my hand, holding down the insect's body with a finger, I feel its tiny claws, and the long legs tensing for the leap that I am momentarily restraining; I lean down to place my eyes almost against its eyes, against its silent mandibles, agitated and furious; I draw back my finger, and the sudden release of the grasshopper sends it five, ten meters, onto the road, toward the low wall, into the fennel; blue wings, red wings.

(from chapter 5)

106 (§ 36) At the end of their mythical age, I gave my gods a language called Peruviac

A few lexical remnants survive from this language of the gods. The first word I recall is not difficult to interpret, since it is (or so it seems to me) a fairly natural neologism in French (perhaps even a real word in the French language. But it doesn't appear in the *Petit Robert* dictionary that I just consulted). It is the word *bouillaque*. This designates that mushy amalgam of primordial pre-Adamite mud (*bouille*), incorporating water (peepee if necessary), sand, earth, a few pebbles, some grass and twigs: a mixture useful (to all children whose artistic aspirations haven't been ground down) for construction, for the molding of statues, or for intimate communion with the flesh of the planet.

The substantivized adjective, "Peruviac," can therefore be interpreted (I am using Leiris's method) as being based—with the help of the suffix *-aque*, which gives "bouillaque" its telluric sense—on a (lost but reconstructed) geographico-mystic substantive designating the land of the Gods, where one also finds in an allusive form the great Inca mystery. My invented language thus allegorizes the difficult and provisional union of natural and transcendental forces.

I will comment especially on three words. (I don't have many others left, since most of those that appear in my incomplete grammar manual are indecipherable. Peruviac is thus rather close to *Cumbric*, the Celtic language that disappeared in the seventh century; only six words remain.) The first is *pétoule*. It designates a magical potion made from vegetable essences and water, used as fuel by the gods. (The word has some sonorous affinity with "petrol.") The recipe for its alchemical fabrication is found in the linguistic document already mentioned, which amounts to saying that it's been lost. I remember the appearance of the finished product, a murky liquid, a little like *bouillaque* but lighter in color, and also a little like absinthe. On its surface, in its multicolored refractions, I read a fleeting and volatile rainbow; it evoked, in a lighter, subtler form, the ones I sometimes came across on the way to school, in the heavy, noxious puddles left by automobiles on the floor of the garage on the "road to Limoux."

The two other words had to do with the fruit of plants no doubt known in ordinary language by other designations (I don't think the fruits themselves, which are totally useless, have ever been given a name). In this case, the names were meant to signify the particular status and dignity conferred on a given fruit by its role in a ritual, in the sacred ceremonies of Peruviac paganism. One of them was full of medicinal virtues, which, however, were essentially symbolic; since the fruit wasn't edible in the usual sense (and was perhaps even poisonous), elementary caution prescribed all but imaginary consumption. But then, especially after being transformed (according to a purely theoretical notion) into a sort of purée or preserve, it took on the prestige accorded to ambrosia on Olympus. Its name was *Op-tida*. It is a little orange ball with a powdery substance inside, and it grows in clusters on an ornamental tree found just about everywhere.

The second was the *pulumuse*, fruit of the *pulumuse* tree: a tiny little pip the size and appearance of a grape seed, and available in several varieties distinguished by their color, depending on the degree of ripeness: green, blue, and brown. The pulumuse was used as a projectile (less aggressive than our cypress shells, it was thrown by the handful in symbolic battles, or into a beret from a few steps away, a game of precision and skill similar to the one played by students in preparatory courses for the *grandes écoles*, who would toss pieces of chalk into the dust-catcher at the bottom of a blackboard), or else as small change, or as a representative of the various commodities necessary for certain games (vegetables for example), but of which it was impossible to obtain multiple examples in reality. Its "mutations," therefore, were manifold. It was a small protean object with a name that rolled off the tongue—a name I continue to use.

My pockets, the drawers of my small desk, were stuffed with *pulumuse* reserves. I gathered them patiently. I counted them. They were the living proof of the real presence, in sensible nature, of the Idea of Great Number, a natural Nuptial Number more directly graspable by the mind than the endless grains of sand or scattered pebbles, or those other pulumuses, brilliant but distant and impalpable: the starry grains of the nocturnal sky.

107 (§ 39) **This is what I would call "autobiographical comfort." It asserts itself unchecked in the novelist.**

One opens a novel. One almost immediately finds a character in it who at a given moment is thinking of his adventures. The pages open and there he is: someone thinking. The justification generally given for these rather unlikely speculations is that the novelist is providing an imaginary elaboration of a character's "possible world." It's all too easy to use this as an excuse. The external point of view of the story, external to its time frame as well as to the inner space of a thinking head, makes it impossible to "treat" such a scene with the slightest coherence. The attempts made by so-called "psychological" prose to be "penetrating" are almost worse, for in such cases one does no more than momentarily push back or translate (in the geometric sense) the same vanishing point—thus propelling into infinity an internal gaze whose real space has a very different kind of geometry.

Nor, however, can one remain within a purely spatial exteriority: describing the radio, the family sitting around the table at dinner, the children already pressing toward the door, ready to go outside to play in the garden, the tension reverberating in the room. Marie is crying. The father speaks, and we read his transcribed words . . .

I don't mean to claim that the novelist shouldn't do this sort of thing. He can do what he wants. But it might be nice if sometimes the narration revealed just the tiniest bit of underlying disquiet, a vague sense of the problem of the adequation (or lack thereof) between the methods of the story, its modes and strategies of narration (on the one hand), and (on the other) the possibility, however minimal, of the other worlds that it thus invites us to consider.

For the novelist is the unconscious victim of a historical shift: the externalization of memories. The collapse in the seventeenth century of the ancestral tradition of the Arts of Memory made way for the proliferation in prose of slow and fragmentary descriptions of objects in the world—so different from the global vision of image-memories in the reality of inner experience.

This development is no doubt irreversible. Older prose, even narrative prose, virtually never had recourse to this same scanning of images, its multiplication of details abruptly snatched from the external world—immobilities strictly inscribed in a well-ordered three-dimensional space.

The mode in which memories function—which is labyrinthine, arborescent, and multidimensional—has been forgotten: their speed, their lack of resolution, their ambiguities have all ceased to be understood. The older forms of narrative never claimed to reconstitute the phenomena of the world. And older poetry did not mimic memory: it brought it forth, it produced it.

108 (§ 39) **In the cities, particularly in Carcassonne, people were very hungry**

The collaborationist "authorities" had invented a very amusing game: on market days, beginning at dawn, or even earlier, when the crowds of housewives (and "househusbands"), all worrying about being the first to reach the displays of scarce vegetables and even scarcer fruit, invaded the elegant rectangular public square with its plane trees centered around the fountain of the "*Roi des Eaux*" (King of the Waters) (although one December day in 1941, there wasn't a soul at the marketplace except a single vendor selling "*fanes de carrottes*" or carrot tops: I retain this generic detail from my mother's account, and because of the word "*fanes*"), they found that barriers had been set up, police style, blocking access to the market by the side streets. This was supposedly for the sake of fairness. At the agreed upon hour (eight o'clock), a bell rang, the barriers were opened, and the candidates for the day's food rushed into the square, awaited by the market gardeners, true masters of the hour. There was some fierce pushing and shoving; a pregnant woman, it was said, got trampled. Global television has since shown us, or now shows us (could show us almost every day) similar scenes, infinitely more tragic. But this was a first, or dare I say a "premier," in Carcassonne in 1942.

Reacting against the general protests, and with their well-known concern for order and "European" humanism, the "authorities" then decided to further control the crowd's access to the precious commodities—still restricted by the barriers—by dividing the women (considered to be the only ones to carry the responsibility of procuring the family supplies (Vichy had adopted the German motto for a wife's duties, the three *K*s (*Kinder, Kirche, Küche* (children, church, kitchen)))) into three groups (theoretically equal). The first were provided with red cards, the second with green cards, the third with blue cards.

There were (there still are) three market days in Carcassonne: Tuesday, Thursday, Saturday. Tuesday, then (let's say), was the "red" day. That day, those with red cards were allowed to enter first, at eight o'clock; those with green cards followed at nine, those with blue cards at ten (and these last might just as well stay home, since if anything edible remained after eight o'clock, the second hungry wave would have left nothing in its wake (except perhaps the "infamous" vegetables of those days: Jerusalem artichokes and rutabagas)).

But, you will ask, what about the sick? what about women who were pregnant (and who had gotten that way "legitimately"), mothers of young children or of a "numerous family" (like ours)? Well, these had special cards (also accepted by the dairy shop, the baker, the butcher) and were entitled to better quality rations (receiving "tickets" for bread, meat, milk): in a word, they had privileges. And the same housewives who went into slobbering spasms (almost erotic, akin to the emotion aroused later, though not in the same people, by Brigitte Bardot's behind) at the sight of the baby-pink face of Marshal

Pétain ("Pink and smooth, legs squeaky clean / Like the ones in a prefect's dreams / Like the ones molded into chocolate . . .") emblazoned across all the newspapers or in the "cinematographic newsreels," felt a surge of vindictiveness in the face of this inequality, this scandal and injustice. One heard their murmurs in the lines, one felt their hateful gazes: "Those women with their 'periority'" they said, "they get everything!"

On Tuesday, Thursday, and Saturday, on market days, the "vans" that wind through the Carcassès region today, whose primary function is to pick up school children (sometimes in the winter, on my return to Paris, in the darkness of seven A.M., I get on at the stop called "Bagnoles Station" (named after the little train that used to pass by there long ago) and sit among the lycée students from Rieux-Minervois, from Peyriac, from Villegly, rather quiet and sleepy at that hour), make a second run around nine o'clock, and occasionally I thus find myself on the square of the "*Roi des Eaux*," on the terrace of the café where my family members like to meet, the rugby café called *Chez Félix*. I look around at the abundance and I make an effort in thought to empty out the displays, and to reconstruct (though the effort is perfectly futile, I know) the memory of that former time of hunger.

109 (§ 39) I devoted myself to my poetic vocation with more constancy, concentration, and conviction than to my studies

More precisely, as it happened, I devoted myself to the essentially dreamy and private activity of concocting poems, in my head and for many hours, during time that should have been spent on more academic disciplines—class time being no exception (and when I wasn't playing at poetry, I indulged in another language game, also mentally: numbering and calculation). Thus, I would begin a poem during Latin, "French," or math class, and I would finish it on my way home, under the protection of my gods of wind, leaves, and sky: a metric and rhyming activity that was more than merely private, or clandestine. It was my own peculiar clandestine world.

In fact, it was also the condition for an exercise in solitude. In being alone, I was, so to speak, never alone. And I had quite naturally chosen those hours of forced immobilization (the hours in school, the pre-nocturnal hours of "homework") to isolate myself internally. This gave me (gives me) all the outward appearances of distraction (distraction in the ordinary sense was (is) habitual for me in any case, manifesting itself in all sorts of forgetfulness). I thus exerted great efforts, within whatever ambient noise there was, in concentration and memorization (but I focused almost exclusively on number-figures and syllables: an external world of language). In this way I approached silence, obliquely: a silence carved out of the surrounding non-silence (from which I sometimes found myself abruptly torn, quite unpleasantly, when a teacher called on me).

Since then, I have continually—whether voluntarily or not (as a soldier, for example)— regained or even reconstructed this state of presence-absence, of invisible absence, of a retrenched camp without a flag, and I have done so pretty much everywhere, in cafés, on streets, at parties, in libraries. It follows that poetry found itself simultaneously associated with and yet participating very little in the institution of education. I have never considered poetry (I mean spontaneously, without reflection) as really belonging to "literature" (which in any case I retained no more than any other academic "discipline." This was not in the least a matter of rebellion, but simply of detachment).

I can identify one exception to this rule of intermittent phasing, as it were, in my formal education (and of the inward migration I practiced within the educational institution itself): English. The English language had everything necessary, on both sentimental and political grounds, to please me. I was able to read English relatively quickly (at any rate, beginning with my first stay in Scotland in 1947), and the opening of this immense continent of reading was a wondrous event, even more bodily, really, than intellectual, and indeed there can hardly be a purer pleasure for me than that of buying a book in a London bookstore, holding it, weighing it in my hands, putting off opening it until a favorable occasion: on a Sunday afternoon, on a train trip, on a park bench, at a table in a café, in a hotel room. I've never really managed to master the language in all its functions (I have, for example, remained very far from the excellence, in their diverse professions, of my mother, my sister, or my niece, Ann): my pronunciation of English is erratic (the stress patterns often escape me, which is certainly an effect of my rhythmical absorption in the language of poetry), and I do not write it. But I read it. I am even more inclined to read English than French: a mechanism meant to protect the language of my poetry, of the same order as the noise that long ago served to enclose my solitude.

I remember Pooh and his poems, which he calls his "hums" (like the sound of the bees of the world around the honey of poetry). I remember Mr. Badger in *The Wind in the Willows*, the young hedgehogs in his kitchen with their little plaid scarves tightly wrapped to protect against the winter snow (I've always had an excessive affection for hedgehogs), and his friend Mole, who inspired me to write a story for my brothers ("The Mole Who Wanted to See the Sea"), and especially a poem, my first poem in English, from which I can only recall a single stanza of three lines, no doubt because of the bizarre use of the preposition *among* that it contains: "Far among / the wind's song / is the Mole."

But above all I hear the singsong of a poem by A. A. Milne (the creator of "Pooh"), which evokes the collective recitation of a classroom:

> Ti-mo-thy-Tim has-ten-pink-toes
> And ten pink toes has Timothy Tim
> They go with him wherever he goes
> And wherever he goes they go with him.

I was intoxicated by the swell of repetitions from line to line, the wave of new lines thrown forward from the crest of the *And*, fascinated by the monosyllabic machine-gun bullets, dazzled finally by the only non-monosyllables, the very un-French dactyls of *wherever* and most especially of "Timothy." His toes are pink, but his eyes are blue: "Timothy Tim has two blue eyes / And two blue eyes has Timothy Tim."

110 (§ 39) **We solemnly performed the tri-monthly ceremony of measurement**

I'm surprised that my father didn't choose instead—as other fathers did—a tree in the garden, one of the pines or the apricot tree: an incision into the tree's bark would have preserved the memory even better, and would have accentuated the vegetal metaphor. That particular tradition has apparently not disappeared, judging from a wonderful drawing by cartoonist Philippe Geluk in his collection *Le Quatrième Chat* (The Fourth Cat), in which his hero, The Cat (his first name seems to be "The"), measures his son in just this manner against the trunk of a tree, and states with stupefaction that the earlier marks (implicitly earlier) are now above the head of the young "Cat." (One might imagine a mischievous tree that had itself grown during the interval between the two measurements.)

But the ceremony of measuring our childhood heights evokes for me, especially now, my old friend from the Rue de Vaugirard, near the Senate Palace on the edge of the Luxembourg Gardens, **that little known Parisian personality, a horizontal copy of Mr. Standard Meter**, and the paradox that threatens all units of reference used in measurements. Indeed, in his *Philosophical Investigations*, Wittgenstein affirms elliptically and enigmatically, as is his wont, that with regard to the standard meter one can say neither that it is, nor that it is not, one meter in length.

Kripke finds that this property of the standard meter in the Breteuil Pavilion (to which I'm referring here) is truly "extraordinary," and he adds: "I think that Wittgenstein must be mistaken." I will not take a side in this weighty philosophical debate, pondered at length by Nathan Salmon in vol. LXXXVIII of the *Proceedings of the Aristotelian Society* in 1988.

For Wittgenstein, it seems, this paradoxical property, which belongs not to the abstract meter but to the standard meter, results from its particular role in the "language game" of measurement: every object has a length, but a measured length is "a meter" only in comparison with the standard. In that case (akin therefore to Lord Bertrand Russell's famous barber who shaved all the men in the village who did not shave themselves), the standard cannot be measured by itself (and yet, like every object, it has a length) (this presentation of the paradox is slightly different from Wittgenstein's: "There is one thing of which one can say neither that it is one meter long, nor that it is not one meter long, and that is the standard meter . . .").

But then what about the copy of the meter, what about "my" meter? Couldn't one use it as a replacement, as a substitute, a double? By what rights would it be any more fundamentally a meter in length than any tape measure, any height gauge? And couldn't one, having verified the perfection of its length, simply ask it to help us, in its turn, measure the standard meter? (Just as Russell's barber, shaving himself in his barber's mirror, is shaving his double.) In other words, to avoid any logical difficulty, shouldn't standard measurements always be considered "**doubles**"?

This is what I was thinking, the other day, walking back up the Rue Garancière, after having evoked in this chapter the memory-image of our measurements and their marks. And I wondered, melancholically reflecting on the downfall of my old friend, who is now but a copy of a fallen god, and whose length (which is certainly no longer a meter, in any case) can no longer even give rise to a paradox, since it got replaced by a wavelength—I wondered, then, if the meter, by changing, by becoming a ray of light, had acquired not only a greater precision and stability, but also a more purely paradoxical status, and irremediably so: for light is not an artifact, and it has no double.

111 (§ 40) As for us, my father had, I won't say Olympic ambitions, but at least the hope of seeing us honorably succeed in the track and field disciplines

I was his first disappointment. I did have a promising start: I ran well, I liked to run, both sprints and longer distances, and I had a certain enthusiasm for jumping, but not much technique (and "without technique, a talent is nothing but a dirty little obsession," as the poet said). I was especially adept at the animal run (on all fours), and the standing jump, disciplines that are not recognized by the *Fédération française d'athlétisme* (French Federation of Track and Field). But neither the inclination nor the desire to pursue sports survived our transplantation to Paris. And I never had the leisure to become a good "wing three-quarter" in rugby (despite a few "intramural" attempts). I contented myself (I still do) with gaining a certain numerical competence in the various Olympic disciplines and in showing myself to be a staunch supporter of the Toulon team (the team my father always favored) as well as the Welsh and Scottish teams (out of a sympathy for the lands of Fife or Carmarthen, and on account of the "Matter of Britain," the medieval legends whose Celtic origins I do not dispute).

Nor was the flame of paternal ambition relayed to my sister. She made a few quite convincing attempts at the long jump, but she soon quit for a reason that was rather peculiar: she didn't mind participating in competitions, but she hated being watched when she jumped. She would have needed to do her trials without an audience or a referee, and with competitors who would turn away at the moment of her "tries." One day she took advantage of the excitement that arose around one particular champion jumper (who must have approached or even surpassed the six-meter mark, a rather rare accomplishment in the 1950s) and tried to execute her own jump on the sly, as it were. She sprained her ankle and had to drop out of the competition.

The spotlight was then turned on my brother Pierre, fifteen months her junior. This was a time when (after some delay) swimming pools began to pop up just about everywhere, if I can put it that way. And it was in this entirely new direction (for our family) that he decided to turn his attentions. He made rapid progress. In school and at the university he reached what was called a "national level" in the crawl, and succeeded even more brilliantly in the breaststroke. This time, the demands of modern training—hardly compatible with studies in biology—were aggravated by the fact that he belonged to a sports federation that competed (politically) with the official one (which didn't make things any easier for him), and by his lack of sympathy for the modes of thought and life of the aspiring champions (we've seen much worse since then!). All of this hindered his path (uncertain in any case) toward a swimmer's glory.

Now on to the next generation. Neither my daughter Laurence, nor most of my nephews and nieces (my nephew Vincent, who works as a teacher and a coach, does not participate in competitions) were tempted to take on the same dream, which by this time was a grandfather's dream (and, it must be said, an uncle's as well). With the exception of my nephew François. After surpassing his grandfather, his father, his uncle, and his aunt—as well as his brother, his sisters, and his cousins—in height (1 meter 98 or 99), he set out to surpass us all in swimming.

He outdid his father, both in the crawl and in the breaststroke, became the French champion at the university level, and might have been able to try his chances as a "top competitor," as one says. He quit, for more or less the same reasons as Pierre, however (and in the realm of the most advanced performers, the atmosphere had become even more suffocating than it had been twenty years earlier. After entering the ranks of the French "hopefuls," his trainer (who was still training the French team at the Barcelona Olympics, at the time) said one day: "Roubaud, he won't stick with it. He's too intelligent!") François had, in addition, a rather peculiar handicap for a competitive swimmer: he hated doing turns. He'd always refused to learn to do them according to the norms and regulations of the period (which have since been eliminated!) and thus regularly lost a half-second each time around. I therefore had to give up my dream of cheering him on at the Olympics, where I had promised to go as a family supporter, if he were to make it that far.

But he didn't give up all athletic competition, turning (with success) to the world of French boxing instead. (My father was a great lover of boxing, during the grand years of this sport, which lasted from Carpentier to Cerdan and from Jack Dempsey to Sugar Ray Robinson.)

112 (§ 40) Look what will happen to their daughters if they keep wanting to run these foot races

Around this time, my father liked to play a little game. He would ask: How long do you think it takes for a fast runner to do the 100-meter dash? The times proposed in response went from one second to one minute. It was particularly striking and surprising for him that our friend Nina was among those who had responded "one minute" (or "one second," I forget), since (my father argued) as a scientist, an astrophysicist, and thus someone in the habit of evaluating scales of numbers and measurements, she should have been in a better position to judge correctly.

Quite the contrary, answered my mother—my mother who'd never had much interest in the results of Olympic events (no more than in those of rugby teams) (much later, however, she did make a superhuman effort to remember the swimming times of my brother Pierre, and then, later still, those, even more brilliant, also in swimming, of her grandson François, son of her son, and my nephew)—quite the contrary, said my mother, more or less: what's a 100-meter dash for someone used to counting in light-years, someone who crosses entire galaxies in thought?

But still! my father repeated, to run 100 meters in one second would require a speed of 360 kilometers an hour, and to run it in one minute is something one can easily do by walking. Yes, absolutely, replied my mother, but why tire oneself working out such a calculation?

Why indeed?

I was very young when I became one of those people who know rather well the spatial or temporal limits reached thus far by runners, jumpers, and throwers from various countries. I watched the "symbolic barriers" fall: the four-minute mile, the 17-meter mark in the triple jump, and even the 6-meter mark in pole-vaulting. No less than the beauty of the great races themselves, such as Sebastian Coe's performances in the 800 meter, or the irresistible sufferings of Zatopek, which I rarely witnessed live, it is the enchanting profusion of numbers (results and rankings) that immediately attracted me to this world, and it was only recently that the obvious perversion of the sports "market"—with its procession of doping, cheating, and sponsorship that's been substituted for the old state-administered force-feeding—finally turned me away from it all.

One of my last great surprises as a spectator was when I saw a woman run the 100 meters in less than 11 seconds: I remembered that I had in fact witnessed (this must have been in 1943) a disputed race in the Carcassonne stadium (where I went more often for rugby matches). The winner (by a very wide margin) was the French champion at the time: a man named Valmy (a highly symbolic name in a time of war), who ran it (well short of his own record (10.5 seconds), it's true) in 10 and 9-tenths seconds.

Women's track and field, as we know, set off in pursuit of men's performances, and the gap between the two has continued to shrink (today the women's record for the 100 meters, that of Florence Griffith Joyner ("Flo Jo"), 10 seconds and 49 one-hundredths, only recently surpassed the French record set by Valmy a half a century ago). Which has recently led certain English researchers to extrapolate from the patterns of records, going back to the beginning, and announce (in *Nature* of course) that a woman will beat a man's world record (I did not note the discipline, but I believe it was a long-distance run, most likely the marathon) around 2028. I would indeed like to see that, if it should happen. But the commentator in the London *Times* was skeptical.

113 (§ 40) **A deeper harmony with one's body and with oneself**

For a long time I thought it possible to achieve this by mastering the high jump. It was my favorite event when I was a child. I aspired to the grasshopper's gift of pure release, having felt their anticipatory pressure in my palm when I held one down by force, pressing with my finger on its brown body. I watched the rubber cord oscillating between the two makeshift poles on the field, set at 1 meter 20 or 1 meter 30 above the sand pit, and I remembered, in the future anterior, the weight of my body in this sand, once the obstacle was overcome. At that point I was *"un athlète dans ma tête"* (an athlete in my head), as my Oulipian friend Paul Fournel says. But I lacked the elytra, blue or red, that I would have needed.

As the effect of some kind of punishment from the gods, or as an elementary lesson in destiny's inventiveness, it was precisely when doing the high jump that I had the second serious bodily accident of my life, out of four or five in all (this hesitation over the exact number comes not from forgetfulness but from an uncertainty about the status of the fourth one). The result was a fracture of the right wrist.

I see the moment very clearly. In other words, I can reconstruct it with such an intensity, such a force of inner conviction, that I say to myself, "that's it!" or "there it is!" I **see** the cinematic endpoint of the event, even though I no longer feel its pain. I unhesitatingly give it a title: Fracture of the (Right) Wrist.

But I should actually write: *second* fracture of the wrist. I can't see the instant at the end of my fall without also seeing another moment that appears to me immediately afterward, also containing the ending of an oblique fall to the ground. **I see the dirt very close, in the garden walkway leading to the washbasin; it is the walkway with the irises; hard iris roots run along the side, protruding just above the ground, and I land on top of one after a jump, or after tripping as I ran; I end up falling and I see with extreme clarity the hard and knotty arm of the iris root (I see that it is an iris, that's how it appears; but I do not see any flower) on which I am about to twist, to fracture my right wrist** (on which I twisted, fractured my right wrist).

During the "regular" hours of "gym" (as distinguished from the long solemn expeditions to the stadium, where the jumping pit was filled with sand), we would jump in the courtyard of the lycée itself. The set-up was extremely rudimentary, making use of metal poles that had been placed there without any athletics in mind: with the elastic cord stretched between them, we took a few steps back, ran, and jumped. We jumped "scissor" style. The "western roll" had just been invented, the "stomach roll" was as yet unknown, the Fosbury Flop was still in limbo. In any case, none of these sophisticated techniques would have been possible in that courtyard: we took off running and landed on cement.

And so, on that day, I jumped and landed poorly, on the cement. **I see it coming. I see the approach of the hard ground streaked with chalk. I also see, standing there** next to the pole (it is a concomitant but separate image), **my best friend at the time, Sicard, known as *Trois Demi*** (for his grade in the preparatory school for engineering). I never saw him again after our departure from Carcassonne (he died, he died young, or so I was told last year by other faces from those years, recognizable in the class photos, not really forgotten, not really remembered, remembered again when I saw them again).

114 (§ 41) The distant news of the war

The war was distant, its destruction far away, as were its dead, its bombings and arrests. Distant and near, it filled the air, filled everyone's mind, their conversations, their silences, their voices, near and far, especially the distant voices that reached us from *there*, brought by the radio. The emblematic music of the war was lodged in my head: the sign for "London" (as one said) was a long melodic fragment of Handel's *Water Music*.

I don't know if this melody was chosen with the intention one might be tempted to see in it: to speak to occupied France in a way that would unify Germany and England, the England of non-renunciation, the England that for one long year was the only thing standing between Hitler and his victory, and the old, civilized Germany—momentarily silenced—in the person of a German musician who had become an Englishman. (This is in any case the significance that I gleaned from it.) I heard it, that fragment, and the war was there. The war reached me through it, together with its future, a future freedom in peace. It was an optimistic voice, joyous and prophetic, announcing Liberation and abundance, the end of hunger.

In a sense, I never stopped hearing it. And I heard it in a way that was certain to make me remember it, as an inner voice, a voice that didn't rely on chance for me to hear it and that I did not have to seek out. It sang to me silently down the streets, from my house to the school, from the school to my house, with the *basso continuo* of the four winds kneeling on Davila Square.

I heard it silently and in silence, for I knew that it was strictly out of the question to sing that melody, to whistle it outside our walls. It was a forbidden melody, a clandestine melody that had to be camouflaged. We painted over it with the night-blue paint of silence.

It accompanied me in the streets turned dark and cold during the hungry winters—
the voice of the Thames in London, the voice of the Royal Navy, of the Royal Air Force,
coming over the Channel that Hitler's ships had failed to cross, just as Napoleon's had
(and I sensed that it was not by chance that my English professor, the jovial Mr. Charles,
gave us a writing exercise based on a paragraph describing the armada of landing craft
amassed by the emperor at Boulogne, for an invasion that was continually envisioned
and continually postponed: the theme was "flat-bottomed barges").

Sometimes, when the streets were empty, when no "enemy ears" were listening to me
from the windows, as I walked with my hands in my pockets (I liked to walk with my
hands in my pockets, my "pilgrim's jacket" over my shoulders, my beret on my head
(whenever I didn't forget it at the house or at school)), I whistled *Water Music*, and I
heard, with the shiver up the spine that music sometimes gives us when it takes control
of our emotions: "*Ici, Londres!*" ("London calling!").

(from chapter 6)

115 (§ 42) **My father set off down the road (on a bicycle) the day after June 6**

(From a "testimony" made by my father, recorded on tape on August 26, 1976, in La Tuilerie de Saint-Félix.)

—I remember, I had to meet some people out toward Quillan. I went to Narbonne first and I made the trip by bike, without taking the time to eat and without even finding a glass of wine in Les Corbières. I was going to meet with the leaders of the *maquis*. I was in the house of a royalist who gave me a place to stay, near the Narbonne train station.

Q: Why wasn't there any wine? Everyone was toasting the landing.

—I wanted some wine because I was starving. I'd left that morning without anything. I had to go sixty kilometers through the mountains, in Les Corbières, then in the Pyrenees, up a lot of hills. The police stopped me. I said to myself: I'll have these guys shot after the Liberation. This idea came into my head, I remember, because, well—to break your momentum when you're climbing a hill! Anyway, my stomach was empty, when I stopped in this village, I forget where, there was nothing, not even a glass of wine. You can't imagine the scarcity in that dry Southern landscape. Since then there have been two droughts worse than the one that year. In '44 I saw wheat only this high, little patches here and there.

This was after the landing—there were parts of the Auvergne region that had already been liberated, Aurillac was still in the hands of the Germans and the militia, Mauriac was free, and the trains were still running . . . with all that this meant in terms of possible provocateurs, spies, etc.

I should mention one thing that stayed with me, visually. I was in a train on the line through Auvergne. I had just verified that a certain other line had been blown up as planned. There were German soldiers coming from I don't know where. No doubt from Italy, on their way to the front in Normandy.

I was in a compartment, and this magnificent-looking German came in, a kind of Beethoven. He must have had some kind of high rank, but wasn't actually an officer. He started exhorting us all to rise up and fight against Anglo-American capitalism. It was absolutely extraordinary. (I had the very same feeling when I read *The Silence of the Sea* by Vercors.)

There were eight of us in the compartment. No one looked at him—it was as though he were speaking into a void. Later I ran into three of the people who were in the compartment. They all felt the same way: the man had been moving, full of conviction, a magnificent fellow. And it was true, Anglo-American capitalism was on its way. But Nazism, anti-capitalist? Just imagine, that guy with his noble air exhorting us in such a moving way, raging against how the French always disdain the grand causes, only ever interested in their own petty little problems . . .

116 (§ 44) **I'm not at all displeased to see the inner certainty of my numerological constancy confirmed**

I can even detect the seeds here of the most constant of the modes in which it later manifested itself: I noted, from the window of the car, not only the number of destroyed German tanks encountered in our chaotic progression toward Lyon, but also the distances to various cities, at that time precisely indicated by kilometer markers on the national and departmental highways (anticipating the next kilometric "message" with the help of the hundred-meter markers) (the fact that I was thus able to measure our approach to the city of Le Puy indicates that, at least on this road in the Haute-Loire *département*, unlike in other regions (where the markers along neglected departmental highways remained mute for quite a long time after the end of the war), these important signs had not been "camouflaged" at the time of the "phony war"—a futile effort along the same lines as the night-blue paint on our window panes).

I have remained interested in these "concrete numbers" punctuating the countryside ever since—these travelers' lookouts, these reassuring and familiar instruments for measuring and marking, for putting the world in order (on the well-kept roads, where the blacktop has no cracks or ruts, the black paint of their uniform calligraphy was clear, legible, clean: I purposely say "was" because I've noticed that they are disappearing. They're growing old, falling over, coming loose, like rotten teeth with muddy roots lining the jaws of the roads. They're disappearing into the grass, into ditches, and are not being replaced).

They bore witness to a time when the roads were not reserved for the exclusive use of one kind of vehicle, when the beautiful black ribbons of the roadways (shimmering, traversed by snails in the rain, doused with receding mirages of puddles in the intense summer heat), lovingly cared for, "kept up" by the Department of Highways (for which our friend Paul Geniet was an engineer), had not yet been taken over entirely and exclusively by motorized vehicles, as they are today.

There were pedestrians, cyclists, horse-drawn carts, and, yes, even automobiles, back when their drivers—not yet perverted by the corrupting power conferred on them by the so-called "market" economy—still felt an obligation to share the road (and had the decency to avoid the hedgehogs)—all of whom needed the episodic but friendly presence of the markers, as reinforcement and confirmation of the maps. The roads were conceived on a human scale, if I may put it that way: primarily, that is, for a human on foot (and secondarily for one on a bike), who alone could appreciate the fact, in its proper proportion, that Villegly was 2 kilometers and 3 hectometers, or that Bagnoles was 0.625 kilometers away (a measurement that only recently disappeared from the blue metal sign at the crossroads)!

At sea level (let's take a theoretical example) a walker, or a cyclist, halting and placing his feet on the gravel on the side of the road, feeling the ground suddenly and bizarrely immobile, would sit down on the parapet next to the marker with its red top (which is all one could perceive from above, winding down from one sharp turn to another during a climb). And it confided to him (I refuse to write "informed," for it provided something more important, more intimate than a mere piece of information) that the village church, in the valley down below, was 3.4 kilometers away, which allowed him to precisely judge the amount of time still separating him from the glass of shandy waiting for him under the lime tree, at the round metal table of the café. But all these small exact decimal numbers are useless, even offensive, to the trucks, the Mercedes, the Volvos.

(On the highways, a graceless set of measurements, technical and functional, designed exclusively for the purpose of providing information to police, tow trucks, and ambulances, can hardly be of any use for a car-passenger like me (when by chance I am dragged into this role by the force of circumstances), except to help me verify, out of the corner of my eye, in silence, that my driver has exceeded the speed limit) (Highway 61, which I followed down along the Mississippi in 1976, has only miniscule green metal signs signaling every mile (one can hardly compare them to the concrete markers I'm describing), and it took me some time to get used to this (during the first days of the trip, the road seemed much longer to me than it was in reality).)

117 (continuation of § 116) **Cities naturally lack any internal distance markers**

Cities naturally lack any internal distance markers, except (here too) along the highways that pass through them. There was a time when I could follow the progression of these roads (the road to Narbonne, to Toulouse, to Montréal . . .) as they entered Carcassonne, and I particularly liked the ones where the city proved its existence by the affirmation of a zero-distance to itself (also a proof of its importance, for it avoided the humiliation of the outlying towns that represent only a hierarchically lower stage along the road and which quite simply disappear from the markers as soon as one is passing through them). The city was not, therefore, completely isolated—cut off from those civilized itineraries traced out on the face of the world. But in 1945 I vainly searched for such reassuring signs in Paris. Which meant that I had to invent other systems for the rhythmic punctuation of my steps.

In cities one can follow the numbers on houses, the different progressions of evens and odds. There are some minimal streets, like the Rue de l'Abbé-Migne, which has only a single number, that of the Blancs-Manteaux Church (are there streets without numbers? can they still be called streets?); others, on the contrary, are so long that their numbers rise far beyond 100 (the Rue de Vaugirard was the first one to impress me with its interminable series). When one wants to know where one is on a long street, when one wishes to arrive at a given number: this is when it is most important to know the golden rule of French address numbers (I have remarked with stupefaction that a good number of my friends and acquaintances don't know it!): **the odd numbers are on the left as the numbers increase**. This means that if (for example) from perpendicular street X one comes out at number 101 on street Y, and if one is looking, say, for number 37 (and if other numbers are not immediately visible), one must place oneself, mentally, on the sidewalk next to 101, with number 101 on one's left, and move backward toward number 37 (or else turn around and move facing the other direction, if one doesn't want to be stared at, or risk unwanted collisions).

(This rule, which I learned from my grandfather, is much more reliable than the one that says that the numbers begin at the point on the street closest to the Seine. For one must admit that the relative positions of the Seine and the street one is on are not, in general, glaringly obvious. What's more, my rule is valid in all the cities of France, even the ones which the Seine doesn't flow through (I only know of one exception: Caunes-Minervois, in the Aude, where a unique numbering system applies to all the houses, which is itself of great interest. Fortunately for the traveler or novice postal worker, Caunes—famous for its marble: in color and appearance rather more like mortadella than the white "Carrara" variety of stone—is modestly sized).

One could certainly criticize the uniformity of this system, its centralizing and "Jacobin" quality, or one could compare it unfavorably with the well-known inventive eccentricity of the streets of London (whose charms I fully appreciate). The rule nonetheless lends itself quite favorably to numerological comparisons, which is not a negligible factor for an inveterate pedestrian like myself. My rule is easy to remember. Especially if one takes note of the fact that it is based on the ancestral association, etymological and derogatory, between left (*gauche*: "awkward," "clumsy," even "sinister") and odd (*impair*: a blunder or a faux pas that one must not commit), as opposed to the moral uprightness of right, natural partner of the noble even (*pair*: in the sense of "*pair de France*," a "peer of France" (rather than in the sense of an "au pair")). Like the punctuation of the roads and highways by the stone kilometer markers, the numbering system used in French cities (and in Europe in general) is humanist in scope: that is, it was conceived on the scale of the pedestrian. It proceeds number by number, house by house (even sometimes dawdling into the occasional "*bis*" or "*ter*" (I don't seem to recall ever seeing a "*quater*," which provides a supplementary proof of the correctness of the TAR(M,m) (Theory of Abstract Rhythm (Metaphysical and mathematized) originated by Pierre Lusson; its cornerstone is the minimal theory known as the "2–3 Theory")) (in certain streets, however, the replacement of the older houses by luxury apartment buildings or low-income housing projects, as the case may be, has sometimes condensed the old numbers, creating such hybrids as "10–18," "17–31," or "14–30," with very unfortunate effects, in my opinion)).

Unlike the American system, then, it never becomes a matter of numbering by "blocks," inspired by an automobilistic way of thinking (even if it existed before the automobile, which I can't say for sure. If so, I would say that it was "automobilistic *avant la lettre*," or even—a much more audacious theory—that such thinking was *responsible* for the rise of the automobile), with the fantastically high numbers on Sunset Boulevard, for example, which stupefied me in 1960 when Bernard Jaulin and I ended up in Los Angeles for an investigation into the emergent forms of artificial intelligence, and I found myself in a hotel in Pacific Palisades, close to the ocean and not to Hollywood, as I had thought (moreover, to reach the seashore, just around the corner, we had to take a car; it was impossible to cross the road because of the ceaseless and uninterrupted traffic, with no red light anywhere to stop it. This was what one calls "culture shock").

At the extreme opposite from the New World (since the malady of excessive numbering extends to the entire continent, as I learned not only from my grandmother in 1942, but also shortly after the war when I wanted to write to Sylvia in Buenos Aires in 1946, and found that her address was "Posadas 1415"), I recently discovered, during a brief stay in Florence, a system of great interest and subtlety: the system of "double numbering." There are blue numbers (for residences, I was told) and red numbers (used for shops and administrative spaces (?)). In the presence of such riches (delightful sources of speculation, adventurous wandering, confusion), the pleasure of an aimless stroll is likewise doubled. I would gladly locate the origin of this distinction in the opposition, at the time of Savonarola, Machiavelli, and the Medicis, between the "little people" and the *popolo grasso*, of which this system would be a "monumentary" trace, in a sense that has been forgotten today.

118 (second continuation of § 116) **In the cities and on the roads, my most intimate enemy is the automobile**

In the cities and on the roads, my most intimate enemy, the adversary of my entire adult life as a pedestrian, is the automobile: particularly the motor vehicles (regardless of type) that clog Paris (except the buses, which I venerate). I have very few weapons to utilize against them, it's true. But with what inner triumphs, as I wend my way through their graceless metallic forms randomly dumped along the sidewalks, do I contemplate the enormous traffic jams of which our capital is so proud. With a few vague ideas gleaned from medicine and fluid mechanics floating through my head, I await the embolism of the Parisian arteries or the great and final absolute freezing of all local traffic (respectively); which, since it would be more pleasant for spectators, I would prefer to see happen some spring afternoon.

For the moment, however, I occasionally content myself with adding new couplets to a song I'm composing (sung to the tune of the popular song *Buvons un coup, buvons en deux* (Let's drink a glass, oh let's drink two)). Here is the refrain:

> *Hymne des automobilistes parisiens*
> *Brûlons un feu, brûlons en deux*
> *Pour n'pas rater les petits vieux*
> *A la santé des Pompes funèbres*
> *Et merde pour ces con de piétons*
> *A qui la guerre nous déclarons!*

Hymn of the Parisian Motorists
Let's run a red light, oh let's run two
So we won't miss the old folks
Let's drink to the funeral homes
And to hell with those bastards on foot
On whom we have declared war!

Until recently I felt infinitely better in London, where drivers spontaneously stop at the protected pedestrian crosswalks (and where, for the sake of the continentals, the direction of oncoming traffic is indicated: *look right, look left*). But during my most recent visits I detected some worrisome signs of contagion there. And what will happen when Parisian motorists infiltrate London, entering like a virus through the open pathway of the catastrophic channel tunnel, and begin to fan out across the island?

On our journey to the USA in the summer of '87, Marie, Charlotte, and I saw yet another tradition at work: the legendary calmness and courtesy of Southern California drivers. Charlotte was fifteen years old (ancient history!). In the hotel—the Inn by the Sea in La Jolla—she and Marie would go up and down in the elevator with its star-specked glass wall. They ordered pancakes and orange juice from room service at all hours, and then, when they consented to abandon these exalted pastimes, they dragged me down to the edge of the Pacific for a few hours of "boogie-boarding." Lying on these planks turned sideways, they were swallowed up, stirred around, and sent flying by a gentle slap from the weary gray waves of the ocean, which seemed to be expending only a tiny part of its might for these amusements; but Charlotte and Marie never tired of this little exercise. (I was unable to find even the slightest point in common between this implicitly enormous body of water and the shimmering blue-green eye of my Mediterranean, as seen from Toulon in 1942.) To go to the beach, they had invented a route with a "shortcut," a descent (and a re-ascent!) down (and back up) a series of unpleasant stairways that, more than anything, were clogged with forbidding garbage cans from the countless restaurants behind which they were stationed: I called it the "Stinking Freeway." To get to it from the hotel, one had to cross the coastal avenue, the main street in La Jolla (there I found the bookstore where I bought the crime novels that I read on the burning hot sand—my head covered by a bath towel—during the boogie-board hours). Charlotte, tanned in her T-shirt and wearing the elegant silky white Bermuda shorts of the California girl she had momentarily become, had invented a game. It was a game designed for a young lady and some passing automobiles: she stepped resolutely onto the pavement of the street, immediately bringing to a stop, out of the pure conventions of courtesy, and at a distance of at least four paces, the immense cars that were rolling down the "Boulevard" as powerfully, slowly, and lazily as the waves in the Pacific. She serenely, sovereignly walked across the street at an angle; then, having arrived at the other side, set out again in the other direction, thus proceeding in zigzags all the way to the stinking stairway, with occasional stops for ice cream or postcards, scissoring her way thus, angle by angle, through the languid summertime traffic. And not a single person yelled at her. (This reminded me of our discovery (I say "our," but this time I'm referring to my brothers and sister and myself. As Charlotte and Marie would say: "We weren't even born yet!"), in 1945, of the mechanical stairs in the Paris metro, with their patient and placid red eye; I recall how amusing it was to set them in motion with a stamp of the foot (as we hadn't quite grasped the role of the electric eye yet), like Kipling's butterfly (reread "The Butterfly that Stamped" in Kipling's *Just So Stories*) or Ali Baba at the entrance to his cave, during the slow hours (of the metro, not the cave).)

But let us return to the sad destiny of the Parisian pedestrian. In order to exorcise the unpleasant presence of cars, to dominate them magically, I sometimes indulge (especially during anxious times) in numerological games. This obliges me (a certain "use value" of this small coin of reverie: prudence) not to lose sight of the presence of the cars, their erratic and hostile movements. These games focus on the numbers found on license plates. For example, I used to try to find numbers that came as close as possible, in one day, to the number 9,999 (maximum) or to the number 1 (minimum). Since it took quite some time for me to approach these limits (as is easily shown by a simple statistical calculation), the numbers located in the first or last tens had to be considered as honorable "performances." But the proliferation of license plate numbers (a sign of the progress of the urban metastasis) led, in certain *départements* and particularly in Paris (the "75" plates), to replacing the usual two letters in the middle of the plate with three, and simultaneously to reducing the number of digits (this was no doubt done, following the experimental psychology of the nineteenth century—which claimed that it's more difficult to remember sequences of more than seven signs (the "75" being taken globally, as a single sign)—so that police or traffic cops could more easily identify the plates in case of a code violation or in a search for stolen vehicles and/or vehicles harboring criminals). But to look for a 999 out of 1000 possible numbers (or a 1) is no more than mildly interesting (since one sees so many cars on a single trip from the ninth arrondissement to the fourth, for example).

I therefore changed the orientation of my game, giving it a very different principle, closer to "life": now, as I move about, I look particularly for the most recent license plate numbers. This allows me to follow the fatal progression of the invasion of the streets. (I began in March 1991, when the trio of letters had reached JJJ. As of today, the nineteenth of September, nineteen hundred and ninety-one (a palindromic date, as today's *Times* of London correctly remarked), my "record" is "15 JNS 75" (which means that more than 100,000 new cars have been vomited onto Paris in the last six months (each change in the third letter representing 1,000 cars; each change in the second being 22,000 (22,000 and not 26,000, for *I*s and *O*s never appear among the possible trios of letters, since they would cause confusion between letters and numbers, just like *Q*s and *U*s (as Marie pointed out to me), though I don't really see why) (the figure of 22,000 is itself only an approximation, since certain triads of letters can be eliminated for extra-numerical reasons: it seems to me that (even if *U*s were used) there could never be a license plate number that reads CUL (ass) on the rear end of a car, regardless of what a recent ad implied with a crudeness & sliminess very much in line with the general evolution of what Renaud Camus calls the "manners of the times." (The elimination of the word CON (asshole) having been assured by the banning of O and I. I don't know if there are any other "bans.")

(My attention having thus been drawn to groups of "meaningful" letters, I conceived a project: a series of short films (each a minute long at the most). For example: a car stops in front of a factory. We see the letters on its license plate. It reads: JAM. Then one sees that it's a factory that makes preserves. The car takes off. It drives onto a highway and ends up in an immense traffic jam, in which all the cars bear the same letters, JAM. It would be a visual pun that crosses French and English—a nice touch. (One could also treat the same theme as a dream narrative, or in a short story.)))))) (if I'm not mistaken, I opened six embedded parentheses, which I had to close at the same time).

119 (§ 44) Somewhere I still have the chronological "framework" of these images

These dates have of course been imprinted in the collective memory: June 6, 1944, the days of that August (the Liberation of Paris, of Montpellier). Even without my grandfather's notebooks and the few bits of my own correspondence that I've found, it wasn't difficult for me to "place" my image-memories of the journey, and of Lyon, in certain very precise "sites of memory," or on certain "floors" of the chronological "elevator to the past" that I possess somewhere (here I'm using an image borrowed from a novel by Isaac

Asimov, *The End of Eternity*: as though these image-memories, mysteriously associated in the brain, each possessed a sort of more or less exact numerical sign (which is also how Robert Hooke conceives them, in his beautiful representation of the mechanism of memory, from around 1680). (The most ancient image-memories almost never have this property.))

One can easily situate ordinary historical events (if they aren't too distant) in relation to the important dates of our own lives (albeit with strange displacements, sometimes). It's clear that, for me, the departure from the Rue d'Assas was just such a date. The years in Carcassonne are enclosed in a time capsule, are a discreet compartment of life, strictly localized in space-time: we are thus like snails inside the space-time shell that a family house becomes for those who lived in it (and it's our memory that allows us to carry it around with us). (But we're also hermit crabs, sometimes, moving into new dwellings, as though stolen from their previous inhabitants (thus do cities behave—even civilizations—arriving one after another on the same points of the earth's surface where they are superimposed like layers of wallpaper). All this is self-evident.)

But one might also use less important events to situate moments in our own lives: such as the change in paper sizes (the shift from 21 cm x 27 cm (the French paper size during my youth) to 21 x 29.7 (the American size). I experienced this as a sort of trauma of writing, and, having discovered the current more "oblong" format during my stay in the US in 1970, I therefore "date" this shift, this traumatizing deformation of the space of the page, as occurring on my return to Paris in May of that year (this may or may not correspond to reality—it hardly matters. In any case, it took me several years to feel at ease again on paper (paper for poetry, not for mathematics; mathematics is hardly affected by these considerations), and the book that I wrote in 1972, *31 au cube*, is in an impossible "format," a compensatory format, forcing the poems to stretch horizontally across two pages. This justification of its "metrics" escaped me at the time).

I have other examples in my memories, which I will present in their time. But, as with the events of History, this phenomena is always a question of an involuntary and contingent scansion. I tell myself that I should have taken note of other examples, deliberately, as a way to mark the punctuation of time, and to populate the vast theater of memory that is life (but no doubt it's much too late for this now, given my age).

Today (nonetheless), I am trying to do it in a deliberate fashion: I note, and mentally insist on the fact (for example) that I've just now discovered how ordinary letters, after the last rate increase, now require an entirely new type of stamp (at least provisionally):

regular stamps are worth 2 francs 50, but the amount isn't marked on the stamp itself anymore, as it's always been up to now. There's only a letter, a *D* (capitalized). (I indicate these things, which are obvious and familiar as I write at present, but which might become obscure in the future, out of politeness to possible distant readers.) I give this fact a date, conventional as it is, and easy for my memory to retain, the palindromic date 19.9.1991. There will be, if everything goes as expected, a "before" and an "after" for this event: the appearance of a postage stamp not marked with its price. (Thus imitating, by analogy, the tickets for the metro. The goal, if this way of doing things continues, is likely the same in both cases: to avoid having to print new stamps with each increase (perhaps in an attempt to render these less visible).) (If this practice is in fact only a temporary expedient, which is likely, I hereby offer this idea to the administration, free of charge.)

For the sake of simplification and reinforcement, I'll also associate another "innovation" with this particular stamp: self-adhesiveness. This gives the stamp a slightly nostalgic tinge: it lacks the charm of perforated edges, which were themselves a decisive innovation in their day, but weren't present on the first stamp to be marked with a price, the preeminent model of the modern stamp (and the history of the stamp is dear to me, since it's indissolubly linked to the life of one of my favorite novelists, Anthony Trollope): I'm referring to the "Penny Black," showing the effigy of the young Queen Victoria, and issued in 1840 (it's so valuable that there are innumerable counterfeits. However, the London *Times* recently announced that, in a "European" spirit, and to facilitate the imminent elimination of customs barriers in the countries of the European Economic Community, it would henceforth be legal to enter England carrying fake stamps on one's person, or in one's vehicle. Now that is reassuring).

120 (§ 45) he promptly led me off to another, whose schedule he'd also noted (a sign of premeditation?)

This was an almost orgiastic excess, an apparently unhygienic debauchery of films (especially for the visual apparatus, which was certainly put in danger by the poor quality of the images: their flickerings, their palpitations). I say "apparently" unhygienic because my grandfather had a theory of necessary excess, a concept that played a role somewhat like that of the *clinamen*—the rare and regulated violation of a constraint—in the theory of the axiomatically restricted writings of Oulipo. Thus, after spending the entire week, when he was alone, content with eating boiled potatoes topped by a tiny dab of butter, on Saturday he would open a can of *William Saurin* cassoulet or sauerkraut and conscientiously eat the entire thing. (It still makes my father shudder just to think of it.) His impatient desire to hurl himself into those darkened rooms also arose, no doubt, from a need to "catch up," and was an attempt to take advantage of our newfound liberty in order to wipe away the cumulative privations of the preceding years.

Yet he had been slow to warm to the cinema. He was a very recent convert to the charms of the seventh art. For a long time, he had answered the "modernist" arguments of my family with an unshakable and impeccably argued conviction that the cinema was no more than a second-rate entertainment. Then, in opposition to this infatuation with novelty, he asserted the millennial and rational hierarchy of the arts, with much the same conviction as his own father had shown in a previous age (according to my grandmother's gently mocking story), when he struck his fist on the table proclaiming: "No, man will never fly! Nothing heavier than air can ever triumph over weight itself!" It was Charles Chaplin (and, rather than "Charlot," the Chaplin of *City Lights*, *The Gold Rush*, and later *The Great Dictator*) who converted him to the cinema, and, from there, in a natural progression, my grandfather soon came to enjoy "mysteries" and "American comedies," not to mention Westerns, much to my joy.

It wasn't until the following year, during the summer of 1945, when the choice of films finally became more abundant, that I finally saw the "American comedies" so vaunted, in nostalgic tones, by the adults I knew. I admired Gary Cooper in *Bluebeard's Eighth Wife* or *Mr. Deeds Goes to Town* (less as a tuba player, in the latter, than as a fashioner of rhymes (proof of an undeniable extravagance (as indicated in the French title, *L'Extravagant Mr. Deeds*) of which I myself was guilty), and out of a natural sympathy for the two eccentric old ladies who reveal to him (as to the rest of humanity) the excellent adjective *pixilated* (which was translated, in the dubbing, I don't really know why, as "*pince-corné*")). And I began a long and unending love affair with Katharine Hepburn. By this time I was already choosing the films myself, and going to the theater by myself, a habit (perilous to one's studies) that I picked up again later, during my student years, when the Cinémathèque was housed in the Musée Pédagogique, Rue d'Ulm, dangerously close to the Institut Henri-Poincaré.

Seeing Charles Chaplin on the screen gave me a sense of "déja vu" (without diminishing the pleasure of viewing). Since we already knew the great sentimental moments in *The Circus* or *City Lights* "by heart." Grandma was shockingly Chaplinesque, partly from a conviction that was at once aesthetic, ethical, and political, but also from the spontaneous sympathy between fellow storytellers and mimes. I must say, the bits of his she chose to imitate, the ones she really did best—like her imitation of "Charlot's" farewell in *The Pilgrim*, with one foot on each side of the U.S.-Mexican border—or of the troubles he encounters, dressed as a clergyman, with a naughty little boy sitting in his mother's arms—seemed almost better than the originals, to us.

But it was particularly the moments that evoked our situation as children living during a war and its privations that made the greatest impression. No doubt also because, in reconstructing them, my grandmother showed a more confident conviction than she would in the merely comic ones: the scene of the "spaghetti shoelaces" followed by the "roast chicken hallucination" in *The Gold Rush*, for example (with the advantage of frequent and limitless repetitions, which the cinema, similar to the theater in this respect, was practically incapable of before the invention of video) (this was until very recently one of the major advantages peculiar to reading—a fact that doesn't bode well for the future of the book); or else when "Hitler" and "Mussolini" try to outdo each other, cranking up their barber chairs in *The Great Dictator* (a film that she'd had the unheard-of privilege of seeing while in the United States).

Upon arriving in Paris we discovered the extraordinary "*petits* Charlots," short masterpieces only a few minutes in length, and we did so in the most luxurious conditions possible for a spectator, which I've never experienced since (at least before video—which, nonetheless, I rarely use—rendered this mode of viewing banal): our friend Harnois, a true Parisian and a lover of innovations had a projector in his home, and he owned a great many films of this type: *Police* and *The Cure*, of course, but also some "Buster Keatons" and, last but not least (whatever the purists may think), an extensive selection of the adventures of Stan Laurel and Oliver Hardy.

121 (§ 47) **This seemed intolerable and unforgivable to my father**
(continuation of § 115: a testimony from my father)

Q: When you were asked to enter the Consultative Assembly, you were offered a more political position than you were used to—though not exactly the position of a politician. What sort of debate did this provoke for you?

—A very short debate. I said to Chambrun [Gilbert de Chambrun was the military leader of the Languedoc region's MLN, of which my father was the "civil" director], "No, it should be you." He said: "No, it should be you," etc. And since he was more stubborn than I was, and was lucky enough to be involved in some kind of military thing, and also because afterward he was going to be a deputy, I went.

—Did it upset you very much?

—Tremendously. I saw de Gaulle's tactic, which consisted of dividing the Resistance against itself. This man who was supposedly against the parties—at least for a moment—did everything he could to prevent the unity of the Resistance. And yet, when I was in the Resistance, I was very Gaullist. Without ever reading any of his books, mind you. It was at that point, in Paris, that I read some of de Gaulle's books—someone gave me *Assemblée consultative, Au fil de l'épée* (The Edge of the Sword), *Vers l'armée de métier* (Toward a Professional Army). I don't have an easygoing temperament. When I read his defense of the people who had seen fit to crush the Commune, I felt my grandfather rising up in me.

I almost resigned after a little while, but it didn't last very long anyway. It was made known to me that I was going to be replaced by someone in the new majority of the MLN, some fellow named Baumel. I lost all faith in Malraux in one blow when I saw him intervene, as a politician, in a Management Committee. Parliamentary life was extremely simple. There was no intervention, it was purely consultative. I understood very quickly that it was nothing but a trompe l'oeil.

—Around the same time, as part of the Consultative Assembly, you were called to be on a High-Court jury?

—I was called as a juror on the High Court for the trial of Admiral Esteva.

—You took part in the Esteva trial, and witnessed the Pétain trial?

—I had an entry permit that allowed me to sit in the audience at the Pétain trial.

—But you were recused in the Pétain trial?

—Yes, I was on the jury in the Esteva trial, but after that I was told, no, you won't be included. I found out, I forget from whom, that I had been recused.

I was disgusted at the way the Pétain trial was conducted. First, they minimized it as much as possible, locating it in a small, side courtroom, as though it were for some ordinary criminal trial. The room and the attendees had probably been carefully "fixed," I don't know how. There was a certain Montgibeau among the judges who did a lot of hand-waving and made every effort to bypass the most serious accusations. And then the people who were questioned weren't really allowed to speak. For example, with Darnand there was a prodigious sleight of hand. Darnand had a lot to say, he certainly did, Joseph Darnand. He was summoned to appear, and one of the judges said to the jury: "Of course we won't be asking a killer any questions." So the jurors didn't ask any questions. [I can see why my father was recused for this trial.]

They could have asked questions, but you have to understand how the judges manipulated people. I'd already seen it in the Esteva trial, there was a majority of jurors who said: "No, we mustn't condemn him to death. He's a good Christian." For my part, I pointed out that we were already shooting people who had fought against the Free French, and I didn't see why the ones who'd actually given the order should be saved.

122 (§ 47) Fragments from a "Treatise on Disputes" (*De Querelis*) from 1946.

25.1 (1) A dispute is an evil.

25.1 (2) A dispute is all the more violent when the wrongs under dispute are shared by a greater number of people.

25.1 (3) Disputes do not leave the family sphere.

25.1 (4) With strangers they are always "childish." Neither party knows the other well enough for anything more.

25.1 (5) Often one dares not go too far either because of one's parents or because there are no "authorities" present capable of judging the conflict.

25.1 (6) Conflicts do not often exist, or they are amicably settled.

25.1 (7) One must always show special consideration to strangers.

25.1 (8) Thus our disputes with the boys in the street were settled with water fights and rock fights. Our disputes were not deep and bitter because there was no long-term "disagreement."

25.1 (9) The deeper the disagreement, the more things get fueled, the more serious the dispute.

(10) Disputes result from a more or less profound knowledge of others. They help us to know ourselves and are based on this knowledge.

(11) They arouse in us an instinct for lying and dissimulation.

(12) Indeed, any mistake whatever (a broken dish, bedwetting, insolence toward authority figures, mstks in the classroom or at home) can fuel the attack against us, awakening old quarrels.

(13) Disputes cannot be suppressed. A dispute that is not completely settled (which is the case 8 out of 10 times), that is, if the discontent is not extinguished on both sides, will engender another, consciously or unconsciously.

(14) However, it is not <u>possible</u> for a dispute to be absolutely settled.

(15) The wrongs are always shared. An investigation that pronounces one party in the right, if the scale tips favorably in his direction, will place him on extremely unstable ground. The other party will harbor resentment and will avenge himself sooner or later.

(16) One always has smthg with which to reproach oneself.

(17) One always has sm evident faults.

<u>Types of dispute</u>

(18) Disputes are essent'ly varied. We must distinguish between: 1) our disputes; 2) disputes with semi-strangers; 3) with strangers (see 4 through 8).

(19) Let us eliminate strangers.

Disputes are limited mst oftn to blows or insults. These insults have no real force. They do not strike one's self-regard.

(20) In a dispute, the disagreement becomes venomous when one's self-regard receives a blow. The latter thus determines evrythg.

(21) I would even say, as a definition of "our" disputes, that in all of these, each party attempts to hurt the other.

(22) When you hurt smone, you have won a round in the battle but this victory "will cost you."

(23) An outraged disputant is more dangerous when he hides his feelings than when he indulges in visible outbursts.

(24) Disputes with strangers are upsetting but do not hit home. From personal experience, I can note that out of nine such disputes my self-regard was harmed only once.

<u>Semi-strangers</u>.

(25) These are already more serious.

(26) A 1/2 stranger is a friend, a cousin, or someone you know fairly well.

(27) These disputes (I mean between cousins in Carc.) are mch more serious:

1) We have greater bonds between us. Thus in Carc. we saw one another almost evry day.

2) One result of this is that we know each other better or believe we do.

The same insults that (19) would not have struck us, in this case hit home more and more effectively.

(28) We do not fear someone, we do not fight with him, when we believe or know that he does not know us.

(29) An insult coming from smone you know is more intolerable than one coming from a stranger.

(30) With a stranger, one retreats into oneself, into one's incognito. One answers with blows, with contempt, or with silence. With someone you know your sensitivity is heightened.

(31) We do not want to and cannot settle our battles by turning them into fistfights.

(31)*bis* Perhaps because the disparities in strength are too great, bt esp because they give no satisfaction, because we're afraid of being punished, because we are all more or less in the wrong, for these reasons there are fights that go no further than name-calling.

(32) Disputes between ourslvs and the people we know are more important also because:

3) (this case is particular to us) it is oftn a q of our prestige. It happens that my cousin Jean is 14 and I am 13, my cousin Juliette is 12 and my sister is 10, Pierrot is 10 and Pierrot R is 9. Thus we correspond roughly in age, therefore we oppose each other. And there is a 4th reason:

4) My cousins are naturally given to mockery, and we are susceptible; which makes the situation ripe for conflict.

Finally, 5) There are rivalries and preferences btwn us. It has happened very oftn, in the general disputes, that the boys find themselves in conflict with the girls or that the older ones, in their conflicts among themselves, make use of the younger ones taking their side in their conflicts, which allows them to attack each other more easily.

(33) As fr me I esp supported Nanet, Denise, and P.M., but Jeannot supports Nanet and Pierrot.

(34) Consequences: these disputes oftn resulted in particular fault lines. Indeed, forgetting our quarrels as soon as our cousins left the garden to go home for an afternoon snack, we made up and blamed everything on the latter. They in any case did the same.

(35) to (25) and (18) Adding people one knows to semi-strangers.

123 (continuation of § 122) **General Plan: 26 January**

(47) General plan: 26 January

Book I: Quarrels and Disputes

[. . .]

(70) I will now begin the main part of this work: "Our Disputes" (see (47)).

(71) Our disputes often result from fundamental origins and causes.

(72) We have already seen (see (13)) that disputes cannot be suppressed. This impossibility is therefore the 1st cause of their existence.

(73) A 2nd cause is (14) that one can never completely settle a dispute. One dispute will sooner or later engender another.

(74) As a 3rd cause there is the fact that we are all constantly together. Indeed, in the course of a day we spend from 5 to 9 hrs together. How much time does this provide for disputes?

(75) 4th cause. Differences in age and in character (see chs. 9 and 10).

(76) 5th cause. Our circumstances have lent themselves to disputes and have favored them.

(77) Indeed, evnts have alwys prevented a solid parental power that might allow for a struggle *against* disputes.

[. . .]

(79) In Carc. Papa's departure from the house and Mama's fatigue from "overwork."

(80) Things are still more or less the same. 1) Papa is very oftn out of the house. 2) Mama is still tired and overworked. 3) The habit sets in.

(81) There are also special circumstances: the cold and the lack of heating here force us to stay together in the same room. When we are no longer doing our work, how will we play, how will we relax? And there you have a new source of disputes.

(82) Boredom is a source of quarrels.

(83) As is life in an apartm.

(84) The 6th cause seems obvious: the number of children. There are 4 of us, which makes it difficult to get along. There's something good to eat? Better leap on it immediately. "P. got more than me, it's not fair." Response: "That's not true." Yet another dispute. Another source.

(86) Whence this jealousy? Unfortunately, it comes from the restrictions. It was the scarcity of good things to eat that gave rise to it, intensified it and made it take root.

[...]

(88) I see no other causes, for the moment. But for now I can draw certain conclusions. The disappearance of disputes can never be complete. However, some of their sources can be avoided. a) the circumstances; b) boredom; c) perhaps also jealousy. Only one way to fulfill this hope: St. Germain. All my hopes lay with St. Germain. May they not be disappointed.

(89) Despite myself, I encourage the disputes. I am disgusted with everything: school, life at home, everything. I no longer have any motivation to learn, not even to read, not even to play. I feel this without being able to fight against it. I want to, but I don't have the strength for it. This worries me.

(90) This digression has taken me slightly away from my theme. I wander rather out of indulgence than out of negligence. And yet it is still relevant to my subject. The disputes and this mental state are closely related.

(91) I influence, I have a great deal of influence on the disputes, sometimes for the worse.

124 (second continuation of § 122) **I must note here, of course, a recurrent and fatal feature of my self-portrait**

I must note here, of course, something like a recurrent and fatal feature of my self-portrait, namely the lack of perseverance that I show in this kind of composition project. No sooner have I begun than I grow tired. And all the future modalities of this malady are clearly present: the moment my enthusiasm for sustained effort wanes, I try to remedy it by laying out plans. In the case of my "treatise," the hypertrophy of its goals already threatens its continuation, and this on the second day of composition. I always notice this myself, at such moments. But no amount of lucidity on this point has ever cured me.

(101) So then let's not put it off. Let's return to a more matter-of-fact examination.

Jan. 27

(102) Further reflection has revealed another cause (see (88)). It depends in large part on the 5th one (see 76-81). It is perhaps even a different statement. This life in an apartment results in a general irritation. This irritation is therefore a source of disputes.

(103) I see that to attain greater clarity I will have to draw up a "technical" dictionary of disputes. This will forestall much confusion.

(104) The disputes have a real history. They go back very far. From this moment, January 27 10 A.M. I will scrupulously and impartially note all the quarrels in order to have a general view and to draw conclusions from them.

(105) I am for the moment therefore powerless to write this history.

[. . .]

January 28

(110) Certain acts, even if repeated often, appear heroic before being executed and facile afterward.

(111) St-Germain, 1st contact. The new is always captivating. The house is odd, the garden not bad. I am quite pleasntly surprised.

[. . .]

(118) Yesterday I had an interview with Denise. What did I learn from it? Nothing very important. I know that Denise keeps a journal. She didn't hide certain details from me, but I can't quite get to the bottom of the matter. I myself was also very

(119) A self-examination, an intimate discussion, inspire one to do good.

(120) Flame that does not last.

[. . .]

January 29

(125) This morning: 2 incidents only. Pierrot and Denise.

That's all. I don't think anything was lost.

I note again, as a new character trait already developing here, a distinct taste for putting things in order, for following a succession of written moments designated by numbers. It's there, unquestionably. I had imagined that I only picked up this predilection for writing in a progression of numbered fragments from Bourbaki's treatises of "harsh mathematics" (to quote Lautréamont), my passion at twenty, reinforced later perhaps by a reading of the *Tractatus*. But that's not at all the case. It was Latin history, perhaps, that served as my model (and I'm still rather glad that my inability to apply myself seriously to Greek prevented me from knowing Aristotle, or the Presocratics, at the time).

As a moralist, the author of this "Treatise on Disputes" locates himself, without illusions, along descriptive, taxonomic lines. There is little "milk of human kindness" or natural goodness among those quarrelsome children, to whom I belonged. An English novel of the '20s, *A High Wind in Jamaica*, by Richard Hughes (far superior to William Golding's heavy-handed, syrupy, and ponderously symbolic piece of plagiarism, *Lord of the Flies*) was, to my knowledge, the first to present an unsentimental and unembellished portrait of a society of children. I read it without surprise.

I see, in the end, that nostalgia is already there in my "Treatise" as well, implicit: never again will there be any occasion to fight, nor, therefore, to play, in the garden in Carcassonne.

125 (§ 48) **These kisses continually set fire to my imagination**

This interpolation is not quite like the others: it's not simply a digression introduced into the course of the story. It's inflective, rather—or corrective. The way I presented Antoinette and my respective positions in our relationship must be slightly inflected. I was a child (preadolescent) in love: essentially chaste, dreamy, and in fact without illusions. And Antoinette was engaged, she was in love with her shy and uncommunicative Spanish boy (whom she was to marry a few months later. By now she must be a grandmother many times over). I made her laugh, it's true, and it's also true that she didn't take my ardent declarations seriously, made as they were in a rather literary style.

Nevertheless, she did indeed let me kiss her exactly the way Tino Rossi kisses Viviane Romance in *The Kiss of Fire* (we saw this film so many times that I was able to study all its variations), and I took advantage of this authorization as often as possible. I remember that one day, when I was kissing her in the laundry house (among the firewood), we were surprised by my grandfather, who made no comment (contenting himself with shrugging his shoulders up beneath his hat, as he always did when faced with something out of the ordinary), and as far as I can tell he never denounced us. In any case, I never heard anyone speak of it. Neither did Antoinette, in fact, who continued to grant me the remarkable favor of letting me kiss her.

But that's not all. I've said that I often, at night, when my brother and sister were asleep, would leave our bedroom (the bedroom of chapter 1), go into hers, across the hall on the third floor, and slip into her bed. And there I not only kissed her again, I also learned to kiss her breasts, under her nightshirt—breasts whose transformations at those moments quite astonished me. My curiosity would gladly have led me toward other regions, but she always forbade it, keeping her rather austere underwear on in bed and responding to my vehement protests with these words: "You never know."

Which leads me to assume, now that I think of it, that she must not have had a terribly clear idea of the reality of certain phenomena that Tino's films left undisclosed (she refused to listen to my physiological explanations, which I had gleaned from the best sources available at the lycée, and that, to my mind, ought to have proved my utter innocuousness, reassured her completely, and persuaded her to allow me more extensive explorations). I also think that she had been so closely watched by her family and so constrained by the rigid rules of conduct imposed on her that she now found herself in a situation where it was impossible to indulge in the joys of a romantic kiss with her designated partner, her fiancé; but also where, in her ignorance, she felt herself moderately attracted, nonetheless, to the physical prospects of marriage. In sum, I was a sort of sparring partner in love. And I made her laugh.

In Paris, she became friends with the maid from the apartment next door (the "service" entrances were across from one another on the stairway designated with the same word), who was four or five years older than she, a pretty woman well acquainted with short skirts and make-up (she even put some around her eyes), and without any doubt perfectly informed about all these mysteries. She gave me condescending looks, and Antoinette certainly must have shared stories with her in private. This maid found me to be "nicer" than the boys she had to take care of for her employers ("stupid idiots," she called them). She "went out" at night to dance with American soldiers and tried, in vain, to "liven up" Antoinette and bring her along for a good time.

I remember a Metro ride one morning with her and Antoinette, and an American soldier, a sergeant, with whom she apparently had a date. I don't really remember where we were going. We were in the back corner of the train car, opposite the door, and, as they exchanged long passionate looks, I saw the soldier slip his hand under her skirt. I couldn't believe my eyes.

126 (§ 49) Volume X of the monumental chronological "Laumonier" edition, where it figures <u>in the second book of the *Meslanges*</u> with the date 1559

In the last line of the sonnet, as I now see, Ronsard actually wrote *"doux souvenir"* (sweet memory) and not *"seul souvenir"* (memory alone). And Laumonier doesn't record any such variant—I prefer it (perhaps because my memory has gotten used to this reading), but it's likely that I invented it. Further, in the first of the two original versions, line 4 was:

> *"Et vos beaux yeux sentoient encore leur enfance."*
> ("And your beautiful eyes still showed their childhood days")

While line 8, also in the first version, reads:

> *"Et vos cheveux faisoyent au soleil une offense."*
> ("And your hair gave offense to the sun")

Which, let's face it, isn't very effective.

Along with the sonnet, I remember three other things that I learned around the same time:

—I learned that this sonnet was a *pièce retranchée*, a piece that had been "cut off," eliminated by Ronsard himself from his *Œuvres*, and then restored by posterity, rescued from an oblivion desired—whether in error or as a sacrifice—by its author. (The term "cut off" likens this condemnation to a kind of capital punishment, by means of an aesthetic "guillotine.") The expression *pièce retranchée* has almost become the title of this poem, and it contributed to the tremors the piece inspired in me (the sort of shiver up the spine that you get from reading certain lines of Shelley, for example).

—But I imagined I understood why Ronsard had guillotined this piece: because of the last six lines, I thought, which are particularly "silly," although no less Ronsardian than the rest (one recognizes (this is based on my current critical judgment) his usual delicacy of feeling: "and if today all your perfect beauties / are no more as they once were . . ."). Such a flaw, which often becomes visible in the genius of a poet from whose body of work only "masterpieces" are chosen for use in schools (and thus were the only ones taught by my professors), was simultaneously scandalous and reassuring.

I discovered almost simultaneously, thanks to Baudelaire, the aesthetic necessity for this mixture of the "beautiful" and the "non-beautiful" in the same poem (which, in certain cases—a supreme "Cusan" refinement—goes so far as to include, as an absolutely essential element of a poem, lines deliberately composed to be the "opposite" of beautiful:

"It's too beautiful! Too beautiful! let us keep silent!" (Rimbaud)): this fascinating terror is similar, for people of my generation, to the one caused by two stockings with runs in them going all the way up two very beautiful feminine legs:

> *Pendant que des mortels la multitude vile*
> [While the vile multitude of mortals]

which is much like:

> *Sois sage ô ma douleur, et tiens-toi plus tranquille.*
> [Be good, my pain, and keep calm.]

For imperfection is indispensable to poetry. (Later still I encountered in classical Japanese poetry a tradition in which this coexistence of aesthetic extremes, the opposition between the weave and the design, is at times placed at the very origins of all composition.)

—Finally, I was struck and enchanted by the double use, at the same place in the line, and in two consecutive lines (crossing the border between quatrains), of a single word with two faces, which acts to avoid a rhyme that isn't really a rhyme: "*encor*," "*encore*" (both meaning "still" or "again"). The difference between the two is minimal and is clearly not primarily a difference of pronunciation. But this double use signals with the greatest possible economy the role of the so-called "silent *e*" in the prosody of the alexandrine. It is counted in the first of these lines, but not in the second. It is, moreover, even when counted, always on the "verge" of disappearing (certainly extremely low on the scale of phonic realization of *E*s according to Milner and Regnault). The first "silent *e*" is in a verse that Ronsard gives the sound of a trimeter—a verse of the future, an "anticipatory plagiarism" of Hugo. The absence of the second one occurs in a line that is a perfect model of the classic alexandrine (thus avoiding a thirteenth syllable), with an "*infante*" falling before the hemistich. Archaism meets anticipation.

I learned this poem—and I was twelve years old. The nostalgia associated with it is especially pure, since it was necessarily situated for me in a time that had not yet come.

127 (continuation of § 126) "She wore no shoes"

That same winter, I learned, and still remember today, another poem, this one very well known by readers of my generation. It is a poem by Victor Hugo, from *The Contemplations*:

Elle était déchaussée, elle était décoiffée,
Assise, les pieds nus, parmi les joncs penchants:
Moi qui passais par là, je crus voir une fée,
Et je lui dis: "Veux-tu t'en venir dans les champs?"

Elle me regarda de ce regard suprême
Qui reste à la beauté quand nous en triomphons,
Et je lui dis: "Veux-tu, c'est le mois où l'on aime,
Veux-tu nous en aller sous les arbres profonds?"

Elle essuya ses pieds à l'herbe de la rive;
Elle me regarda pour la seconde fois,
Et la belle folâtre devint pensive.
O! Comme les oiseaux chantaient au fond des bois!

Comme l'eau caressait doucement le rivage!
Je vis venir à moi, dans les grands roseaux verts,
La belle fille heureuse, effarée et sauvage,
Ses cheveux dans ses yeux et riant au travers.

Mont.-l'Am., June 183X

[She wore no shoes, her hair was unkempt,
Sitting barefoot among the lilting branches:
To me, passing by, she seemed an enchanted fairy
And I said to her: "Will you come with me to the fields?"

She looked at me with the supreme gaze
That remains to beauty as we triumph over it,
And I said to her: "Will you, it is the month of love,
Will you come away with me beneath the deepest trees?"

She wiped her feet on the grass of the bank;
For a second time she looked at me,
And the beautiful mad woman became pensive.

Oh! How the birds sang deep in the woods!

How the water gently caressed the riverbank!
I saw her come to me, in the high green reeds,
The beautiful happy girl, terrified and wild,
Her hair down in her eyes, her laughter trembling through it.]

The large edition published by the Club Français du Livre notes here, with a discreet irony, it seems, the following date (if not the date of composition, it is at least that of the poem's entry into the manuscript of the <u>Contemplations</u>): "12 April 1853"—and then goes on to say, "V. H. does not seem to have returned to Montfort-L'Amaury after 1825, except during the first week of August 1830: the fictive date remains obscure." No doubt. And yet, something in these stanzas points, fictively perhaps, but effectively, to the poem's past—namely, its versification.

This poem contains no enjambments, no romantic trimeters, no disjointed hemistiches. In it Hugo uses the "simpleminded" alexandrine of his youth, the one he used, for example, throughout *Les feuilles d'automne*, from 1831. In that respect, this poem is indeed something of an "<u>Old Song from the Times of Youth</u>," even if the real date of composition (which I don't know) must have been much later.

Poetic prosody always indicates its moment in time—archaisms as well as contemporaneity and innovations—with numerous signs that a patient effort at analysis can enable one to partly identify, and which give the poem a large measure of its color and its power. The considerable distance between the alexandrine of this poem and the one that's ordinarily used in <u>The Contemplations</u>—in "<u>Réponse à un acte d'accusation</u>" (Response to an Indictment), for example, or, to remain in a lyric register, in "<u>A celle qui est restée en France</u>" (To Her Who Stayed in France)—contributes in a decisive manner to our reading of his intention.

The old alexandrine marks the lost youth of the moment. And it does this all the more in that, for someone who reads it later in history, and after more than forty years of involvement with what is called "free" verse, the irremediable nature of change, of aging (which was accelerated by Hugo himself) in the nature of the alexandrine, adds its own commentary *a posteriori* to the nostalgia of the line:

"*Vos beautés si parfaites / Ne sont comme autrefois.*"

("Your perfect beauties / Are no more as they once were.")

128 (§ 49) **The *Sempourgognics***

The *Sempourgognics*

With the exception of a few fragments, the work of M. P. Dataficus, which extended over a period of 107 years, has been lost. This immense work was divided into nine <u>dodecades</u>, each of which narrates the events of a twelve-year period, and each of which is divided into nine books. Of these eighty-one books only the following survive: Books I, III, VII, and IX of the first dodecade, and then XII and XVI, all recounting the conquest of Peruvia; then, Books XVII, XVIII, XX, XXX, and eleven chapters of Book XXXII, of the 2nd, 3rd, and 4th dodecades; nine chapters of the summary of the 5th and 6th dodecades; Books LV, LVI, and LXI of the 7th; and Book LXVIII, all narrating the reign of Sempourgogne. Finally, book LXXIV on the reign of Ipir I, and the last three books of the work.

We cite here excerpts from books I, III, XVI, XXX, LXVIII, LXXIV, LXXX, and LXXXI.

The *Sempourgognics* most likely appeared in 126. Dataficus died in 134.

The Greatness

of

SEMPOURGOGNE

Emperor and King of Peruvia, from

the Year 22 of His Era Until the 89th Summer of His

Arrival,

By the Grace of the Gods

Garenne and Goguelu

(Goguelu is no doubt another one of my gods, but a forgotten one.)

A very truthful and marvelous work of Master

Marcus Publius Dataficus

Perceptor [sic] *of the worthy son*

of the Lord Count, Viscount, Duke, and Archduke

Johannus of Bessinguya

HUJUS MAGNI HEROIS

NEPOS

this 17th of April 126 at
Licoll.

EVENTIS DE QUIBUS SECUTUS EST ADVENTUM IN PERUVIAM SEMPOURGOGNI MAGNI

I (1) A fortuna missus in Peruviam Sempourgognis Magnus, primo statim adventu illius populi[1] feros cultores,[2] quorum habitus ac lingua singularis erant, obstupefecit et cum e suis navibus, ubi praesidium collocaverit, egressus in superiore loco sua castra posuit, facilius sibi instantes hostes fortuitos sustinendos; itaque ergo placide, ibi, pernoctavit.

(Sempourgogne the great, sent to Peruvia by heaven, upon his arrival astonished the savage inhabitants of this region whose ways and language were singular. And after quitting his ships, where he left a garrison, he set up camp in a high place in order to be able more easily to repel any possible enemies; thus he spent a peaceful night.)

(2) Deinde, ubi primum stallarum lanearum pallescit fulgor, dum superbi solis erumpit lux, tunc Sempourgognus Magnus, castris motis agmen suum in planum demittit, suumque caprafelem, cui animali nomen dederant Peruvii capracatem (quod erat fama a Garene generatum deo ac e cappelis felibus que fictum) equitat, donec ad utilem castris locum prevenitur.

(3) Ibi, tum, non solum flumen sed castella duo quoque conspexerunt et manum eis quae incolis victus peterent atque commeatum misit Sempurognus, sapienter, Magnus, ac autem prudenter, ipse, cum robore caprafelitorum[3] progressus (dum stabat agminis Gallorum[4] maxima pars),[5] lenteque hanc manus insecutus.

(4) Paulo post oratores, ad illum celticum ducem venerunt et, dum eos rogavisset benignissime id quod, ut victus, sibi concessurum possent, respondisse:

(5) "Quis es? unde venis? quid agere vis? o advena flava coma et ideo nobis similis, si tua bona erunt consilia tui amici erimus. Responde, o dux, dic nobis qui nomen sit tibo et quae acciderunt." His dictis tacent Peruviaci duces.

(6) At ille: "O, jucundae hujus regionis . . .

(Later, when the fuzzy shining of the stars disappeared, as the proud sunlight broke in, Sempourgogne the Great raised the camp and led his army into the plain sitting astride his <u>caprafelis</u> (which the Peruviacs call *Goatcat*, because it was conceived by the god

Garenne from a mix of these two animals) until they arrived at a favorable place to set up camp.

They saw there a river and, in addition, two villages to which Sempourgogne the Great wisely sent someone to garner provisions from the inhabitants and to secure permission to pass. He himself, however, with the elite of his caprafelites, cautiously advanced, and though the greater part of the Gauls stopped, he slowly followed this troop.

Shortly thereafter, some ambassadors came to meet this illustrious Celtic chief, and as the latter asked them what they could offer him by way of provisions they answered:

"Who are you? whence come you? what do you want here? Oh blond stranger, who in this is like us. If your intentions are good we will be your friends. Answer, chief, tell us your name and your adventures." That said, the Peruviac leaders fell silent.

He answered: "Oh chiefs of this fine land, hear me . . .")

1. *Populus* = region

2. *Cultor* has here the sense of inhabitant.

3. The caprafelites are elite soldiers.

4: Sempourgogne, like the Peruviacs, is of Celtic origin.

5: Fragment of doubtful authenticity.

Sempourgogne then gives an extremely brief account of his adventures. The Peruviacs listen "as pupils listen to their master" *(sicut discipuli magistrum attendunt)*, and according to whether Sempourgogne the Great speaks loudly or softly, draw near to him or shrink back *(et utcumque Sempourgognus Magnus aut fortiter aut languide loquebatur, aut propinquabant aut discedebant)*. The hero then falls silent (and "nature itself increased the silence") until the native chiefs offer to lead him and his troops to their *oppidum*. They arrive at a great wall that seems to be impassible, and the "Gauls" fear that they have fallen into a trap. Then

(14) Sempourgognus tunc Magnus alienum ducem adlocutus, saxtumque invium ostendit et iter designare eum jussit. Statim Peruviacus saxo appropinquat, ac, lapide ingente diducto, exitum detexit qui mirati Galli conspexerunt mobile mare.

(Sempourgogne the Great addressed the foreign chief and, pointing to the impassible stone, ordered him to show the way. Straightaway the Peruviac approached the stone and, ordering an immense rock to be turned about, uncovered a passage through which the wonder-struck Gauls perceived the movement of the sea.)

With this *coup de théâtre* inspired by the best authors, section I of this chapter comes to a close.

129 (continuation of § 128) **The incidents of the second section are far from memorable**

The incidents of the second section, which serve above all as a training ground for certain difficult syntactic constructions (no doubt recently acquired by the author), are far from memorable. Let us jump straight to the third part, then, devoted primarily to a physical and moral portrait of the caprafeles, those hybrid animals so dear to the heroes of the *Sempourgognics*.

[. . .]

III (2) Peruviaci, maxime, caprafelibus detinebantur; alii mulcebant earum mystaces, alii trahebant eas. Illae sinebant illos, benignissime.

(The Peruviacs were especially busy taking care of the caprafeles; some were caressing their mustaches, others were pulling on them. The animals magnanimously allowed them do this.)

3) These animals have curious ways, as one would expect. If most of the caprafeles have four feet, one the size of a goat's and three that almost touch the earth, the Great Sempourgogne's caprafelis, which the soldiers called the Witch, was the size of a man and had five feet. She was so, it was said, out of pure caprice.

(*Quibus animalibus sunt, scilicet, singulares mores. Sicut caprafelibus plerumque quattuor pedes et caprae statura est, pedesque tria fere qui terram tangebant, ita capracati Magni Sempourgogni, cui nomen dederant milites Incantatrix, erat tamen hominis statura atque pedes quinque. Caprafelice ita fuisse dicebatur.*)

(4) Among the caprafeles whose bodies conform to the norm, the tail and the head are those of a cat. According to tradition, however, a certain breed of caprafelis has the nose of a goat. Moreover, the caprice and perfidy that most certainly belong to women are also vices specific to these animals.

(*Capracatibus semper corporis convenientis habitu, cauda caputque felinum est. Fama, tamen, caprafeli cuidam nasum caprinum fuisse, est. Ceterum, ut libido ac perfidia certo mulieribus, ita, animalibus illis, ista vitia sunt.*)

(5) Caesar had had one long ago, and it is said that one day when it asked him why he had dared to vanquish the Gauls, and he had answered that it had been his duty as a Roman, it replied to him that he was a stupid beast.

(Caesarem unam earum habuisse, atque quondam eam, cur ausum esset Gallos vincere, eum rogavisse et, cum illi respondisset officium fuisse Romanum, eam declaravisse Caesarem stupidem, aiunt.)

(6) These creatures are indeed very garrulous women who have been punished by the gods and are able to speak only when they are questioned.

(Nam bestiae eae mulieres garrulissimae sunt quae deis punitae et ubi rogantur, loqui tantum possunt.)

(7) But their defects are compensated by great virtues. They always serve good masters, and moreover are resistant to fatigue—though while they do not easily go to sleep at night, they wake only with difficulty in the morning.

(At quoque, magnae virtutes aequant earum vitia. Et ad bonos, semper, dominos se applicant, et, insuper, sudori cuilibet resitunt et, ut vespere somno haud facile connivent, ita, mane, haud facile exitari possunt.)

(8) This is why Sempourgogne the Great would send, early in the morning, official delegates to awaken them. These rites were known as *le Grand lever* (the Great Early Rising).

(Itaque mittebat semper, mane novo, legatos publicos qui eas expergefacerent, Sempougognus magnus. Ritus illos, Surrectionem Magnam, vocari.)

(9) The caprafeles do not have an even temper during the day and at night. They usually eat well, and a lot. They graze on budding plants and tender leaves: they like tastes that are sharp but not bitter. During meals they are calm or raucous. After a good lunch they sometimes smile. But most often they are unhappy with the cook and chase after him throwing stones.

(Illae die noctuque non civiles. Multum esse solent benque. Oculos pascunt ac tenera folia. Acrem sed non amaritudinem amant. Inter cenam aut placidae aut accensae sunt. Post jucundum cibum nonnunquam arrident. Saepe autem in coquo offendentur brevique lapidibus eum appetunt.)

(10) However that may be, the caprafeles were highly venerated . . .

(*Quamquam magnopere colebantur caprafeles . . .*)

(The story obviously didn't get much farther than these few chapters.)

130 (§ 50) **Leningrad, Stalingrad, Orel, Kursk, Velikiye Luki, Bryansk**

These names will never change for me. They no longer designate the actual cities, neither the archaeo-retro Saint-Petersburg that returned in 1991 (ah! the good old days of Holy Russia, with its Tsars, its *barines*, its muzhiks, its pogroms!), nor the ridiculous Volgograd of the Krushchev era, but the battles that were waged there (the defeat of von Paulus's army, the terrible siege in which the poet Kharms died). These are <u>sites of memory</u>, and it's better if the "sites of living" are kept distinct from them.

If I end the above enumeration with "Bryansk," it's because of a "generic" memory of the time, when the decisive retreat of Hitler's armies began: I had gone to the barber with a book and on the Vichy radio I heard the announcement of a new "elastic retreat" (the cheerful expression of the German "Propaganda" services), the evacuation of Bryansk, precisely, in a westward displacement to "positions established in advance." I hurried home to share the news. And this time "London" was lagging behind, announcing the news only later that evening in their usual information bulletin, "The French Speak to the French." This shift from the denial to the anticipation of retreats was an excellent indication of what was to follow for our enemy.

"Velikiye Luki" is a Byelorussian city, I think. And the (Russian) name means "high plains." Around this time, Georges, the brother of Nina Morguleff (whose testimony you read a little earlier), also found refuge in the Carcassonne region, and had "entered" the Resistance, as one said.

(From my father's testimony (§ 115):

Q: Who was Georges?

—His parents had emigrated from Russia to Germany. Then with the rise of the Nazis his parents said: "We have to go to France." They arrived in France, he and his sister. Georges Morguleff is a fellow of tremendous intelligence, so much so that, as we learned through some friends, he was first in his class in French only a year later. An extremely brilliant fellow.

At the beginning of the war he was an officer cadet in the French army. He hid out in the Tarn region. We knew him through the family in Lyon. I secured his return and he became my secretary. Finally, when Myriel was killed he became an FFI commander in the Aude. His sister was secretary to Marc Bloch, who was responsible for the sharp-shooters in the Lyon Region.

Q: He lives in Paris now?

—Georges? Yes, with his sister. Later she became a journalist for *Midi libre*. She's an astrophysicist.)

Georges and Nina tried to teach us how to pronounce the impossible liquids of those two words, "Velikiye Luki". We never could. No more than we were able to correctly pronounce the "r" and the final "l" of "Orel," the city whose name means "eagle."

131 (§ 50) **I had admired the anti-Pétain demonstrators in 1942**

(Again from my father's testimony: § 115 and elsewhere)

—The first organization was set up by Picolo.

—I'll skip the childish preliminaries. In the beginning we played around doing things like going off with a hunting rifle to scout for places where we might lay an ambush, things like that.

—He knew a lot of people. His pharmacy was a meeting place, but it was a little too open.

Q: He was a pharmacist?

—His wife was a pharmacist, he was a physics professor at the lycée in Carcassonne. He was dismissed from his position; he had been the Socialist candidate for the district.

—Well, he was the one who put together the first organization. I got a visit from this man named Stéphane. I said: Come back tomorrow.

Q: This was in 1941?

—1941, yes. He had such a mysterious air. I was on my guard; he had all our names written in a notebook. I phoned a friend who said: "You're completely crazy. I have some Spanish refugees at my house, we've been under surveillance for a long time." Picolo, however, made contact. And he began to organize "Combat," or at least something that was later called "Combat."

—He did something that caused quite a stir in Carcassonne. He tore the bouquet of flowers out of the hands of the German who'd come to give a lecture on cultural collaboration, in the Carcassonne theater. People had presented him with a bouquet, out on the main street, and Albert Picolo tore it from his hands.

—It's true that his organization wasn't well-structured, but it had a far-reaching influence. I'm thinking of July 14, 1942—of Barbès. Armand Barbès was one of the glories of the region, a revolutionary of 1848. His tomb is in a very beautiful wood in Villalier. This is the village where Joe Bousquet is buried. There was a statue of Barbès on one of the main thoroughfares in Carcassonne, the Boulevard Barbès. It was made of bronze. The Germans took it down. The next day, someone had written in its place: "Barbès, we will avenge you," or something like that. And on July 14 there was an enormous demonstration, July 14, 1942.

—Albert wasn't there, he had been arrested, then he went to Lozère. Word of mouth traveled very quickly. I remember that we were with Albert's wife, Odette, in the garden, there were a few of us, we left to go to the demonstration, we didn't think it could ever be so beautiful. The streets were completely full. Even the notables were there: Father Bruguier, Dr. Gout, the public prosecutor Moreni. Moreni was deported and died.

—When the police contingent from the legionnaires came, there was a huge crowd. People sang the *Marseillaise*. In a parallel street, Father Bruguier, Dr. Gout, and Moreni were leaving the demonstration, and at that moment the legionnaires arrived and tried to beat them up. There weren't many Pétainists, but there were enough, in full attire. We got word of it and headed down there as fast as we could; there was a confrontation. They backed down.

—What amuses me most about this story is that we'd just had a rugby match, the lycée professors versus another team, and there was this kid who seemed to be a bit of a thug, and who got into a fight with a professor, a "prop forward," and yet here we were again, this time fighting together. He said to me, "Hey—what are you doing here?"

bifurcations

Bifurcation A

The Monster of Strasbourg

132 (§9) I see this immense title, <u>The Monster of Strasbourg</u>, against a cinematic background of chimneys and rooftops

I see this immense title, <u>The Monster of Strasbourg</u>, against a cinematic (anachronistic?) background of chimneys and extremely steep rooftops, with a stork popping up here and there: their nests against the chimneys, their long white or pink feathers blending in with the snow, their interminable legs; iron rooftops, covered with flat metal plates, wet leaves of tin turned green; a setting: a living, moving title page. The indescribable "Monster" is certainly in the picture too, behind the chimneys; it's because of him that the storks soon fly away. I see his invisibility; I can almost feel the fear he causes, the slight fear I felt when I told a scary story in our bedroom, where it's already getting dark: the fear held in a bubble of night, blown by the teller, by myself, around the room, around the three beds, around my own; around our heads, around my own, inside my own; containing a moon. ("When the storks of the Cayster / Fly away with the breath of evening / When the moon appears, sinister, / Behind the great black domes . . ." (Hugo).)

I'm in the same childhood bedroom, in Carcassonne, on the Rue d'Assas, in the evening: an evening when night is falling rather late; it's a summer night, or one at the end of spring, or the beginning of fall, after classes have begun again; the bed in the dark room, the three beds; the lighter sky through the window; an evening sky, almost night.

As I lie down, the two other beds are to my left, as I said → chap. 1. I <u>bifurcate</u> in my memories, shifting from morning to evening, from winter to summer, in another very natural and effortless leap, whenever the vision of the frost on the window, its contact with my finger, comes to me—whenever I let it run. **At this moment, which should be a moment of sleep, of preparation for sleep, I tell stories instead.** It's a **story night.** And it's true that I neither see nor hear myself telling stories. Nor do I know which story I tell. But a memory of doing this has been transmitted, externally, to myself. The stories we told then have been retained for a long time: if not their details, at least their atmosphere. The Monster of Strasbourg was a story, a fantastic story, drawn out into various episodes—in other words, a "serial."

If this story ever had any other titles, only this one remains. And this same title—which too has effaced almost all the other titles of all the other stories we told in those moments, in those years—has also become the title of this particular family of memories, those of the summertime bedroom, in the evening: The Monster of Strasbourg. A gothic horror story, inspired by *Notre-Dame of Paris*, for example, or by *Quentin Durward*, or *Ivanhoe*, or *Guy Mannering*, or *The Bride of Lammermoor*—one of these, certainly (and there's little danger of my being mistaken: I was a devoted reader of Hugo's novels and even more of Walter Scott's). For the "Alsatian" local color implied by the "Strasbourg" of the title, one would have to look towards Erckmann-Chatrian (*Madame Thérèse, Le Conscrit de 1813, L'Invasion*); and, for the story's fantastic contents, to Edgar Poe in Baudelaire's translation (*Les Aventures d'Arthur Gordon Pym de Nantucket?*) . . . But then there would have been plenty of possible inspirations.

As for the later episodes of my serial, if one moves forward to the fall of 1943, I would have to add the Rocambole novels of Ponson du Terrail (§ 144–145) (and, perhaps because it invoked the name of the author of this enormous series (and probably not entirely by chance), I have retained an insistent "personal message" that was broadcast by London radio—one of those enigmatic and recurrent phrases that, through repetition, used to ring out with all the fascination of proverbs, leitmotifs, great quotations. We listened to them as though they were poetic or prophetic voices (as indeed they were, though in a sense that was beyond us), never understanding their function: "*Ponson du Terrail is shaking up the neighborhood. I repeat: Ponson du Terrail is shaking up the neighborhood.*" I learned later that the voice was announcing an aerial arms drop, or a bombardment: the business of the "Resistance").

Reconstructed in this way, however, this memory no longer has anything "gothic" or sinister about it. And today, nothing, or almost nothing, remains of its "aura" of romantic mystery, which back then was always present, constantly deferred, suspended, and then renewed in our suspenseful nightly sessions, with sudden twists and resolutions punctuating each of the story's "episodes." I held onto this aura for a long time, like an echo from those years, and as an irrefutable testimony (since I wasn't the only one of us who remembered it) to an ancient pleasure in telling "stories" that generated particular effects. I will confess here that in **The Great Fire of London** I would indeed have liked to reconstitute some part of it: at least an "approximate value."

But the halo of mystery surrounding my terrible but harmless childhood monster appeared to me one day as being much stranger than I'd previously thought—even disturbing. It was as though the entertaining **mysteries** of the tale had merely been the displaced effects of a certain **riddle**, whose answer, with time—after years of concealment and hesitation, and through an unlikely, contingent, absurd, but irrefutable conjunction of images—finally revealed itself to me as the dark and sinister thing that, in truth, it had been all along. This process began one evening in 1983, some time after Alix's death; I had lain down once again on her deserted bed, in the corner, alongside the strip of mirror fragments attached to the wall that she had put there to reflect the sky and the clouds. The clouds, as was their wont, emerged from nothingness, emerged in the silence that had settled in behind the Blancs-Manteaux church, in the bay of roofs between the church and the houses on the street.

The clouds slowly bore down on the church, on the trees in the square, heralds of evening, bearers of the desolate waning light; they drifted through their fragments of mirror, disappeared, with their silent sky-bound tranquility, with their intolerable indifference. And I despised myself for being there again, for being unable to stop myself from being there in my suffering and in the abandonment to absolute suffering that being there signified, as the light, unforgiven, fled beneath the door, withdrew from the wooden floor, from the windowpanes, from the ceiling, the books, the chair, from my hands, from my eyes, from all my attention to the sky, gathering in the clouds, in the still very luminous estuary of daylight between the rooftops.

In the movement of the clouds, then, in the image of the outline of the church's spire, where they first appeared to me, shaped by the stone, I felt the presence of a monster, coming from far away—from very far away: a presence I felt I knew, but that I could not as yet identify. And it was only later still—when I pointed out those clouds to Marie: their sudden arrival out of the oblivion of the upper corner of the window—that its origin came back to me. What was there wasn't a monster, but that monster, the **Monster of Strasbourg** from my childhood: the improvised invention of my novice storyteller's imagination, and now no longer the least bit friendly.

133 I open the door at the far end of the bedroom

I open the door at the far end of the bedroom; I open it in the very early morning, in an uncertain season—it doesn't matter which—while it's still dark outside; the bedroom is lit by a naked bulb hanging from the ceiling, not quite in the middle of the room, closer to the door; the open door draws the yellow light of the bedroom outside, annexing part of the space above the door, all the way over to the opposite door, across the hall; which I do not open; like an image from a Hopper painting; in this yellow light of a naked bulb, the bedroom spills out of itself, overflowing through the door and through the window; it fills a pocket of space, on one side suspended in the garden air, on the other hemmed in by the wall, the other door, and the floor, which is interrupted somewhere by the top step of the stairway.

I go no farther; for the moment I do not enter the other bedroom on the third floor (across from the first, the one I just left). This was Marie's room (then Antoinette's, after Marie's marriage and her departure for the Minervois, for Villegly); **I stop at the top of the stairs. I lean out into the darkness of the stairwell: below me, a half-century, in darkness.**

I linger at the top of the stairs as though it were the edge of a well, or a pit—another well besides the condemned one in the garden between the terrace and the bench. I stop. I wait for some kind of truth to come up out of this well. But what kind? Not a lesson, I'm certainly not after any lessons. (A moral? "And what's the moral? There isn't one" (Charles Cros).) What I'm looking for is a new continuity of images in order to move forward on this path, to reach the end of this bifurcation (I have a specific goal). I've arrived quite easily at the point where I lean out into the ancient darkness of the stairway. I have closed the door behind me. No light reaches me from the sky, and there's no water in the bottom of this well to reflect my image back up to me (but then, in the past, no water from any well ever reflects my face back up to me). And I'm confronted here not with a motionless and impenetrable obscurity, but rather with a dense and weltering profusion. As if all the darknesses of all the stairwells of all the houses I've ever lived in are pressing together below me, merging together and releasing a great cloud, a vapor of visions.

To progress, I must undergo the intense effort of methodical separation: not this image because it leads directly into that one, and not that image because the banister there is made of iron, and then not this one because its steps are made of stone; not that one because its stairway goes straight down without curving. What I need to see is wood (both rail and steps) and a spiral. I don't really understand (or I understand only too well) this resistance to identification that I'm trying to overcome (a stubborn resistance that I've been fighting against for three mornings now), the unsystematic proliferation of remembered images constantly covering up the fragments of clear and certain vision I would normally rely on (it hardly matters whether this certainty is well founded or not): propelling me, for instance, all the way to the (dizzying) heights of the Scott Monument in Edinburgh (which is what just happened to me) as easily as into the stairways of the other houses where I've lived.

But I continue to insist on moving down this particular path—despite the involuntary but tenacious reticence of my brain, for which I can find no external justification. I insist, and do not give myself license to accept any of the random diversions that emerge from the dark, or to embark upon another interpolation in order to return, by an oblique path, to the same point of departure. I need the spiral of the stairway: because it's similar to the journey-via-levitation that took me from the bedroom to the garden, and because a spiral is also a loop: because as I gaze down toward the discontinuity of the stairs, toward the continuity of the banister, I know this is not in any case a real descent, neither in space nor in duration. The points of departure and arrival are the same, just as two dawns are the same, or two first days of winter, or of the year, or of spring.

I insist (I have insisted for almost six months: between this prose-moment and the preceding one there has been a six-month interruption. But I needed all this time: as though I had set out to dig a tunnel with a very thin and precise needle), I fiercely and unremittingly persevere until I finally receive the truth of this profusion: that in leaning over the dark spiral of the staircase, my gaze had sunk into a whirl-pool, the endless coils of a whirlpool, in which a proliferation of images was the rule. Impossible for me to separate, to distinguish, to organize. The images thus "compressed" together, endlessly, one on top of the other, demonstrated another condition, another modality of past time, to me. I could hardly refuse it.

To climb onto the wooden banister; to slide down to the bottom; down to the doorstop; to climb back up, to slide down again. A game. The essence of the game is to become absorbed in the spiraling movement; **the pressure of the wood, the moment of perceptible acceleration occurring at the point where the stairway turns, where the friction begins to warm the palms, the thighs; centrifugal speed, scented with wax.**

Or else another game: **to climb onto the first step, to jump; to climb onto the second step, to jump; to jump from the third; to go higher still, to put one hand on the wall, the other on the railing; to reach for the lowest grasp-able point on the wall, on the railing, from the chosen step; to slide my hands down little by little, to press forward with my toes (naked?) and to spring from the tip of the ninth, tenth step, to draw my legs up beneath me in a leap; to go past the corner of the wall, then to thrust my legs forward, so that the highest jump begins at the turn in the stair, so that the arrow of my fall changes direction before flying toward its target, the floor.**

Thus, utilizing this game's double movement, both discontinuous and continuous, my body easily crosses the distances that so long remained an impenetrable obstacle to my gaze. I accept the lesson. I will not restage the experiment when I reach the second-floor landing. I might get stuck there indefinitely.

134 Here, three paths lie before me.

Here, three paths lie before me. Across the landing there's the door onto the balcony, and to my left is our parents' bedroom (I don't go in there). On the right, the "study." I will begin there. (The door to the balcony is a "French door." The light enters much more easily here than on the floor above. But the stairway itself nonetheless remains populated and impenetrable at the same time, "a Trophonian cave full of cloud and shadow," full of oblivion.)

In the study I see the desk, across from the door, between the two windows (the first on the left, looking down on the terrace, the second likewise across from the door, looking down on the "greenhouse" and the "vegetable garden"). On the wall, between the windows, books on a shelf, piled up to the ceiling. (Books also on the wall to the left, between the door and the window, but not all the way up.) I tend to see this room from the "head" of the sofa, against the wall to the right of the door, nestled (on two sides) by a piece of furniture we called the "cozy-corner."

The desk was massive, made of heavy wood, so heavy that it seemed to be attached to the floor; its general form was that of an Arc de Triomphe, flat on top, covered with a sheet of glass (beneath which there was sometimes a layer of blotting paper: pink, green); each of its two "legs" was elephantine, and hollow: the one on the left had a door; the one on the right had three drawers, almost impossible to budge, to open; between the two "legs," in the center, yet another drawer; the left-hand door had a lock; as did the middle drawer. The desk was the very essence of the study; the study *was* the desk.

It was an obligatory companion to the humans in the family and accompanied them over the course of several moves. And yet, looking back, I don't see it in Paris (on the other Rue d'Assas) or on the Rue Franklin in Saint-Germain-en-Laye. It resurfaces, visually, unchanged—although with its proportions having been reduced by age (my own)—only at a later period, in Paris, Rue Jean-Menans, where, hoisting it as was necessary up to the sixth floor—quite a feat even today, without some advanced tools—it seemed as light as a wisp of straw for a crew from that heroic generation of movers whom I still visualize in their overalls, like the ones from the beginning of the Third Republic, singing in chorus the refrain by Courteline: "On our shoulders and on our backs / load up, sirs, load up the heavy sacks . . ."

After that, the desk didn't go to Saint-Félix, near Carcassonne, but, out of pity for the French National Railway perhaps, only as far as Villejuif, whence it was once again extracted so as to be installed in my bedroom, at 51 Rue des Francs-Bourgeois. When I left there, Charlotte claimed it, intending to give it a long and dignified old age (she was attracted too, I think, by the luxury of deep and secret drawers). Then, however, it finally made way for a lighter and more modern arrangement, one more in agreement with the aesthetic demands of a sixteen-year-old girl.

For me, however, in 1940 and afterwards, the desk really didn't actually consist of its solid and material parts, but rather of the space—more or less cubic—contained within its arch. I constructed a kind of dwelling there—something between a hut, a palace, and a nook; and all it took was a bathroom towel, a shirt, or a few odd rags to render this space inviolate to the world, securing us a place to whisper in dark seclusion whenever a need for this was felt by one or several children (each one of us taking up very little room on his or her own). Looking out from this keep, **I see the underside of the lowest board on the shelf, the dust bunnies clinging to it, the bottom of the sofa, and the lower edge of the door; I feel the hardwood floor with its oblique grooves under my knees.**

The "office hours" in the study came at the end of the afternoon, before the evening meal, or else during the slow hours on rainy Sundays (and perhaps not even rainy ones: Sunday evenings precede Monday mornings, and are the last chance to do the grading that's been put off all weekend). Hours for grading homework: English compositions for my mother, exercises in philosophical argument for my father. As for me, heir to various bundles of old and now useless papers, there were tests to grade on every conceivable subject, real or invented.

Within the protected cube under my wooden ceiling (and with the papers piled up on the floor), I took on in my own peculiar way the problem of evaluations, class rankings, and averages. I added my own remarks to the marginal annotations already present (I used my own ink, made from elderberries), and to the final judgments written at the top of each paper's first page, in red ink, next to the final grades. I paid close attention to the length and the overall appearance of the writing, as well as the onomastic qualities of the students—especially their first names. I imagined how they looked, pictured their faces. (I had a few surprises when I actually met them (which did happen on occasion). Sometimes they seemed like they must be frauds, imposters; other times, on the contrary, they looked exactly as I'd expected. (Their grades came to reflect this.))

Grading papers, thus conceived, was in no way a chore, but a veritable delight. We even sang songs: original compositions or else adaptations by my father (for him this was most likely a form of distraction, or perhaps an exhortation, or else a way to celebrate the completion of a task that was unavoidable but in itself not particularly fun.) Thus:

"*Les cloches du grand Séminai-ai-re / m'appellent au pied des saints autels / C'est là que mon coeur à la te-ê-rre / fera ses adieux éternels / les boucles de ma chevelure / ne tomberont plus sur mon front / et le ciel sera ma parure / et le ciel sera mes amours / tou-jours, tou-jours.*" ["The bells of the grand semina-a-ary / call me down to the holy altars / There my heart to the ea-earth / will bid a long farewell / the curls of my hair / will fall no more in my eyes / and the sky will be my jewel / and the sky will be my love / forever, forever."]

Or else, to the tune of a well known hunting song:

"*La calvitie préco-o-ce / de la reine d'Éco-o-sse / la fait paraître ro-o-sse / les Zécossais sont tous dé-concertés!*" ["The premature ba-a-ldness / of the Queen of Sco-o-tland / makes her look mea-ea-n / The Scots are all up-set!"]

135 Second magnetic pole of the study: the pillow at one end of the sofa

I move now to the second magnetic pole of the study: the pillow at one end of the sofa. Its proper time was the time of illness, with the eruption of any of the various childhood "pathologies" (flu and sore throat, chicken pox, measles, mumps. All of us got them all. It was an obligatory rite of all our childhoods). The patient was automatically installed on the sofa in the study, where he or she could enjoy the solitude necessary to their state, but could summon immediate assistance in moments of distress or high fever (and would also (though this was in general a completely futile hope) thereby avoid spreading germs to the highly receptive organisms of brothers and sister). I had my share of these sojourns. Despite their relative rarity, they all left traces of an intensity wholly incommensurate with their durations. (Much as with periods of snow—those inverse fevers of the climate.)

One summer morning when my fever was abating, I opened my eyes to see the sun, and heard the sound of buzzing flies coming through the study window. The faculty of language and even the poetic function having been stimulated by the intoxication of my fever, I pronounced (or so I was told), like an epigram and with slow, firm conviction, the following words: "The very first flies, the buzzing echo of flies!" [trying to "echo" JR's regular meter]

The flies came in, with the morning air of summer and the sun, humming in their undignified commotion, they flew through the luminous air amid the motes of dust following irresponsible Brownian trajectories, landing wherever, marching gravely across the page of an open book, along the windows; with my naked arms lying on the covers, I waited for the ticklish irritation of the flies' legs scuttling over the thin hairs on my skin, or else, with both eyes trained crosswise on the tip of my nose, I watched their hairy gray abdomens distended by this hyper-proximity, inept; on my hand, a little gray reflective fly raised two legs, touched them together, rubbing them against one another mechanically; I tolerated the tickling sensation made by their desultory movements for as long as I could ("Does it tickle or is it itchy?" ("*Ca vous chatouille ou ca vous gratouille?*" (Jules Romains))), then I shook them off, scratched myself; they flew back toward the ceiling, the walls, or, as though gripped abruptly by the exterior light, suddenly flew out of the room into the rustling garden.

During the hours of heavy fever, of contemplative, involuntary, stupefied immobility, **I saw, lit by the slanting light of the lamp that was left illuminated on the glass surface of the desk, an austere geography, made up of zones of shadows, cracks, stains, and fissures in the flat whiteness of the ceiling.** I still have a "geographic feeling" of this room, not in the way one apprehends landscapes, architectures, herds, and fields, but as of maps one has studied—whether imaginary or real—and of an extraordinary abstract space.

I identified streams, rivers, and oceans, islands and chasms; or else, beginning with the same signs, but abruptly inverting the imaginary reference points, I distinguished countries with their various borders and cities; countries at war or about to go to war, with their Manichaean armies clashing in titanic battles. Good and evil could be easily separated then.

Taking advantage of the general calm, steeped in a medical aroma of syrups and infusions, the scuttling spiders emerged, cautious and grave, from their recesses; they moved swiftly and decisively across vast tracts of ceiling, Soviet or Libyan, and busied themselves in the corners and angles strategically recommended by some arachnid Clausewitz for the patient annihilation of the legions of flies (all my sympathy was with the spiders in this); I wasn't afraid, I felt no revulsion at their black hieroglyphs, which were rarely set in motion; I hardly moved, so I didn't bother them.

And I closely observed their descents, as perfectly vertical as a plumb line, along those infinitely thin cords of biological steel that they extracted from themselves as they went, like string unwinding from the belly of a yo-yo (an apparatus that would have been perfectly suited for the escape of a heroic prisoner), stopping in a micro-instant just above the floor as though to reconnoiter the terrain in minute detail (a slight movement on the part of the observer could cause this interrupted descent to be resumed in slight oscillations, or even abruptly transform it into a re-ascent toward its origin, the ceiling, like a prisoner hurriedly climbing back up into his cell, twining his rope back around himself as he goes).

One night a spider came down toward the edge of my bowl of soup, perhaps to drink from it; frightened by the door suddenly opening, it hid under the collar of my pajama top. I sat very still, imagining (?) with delectation that I was immobilized on my bed beneath the innumerable tiny cables secured by a population of miniscule Audois Lilliputians, and I was proud of this remarkable sign of insect trust. After a moment, once calm was restored, it came out of its provisional Gulliverian shelter and, taking in military fashion the thalweg running along a fold in the covers, vanished beneath the "cozy-corner" at my feet.

This particular piece of furniture, made of a wood that harmonized with the desk, consisted of a small sofa with a cabinet on each side, each raised up off the floor at a certain height (and with doors that swung all the way open; the interior space closest to the door contained balls of wool and other instruments for knitting), so that between the mattress, the frame, and the wall, there was a space wonderfully and utterly lacking in practical utility. Two or three of us could squeeze in and sit comfortably, knees together, arms around our knees, in silence, in the delicious semi-illusion that we were being ignored by the world, that we had disappeared, that there was no one who knew we were there.

136 It seems to me that it was there that I acquired my three passions: the passion for numbers, for poetry, for books.

It seems to me that it was there, precisely there, that I acquired three of my main passions, "fundamental passions" that have never left me: a passion for numbers, for poetry, and for books. These were and are three mental passions, and like all passions they have two sides: a side of joy, of happy absorption, and another of suffering: an always hidden suffering, covered over, fleeing, obliterated, born from one's terror of another great passion—one that is, for its part, made up entirely of pain, or in any event an unwholesome kind of joy & torpor—a philosophically fundamental passion: <u>boredom</u>.

I acquired my three passions in those extended times of illness, cut off from ordinary time. (As with all trinities, there are really four elements: My passion for <u>solitude</u> accompanies them. They are never separate from it.) In ordinary time (including school-time) I was perpetually on the move among the things and creatures of the world: My time of being-in-the-world was a time of motion. Which means that the imposed immobility of illness would have been subject to the axiom of boredom. Later on in life, however, when confronted with other people's complaints about boredom, I could always claim in all sincerity: "I never get bored!" Indeed, whenever an insidious and ugly boredom arises in me, I can always start counting.

And counting is my first recourse: an automatic reaction in the face of potential boredom (that's why I placed that passion first in the above list). These are the origins of my particular rapport with numbers, and it still shows: it is because of these origins that I still see numbers above all as whole numbers, not excessively large; having taken on, in those days, the habit of sharing so many moments of my life with entire populations of whole numbers—numbers in action, in perpetual motion, a motion inspired by counting. Numbers, as I learned them in the beginning, and certainly once I made them my own, are inseparable from those mental entities dressed in the garb of language that we call "digits." I recognize the distinction between number and digit, of course—I learned it as a student; I just don't find it very interesting. (More seriously: between 4 (decimal notation) and 10 (binary notation) there is synonymy. But this synonymy leaves me cold. I prefer the homonymy of the two interpretations of the digit 10.)

Which means that I'm not naturally an arithmetician, and even less a natural mathematician. My effort at gaining comprehension and control over even a minimal conception of mathematics (for professional purposes) was no more than a belated superimposition by force of will onto this ground of irresponsible passion. There was always some chance that I could really have devoted myself to a purely mathematical passion, much as I'd turned, spontaneously, toward a passion for poetic composition or for reading, but that never happened. Doubtless because being a mathematician is no longer really possible, except as a member of an academic institution, with which I have always been rather hesitant to associate myself (poetry, on the other hand, takes place almost entirely outside academia).

It follows that these mental manipulations of number-objects (whole numbers in their written decimal form, and, very exceptionally, fractions), which I absorb myself today almost as intensely as I did back then, are the same ones that were first possible for me to do in my head, the head resting on its pillow at one end of the sofa, in the crook of the "cozy-corner": enumerations, series, elementary operations, sums, comparisons, division (with a particular delectation—a consequence of my variety of numerical passion—for those "originals," those hermits of division: the prime numbers), explorations of the calendar (on what day of the week will February 2, 2020 fall?), all "inner/oral" operations executed entirely without paper, except occasionally to keep a record, in order to continue my games beyond their initial moments.

Since I had a passion for these activities and devoted every moment of potential boredom to them (there were numerous opportunities), I quite naturally acquired at a very young age a certain virtuosity in calculation, a few remnants of which—albeit much slower and more prone to error—remain with me today (which leads people who know no better to readily accept, based on faulty reasoning, that I am a mathematician). But this talent was never really anything particularly exceptional.

It seems to me too that when I left Carcassonne at the age of twelve I had already acquired all the arithmetical baggage I've relied upon since. Only a very small portion of later mathematical knowledge has ever managed to find a place in my number games. (The acquisition of which knowledge represented one of the rare enlargements of my "numerical family"—something that's only happened on two occasions, but that nonetheless has a certain importance for my purposes in this text, as we'll see in two later branches.)

And I must stress that it was a matter of "true" numbers, number-individuals, known and familiar, and not of groups, types, or tribes of numbers. In my passion-fueled numerical activities, I've almost always remained at the archaic stage of the exclusive manipulation of examples, a "pre-Vieta" state of negligence, if not disdain, for literal notation (except as part of a personal "Gematria," in which letters are treated as digits or as the pseudonyms of clandestine numbers).

I counted the flies, as they crossed back and forth around the lamp, in the bright morning sunlight (idle hours, not in school; idle flies, patient sun, calm and warm); I counted the geographic fissures dividing the ceiling in the feverish night; the numbers overflowed in my head; one morning I said: "I have an ache in my digits."

137 I put poetry second on my list of passions, after numbers

I put poetry second on my list of passions, after numbers, in order to mark a chronological dependence (a direct, concrete dependence—counting was necessary for me to write poetry (it still is: I'm not a "free verse" poet)). But I didn't put it last, after reading, because in this case I want to indicate a lack of dependence: I think of the passion for poetry as an activity, not as a passive passion (poetry that is to be or has been read). It's an affair of memory, pure *cosa mentale*.

I say activity, but certainly not "creative" activity—at least if the slightest hint of aesthetic value might be associated with this adjective. As "creations," my first experiments in poetic composition (much of which has unfortunately been preserved) are strangely similar to everyone else's, and certainly don't deserve to be placed under the pompous rubric of "creation." The natural linguistic production of a child expressing him- or herself in the ordinary circumstances of life (in that aesthetically uncertain zone located between uncanny error and involuntary discovery) offers infinitely greater satisfactions.

Intentional constructions, however, are dominated by preferences and habits learned in school. In them one verifies, at best, whatever progress may have been made in lexical or syntactic mastery. Nothing is more touching, and perhaps pedagogically useful, than those notebooks of student poems that are requested, collected, and assembled by a teacher from his or her class. And nothing is more distressing than to see these same compositions presented as "models" of what poetry should be, of what the "poetic function" would be capable of, or so we're told, if it didn't have to be perverted, falsified, blunted by age and knowledge. The notion of children's poetry as a pure fount of limpid gold is nothing but a mirage.

As far as I can tell, anyway, I took up poetry—which was introduced to me in the form of examples proposed for classroom "recitation," and thus was absolutely inseparable in my mind from the nineteenth-century tradition of strictly counted and rhymed verse—as an unforeseen terrain for my original if sometimes recalcitrant application of the numerical faculty. It was indeed, first of all and for a long time, a game of numbers. (No doubt it still is.)

I have retained, who knows why, two poems that I "date" in my memory as my very first compositions, separated from each other by a year. I must have been seven or eight years old. Here's the older of the two in its entirety:

> *Le petit lapin*
> *Qui d'un air malin*
> *Mange le matin*
> *Un peu de sainfoin*
> *Sort le bout du nez*
> *Du petit terrier.*

> [The little rabbit
> Who with a knowing air
> Eats in the morning
> A little sainfoin
> Pokes the tip of his nose
> Out of his little hole.]

(I can't guarantee that the spelling matches the manuscript version. In fact, I'm almost certain that the original of this work (no longer extant) must have contained a few glaring errors.) If this remarkable text is truly and exclusively a product of my own invention (which I believe to be the case, but perhaps I'm presuming too much), it has one and only one undeniable virtue (given the poverty of the rhymes): It is correctly counted. It is a sestet of pentasyllabic lines, and each line has exactly five "syllables," according to the traditional count. For instance, the third line only reaches this number by means of a "counted silent e," at the end of "*mange*": a significant fact that establishes the mastery of prosody clearly demonstrated here by the poem's author.

I will provide a point of comparison (in a quite similar aesthetic register). This is a poem that I often read (since I pass by it regularly as I walk from where I live on the Rue d'Amsterdam to the Rue des Francs-Bourgeois), in large proud letters, on the front of a *boulangerie* (founded in 1902) on the Place des Petits-Pères, near the Bibliothèque Nationale (I also often see it through the window of the number 29 bus, which then turns down the Place des Victoires, on its way to the Porte de Montempoivre):

> *Le bon pain*
> *Au levain*
> *Se cuit toujours*
> *Comme autrefois*
> *Dans un four*
> *Au feu de bois.*

> [Good bread
> With leaven
> Is always baked
> As in the past
> In a wood-
> Burning oven.]

Compared to the "sainfoin poem" (my own), the "leaven poem" features a superior and more sophisticated rhyme scheme, in three variations (both are sestets, in the grand French strophic tradition): aabcbc. (This is the conclusive "scheme" of one of the two dominant variants of the "French sonnet," which I have called (in a work devoted to it) the "Peletier scheme" (after its first devotee, the poet-mathematician Jacques Peletier of Le Mans).) In my case, I use an "awkward" scheme, with two rhymes: aaaabb. The "quality" of the rhymes (poor in both cases) is comparable. But I must say I suspect the poet-baker of an imperfect mastery of the numerality of verse, and his oscillation between tri- and quadrisyllables to be involuntary (he carefully avoids the silent "e").

Which means that, on the whole, the technical quality of the two works seems about the same.

If I turn now to my opus no. 2 in the realm of poetry, there is some visible progress (in no way a question of progress in "poetic value," which is still non-existent, but of progress in the appropriation of the forms of versification). It consists of two quatrains; here is the first:

> *Lettres d'or qui faites les mots*
> *Vous qui rendez joyeux ou triste*
> *Vous me soulagez de mes maux*
> *Car vous êtes des humoristes.*

> [Golden letters that make words
> You who bring joy or sadness
> You relieve me of my ills
> For you are humorists.]

Progress, I need hardly stress, in all matters "technical": a shift to the octosyllable, longer lines, a "crossed" rather than a "flat" quatrain, rhymes that are adequate and even somewhat recherché ("*mots*"-"*maux*"). Inspired by Lamartine and Victor Hugo, my ambition could only go on, after this, to embrace the alexandrine, which promised long hours of introspective absorption, as well as plenty of counting that wasn't restricted to arithmetic and involved a completely different kind of subtlety.

I felt obliged to note here the extremely modest origins of this progression.

138 I see a book: an atlas

I see a book, but one that lies open for me to read before I am able to read (it must be a very old book; I learned to read at five, at the latest): I see that it is **an atlas**. Not a geographical atlas, but a book with fold-out pages, representations in color of typical natural sites. It is a "multiptych" with ten or twelve panels, **an altarpiece showing the life of a river, from its source to its enchanted dissolution in the deep blue of the sea;**

it is born as a spring, between two rocks high in mountains heaped with white like ice cream cones, enormous, intense, soaking in the soft blue embracing sky with its reassuring yellow sun; around the baby river, in its cradle of watercress and reeds, there is neither ox nor ass, but a sort of chamois, hesitant as a leaf, and three trees with perfectly round crests, three vegetal Magi adoring a new divinity: the River, no doubt, but especially the God hidden behind it, the Book;

the river flowed down; it gushed onto another panel (thick stiff pages with bright colors), descending steeply from the horizontal line at the beginning (top ----> bottom of the page; left ----> right) (coming to an end almost in a flat line as it meandered toward its goal), its narrow course, lined with arrow signs and large rocks beneath which trout or salmon, suspended in their inverse flights, leapt against the current; it encountered cottages, pine forests, pastures high and low, plowed fields, cows dripping milk, sheepdogs caught in the midst of their virtual barking, daisies, buttercups, marguerites for first loves, for "she loves me" (one petal) and "she loves me not" (the next); hedges, ditches, paths; its first few villages, small towns, their peasants in overalls, in hats, behind plows, pushing carts; roads and their kilometer markers red on top like boletus mushrooms, or yellow like half-moons, or white like sugar, milk teeth, or chalk parallelepipeds, accompanying it along its path; locomotives pulling train cars with travelers all arranged in their proper places on wooden benches; now passing through cities, now under bridges, now receiving the homages and tributes—quite so—of its tributaries: streams as thin as needles, modest rivulets, green veins; it grew, spread out, took on a broad calm surface, majestic, edged with sandbanks, islands, willows, murmuring with poplars; it entered the plains with all its arms outstretched, took a broad turn around a bend overlooked by steep cliffs, it buoyed tugboats, canoes, sailboats, rowboats, paddle wheels, steamboats; it sank into a sovereign and powerful lethargy, hesitating, hesitating, until it ended, finally, in the sea.

I've held onto the intense profusion of images from this picture-book, a profusion all the more ancient and precious because, once I was armed with letters (those "golden letters that make words"), once I had crossed the threshold of autonomous reading into a personal relationship between eye and book,

I was no longer interested in images: I stopped looking for them and retaining them. The atlas has thus remained for me my only book-before-the-Book, before all books. Just as its river cautiously abandons itself to the confusion of the sea, this book became lost for me, though never forgotten, in the ocean of books that I've read since. With very few exceptions I never felt the need for "illustrated" books, becoming entirely absorbed in letters, in lines and pages of reading—though some of these pages have left me with a visual memory just as intense as that of the river depicted without words in my "atlas."

One learns to read, but one doesn't necessarily learn, after that, to read for oneself, for one's own purposes. I associate the crossing of this border—beyond which one finds oneself in another world, never to return—with the same place, the same circumstances, as with numbers and poetry: sick on the sofa, convalescent and idle in the shadow of boredom. Much later, in a poem by Baudelaire, I found a justification, or anyway a sort of sensual rationale, for this repeated state of total absorption in books (in which I have continued to lose myself again and again, without hesitation, throughout my life), for hours on end, without any pretext of studying (or, in any event, for totally "gratuitous" studies that were in no way obligatory): "*Et mon esprit subtil que le roulis caresse / Saura vous retrouver, ô féconde paresse / Infini bercement du loisir embaumé.*" (And my subtle spirit caressed by the rolling swell / Will find you again, oh fecund idleness / The Infinite rocking of sweet-scented leisure) (in these lines I understand the word "leisure" to mean reading, an interpretation I know isn't justified by the text). But in the end I don't think this "excuse" holds up. I read, that's all.

In any case, the reading that comes back to me from those days is all of novels. And I would read very quickly (a habit that was extremely difficult for me to shake off, when I began the serious study of mathematics). Since it didn't take long for my passions to "grow out" of their place of origin in the study, my consumption of books grew rapidly. My parents used to make their book purchases in "the" bookstore in the city, the only one at that time where one could find real books (that is, aside from school books or technical books). And they were friends with the owners, M. and Mme. Breithaupt.

I often went with my father to the Breithaupt bookstore, and when I did I would get to choose a book—usually a novel in the *Collection verte*, which were all in hardcover (there was another series too, but I've forgotten the name: they all had paper covers with an illustration on them, but these were less resistant to harsh treatment). With the book in my possession, I stood next to my father, unaware of what was happening around me; I opened the volume and read. I began reading the moment the book had been purchased, continued to read as I walked out into the street. Occasionally it happened that I finished my book before we even got back to the house.

There aren't many of these books that I've forgotten: not Jack London, or James Oliver Curwood (*The Grizzly King*), or Mayne Reid, or Jules Verne (who, I admit, wasn't my favorite), or Gautier (oh! *Captain Fracasse*! oh! *Avatar*! oh! *Jettatura*! oh! *The Romance of a Mummy*!), or Mérimée ("Matteo Falcone" more than *Carmen*, the "point" of which I found difficult to grasp), or Hugo (abridged, I'm afraid), or Edmond About (*The Man with the Broken Ear*, "The Notary's Nose"). Fenimore Cooper (ah! *The Last of the Mohicans* and its sequels!). I'll stop there; despite my passion for the poetry of lists, this one, which could be quite long, is rather banal, given the period. I didn't read much "beyond my years" (as one says).

I made and will make an exception for Edgar Poe, however, in Baudelaire's translation. This was a book "for adults," which stood alongside other "precious" volumes (numerous works by Paul Valéry; Joyce's *Ulysses* in English (with a blue cover) (one of the first editions) as well as in the venerable French translation by Larbaud . . .) on the higher (but accessible) level of the little bookshelf that sat on the right when one entered the study. **I see it, a gray-green hardcover, sitting closed on top of the "cozy-corner," set down after its most recent reading** (I reread a lot, if only because of the continual and rapid exhaustion of newly stocked items), **"The Fall of the House of Usher," "The Pit and the Pendulum," and most especially, "A Descent into the Maelström"; as intense as the image of the river in the Atlas, I see this one as well, created in me by my reading: an image of the black and white gulf of a whirlpool, like a gigantic washbasin, like a bottomless pit, like a staircase in possession—and forever jealous—of time.**

139 The dining room on the ground floor was quiet and dim

The dining room on the ground floor was quiet and dim, though its darkness was relative, accentuated by the near-continuous brightness outside in the garden and by its location beneath the pine trees that stood next to the terrace. One window opened onto this terrace; another side faced the greenhouse. Looking directly at the house from outside, as though it were a face looking back at you, the dining room was on the left, like the bedroom on the third floor, like the study on the second. Therefore, in this <u>bifurcation,</u> I have as yet only entered into (cannibalized) the left cerebral hemisphere of my memory.

In the summer, it was a place that remained relatively cool; in winter it was very cold, during the first hours of the day at least, before the stove warmed up. **The stove was covered in brown ceramic, and had a little window made of mica; when someone opened it to clear out the ashes, the unburned wood residue, and the remnants of burnt coal, the smell that escaped was the smell of night, of winter nights, the smell of cold; the fire had gone out during the night, its soul had flown around through the mid-night, and what escaped into the dim room was its phantom.**

My father filled the empty belly of the stove: first paper through the open window, the pages crumpled into a ball one by one from the newspaper, which I held for him; then the "kindling" on top, tufts of pine needles and twigs, white branches from the boxwoods, from the spindle-trees, the top layer of bark gnawed away by rabbits; and on top of that went the coal, poured from above; the round anthracite nuts in black ellipsoid shapes, each ringed with a hard line, a continuous reinforcement around their equators (their widest circumference);

the room filled with white smoke; with the first yellow flame, the first feeble winter light retreated, overwhelmed, and the night reasserted itself around the rising fire and its own light, the only light, its smell of morning;

then, the window of mica was closed, the anthracite began to burn, each eye of incandescent coal a red star, white-red, radiant almost to the point of vertigo, each ellipse a wide drop of fire casting a shimmer just beyond its surface, surrounding it like velvet; the paper caught fire almost without a sound; then, when the wood started to burn, to "catch," sometimes resisting at first, covered as it was with the moisture of newly erupted sap, it was with a violent, urgent, imperious voice, muted by the closed window—a contained fury; as for the coal, it purred; no flame, no incandescent blaze appeared through the mica window, which wasn't really transparent— merely translucid; what one saw was a hot, furry sheen.

As compressed as an anthracite nut myself, I huddled up as tightly as I could to absorb every possible bit of warmth in the armchair, facing the red fire, the white fire, as I listened to the voice coming out of the radio, the "wireless," its distant origins made manifest by its constant fadings-out, its intermittences, its explosions of clarity followed by abrupt silences; it was the voice of "London": "The French speak to the French," it said, it said to me. "*Radio-Paris ment! Radio-Paris ment!*" it sang, in five notes (three horizontal, two rising). "*Radio-Paris est all'mand!*" ("Radio Paris lies! Radio-Paris is German!")

But this broadcast did not lie—it spoke the truth to our avid ears, the truth of our just war against Nazi Germany, and against its French supporters. I didn't have the slightest doubt about this. The truth always came from elsewhere—from heroic England, and from the Soviet Union and America, its allies; from the French sheltered by England, from the General and from Pierre Dac who spoke in their name. But it came above all from England, from Churchill's England, and with a certain maternal inflection (my mother taught English): it was from London that all their voices came to us, the voices that told the truth about the war.

Today I hear it as an entirely optimistic voice, perhaps because I didn't really begin to listen to it, to really discern or understand the meaning of what it was telling us, until the moment when, after Stalingrad and El Alamein, it had nothing but victories to report.

I heard the signal, the joyous and virtuous melody of Händel's *Water Music*, countless times—several thousand, perhaps; confident and irrepressible, the broadcasts moved ever closer to their goal, and with ever greater certainty: each time predicting the forthcoming celebration of its own obsolescence.

140 **Looking through the window, as I sit on the piano stool, I see the Sunday pine trees swaying in a gentle wind**

Looking through the window, as I sit on the piano stool, I see the Sunday pine trees swaying in a gentle wind, the air cheerful with birdsong, the full and impalpable play-space outside. No regret is connected with this image. Or, rather, the contradictory currents of past boredom and present nostalgia have canceled each other out, and I can revisit this moment with neutrality, as something drawn from my reserves of vision (indeed, almost all the images that I'm reconstituting as part of this section are affectively neutral, at least superficially (the effort required to cross certain thresholds of visibility indicates to me that this is almost certainly no more than a surface neutrality)).

I practiced on the piano's black and white teeth. The piano, and music in general, were a part of my mother tongue, my mother's language (on my father's side there was another kind of music, another kind of practice, equally mental and physical, associated with water: swimming, the sea, the Provençal *mar*). I never got to know any other instrument: only the black and white of ivory keys spread out beneath the black and white of the staves and notes.

The disruptions that occurred in the last months of the war, followed by our departure, meant that only the older children of the family, my sister and me, had gotten the opportunity to play the piano. She's the only one who still plays today. I didn't stop voluntarily, but I had to give up, betrayed by my right hand after it was injured in an accident. Chance thus produced a kind of intergenerational transmission—a striking symmetry—since the sea had also "punished" my father on his right hand as well.

Music to be listened to as music, however, didn't come from fingers on a piano (I rarely managed to play well enough for anyone to really want to listen to what I was playing), but from the "phonograph," from records turning on the "pick-up" to the right of the sofa ("pick-up": an old name for a "record player" (itself an old name for a "stereo," also called a "*zinzin*")): violins, cellos, orchestras, and voices (Marian Anderson in a "siciliana" by Händel, arias from *Don Giovanni*), trios and quartets by Mozart and Beethoven, sonatas, impromptus, some harpsichord (the very first recordings of Wanda Landowska), the *Brandenburg*s, the *Suite in B minor*.

Eyes closed, my hands gently cupped over my ears, cramped in the far corner of the sofa, on its rough gray-green "upholstery," nearly against the wall, I heard the regular hiss of the needle spiraling over black wax like a *basso continuo* beneath the prodigious edifice of Beethoven's fourteenth string quartet, or beneath the cheerful surface of the rondo of sonata K. 331, until the sound of the final skid, in extremis, brought to a stop when my father raised the "arm," propping it on the side of the machine, return-

ing the completed record to its sleeve, then once again moving the needle over and down for it to scratch through a few preliminary grooves, until finally, and again, the music returned, filling the shadows under my eyelids, filling my fingers with rhythmic compulsions, filling my head with a sensual hope that the sound would never stop.

The state of the art of recordings before the war (always the same recordings, but inexhaustible in their effects) was such that the whole and continuous form of any given work always eluded me almost completely (one side of a 78 lasted two or three minutes at most). I experienced almost nothing but autonomous musical "moments" (which often didn't even cover one entire "movement" of a sonata), punctuated by the preparatory or concluding rituals of the placement—or, as the case may be, the removal—of the record in question on—or from—the peg on the turntable, covered with a cloth-like material, and the "overture"—or else the final chord—produced by the needle's entry onto—or removal from—the sonorous scene. These punctuations so inviolably circumscribed the duration of the music, and were so inseparably associated with it, that they ended up (like the applause at the beginning of Stockhausen's *Momente*) becoming, for me, an integral part of it.

Thus strictly defined and delimited, all these varied music-events were brought into the same general musical family by the almost perfect equivalence of their duration, of their beginnings and endings, and as such they were grasped by my mind, intensely and in a single stroke, as so many separate *now*s—that is, these discreet moments were grasped by a mind that, after innumerable repetitions, was certain of possessing them in their totality, and which, in a movement of memory that was both anticipatory and projected back from their endpoint, incessantly and palindromically went to meet their unfolding movements halfway. I have never lost them.

There were other records too, no less precious, but they belonged to a very different category. They were precious because English (or "American") was sung on them, and they belonged therefore to that future freedom that we dreamed of and that came closer every day (they were precious for our parents too, for a different reason that didn't entirely escape us: because they represented a recent past that was nonetheless irremediably lost with the war—the years "before us").

We didn't listen to these other records in the darkness of some solipsistic intensity. No, on the contrary, they were the occasion for impromptu accompaniment, frenetic gesticulations, somersaults on the sofa, laughter, and more or less accurate imitations, in our shrill or piercing voices.

Thus: "There are no flies on Auntie / On Auntie / On Auntie // There are no flies on Auntie / And I will tell you why / She's not what you'd call hideous / But the flies are so fastidious. // There are no flies on Auntie / And that's the reason why / Oh! there are no flies on Auntie . . ." This was one of my favorite songs (and I still sing it today to the children of my friends and my family, not without a certain success).

Thus the sentimental marshmallows of the Whispering Barytones: "She's got eyes of blue / Who ever heard of eyes of blue? / But she's got eyes of blue / That's my weakness now!"

And then sometimes I listened dreamily, with something like an anticipatory nostalgia for England, to this: "The first weekend in June / A sentimental tune / Awa-a-kes in my heart / . . . / The clouds have all passed by / The sun is in the sky . . ." For this was a different sun from the one we knew: gentler, milder, one that knew how to talk to the moon ("And the sun will tell the moon / That the summer will be over / very soon"), to the clover (in the next rhyme), to the grass, and to the roses, after heavy rains.

141 I can without fail enter this room populated by voices, especially musical voices

I can without fail enter this room populated by voices, especially musical voices (and when I choose this path, the image it leads me to seems stable to the point of indestructibility) by evoking (I've mastered this) (though sometimes I hear it without wanting to, suddenly, wherever I happen to be, in my head) a dance from one the *English Suites* by Johann Sebastian Bach: to be precise, the first "*Passepied en Rondeau*" from the *Suite no. 5 in E minor,* BWV 810.

This musicological precision is of little interest in the absence of the music itself, which there's no real way to evoke in written prose, aside from such a designation (it would be easier in the course of an oral performance, a "reading", but not necessarily any more enlightening, except as a way to stress the "truth effect" of my story). But I did take the trouble to verify it by finding the exact position of this fragment in the suites for harpsichord (I was unsure whether it was one of the *French Suites* or one of the *English Suites*, my preference being for the latter) yesterday afternoon, June 8, at 51 Rue des Francs-Bourgeois.

It was there, somewhere on the final side of the recording by Glenn Gould. Marie stopped the record, counted the slightly discontinuous "tracks" of grooves on the surface, and announced that "*passepieds* 1 and 2" came just before the final *gigue*. I immediately noted this information in pencil on a torn sheet of paper, alongside some formulas of propositional calculus, these being the correct solutions to an exercise in algorithms I had given as a second midterm to my (rather numerous) students in "Formal Languages," and which I had just been correcting. I noticed, at the same moment, as I tried unsuccessfully to whistle the notes at the speed of Gould, that my ear automatically changed the timbre: What I hear is always the old-fashioned harpsichord of Wanda Landowska.

I found it impossible not to take steps to verify exactly which piece I was referring to, initially, which, however (on the one hand) caused me to step outside the strict time frame that I imposed on myself from the beginning of this work (and that I indicated explicitly in branch one, chap. 1, § 5, and (on the other hand) violated an almost obligatory consequence of my principle of writing "in real time," without preparations or revisions (a deviation that I immediately tried to "make up for" by interrupting myself yesterday at the moment when I wrote "a dance from one of the *English Suites* by Johann Sebastian Bach: to be precise . . ." and by picking up again today where I left off, with the story of the circumstances of my identification): I must not to try to erase the weaknesses of my memories.

But this exceptional treatment is perhaps appropriate to the nature of the "case," which is itself quite singular: what appears as an exception, or a counter-example, if you like, to my hypothesis (only a narrative hypothesis, to be sure, but one stated with conviction, despite everything) concerning the inevitable and rapid disappearance of memory images as soon as they are actually "brought to light" by memory.

For I have heard this melody innumerable times (internally, so to speak, or externally, from that old record) (or else by whistling it (poorly)), and the reconstitution of the old site (the sofa, the record, the precise attitude of my listening) is always just as immediate and absolute for me as the melody. And I don't even need to hear (or whistle) the entire melody to summon the accompanying image—the first six notes are enough.

(I say six notes out of caution. I have in my memory several "airs," the first four notes of which coincide with this one (one of Beethoven's piano sonatas, for example). In fact, I think that a single note, the first, if heard with its particular timbre (not only of *a* harpsichord, but of *that* harpsichord), would be enough. For the inner qualities of this "G" (I say "G," but this designation is likely wide of the mark, because of the "discord" permanently fixed in my ear from our old piano in Carcassonne) are the result of a previous listening, lingering silently in my mind, with memory, as I said above, both anticipating and projecting back from the end of the melody, ceaselessly encountering its own unfolding—making itself available for an explicit repetition. The opening note is only a recapitulation of this repetition.)

Among all the music that survives there, in my mind, why this one in particular? why not the *Suite in B minor* by Bach? a sonata by Mozart, by Beethoven? a song in English? other melodies that I can also retrieve and place in the same room, at the same time? I don't know. I simply observe that the <u>essential effector of memory</u>, in this case, is a piece of music, this piece of music.

The infinitesimally decisive factor is perhaps the harpsichord (a consequence of the antagonistic harpsichord/piano duality, and of the interdiction that, after the accident with my hand, barred the latter to me?).

142 The position of the kitchen, the last of the six rooms, can easily be deduced from the rest of my description:

The position of the kitchen, the last of the six rooms of the house (not counting the *envoi*, the *tornada* of this song of the childhood home—an "add-on" stanza, as it were: the external bathroom), can easily be deduced from the rest of my description: with the house divided into two halves, the two cerebral hemispheres of my memory, as I said, and separated by the gap of the stairway, and since I voluntarily left two rooms empty, on the second and third floors to the right: the kitchen is opposite the dining room on the ground floor, with a window opening onto the terrace.

Here too, the "rational" mode of entry—through a doorway—has nothing to do with the mode by which I reconstitute or reoccupy each of these spaces with my phantom body, which places itself in a room with an almost ubiquitous multiplicity of "points of view." (And, incidentally, I note that the first images that come to mind of the two bedrooms I won't be entering in this particular prose-moment have me stationed in front of their closed doors—on the outside.) It's still a question of seeing (even when I'm on the sofa, listening to the harpsichord with my eyes closed, I'm seeing), and of a shifting family of unequally distributed lines of sight; but these are unequal in terms of sharpness, clarity, and sentimental or sensual importance. The sense of sight orders this world, in accordance with the meditative hierarchy of the full five senses at my command.

But another sense always and necessarily accompanies sight (which is to say that as I reflect on this process for the purposes of description, I become aware that another sense is always involved. The remaining senses are no doubt also present, but are usually inaccessible). It is this other sense that serves as an <u>effector of memory</u> (just as every image I review plays this role in relation to the other images that it then calls up). In the bedroom where I found myself so abruptly at the beginning of this branch, it was the sense of touch that was at work, implicated there in a subterranean manner by the content of that first memory: the frozen mist on the window.

The initial image of the desk, which I chose not to place at the beginning of this bifurcation—it's rather a starting point for thinking through the space of the study and thus serves an introductory function in the reconstitution of that room (I almost always find only one such productive image)—this image is made effective by the sound of the Brownian movements of the flies around the lightbulb on the ceiling, in the morning sunlight—by the sense of hearing, then: my second sense. And the timbre of the harpsichord note from the *English Suite* also brings hearing into play.

Searching further, I find that the sense of taste intervenes in the **Oranjello** of the **Wild Park**, and in the penneque fig of the **Basin** (see Chapter 4). But nowhere has there been the slightest smell (it's my weakest sense, at least now). (This observation satisfies me; let it serve as the prelude to a "theoretical justification" of my hierarchical scale of the senses, generally and in particular.)

I stopped for this brief inquiry because as I was about to enter the kitchen I came up against two nearly simultaneous images (more precisely, my repeated efforts to think through this entry placed me in the presence of two alternating and independent images, and I was unable to decide which one was "semantically" primary): one is purely a matter of sight (in appearance at least), and the other on the contrary is deeply marked by a tactile sensation.

Up to that point I had not encountered any hesitations, or perhaps had automatically eliminated them as extraneous, unworthy of reflection, because I was solely preoccupied with moving forward on my path. I note, however, that they raise a different question, which I already raised in an earlier interpolation (§ 90), leaving it suspended there: What is the nature (unforeseeable and random, or not?) of the initial position in which one finds oneself in a room, in a memory—when the gaze, unnoticed, takes up its place? No hypothesis presents itself.

My choice, in this case, is between two possible positions:

—a makeshift bathtub is occasionally placed at one end of the kitchen table; contact with the hot water both revives and calms the pain of stings and scratches made by thorns on bare legs, got while running all day down the paths, through the vines, of the "*bois de Serres*" or "*Gaja*," our names for two ludic escape routes leading towards the outskirts of the town. As the burning water slowly cools, as the immense well-being of the bath seeps into me, I see the skin of my fingers becoming wrinkled and turning pink, as they do after long immersion in the washbasin in the garden, playing my maritime games.

—A window onto the street looks toward the Enclos du Luxembourg; other children are playing; sometimes, rarely, a car passes by.

143 this time I let myself open the door onto the balcony

I climb back up to the second floor landing, and this time I let myself open the door onto the balcony. Here, then, is the balcony: it leads to the left, toward the bathroom, which was a later addition, an extra room attached to the house at this level and supported by the hallway below, which leads out into the garden. (This is the real entryway to the house, through the little door where the hallway leads out to the terrace; the official entrance to "7 Rue d'Assas," the gate to the street, is almost completely out of use.)

I walk on the balcony, and at the same time I look at it from below. **I see,** almost simultaneously, **the garden from above (the bench, the terrace, the few steps that join them from the entrance) and the balcony from below.** Each of these views is immediately reversible.

That is, I can't see the balcony again without also seeing it from another spot, a spot more or less exactly situated on the bare ground of the garden, at the top of the steps, where the central walkway begins, between the two "hills" with their trees (the part of the balcony that's in the center of this view is a little to the right of the door, in front of the first window). But, then, having seen this, I can't avoid looking from the other direction as well, and immediately— toward the ground of the garden, toward the steps, the trees on each side of the walkway—an inversion that would be impossible to achieve in real time, an infinitely accelerated exchange of perspectives, which continues in oscillations and would go on doing so indefinitely if the vision didn't become blurred, quickly eluding me.

But all around, **it is summer; the table is set outside; looking up from below, toward the balcony, toward the windows of the back bedroom; following some childish commotion, a voice asks: "Are you asleep?" A naive voice answers, "Yes."** I was so seduced by this logical trap that I've held onto it, preciously, ever since, wrapped up together with the sun-drenched table, the tablecloth, the glasses on it; with the laughter, the silence of the windows, their curtains drawn for the afternoon nap of my youngest brother, Jean-René.

The question posed to the sleeper is a riddle. I can't say, "I'm asleep." If I say "I'm asleep" without lying, then I can only be answering myself, for myself—I am dreaming. The implicit question asked by the dreamer is similar: "Am I sleeping?" This is the question that disturbs and paralyzes Perceval before the Fisher-King, in the Grail castle. But one must never try to answer such questions. One must never decipher these riddles. One must let sleepers lie.

The balcony continued off to the right (as seen from below), though not as far as the windows of the study. And at its far end two steps went down into the bathroom, that curious addition appended to the main building. The bathtub was right at the bottom of the stairs, and the floor was covered in cracked linoleum. There was a sink and a mirror on the opposite wall, and a window to the right, directly over the terrace.

In the back of the bathroom, on the right, in an even more audacious architectural outcropping, was the "stall," in which some reading treasures were set aside. A pile of books had in fact been placed there to make up for the lack of an adequate paper supply for this sort of place (one effect among others of the general penury). The fleeting and fragmentary knowledge that one could glean from them (but rarely find again) was rather tactile in nature, something like an extreme version of the "paroptic vision" that once so fascinated Jules Romains (which *Le Canard enchaîné* had summed up in a lapidary visual way with the following: "M. Jules Romains reads his newspaper by sitting on it"). The choice of books thus consigned to such a "muddy end" tended not to inspire one to linger over them.

But one day in the winter of 1944 a cover caught my attention; it showed a sort of swimming pool in violent, expressionistic colors (actually, I think it was a reservoir in a basement (?), or maybe a water tower (?)), its water tinted red from the victims stabbed by a criminal wearing a sly and sardonic grin, frozen by the artist's pen at the moment when, his evil deed accomplished, he's climbing up a rope ladder to rejoin the world of the living (and so to carry out further crimes); one of the victims is rising up with a gesture of surprise mixed with vain supplication, whereas the others already show the limp indifference of those who have been both drowned and bled.

The cover struck me as promising; I too plunged into the bloody water of the story, which I took up in the middle, since at least half of the pages had already been torn out. It was one volume (and luckily not the only one) of an exhaustive edition of Ponson du Terrail's Rocambole novels. **I forgot the cold; everything began** (in my reading everything began) **with a letter.**

144 Rocambole, as you no doubt recall, passed himself off as a viscount

Rocambole, as you no doubt recall, passed himself off as a viscount, under a name I can't remember at the moment (I must not be so careless as to confuse him with the Duke of Château-Mailly, whom the criminal will dispatch within a few chapters (as his rival for the beautiful woman), by injecting him with "anthrax" by means of a needle perfectly placed in the mane of his favorite horse: pretty clever, no?). The real viscount, absent for several years (did he leave on a world tour after an unhappy love? to spread the Gospel to savage tribes? Perhaps he's dead? perhaps killed by Rocambole when the latter escaped from the

penal colony? Perhaps he'll return to denounce the imposter (which is indeed
what happens, I believe, a few hundred pages later))—the real viscount, I say,
has involuntarily loaned his identity to Rocambole, who thus gains a foothold
in Parisian high society. But Rocambole will not stop there.

  And so he courts the beautiful Concepción de Sallandrera, daughter of a
powerful Spaniard, himself in possession of an unspecified but considerable
number of paintings by Zurburán. Rocambole is at his club (playing whist
perhaps? (one of the games my grandfather savored, almost as much as *ma-
nille coinchée*, a less noble pleasure certainly)) and here comes someone bringing him a sealed envelope. It's a letter from Concepción! The envelope is perfumed, he casually weighs it in his hand (he's in no hurry), doesn't open it right
away. Why should he? Even before he reads the words traced in a trembling
virginal hand by the proud and beautiful girl, he thinks: "It's several pages
long! She loves me!"

  I was greatly impressed by this astonishing sign of acuity, this ability to
touch the very depths of feminine psychology (whose laws no woman could
escape, not even the daughter of the lofty Duke of Sallandrera) on the part of a
thief who was raised—dare I say—among the "bandits" stalking the "customs
barriers," and who joined up for a life of crime with the ignoble Venture and
the diabolical Baccarat. "Ah, the lessons of Sir William have been fruitful," I
thought—unless Ponson du Terrail thought it for me.

  But, to tell the truth, I not only admired this—the indication of psychological perspicacity as revealed by Rocombole—I also avidly absorbed the truth
of this basic law of the soul: "Six densely-written pages! She loves me!" For
although I was in love myself, I was hardly in a position to receive such a confirmation in return. This was the winter of 1944, and I had the good luck of
being able to discover these precious truths in one of the large volumes of the
Fayard (?) edition of Ponson that I found in the "stall," to which they had no
doubt been relegated on account of their literary unworthiness, compounded
by the scarcity of paper.

  **The light, during a gray afternoon when school was out, reached me
through the small side window, where the bare branches of the fig tree
swayed**. I would dearly have liked to see Concepción de Sallandrera fall in
love in a more palpable way, which would have been even more instructive,
but this was a possibility that the general superficial prudery of the work could

hardly allow one to anticipate (and besides (very morally) Rocambole fails in his megalomaniacal and titanic enterprise).

After returning from a hard-labor colony, Rocambole becomes a good man (and simultaneously a very boring one, it must be said). With the help of Wanda, the young Russian woman who is his disciple (a sort of rehashed version of Baccarat, unavailable since she became the Countess Artoff) (I saw her too in the guise of Nina, whose name, when she wasn't in hiding, was Morguleff), Rocambole foils the plans of a few minor scoundrels who, though much duller, are quite similar to what he himself had been before his reformation.

During that winter, the last of the war (when the bathroom couldn't be heated), another scene, infinitely more gruesome than that of the letter from the innocent Concepción, but strangely appropriate to the atmospheric circumstances of my reading, kept me shivering but fascinated: the scene in which Wanda, the cold beautiful Russian, insulted by the beastly desire of a wretch, the steward of the domain of X—, a few versts from Y—, I think (alas! the imprecision, the vagueness of those ignoble desires!), carries out a terrible act of vengeance, worthy of Sir William: pretending to yield to the demands of the wretch, she arranges to meet him deep underground, at the very bottom of an empty water reservoir. Once there, she disappears for a moment (supposedly to prepare herself for the worst?) and seals him up inside (it's a covered building with a single door, protected by a lock whose key she has stolen). Then she opens the taps.

The basin fills with tepid water, which slowly rises to the steward's shoulders, but only to his shoulders. Only his head is above water. At first he laughs, then becomes worried, thinks there must be some mistake, shouts, screams, begs. He's reassured for a moment when the water first stops. It was all a bad joke! He's not condemned to die by drowning! But it is winter (a Russian winter, which I imagined perfectly, by extrapolating from the temperature in the stall and from the news heard on the radio: the Red Army was entering Budapest. A few photos of the fate of Von Paulus's soldiers at Stalingrad had begun to appear in the newspapers). The sunny afternoon is already coming to an end. The water is growing cold. The sides of the basin are smooth, and the unfortunate man claws at them with his nails as he tries, in vain, to climb up and escape from the deadly grip tightening around him.

145 **because the water, growing cold in the Siberian night, will soon freeze**

Deadly, you see, because the water, growing cold in the Siberian night, will soon freeze, and when it freezes (and I'm not unaware that this physical law had an unfortunate effect on the Titanic) it will undergo a terrible increase in volume, crushing the man in its purifying embrace, in horrible retribution for having dared to think of that other embrace, to which he had wanted to subject Wanda (whom I nonetheless imagined succumbing—in some nice warm water that nature would surely provide—to my own not very honorable embraces).

I seem to remember that Wanda peers through a chink in the wall or some Russian skylight in the roof in order to witness the criminal's agony (she herself is warmly wrapped in superb furs, outside in the twilight cold of the steppe, which enhances her blonde, icy, Slavic beauty all the more). But this is perhaps only a refinement of my own wintertime imaginings, incontestably enflamed by Ponson du Terrail's sublime scene. Later, when I gave Laurence a new paperback edition of Ponson's work, I was unable to find this chapter again, much to my regret (but then I made only a feeble effort: rereading it then, I found it really boring).

There were at least ten volumes. To forestall (as it were) the premature destruction of all my Rocamboles, which I couldn't read in one sitting, I carefully stashed them in the "reserves" behind the sink and replaced them with old and outdated philosophy textbooks, whose powers of "suspense" I found distinctly inferior, and which could be sacrificed before the rest without causing any harm. I was able thus to read most of the adventures, with the exception of the very beginning of the series, in which the awful demonic genius of Sir William reigned supreme.

(But fortunately I didn't miss the scene in which the arrogant Rocambole, believing he's learned all he can from his master (now blind and stuck in a wheelchair), throws him off a cliff to get rid of him—so that he can fly with his own wings, so to speak. And at this moment (midnight—thunder and lightning), he remembers, in capital letters—but too late—Sir William's warning: I AM YOUR GOOD STAR. THE DAY I DIE YOUR GOOD STAR WILL GO OUT!)

The wretched man (I'm virtually certain that Ponson du Terrail calls him "the wretched man") then falls to his knees at the edge of the enormous cliff (on the Cornouailles coast? Perhaps I'm confusing it with "Tristan's leap" at Tintagel) and says: I AM AFRAID! OH! I AM AFRAID! And he's right to say it. After this, things don't go well for him.

Whenever I finished one of those voluminous adventures, I abandoned Rocambole, his accomplices, his diabolical schemes and infamies, to their no less infamous fate.

And after I had set down one of those books with its pages already falling out (pages bound for an ignoble end), I hoisted myself up to the edge of the little side window, stuck a leg through, and slipped cheerfully into the garden through the branches of the fig tree.

The fig tree which, in my field of vision, appeared to the far left, next to the wall, along the same horizontal line as the bench (as in the game of **Go-Creeping**).

and this image—if one adopts the suggested path of reading this volume, according to which this <u>bifurcation</u> follows the first chapter—will lead into chapter two of the present branch, the title of which is, precisely, <u>The Fig Tree</u>.

Bifurcation B

Fore-life

146 I mark out a border in time, I think of the beginning of my life:

I draw a border in time here, and I think of it with a certain solemnity as marking the beginning of my life: an image functions as its border post. In this image, **I enter** (all five of us enter) **the garden on the Rue d'Assas**. And it is indeed the garden on the Rue d'Assas—I recognize it. But now it is a garden in which we've never set foot before: a pristine site for our activities. This last assertion is derived, very simply, from the fact that **the ground of the walkways is covered with sand; fine sand, almost white** (the thoroughly innocent whiteness of this sand is certainly exaggerated in the image). In the time that followed our crossing of this threshold, the sand disappeared entirely. The dull trampling of legions of children, in their races, on their bikes, and in their games, with their spades and pails and scraping and splashing, quickly got the better of that thin layer of decorative sand. The real ground—rough, rocky, and dry—simply swallowed it up. It was there, it was with this (?), that my life began.

Of course, I wasn't born (like some new Dr. Faustroll) at an already "countable" age—in this case, the end of my fifth year, in September 1937. Nor was I born six years old (if I allow for the few months that would have been necessary to create the garden's new, sandless landscape through the destruction of the old one). But the inner conviction that one has of being oneself (that is, of possessing the central imagination of a seeing, sensing ego, that of the average sensual child) necessarily presupposes, via a reversal in time—an inverse return—the <u>continuity</u> of one's memories, and thus a faculty of **memory**. And mine begins there, on the Robinsonian sand. With regard to the quasi-totality of what preceded the moment when I set my bare foot on those walkways, I've been struck with amnesia. Everything prior to that moment is like the dream of a prenatal life, or like a collection of reminiscences entirely outside the duration of time, discontinuous and belonging to my **fore-memory**. To live, and to live as a unified whole, requires that one be able to think a continuity of being, it requires the certainty (illusory but persistent) of having lived without interruption. And this certainty itself requires a setting, a framework, a background both geometrical and temporal, without discontinuities. For a "self," the real beginning of life isn't birth (which, strictly speaking, is as internally unthinkable as death)—and is even very distant from birth. Everything that precedes the beginning of a "perfect" time (perfect in the topological sense: a closed set with no isolated points) belongs to a border-zone of existence, like sleep, and not to life at all (which, topologically, is an "open" set). Thus, the entry into the garden designates the end of my **fore-life**.

The preceding years, from December 5, 1932, to September 1937, are external to me for this very reason. 1935, for example, and 1936, "resemble" 1930 (when I didn't exist at all) much more than they do 1939. As a result, I can turn toward this period of my life with an almost "objective" gaze—by way of photographs, for example—and thus with much more calmness and with less distrust than with respect to what came after: practically no interference with the certainty of my identity is possible. The rigor of my narrative constraint (which dictates that, in this prose, my memory must act, as much as possible, without any assistance) doesn't run any risk of being compromised on that account.

I lie down on my bed with the gray file in which I've gathered just a few of the letters and photographs that make up the more extensive mass of my "family archives" (everything that has survived the various forms of destruction that have befallen it). I keep it all in my bedroom, the "bedroom with the copper bed," in the Minervois (and after I'm finished I will return the contents of the file, as is customary, since these documents are meant to be available to everyone (though for the moment they don't seem to attract much curiosity)). I will pick out a few photographs, a half-dozen at most. That will suffice.

I'll look at them at some length. I've never really looked at them for very long. They are true childhood photographs: their emotional charge is pure, of a strictly private order. And they are perfectly banal: rather small, on the ordinary paper used for black and white family prints in the thirties; there they are, slipped (having been divided at random) into two small yellow-beige (and yellowing) folders. On the first of these I read:

PHOTOGRAPHIE

A. GAMMONET

86, Avenue de Saxe - LYON

Above this, a dark blue diamond in which is written, in fake italic hand-writing:

Agfa

with the diamond topped by a small red figure: a young woman with a pink face, her hair hidden in a woman's hat from a film or fashion magazine circa 1930, her republican right hand raised, a red muffler lifted by the wind like a left arm opposite it, which, along with the first arm (the real one) forms a V for victory; while a longer scarf juts straight out from her neck (thanks to that optimistic breeze), which is itself perpendicular to the arm and muffler (the whole thing resembles the three axes of the orthonomic frame of reference used to work out problems in cinematography). Below the scarf, finally, is the second arm of this young allegorical personage: it is holding a camera, a black rectangle from which a round white eye contemplates us.

On the back of the folder someone has written the customer's name in black ink:

Nom: Molinaux [*sic*, for "Molino," the name of my maternal grandparents]

Developing:	1	2.40
Printings:	8	5.60
Enlargements:		____
Total due:		8.00

At the very bottom, in tiny print:

Pochettes BURLET 30 Rue Saint-Merri Paris

The prints are in the inner left pocket of the folder, the negatives on the right (some of these were never printed; as far as I can tell, they are only slight variations of the prints themselves). The edges of the prints are not straight, but undulate slightly as on postage stamps (although more irregularly and crudely). I run my finger along these edges.

I lean back on the four pillows lying at the head of my bed, against the bookshelf, my feet beneath the protean duck-feather duvet that Marie ordered for us from La Camif (a mail order service for teachers only) (it's June, but not really very warm). I take out the first two <u>pictions</u>, then set them down in front of me. In each one I see the inner facade (facing the garden) of 21 *bis* Rue de l'Orangerie, in Caluire, where I was born.

147 My grandparents moved to Caluire when my grandfather was given a position as a primary-school inspector

My grandparents moved to Caluire when my grandfather was given a position as a primary-school inspector (inspector, that is, of the teachers) in the *département* of Isère. Caluire is next to Lyon, between the Rhône and Saône Rivers. The Rue de l'Orangerie is at the top of a hill, above the Rhône. Numbers 21 and 21 *bis* were immediately adjacent (it's the same building (?)), but they were unequal in size. 21 *bis* was smaller than 21, only including a narrow, and not very long, section of the immense garden, which was separated from the rest of the plot by a fence of wooden stakes. From the moment they moved in, my grandmother (who had four school-aged children) began to pursue the ambition of moving next door, from 21 *bis* to 21, which was far more spacious. Her will was virtually irresistible: It took her several years to convince the owner, a rugged Swiss fellow, but she finally did. But this decisive victory didn't take place until shortly after my birth. I was born in 21 *bis*.

My father had done his (deferred) military service in the Alpine Chasseurs, then began his teaching career at the middle school at Arbois, land of "yellow wine" (with which, he told me, I was "baptized"). My mother had received her *agrégation* certificate in English after returning from Oxford and had begun teaching in Bourg-en-Bresse. She went there every day by train. She would always leave at the last minute, to the disapproval and anxiety of her father, a fanatic when it came to punctuality. She would run down the Rue de l'Orangerie, then down the long Rue de l'Oratoire—at that time bordered by a very long uninterrupted wall—to the small Cuire train station (the town is

called Caluire-et-Cuire), where she would arrive out of breath at the same moment as the locomotive. She rushed over the grade crossing to the platform,
and, at the very last moment, the stationmaster would hold out the ticket he
had already prepared for her. I waited in my cradle, in the company of my
grandmother and my aunt Renée.

It wasn't difficult to assemble, and to concentrate into a few sentences, the
various elements of the above description of the circumstances "surrounding"
my birth. I didn't need what I will call <u>external memories</u>—that is, physical
documents, or images fabricated from stories—I have succinctly reported exactly what I've been told; this much is what I've retained from various statements collected from various people at various times. But I have retained
nothing of the statements themselves, nor of the moments when I heard them.
I know all this in as impersonal a way as I know the fine schoolbook alexandrine: "*La Loire prend sa source au mont Gerbier-des-Joncs*" ("The Loire has
its source in the Gerbier-des-Joncs mountain"). In the new school of what's
called "ecological memory," this is referred to as a "generic personal memory."
According to my generic personal memory, I remember that I was told that I
was born under these circumstances.

I know nothing of these circumstances "on my own," of course. My fore-life
is almost entirely invisible and inaudible to me. Nor, as I said, does anything
remain of the statements that first informed me, "it was there," "that's how
it happened." I believe them (I believe that what I have retained of them is
true), but neither more nor less than the similar statements that taught me,
for example, about the catastrophe of Hitler's triumph in Germany, which was
nearly contemporaneous with my birth.

More generally, I don't ever seem to retain any exact recollection of things
said. To once again borrow a comparison from "word processing," I virtually never apprehend language events in "image mode," but on the contrary
as "digitized" traces (or rather, I should say, following Milner, "literalized"):
that is to say, recomposable, transformable at will into other forms that are
specific to me, operative, and calculable (capable of undergoing a "calculation"
in the mind). (For me, language is never "cooked language," except for the
language of poetry.) All the images that I have preserved are, therefore, "out-
of-language." Everything that I "know" (and therefore everything I remember

in this specific sense) is "in-language." My <u>internal memories</u> (in the "image mode" of my memory) are strictly distinct from these other, external ones (in the "literal mode").

At that point in my perception of the past where the sense of a personal continuity first appears, I can place these two modes (along with the worlds that they constitute in me) parallel to one another, and I can compare them (to the inevitable detriment of the first, the <u>image-world</u>: when language takes hold of images, it undoes them, recomposes them, destroys them). But before that, there is practically no passage from one mode to the other: the visions, the images, which are very rare, seem "out-of-the-world," strange, unlocatable. They hover suspended, deprived of the supports provided by a formed world, by a geometry and a temporal axis.

The Gammonet photography studio prepared eight prints (which it called "printings") for its customer, "Molinaux." I have in front of me the third and the sixth (if I can trust the numbers written in pencil on their backs). They both show "21 *bis*" (as it was called in our house), more or less from the same angle. In one case, the view was taken at a certain distance, from the garden. One sees the entrance, the two upper floors, the roof, and, on the right, part of the house at no. 21 (but we never said "21." We always said "21 *bis*," since for my grandmother it had never been anything but a *bis*, an *ersatz*). There's a face in the highest window, perhaps my aunt Renée, but I can't tell for certain.

In the other photograph, the facade is cut off just above the windows on the third floor. It is this view that I look at more closely, with the eyes I have today:

the window on the second floor is open, and against the black background inside the room I see my parents. My father is standing. My mother, at his left, is leaning with her elbows on the windowsill.

148 I take out another photograph, in which the "subject" is myself:

Now I take another photograph from the same folder (it shouldn't be there: it's a later parasitical addition to its contents), in which the "subject" is myself: in a leafy sloping walkway, perched on a tricycle, turned halfway toward the photographer. My surroundings are poor in detail, but I still know where I am.

In the window of 21 *bis*, Rue de l'Orangerie, I immediately recognized my parents (even though the figures aren't very clear, the dimensions of the photograph are small, and my eyesight isn't as good as it used to be): I'm not an orphan, after all, I've never gone very long without seeing them, will see them again in a few days. I recognize them without any difficulty in this window of my fore-life, by what is, in a way, a palindromic extrapolation.

But how does one recognize oneself? I am not at all certain that I don't actually have to depend for this recognition on those external memories provided by photographs, and a certain number of photographs can constitute an ordered documentary sequence, punctuating the years at not-too-distant intervals: stable witnesses to time, much less subject to doubt than internal memories, but far more indifferent. (And this is independent of the fact that photographic representations look at you from the outside, and present a different face from the one that we see in the mirror.)

In fact, I find them at once strange and unconvincing, with their spaces that resemble nothing real, their dull geometry. My spontaneous reluctance to accept these supposed supports of identity as authentic (however conventional they may be now) doesn't go so far as denial (one must be reasonable, after all!), but despite everything I feel that they are "outside," artificial, factitious (and I could continue this list of pejorative terms).

It's not just that they're usually incapable of facilitating access to one's internal images (internal memories being the only "real" ones, according to an unreflective conviction of mine): I look at them, and the flat apparition of this form that is meant to be "me" says nothing to me, gives me no access to any movement of the past, no access to any vision. They are perfect proofs of the idleness and sterility of pictions, those *ersatz* images.

But also, and more generally, they're like the statements or writings that transmit to us, inside us, the knowledge of a language (another family of external memories), for when they become internal (one looks at them, one has seen them, one memorizes them involuntarily), they too end up disturbing our other memories, and replacing them. Quite often, when I try to evoke a face, I find that only a photograph comes to mind, only the poor and unsatisfying image of a piction. (And progress of the televisual "image mode" & of "tele-existence" will render the faculty of memory even more artificial in the future—when I will not exist. Their poverty is not due solely to the artificial character of such images, but to the fact that the natural images retained by our memories have a much more complex and vast geometry, are not limited to the three conventional dimensions, and are in fact not entirely oriented toward the sense of sight (as such images are even when they're augmented by sound, for these sounds are merely plastered onto their surface, like color slapped onto a wall).)

This time, the place designated by the paper rectangle is Tulle. At this point, my father had already made several unsuccessful attempts to secure a teaching post—this was partly because of the extreme scarcity of the positions available, but also because of a few conceptual quarrels with his committee, which were complicated by his persistent ignorance of Greek—but when he received his *agrégation* in philosophy, my parents aspired to that great luxury desired by all teacher couples: a double position, that is, an appointment in the same city, where they could set up house as an autonomous family.

But the possibilities to choose from, even for teachers coming from the École Normale Supérieure and holding the *agrégation*, were slim: the perpetual and pendular motion of recruitment policies in our country, which swings (usually quite abruptly) from brutal Malthusianism to unrestrained laxity, had at that time (with help from the global "crisis") stopped at a level close to zero.

The administrative dice were cast: they went to Tulle, Corrèze, a small respectable city whose climate, however, was starkly different from what one finds in cities near the Mediterranean. But nothing was available farther south. They spent five years there. My sister Denise was born in Tulle in October '35, my brother Pierre in January '37.

149 I can only recall a miniscule number of images from my fore-life.

I can only recall a miniscule number of images from my fore-life. Incredibly rare, they emerge only with difficulty, almost painfully, from my **fore-memory**, from its populous oblivion. I admire (with a skeptical reserve that I usually keep to myself) those who can relate memories from when they were two or three years old (some even believe they can go back to the end of their first year, or even further). I am persuaded (extrapolating, no doubt improperly, from my own particular case) that in most of these instances the primordial scenes in question have their (composite) source in stories told by adults, and in family albums, when they haven't quite simply been backdated and inaccurately situated in space. These are external memories that have been internalized, or else ordinary memories that have become disoriented—the "displaced persons" of memory.

And since such images as these appear without any support—that is, most often, without the objects, persons, or landscapes that would allow one to identify or date them with any certainty—I'm not really sure that I possess even a single one. I will therefore refrain from entering the race to break the record for "earliest memory," into which autobiographers have thrown themselves ever since some first pioneer among them came up with the idea and decided that that he possessed this fabulous "thing," a "first memory" (I don't know who this was, or even when it happened: who is the author of the first "first memory"? (a written memory, that is)) (Robert Graves seeing Queen Victoria at the age of one, or Tolstoy in his little bathtub at two, are among the most ridiculous I have ever read). Conversely, it may well be that other images I encounter in the course of my wanderings in memory (intense images, but without an indisputable "address") do in fact belong to those years in Caluire or in Tulle. But I've never been able to verify this.

It's clear that the perfection (in the topological sense) of a segment of the past hinders the reconstitution of singular moments: otherwise, the isolation dissolved by this perfection would protect them from interference on the part of other associated moments, at once close together in time and situated in the same locations. Instead, a phenomenon of "super-imposition" occurs (only the emotional inequality, the selective insistence on a few focal points, prevents the whole aggregate from sinking into a vague neutrality).

I've also noticed, in my attempts to resuscitate this bedroom, where I am today—where I was for many years, and to which I've returned after still other years of interruption—that the details and the places in which I was best able to revisit some former version of myself were not only the ones that had changed the most (the brown carpet on the floor which has been transformed into yellow linoleum, for example, or the position of the bed), but also the ones that had changed very little, or not at all: the wardrobe, and, of course, the size of the windows (but in this case I am far from certain that my temporal evaluation is correct).

I wake up in the half light of an immense bedroom (this is the perceptual "proof" of this memory's old age, its archaic status), **I open my eyes and see two enormous windows** (and the fact that I see them in this way is a sign that this old memory has been penetrated by its future: I see a fragment of the past with my eyes of the past, but I judge it with my eyes of today, or else with those of another, later past. I view the image with two different sets of eyes, so to speak—and I squint. Because in this strange family of images, which we all have and which more than any other gives us the acute feeling of gaining access to the remotest reaches of our existence, the obligatory penetration of the past by the present is always there, made obvious by a change of scale that testifies, for us, to the fact that they come from the land of what-was-before: why would I see the windows as "enormous" if I wasn't also seeing them now?); **and at the very moment when I open my eyes to see, the windows move forward all at once, until they almost touch my eyes; then they recede, and I see the curtains on the windows in a dim light, silent and gray.**

I do not "possess" this memory as freely as the others (that is, most of the ones I'm interweaving into this branch, in a calculated sequence). It comes to me in a recurrent manner, from year to year, when waking from a half-sleep, most often in the afternoon. But it's impossible for me to recall it at will.

I know enough about it, however, to be able to describe it in this way (succinctly), but I am unable to add anything to it by "freezing" it and questioning it, since it always vanishes almost immediately whenever I encounter it (like the images in dreams, as one says—but not in the dreams I dream). Still, when this memory comes to me there is no mistaking it. I see the two immense windows facing me (even if, in the present, there's only a single window of ordinary size in front of me, or a wall). I recognize it.

And every time it appears, I feel the same certainty about its ancientness and setting: Tulle.

I chose it—arbitrarily, with respect to memory, but necessarily, with respect to my story—in order to insert it into **"the great fire of London"** as being my first memory, the oldest **memory-sign** of what has been forgotten.

150 I am looking at a patch of grass in the garden of 21 Rue de l'Orangerie (this time it's 21)

I am looking at a patch of grass in the garden of 21 Rue de l'Orangerie (now it's 21 proper). It's growing in the foreground of a photograph, taken at a time that I have completely forgotten, between my life and my fore-life: the grass was always dry after the summer of 1938, dry, gray and white. It is summer, I'm certain of this: the weather is fine, our clothes are thin and light. It is 1938, as indicated by our respective sizes (my brother Pierre, my sister Denise, and me). It is 1938, since there are only three of us.

My mother, on the left, has placed her hand on my brother's shoulder. He is standing, she is sitting. She's pointing something out to him, which can only be the photographer (who is it?) and the camera. But he is looking down, the sun is too intense. My father is sitting next to my mother and is turned toward my brother. I see that he's beginning to lose his hair. Behind them, a low table, with a tray, a teapot, three cups, and something that may be a tea-cozy. If it were a painting it could bear the title *Le Thé sur l'herbe*, Tea on the Grass.

On the far right my grandmother is in a chaise longue. Her hand is tapping nervously on the frame of the chair, as though on a piano. Obviously I don't see any actual movement in her fingers, but I know they are moving. She has my sister on her lap. Denise has a white headband in her hair. She is looking at us with a certain circumspection. The chaise longue appears to be firm & stable (only a small part at the end of it is cut off at the edge of the picture). I don't know whether it's one of the prototypes of the "untippable" chaise longue constructed by my grandfather. Since "chaise longue" and "grandmother" were two constants often associated with my early years, their common presence gives the group of twelve figures posing on the gray grass (at least eight of them are still alive today, fifty-three years later) a kind of serenity.

There is someone standing exactly at the center of the photograph whom I don't recognize. He is a man of about thirty, his left hand raised (perhaps holding a cigarette), his right hand in the pocket of his pants. I am in front of him, propped on the shoulders of my uncle Frantz (who is sitting in the grass) with my arms around the front of his neck. I have short hair, which is still visibly blond.

On our right is my grandfather. He already has an old man's thin long face, which he will still have almost thirty years later (here he's just past sixty). He has covered his absolute and intransigent baldness with a beret, to protect it from the sun. He is holding his left wrist with his right hand. His expression is slightly astonished, or reflective, or quite simply disturbed by the excess of light. I recognize this expression perfectly.

Between my grandmother and her son Frantz, sitting up very straight in a chair (one can only see the tip of its back), is Mlle. Chauvin, known as "Taia," an old teacher friend of the family, a woman of great kindness, of infinite and modest kindness. At her feet, side by side, my aunt Renée and my (then future) uncle Walter. My grandfather and he are the only ones wearing a tie. These are the twelve people in the photograph.

This photograph shows me the first form of the invisible: that of oblivion. For I now remember nothing of this moment on a summer afternoon, at the far end of the garden, a year before the Second World War—though I see that I was there, that I too looked at the photographer, and I see those familiar, beloved faces, some of them gone forever.

Instead of those faces, instead of the grass, the dark trees in the depths of the sunlight, the teapot, today there's only the paved-over courtyard of a nondescript "apartment complex." The grass will never grow back.

I can recall, however, a moment very close to this one, in a place that is very close as well. But in this case I am alone. **I see this grass**; or if not this grass, some very similar grass; **I perceive the bustling, obstinate, incessant movement of ants between the stalks, climbing the scaffolds of graminae, the cathedrals of clover; next to the ants, those other insects, red with black markings, called "*bêtes du diable*" or "devil's beasts,"** but I gave them (so I've been told) a briefer and more generic name, *bêtten*, with a strong trochaic stress on the *ê*. And I even claimed that they were edible (a claim that was immediately put into action, to my grandmother's horror). **I see an ant stop, hesitate, on the tip of my finger**.

Bifurcation C

On Clouds

151 On the ground floor of the house, there was a window looking out

On the ground floor of the house on the Rue d'Assas, there was a window looking out. In this image, I and a window were both looking out: the look, and the
windowpanes, opened onto a downward sloping space, unpaved, wider than
a street, going down toward a street that ran parallel to the window: the "Enclos du Luxembourg." **It was raining; I look at, and I see, the water streaming over the ground, flowing away along the slope, following its downward
path, like all water, all rain; in front of me, outside the window, is a puddle;
and in this puddle of rainwater, whose surface is being stippled, riddled,
bombarded by tiny pellets of rain, I see the clouds.**

I lean against the window and I look through the glass; and immediately
the image is imbued with words, it becomes as much an "aural" image as a
visual one; **I struck a pose, sitting on the inner ledge of the window, and I
hear, in silence,** at the inner edge of the image that is in my memory. What I
hear isn't anything specific. I cannot say: **I hear that**, but only: **I hear.** I hear
and only later do I recall a poem, or more exactly I am "recalled" to some
verses, some of the insipid verses with which—in my childish determination
to "be a poet"—I covered my notebooks in those years: *Je regarde couler un
torrent de nuages / Dans l'infini des flaques d'eau.* (I watch a torrent of clouds
flow by / In the infinity of water puddles.)

(This is the beginning of three quatrains in alternating 12/8 time, inspired by the
Stances classiques (?), from Corneille's *Le Cid* (?); and farther along (in the notebook),
and at a later time (in my ears, today)): *Je n'ai qu'un horizon de fils télégraphiques
/ dans la lumière insipide des réverbères* (I have only a horizon of telephone
lines / in the insipid light of the lamp posts) (but did I really write "*insipide*"?
or is this a judgment of insipidness made by a present "ego," who, as so often happens in
oral transmission, uses this metrically quadrisyllabic adjective in place of another that's
been lost?)

Out across from where I am, farther away, farther than the dirt-covered "*enclos*," which is wet, claylike, and full of pebbles, on a facade on the other side of the street, I see something green, a slightly pale green, a sign that doesn't quite enter into this image, but that has something written on it; something is written there, on this facade, that much is certain, something green, "green" expressed as a light green; in which I decipher something like "Ferrand," together with something like "marble"; is this true? Or: is it plausible? Certainly, it's plausible.

But what is implausible, then, in this same <u>memory-image</u>, is **to see**, also, and even more distinctly, **in the sloping dirt of the unpaved "*enclos*," between the few scattered tufts of grass, some borage plants, rough borage with its blue eyes**, an implausible element born from a visual leap of memory, a memory that no doubt originates from Les Corbières (the area of Les Corbières that appears in my story (chap. 4)), making for a totally unjustifiable element in this current memory, a parasite plant suddenly sprung up in this ground.

The path that I'm now about to follow, onto which I've been led by this vision established by a few old poems, opens onto one particular "way" through my memory landscape. Along this way a very peculiar space lies before me, entirely contained in the "left" axis of my vision and of my <u>mnemonic field</u> (I call it "left," but "left" is only a relative term, not the subjective dimension of a semi-trihedron that would be opposed, in this field, to a space on the "right"). I open the door to a space that is a space in itself, largely independent.

(The other "way," the "right way," which also has the dimension of an "after," and which opens into other years, is the one I would reach at the bottom of the same slope by turning not to the left but to the right. I can't, in fact, turn to the right at the bottom of the slope, or not anymore; I can no longer do this because I've forgotten, and I see nothing. I can reach the "right" space only by another route (according to the structure of the reading that I'm offering you, it opens at the end of this <u>Bifurcation</u>, which leads into chapter 5 of the Story, titled "**Davila Square**").)

If, in order to name that "left" space in the sky of my memory, I were to choose a formulation of the type "the X way"—following the well-known example of M. Proust—it would be the **Primary School Way**. And the opposition between the two "ways," between the "left" space and the "right" space outside the window, is also a sentimental opposition: between "primary school" and "high school," or lycée. Primary School is very different from High School (which is in the right-hand space, the **Davila Square Way**), since it doesn't seem in any way—as High School does—to be a place of confinement. I don't at all have the feeling, for instance, that it belongs to the same family of places as hospitals (of which I have some experience) or prisons (which I don't know much about, but which I'm able to imagine quite precisely at the moment, thanks to the stories of my daughter Laurence, who is doing one of her internships in the hospital of the Fresnes Prison). Thus, Primary School can naturally appear in close association with the space of the garden, an outside space, a space of movement.

And, with the passing of the years, it's appeared to me more and more as belonging to an amiable and happy time, a physical and animal time inseparable from the time of games: vacation time. During those years in primary school, on the "Primary School Way," it's almost not even wartime. There is no anxiety, no privation. (And yet I was there during the first year of the Occupation, which was my last year in primary school. But I no longer remember anything about it, and it seems to me that I didn't have any real perception of these circumstances then.)

152 we played war games in the school courtyard

Except that we played war games in the school courtyard. Like the Hellenic warriors in Giraudoux, we exchanged not blows but insults. We gathered in the play area, and after the more serious physical ball games or *jeux de barres* (similar to "prisoner's base"), we would stop, giddy from all our running, to rest and to talk. Pressed together as though in a Carcassonnian *agora*, we held forth with the rhetoric of warriors' speeches.

In this game of words, some played soldiers and others played commanders. As for me, I played and recited in the role of Churchill. This role was reserved especially for me. I always claimed it and it was my right to do so, by a tacit agreement, because of my stated convictions and my parentage (since my mother was an English professor, I could already pronounce a few words. And it was well known that my parents had rather unfavorable "opinions" regarding the "Axis Powers").

I recall too that it was very difficult to find volunteers to play the enemies, or the traitors, in this game: Hitler, Mussolini, Laval, Pétain. These had to be assigned and imposed. De Gaulle and Stalin were little known to us (likewise the Japanese. However, the empire of the Rising Sun must surely have come up from time to time in the "radiophonic" air, for we—little students that we were—were enchanted by an irresistibly comic phrase: "*Le général Yamamoto a été mis à pied*" (literally, "Generel Yamamoto was set on his feet," which meant that he was suspended from his position, but we only saw him being knocked off the "moto" (the motorcycle) in his name) (this happened in the spring of '41 no doubt. I see that the weather is fine, but it's still during the school year. The Germans have not yet launched "Operation Barbarossa." Everything happening in the war is far away, and for me it's a battle fought by England, my Arcadia, against "them," our enemies).

In our school, non-collaboration (rather than Resistance, an idea still awaiting its birth) was "hegemonic." The fear of denunciation—and the accompanying silence recommended or imposed on wagging tongues—were still to come. (Generally speaking, the wine growers in the Aude region didn't have much sympathy for Vichy. The Aude was a "secular" and "radical-socialist" department, with a streak of discontent and a fringe of deep "red," inherited from Marcelin Albert, Dr. Ferroul, and the rebellious wine growers of the beginning of the century (a time when one heard the song "We salute you, We salute you, valiant soldiers of the Seventeenth!" (this was the regiment of wine growers' sons who had refused to shoot at their own people)).)

(Not long ago, my father suddenly remembered (the reemergence of old Vichy demons in France brings these times back to the surface of one's thoughts) the recommendation of the principal at the Carcassonne lycée where he was teaching philosophy. It was October 1940. The new "authorities" had demanded that the principal of the lycée for boys choose someone to give a speech before a gathering of professors and students assembled for this purpose on their first day back to school (as a sort of "solemn recommencement," like those one might have seen in the old days at the University). The speech was to be conceived, in the Vichy spirit, as the supposedly expiatory "counterpart" of the patriotic speeches given the year before (the year of the "phony war"), and to accompany some "false prizes" that were to be handed out. The principal entrusted this task to my father, saying: "At least with you there won't be any risk of praising 'those people.' ")

I spent four years at the École Annexe. That's what we called the primary school attached to the École Normale d'Instituteurs, where the teachers were trained (an institution that, after more than a hundred years, only recently succumbed to the flailing blows of the reformers). The "master-students" worked under the direction of a respected and experienced teacher, trying out their first pedagogical weapons on us little guinea pigs. When I left the school in July '41, almost on the verge of tears, I was eight and a half.

Being a student at the École Annexe was a didactically luxurious situation. There were very few students (only two classes, in fact: a class for the "little" children and a class for the "big" children, some of whom were not going on to the lycée but were studying for the *certificat d'études* (awarded at the end of a successful completion of primary school (usually before entering the work-force), this was a formidable obstacle in the imaginations of the children in our school; having entered the lycée prematurely myself, I never had to take that particular test, a fact that for a long time left me with a vague feeling of in-adequacy, as the grandson of two primary schoolteachers)). What we learned was (more or less) grammar, spelling, arithmetic, history, and geography. We were well treated, and content (I believe that I was, in any case).

Given my continual interest in reading and arithmetic, particularly in the form given the most prestige among school children, "mental calculation" (in writing this I now remember, with an immediate clarity, that my best friend had a "numerical" name: he was called Quintaine), I didn't stay in the "little" class very long.

Our teacher was M. Castel. He was a breed of teacher that today would be described as being "of the old school," an expression used with a mixture of regret and condescension ("People who believed in what they were doing, just imagine!"). One speaks of such teachers in the tone of voice reserved for bicycles (which were not yet "bikes"), advertisements (which were not yet "ads"), wheelbarrows and carts, but also (and this time with longing) for non-pasteurized cheeses, "raw" milk, and Reinette apples (the ones that were but are no more, and which in any case are not to be confused with the bland, hyper-healthy, American Golden Delicious, nor the Australian (?) Granny Smith with its skin waxed in chemical green). They belong to the same epoch as bread "baked in a wood-burning oven" (which one misses and longs for. A missing and longing that opened the way for brilliant and successful exploitation by a clever industrial chain, whose products are nonetheless just as mechanized and "instant" as every other type of mass-produced food, and have only a passing resemblance to the results of the old methods; their success was in essence purely onomastic, a result of the decision to call themselves "*Fournil de pierre*" (stone bakery)—the better to sell the "fast breads" they offer.) One tends to add that the mold in which these artisanal teachers were formed has since been broken, and that they don't make them "like that" anymore. Let it suffice for me to say here that M. Castel belonged to this breed.

153 During these blessed years

During these blessed years, "arithmetic" and "recitation" were and remained my "strong points." It was no doubt my facility with mathematics, as well as the collateral speed with which I could memorize poetry ("number" subtends the recollection of verse), that earned me the (perhaps excessive) indulgence of M. Castel in dealing with (or rather not dealing with) my primary scholarly deficiency: a paroxysmal disorder in the completion and presentation of my written work.

(My educational experience never once placed me in the presence of one of those harsh teachers found everywhere in the literary tradition. Quite the contrary. A model teacher who was close at hand, at it were, was my grandfather: indulgent, and with an almost proverbial indulgence. Mistakes made him suffer. He had so much "sympathy" for a student who uttered them that it was all he could do not to give the correct answers in his place. (At times he also exhibited this propensity in ordinary conversations with adults, to the despair of his interlocutors.)

Much later, when I was studying mathematics at the Institut Henri-Poincaré, I took a course in arithmetic with Prof. Salem. It was said that he was a former banker who had suddenly converted to this abstruse discipline, in which (to paraphrase Mallarmé) one gives a purer sense to the words of the tribe of numbers (my old friend Pierre Lusson, who like me has forgotten Salem's first name—which I first left blank on my screen with the intention of filling it in later, since it bothers me to designate him here with the much too familiar nomination "Salem"—my friend, then, does not remember his first name either, but believes that he had been a manager for the Banque d'Indochine). This eminent mathematician was literally incapable of "flunking" a student on an exam. There was a story about him conducting the oral section of one unfortunate student's exam in what was called "General Mathematics." This student stood completely silent in front of the blackboard on which the equation he'd been asked to solve was written. And Salem, with infinite care, speaking in his gentle voice, which he made even more gentle so as not to frighten the poor creature, said: "Let's see now, what kind of equation is this?" Silence. "The equation," Salem continued, more and more gently, "the equation is a diff . . . ?" At which the student, suddenly radiant with comprehension, completed the word, as legend has it, not with the expected adjective "differential" but with "difficult." "The equation is a difficult one!" said the student with conviction. And Salem, in a transport of benevolence and relief, said: "That's very good, very good, a difficult equation. That's certainly the case. You pass.")

Writing was for me an infinitely unpleasant exercise, almost torture. In those days, students still wrote with liquid ink, using penholders dipped in an inkwell. Each child's table, each downward-slanting desk in our class had a white porcelain inkwell (whose shape was located, in the general field of shapes, somewhere between a flower pot and a chamber pot (more flower pot in its geometry, more chamber pot in its contents)) on the right (a supplementary ordeal for my spontaneous "leftism") filled with a purple or black ink that was dreadfully inky, sticky, tenacious, persistent, wet, staining, and virtually indelible.

Into this pot one dipped a steel pen with a sharp blue or white nib (itself an object of dread), after attaching it, with great difficulty (you can't imagine!), to the penholder lifted from the little box with a sliding cover, also full of chewed-on pencils and erasers. It was virtually impossible for me to carry out the indispensable transfer of a drop of ink from the pen to a page of my notebook without drips, splashes, spills, smudges, and other messy aberrations.

The sharp pen-nibs would bend, spread apart, get lost, break, or set off down the wrong line, or else the ink suddenly refused to flow, then flooded out all at once, the pen scratching or splitting or pouring its ink into an irregularity in the paper—letters, words, and sentences merging together. My fingers turned blue, black, purple, my blotters could absorb no more, there was ink on my smock, on my textbook, on the notebook of my neighbor (who had urgently asked me for help with a multiplication problem). There was ink on my smock, on my bare knees, on my nose and my ears, in my hair and on my socks.

One day when I had been particularly negligent in the manipulation of this secular ink, republican and compulsory, M. Castel had a rare attack of ill humor, and I suffered a humiliation that I have never forgotten. He dragged me, sobbing and debased, in front of everyone, into the class for the "little" students, where **I stayed** (I feel this more than I see it) **an entire morning, petrified with shame, my ink-colored tears hidden on my face, which I covered with my arm; my nose pressed against the rough wooden table**.

My handkerchiefs (which I constantly mislaid, like my berets, like my sandals or even my shoes, which I took off as soon as I possibly could once I was outside, so that I could walk the way one naturally walks, with bare feet), my handkerchiefs were always completely recognizable by their ink stains. Ink flowed from me ceaselessly, from that part of me so inexplicably resistant to my will: my penholder.

I was as helpless with ink as I was at the sight of the blood that sometimes fell vertically and irrepressibly from my nose after being struck by a fist or a rock. (It's still just as unpleasant when (as sometimes happens in autumn) I begin to bleed from my nose while in the metro or on a bus, and I feel just about as helpless, ashamed, and annoyed.) The blood oozes like the old ink into a Kleenex-blotter.

154 The ink, the blood of wild blackberries, was very different

But the light red ink, or blood, from wild blackberries was very different. It only stained one's fingers, and one's legs, where it mingled with the enigmatic writing of real blood that darkened into scratches and scrapes. This, no doubt, is why I was so fond of fake inks, made from clusters of elderberries squeezed between my hands into cups of red juice, then wiped onto my clothes. It was elderberry ink that I chose for the voluntary servitude of my other, secret writings—poems and stories—soon faded, soon effaced on the page, and of their own accord, whereas anything written with the ink at school seemed eternal, eternally destined to denounce my spelling mistakes and my clumsy hand.

The ink from school that had dried in my notebook—as though eternal—perpetuated the irreducible childishness of my writing in an almost illegible form, and this was something I was ashamed of without being able to remedy it (ashamed especially in front of my grandfather, my model, with his perfect calligraphy—whereas a hurried, erratic, and illegible script was characteristic of my grandmother, whom I loved less).

But sometimes, **at the foot of a plane tree, I sat with my notebook thrown open on top of my satchel, the large drops of a sudden brief rain restored a momentary fluidity, and I saw**, as in my fascination I delayed the moment of closing the notebook, in order to protect the math or grammar exercises from a premature dissolution that would doubtless generate future familial or academic difficulties, **I saw the black ink turn blue, become diluted by the water, attenuated; it began to move on the page, to form tiny bridges of streaks between the lines of writing, to annul and confound my clumsy downstrokes, my crossing out, and to restore to the words or numbers all the mysteries of indistinction, by mixing them all together.**

Our school had a courtyard, and in this courtyard there was a /*préau*‘, a small play space that was covered but open.)I enclose the word *préau* (and a few others, skimmed from this particular layer of time), between two written wings, thus: /‘, for it has (they have) almost joined the dead souls of dead words in the limbo of language, and with this typographical innovation I mean to give them an "angelic" status: an innovation that, at the same time, in order to signal its initiation here with a brief interpolation explaining its usage, I follow with text between the two ordinary signs for prosaic interpolations, open parenthesis, "(", and close parenthesis, ")", the *lunulae* or "little moons," those inventions of Erasmus; but, in another innovation, I here invert the Erasmian order of the parentheses, which is associated with the lunar phases (and I notice that, strangely, it does not in fact proceed like the calendar, from the first to the final quarter, but in the opposite direction). Thus by reversing the direction of a parenthetical notation, I would like to mark, occasionally, as here, the retrograde pathway of recollection.(And in this /*préau*‘ we hung our /*pelerine*‘ jackets on hooks, and our /*berets*‘ (objects that, fifty percent of the time, I forgot to take with me when I left).

I see October; the ground is marked with reddening leaves; I see the air, I see the cooling off at four o'clock of the autumn air, the insistence of the

**trees against the sky; the afternoon is about to become a deeper blue, to
become evening; I see the urgency of the air's deepening blue, of our game;**
this is a moment like the one, ceaselessly reiterated, that identifies for me the
game we played, after four o'clock, four o'clock in October, in the courtyard of
the school: /*jeu de barres*'; a game of Zenonian hares and tortoises, in which
there are, however, several hares, several tortoises, and in which there are two
sides. But not with hares on one side and tortoises on the other, because we
do not know "*which is which*"—because the hares and the tortoises in this
game don't have their role assigned once and for all in a geometry of regulated
gestures: whoever is the last to leave his side is a hare, and the last hare always
becomes a tortoise.

(Isn't this exactly how I play in these pages? Here I'm playing a Zenonian *jeu
de barres* of recollection. Temporary hares sometimes join up with temporary
tortoises, and sometimes not. But what can never be brought to completion,
what is properly Zenonian in my game, isn't their race: it's the gesture of pursuit, taking place now, a gesture that is endlessly exhausted, that is annulled
in being completed, and that is endlessly repeated, as though a Carrollian tortoise were about to be overtaken by a no less Carrollian hare, and demanded
ceaselessly, before conceding defeat, to see a replay of the race and its "photo-
finish" one more time, to have a verification, and to have a verification of the
verification, without end.)

The perpetual moment of primary school is thus the moment when it begins, its first autumn days: **after the game came a moment of dark red; the
green burrs of the horse chestnuts, prickly as hedgehogs, had fallen from
the chestnut trees with their dark red leaves turning redder; the sky soaked,
rippling with clouds, swift shadows in the puddles, cottony skiffs, a creamy
sky, the color of mud;**

**another identical moment of dark red; the green burrs of the horse chest-
nuts, prickly as hedgehogs, had fallen from the chestnut trees with their
dark red leaves turning redder; the sky soaked, rippling with clouds, swift
shadows in the puddles, cottony skiffs, a creamy sky, the color of mud;**

**the color of mud, creamy sky, cottony skiffs, swift shadows in the pud-
dles, rippling with clouds the soaked sky, from the chestnut trees with their
reddish leaves turning redder, hedgehogs, horse chestnuts had fallen, the
green burrs, prickly, a moment of dark red;**

155 Positioned in the window, watching, looking out toward the Enclos du Luxembourg, I see the city as an amplification of the garden.

Positioned in the window, watching, looking out toward the Enclos du Luxembourg, I see the city as an amplification of the garden. With its boulevard-streets and opaque house-trees, and in anticipation of its various routes and pathways, it presents a lacunary topology of large concentric circles in which to wander—whether by looking, walking, or running. Taking the "Primary School Way," one can leave the city by two "roads": the road to Montréal (where the school is located) and the road to Limoux. It didn't take long to leave the city in those days. Very soon the houses one passed were no longer city houses with street numbers on cream-colored, yellow, or yellowing porcelain painted with blue, or on enamel plaques with black numbers, but, rather, islands: islands protected by walls, by low walls. The gardens and houses became more and more distant from one another, the vines took over.

I would go down the slope of the Enclos and turn left, where the street continued on its downward path. At the point where the two roads separate, or begin, **there is**, there was already, a garage. I looked, **I look at the mesmerizing rainbow colors of the gasoline spilled on the cement, the oil spreading out like flattened licorice**. The road to Limoux, as it was called, soon reaches the Aude River, which having come down from the Pyrenees, flowing north, takes a sharp turn to the right at Carcassonne, to the east, and from there flows off to the Mediterranean.

Between the road and the river there were truck farms, paddy fields of melons, tomatoes, reeds, trails, brambles. All this has disappeared. My vision rebels. But if nothing had changed, or almost nothing, would that be better? Returning to a remembered place confronts you with an alternative between two difficult situations: either everything is there, recognizable, and you are no longer there. Or: now nothing is there, nothing resembling what you remember, but there you are, you yourself, once again.

On the road to Limoux, at a point where you've almost left the city behind—just before the path began that we often followed to the river's edge, on certain afternoons in June, or July, or September, hot afternoons during the school vacation, or on Thursdays when there were no classes—my grandfather sometimes stopped with us at the café on the right along the long straight section of the road, before it turns and takes leave of the Aude (to join up with it again much farther along, near the town called "Madame"—but that was beyond the reach of our walks). We would sit down **beneath the arbor, at a white metal "garden" table**, on **chairs with green slats, a decimated worn-out green**. We would sit in the **hot shade traversed by flies, butterflies, wasps in August and September, attracted by the grapes, and likewise traversed by the sun, which made the white pebbles on the ground all the more brilliant**, and my grandfather ordered lemonade for us, and for himself a *panaché*, made with a beer produced in Carcassonne (Ruoms? or Fritz-Lauer? These were two of the beers available at the time—and the worst ever, according to my parents).

He drank the moderately frothy mixture of lemonade and beer slowly, for it's not prudent, it's not hygienic, to drink too much or too fast when one is hot. It is imprudent, and it does not even quench one's thirst. He drank the **very pale yellow liquid from the glass** (there was very little of that beer, itself almost without alcohol, in his lemonade). He drank the bitter-sweet liquid slowly, his **cane leaning on the table next to him, as he sat up very straight**, without removing his **boater hat** from his head except when he greeted the café owner before placing our order, or to acknowledge him once again when leaving, **after looking at the time on his round fob watch, after taking his wallet out of his vest pocket, and then the coins from the wallet, setting them on the table**, the exact amount required, supplemented with a tip (but only if we had not been served by the owner).

We sat under the trees, or under the vine in the arbor, but he still wouldn't remove that quasi-permanent protection from his head, depriving himself of any natural defense against the sun's rays, which he considered to be quite capable of passing through the unreliable screen of leaves above us. In fact, I have the impression that he kept his hat on almost all the time, even when he was at our house, for he was a Dauphinois who remained distrustful of the extreme aggressiveness of the Mediterranean sun, which could even seep into the air indoors.

(I don't think it was out of vanity that he concealed his absolutely bald head. For at home, in Caluire, in his study, in his studio, and of course in the dining room at mealtimes, he appeared comfortably bare above the eyebrows.) The lemonade left a delicious sting on our tongues and sometimes—mysteriously rising up into our foreheads—between our eyes, produced a prickling sensation in our brains, a fake "head cold," as occasionally also happened when we kept our heads underwater in the river and accidentally let some liquid enter our noses.

Because, on these walks along the road to Limoux, we often went all the way down to the Aude to swim. There was a spot on the river with a small waterfall, where the current was rapid but the water shallow. And when my father was confident that we were able to do the breaststroke, and especially to swim underwater without panicking and with open eyes, and capable of remaining there for some time, the river was ours. The (relative) rush of the water between the wide flat stones formed a natural toboggan that launched us head- or feet-first into a clearing of calm water; from there we could easily make our way out with a few strokes, and then walk back up along the bank, dripping with water, to the origin of those "rapids," wilder than any the Last of the Mohicans had ever encountered. There was a kind of small wood there too, of poplars and elders.

The poplars covered the water with their leaves, filled the air with their personal odor, tinged with honey. And, especially, the **miniscule capsules of their fruit** (?) spilled forth, and **the fine, silky, shiny down of their "cotton" snowed down onto the river.** We brought back veritable harvests of these pods before they burst open, putting them in our pockets, in our school smocks, in Marie's basket, so that later we could send them floating and shivering through the air of the garden, or so that we could on the contrary hoard them away to make a pillow, unimaginably soft: a thrilling prospect, but one that went unfulfilled every summer.

156 One could also reach the Aude by the Rue d'Assas

One could also reach the Aude by the Rue d'Assas, as we did on the road to Limoux. My "reconstituting" vision grasps, as though by pincers, and from very high up, the unknown gardens sloping down the hill, the opaque houses between the two itineraries in view: the first leading off from the rainy window onto the Enclos du Luxembourg, the second arising from the summer freshness of the "laundry house" in the heat of the afternoon sun as it melts the blacktop encrusted with gravel in the street (§ 29) (I also "jump" directly from the garage to the street, from oil to tar, by following the path of the word "licorice").

The two paths join together, as **I see; Rue d'Assas descends rather abruptly; at the height of the summer afternoon, siesta time, it is empty, à la de Chirico. To the right, in the direction of the river, a cascade of steps, then a trail, a hot trail, rustling and resounding with light, with the buzzing of insects, with footsteps in the sandy dust along the gardens full of vegetables; the Aude over there, getting closer;**

a trail rustling with grass no one ever cut; long grass stems and false oats, nettles; fennel (sprigs chewed to fight off thirst, the taste of anis, of lemonade); especially the spiky ears, ears of grass, not of wheat, ears without seeds; we look for the longest ears, the longest one when they're placed side by side wins, then we keep the winner to test its successors, later;

picked when green, flexible, soft, tender, when the grass is still fresh and sweet, they turn yellow later, grow hard in our pockets; then they fly straight through the air and get stuck deep in our hair, in the wool of our sweaters, which they hook onto, becoming more and more tenaciously embedded, like fish hooks, before finally falling apart (made up as they are of separable elements, similar to the "chevrons" designating "elevated areas" as more or less steep, on the scale of the Michelin Map), coming apart in the wool, and sometimes we don't notice them, but then they show up later, on the inside of a sweater (already saturated with "burdocks," scratching the skin);

the nearby subterranean wetness of the river, of the watered gardens, nourishes the oddest fruits along the trail: cucurbitaceous plants, wild vagabonds and rogues, miniscule compared to squash or cucumbers (but one feels, one deduces that they belong to the same family of plants), dark green rugby ovals, furry and rough, dry as dust on the outside, and yet full of juice and seeds, an intense liquid pressure, a compulsion, a hereditary *impetus* to eject their profusion of seeds, grains teleologically invented by their ancestors for the perpetuation of the plant, a pressure maintained within the fruit in a tension so fierce, so violent, that when they are squeezed hard between two fingers, they burst open, spraying as

far as a meter, two meters away, a missile marvelously suited for our wet skirmishes, for ambushes,

or for the simple joy of provoking the sudden spurt of their reserves of water & small seeds, bursting out as though from an artesian force, as though it were alive, animal, akin to the pressure, the sudden impulse, of the tiny claws of grasshoppers flying from one's palm into the hot trembling air (as when from a fist squeezed shut on the surface of a hot winter bath there rose a vertical fountain surrounded by steam (to limit myself to this one comparison, not biographically anachronistic)); the ripest of these ellipsoid fruits, once they've become a little yellow, a little darkened on the vine, with their pointed tips like crumpled straw or paper, loosen their hold on their stems and tend to explode on their own, when one touches them, when we touched them: green grenades, their pins pulled out by the sun.

We also found them in the ditches of the medieval Cité, along with the grassy ears, as well as the hooked spines of the burdocks, at the foot of the Viollet-le-Duc towers, with pointed tips like the poulaine shoes on the medieval figures in Samivel's illustrations (in the *Roman de Renart*). Here too they functioned as missiles, but this time they were launched from imaginary cannons, in scenarios inspired by Walter Scott, in which our assault, designed to liberate the prisoners from the Tower (any tower), added volleys of arrows to these explosives, shot high from palm-branch bows into the slate colored sky above the similarly colored rooftops (which gives the Cité its exotic allure—like an arbitrary implantation, a Nordic crossbreed. Back then, the builders in the Aude generally preferred the rounded ochre pink of tile roofs).

One trail, then another, rose up from the ramparts toward the woods where we went on our schoolboy excursions, to a spot in the woods that we called **Gaja**; and on our way there, the enormous Cité massed together as it receded, became condensed and more comprehensible, seemed more vulnerable from the height and distance of the hills, and along the path **beneath the low walls of dry stones a little flower grew with very blue clusters, a very heavy blue, full of a dense smell, heavy and persistent, a musky odor contained in the name of the plant, <u>muscaris</u>, or grape hyacinth; I rubbed them between my fingers; their smell stayed with me into the night, in my bedroom; it rose into the dark air, accented with all the smells—vegetal, leafy, and floral;**

earthy clay and mineral smells—that had been deposited throughout the day on my dusty, scratched, ant-eaten skin, and caramelized by the sun; the day was condensed into all these smells, they composed a melody of the day, a melody liberated by my naked limbs in the sheets,

and above the aroma of the grape hyacinth, just at the moment of dropping off to sleep on my pillow, the screeching eddy began again, flying off into the night air, the long restless train of black crows ceaselessly whirling out their vehement but feigned protests around the tower-tops stuck onto the shoulders of the Cité ramparts.

157 Eleven years ago, I ended a book of poems with a "song" borrowed from the Chippewa Indians

Eleven years ago, I ended a book of poems with a "song" borrowed from the Chippewa Indians, one of the "birch-bark songs"—which, to me, are poems, according to my own idea of what poetry is. It is a Song of the Clouds, which I took for my own purposes in order to make it the last and shortest poem of that book, which is titled *Dors* (Sleep), published with *Dire la poésie* (Saying Poetry) (it's also the shortest poem I've ever written). It consists of three words, in two lines separated by a blank:

Song of the Clouds

The clouds
change

To present these words as a poem is (again, according to my idea of poetry) to place them **"out-of-time"** and **"out-of-space."** Which means placing them in the **"here-now"** of a page (for the eye of a reader of poetry) or of a volume of air (for the inner ear of an auditor of poetry). (Though, to be even more precise, perhaps I ought to have marked the isolation of these terms within language by using the typographical convention I invented earlier for certain vocables tinged with the past, in order to give them a new present, and thus written them as **/out-of-time'**, **/out-of-space'**, **/here-now'**.)

"The clouds," sang the Chippewa birch bark, somewhere near the Canadian border, where the song was recorded onto a wax-cylinder by Frances Densmore around the end of the last century: "The clouds / change." They changed, they change, over the bison-covered Minnesota plains no less than in the valley of the Aude in 1941, but what my poem does with these words is extremely close to stating—simply by having become a poem that encompasses them, that situates them—is **the permanence of their change**.

A similar definition was proposed for memory: "permanence of change." And I would be inclined to subscribe to this characterization, adding (this much is implicit): "in us"; except that this definition seems insufficiently specific to me, because all it really says about us is that we are objects in the world, and what do all the objects in the world have in common if not the fact of being—and of being nothing but—the provisional permanence of certain changes.

Clouds already tell us this in the purest, most serene, most trying manner possible. This is the inexhaustible source of their fascination. I understood the Chippewa (I dreamt that I understood them), I was grateful to them—to the point of stealing their words—for having grasped this message as the ultimate song of the clouds: the hypnotic persistence of their changes, of their changing continuity, in all the vast generality of the sky, above the ocean of particularities, above the grasses, pebbles, ants, mud puddles, quintessentialized lakes of rain.

Because it is always the clouds that I find again, on these pathways from the school to the river, from the river to the Cité, from the Cité to the hills. They accompany me with all their formal indirection, with their shapes, of which one could say nothing stable, nothing precise, of which one could say nothing at all before they were classed, nimbed, stratified, cumulated into their families, around 1800, by the Quaker pharmacist Luke Howard. (But this in no way renders the Chippewa lyric obsolete. It remains entirely correct: The clouds / change.)

The thick clouds accompany me into these outdoor territories, enveloped and preserved by the wind that drives them on, breaks them apart, lifts them up, tumbles them over; and beneath these clouds, and only beneath them, can I be certain of the myopic proximity of the nettles, the elders, the bubbles rising in drinking glasses, the chestnuts in their dark red burrs, the pages with blue ink, and then black and red and purple, wet and smudged—especially the blue and black of the grape hyacinths—the magpies, the crows: memory-images as intense as though they'd been pasted onto my eyes. Without the clouds flowing across a table of sky, there would be no way these memories could have survived.

Thus, I imagine them present for me, guardians of my memory, guarantors of my memory, even if it's impossible for me to place any of their specific shapes here or there, precisely, in my mind: neither the handkerchiefs nor the scarves, neither the broad boats loaded with gray nor the spume, not the flakes, the needles, none of the variations of their beings, of their *inscapes*, which I saw at one moment or another in those years, saw and absorbed, recognized, happened upon, my head tilted back as I walked so as to only perceive the sky in them, only them in the sky, or with my hands cupped around my temples to block my view of the ground, the houses, the electric wires, so as to fix my gaze on nothing but their rapid passage in the water, in the water of a puddle, somewhere. Right outside the window looking onto the Enclos du Luxembourg, perhaps.

158 Between Villegly and Sallèles, in the Minervois, a little to the north, or northwest, of Carcassonne

Between Villegly and Sallèles, in the Minervois, a little to the north, or northwest, of Carcassonne, there is an unpaved but "passable" road (on which wagons were able to travel, and where cars travel today, albeit infrequently); it crosses through the scrub along a tiny river, the Cèze, which comes down from the Black Mountain, irrigates Sallèles, and goes on to hurl itself (dare I say) into a stream of water, in Villegly, that's hardly any larger than it was itself, which bears the proud name of Clamous, itself a tributary of the Aude.

Not far from this road is the house where my parents went to live when they retired, which has belonged to them and to us, their children, since the beginning of the fifties, and which is called the Tuilerie de Saint-Félix. It's a "country place" on the Minervois road, near an intersection that heads off in four directions, each designated by the name of a nearby village: "Conques-sur-Orbiel, Villalier, Villegly and Bagnoles."

(The intersection was long known by the name "Gare de Bagnoles," in memory of a small train stop (a train used to pass by there, long before us; Gaston

Bonheur mentions it in his *Souvenirs*. We never knew it when it was active, but the rails were still visible in the pavement for several years after the war). The youngest drivers of the school "vans" that I sometimes take into Carcassonne to catch the train—very early on winter mornings—have already never heard of it, and the last lingering onomastic trace of that little train of the Minervois recently disappeared from the "schedule.")

This road, the beautiful sloping village of Sallèles (which, after being almost abandoned ten years ago, was converted, atrociously, into second homes for people from Carcassonne), the scrubland on both sides of the Cèze, across from the Black Mountain, against which Sallèles abuts, turning its back to it—these are all places I've known for fifty years. I ran there, jumped, rolled, clambered, and climbed there as a child, and I still walk there—albeit with less speed and more circumspection today—when I go to the Tuilerie.

The scrub grows quite high on both sides of the valley (it's the end of one of the many zones of scrubland that begin in the Hérault region and come to an end there, or almost, interrupted on their left side (facing north) by the Orbiel River valley, and on their eastern edge by the narrow strip of low vine-growing land that separates them from the Black Mountain and from the lower edge of the Massif Central). I have a habit (an almost Lamartinian habit: "Often, on the hill, in the shade of the old oak . . ." (though we would have to replace "oak" with "pine" . . .)) of stopping somewhere in one of these high places and sitting down on a flat stone or a cushion of pine needles (between oaks that provide no shade, since they're only very small holm oaks) in order to stop and look at the clouds.

I go there—especially on days when the great west wind, the *cers*, is blowing, but in fine weather—for a long contemplation of the clouds. I located my lookout point there, my center of reconnaissance, a site for the memorization of their shapes, their movements, their changes. I'm not learned when it comes to clouds: I have a poor knowledge of their classes, their species, their genres, their varieties, the "Thomist" catastrophes by which their mutations can be interpreted. The cloudy science is (or at least was for a long time), like astronomy, an "observational" science (according to the ancient distinction); that is, lacking any possibility for experimentation. The clouds (like the stars) go their cloudy ways without any interference, except perhaps from eagles or airplanes.

And in the lightness of the soft blue sky I see them emerge, themselves light, white, distinct, cottony, supple, rounded off and driven on by the sharp, determined wind. They appear, driven to the edge of the Black Mountain, they hesitate, then set out again, descending slightly, throwing themselves into the sky's vat of blue water. And I follow after them in their continuous navigation, from the left to the right of my view, until they disappear, on my right, into the uncertain distances of the Mediterranean.

I let time pass, and clouds, counting the time not in minutes or in hours, but in units of contemplation, in **cloud-hours**: a cloud-hour is the time it takes for a given cloud to cross the width of the sky. My memory is full of these images. They come to me from the very distant past, always from the same point, in the same circumstances, these images of the slow circulation of the clouds on the Minervois horizon: they emerge in the lightness of the soft blue sky, themselves light, white, distinct, cottony, supple, rounded off and driven on by the sharp, determined wind. They appear, **cloud-hour** after **cloud-hour**, driven to the edge of the Black Mountain; they hesitate, then set out again, descending slightly, hurling themselves into the sky's vat of blue water.

And sometimes I wonder: what if the clouds coming to me now from the past times of these images, accentuated with all the emotion of recollection, have undergone a kind of Zenonian deceleration; what if the distance they manage to cross during the second minute of that old and real time was only half the distance they were able to cross during the first, and then again, during the third minute, only half of the distance of the preceding, thus extending the true time of a **cloud-hour** indefinitely; in that case, wouldn't I be—I who look at them again at this moment with my interior gaze and force myself to contemplate a limit and an origin—wouldn't I be (as we all are in our memory) now at a virtually infinite distance from them?

159 **We lived in Carcassonne, as I have said.**

We lived in Carcassonne, as I have said. My parents arrived from Tulle with their three children in the fall of 1937, having been given a "double post": a rare commodity for two teachers during this Malthusian post-crisis and pre-war era (my father as the "Chair of Philosophy," replacing the eminent Descartes scholar Ferdinand Alquier; my mother as a professor of English). They were also accompanied by a young woman from the Corrèze *département* (not all that young, really, since she was the same age as my mother: thirty), Marie Noilhac, from Souillac, Corrèze—but for us, and always, until her death last year, she was "Marie."

One Sunday in 1943, I believe, Marie met a wine grower from Villegly, in the Minervois, a man named Antoine Bonafous. He was a wine grower but also had a passion for horses, in whom he inspired great trust, and which he sometimes accompanied on their long journeys to new owners, to guide and comfort them along the way. He was in no way a horse dealer; he didn't own any, nor did he sell them for profit, but he took care of them, fed them, and comforted them on their travels on the "iron path" of the railroad, for a modest fee. The rest of the time he spent in his house in Villegly, in his cellar, in his garden at the edge of the Clamous, in his scrubland vines.

Antoine and Marie talked together, I think it was on the parade grounds, on the Allées Barbès, on several following Sundays, for a few months, in our absence. Antoine asked for her hand in marriage, and she accepted. She took leave of my parents, of us children—of Jean-René, called "Nanet," who was the youngest, and whose birth she had witnessed—on Saint John's Day in 1939; he was her favorite (an obvious preference, spontaneous and without malice, for which no one ever dreamt of reproaching her (the testimony of a secret note written by my brother Pierre that was "discovered" one day behind a "cozy corner" in the study during a cleaning: "Marie is a kind girl, but very often she scolds me when Nanet is the one she ought to blame" (I note this "from memory," as one says, which is to say that I have completely forgotten the strange spellings of the original))).

Marie was tall, very upright, with that posture which in Provence makes people say: "She's a 'fine woman.'" She was from a peasant family in the Corrèze, rather unpleasant people, from what I understood, whom she had left behind, boldly & without regret, in order to stay with my parents, against the will of her own people, who had kept her in a situation of almost slave-like dependence, deep in the distant and murky corners of the Aude region. She never really took up with them again.

She didn't get much schooling; she read little, but had a sort of intense and spontaneous aesthetic apprehension that, on one occasion, when the music of a sonata for violin and piano by Mozart rose from the "pick-up" for the first time, led her to react by rushing in from the kitchen to say: "Oh, how beautiful!" (She was similar in this to certain (mythical?) Amazonian Indians that used to be invoked in psychology courses (an argument naively (?) presented in favor of a universal component of musical "taste" and, likewise, for the superiority of tonal classicism in its Mozartian form).)

Thus, in 1943, she left the Rue d'Assas to set up house on the main street of Villegly, which is quite simply the Minervois highway. Antoine was a few years older than her, and was a widower. He lived with an uncle of his first wife, known simply as Uncle, with whom Marie had a few disputes, but not for long, since he was a decent old man, grumbling and surly but not mean-spirited. He proposed, once, that we children drink a toast with him, and as we did so we raised our voices with him, lifting our glasses (ours full of lemonade, his of wine), and saying: "Dragons, curl your mustaches!"

Marie and Antoine's house took turns with my grandparents' on the Rue de l'Orangerie in Caluire (but not without a little jealousy) as a place of refuge and a getaway, which it remained well into the middle of the fifties. The "Tuilerie" where my parents live now was chosen by Antoine, and he would have been its counselor and protector were it not for his untimely death. (But I won't "bifurcate" again here in my "recollection.")

The front door of the house opened onto the sunny street-highway (which one could cross without risks, so rare were cars then, in order to reach the "shed," where the boarded horses were kept, along with rabbits, wine, and some supplies), and it was a wooden door cut out of a large wooden gateway that could itself be opened to allow a cart inside. The stairway rose on the right, up to the floors with living quarters.

Up toward the top, a little daylight entered the gap between the gateway and the wall, and I sat on the stairs and watched for a long time, in a miracle of optics, as the passersby and the wagons were reflected in inverted silhouettes on the ceiling, while the voices, the steps, dull, indistinct, and refracted by passing through the thick wood, underscored this train of passing shadows.

160 With Uncle, Marie, and Dick the spaniel, with reed baskets lined with grape leaves

With Uncle, Marie, and Dick the spaniel, with reed baskets lined with grape leaves—for tomatoes, for strawberries, for melons—we went down the Minervois highway to the garden, "Antoine's garden." The road was always pretty much devoid of cars, and the rare ones that did pass by were slow, wheezy "gasogene" cars, almost as slow as the wagons drawn by modest horses. The rare cyclists that hazarded this route, under the intense June sun, were visible from quite far away as they approached from some distant horizon, from Villeneuve- (or) Laure-Minervois, from Rieux or Caunes.

One day, returning up the road from Antoine's garden, we saw a bike coming toward us in the distance, set off against the dazzling sun, and my brother Pierre immediately said: "It has to be Papa—he's the only one who goes that fast!" He was right. We ourselves weren't greatly surprised, but he wasn't expecting to see us at all. He shouldn't have been there in June 1944, a few days after the "landing" in Normandy, but somewhere else, on the Rue d'Assas, or in his class, for example. Still, we paid no attention at all to the flagrant incoherencies in the stories the adults told us. It was perfectly natural to encounter our father on the Minervois highway. The important thing was that he was going really fast. <u>That</u> was well within the proper order of things. And in any case, Antoine and Marie—who felt the same as my father did about the war—were just as unlikely to offer any astonished commentaries concerning this apparition. They felt the same: there was no other possibility. Uncle did too, although he had a tendency to confuse all the "Krauts," past and present, with the same sweeping disapproval: "Dragons, curl your mustaches," he repeated to us, lifting his glass in an invocation of Victory (not of Liberation). (He kept his rifle hidden for the right moment. The Minervois area was strongly represented among the Maquis of the Aude.)

The Clamous (or Clamoux) River began there, in Antoine's garden, and its territory, its very existence insofar as it concerned us, extended as far as the village, then beyond the village to the boundaries of the small neighboring village, Bagnoles: a tiny little river with a triumphant name, which one is apt to make fun of in ordinary times when the continuity of its course almost disappears due to the dry climate, but that sometimes gets filled, with an almost

Provençal violence, all of a sudden by storms. On such occasions, even if only for a short time, it does complete honor to its name (which one must then pronounce "Clamou-sss," or "Clamou-ks"). Along the banks of the Clamous there were poplars, soapwort, and nettles, and therefore blackberries. And in the Clamous there were fish.

The Clamous had its inhabitants, its population of fish. In the clear shallow water, we saw them moving around, bustling, darting around or thickly hovering, disappearing in fright at our shadows, scrambling under the water-lapped riverbanks and beneath the rocks. Their size was more or less proportionate to the volume of the body of water they lived in. The largest were the length of an *ell*, the medieval unit of measure that measures the distance between the crook of the elbow to the end of the fingers (a measurement invented by fishermen like us—fishermen without accessories, that much is certain). But it was an *ell* adequate to the Clamous and, at my age, a very short *ell*. There were, nonetheless, in the well-hidden hollows, a few rather imposing specimens of what we called *cabots* (striped mullets).

Anyone fishing with a line disdained the Clamous, which sustained no noble fish, unlike the torrents of the Black Mountain (and even the Clamous itself, near its source up in the mountain regions), nor a sufficient abundance, like the Aude, the Orbiel, or the Canal du Midi. Small and shifty, its fish prospered in their trembling agility. There were also a few water rats, and a few crayfish. And, once (but only once, alas), in a section of the river where we almost never went, upstream from the garden, I saw **an otter**, a British animal if there ever was one, straight from the stories of Saki or out of *The Wind in the Willows*. It was a brief but indelible vision, promptly tucked away like a treasure. **The animal was slumped like a dark mass of leather on a large sun-drenched slab of rock, and I barely had time to see it slip lithely into the waiting surface of the water, its kingdom, and disappear forever**. And when I finally saw it again, when I saw its astonished head with its round eyes, it was in Berlin, the Berlin of a book, in Walter Benjamin's *Berlin Childhood*. And I recognized it immediately: it was her, the "good virtuous otter / who resists all the poisons" (as Éluard wrote) of oblivion.

I don't know how I conceived an ambition to fish—no doubt from the stories my father had told during our trip to Toulon. But there was only one possible way to fish: by hand. So I fished. I fished for hours in cool or warm water, in the shade of the poplars or in the burning hot air. I caught nothing but barbels, speckled barbels and *cabots* (almost the only species found in the Clamous. Trout never went that far downstream). But for me they weren't prey, weren't food (though, later on, we sometimes made them into food, my brother and I, despite the lack of enthusiasm, in the family kitchens and at meals, for their particular blandness spiked with bones). They were my partners in play, at root rather analogous to the *jeu de barres*, to *chat perché*, even to the game of Go-Creeping (with the difference here that the other players, the fish, were not the least bit willing).

My goal was to catch them and take them out of the water (and then to restore them to their element); theirs was to avoid being caught. Anyone who's ever tried to grab hold of a fish in its element will think my ambition insane. And, it's true, grabbing a fish in a pool of water with smooth sides is virtually impossible (except by making it jump up onto the edge with a "handful" of water surrounding it, a very difficult feat (though not for cats)). But the Clamous wasn't a smooth pool. There were all kinds of stones and rocks in the current. And there were the banks along the water's edge.

The tactics of the fish were simple. Once my hand was in the water and was drawing nearer to them, they took refuge under a rock, or under the muddy bank, low and heavy, entangled with grass and roots. They pressed against the rock wall or sank as far as possible into the mud along the edge, and didn't move.

My tactics were no less simple. I slid one hand gently toward them until I touched them—using my other hand, if possible, to discourage any notion of fleeing toward other stone refuges, other holes in the water, toward the shelter of other roots. I touched them as lightly as possible, in order to register their size, their position. Very gently, with the tips of my fingers, so as not to goad them towards all the disorderly actions inspired by panic, and which in fact would have been the best means for them to escape. But if my approach was sufficiently discreet, they were easily persuaded (or at least I was persuaded that they were thinking along these lines) that they were safe, and that absolute immobility was their best defense. I encouraged them in this opinion.

161 I encouraged them to believe for a moment in this illusion of security

I encouraged them to believe for a moment in the illusion of this womb-like security. Then, still very slowly, cautiously, gently, I moved my hand the entire length of the fish's body, parallel to its smooth scaly body, without touching it, toward its head. The decisive moment, the "Machiavellian moment" of the capture, was approaching.

There is one and only one way to catch a fish by hand: grab it by the gills. Grab it behind the head, by the gills, and keep this grip firm and steady, against all its outraged protest, against the vigorous lashes of the tail which it will use to intimidate you and break free—lashes that become particularly violent and energetic when it feels itself plunged into the suffocating (for it) element of air. A steady grip is the only way to attain victory.

The fish in the Clamous were ardent and courageous fighters. I needed enormous reserves of patience to bring the most stubborn of them out of their hiding places. When my hand made its way closer to their heads, they would sink deeper into the tangle of muddy roots along the bank, press themselves even more intently against the inner surface of the arched hollow rocks. Sometimes, if there was still a little room in the space of its refuge, a *cabot* (the most dreadful opponent) would simply slide the length of itself inside, and I would have to start all over again. Whenever they could back up or sink farther into the bank, I was lost. The water was already lapping at my chin. Finally cornered, I felt my quarry of the moment tense up, ready to change its strategy—counter to all its instincts and to all the lessons of its parents and ancestors—and to try to flee. That's when I had to act quickly, decisively: without a single false move, grasping the one and only spot, to grip it, to pull it toward me. An old *cabot*, the biggest I'd ever seen, and in the deepest trench in the river, resisted me like this for more than an hour. But I got the better of him in the end.

The trout, it is said (the English say), is a *gentleman*. They would gladly invite it to dine at their club. But this is something only a line fisher would say. For someone who fishes by hand, nothing is more ridiculous than a trout. It's such a snob, and so infatuated with itself, that it doesn't imagine for a moment that you might be able to lay a hand on it. To do so would be a crime of *lèse-majesté* (it no doubt thinks of itself as a queen). In reality, there's only one thing it really knows how to do, aside from evaluating its own pedigree: it can resist the temptation to swallow the fly thrown to it by the old *gentleman* with a brick-red face sitting on the riverbank with his pipe and a handkerchief folded on his head to guard against the sun. I discovered this truth of "natural philosophy" in Scotland in 1947. I had climbed a small hill of heather and bilberries with George Lugton, overlooking a small loch; a stream was flowing by, and with my practiced handfisher's eye, I caught a glimpse of some trout in the water. I immediately set out to capture one (despite the bracing cold of that transparent and syrupy water). Familiar with the trout's reputation, I was expecting great reserves of shrewdness on its part, to the point of making the *cabots* and barbels of the Clamous seem like unsophisticated bumpkins. But all I had to do was hold out my hand, as it were. I was so surprised that I almost crushed it as I gripped its neck. My esteem for the trout instantly fell to zero. And it has never risen since.

I haven't mentioned the existence of another inhabitant of the Clamous yet (and my rival in capturing the smallest fish): the grass snake. Or, rather, in this case, the water snake (one of its alternate names), since I'm not referring to the long gray-green grass snake which lives in ruined walls, and which to its great shame is often confused with its cantankerous cousin, the adder. The water snake is short, the approximate length of an *ell*. It zigzags on the surface of the water, sticking out its little forked tongue with indignation when one captures it, after which one coils it around one's neck and takes it to the village to terrify Marie or her neighbors (when I think of the journey that these unfortunate beasts then had to undertake in order to return to the banks of the Clamous, I blush with shame, in retrospect). One hardly even captures it: it's enough to grab one directly from the water, nimbly and decisively.

After the war, and especially after the purchase of the Tuilerie, when we returned to the region more regularly and for longer periods of time, my brother Pierre and I continued to fish by hand (we also fished in the Aude, where I was quickly outclassed, not being as good a swimmer as Pierre, and finding myself incapable of remaining underwater as long, in order to have it out with a recalcitrant fish (my brother even managed to catch an eel, twice!)). One day, not quite twenty years ago, already feeling the years accumulating on my shoulders, I said to myself that the time had come to transmit my knowledge of fishing by hand to someone ready to receive it, so that the tradition wouldn't disappear from the family. And, according to the well-known example of the medieval romances, it was from uncle to nephew that these lessons had to pass. One August afternoon, therefore, I invited my nephew François (who was then the same age as I had been at the time of my initiation into this sacred ritual ceremony) to accompany me to the river. I taught him the art of selecting the stones, of approaching the fish, and of taking hold of them. We proceeded slowly upstream, as I gave myself over to didactic instructions and to reminiscences, and we gradually accumulated our catches in a plastic bag from the Cité bookstore (in Carcassonne) so that the family could enjoy (?) them at the evening meal, cooked over a fire made from vine clippings.

The narrative action then shifts, abruptly and dramatically, to the Tuilerie itself. There, as my mother tells it, she suddenly saw François appear, pale, beside himself, out of breath (he had been running); having been sworn to utmost and absolute secrecy, refusing to explain himself, he demanded that she immediately give him my identity card, which was in the left-hand drawer of the table in my bedroom. I am, said François mysteriously, in urgent need of it.

Indeed. So absorbed had I been in my demonstrative ardor, I'd forgotten the first rule, the golden rule of fishing by hand: WATCH OUT FOR THE POLICE! And so it happened that, stupidly, for the first time in an honorable career of fishing by hand that had spanned some thirty years, I was caught. There's no doubt about it, of course: fishing by hand is strictly and absolutely forbidden (only a few biologists who, like my brother, are fish specialists, are exempted); the law considers it to be a form of poaching, and the official fishing societies are the "civil plaintiff" in the suits brought before the courts, indifferently and without distinction, against dynamiters, people who use underwater lights to fish, people who poison the rivers and other polluters, and the unfortunate hand-fisher alike. Two officers hired by the fishing society of the Aude region had set up an ambush (on the lookout, in fact, for some prey other than myself), had followed me and caught me. I was made to pay a fine. And I was promised a stay in a "correctional facility" if I should be guilty of another infraction. In my humiliation (compounded by the presence of François, and compounded again by the fact that I had no one to blame but myself), I had only one very small consolation. Since the bag in which I'd stored my catches was being used for didactic purposes (I'd been catching fish of different species and different sizes), I had added a crayfish or two, and, most importantly, a few water snakes. One of the terms of my condemnation, as the secret agents of the Fishing Society of the Aude explained to me, was the immediate confiscation of the illegally acquired products that, I suppose, would then be donated to an orphanage or a halfway house for single mothers. Well, those gentlemen seized the bag of evidence avidly, which I held out to them with a caustic grin, and when they opened it to inspect its contents (which was sufficient proof of the crime), they jumped back in horror at the discontented and agitated snakes, who manifested their fury by sticking out their extremely viperous tongues. I gave the officers a friendly smile and removed the snakes one by one, setting them free, with the law's wholehearted consent. Such was the shameful conclusion of my career as a hand-fisher (I no longer fish, at least not officially. But I'm uncertain as to whether my crime is covered by the statute of limitations).

A few years later, after the publication of a book bearing the title *Les Animaux de tout le monde* (Everybody's Animals), I was invited to give a poetry reading. It took place in an institution of secondary education in a rather modest suburb (this detail is important) of Roanne. The audience was made up of a few classes of young students (from about seventh to tenth grade, I believe) in the company of their teachers. Everyone attending had been allowed out of class for the reading, and so they listened to me with good will. I read, among others, a rather mocking poem about the trout ("The Trout": it's a dull poem. It begins like this: "The trout is a gentleman / as the English say"). And to explain the casual way in which I spoke of this noble fish, I succinctly recounted what I've just related here, albeit at greater length, regarding my experience with fishing by hand. And when I arrived at the "Golden Rule of the Hand-Fisher," I interrupted my story and asked my audience: "Who can tell me what the golden rule for a hand-fisher is?" The teachers' faces betrayed a complete ignorance of the matter. But the students, for their part, did not hesitate for more than half a minute. From which I concluded that one must not lose all hope in future generations.

162 **It was the midday hour, on a summer day**

It was the midday hour, on a summer day, and this very choice of words ought to illustrate the ardent atmosphere (so to speak), which so much light had sublimated from the stones themselves, from the almost exhausted sun, from the white wall of the little drystone hut, dust-covered and silent. The moon melted into the sky like a whispy cloud.

Antoine's "possessions" essentially consisted of his vineyards, as was usually the case in the Minervois. And like everywhere, the process of dividing up family shares, of exchanges and buybacks, had dispersed these vineyards more or less at random across the scrubland.

Between two crests of scrub, on slopes with hollows furrowed in each side by the storms, there were also some smaller vineyards, all laid out in the same way, with a small wooden hut at their bottoms, and an entrance for carts, plows, horses, and grape vats, and a wide path forking off into the capillary network of trails running through the vineyards themselves. Each of these vineyards was designated by a name associated with its particular location. I can remember several of these, and one especially, with an almost painful acuteness, as well as a sort of "generic" moment situated in one of these places, the **White Quarry**.

In the striking immediacy of this moment, I see Antoine behind the plow, and the horse pulling it. At the bottom of the vineyard, on a slope, there was a well, a stone hut, some fig trees, some peaches (*pêches de vigne*), some cherry trees.

There was a tall cherry tree with big fat cherries, white and pink, bigarreau cherries. Between this vineyard and the next, there was a small wall, and some nettles. The horse went back and forth in the vineyard, and we sat with Marie around a basket draped by a cloth; in it were the water bottles and glasses.

The dog, Dick, was sitting at our feet, his tongue hanging out in the heat, his curly brown fur full of what we called "*agafarots*" (those very small sticky balls that get caught by the hundreds in clothes and fur): on his belly, on his back, and along his ears, which had flopped like shutters over his eyes.

It was, in this memory, the midday hour, in the full incandescence of summer, bristling with insects and intense heat. It was noon, the highest point of the day, and yet the moon appeared in the sky. An infinitely light, pale moon, flaky and thin. I found it hard to believe.

As though the moon had forgotten itself in the sky above the White Quarry.

It has never moved from there.

163 These days I rarely stray from the valley of the dam

These days I rarely stray from the valley that passes through the scrubland in Sallèles, the valley of the dam, once so thick and green, before the fire that mangled the pines. A half-century ago I wasn't afraid to cross through the tangle of reeds and nettles that hid the water. Today I won't leave the path. But the clouds haven't changed. I see them, now and once more, my head tilted back as I walk, flowing over the surface of the waters of the sky.

The dam formed a pond, but I've almost never seen it full, with its water flowing in cascades over the large stone parapet. In the past, it must have collected not only the trickle of water from the Cèze, but also the runoff from storms. Long ago, as I remember it, the stones of the dam weren't quite as dislodged as they are today. But already, after the first weeks of summer, it was always almost completely dry.

Most often, **the sun weighed on the shrunken surface of the water, a refuge for carp, as mythical as they were ancient, the water almost invisible under the reeds; and the bottom of the pond, abandoned and dry almost everywhere, had split apart into large slabs of clay curling up at their edges; it took us hours to get across, from one zone of scrub to another, climbing down the stone ledges from the top and opening a path for ourselves, legs scratched at every step, striking with stick swords into the thorns and the (to us) immense reeds, the long cutting leaves; the water snakes fled with a hiss; flights of huge dragonflies with diamond eyes, frightened partridges, or ducks flying away just above the reeds, the clumps of stalky grass sprinkled with gnats; aspens and ashes; leaves with near-white undersides; here the smell of the poplars was a smell of dense honey; neither the path nor the scrub was still visible from the interior.** We called this place of trials and exploration: the Gobi Desert.

Farther along, after the path has gradually descended toward the bottom of the valley, it crosses the water, begins to follow it on the other side (though the Cèze is never larger than a stream, contrary to what one might be led to believe when viewing, from above and at a distance, the profusion of trees and grasses that stifle it). And there, just a little way down from the path, **trees uprooted by the wind and eaten with decay created a sort of dike. Alders, aspens, and poplars had taken root there: a green wall, an impenetrable green vegetal wall; however, the Cèze filtered through the debris; it came out lightly topped with foam, to form a natural pool of great purity. There the light laid an almost black sky to rest, complicated by little clouds.**

At the point where the valley widens, before the vineyards begin, before the path crosses and then curves back to join the Villeneuve Road, which passes below Sallèles-Cabardès village, the scrubland on both sides is at its highest; and it's there, at this highest point, that I take my place to look at the clouds, at the point where the *cers*—in December, when it's strong—is at its strongest, and fills one's mouth with such a racket that you can hardly take in any air.

But in August, when the air is almost immobile, when the sky, the heat, the sun, and the dryness are punctuated with insects, with rustling thyme, with lizards, hums, and buzzing, I look out from the other side of the Cèze—at once distinct, visible, and far away, as though inhabiting a space entirely different from my own—and I see the large farm set there on the slope, at the mouth of the valley. I never got any nearer to it than one or two hundred meters (the distance separating it from the path), and year after year, looking at it from above as I go down the hill directly across from it, I perceive the same layer of tilled earth with its variations in color, on which, in a darker shade, is outlined what I imagine to be the contours of a deep body of water, but which in this geological border zone is perhaps only the sign of a change between two kinds of terrain.

The ground drops abruptly beneath me, and there, before the little patch of woods consisting of a few pines, once inhabited by a buzzard, one finds **a trench in the slope, an almost vertical ravine of pure clays in different colors: a Sicilian cassata of different kinds of clay, their veins of green, and yellow, ochre, and red, pressing up from the depths of the scrub in a sort of lively frozen cascade, separated into three stages by short flat strips run-**

ning lengthwise, the first almost vertical, the others at slightly lesser inclines.

We would slide down on the soles of our sandals or on the hard bare skin of our feet, from the top to the bottom, crouching down on our heels, leaping at each flat level in order to come into the next section in the same position, breaking and turning abruptly at the bottom of the last one to avoid the rocks immediately beneath it. Once we had reached the bottom, we shook the clay (powdery in the hot air) off of hands, our legs, our clothes, and again we scaled the slope on one of its sides, grabbing onto the hardened tufts of thyme, the roots of the little cork oaks, the sapling pines, before regaining our position, one after the other, at the top of this toboggan of natural colors, ready for the dizzying speed of another slide.

Some time ago, as I carefully descended this same slope in order to reach the path more quickly (I had lingered at the top in contemplation of the clouds, and the day was already disappearing), I wasn't surprised to find that their colors had grown duller, that their steep inclines were lower and flatter. I wasn't surprised by this, but I didn't for a moment feel inwardly that there was any error in this memory.

164 That evening, I had gone to sit beneath the pines, across from <u>Sallèles</u>

That evening (a summer evening, two years ago), I had gone to sit beneath the pine of my "lookout point" across from <u>Sallèles</u>: the evening was fine, the air silent, calm, the sunset was red, cloudless. Everything seemed fixed, illuminated, immobile. And for a moment, raising my eyes, after having lingered for a long moment on the crisscrossing pine needles I was sitting on, I had the forceful illusion of seeing a form already perceived once before, during my childhood, in the sky.

Clouds are supreme <u>conductors of memory</u>. Abstraction is their form, since the extraordinary lightness of their content gives it no consistency. At the beginning of that summer, my days had been poorly occupied: they provided little satisfaction to my intelligence. It wasn't only that the tasks I'd promised to see through and then put off were making me anxious—and, in making me anxious, were paralyzing me even more (such periods are recurrent throughout my life): even the slightest reflection would have demanded that I divide up my time in a different way. But the clouds contented the present, they exerted their sky-bound authority—their progression seduced me, and, if necessary, at certain moments, even changed the entire aspect of the world for me. This is why, in the evening heat, I tirelessly crossed the distance separating me from the scrub; I climbed back up onto the dry shoulder of stones, of dry oaks, junipers, and pines, and found the same tree again, an umbrella pine. Since 1943, I've never gone more than six months without sitting beneath it, on its carpet of needles, abandoning myself to the same empty, peaceful, and overwhelming contemplation.

To seek to extinguish one's thought, to approach the one and infallible absence that absorbs all things—wouldn't this be one way to participate in the duration of all beings as a whole? Gradually, as I stared at them, several forms became visible in their rushing indistinction, various rapid and incalculable combinations, shifting too quickly for my limited awareness, my heart constricted by the oncoming night.

The air without depth, without shade, the solitude of the dry stones on the slope below me—these kept me from moving. The slope angled down, it slid down in layers of ochre clay, almost red, with green veins (a paradise of ruined colors). I lay down, my head on the tufts of thyme, on the false lavender, my heels on top of a *restanque*, a low wall of now dislodged stones. That evening the sky was full, parallel, almost vertical, dotted by a single cloud, round and white.

The next day, on the contrary, a driving wind had drawn them en masse toward the lower edge of the Black Mountain, and from there they slowly descended, as though coming toward me while I tried to take them all in, one after the other, in all their singularity. I repeated to myself that, as limited beings, they necessarily had to differ from each other by some formal index, since otherwise they wouldn't have appeared distinct. And yet they didn't manage to form, in my eyes, anything other than a whole—at least not when I tried to see something more than their overall mixture, to reach some kind of comprehension of them. From time to time, then, I shifted my view, and was soon vanquished by the curvature of the earth.

My sight had always maintained possession of all the visions I had collected of them—of all the looking that I'd directed at them, almost from the same point, for so many days and so many years; and now I sought to recognize

distinct classes of those _equivalents_ on which Stieglitz had carried out a photographic meditation over a lifetime of visions at Lake George, where he'd
captured the images that had propelled me—by analogy if not by emulation—
into this conscious activity of contemplation. I said to myself that each of the
classes of cloud might provide the identifying mark of an autonomous region
of the past.

And whenever one of them hesitantly reappeared in my field of vision, I had
the feeling of recognizing it. How could a form, an arrangement of air that
had remained entirely foreign to my conscious reflection, even after appearing
hundreds of times—how could such a thing have had so much of an influence
on my thoughts? Was each one of them the sign of an instant that my memory
hadn't entirely succeeded in relinquishing, or only of a mood, an emotional
aroma of the past itself, which chance alone allowed me to regain on these idle
evenings of days spent in neglect and disarray?

The clouds, however, offered me their variety without reticence. Here they
had a free sky to pass through. The solitude suited them. They were not ir-
resolute, in this regard. But there are different ways of gliding through the sky.
I would never have thought that so much gentle, billowy concentration could
be reconciled with such demanding geometries. The least favorable, however,
were the low-flying ones, small and monotonous, so unnecessarily profuse.
Their approach filled me with anxiety. But I didn't hear any torrential murmur
in those vast, incompressible caves of air: in other words, there was no storm
coming. I was witness then to nothing more than a shifting of planes. They
eluded my tightening grasp, fleeing into infinity, and they added to the anx-
iousness of my precarious days. Even when their shadows had come to a halt,
by chance, on the ground.

And so, evening after evening, I found myself again and again under these
pines across from Sallèles, recurrent target of my local sadness. It wasn't only
acedia I was suffering from, but also from having to remember—there in the
deep space between the sky and the mountain, almost entirely flooded with
clouds. Seeking to extinguish my thought, to approach the absence of this
cloudy sky, I lay down, my head on the tufts of thyme. And still the clouds
didn't manage to form anything other than a whole in my eyes, a whole in
which the light—like so long ago, at the foot of the vineyard in the White
Quarry—laid an almost black sky to rest.

Bifurcation D

Montée de la Boucle

165 the Perrache train station laid a trap for travelers

In Lyon, the Perrache train station had laid a trap for travelers whose loving and anxious families were awaiting them there: it had two exits, virtually indistinguishable from each other—a North and a South exit that divided the numberless throng, the tumultuous flow of travelers (easily enough people to fill at least three pre-war trains), into separate groups. These travelers moved forward—a mass of individual particles, tired and exhausted by the heat, soiled by the black soot of the locomotive smoke that came in the windows of their compartments, their brains haggard from a long and uncomfortable night, their bodies bruised by their neighbors' enormous and unwieldy suitcases (sharp edges on every side)—rushing along like the famous sheep of Panurge's enemy, the merchant, and thus stampeded at random and without thinking toward one of the two exits.

Like the electrons in that famous experiment, given two points of exit, two miniscule holes under constant surveillance, they passed one by one through the two narrow checkpoints, each leading to a different way out, slowly finding themselves back outside, some at the South exit and some at the North; but, like those same electrons, under the gaze of their observers, following a totally unpredictable distribution. I was eight years old. I followed them.

Before my departure from Carcassonne, I had indeed been warned about the existence of those two irreconcilable paths, and had been told that my grandfather would be waiting for me at the North exit (or perhaps it was the South exit. I don't remember). But by the time I arrived, I had forgotten which one I was supposed to "take." Hesitating on the platform with my little suitcase, the two paths looked strangely similar to me, like twins even: for me, one was Tweedledum, the other Tweedledee.

My grandfather, however, who had come down from the hills of Caluire with his cane and his boater hat to greet the eldest son of his eldest daughter, and, as was his wont, had arrived at the Perrache train station a good half hour early, was likewise gripped for a moment with an uncertainty symmetrical to my own (as he later confessed, much to his shame). But then at last he thought he distinctly recalled that he was supposed to go to the North exit (or perhaps it was the South). Of course it wasn't the right one.

But let me be clear. The exit in front of which he decided to stand and wait for me was not the one to which he should have gone, according to my grandmother's instructions, which in fact she had transmitted to my mother in a timely manner by letter (the telephone was still, in my family, little more than a futuristic object seen in American film comedies). During the rather lively discussion that followed my grandfather's return, and that was sporadically reprised over the following weeks, he was obliged to admit that this was the case—much to his vexation, since it was very rare for him to make a mistake concerning the "immediate data of consciousness" and the algorithms of practical life, and unlike my grandmother, my mother, and myself, he was not the least bit absentminded.

It's at this point that things become complicated. Later, when my mother learned of this adventure, she pointed out that the exit indicated by my grandmother as the one where my grandfather *should* have gone to receive his grandson without incident (assuming of course that the latter went that way himself) was not the one that had previously been indicated in the letter she (my mother) had received on this occasion. Now, my grandmother, as I just said, was indeed absentminded, and in fact lived in an extreme state of distraction, of which I shall no doubt have the occasion and pleasure to relate a few examples. It was therefore perfectly conceivable, perfectly natural, even ordinary, to think that she might have directed my grandfather to an exit other than the one she had stated a few days earlier, when she had written her letter to my mother.

My grandfather was pleasantly surprised at this unexpected turnaround in the situation, and did not fail to emphasize the point. To which he received the retort, however, that this revelation made absolutely no difference with regard to the fact that he had, after all, make a mistake, and thus that it was purely by chance that he'd found himself waiting at the right exit. "The right exit? Well then, which was the right exit?" my grandfather asked, with a slight hint of bad faith. This question (and especially the tone of voice in which it was formulated) was judged to be specious, a sophistry, inadmissible, an attempt to sow confusion. He had been told to go to the North exit (though perhaps it was the South exit), and he had gone instead to wait for the child (me: a finger pointed at me) at the South exit (or North, as the case may be). No logic, no hairsplitting arguments could change this fact. My grandfather, shrugging his shoulders, then fell back on the other element, in his view undeniable, of the equation: that he hadn't been the only one to make a mistake. My grandmother's share of responsibility was at least equal to his.

But was this really so certain? In other words, had my mother read correctly what her mother had written to her? Since the two exits were distinguished by a single short word (four letters for *Nord* (North) and three for *Sud* (South)), had she identified the right one? A second characteristic of my grandmother's explains the relevance of this question: her handwriting was virtually illegible, much worse than that of her physician, Dr. Bouchut (who now has a street named after him in Lyon, near the new Part-Dieu train station). A critical analysis of the document in question did not resolve the question. My mother had read "South" (or "North"), no doubt, but had my grandmother actually written "South" (or "North")? As she was almost the only one competent enough to decipher her mother's handwriting (we always turned to her when our grandmother wrote to us), my mother had relied on her long experience, and had not hesitated.

But looking more closely at the letter, in light of subsequent events, she was no longer so certain about her interpretation. The simplest remedy, in this case, was naturally to put the letter before the eyes of its author. My grandmother, then, having identified (not without difficulty, as usual) the place in the house where she'd left her eyeglasses, put them on, looked attentively at the incriminating passage, and was obliged to admit that she did not know.

166 And yet

And yet (going back a few days now, to the morning of the confusion itself), having passed through the exit (wrong in any case), held out my ticket, and looked around for my grandfather in the crowd, I soon made this undeniable observation: he was not there. I did not hesitate either. I would not ask for help from the railway authorities. This was the call of adventure, and I would not refuse it: I would find my way to 21 Rue de l'Orangerie on my own.

I don't know why (perhaps because it seemed less complicated), but between the two possible itineraries that came to mind, I didn't choose the one that would take me by streetcar "4" to the bottom of the street called Montée de la Boucle (across from the bridge of the same name), but the alternate combination of the "8" (through the Croix-Rousse area) and the Rue de l'Oratoire. I boarded an "8," paid my fare, proudly took a seat (I was in the midst of a great exploit), and began to enthusiastically absorb the scenery (I loved streetcars, those inner-city railways. There weren't any in Carcassonne). (The disappearance of streetcars, which fell victim to the invasion of the automobile, was one of the great tragedies of urban life in the 20th century, and only now is the extent of this tragedy being appreciated. And one can only applaud the initiative taken by certain pioneering cities, like Manchester, that have decided to reintroduce them. I was unable, alas, to be present at the beginning of this year, 1992, for their re-inauguration—one of those symbolic events that, in a modest way no doubt, but nonetheless quite distinctly, manages to restore one's faith in humanity!)

It was morning, an early morning in summer. The air was still cool. The train climbed, turned onto the main street of Croix-Rousse. Travelers got on, got off. With my suitcase on my knees, I watched the travelers getting on and off, the shops and pedestrians approaching and receding. More and more passengers were getting off and fewer and fewer were getting on. The landscape became less and less like that of a busy city. This didn't worry me at first, because our usual stop on the way back from running "errands" in Croix-Rousse was virtually deserted. The streetcar was now almost empty, however, and I could find nothing familiar in this landscape. I got out at the end of the line (somewhere in Cuire), and decided to return on foot in the direction from which I had come. No one paid any attention to me, no one was surprised to encounter an eight year old child like this, alone with a suitcase. No one asked me where I was going, whether I was lost. It strikes me that such an adventure would no longer be possible today.

Now, as I walked, I found my way. The relief, perhaps, at no longer being lost, at being close to my goal and to relief (I was hungry, I was hot, I needed to pee) gave the long, long Rue de l'Oratoire an indestructibly joyous appearance (which could only surprise those who knew it then, in all its austerity). It was empty (it was almost always empty), and I moved forward under the sun, between high walls only rarely interrupted by small secret doors opening into invisible sumptuous gardens, closed and locked tight, walls whose tops were planted with shards of broken bottles, to discourage intruders (a characteristic detail of this supremely closed off, involuted city—as far from the Mediterranean style as possible—in which all architecture is turned inward).

At the end of the street is the Oratory (the convent that gives the street its name). It stops there suddenly at the edge of a slope, an abrupt slope that descends into the Rhône. The Rue de l'Orangerie ends there as well, perpendicular to it. Just a few houses to my right, then number 21 *bis*, then I arrived at last at the small iron door, to the right of the gate.

Walking along the Rue de l'Orangerie, you could not see the Rhône. As on the Rue de l'Oratoire, an uninterrupted wall on the left (behind it a garden, on a steep drop-off: wild vines, fruit trees, herbs) blocked the view. And farther along, after number 21, began the modest houses of the Clos Bissardon area.

Walking in the street, beneath the blind wall, one saw nothing of the precipitous drop or the Rhône down below. But above the wall of number 21, on the other side of the terrace into which the gate opened, covered with paving stones furrowed by geometrical lines, there was an unlikely "pergola" perched on the top of a large rock (aesthetically similar to the artificial wilds in the garden of the Buttes-Chaumont, in Paris), which one reached by a stairway twisting upward through the stone (or, preferably, at our ages, by climbing up the craggy rock-face itself, covered with hanging ivy and hollowed out by a false grotto with a fake spring trickling into a cement basin). A small parapet jutted out over the street, and from there, now that the view had finally overcome the obstacle of Lyon's stubborn retentiveness, the city's cold and evasive passion for secrets, one could gaze out over a distant leafy Arcadia (I never entered that garden), into its profusion of trees and flowers rushing down toward the rapid brilliance of the river beyond it.

Later, I passed many vacant summer hours in that spot, reading, looking at the Rhône, at the hill populated and buzzing with insects, with the rising murmur of the city spread out in the distance. It was the site of "a self-renewing vegetable bliss" (as William Herbert, Lord of Cherbury, put it).

A fragment by Hölderlin remains irresistibly attached to this space—reveals it and wrenches it away from all oblivion: (I will cite Pierre Jean-Jouve's translation, as I remember it, since it was his version I read first.)

> *Et moi*
> *L'homme de nulle part*
> *Devrai être enterré*
> *là*
> *où la rue tourne*
> *au sentier des vignes*
> *et résonnante au-dessous des pommiers*

> [And I
> the man from nowhere
> will have to be buried
> there
> where the street turns
> on the trail of the vines
> and echoes beneath the apple trees]

167 Not long before her death, my grandmother

Not long before her death, my grandmother, then eighty-three years old, wrote down some of her memories and had them transcribed for us, her six grandchildren (three each from the Roubaud and Molino families). She had long been asked to do this by those of us who had heard her tell stories at one time or another. The text, of which I have a copy (just shy of forty pages typed in purple on an American typewriter, with the accents added by hand), was written at the home of her youngest daughter, my aunt Renée, in Cambridge (Massachusetts). Here are the first pages (without omissions or corrections):

MEMORIES
1900–1945

Mme. B. Molino
Cambridge, December 1963

"This is written for a young schoolteacher in the year 2000 who is curious about the past of her profession and who has perhaps read *L'Histoire d'un sous-maître* by Erckmann Chatrian dating from 1816 [sic: 1871] and can appreciate the progress that has been made.

On October 11, a young woman of nineteen was about to enter the path of her first position as a teacher. Whence did she come? Where was she going?

She was the daughter of a teacher from Marseille, and her mother was a simple homemaker. Three months earlier she had taken the examination for entry into the École Normale d'Institutrices in Aix-en-Provence, and she had succeeded, thanks to the serious efforts that had become necessary because of the considerable number of candidates (80 for 8 positions).

The only city she knew was the big city of Marseille, which had made the greatest impression on her during her walks by the seashore, on the happy fishing trips, for which her father had a great passion, and in the touching friendship of a dog raised in part by her.

Her entry into the École Normale, with its austere edifice and austere house rules, made it difficult for her to appreciate the charms of this small provincial city and its ancestral beauty. The few walks outside the town were indeed marked by a certain relaxation of discipline, but the few, and dangerous, chance encounters with the male residents, particularly the Normaliens or the terrible 'Beaux Arts' students, brought the impeccable rows back into order, in the dignified silence of strictly surveyed young ladies. To maintain this good reputation 'extra muros,' it was even necessary to be on guard against the few isolated strollers. Why, on one of these walks the Rector of the Academy had even heard a few independent souls set out on the road singing, '*Viens, Poupoule, viens!*' A memory that found its way into the dreaded director's Sunday-morning speech.

But from these harsh ways, these outmoded rules, one should not conclude that the instruction was deadly or deadening. Our young lady remembers the excellent courses given by the experienced and conscientious professors, who devoted themselves to their tasks with all their knowledge, with all their soul, one of whom she preferred to the rest, but all observing a spirit of complete neutrality (freedom for religious services).

Outside this full but theoretical life, what did she know about real life, the one awaiting her in a Provençal village, or about life in the country, where she had only ever made a few brief visits during vacations? Her father, a fervent republican, placed all his faith in the defense of the new regime which he had seen come into being and prosper, and the elections, the lavish celebrations of 'July 14,' had been the bright sparks of her youth, which in other ways was carefree and full of so many diverse interests.

168 So let us follow the young lady along the road

So let us follow the young lady along the road that led to her post.

Having arrived in Salon-de-Provence by train, her suitcase stuffed with the necessities . . . and with hope, she found the Miramas-Lancon stagecoach stop. The coach was there at the stop, surrounded by groups of women loaded with supplies from town, in hampers or baskets covered with cloth. Salon is a capital, the capital of oils. The waiting people chide the young conductor, a handsome fellow from Provence, calling for him as he blithely prolongs a lover's conversation with the girl who will soon become his wife.

Finally, we take our seats. Without any doubt, the young stranger has already distinguished herself when, as she sits down, she politely asks the driver to stop near the Écoles for her. This bit of information confirms the general opinion of the travelers who were looking at her on the sly, whispering to one another, and allowing her to hear these few words: 'But she's so young!' Up to then she was proud to take up her duties with all the dignity she believed she projected from her person, but already her self-confidence and her hopes were shaken!

The oversized Tintin of a driver, always late on the return trip, and with good reason!, whips his horses without pity. The windows of the car tremble while outside the olive trees shaken by the wind from the Crau pass by in waves of silvery branches on which, it seems, one can distinguish a few olives.

The coach stops before a rocky uphill path: this is the path that leads most directly to the Écoles, and our young teacher, carrying her suitcase, begins to make her way up the road, followed very curiously by all the travelers who, for their parts, will get out in the village itself, without neglecting to spread the news.

Next to the little house, at the entrance to a street leading up a hill, two twin buildings beside a very large grassy square beckon the young lady of their own accord, but everything is closed up, there is no sign beckoning her in. Fortunately for her, on the threshold of the house next door, a woman gives her a glance which she takes as an invitation to approach. This is the person with the keys. She can give out the information most needed on arrival. A welcoming face, certainly sympathetic to the teaching staff (the old female staff had been automatically renewed because of a serious lapse in their duties). [? J.R.]

Here, then, is the young teacher earning her living in complete independence, in the full bloom of her youth, about to take possession of her personal lodgings.

The apartment is on the second floor: a bedroom and a kitchen. The young lady first opens the kitchen window looking out over the 'Champ de Mars' with its historic name. It is very large, and through the sparse trees, still covered with their autumnal finery, one distinguishes a statue covered with verdigris: it is the poet Signoret, a native of Lançon. Just outside the window, on the other side of the path, the fountain lets its water flow, and the wind, the terrible mistral, blows it every which way. In the kitchen, a thin cabinet will receive her personal effects, as the bedroom with the flowery tapestry does not have one.

After standing at the window for a long time, the window facing the 'Champ de Mars,' in the midst of arranging her affairs, the young teacher gives a start upon hearing the knocker on the door of the first floor. There she is in front of a man with young features, rather short and dry, with a resolute face. What was this about? Word had spread throughout the village and the Mayor had come to introduce himself. Then came the customary introductions and compliments: wishes for a comfortable adaptation to life there, for getting along well with the townspeople, the opinion that the new Director would soon arrive from a neighboring hamlet to greet his new assistant.

But the visit had another pressing purpose, which was to inform her that everyone at the Écoles would have to be present the very next day (a Saturday) at a funeral. The young lady showed the customary concern and asked for a few details regarding this loss. Here, word for word, is what was said to her:

'A stillborn child will be carried to the cemetery, a child who, if he had lived, would have been a student here at the secular school. We know the family, there can be no doubt on this point.' "

169 **We were sorely disappointed.**

We were sorely disappointed. These pages, written in the style of the old "Read-ers" used in the secular schools at the beginning of the century, and bound in the corsets of their narrative conventions, show no trace of the vivacity, the spontaneity, the irresistible humor of the stories that we had heard so often and so often asked to hear again. The story of the "Affair of the Secular Burial of the Stillborn Child," a prelude to the ultimately triumphant confrontation between our grandmother and two conniving figures, veritable allegories of sectarianism and bigotry, had in fact been one of her most reliable successes.

(As were the story of the mistral and then the one about the child knocked down by the wind (who then exclaims in Provençal, "*Ren que per aco rest'aqui!*" ("Well then, I'll stay here!")); these don't figure in the typed "Memories," per-haps because they have nothing to offer to an "ideological" interpretation. For, you see, the text has two parts: the first exalts a "pure," apolitical conception of secularism. The second praises the struggles of the "Resistance," which my grandmother joined, forty years later, with the same intrepid character that she had shown at the age of nineteen in her encounter with the politicized mayor of Lançon-de-Provence.)

She was constantly telling stories. She recounted life as it went along, pass-ing from the most recent incomprehensible disappearance of her eyeglasses to distant scenes of childhood. (At four years old, perched on the table by her father after a Sunday meal, she had sung for the guests, with tremendous suc-cess: "*Va petit mousse / Le ventre pousse . . .*" ("Go little ship's boy / My belly is growing").)

In fact, she often repeated this particular success with us, her grandchildren, sixty years later. And sometimes when she sang other very old songs, like "*Au revoir bon voyage / ne sois pas triste ainsi / . . . / Donne-moi un peu de courage / Pour rester seule au nid . . .*" ("Goodbye, safe journey / don't be sad like that / . . . / Give me a little courage / To stay here alone in the nest . . ."), she showed us that her triumph back then had been due less to the musical qualities of her voice, which remained mediocre, than to the mistakes she had naively made with the words (which should have been: "*Le* vent te *pousse*" ("The wind drives you on")), and thus that the applause which had been lavished on her by the adults was simply mockery.

(At this point, she could have employed a technique that quite a few autobiographers—Sartre and Leiris for example—certainly don't refuse themselves; she could have inserted the moment of a conscious and deliberate decision into this childhood memory, a firm resolution to avenge her father's mean trick, to "embrace" the career of a teacher and thus to become someone who would possess the "truth" of the language in its proper form, and who would inculcate it into the children of coming generations, so that they would never fall into the same trap. But her oral "performances" didn't contain any hint of the highly moral coloring that marked her actions and judgments in other respects (I would say that she had a hypertrophied sense of the ethical component of existence). Her performances were essentially concerned with the pleasures of storytelling, with a ludic relaxation. At least that's how I remember them.)

These, then, were the sorts of moment we'd expected to find in her "memoirs," and that, as adults, we had asked her to set down for us (the tape recorder, alas, came too late, as did video of course). One other *exemplum* figures in the text that I have in front of me now (it may give you a rough idea of the "oral" version): a visit from a school inspector (I note this bit of praise, found in the "inspection report": "Satisfactory. The children look their teacher in the eye.").

"The inspector paced before the first rows, the teacher remained at her desk. 'Let's see,' he said, addressing the entire class, 'which animal is the first among the mammals?' Various responses fly off, like 'the wolf, the dog, the horse, the monkey.' The teacher strains to hold herself back, does what she can to rescue the situation. Alas! Nothing comes! The inspector, suddenly overcome with anger, shouts at the terrified students, tapping himself on the chest: 'And what about me? Am I not a mammal?' The entire class, in a state of panic, stares with incredulity at this mammal—rather hairy, it's true—but whose flat chest offers no hope of any nourishment for its young."

She always arrived home from a walk, or from America, with a bag of supplies or else suitcases full of stories. We expected no less. But the rest of the time she was self-absorbed, distracted, doleful, silent, absent. In the photograph described at the end of the chapter on my "fore-life," she can be seen sitting in a chaise longue with my sister on her knees, looking at no one in particular. If I set aside all the moments of her storytelling, in which she al-

most seems to be another person, it is indeed like this that I see her, according
to three distinct modalities:

—reclining in a chaise longue (or in the "rocking chair" on the veranda, in
Caluire) reading, or knitting, or dreamily tapping her fingers on the arm of
the chair;

—coming and going all alone on the large walkway in the garden between
the mulberry trees, a letter in hand, or with my mother, or else with her sister
Jeanne, or most often with her old friend (even smaller than she), Mlle Chauvin: "Taia" (my grandmother does the talking, Taia nods her head, says two or
three words, states an opinion);

—lying on her bed, her head on the pillow, in the dark bedroom, with its
heavy curtains and medicinal odor, which we entered only rarely, speaking
only in whispers.

170 There were a great many teachers in my family

There were a great many teachers in my family, virtually all of them on my
mother's side. To be sure, my paternal grandmother, whom I never knew, was
a teacher as well. But she was the only one in that branch of my genealogical
tree, and in that generation. In a certain sense, my father skipped a transitional
stage, one represented perfectly, typically, by my grandparents' generation.
Our family is a true sociologist's delight.

In the beginning, like everywhere else, one finds the land: the vines of Soliès
or of the Nissard back-country on one side, mistralian Provence or Piedmont
(Villanova d'Asti) and Savoy on the other (I won't go into the details here). But
then comes an almost absolute convergence between both sides. Which is to
say that the choice (?) of lifestyle wasn't made in favor of material wealth: neither land, nor commerce, nor business. Each side avoided (either deliberately
or otherwise) both the immobility and the general course of life described by
Charles Cros in his poem "*Le Propriétaire*" (The Property Owner):

"Born in some unsavory corner / Of Auvergne or Limousin, / First he tills
the ground. / Humble, without desire, without a goal, / These are the modest
beginnings / Of the Property Owner. / [. . .] At first to earn his bread / He
sells his rabbit skins / Although this business makes him thirsty, / He does

not drink his money down / For he is intelligent / The Property Owner. / [. . .] His pile of money, small at first / Very slowly grows fat / In great calm and mystery, / Then, at peace with the law, / His gold makes him almost a king, The Property Owner . . ."

(The poem is set in a different climate, but the general trajectory isn't dependant on that.)

My grandmother's father, Paul Devaux, was a teacher. Her mother (*née* Boeuf: we always very much enjoyed reading on Blanche Molino's birth certificate—which she showed us with a laugh—that she had been born the daughter of ". . . Devaux, *née* Boeuf" (which sounds like: "Of veal, born Beef"!)), as we've seen, was a "homemaker": a housewife and a cook from Marseille, expert in "*pieds et paquets*," in "*alouettes sans tête*," in "cannelloni" or "ravioli" (Marseille style), and stews that she prepared for her husband, an irascible, food-obsessed tyrant (who would rise trembling in the middle of the night to check on a pot in the midst of a very long, very precise, very delicate, and very difficult simmer).

Either my great-grandmother wasn't so completely tremulous and submissive as family tradition has it, or she actually was to such an extent that she became a forceful counterexample and thus incited her (not very numerous) descendants never to repeat this same configuration—but in any case, her two daughters, Jeanne the elder and Blanche the younger, emancipated themselves from this exclusive slavery to housework by becoming teachers like their father. My great aunt Jeanne inherited some culinary talents (my grandmother's ambitions in this domain, at least during the years when I knew her, went little further than soft-boiled eggs and pots of hot milk for tea, which in any case she naturally forgot on the stove, leaving them to burn half the time). After a youth that according to my mother was quite stormy, and some long "emancipated" years as a clerk in the "Nouvelles Galeries" (her younger sister helped her prepare her entrance into public education), she married a teacher named Pierre Thabot, a man who liked his peace and quiet. They worked, lived, retired, and died in Marseille. They had no children.

What was for her sister only a snug and comfortable solution (Uncle Pierre was anything but a domestic tyrant), my grandmother saw as a choice that was necessarily as theoretical and ideological as it was personal, in line with the

"1900" style of feminism that she never relinquished. She got married (to the brother of one of her École Normale classmates), became an assistant teacher, then a teacher in her own right, in Lançon, then in Fuveau, where my mother was born. After that she became a school principal (in Digne (a *département* in the *Basses-Alpes*, or Lower Alps region, as it was called at that time)). She raised four children: two boys (my uncles Maurice and Frantz) and two girls (my mother, Adèle Suzette, born in April 1907, and then youngest child, Renée, born rather later, during the Great War, after my grandfather received the wound that no doubt saved his life, in 1916).

I just wrote, very naturally and without thinking: "she raised." Indeed, everything in the family story seems designed to displace my grandfather, nudging him gradually into a "side" position, as though the motivating responsibility for events (in every domain except economic, particularly in light of the financial improvements that came when my grandfather secured the position of primary-school inspector) was the exclusive privilege of my grandmother. This very particular inflection of the past, which was entirely adopted by my mother (I can make no declarations as to its truth, which eludes me), is also found expressed in the text of my grandmother's "Memories," almost in the form of a caricature (with this in mind, I will underscore the significant use of pronouns in this new excerpt):

". . . the life of a woman who is both a mother and a teacher is illuminated by the joy that a special authorization has given her: that of being able to place first one and then the other of one's two oldest children among a large class of girls, such that one's natural and perhaps atavistic pleasure is compounded by the impetus that one's role as an educator brings to completion with them. It is their dear presence that often animates and illuminates one's lessons . . .

"From this moment on, the life of one's children has taken on so much importance in daily existence that it naturally leads to the use of the word "us," since "I" has now become impersonal. When the teacher's career takes us to Digne because of their father's new title, it carries me with great fear to a position as principal of a primary school in Digne (Basses-Alpes) . . ."

171 My grandfather's father Robert Molino was a stationmaster in Poliéna.

My grandfather's father Robert Hyacinthe Molino ("born in 1840 [1835, in fact], died in 1916," wrote my grandmother on the back of his portrait, a full-length portrait showing him with a beard and a gilt cap, still kept in a large box of drawings beside my bedroom dresser in the Minervois, between the dresser and the bed) was the station-master in Poliéna. The walnuts from there, or so I was told as a child, are the best in the world. (His father, my great-great grandfather Joseph (Giuseppe) Molino, carabiniere then a common carrier, had left Villanova d'Asti, in Piedmont, and crossed the border into Savoy (not yet French) to marry a young lady from the village of Les Marches, my great-great grandmother Maurizia Bal, "a former schoolteacher who did domestic work," and a "*Marcherue*," then, as one calls the people from her village.)

The oldest family document in my possession (though what I have is in fact a later copy) comes from the mayor of Les Marches (Savoy):

Excerpt from the Public Records Office
of the Commune of Les Marches for the Year 1839

In this year eighteen-hundred thirty-nine, on the twelfth day of the month of September at eleven o'clock in the morning, in the parish of Les Marches, commune of Les Marches, there was presented at the Church a child of feminine sex, born the eleventh of September at five o'clock in the afternoon in this parish, daughter of Maurice Bal, farmer by profession, resident of Les Marches, and Marguerite Ferreros, his spouse in lawful marriage, ⸻

The child was baptized by me, the undersigned rector, and received the name of Marie ⸻

Named as godfather was Claude Ferreros, tile maker by profession residing in Les Marches, and as godmother Péronne Bal, laborer, residing in Les Marches.

My great-grandmother was Marie Bal, daughter of Maurice Bal (born in 1812, the most remote date reachable in this genealogical movement back in time, without the aid of archival research) and of Marguerite Ferreros (a midwife), who later married her cousin Robert Hyacinthe Molino, son of Giuseppe Molino and Maurizia Bal. Marie Bal had very long hair, and only her husband could comb it.

Their numerous family consisted mostly of girls, all of whom, without exception (except for my grandfather's twin, who died at three months from whooping cough) became teachers. All but one of the girls remained unmarried. All but one (the same, Louise: married name Glodas) died of "consumption" (translation: tuberculosis). Joséphine was the first to die: at nineteen, in 1900. Adèle cared for Joséphine, then died of it in turn. Finally, Marie, the oldest, fell victim as well.

In what seems to be a recommendation as to the beneficial effects of marriage, the only survivors of this typically nineteenth-century hecatomb were the children who got married: for one of them the role of house-nurse was simply impossible, since he had his own family to take care of; and the other, my great aunt Louise, refused (out of "egotism," according to the family tradition—a tradition that is willfully Spartan and sacrificial). (My grandfather also made it through the war with nothing more than relatively benign leg-wound received in 1915, compounded however by the loss of his first watch and his first pen.)

The threat of death weighed heavily on my mother's childhood. It was a sort of curse—originating, it was thought, in hereditary traits, and creating a predisposition to illness in successive generations, a "fragile constitution" that could be fought only with a regimen of vigilance and hygiene (a hygiene of cleanliness as well as diet: a veritable secular passion), whose precepts (taken from the "bible" of the teachers of the time, the at-once Hippocratic and "progressive" works of the doctor and republican Raspail) were vehemently adhered to by my grandfather, as strictly as the rules of so-called "logical" orthography and syntax, until his death at the age of ninety one.

All her life, my grandmother remained convinced that her children had only survived by a miracle. (Her two daughters, however—my mother and my aunt—are now 84 and 75 years old, respectively. Her two older children did die prematurely, but by accident.) Thus she wrote, in her text from 1963:

"The move to Marseille is marked, alas! by the sad effects of a deadly epidemic of measles that gravely compromised the health of our children, which adds a chronic anxiety to the daily work and to the worries of the job, casting over our family, and <u>especially over their mother</u> [my emphasis] a veil of sadness for the rest of her life."

She herself was a chronic invalid, especially after 1938 (the year of my uncle Frantz's fatal accident), and her sufferings—physically quite real, according to the doctor—were certainly intensified by this permanent state of mourning, from which she never emerged.

172 the striking dissymmetry between my grandparents' reactions to illness

At the same time, the striking dissymmetry between my grandparents' reactions to illness can't really be explained in terms of a greater susceptibility on my grandmother's part to the appeal of irrational explanations. Their intellectual formation was similar in its positivism, and their general outlook and ideas were very close. But whereas for him the specter of hereditary morbid fatality took on the guise of "consumption," the illness that had struck down his sisters, for her it had another aspect, more obscure, more terrible, and more hidden: that of a moral curse.

Indeed, it wasn't until the time of my mother's engagement that my grandmother finally resigned herself, for honesty's sake, to confessing a terrible secret, a shameful fact that, moreover, she considered to be dangerous: her own father had been syphilitic (and had conjugally transmitted a lovely case of tabes (a disease of syphilitic origin, characterized in particular by a hardening of the dorsal columns of the spinal cord, disturbances of motility, and the suppression of reflexes, all this as described in the *Petit Robert*) to his wife, my great-grandmother Boeuf, who already had the distinction of being the daughter of an unmarried mother (the father was a "young man of means" from Lançon-Provence, in fact, where my grandmother later began her career as an assistant teacher). (I note by the way that even though she joked about her mother's fears (half-medical, half-moral), my own mother didn't "reveal" this fact to me until fairly recently, and I don't even know if she's ever mentioned it to my brother or sister)). There can be no doubt that, in the implementation of her educative strategies, this fear of my grandmothr's reinforced the ethical dimension of her demeanor, as well as her prudence regarding hygiene.

She subjected her four children to a strict program of study, which they absorbed apparently without difficulty. (Despite my doubts, I am implicitly adopting our family's traditional portrayal here, in which the responsibility for the impulse behind this regimen is attributed solely to her. My grandfather certainly participated, but his role is considered to be more "technical" and intermittent, if only because of the war, and later because of his "tours" of inspection, which often took him far from home.)

Thus, my grandmother had conceived a totally new ambition for them, along with new goals and horizons, which the preceding generations could never have imagined: she had become a schoolteacher, an instructor in a primary school, but (unlike her older sister), she had achieved this by taking the most difficult and the most "elevated" path: that of the École Normale. Her children, however, would be professors, and they too would take the most difficult and the most "elevated" path: that of the École Normale Supérieure. (I put "elevated" in quotation marks in both cases, since for my grandmother it was only a matter of an intellectual hierarchy, related to the difficulty and the complexity of the studies involved. The social "elevation" that would possibly result from taking such a path was to her mind a legitimate and worthy goal, but I think it was secondary (and yet she never saw it as what it appeared to be later: illusory, not only economically but also symbolically).)

I don't know whether her "program" was fully conceived from the start. My uncles Maurice and Frantz were without any doubt brilliant students, and their lycée professors most likely encouraged them to continue on to the "*khâgne*," the preparatory class for the exam required to enter the École Normale on the Rue d'Ulm, after the baccalaureate. But I believe that we can without risk of error credit my grandmother, and her feminist convictions, with the extremely original idea (at the time) of allowing her oldest daughter (and later, quite naturally, her youngest as well), to do the same (and not to aim for the École de Sèvres, a school for girls, but to compete with the boys on their own terrain). To send all her children to the "Rue d'Ulm"—this was her project. She conceived of it as her life's work, her magnum opus. She almost completely fulfilled her goal, and later she was extremely proud of it (she told me so, though not without pointing out that there was a risk of familial decline, since only two of her grandchildren achieved the same results). (And I don't doubt that she saw the two tragedies that struck her a few years later, and only a few years apart, as a return of the old ancestral fatality—as a sort of revenge of death.)

It's difficult to imagine just how unusual it was for a young woman, in Digne at the beginning of the twenties, to presume to present herself as a candidate for the baccalaureate. My mother became one of the first, despite all the internal and institutional reluctance. She benefited from the lessons and example of her brothers, who were just a little older. It's clear that she loved and admired them passionately. It's also clear that she considered herself to be intrinsically inferior to them. (Of course, they were older, and they were far from being idiots, or ugly, or timid. And she considered herself to be stupid, not very pretty, and devoid of courage.)

But that's not the only reason she thought this: the notion of the equality of the sexes still had a long road to travel before becoming inwardly natural. And, however much of a feminist she was, it's clear that my grandmother had a tremendous love and admiration for her sons (she certainly had love for her daughters too, but perhaps less admiration).

Nonetheless—this acute feeling of inferiority did not have any kind of paralyzing effect on my mother (it seems to me that she's always derived confidence—as though from below, I would say—from a curious mixture of her desire to do the right thing and what I can only characterize as a pride in being right). She received her baccalaureate, went on to the "*hypokhâgne*" (the traditional nickname for the "Première Supérieure" class, the first year of literary "preparations") in Marseille, then on to the "*khâgne*" in Lyon; she got help from her brothers in preparing for the exam, in the very same house I've already mentioned on the Rue de l'Orangerie, and after a first failure (as I recounted elsewhere), she was accepted to the Rue d'Ulm.

My aunt Renée no doubt could have followed the same path. In fact she came very close to doing so (as was the rule for the top scoring students among those who "flunked" the orals, she received a scholarship, a "*bourse de licence*"). But she didn't persevere. It's true that it was no longer a very favorable time (this was a little before 1939) for such aspirations.

173 From their house in Caluire (which was still number 21 *bis* Rue de l'Orangerie

From their house in Caluire (which was still number 21 *bis* Rue de l'Orangerie, since the "conquest" of number 21 didn't take place until shortly after my birth, by which time my grandfather had retired (at the age of fifty-five, a privilege of those in "active service"; one advantage schoolteachers had over professors, which fact angered my father)), Inspector Molino would depart on his required visits to his "district" in the Isère *département*, with his cane (his war wound had given him a slight limp) and his hat, always rising very early, even in winter, in order to surprise the mountain schools at the moment when classes began—eight o'clock during the entirety of the Third Republic—and in all weather. He didn't do this out of spitefulness or in order to disorient his "constituents" (he was strict, but indulgent), but rather out of an absolute belief in the pedagogical virtues of setting a good example (no "sleeping in" for him any more than for the "schoolmasters") and of punctuality.

As for my grandmother, with the enterprising spirit that always character-ized her, she had, as one says today, "returned to private life." Here is how she "explains" it in her "memoir": "It was in Lyon that, concerned with my duties toward our adolescents who had become advanced students, I thought it necessary to leave public education and, by inclination as much as out of economic necessity, to undertake some scholarly rectifications, which led me to understand the responsibilities of parents too estranged from their task, and to understand as well the considerable percentage of students who, sup-ported or corrected in time, manage to put on a good face in their class, some of them as well as my own children who, here too, were my support and who raised me up with them."

I have occasionally wondered, when faced with a few absolutely incom-prehensible manuscript lines, how my grandma (we said "*grand-maman*" and "*grand-papa*," which was hardly original, but our cousins said "*bonne-maman*" and "*bon-papa*" ("good-mama" and "good-papa"), each family thus distinguishing its own pair of grandparents as entirely theirs, at least in name, without having to share) had been able to teach young children how to write.

She no doubt underwent a progressive deterioration during her later years, brought on by age and by her withdrawal from teaching a variety of subjects (otherwise, if she had always had such bad handwriting, I don't see how she could have taken an exam like the one for the École Normale d'Instituteurs, and then have had a career in the "secular monastic order" of primary educa-tion, where the proper formation of signs on paper is an indispensable ingre-dient of the profession).

It also seems to me that, with passage of time, the contrast between her and her husband was reinforced on this point as well, since he was always an extraordinary master of the secular and republican regime of handwriting. (I can imagine the exasperated shrug with which, in his bedroom on the third floor, he must have received and perused one of the justificatory and indecipherable missives from grandma (which she often left for him following one of their disagreements or even quarrels), in which the aesthetic wound of her handwriting could only have aggravated his sense of the basic logical incompatibility between their arguments.)

With the minute care of a joiner, in an infinitely careful and precise pen, using various inks (blacks, reds, greens, blues, and purples), he crafted, in his workshop (his perfectly ordered desk, its drawers veritable strongboxes of pencils, blotters, pens, pen holders, paper, notebooks, and envelopes) a series of small and original reading-writing booklets, designed with increasing levels of difficulty in handwriting and pronunciation, in three versions (capitals, small block letters, and small cursive letters), designed (and individualized) for the various children entrusted to his care, and above all for his grandchildren.

All of us, I believe, learned to read according to his (pre-Oulipian) "models," in which every letter and every sound received its own special treatment, in a text giving it both a quantitative prominence (the number of words containing it) and a qualitative one (the choice of a specific color reserved especially for it):

> "*TOTO PORTE LE POT. TOTO TOUCHE LE CHOU.*
> *Toto porte le pot. Toto touche le chou.*
> Toto porte le pot. Toto touche le chou.
> *Lili finit de lire le livre.*
> *Jaja le chat marcha dans le plat . . ."*

> (Toto carries the jar. Toto touches the cabbage . . .
> Lili finishes reading the book.
> Jaja the cat walks on the flat . . .)

(And later still (this must have been in 1964, not long before his death: he was eighty-seven years old!) he came to my apartment on Rue Notre-Dame-de-Lorette to give handwriting lessons to his great-granddaughter, Laurence, my daughter (who had just turned four). He constructed a "writing book" especially for her, just as he had always done, but his hand was no longer as steady, his powers of concentration and his authority were not quite adequate to the job (I believe too that Laurence was a little afraid of this very old man (so she told me)), and he had to give up after a few fruitless attempts, much to our sadness and embarrassment.)

I'm afraid I myself never really did him much honor, since I never succeeded in mastering inks, ink bottles, or quill pens (or, later, fountain pens, which I handled with astonishing awkwardness: they spread their ink all over my fingers, in my pockets, on my papers, always in more and more surprising, unforeseen, and exasperating ways. It was the arrival of the "ballpoint pen" and then, much later, "felt-tips," that saved me from what had been a veritable torture throughout my school years. It was only then, before I ever sat in front of a typewriter or a Macintosh, that I made some tremendous and conscious efforts at good penmanship (conscious also in their attempt to honor my grandfather, and to make amends). But today, once again, my writing has become what it was in my notebooks in those early days: illegible).

174 The house at number 21, which I finally reached at the end of my long wanderings

The house at number 21, which I finally reached at the end of my long wanderings from the Perrache station in that summer of 1941, is almost more visible to me—more distinctly although less violently present—than the house on the Rue d'Assas. Or, if not really more visible, then closer: the difference being that my visits there stretched out over a period of more than thirty years. It wasn't abandoned by us (I mean sold) until my grandfather's death in 1967. (How I regret this! even though it had already been amputated of its enormous garden, to my grandmother's understandable despair.)

I saw it for the first time, then, from my crib (if it can be said that I perceived an object of such dimensions), or in any case as a child—from year to year, from one vacation to the next, and then in adolescence; the last time I was inside it, I was more than thirty years old. (I passed by with Marie five years ago, along the Rue de l'Orangerie. The house was still there, unchanged, at least superficially.)

The result is that, in my memory, it has become the projection of a solid that not only has four dimensions, one of which moves through time, but also a bizarre topology: several simultaneous "metrics" contract or distend the same fragments of its space, numerous discontinuities fracture it, and a multiplicity of points of view collide in it, creating a geometry so complex that a cubist pictorial representation would appear exceedingly "naturalist" in comparison. (At the time of my novelistic ambitions, in order to develop my characters, I attempted to construct a model based on Jacques Tits's theory of "buildings." I called it "Coxeter's Apartment" (branch one; chap. 5, § 83).)

Against the front of this house, facing the little rocky hill, on an area paved with cement, bounded on the left by the edge of the garden, on the right by the gate and the little door, to the rear by the large rock, we played our own particular version of "real" or "court tennis," which we called "*pelota*": a tennis ball bounced off the wall (which took the place of the net) (the ball was supposed to hit the wall above a minimum height marked by a natural division in the surface of the wall, and then land within the boundary marked behind us by a line parallel to the wall, traced like a furrow in the cement), to be knocked back by hand by each of the two players in turn. **(I felt the heat of the shocks in the palm of my hand; I see the gray, worn out skin of the ball.)** We kept score as in tennis, just as my father (who admired the "three musketeers," Cochet, Lacoste, and Borotra, as well as Tilden and Suzanne Lenglen) had taught me to do: "2–0," "6–3," "40–15," "advantage!" "deuce!" "set point!" "second match point!," etc.

Something strikes me when I enter by the door on the right, to the right of the very small window of the "privy" on the ground floor, when I "simulate" an entrance into the vestibule, toward the kitchen across from it, the stairway with waxed steps on the right after the bathroom, the large sideboard for plates and napkins to the left of the kitchen door, when I allow myself to enter this very familiar configuration, so heavy with what I would be tempted to call the smell of half-light (there being no direct opening there for outside light):

everything I see, I see from down below, as though I were moving forward while sitting, or on my hands and knees, or crawling. I move forward in the lower layer of this space, less than a meter above the ground.

I'm not tempted to draw any hasty conclusions from this concerning the pure anteriority of my vision, or to situate this gaze in the extremities of early (or even later) childhood. Still, my memory undeniably privileges a certain way of locating myself in this space, which would be very unnatural if it were the vision of an adult or even an adolescent.

The horizontal line that divided the wall into legal and illegal zones in our tennis game was already excessively high, by the same criteria (I'm able to discern this because I <u>also</u> possess, although less naturally, and as a second choice, as it were, another way of seeing based on my present size, with my eyes above the ground at a distance that hasn't varied since around 1950).

But when I enter the house, this part of the house (I forbid myself for the moment to go elsewhere), I "fall" even farther down. Here again, as on the terrace, it's not that I can't also see at a reasonable height (that is, as I see everything now) but that, on the one hand, I do not situate myself at this "correct" height right away—I have to make a conscious effort to do so—and, on the other, when I make myself see this part of the house "standing," or full grown, I see less, less clearly, and even (the effect is the same) with greater indifference.

It seems reasonable to me to assume that here, in the above conditions, I possess something like an indirect proof of the geometrical persistence of my <u>fore-life</u>—in the sense that I previously gave to this expression. But from this I draw nothing more than a rather moderate satisfaction.

175 <u>A smell of half-light so familiar that it was mixed with wax</u>

A smell of half-light so familiar that it was mixed with wax, with the wax of the first immense steps of the staircase, as though the cool ceramic tiles were themselves waxed—waxed, shiny, and smooth, on which one could slide one's bare feet, absorbing the coolness after the scorching heat of outside, in the stifling August streets of Lyon, the Place Bellecour, the banks of the Rhône. The design on the tiles escapes me, something in red and black. When I touch the same kind of tiles now, and bring these old ones out of oblivion, they awaken the waxy odor and the half-light,

awaken the mystery of the infinite emotion evoked by the incline rising between vestibule and dining room, a strange flat section on an incline, rising in the passage, without interrupting the design on the floor, without fracturing the tiles, raising them very gently at a slight angle on which our marbles rolled—the clay marbles painted red, green, blue, or the "agates" veined with spiraling yellow, red, blue—all the way down to the first step of the staircase,

the mystery above all of the passage into the other room, the sitting room, through an enclosed compartment between two heavy doors, dense with total darkness and with coats hanging in the heights rustling thick with cloth: a hiding place, the soft shadow of a secret solitude, but one without terror, protected by all the familiarity of nearby noises, the commotion of dishes, household bustle, the clinking of glasses, muffled voices, footsteps,

the large clock speaks peacefully. I see that. I see it, but what exactly do I see, with my eyes in the Arcadian darkness of the compartment between its two doors of heavy, odorous wood? I'm not only asking myself that skeptical Wittgensteinian question, which takes aim both at shapes and at colors (§ 70: Can one speak of a pink rose in the dark and of a red rose in the dark?). I'm also asking a question about the moment's imprecision: the image without vision that I am reconstituting—was it accompanied by fragments of the visible past, by sounds emanating from the surrounding space? Was this image already a whole, the whole of what I imagined then, or is it a contemporary construction of my mind, an association of images widely separated in time and in origin? And what sort of experiments would allow me to decide between the two explanations?

In the kitchen, I go toward the two windows to the right of the entrance, looking out onto Rue de l'Orangerie. The door to the basement is at the far left, the table stands before me, on it there's a teapot. The water is warming in the kettle on the blue flame of the stove, between the door to the basement and the sink. My grandmother and her friend Taia are standing in front of the table, having a discussion as they wait for the tea to be ready. "Discussion" is not quite the word. My grandmother talks, recounts; Taia listens, objects, comments, or asks brief questions.

"Now where could I have put my glasses?" asks my grandmother, suddenly interrupting herself in the middle of a story. The "question of the glasses" is a vexing, primordial, recurrent question. To be sure, my grandma's distractedness has a nearly universal application, but it has one particularly privileged domain—namely, her glasses. Her glasses are never where she thinks she put them. It is in this domain that her distractive creativity shows itself to be quite especially active, necessitating long investigations, exasperating as they occur, but later a source of pride, and of great mimed reenactments (Grandma tells stories like a marionettist, with her hands), when the danger of having actually lost them for good is past.

"Let's not get worked up," says Taia. "They can't be far. We must proceed methodically. You had them when you came back in from the garden, since you read Renée's letter to me. You must have set them down by the door." But Taia knows, and they both know, that method can do nothing against the demon of the unforeseen. The glasses are not by the door, where my grandmother in fact remembers having put them. For her "evil genius" is much less megalomaniacal than the one in Descartes's "thought experiment": it doesn't at all try to persuade her, falsely, of the existence of objects in the external world, but contents itself with offering her completely erroneous visions of the probable location of her glasses. Nothing more is needed to satisfy it.

Since her glasses aren't by the door, Grandma tries to convince Taia that she herself must try to remember the place where she, her old friend, whose proverbial distraction she knows well, left them. Taia remembers nothing. She knows that the distractor demon can only laugh at her vigilance. It's better to undertake a systematic search. After all, she remarks, there are only so many places in the kitchen where "they" could be hiding. This is meant to be a show of optimism. But Taia is usually calm and optimistic. This is why they get along so well, and have for so long, since my grandmother is neither calm nor optimistic.

The "systematic" search consists of thinking of all the places where the glasses have turned up in the past after one of their previous escapades. This is a misguided strategy. They should know better (I myself know better, I who am only watching the scene—an imaginary scene this time, if ever there was one, reconstructed from a few real remembered moments and some of my grandmother's stories). The place where the glasses are hiding at present simply cannot be deduced from the previous places. The place where they're hiding now does not resemble the earlier places, and is not a place where the glasses are habitually found when they go astray. Neither habit nor resemblance are adequate concepts for taking account of the free exercise of distraction as practiced by Blanche Molino, my grandmother.

176 In conducting their search, they ought to have taken into account (by anticipation, as it were) Chomsky's famous argument

In conducting their search, they ought to have taken into account (by anticipation, as it were) Chomsky's famous argument for the creativity of man's linguistic function: the probability that a given sentence, having been pronounced by someone, has already been pronounced by that same person, or by someone else, is virtually zero. It's neither because our sentence resembles another sentence that we've already heard, nor because we're in the habit of saying this sentence, that we suddenly come out with it ourselves. We create sentences thanks to a mechanism ancestrally implanted in humanity, and hence in us: a syntactic model that we inherit and have learned to use. Thus, for my grandmother, the distractive faculty was capable in each case of creating new, non-habitual, and unheard-of hiding places, each of which resembled none of the ones that had previously been invented in her (my grandmother) by this faculty (that is, the faculty of distractive syntax, the actualized model of this faculty of distraction. What the structure of this model was, I couldn't say; but it certainly wasn't independent of the context of daily life, was no more "context-free" than is the syntax of ordinary language).

After doing the rounds in the kitchen several times, opening cabinets, peering into the sugar tin, into the oven (where Grandma's pocketbook turned up one day (but never her glasses!)), rummaging through the refrigerator (I see them rummaging through the refrigerator, behind the vegetable compartment, behind and in the butter dish, which proves that this "scene" couldn't have taken place in 1941, at the moment of the visit that led to this narrative bifurcation), they return, somewhat discouraged, to their point of departure: the glasses have never held out so long before (but then, at the same time, they've never been completely lost).

Then I hear Taia say, with her gentle little voice, never irritated (she is one of the most absolutely good people, and most free of malice, that I've ever known): "Oh, now look at that!" "What?" asks my grandmother. "You have them right there on your nose!"

This episode represents, as it were, the masterwork of the "demon of distraction." That day this demon so surpassed himself that he was never able to do any better (which likewise makes it unnecessary for me to give other examples of his inventiveness): in the set, ordered by strangeness, of the places where that accessory of sight had gone missing, it was in the end a question of a "greatest member," an "internal upper limit," as one says in the idiolect of the basic theory of ordered sets. This demon was perhaps a reader of Edgar Poe (and, as a demon, escaping temporal constraints, also a reader of Dr. Lacan, or even of Jean-Claude Milner (who, as I recall, composed a marvelous "fictive deduction" around the tale of "The Purloined Letter" (my grandmother, for her part, was an avid reader of Agatha Christie))). (One might be amused by the distribution of roles in this analogy: the demon in the role of the minister, Taia in the role of Dupin!)

A contemporary incident (contemporary, that is, with the screenic composition of these lines) has perhaps launched me into this digression (I did not set out to occupy myself with eyeglasses, but to cross the kitchen on the way to the basement of Rue de l'Orangerie, to which I will return): I was walking through the inner courtyard of 82 Rue d'Amsterdam, where I live, my ring of keys in hand (I keep it in my hand until I reach the street, so as to be sure not to forget them too often in the door, or in the lock of the mailbox). I do this just before going out into the street and then to the Saint-Lazare train station, from which I take the regional line to the Nanterre-Université station, where I leave the train go to the "Mathematics Department" of my "UFR" (or "Unité de Formation et de Recherche" (Training and Research Unit)) on the fifth floor of Building C. Outside of rush hour or counter-rush hour (if I can put it this way; I refer to the rush hour, or hours, that come later in the day), there are four trains per hour at that time: 04, 19, 34 and 49 minutes after each respective hour. It takes me ten to twelve minutes to reach the platform after buying the day's London *Times*, and so I leave about 25 minutes before the hour in order (as is my habit) to "miss the train before," in keeping with the precept upheld by my grandfather.

In the courtyard I ran into Mme Jacquet, the concierge, whom I greeted amiably but briefly, since I didn't have the time (I was a little late in my earliness) to engage in one of our usual conversations ("Will it rain today?" "I'll tell you this evening.").

Now, Mme Jacquet, in a way that fell completely outside the tradition of our exchanges, and that halted me in my progress toward the entrance hall of the building, asked: "And where are you going like that, M. Roubaud?" "I'm going to do my course at the University, and I'm late." "Are you sure you want to go there like that?" I was sure—but I was wrong, since I was wearing my slippers.

This proof of distraction, perhaps only a little more extreme than usual, did not unduly surprise Mme Jacquet (after all, I'm a mathematician, am I not?), and could never compete with my grandmother's own total and perfect feats of distraction.

I relate this incident not only because it was doubtless the indirect cause of my digression, but also because it leads me to observe (and this gives me no particular pleasure) that since my father too is a little distracted (my mother a little more, but not as spectacularly), and since my grandfather was not, if one admits (in a purely fictive hypothesis concerning the heredity of character) that the demon of distraction changes hosts within a family from generation to generation (and often skipping one here and there, as with other hereditary traits), it was from my grandmother that I received the demon, whereas the model that I've always consciously and constantly cultivated was my grandfather, her opposite in almost every way!

177 My grandfather considered the temperature of his basement to be ideal

My grandfather considered his basement to be ideal in every respect, particularly in terms of its temperature, and therefore ideal for storing food, and consequently too for the pleasure of the palate, which can only delight in what is devoid of extravagance. Fruit, water, and dairy products can only be appreciated, according to him, at a moderate temperature, which was precisely the temperature found naturally in his basement. It remained the same, with minor variations, throughout the year.

Thus, it was cool in summer, compared to the often torrid August in Lyon, and it was almost warm in winter, when he went down to fill the coal bucket in order dutifully to feed the overheated stoves (producing a temperature much higher than what he considered hygienic, which was the fifteen degrees Celsius that used to be marked on nineteenth-century thermometers as the "inside temperature." But his wife, my grandmother, was always cold, always wrapping herself in her dressing gown even in the kitchen. So he filled the stoves completely to their tops with coal and opened the window of his bedroom). It was only after great hesitations that he allowed the refrigerator's polar brutality to invade his home (what would he have thought of the freezer!), and despite its presence, he always kept a few precious supplies in the larder downstairs.

In the basement, where I follow him in thought, I see it, this larder with wire netting on its door, and the light-colored butter, firm but not too cold, sitting in a saucer, which also contained a little water. The temperature of the basement and the relative humidity maintained by the water vapor kept butter in the most optimal state for consumption. From the refrigerator, on the contrary, it emerges cold and hard, both unyielding to the knife and devoid of flavor.

(My father recently rediscovered a taste for catalogue shopping (once he got over his disappointment at the demise of the Manufrance Catalogue), and while buying a drill for Marie—in whom his practiced eye recognized an authentic handywoman, after she set about restoring the irrigation walls of the *restanques* last summer (I myself am no handyperson, nor is my sister; and my brother Pierre, according to my father, is a fanciful and unreliable one at best), and therefore as someone capable of taking over for him in the immense battlefield of the familial domain, Saint-Félix—when buying this drill, then, he also acquired a "butter bell" constructed on the same principle as my grandfather's saucer (similar, in fact, to the porous clay water jug in which people used to keep fresh drinking water).)

I see the "*faisselles*," the soft fresh cheeses purchased from the dairyman in Clos-Bissardon, in their metallic strainers full of holes, which, once the mold was removed, held on to little specks of cheese. Before biting into one, one's tongue felt a rain of sugar, first white then clear, like slowly melting snow, and beneath this, in anticipation of the pleasure, the physical presence of its white flesh, thick and trembling. They disappeared with the scarcities of the war and never did reappear in the same abundance, rendered obsolete by modernization and by the death of the small-time dairymen. Then, under the effect of a commercial response driven by nostalgia, we saw their return not long ago, but as caricatures of themselves, enveloped in an unappetizing plastic. And smooth!

The larder in the basement also stored whatever fruit was in season, especially my grandfather's favorites: rennet apples, peaches, and pears ("Peel a pear like your friend, a peach like your enemy," he said, to explain the different treatments to which he subjected these two fruits). Before peeling them, and slicing them, as he also did, and likewise before spreading a moderate and even layer of soft butter on his slice of bread, he took his Swiss Army knife out of a pocket on his vest and flicked open the appropriate blade; then, after using it, he wiped it at length on the white insides of his bread, folding it back into its handle, with an eminently Helvetic fastidiousness, only when it was shiny once again, impeccably new, and clean.

During these operations, as in all those that demanded a certain manual application, he proceeded slowly, with the care and attention of a calligrapher, or a joiner. He let his tongue stick slightly out of his mouth as he lay out a quartered peach around his plate, each piece separated from the pit. Of course his peaches had to be neither insufficiently nor overly ripe, but also full, healthy, aromatic. The ones I see are peaches from their garden, the real peaches of long ago, drawn from this garden's inconceivable, prodigious and anachronistic profusion.

But he left the pit abandoned on his plate (and I regretted this for his sake), with a little juicy flesh still clinging to it, but above all enveloped and entwined by those numerous fruity filaments embedded in the maze of the pit's woody grain. Many long minutes would be required to flush out their ligneous pulpy convolutions with one's teeth and tongue, thus prolonging the pleasure of the fruit by keeping the pit in one's mouth or held between two fingers, before finally throwing its pale remainder under a mulberry tree along the garden path. But for pears (and apples, which he also peeled), he proceeded otherwise, cutting slices from the fruit and eating them immediately, so that they would not have the time to oxidize in the air, to rust. (With peaches, he also drank a drop of pure wine.)

My grandfather didn't follow the usual strictures as to fresh bread. He even preferred it a little stale. Bread and butter, in moderate concentrations, together with a moderate amount of coffee (of moderate strength (to avoid any abuse of stimulants)), tempered by a reasonable dose of milk, were the sober constituents of his very early breakfasts, taken before seven in the morning in the kitchen. It was there, too, in undisturbed peace (since my grandmother, an insomniac, didn't come down until much later), that he performed an operation that I found magnificent: he shaved with a "straight razor" in front of a round heavy-based mirror with a slight magnifying effect. He then rinsed his face in the sink, wiped it, made sure to eliminate every trace of his passage, put his vest back on, and soon thereafter closed himself up in his room for his morning work. I too rose early, and I would watch all his movements closely, leaning my elbows on the kitchen table, in silence. I did not disturb him. Much later, I developed an intense admiration for this mark of discreet autonomy, made up of order and habits. At the time, it was simply a fact, one of those facts that constitute the world, and are expressed in calm propositions.

178 My grandmother's hour was, on the contrary, as far as possible from dawn, at teatime

My grandmother's hour was, on the contrary, as far as possible from dawn, at tea-and-toast time, which was also the time for conversation. I would almost be tempted to give this hour the title of a novel by Christina Stead, *A Little Tea, a Little Chat*, if not for the fact that "chatting," as my grandmother practiced it, was most often *one-sided*, an opportunity for her to tell stories to a small audience. This English expression, "one-sided," comes to me now as a mark of the ritual's particular Anglo-Saxon air, which was undeniable. In fact, my uncle Maurice had studied at Oxford during his years at the École Normale (as had my mother, a little later). I might be tempted to put forth a hypothesis here concerning the influence that may have been exerted by the children, in this instance, on their mother, in a direction contrary to the usual one.

But, contrary to this hypothesis, I've remembered the story of an episode that was heard and appreciated several times, to the point of developing its own "formulaic" variations: a "recitation" from my grandmother's "Odyssey of Distraction," in which she was both Odysseus and Homer, and which demonstrates indirectly the extreme antiquity of the ritual.

One morning in Digne, sometime in the 1920s (?), she had written two letters (she was a relentless correspondent, always turning out long pages of shaky, hurried, almost indecipherable writing): the first was to some old friends, the d'Argences, in their distant exile in "Indochina," while the second was to some other friends, whose name I've forgotten, the Xxx's (I'm not even sure about the spelling of the first-cited name, "d'Argences," which I only know from having heard it, and which I'm confusing, perhaps, by a kind of contamination, with the name of that eighteenth-century "polygraph" (in the original sense) on whom my older cousin, Jean Molino, once did a "thesis"—a project that provided him with the occasion to write a series of encyclopedic monographs on that encyclopedic century par excellence).

The Xxx's, then, were somewhat taken aback to receive, with an extraordinary richness of detail, news of the entire family, who lived in the same city as they did and about whom they didn't consider themselves to be quite so ignorant. As for the missive that went astray somewhere in the China Sea, it was an invitation to tea, on a day in the near future (what the d'Argences thought of it is not related in the story).

The treatment of the butter at my grandmother's teatime was marked by an exuberance in stark contrast to the almost Jansenist sobriety of Grandpa's morning bread: waiting in the saucer, and already considerably softened by the proximity of the red hot grill of the ferocious toaster, it rapidly lost all pretensions to solidity as it covered the toasted slices of bread, which soaked up its soft and glistening yellow (these slices were first scraped of their now-blackened crust, for they were regularly forgotten inside the burning hot appliance, whose nonetheless peremptory warnings didn't reach the inattentive and forgetful ears of the storyteller, or indeed were considered to be negligible in comparison with the much greater interest of her tale).

When they were topped with an added layer of creamy honey or bitter orange "marmalade" (anachronistically, I would add *lemon-curd*, for which I developed a taste much later, after our mother—whom we had heard praise the wonders of this delicacy, which she had first tasted during her time at Oxford—was obliged to try producing her own; I don't believe it had a place in the teatimes on the Rue de l'Orangerie), I knew nothing more delicious, more luxurious than those sweet crunchy mouthfuls. And the long years of scarcity (extending far beyond the interval of the war, even beyond the continuation of the official restrictions, so habitual had they become in our minds) only added to their prestige. **In the teacups, I watch the milk invade the pale tea like a lazy fog.**

In the climatic extremes of the dog days of August, the butter completely melted in its plate; then, after cooling again, it coagulated into strange lumps. I have sometimes tried, in vain, to recreate the irreducible difference in taste that resulted from this physical transformation. I no doubt lack the now long-past but necessary harmonics of the place: the shadows, the steady drip of voices in the kitchen, the swaying of the rocking chair on the veranda. I never had much success in my attempts, in the mornings, to combine these two antagonistic models for the treatment of butter. I do have a toaster, here where I live, on Rue d'Amsterdam. But I never think of using it when I wake up, at five o'clock in the morning.

The veranda maintained a heat as constant as the coolness in the basement (I like this symmetry, which in fact seems quite plausible: the pale winter sun "helped out" the crackling stove. The "greenhouse effect" added to the summer sun). **In the veranda the rocking chair with the stiff straw seat rocks back and forth, in a perpetual motion, accompanied by Grandma's fingers moving incessantly on the brown wooden armrests.**

I leave the kitchen, walk barefoot over the painted tiles of the entrance, the tiles rising slightly at the entrance to the dining room. This is a room of formality and ceremony. I see, without surprise, the end of one of our meals (at dessert, the obligatory photographic moment of family gatherings).

179 Very soon, in the months that followed the effervescence of the Liberation

Very soon, in the months that followed the effervescence of the Liberation, my grandmother was forced into a period of inactivity and rest that wasn't entirely pleasant after the anxieties, dangers, and tragedies—but also the adventures—of the war. Walking distractedly (with her glasses in her hands and her hands behind her back) along the deserted paths of her immense garden, she saw it as she had perhaps never seen it before, and found it unbelievably beautiful (which it was), very precious, but neglected. I don't think that she felt then the threat that might have weighed on her, stemming from the fact that she (that they, she and my grandfather), as a mere tenant, was no more than a precarious occupant of this miraculous place.

The war had overturned lives, sown death and destruction, exiled and dispersed friends and loved ones, but the fact that the age-to-come would be an age of developers and property owners, of increasing scarcity and an explosive rise in the value of urban housing—of this I'm afraid she had no idea. (It was a fact that did not, on the other hand, escape my uncle Walter—who had meanwhile become a prosperous chemist in Massachusetts and an American citizen—when, after normal communications between the two continents had resumed, and were even accelerated by the progress in aviation, he came back home to see the trees beneath which he'd become engaged to my aunt Renée (on my desk, to the right of the Macintosh, I have a few photographs of this garden, taken from various spots and at various times, with various people, and in one of them my aunt and uncle are sitting on a bench, looking at one another, with the sun of 1939 illuminating the picket fence behind them, between number 21 and number 21 *bis*, deeply sunk in its leafy, vegetal shade—like the past). Unfortunately, he was not there at the decisive moment.)

But when, one day, she went into the neglected wooden building that had previously been the orangery proper, in the days when the Rue de l'Orangerie had merited its name, she discovered the old account books of what in some distant era had been a prosperous business dealing in I don't know what exactly (I have a vague idea that it was silk, but this seems too simple and is perhaps merely an unconscious pseudo-deduction based on the majestic presence of the mulberry trees). And my grandmother then had the idea, which seemed perfectly natural to her, to turn her garden into a dynamic business, a fruit-producing orchard (half the garden only, to be precise: the section past the largest trees, the farthest from the house).

I therefore offer the following hypothesis (hypotheses come cheap): the discovery of the account books, as proof of the former and active prosperity of the orangery building (and in particular the discovery of a considerable quantity of large blank account books) provided the decisive impetus for the creation of an informal association (with bylaws, a president, and an office, of course—though I doubt that any of this ever had the least legitimacy as an actual legal entity, a proper "association" under the "law of 1901" registered with the Rhône authorities, etc.)—an association uniting a number of friends, retirees, and neighbors around my grandmother for a new educative task: the maturation of fruit.

The meetings of this association took place in the orangery, which was dusted off, patched up, and furnished with comfortable lawn chairs from the garden. I remember it: I see the large thick account books. The question up for debate that day: what names to give the pear trees, what varieties to choose, and who would sponsor the young trees? I was there. And I wrote it all down:

NATIONAL CONSTITUTIVE

ASSEMBLY

LYON, 11 JULY 1946, 10 A.M.

dear maman, dear Denise, I arrived yesterday at 5 P.M. at Rue de l'orangerie after an excellent trip. after Dijon there were only five of us in the compartment and the train arrived on time. I found Grandma in the garden and she told me about the great transformations it will undergo. The work of the PP-PCAFV Society has in fact begun [divine for me please, dear readers, what this abbreviation could mean—I no longer have the slightest idea]. Two superfluous trees have been cut down, the lawn has been raked, and the middle pathway is delightfully green. Holes will soon be dug for the new trees: P.P.P.C.A.F.V.

Grandma then told me about the debates of the society during its plenary session which took place a few days ago. Raymonde and Emile Sermet are supposed to write up a report of it and Grandma asked me to spread the word to Madeleine, Armandou, and co., in order to recruit a few honorary members.

Now I will ask Denise which tree suits her best because I hope that the state will sign up for one or two babies at an average price of 150f. The state has an interest in taking them since in the regulations of the Society, half the fruit will be ours while the other half will be sold by the PPPSAFV at reasonable prices in order to fight against the black market. Thus we can either eat what we harvest or else collect whatever the sales bring in.

In a little while I'm going to do my gymnastics and Emile Sermet will examine my fingers.

[. . .]

(at the bottom of my letter I can decipher a few words added by my grandmother:

"Jacquie [that's me] forgot to say that he already worked on his German with
Holl, who says that his accent is excellent.")

Who, indeed, had "raked the lawn," and who was going to "dig holes for the
new trees"? Of course, there had to be a secular arm, an arm equipped with
spade and rake, for this new church of fruit-growing souls. And indeed there
was one right there, on-site: a German named Ludwig Holl.

Holl was a laborer from the Ruhr, a German communist. He fought in the
streets against the Nazis in 1930, '31, '32, up until the beginning of '33. Then
everything fell apart: "Nobody wanted to fight anymore," he told us, in his
hesitant and raspy French, when we went to sit with him among the furrows,
on the dry earth, in the scorching heat of late afternoon. "Nobody. They all
fell into line. All of them." But he fled to France. He fought in Spain, outside
Madrid, at Teruel. He was taken prisoner by Daladier, escaped, went into hiding. He was caught while working with the *maquis* in the Savoy. His enemies,
his compatriots, didn't kill him on the spot, but took him to Paris, tried him,
condemned him to death, and then pardoned him: he was German, after all.
They sent him to Buchenwald, to be rehabilitated through work. He related
all this to us, not in order to boast, but so that we would understand, so that
I, the eldest, would understand. Was that the end of the story? No, that wasn't
the end, he said. At Buchenwald his work was to maintain the electric fences
around the camp: electricity used to be his profession, in the past. But toward
the end, as the Americans approached, he managed to be forgotten there one
evening, hidden between the barriers. He stayed there for two weeks, feeding
on raw snails and grass. And he didn't go back to Germany, or not yet, but to
where he was now, to Lyon.

And because during the war my grandmother had hidden people who
needed to hide, she took Holl in after the war. He lived there, ate there, did
the gardening, participated in the great fruit-growing project (which made
him laugh), regained his strength. He was waiting. A few months later, he left.
I never knew for where, for what kind of life, in which German city. But during that time, beneath the mulberry trees of Caluire, in the evening, he sang
for us:

Wir graben unser Gräber
Wir schaufeln selbst uns ein
Wir müssen Totengräber
Und Leich in einem sein

(We dig our own graves / We bury ourselves in them / We have to be gravediggers / And corpses all in one)

(Today, at times, I hear his heavy voice again. And I think of the harsh metaphorical irony of this deportees' song.)

180 I see in the garden, at the heart of its luxurious immensity

I see **in** the garden, at the heart of its luxurious immensity. Now, now that it has disappeared from the face of the earth—leaving only these images that I call up within me and a few pictions that I spread out on my table, to the right of my screen—I possess it wholly, finally, and among my various imaginary possessions it occupies a very particular place, with no equivalent in any other location: not in the house on the Rue d'Assas, in Carcassonne; nor in the Impasse des Mûriers, in Toulon; nor in the Wild Park, in Les Corbières; nor elsewhere (in Villegly for example), nor *a fortiori* in any of the places I would come to know after the end of World War II.

I feel this singularity, internally—that much is certain. And I won't resist the urge to interpret it: the fact that I was born at 21 *bis* Rue de l'Orangerie, **next door**, in a separate but contiguous space, that I learned to walk on its paths, beneath its trees, that I first stood on my feet there, that I first conquered the surface of the earth at the same time as my grandparents were taking over the garden, settling into it, creating the long-term moment of a familial continuity there—because of all this, the images of this place that I bring to light are never simply contemporary with the moment of their perception, but come in the wake of a continuous immensity of buried instants, of faces and gestures, all of which took place **there**. When I feel that I am there, when I see it, I feel too that I've always been there.

More than that, the local identity of the circumstances of this memory and fore-memory is not, for me, divided; in particular, it's not divided in two, it doesn't have two sides: this means that it imposes what I would call a matriarchy of memory. More to the point, like the invention of the "PPPCAFV" related above, the garden was preeminently my grandmother's domain (my grandfather was never invited to the association's meetings. The only part of the garden that he made any use of was his carpentry workshop, which was sheltered from any interference or curious eyes, being well off to the side, at the foot of the little hill). Thus the garden, and my childhood, are to a large degree under the sign of what was, in fact, a "grand-matriarchy."

During our first years in the Minervois, during the fifties, my grandmother had a room in our house, equipped with two large glass-covered photographic portraits of her deceased sons, my uncle Maurice and my uncle Frantz. A poorly done bust of herself was exiled to the top of the wardrobe, and a bad painting in a frame hung on the wall, a medium-sized painting showing one edge of the garden, with a view of the house, the terrace, the veranda, two insipid female figures sitting on a bench in the middle of the image. It was the work of an artist who had taken momentary refuge there, around 1942 (in this it was like the bust, but by a different "hand"). (This is the "painting that shows a garden of an old house sunlit from behind" in branch one, chap. 3, § 38.)

All this means that my "immersion" in the immensity of the garden, because supported and protected by familial time, secures a certain stability for the images I extract, a density and autonomy that no piction can breach. I recognize that in the photographs I am looking at the same territory, but for my part, I still see it in my own way. I owe them nothing.

I set out a few of these photographic "statues" from various periods, scatter them somewhat randomly on the floor:

—Uncle Pierre (Pierre Thabot) and Aunt Jeanne in front of the openwork fence along the border with number 21 *bis*; he is standing, with a beret and a mustache, she is sitting. Their feet, the ground, the entire foreground is beyond blurry: it's completely effaced, leaving only a block of gray and a white oval, the sun.

—Grandma in front of the veranda, her hand on her friend Taia's shoulder, at their feet Coqui, my brother's collie: very fine, very noble, somewhat subdued by age. (A later moment, then.)

—A little farther down the path, and many years earlier, Grandma again, Taia again on her right, but this time my mother is with them, young.

—A table set for a meal in the garden during the summer, bright sunlight on a leafy wall. This is an even earlier moment, my aunt Renée isn't much more than ten years old; my grandfather has his hat on, my grandmother is tilting her plate up with her left hand.

—The house behind the trees in winter, the bare branches of the mulberry trees.

—My grandfather and I sitting beneath a tree. Violent sun. Grandpa has his eyes closed. I (seven or eight years old) am wearing a knit jacket with buttons, am turned toward him.

181 Immersing myself in the garden, turning from the mulberry trees toward the house

Immersing myself in the garden, turning from the mulberry trees toward the house, the terrace, the veranda, I am implicitly surrounded by all its immensity, as though it were a piece of clothing around my shoulders. I think, and I see, the mulberry trees, truly enormous, venerable old creatures of vegetable life. They had lived so long that the damage from the storms, or the exaggerated pressure of their sap, or simply the weight of their dark green crowns of wide leaves, had burst open some of their trunks, and thus they had been rigged with stonework bandages, cement cataplasms, stone gauzes that, strangely, made them look like immobilized animals rather than trees. They stood watch over the walkway, up to about the middle of the garden viewed lengthwise (107 meters by 40 meters), before one reached the orchard that had engendered my grandmother's utopian dreams.

The trees, as one would expect in that town (Caluire-et-Cuire is next to Croix-Rousse, where in the nineteenth century the "*canuts*," the Lyonnais silk workers, rebelled ("We weave for you people of the land / and we poor *canuts* without a flag, they bury us . . ."), and where despite this the silk manufacturers prospered all the more ("We have no more money to bury our dead / The priest is there, tallying up the price for our funerals . . ." (Marceline Desbordes-Valmore)))—the trees were mulberry trees intended for silkworms, and their fruit was the white, hairy, sickly-sweet mulberries, which after falling to the ground turned to rust and were immediately imbibed by the ants.

(I later discovered the red mulberries of Delphi, exploding with a wine-red juice, which when they fell left bloody stains on the tiers of the ancient stadium, like silent prophecies.)

The high wall at the far end led out to another narrow street, through a small door, and then immediately onto other small, steep streets, toward the large Pont de la Boucle, the "Loop Bridge," and the Vaise streetcar stop, and on each side of this door was a thick bushy mass of slow, heavy "Burgundy" snails, clumsy as tanks (far inferior to the agile "little grays" of the Carcassonne area: along the Aude, or in the ditches of the Cité).

M. Nithard, the sour Swiss owner of the property, died in the middle of the fifties (during the time of 21 *bis* (that is, before my grandmother was able to extract from him, through the sheer authority and insistence of her desire, our "right of entry" into number 21), his renters, the Calames and then the Pasquiers, had all been Helvetians, like him), and his heirs, uninterested in Caluire, anxious to divide up their inheritance (they didn't get along) and apparently at least as indifferent to the future of real estate (as blind, that is, in their foresight) as my grandparents, offered to sell them the whole thing, house and garden, for such a ridiculous sum that we still blush to think of it.

Certainly, my grandparents didn't have it. But it's no less certain that they could have borrowed it from my uncle Walter, who would have been glad to lend it to them and who would hardly have felt its loss, given the exchange rate for the dollar at the time. But my grandfather decided against this (he made this decision on his own, unilaterally, thus demonstrating a patriarchal mentality that was so uncustomary for him in other domains). "A renter he had lived, a renter he would remain."

Certainly (a third "certainly"), I can't help but retrospectively admire the firmness of his convictions (in which were mingled, perhaps less admirably, a certain propensity to avoid changes in habit, after the tumult of the war, as well as a horror of being in debt, of owing anything whatsoever to anyone else). But still! (It's difficult for me to understand how Grandma didn't manage this time to push the sale through, regardless of his objections. Perhaps she wasn't completely aware of the stakes involved.)

Years went by. And the inevitable happened. The Swiss decided to sell. They didn't even offer to sell it to my grandfather, this time: the price would be determined by the current market value. Since the "law of '48" specifically protected renters who were almost octogenarians (and who themselves rented out two rooms, for security, and for a song), they only put the garden up for sale. And so in place of the mulberry trees, some modern apartment "blocks" arose less than twenty meters from the house. That was the first blow.

And not long after that, the house itself, whose facade made the Rue de l'Orangerie particularly narrow, was, as one says, subjected to "modification" in order to make way for a wider street (but as anyone can see, the house is still there, thirty years later). To avoid expulsion and relocation who knew where, there was no choice but to finally become the owners. The price wasn't too high, and this time my uncle Walter was indeed asked to participate (amply) in the purchase. (In 1967, when Grandpa died, I remember trying to prevent the property from being sold, even imagining for a moment that I might live there myself (I had just been given an appointment in Dijon after completing my thesis). It was no use. But in any case, the garden was long gone.)

Bifurcation E

Childhood of Prose

182 **Throughout the writing of this <u>branch</u> and up until today**

Throughout the "screenic" writing of this **branch**, and up until today, I have had the necessity of this bifurcation in mind. To its single **moment** I provisionally assigned the "theoretical" mission of gathering together all the useful elements in the general economy of my undertaking, the **memory-images** that have accompanied me in the story (not a question of the images themselves, of course, but of "pictions" of these images, laid out in a descriptive sequence), and of establishing a parallel between these images and the **assertions in chapter 5 of the first branch**, which constitute a fictive deduction of what "**the great fire of London**," among other things, still finds itself in the process of recounting: a **Project** and a **novel** that originated in the **axiom** of a **dream**, and whose title would have been **The Great Fire of London**. I also wanted to examine, in this bifurcation, the situation of these images, of this family of images linked precisely by a "family resemblance" within the **Project** (a project involving both poetry and mathematics), and then consecutively in the <u>novel</u>.

But as I continually found myself somewhat overwhelmed by the accumulation of this material and of the elucidations it seemed to demand along the way, I've never, therefore, been able to properly "prepare" myself for this moment, which, if I kept to my initial goal, would subsequently risk expanding to extravagant dimensions (in comparison to the others): a veritable "theoretical hernia" within a continuity that elsewhere is numerically controlled, on the whole. It would also risk never even reaching the starting point of its own "intention," which is to provide a foundation for the kind of "correspondence" between **assertions** and **images** that constitutes one of the principal formal links between the two first branches of my memoir. For these reasons I gave up on it (or, more precisely, I shifted the set of divagations that resulted from it into what I've called **inter-branches**).

Nonetheless, the "narrative situation" of this fifth bifurcation remains eccentric. But this is not without some advantages. What survives from the threat of my "theoretical digression" will thus appear more inoffensive, less rebarbative than its homologue, chapter 5 of the first branch, "Dream, Decision, **Project**," for which I have often been reproached by some of my readers. As the penultimate Bifurcation, its place is less visible, and will also make it much easier for the reader to carry out the "excision" that I recommended then (in a way that might have seemed merely provocative). Its numerical arrangement even facilitates its isolation. It is no more than a single **moment** of the text, in the particular sense that I've given to the word "moment," but, unlike the others, it is not a moment uniquely circumscribed, temporally speaking, by the composition of the text.

I will affirm no more than this: all the constitutive images of this branch, the particular image-memories that have become **memoir-images** by being inserted into the constructive continuity of the narration, are all situated within a threefold past anterior made up of the dream, the decision, and the **Project,** at the center of the first branch.

I now come to the place occupied by this bifurcation, the fifth. It is as follows: it begins at, is inserted into, the end of chapter 3 (**Rue d'Assas**), and ends at the beginning of the sixth and final chapter (**Hôtel Lutetia**). If one were to envision the six chapters of the part of this book entitled **Story** as a continuous and rectilinear path of prose, this bifurcation therefore constitutes a "**loop**." Likewise for the other bifurcations: each of them constitutes a possible loop in the story between the end of one chapter and the beginning of another (the title of the present Branch, **The Loop**, is thus partially explained). Bifurcation A, the first, "goes" from chapter 1 to chapter 2, Bifurcation B from chapter 2 to chapter 4, Bifurcation C from chapter 4 to chapter 5, Bif D from chap. 5 to chap. 3, Bif E, as I just said, from chap. 3 to chap. 6, and the last one, Bif F (which is located after this one in the book, and completes its linear development) creates a final "loop" by joining the end of chapter 6 to the very beginning of the first chapter. I leave it to the reader to visualize the geometric "figure" this proposed path of prose might form, if traced out.

This branch, as I said back at the beginning, represents a pathway of my **Fore-Project**. It's also a description of childhood, according to the model of the medieval narrative, the <u>childhood of prose</u>. And its construction mimics the space in which I lived during childhood. The topology of this space (which is also that of **memory**, as I've conceived of it in this book) is quite remote from the one in which we imagine we live later on, once we've become accustomed to the ordinary and consensual perception of the world. I will evoke it here only through a fragment of a text by Italo Calvino, "From the Opaque," the last of six "memory exercises" that make up the posthumous book published under the title *The Road to San Giovanni*:

"If they had asked me how many dimensions space has, if they asked that self which still does not know the things one learns so as to have a code of conventions in common with others, and first among these the convention according to which each of us stands at the meeting point of three infinite dimensions, skewered by one dimension that goes in through the chest and out from the back, by another that runs through us from shoulder to shoulder, and by a third that pierces the skull to come out from the feet, an idea one accepts only after considerable resistance and frequent rejections [. . .] if I were to answer [. . .] about the three dimensions which by dint of standing in the middle of them, turn out to be <u>six dimensions, in front behind above below right left . . .</u>" (my emphasis, J.R.).

In the tradition of the <u>Arts of Memory</u>, at least one author, from the fifteenth century, <u>Lodovico da Pirano</u>, seems to have had a similar intuition, organizing his mnemonic space according to eight dimensions associated in pairs along their respective axes, each of which is illuminated at both ends by a sun.

And it is indeed in these terms that I represent myself here, as a child **seeing** the world: as the center of a kind of vision for which what is behind is not the virtual continuation of what is before, but an entirely other dimension, another "before" completely distinct from the first, to which one gains access by inwardly turning oneself around (just as one does then, quite naturally, without thinking about it, in the act of remembering); and it's the same with above and below, right and left and before and behind, as dimensions of past time.

I'll add too that in each of these <u>eight dimensions</u>, inner space is doubled, folding back upon itself by means of its own reversibility.

One is born into this space at the moment when one acquires—at same time as language—the inner sense of these dimensions, as well as their irreducible distinction. As an adult one forgets it (perhaps never completely).

It is this lived space that I inhabited, then left behind (to find it again, as an imitation of itself, only in mnemonic space), by losing the garden on the Rue d'Assas.

Bifurcation F

Boulevard Truphème

183   Saint-Félix Eighteen December
The right side of the house is reserved for lanmlordMadame

Saint-Félix Eighteen December

The right side of the house is reserved for lanmlordMadame

Atjer I see her faec again   flabby   shivelled and

pale When she xxxxxx   speaks she often raises her

eyes to heaven and blinks her eyelids She is a widow   Leives

alone and sees no one   She watches over us to make sure that

　　　　　Dear friends

we don t encroach on her territory   Ball games

on the terrace   are strictly regulated

　　　　　The calissons from Arles arrived this morning Just in time f

We have water from the sink in the kitchen   No gas

　　　　　for us to enjoy them with two of the children and grand

no electricity   Meals are prepared over a woodburning fire

　　　　　children who will come to see us this Christmas Thanks for them and who

on the potager or on a spirit stove Evenings we turn on

　　　　　for usPaul isn t the only one who likes sweets

the ceiling light in the dining room if we decide we really want to which

　　　　　We will have on ly a fraction of the family here

is rare or gas lamps   which don t   smell good

　　　　　Anne will start all by herself on Thursday She will stay only

and are quick to start smoking if one does not control the

　　　　　until the day after Christmas and she will show her taste for

length of the wick The only source of heat that I

　　　　　independence by taking the train for Paris that very day

remember is an gas stove with a blue flame that

　　　　　where her mother will take cxxxxxxxxxx her train in the opposite directionx is used especially for Frantz when he goes to sleepBut I

They will meet up during the nightDenise will give us only

am not aware of ever having been cold

the last week because she doesn't want to leave Anne's grand

The two bedrooms on the one and only upper floor have

mother alone on Christmas dayPierrot is bringing us

the same layout as the rooms on the ground floorI often

only half of his progeny There are two who won be there

wondered how we were able to live there four of us

Clairette and Vincent   one is on a language learning trip

at first no five we three mother and grandmother There must

living with a family in the GDR the other is paying her own way to Mars eille

have been a third room but I don't see itWe n

with some friendsA ll th se kids have an odd case of the xxxxxx

---

fidgetsFrançois will have just returned from a trip to London

Life at school is from eight to eleven in the morning then from one

in order to drive down n his father's

to six since we stayed late for afternoon study prep

car for the sake of economy

This period after our freedom in the lovely

We have begun a wintertime diet   with all the more reason to

ountry now seems to me like a

day since the weather has cooled considerablyThree sources

prisonEverything was small petty ugly The return from school on

of heat thenThe big fire in the fireplace is

winter evenings theby the Bd lt was gloomyThe gaslamps

what we most enjoyWe will be ecen better

were dimIt was then that I had

protected from the cold when the stone mason has finished insulating

my first impressions of doldrums and of oppression that were all

the roofing in the attic with glass wool and hardboard

contencrated in the cry of the street vendor selling just abou every sort of

Lucien recovered from his lumbago sciatica and after that he
chestnut flour crepes   dripping with oil The merchant
suffered only from his normal pains so to speak
let out two long notes always the same Fa mi
Whole stretches of my days are left empty by the extreme pov
the second lower than the first
erty of the radio programming I fill them by llistening to cassettes Barrès
the onlyx significant events were the times
together with Colette Baudoche are to me such perfect examples of the
when we swam in the sea on Thursdays by the oast in
revenge-mongering jingoistic nationalism that reigned before
MarseilleA heated pool in winter The whole year for
nineteen fourteen that I could tolerate little more than the beginning and the
endx
Frantz Not for Maurice and me we went into the water
I also couldn't get through a particularly de
in the space closed off by ropes M learned to
pressing piece by Samuel Beckett   Our friends the rollands
swim not meWe returned on foot by the Corniche and the
put me in contact with a recording-library in Grenoble
Prado until we reached the first tram
Unpleasant memories also of the return to Le Canet in the evening
af ter running errands in town in the streetcar xrammed and stuffed together
in front of the Fournier Gandle factory on the outer Boule
vard sickening air The large horse-drawn hauling carriages loaded with xx
sticks of sulfur made an infernal noise   on the irregular paving sx
stones Sparks flew from the horses shod hooves

184 Not long before she definitively gave up her typewriter

Not long before she definitively gave up her typewriter (the keys of which my brother had adapted for her blind and uncertain touch) (she gave up when she became convinced (wrongly) that her typing had become unreadable), my mother undertook (in a prolonged wintertime effort that required great exertion on her part) to reconstitute a few moments of her past on paper. These notes cover (at least in the few pages I have) the time between what she designates as her first memory (dated October 1910: when she was three and a half, therefore) and the spring of 1916, in the middle of World War I.

In preparation for this final <u>Bifurcation</u> of my book, which I thought (without having considered its contents in other respects) I should insert between the last chapter of the section entitled <u>Story</u> and the first chapter of that same part, which begins the book (thus completing, at least in spirit, the entanglement of the "memory loops" of which this branch consists, by returning to its first moment), I opened the flap of the flexible red folder where I'd placed her writings and found the above pages, this chance mixture of a description of Marseille before 1914 and a letter sent shortly before Christmas in an unspecified year (which was of course the same year my mother was attempting to reconstitute her childhood) to our friends the Geniets, in Arles.

When, in order to write this letter, she went looking for a piece of paper in a drawer of the little desk where she kept her typewriter, she went into the wrong drawer by mistake (this is how I interpret what I am reading) and took out a sheet of paper already covered with one version (among others) of one of her place-descriptions (she constantly reworked them, always unhappy with their style, their gaps), and without realizing it (for obvious reasons), she superimposed the two texts.

But, again by chance—this time the chance of inserting the paper into the roller in a certain way—the lines were not, in fact, exactly superimposed, which would have rendered the whole thing illegible, but slightly staggered, and that's how I've reproduced its opening. (The alignment of my "word processor" is perfect, obviously, and the typographic layout will also be perfect, but this is not the case in the original, where the lines of the two texts, without quite overlapping, are not precisely parallel, and at times begin to encroach upon one another.)

It occurred to me, then, that I couldn't really do better, here, than to reproduce this attempt by my mother, in part, and to let her speak directly, since I've also let other people speak in other sections (even if it's only a "written-speaking," and according to different modes in each case), namely my father and my grandparents—or at least my maternal grandparents, the only two I knew.

For this involuntary typewritten conjunction of past and present is like a brutally simplified but highly revelatory illustration of my own attempts to decipher memories (attempts that have in fact been pursued throughout the pages of my story, my interpolations, and my bifurcations in even more uncertain conditions of legibility, and in which the lines of vision not only pile one on top of another, merging together (as one might say, to extend the comparison), but are no less murky, confused, and incomplete than her own).

There are three parts, three places evoked in these memories: the Campagne Jolie, the Boulevard Truphème in Marseille, and the Boulevard Thiers in Digne. I have not corrected the text. I left in all the typos, the crossed-out words, the omitted letters she left uncorrected (because for her these omissions were unfelt, unseen, and irreparable, because letters were forgotten or keys were not pressed hard enough) (although the omission of apostrophes, after an "n" (in a negative contraction), for example, is so systematic as to suggest either a deliberate omission or a glitch in the tired old machine, rather than a simple "negligence of the fingers"). I preserved the irregularities of the line breaks, which sometimes come too soon. Words were sometimes lost on the roller past the edge of the paper (or even past the bottom of the page), and I have made no attempt to fill these in. I did impose a flush-left alignment, but I've retained certain excessive blank spaces between words. I didn't restore the (nonexistent) punctuation. I've also preserved certain repetitions, false starts, contradictions. I cut certain small details and developments in the third part so that we're left with nothing but visions, almost everywhere, in this reconstitution. (No doubt I've inevitably added some errors in the process of transcription.)

All these particularities of the text present obstacles to reading, and they cause the eye to stumble, I know. They do not, however, affect the comprehension (rarely is a word completely deformed). And I leave them here most especially because they are signs, persistent signs that I do not want to omit, of the circumstances of composition.

And of the fact that every vision of the past is a vision of the blind.

185 **Campagne Jolie,** Sheet 1. Preceded by: **My first memory October nineteen hundred ten**

I remember nothing about the village where I was born Fuveau   a village of
miners in the Gardanne Basin And nothing about that apartment building
such a cheap ugly mod ern slab where for a time my parents

occupied the sixth floor when they had been appointed
to Le Canet   a working class suburb north east of Marseille Our family
historu relates something my father said During an earthquake

that did considerable damage in Provence the house on
Place Casemajou began to rock very preceptibly during
the night When maman was nudging him and shouting The house is shaking he
answered, Well, let it shake and he turned over and went back to sleep
The family was going to move out of this cramped apartment undi nto one battxr
situated on an enormous piece of land, like there used to still be at that
time just outside Marseille
we were standing at the window my brothers and I no doubt
but I recall only the presence of maman Far off toward
the north is   in the middle of the felds and trees two columns
of smoke are rising Two fires of deadl eaves Maman said look
over there the house where we are going to live Maybe that's the housse
that's burning   We laughed

Le Canet La Campagne Jolie

From Parseille one reaches Le Canet by the rue d Aix lined with second
hand shops with their clothes hanging outside in the open air ther displ
racks of old shoes The street goes u hill an Then the pxxxxxxxxxxxxxx
Porte d Aix a vast square whose name I've forcotten a wide boulevard
ghat one takes perpendicularly to the right It already smells like the suburbs
Somewhere around there axxx   the large Fournier candle factory oThe
streetcar turns to the heft heading north east and climbs a street with un
even pavement to the last stop at the main square in Le Canet it still had a small town
feel

---

the image has always remained in my mind of the large bend that
looked like a dead end wherm we stopped in front of a small door
on the right It wasn t a dead end since the narrow street went xxxxxxxxx
continued on to the little railroad which that came out of a tunnel

north of that area   and went down into a deep trench that
frightened me

                    We were in front of the little door never x
locked only closed with the latch From the top of a small stone landing we
went down about twenty steps also stone also
and without a rail and from there we came out onto an immense sl pe with
rolling hills and all sorts of green spaces
The house was to our left entirely down below
the road that cuts across up above where one can still see the xxx   the top
of the pines from this bend in the road where the mistral blows so much that we
call it the North Pole

the house

a sort of buffer zone separates it to the north from the
road cutting across a narrow dark moist space where all sorts of rubbish
was thrown where we will throw my puppets the ones given to me to
develop in me an instinct which it seems I lxxxxxxtack x
my brothers helped me tear them apart an that is where they
ended up

                    On that west side of the house there was a window only on the
second floor Passing along the wall   we arrived on the terrace   rather
like a platform which domainated the green spaces of the area farther xx
in the distance the roofs of marseille then the sea almost always obscured by the
smoke from the factories xxxxxx
I have no precise ision of the outh side As far as I can rem
ember it was plastered over with a slightly dirty hellow which really
struck me   ther s a bull's eye window at the top The word itslf surpri
sed me like the roudness of this opening I don t know what it led

---

186 Sheet II

to I never had any access to anything at all
resembling an attic

The inside

I will speak of this first since it is eclipsed by far by the w
wonders of the outside The layout of the i rooms was banal simil
ar to that of many houses in Provençal houses It s also txx
the same layout as St félix a small doorstep with a few steps A central
hallway On the right the dining room lower down a door to what is
here the cellar I believe it had two windows one facing south the
other xx facing east On the levt something that was supposed to be a sitting room It was
used as a junk room We called it the bthroom because a zinc
bathtub was put there and we were given our baths in it I have no idea
how the water was heated or where it came from
I see myself there in front of a large panel   representing the letters
of the alphabet with some corresponding syllables My mother pointed
to them for me with a long bamboo stick She said to me now
you know how to read

                              At the end of the hall on theleft indow facing west Since
the house was down the hill the room was tark A rather large chi
mney in which we rarely built a fire Rustic in appearance A
cooker beside it on which clay casseroles sometimes simmered ox
on the wood coals several peasant storie some
fairy tales were of course perfect for such a setting Particularly
the three wishes We always ate in the kitchen except for thexx
rare occasions when there were guests That is where we did our homework
where we washed up how did we heaf fhe room I don t remember ever
being cold there A certain corner where I sat brings back x
voi voice of my father for the occasion low and dramatic   reading x
a description of the pyramids for   sake of my older brother in the lycée
fifth grade I still have that voice in my ears
               the dining room remained nearly empty for a lont time
until the day when the set was delivered from the Nouvelles Galeries in Marseille
of which the serving table in the hall on the br und f"oor
in st Félix is the last survivor An overly ornate side table l
like the one from Aunt jeanne at denise's but much more simple
however the six cane chairs with the ornane backs and the top

of the serving tabl made of very shiny marble seed to me the height of luxury
A fw chairs from this set are still scattered in the house here
in various places

         The staircase climbs up to the end of the hallway and turns to the left like
herexx
three bedrooms on the upper floor My parents' room seemed large to me Frantz
slept there because he was ill so often after catching the measles broncho
pneumonia qhich had taken almost nih children out of ten in the
Casemajou Square neighborhood

We Frantz and I were often alone while my paretns and
Maurice were at school in Le Canet It seems that there was
always a woman there to watch us but they have
no existence in my memory Frantz was often in bed He was
always cheerful and sang in bed One of our usual games
sonsisted of him trying to guess which step on the stairs I
managed to reach by climbing up from the bottom as silently
as possible Or in the bedroom where the windows were decorated with pink
curtains with large leafy patterns a gift of my aunt Adèle who died
died before I was born and to whomI owe my real first name so in
the bedroom we read or he read to me poems from a coleection of
selected works by V Hugo

                                    his bedside book for many
years later Maurice and I slept in two cramped
bedroom x which I cannot situate in relation to the large bedroom
but on the bed there was a large red down cover very puffy   We
called it puff pastry in fact I like to believe that theo ne
at Saint-Félix that the children fight over is the same one

         It in within this injterior that I also place the memorable arrival
of the friends from Indochina   the d Argences   with their five children more x

or less the same ages as us and their Annamite maid with teeth varnished
black Some oriental gifts arrived with them   and others
came in the mail for many years Their smell
　is still familiar

The exterior
　　　　The place of wonders the weather was always beautiful there The large terrace
in front of the house was bathed in sunlight shaded only xx side x
noon It jouted out over a large wash basin where later I always imagined
my arithmetic problems about faucets taking place On the low wall above
it my mother often washed the dishes in large shallow glazed bowl
straw yellow I was sometimes granted this honor

---

187 **Sheet III**

on the west side we were separated from the neighboring property by a hedge
jqixxxxxxxuCthere were openings that allowed us Maurice and me to slip away
to go prowling for strawberries for which we were severely
punished   n a pile of sand nearby I played Lilliput by m rking out
paths and planting broken branches to stand in as trees
I leave the terrace to go toward the east near the house a x
large St Fohn's pear tree produced a lot of pears which we
weren t allowed to eat fallen on the ground Thee spread
cholera Along the edge of the wide xxxxxwalkway that led to the houses of the
market gardeners therewe re all sorts of tall trees One of them had
a swing on it my brothers played at pushing me as high as I could go

I was not too scared but I felt seasick when I got downThe
the maket gardeners lived in a lowlying house that included sev
eral separate apartments some uninhabited

　　　　　　　　　　　　　Through the large gate at
the end of the walkway wes aw one day a carriage enter drawn by a white horse h

or horses It was bringing my parernal grandparents who o
were coming to live in the dwelling closest to oursWhen my
grandfather died

                    Grandmother came to live with usShe was
tall and upright Her blonde hair without a bit of gray was
divided by a part in the middle and flipped up at the bottom on both sides Sxx
Shehad hazel eyes and high heekbones

                                        She was very
kind I liked to go to her part of the hosue to play xxx in the room
on the ground floor that looked directly out onto the terrace The main room was
dark and the celings were low

I no longer recall where the clock was myxx
grandfather made the casing out of walnut from Isère but I could
hear it ringing all the way in the Rue de l Orangerie My grandfather
a short thickset man was not as gentle He made fun of me when I
cried

Sitting on the low wall that begins at our terrace and continues
up to that pount I saw the pomegranate trees in the midst of a tan gle of other
s ecies The red of their flowers their slightly fleshy)etals at
the base gave me an extraordinary sensation Down be ow xxx
clombed the olive trees Their lower branches were easi
accessible And I could climb as well as my brothers

The market gardeners went down toward the house of the ownxxx
owners the Villaldacs Athe corner of the retaining wall we had our
sunny heat well protected from the mistral

                                        I seem to recall
some
workers gardeners who worked sometimes in the flower beds

———————————————————————————————

188 **Campagne Jolie (second version), <u>Sheet III</u>**^{*bis*}

<u>The gardens</u>
I use the plural   It was in reality   a very splendid proper
ty that included paths a park large market gardens sloping meadows
pine trees watering basins overgrown bushes In my memories
the whole thing is larger then the garden of the OrangeryI have a vision
of my fatther and my mother walking on the path leading to the
path leading to the hunting lodge among the pines They appear
extraordinarily small as I see them and I cannot really tell
if they are walking

let s begin from the house Making a   in the esplanade already circumscribed bye a
wide path flanked on the   lieft by shady areas like in Lyon
At he corner of the house   a large St Fohn's pear tree from which we
were forbidden to eat the pears that fell on the ground we were told they could
give us cholera F rther along was a swing hanging from the branch of one of the beautiful
trees   I don t know what kind

        Several magno
lias I recall the feell of their thick flowers their thick petalsx
that turn brown and begin to wilt as soon as   one rubs them a littleAnd the smell
Between the park and our terrace there was a large wash basin since then
I have always placed my water faucet problems there At the exit from the
park in the sunny areas some pomegranate trees on the right

<u>Campagne Jolie—forgotten details</u>
   How one reaches the property
we follow a suburban street that leads farther
e st than the one the tramway goes up.In fact it

goes around or rather skirts the circumference of the vast

vague wasteland where the Bd Truphème will end in the westThe xxxx

houses and the rather pitiful stores are both

interrupted We were on a path I cannot

specify at what point this path changed into a "Cut-across"

This is the word used in the Marseille suburbs to designate

those tortuous narrow streets running between large walls interrupted

less and less frequently by doors that open into

the vast PROPERTIES they are only very small doors

The main entrance must have been located n nother xx^

xxxxxx side Our cut-across was called La Traverse de la

Mère de DieuIt was much narrower than rue de Mx

Margnoles in Caluire I always thought of it x

when I read in Les Misérables about the path taken by Jean Valjean

and Cosette when they are pursued by Javert in the area aro und xx

Petit PicpusBut here there were no lights At first

we walked on it every evening Not all of us xxx

o ly Papa Mama and Maurice when we left school late after study prep

around six o'clock in the e vening my father had a lanter in

one hand and in the other a pistolWhen the cut-across turned out

to be mre peaceful than the inhabitants of le canet

xlaimed it to be there was no more question of these two objects which

I do not remember ever heeingBut the impression

that it was not safe and the sinister aspect of those long blind xxx

walls nevre entiely left meWe were vx

very close to the house when at a turn the narrow passageway

widened a moment before narrowing again immediatelyx

behind the wall on the left the ground must have been raised

for one can see enormous aloe plants and tall pinesThis area

was what we called the North Pole On days when the Mistral came

the wind rushed through in whirls and the iontense blue sky

was even more frozen than anywhere elseOur pilgrim jackets rose

up over our bare legs adn the air chilled our thighs

But a small door on the right would lead us back home

At the bottom of the stone stairs we were immediately pro

tected   —Sea preceding pages

I do not know the names of the trees that make up the parkThere

were a lot of them very tall and bushyThe whole park smelled ofxxx

cool air and dead leaves Especially in cxxxxxx

ontrast with the olive trees in rows farther downI never

did climb a tree in the park   but the olive trees were

completely accessible to usFrantz fell fxxx from one of their

branches he seemed to have gotten a wound on the head

bleeding slightly It was me so I was told who had ixxxxxxxxxx

suggested that he must have crushed a ripe olive

The fields   Or rather the meadow It was immense went downhill

first abruptly then more gently all the way to the lower end of the property

v ry far very farWe would roll down pretending to be bxxxxxxx

barrels

I have always kept the green of the grass in my eyes

one sunny morningwhen the intense color of the grass of the

daisies and dandelions hurt my eyes xxxx

while we sang A green mouse . . . etc

From the tops of the olive trees one could see tha sea but it

never through the fmoke rising from the city   that

extraordinary blue almost purple almost solid that xx

I saw the first time I was taken on a

ride along the coast at the moment when   the uncovered trailer tha

the houses and let see the sea

The green   and the blue   now I place them during the time

of La Campagne Jolie As I do   the thick frosty transparent

blocks transported by trucks to

the cafésThis first visual notion of refeaction

is associat d for me with the tapioca seeds in the whiteness of t

the soup

Illness

I believe I had chicken pox I was kept away from my brothers Then being sick

meant austerity do not stick your arms out from the bed so as not

to catch coldNo books No reading just teaThe wall hanging

with little flowers is dull in the garden I heard

the soung o f little bells running by I imagined that my

parents had adopted a dog I learned that it was the ells

from the guide dogs that had been given to my brothers to play horse

Frantz s room was heated with a gas stove that produced

a blue flame and did not smell good

189 Le Canet II—Bd Truphème

If I can trust the mental topography that I have

maintained since that time coming from le Old Port o

one takes the Rue d Aix La Porte d Aix is at the end of th

that street with its avundance of second hand clothes shops All sorts of bulldings

hang over rue Bd d Arenc One saw

the Cournier Candle factory which burned down

during those years and stirred up great emotion in the whole

neighborhood and for several days left lixx

little flakes of soot all over the area We took the street that goes up

toward Le Canet heading borth east I think It was covered

with large wide paving stones A major route for large loads drawn by horses very

noisy sparks flew from the horseshoes

on the w y upBehind them we often picked up x

sulphur in the shape of little tru cated cones fallen from the

trucks The streetcar that came from the Old Port ends at the square

center of the village and the usual plane trees of thes proven

çales squares Bd Truphème is the last stop an optional stop

before the end of the line

First on each side small villas very shabby

set in tiny gardensThen on both sides long dirty

walls that hide factories or warehouses and

other more and more shabby houses except at the ofher end where xxx
the small houses begin again or the rented residences
wlth three or four floors The large municipal school the secular school
for girls was on the rightthe
Boulevard leads into a large wasteland and disappears there
Our house was the ne t to last on the heft

The house
   It had only two floors. The entrance opened onto a
hallway with the staircase to the second floor at the endSame layout
as in Toulon The owexxxxx owner occupied the
section on the right We had the other On the ground floor along the street a
tiny dining room even for the seven year old I
was then The kitchen led out to what it would be a stretch to call
a garden it was smaller than the one in Toulon
At the end to the left a shed The privy I don t seem to recall
there being any trees It was ugly and dilapidated the only pleasant
bit of greenery A trallis but
what kind Surely not a grape vine or a Virginia creeper
it darkened the terrace arong the entire back part of the house
and there was not much dayl ight in the kitchen which was always
dark it was bright in the front which I believe faced south
Two bedrooms on the second floor Same layout as on the ground xx
xloorAft!r the space of la C pagne jolie we felt like we
were in a tiny hovel

Sheet II (another version of Bd Truphème)
Our house is one of the last ones on the left a little below street level
since the voulevard is on a slight incline We are really at the outer limit of the
inhabited part of town like at the student housing complex in twenty seven
at the far edge of the central zone We went up and down this gloomy bou
vard to go to school or to the village square we see the
same sinister looking houses as the ones on the tiny streets that intersect it

usually bordered by the endless factory walls like the Lyon Photos factory

repeated in black on a dingy gray background Post No Bills the bottom is

often strewn with animal or vegerable wasteAt nightfall we

see the lamp lighter arriving on a bicycle or on foot with his

long pole It was always an exciting diversion for the neighborhood kids I

no longer reca ll how he opened the glass door on the lanterns x

but from the end of his pole flew the spark that lit the

blue flame of the gas that is soon blue no more letting off a dim

yellow greenish light that does not shine very farThese evenings when we returned from

school around six in the evening because maman and I stayed late for study

prep left me with gloomy memories made even worse on those nights when the

roving peddler passed by selling a sort of thick crepe made of chestnut flour cooked in

a poet and thoroughly soaked in grease more or less rancid His shouts

have remained in my ears and his descending third sung in a

trailing voice reinforced the miserable aspect of the street

this little neighborhood left me with no impression of color except

the red curtain brightly illlit from ixxxxxx inside and it is the color

of a feared authority simce that is where my teacher lives

Mme Ricoud with her blotchy ruddy face not very appealing at first sight

The school where my mother takes me and where she teaches sits between the walls

of a factory a little farther xxxxxxxxxxxxxxxxxxxxxxxxxxxxxxxxxxxxxxxxxxxxxxxxxxxxxxx

a little up the hill from our houseIt is large has three floors and about a

dozen classrooms Between four and five o'clock during the evening recreation

the courtyard and the covered playground dxxxxxxxxxxxseem dark and dangerous

O eat my sneck there usually an oranhe and some breand The irrxxxx

The inritation of the acidic orange eaten with brea makes me grind

my teeth when I think about it

the nice moments moments came on Thursdays when we went to the sea not

the days when we left only to run errands. As soon as we reached the

Old Port after walking down rue d Aix where on both sides we saw

the clothes hung up by the second hand stores our pleasure began We watched the

unloading of the feluccas full of oranges from Spain

Sheet III

I don t know when I saw the sea for the first time butbut what has remained with
me is the su den apparition of an expanse of blue so intense that I imagined it
was made of an almost solid matter its smell then was henceforth invincibly
linked with that of the black oilcloth bag that contained our
bathing suitsWe stopped at the Roucas Blanc Public Baths Franz went
inside to take a hot seawater vath Maurice and I
went to swim in the area where the water was marked off by ropes outside
Maurice learned to swim all by himself I admired him as I clung to the r
ropesNot far from me an English gi l was making a big fuss as she got into x
the water and I had a revelation about nglish diphthongs when I heard her
drawing out the o in it is cold Like the floristfromin
xxxxxxxxxxxxxxxxxxxxxxxxxxxxxxxxxxxxxxxxxx

when I heard her drawing out the o in it is cold like the florist at the beginning
of PygmalionAfter our swim we were ravenous The one chocolate croissant
that we had was exquisite but much too smallWe returned returned
on foot along the open beach by the big waves of wrackand They
were already covered in filth We turned left at the pradoAlong
the way The fine homes in their garde s the chestnut trees with their white
or red flowers impressed us with their luxuriousness and their beautyThe
way back by train was not so nice the train from Le Canet was full and
we had to squeeze together on the platform Le Canet seemed terrible to us

190 We took piano lessions at home

We took piano lessions at home because of Franz who
could rarely go outMaurice went by himself to his professor s house Frantz and I
waited at the house on the table mother had prepared a platter
three glass platters made of crystal decorated with a golden bird and axxxxx
a small carafe in the same style plus a plate of cookies called champagne cookies
Mlle Balardini arrived she was very elegant discreetly perfumed She drank a

little Malaga wine after the lesson I went with her back to the tramWhich afforded me

the extraordinary spectacle of seeing her climb into the streetcarHer tight stiff dress

that was the style in nineteen fifteen so her dress made it difficult for her to move

her legs when on the same vertical planeI heard the rustling

of her calves against the thin cloth

we went to spend the summer of fifteen at the house of some friends

t eachers fro the Dauphiné region grandmother was ill She had a mad wish

to return once again to her dear Dauphiné almost a native For the journey beneath her

long

black skirt she kept on her blue kitchen apron with her vegetable

knife in the pocket

The owner's name was Mme Atger She lived in the right section

of the house exactly symmetrical with ours She reigned over every

thing Eve when we didn't see her we knew she was there behind

her shutters always propped open slightly in the old Provence style We dared not

let the ball roll over to her side of the terrace and it

was always unpleasant to cross her path

She was a widow I wonder why I see her face so clearly

with its dullgray tint She had fleshy drooping skin

thick flaccid cheeks When she spoke   she constantly blinked

her eyes and often raised her eyes to heavenWe knew that she had two

pet toads in the garden and for us this was a fitting

complement to the personage and the place where she lived where we

lived

xxxxxxxxxxxxxxxxxxxxxxxxxxxxxxxxxxxxxxxxxxxxx of Easter fourteen

Even though it last   for me only from October of fourteen to

Easter of sixteen this period is associated in my memories

with a general impression of sadness imprisonment

ugliness and a small narrow life with a few moments of real

depression especially in winter in the evening between six and seven coming back after

studying late the gas lights hardly shed any light it is often almost dark when the lamp-

lighter comes by to light them

with the end of his long poleCertain days

                    same impresion in the schoolA large

slab a flat front nos shutters blinds

instead made with slats of orientable vood The courtyard was not lare and

its covered playground   at the end with its iron colu s and its row of

bathroom sinks was always gloomy

There were few opportunities to leave this routine In the spring

the no an s land that separated us from our Campagne Jolie had some

very green gre en grass that did not live long the side streets were

dirty and gray often flanked by long factory walls Post

no bills penal code no   Few shops and they were generally quite

shabby like the tiny grocery store called chez jacque very

similar to the Portepots in the Clos Bissardon (in Caluire) I went there

by climbing the little hill almost directly opposite our place

I liked it especially because of its old fashioned jars filled with

a kind of ca dy called Mistralets becaus of the freshness their

mint.They looked like sealing wax

whi e or red

Maurice was at the lycée and did not come home until eveningFrantz

stayed at the house with grandmotherOur rips to arseille

happened more and more nfrequently for errands we ran as quickly as possible from

xx

---

there we returned lape on the stuffed tramway from Le Canet

no doubt the atmosphere od the war added to this dreary

feeling my schoolmates talked about it at school two teachers

saw two policemen enter the school courtyard they were coming
to inform them of the death of their sons at the front

b ut after this purgatory a new happier period began later when
we lived on Thiers Bd in Digne Papa waswounded in the spring of fifteen Txxx
The telegram ran thusSlightly wounded Hospitalized
Autun drove grandmother to tears it had to be explained to her
that it was good news xxx One year later we left
Bd Truphème

191 Easter nineteen hundred sixteen
   Departure for Digne

Papa was wounded din in the leg in the spring of fifteen by an exploding
shell it healed and could walk with an xrtho orthop dic
shoe He was named primary school inspector in castellane with a residence in
Digne   We left Marseille and Bd Truphème

Railway line from Marseille to the Alps Stop in St Auban ugly
little train station reeking of chlorine from the factory next to itThe xxx
surrounding vegeration had been killed The little that remained was
shriveled up
Three stations on the short line to Digne Malijai malemoisson
champtercie Digne was the last stop
no taxis in front of the station of course but there were
cars from the two hotel the Boyer Mistre and the Grand Paris
We went on foot toward theCi tyA good fifteen minute walk A
long very high wall on the left then the rocky path
on the heft leading through the olive trees and the
almond trees to the hamlet of Courbon half way up the hill

T hen we walked along the Bléone river up   stream
to the one large bridge that connected the neighborhood
around the station and the city itselfthe bridge seemed very long

it is indeed in order to span the wide bed of the
Bléone which can rise to the top of its banks when there is a storm
At the end of the bridge we walked past the Place du Tampinet
on the left and continued down along the river on Gassendi Bd with
its plane trees Almost like a continuation of the
bridge this was Bd Thiers

The wall of our garden its large gate
almost always open Nu mber four Our house
A double row of plane trees Open space all the way to the parapet
of the Eaux Chaudes river a vista toward the south the trees
of the public parkThe large gray buildings of the boys'
Lycée
the Caramentran hill in the foothills of the Cousson mountain a little bridge
over the Eaux Chaudes
after the bridge the oulevard narrows
becomes Rue Pied de Ville rue de l Hubac in the
old city.

On the ground floor the office of the notary Pierre
Mouraire our landlord
thee garden wall its large gate that obened
almost directly across from it a fountain with running water al ways
cool   the one where Jean Valjean stopped to take a drink
no knocker one had to pull on a bell One ring for us
two rings for the upper floorThe door opened by
a system I have forgotten
a wall with a window First flight of stairs wide gentle
ascent first landing on the outside steps leading in from the garden
the superb wooden banister wide and flat with a round molding
the wood was a beautiful dark brown almost mahogany covered with an
impeccable varnish without a scratchYou would think
it was made of glassThe only drawbackwas that the rectangu

lar shaped turn made it impossible to slide on it all the way down to the
ground floor You had to jump off at the turn

All the windows eight of them looked onto the boulevard
without any direct view of the Eaux haudes river the trees
of the public park on a small plateau a dark fountain far away
the inscriptio A SOUSTRE from the Basses Alpes in recognition

---

My parents larfe bedroom One smal l
bedroom The study of Monsieur l inspecteur our father a small room
opening directly onto the stairs
the large sitting room with three windows the previous tenant
held receptions and ballsOn the
ceiling angels made of molded plaster
one could enter the kitchen through a sort of outdoor
fallway forming a verandah Its zinc
roof clattered under the rain during heavy storms from the hail That
is where we washed off our feetA
small back kitchen with a small xink and a gas
sto veA hidden stairway allowed us   But of this later
all this in a jumble I shift around without any hesitation xx
in my memories A plan would be easy   but

the marble chimney was draped this was the fashion with a sor of
silk shawl embroidered with ribbons actually embroidered by aunt J
jeanne It sent me into transports just looking at it
An wardrobe with a mirror with a door I do believe it was this one which
horribly painted blue by the Italian tenants of
the orangerie here it became the cabinet for preservesThe bottom drawer
is hard to open and close It annoyed me every time x
I went to look for a pair of socks in it

The bookshelf the work of m y grandfather which was

until this year in the attic its windows broken
the large clock that belonged to grandfather was given
to Pierrot Molino
the rocking chair
I still have the smell hovering in the dining room
in my nostrils I have never encountered another like it It was
of old walls with a touch of slightly worn varnish
it turned your stomach but it never smelled like a stuffy interior
Papa made sure of that

192 **It was an enchanting spot**

(the privy) It was an enchanting spot Sitting on the seat by the
window on the right noxxx one could see al the greenery of the g
garden and farther out on the right the old town the xx
set against the big stone we called the nine o'clock rock Classic xx
since there was no good translation of the Provençal word   The whole sprawling
mess of rooftops with their round xtxtiles the color of undercooked breadx
on the cathedral's bell tower of forged iron To
xxxxxxxxxsssss   To see this wonderful view no
need to open the window We had scratched with our fingernails
on the paper glued to the window mostly red and blue
and opened a few places where the glass was bare

the veranda was covered here and there   by the virginia creeper it
created a leafy shade over the steps up to the garden the stems and the xx
leaves cast shadows on the window paper Or if one
opened one or two vindows the curtain of creepers looked
at first like a book of the Saints' Lives provided
toilet paper but its leaves had been
cut by papa and I was never able to reconstruct
a Saint's life in its totality after that only some
pedagogical journals were there for our use I found them
rather stupefying but I read them all the same

I was wonderfully coo l in the summer but in the winter it
was best not to linger

spending a hinter in Digne was like going through an ice age In
the kitchen where we did o ur homework it was nice In the evening
we sat in a circle around the stove in the dng rm On kitchen chxx
chairs There was not a single armchair in our houseOn the stove
we warmed small flat pebbles that we had gone xxx
to collect in the riverbed the smell of newspaper
around the burning hot stone in the bed it took a good little while
before you finally decided to stretch out your legs Only the sector around
the stone was a little warm It happened sometimes that I would
wake up in the morning with my feet as frozen as when I went to be

Since the primary schools did not begin vacation until

---

until Ju ly thirtieth we spent that month in Digne it was
dry and very hot in the city hemmed in by the
mountainsThe southern facade was in the sun all day But there
was the shade of the plane trees part of the dayin the diing
room the open windows together with the back
stairs and the terrace created a pleasant crosscu entEntering
it you always had a sensation of relative coolness
the window shades stayed unrolled all the way downThey were
made of thin rods of unfinished wood it is in the
 of fresh wood even at night the rooms on the north side
were hot I went to bed without a shirt on the xxxxxxx cold flx
flat stonesoutside in the garden in the trees the oxx
owls let out their two fluty notes You could hear
very distinctly thxxxx the clock of the cathedral that
rang twice each hour and on the half hour

The terrace

esposed on the north side and the east side   the back wall of the sitting room

shaded it on the north side   sloping downward   toward the

first ranches of a lime tree it was possible to pick its

flowers by straddling the iron banister   too bad

if we broke a f w of the round tiles when we walked over them

The terrace was the way we ordinarily took to go out

into the garden on the west sideNothing could be easier since

the windows of the ground floor where the study was were

covered by iron ba sThat is where I had my memorable

fall in the summer of sixteenNo memories of any pain papa

picked me up a good dozen meters awayI awoke on

my parents' bed in hardly any pain

but since then what a nose

It was on the terrace that w e ate our dessert

while playing hopscotch or with a big bouncing ball No a tennis ball Against

the wall and jump rope for girlsOn the ground   In the Hands   Whirlwind

No Talking   No Laughing   No Letting Go

our side of the house had some hidden passageways and rooms in the second

vestibule of the entrance a small door opened xxxxxx

on the left It gave access to a narrow dark and humid

hallway that led to another similarly small door

which opened on the right onto a long deep room

through which one went out to the garden It was used as an eating place for the

domestics during the bourgeois period of the house when

the Paymaster resided there It was ours to use

but we didn t do much with itA rather large recess

beneath the sloping roof that went down from the terrace toward the

lime treeAn opening I hesitate to call a window

It had neither glass nor shutters I could just barely fit through if I

slid twisting head first then pulled the rest of my body

through and jumped into the garden I did it

one day upon his request in front of the young lady proprietor
M ouraire Angèlequi wanted me to carry out this performance
to amuse a lady friendbut I prefered to access the garden by other

---

a small landing led to a sort of large
cavernous shoulder-high nook between the second floor
and the ground floorIt was supposed to serve as storage space for food Wee
put stores of potatoes in it they were covered xx
with a veritable tangle of long pale stalks when spring
came We had the chore of removing by hand these
long sprouts which then left the potat oes wilted
wrinkled and flaccid

occasionally the laundry was done in that dark
humid servant's spaceA large wooden tub with a hole in
the bottom was set on the cooker The bottom was covered with vood
ashhe very clean no chestnut shells no rusty xx
nails The dirty laundry was piled up in folded layers
xxxxxxx almost all the way to the ceiling Water was poured in
cold at first It f lowed out through the hole in the bottom into a xx
large bowl this water gradually heated and poured out hotter
and hotter onto the already soapy laundry and becomes the wash
liguid a murky yellow green color filthy It took a whole
afternoon to rinse out the soap I helped by carrying baskets
of steaming laundry all the way to the Eaux Chaudes river where the woman
who does the washing would rinse it in flowing water during the months
when enough water had run down from the big ridge on the
mountain   the ridge of les Dourbes that one sees sticking up on the hor
izon in the east far in the distance

Fourth floor
for there was yet another level a fourth Aside from the attic xx

properly speaking where we went only rarely   rarely

only to bring down the trunks to pack for vacation

xxxxxxxxxxxxxxxxxxxxx   in the Dauphiné we were still able to use

the maid's room a real room without a sloping ceiling No one

lived in it It was used to store fruit In one corner the chestnuts

piled up on the floor in another the mound of little xx

red apples on one side and yellow ones on the other which we ate or they

were baked in the oven by the cooks Also the pile of pears

stewing in syrup the ppples belonged to the species

called changarnier But what species were the pearsThis fruit

came from various parts of the basses Alpes region where   on his various trips

for inspections P apa had the opportunity to order them

I was often given the task of going to that room and bringing back the

amount needed for the day's consumption Toward the end of Oxx

October we brought down the large pot of chestnuts f

for the chestnut fpread that we made as a family A fter dinner

on Thursday the whole family was enisted to peal the

burning hot chestnuts and to strip off the inside skin

193 Here the jarden was entirely enclosed by walls

Here the jarden was entirely enclosed by walls they were very high

but they surrounded a space too vast for us to feel enclosed in it

we were in the vity but removed from it Just a few steps and we were

at the riv er We came in We went out To the west the new part of the city and the

shops on Bd Gassendi To the east the old town that goes up toward the

cathedral with its bell tower made of wrought iron the roofs with soft pink

Roman liles spread out at different levels below it with the Nine o'clock

rock that vounds the horizon to the north is the Chevrier hill

le Cousson dominates the vall y and the ity without imprisoning

themAnd to the sou west there is a vista of the Bléone river x xx

I always had the impression tht th s valley wxxxxxxxx   was going

to open out onto the sea

The garden was roughly the shape of a re ctangular trapezoid
the base would be Bd Thiers I cannot give any estimate of its surface I believe
I heard it said that it was at least s large as the park
of the orangerie
the grand exit from the house was down the front steps
We preferred   the other more original exits
by the terrace where one glimbed over the
balustrade and then scaled down the iron bars on t he
windows

The front steps shaded during the summer by the immense rede Virginia creeper that
climbs up the veranda privy   Five or six steps down and One is standing
on the gravel that surrounds the house
one can take the country road by the old sheds
and the little coal rooms
or the central walkway straight ahead it runs   more or less
along the border of the Mouraires's place A large rectanbular meadow that ended in
a stand of trees A very ald and tall weeping willow
Climbing onits bra ches
and falling back to the ground one can swing all the way to the back wall

---

so that the ends of the branches were almost constantly stripped
of their leavesWe were not allowed to walk in the meadow txxxx
the currants that we glaned on the sly
they were not ours then our side began by far the
largest and the most beautiful   varied   leafy full of
little hideawaysHow others besides me
reassemble its pieces geographically I only turn
around and around in m y memories

the plane trees   There were two they shaded a sort of
Provençal vollage squareOn the trun at a point

low enough for us to be able to climb up

the large branches cut in such a way as to spread out

horizontally in overlapping rows We climbed up to

forking branches perfectly shaped for xx sitting

straddling in the midst of the leaves Excellent

for reading or resting

At the foot of the plane trees noxx

vegeration The ground was like the courtyard of a school no cement

A large gate open at the corner of the house and the wallThat was

the entrance for piles of wood that would be sawed in that courtyard

the catalpa grove

Entangled shrubs slipping through an opening in

the branches one entered a space apart completely covered

by a canopy of leavesWe had a table there I worked on my

Latin translations leaves would fall onto my old Quicherat

dictionary that I kept all the way up through Khagne To pass the time

I would catch the l ong brown seed pods falling from the catalpas that rose up over

the shrubs

The Chestnut Tree

it was in the center of the park very wide difficult to climb

A large branch stuck out almost horizontally

We hung a lamp on it when in the summer we had dunner beneath

this chestnut tree surrounded by axxxxxxxxxxxxxxxx   an xxxxxxx   a

clearing on the ground covered with gravel Then a very large round flowerbed

from the time of the Paymaster's wife and her

splendors Itwas surrounded by a very dense ring

of periwinkles In the spring red and ellow tulips and a number of crocuses

were still coming up

the florists sold them in pots but their smell was
faded   just as the fussy tulip
bulb s had lost thexxxxxxxxxxxxxxxxxx were a
caricature of the tiny sim ples blossoms so every
time thxx
it's Digne that I am reviving

194 to the left of the clematis the back wall

to the left of the clematis the back wallA little
behind it the backs of the houses setback a little from Bd Gassendi We
saw the narrow windows but under the trees
we could not be seenThey were all dark trees

my very tall fir tree with its jorizontal
branches that formed a very handy ladder
I climbed on it often higher than my brothers By
climbing almost all the way to the top I worked out an accessible
path but I would still get caught
on the needles that still remained close to the trunk and
when I came back down my hands and hair would be allsticky with
sap a tenacious odor but the sxxxxxxxxxxxxxxstains
did not come out easily and the clumps of hair stayed stuck together
difficult to untangle It was on the branc of this fir tree on which
the branches began at about the height of a person that I
tried to demonstrate in practice for my brothers
my famous theory of perpetual ascent

(My mother's theory of the vertical walk: a reconstruction)
It was very simple. "I thought about the problem of
the vertical walk and I found a satisfactory solution,"
I told them. "When we walk in the ordinary way we
proceed, as you know, in the following manner: we
place one foot on the ground, the right for example, and then, when
this foot is solidly planted on the ground, we lift our

other foot (the left in the example chosen) and place
it in turn a little farther along in front of us. You
follow me?"
"Yes"

"Good. Now suppose that I want to walk on
the trunk of the fir tree which, however, is vertical. I place my left foot,
for example, on the trunk, like this, then, as when
walking, I raise my right foot and . . ."
"And you fall to the ground"
"And why do I fall to the ground? Because of
gravity, which pulls my left foot downward. It falls, and
I fall with it. You still follow me?"
"Yes, yes."

"Alright, but suppose that before my left foot
has had time to fall, I have nimbly moved my right
foot from below, like this, and I place it very quickly
above my left foot on the tree and before this left foot
has in turn had time to fall I do the same with
the other foot, and so on, what will happen?"
"Go ahead," they said, "Show us."
They had a good laugh.

in that part of the garden the ground is black from the humus of the lexxxxxves
no green grass in the few holes a little brighter there
some swallow-wort it is said that the yellow juice is supposed to cure
warts the smell of rotting   moldy pine needlesA vaguely
disquieting impression of the numerous plaster moilds
of dentures that the dentist's assistant
Besaudun an uncle of m y schoolmate germaine Besaudin threw
out the window of his officethese molds were used to
draw lines for hopscotch on the terrace when
we emerged from that shade we found ourselves in the bright
light of the clearing

the shrubs with little white buds
a type of viburnum I don't know the name you see them in
Saint-Félix but thinhner and more shrivelled than the ones in
Digne They formed a sort of hedge the height of a child's
shouldersbut they left open a space to pass throughThe white buds
that sprouted after the little pink flowers were wilted off smooth
and full of juice We used them as projectiles for
the assault on the hideout in the laundry house eiquipaed with a sink
made of stone and a faucet the attackers threw their balls
through the little vent marrow as an arrow slit which only I
was able to pass through the defender threw pots full of water
through the slit or the spray you could
make by holding a finger partly over the hole on the faucet

---

the periwinkles
their   astonishing blue
The
tiny yellow smell The round corolla from which all the petalsxxx
made of petals its oblique outer edge iin the same direction
Several shades of tulips bright red and yellowxxxxxxxxxx   Tx
their shiny petals Their curious pistils I see them as black

Near the white grass some blue larkspur s that
would reseed at random on their own ike columbine
pink mauve or purple their blossom squar like
lanterns with strange cones on each corner
In the central area covered with gravel suddenly
and for a rief period yellow and red crocuses came up
between the pebbles very low to the ground I
think but I'm not sure Perhaps also some mauve ones like
autumn crocuses

for the scent alone the fragrant lime tree

195 How could I forget the bamboo

How could I forget the bambooThere were two or was it
three   extremely dense clumps of them Black or white
stalks one day I wanted to offer one
to Mlle Giraud head teachr of the fifth grade for
her demonstrations on the blackboard Impossible to cut the vood
with my little pen knife
From the first dry days of summer and all throughout the
vegeration down at ground level dried up but the garden remained
full of shade

<u>Various impressions</u>
I will gather a few together here at random Perhaps I havealready
mentioned some of them elsewhere Too bad if I repleat myself

<u>Enjoying food</u>
after the profusion of sweets with the thirteen Christmas
desserts the scarcity returned There were still a few pieces of
the Provençal cake called "pompe" sent from Lançon every year A treat for
breakfast I swiped a few spoonfuls of honey from the large jar
not the big bucket from Lambruisse   With a spoon
I would take just enough so that
the level of the preserves waiting to be
covered would not go down This was difficult to do when
the contents had firmly congealed
The sweet acidic flavor of the little red and yellow
apples the changaillards that we went to get in the
thi rd floor bedroom where there was a whole pile of them
We were given them for our snack Cxxxxxxxxxxxxx
After the apple every bite I take from the bread
makes me grind my teeth

The market

I liked going to the market which was located in front of the cathedral

and in a rather wide street that begins at the square the vendors

in black or in dark clothes standing behind their baskets

Small baskets I recall the year when I went regularly

with the little maid Marie Jacob a pale and sickly

orphan with a black scarf on her head To me she seems like an adult

but I think she could not have been m ore than sixteen It was with

her that a peasant woman sold us by way of future

egxxxxx egg-laying pullets a young rooster and a

blind hen Only after the fact did I understand the

sly smile she had hen I asked her whether

they would soon lay eggs

Rainy Easter

that year I must have een around twelve or thirteen

We were waiting for a group of friends for a big afternoon

of games in the gardenin the morning the sky was absolutely clear

I was impatient for the morning to be over I scanned the sky around eleven

i'clock the edge of a cloud was rising behind Caramentran and

Le Cousson coming from the east I xxxknew this threat but I

didn't want to believe it I watched I watchedthe cloud grew larger Another

followed it another and yet another the sky was now

completely coveredA little after noon there was a downpour

a real Provençal rain that falls for several days

in a row around the time of the equinox

Cold

The cold in the house where in the evening we huddled around

the only pot belly stove in the dining room

the cold to get into bed with the smell of the overheated

newspaper pages wrapped around the tiny flat pebbles

that we brought with us to go to bed

that heat

spread only a few cmsIt took me a good while to

gather the courage to stretch out my legs in the linen sheets
The cold when getting cleaned up in the morning at the sink in
a little washbowl   of ice cold water Chilblains
The cold on the way to middle schoolmyxxxx   wool stockings
which I wore on the coldest days only came up
over my knees and left my thighs bare under my
skirt and my short coat No gloves The hand
holding my satchel was so numb that sometimes I even
cried in the coat room when the blood began to recirculate
in my fingers

Freedom
outside the very strict times in our house for
meals and school work during vacations and on xx
Thursdays and Sundays I was free to do
as I pleased Games with my brothers reading   ous loud But
especially I went in and out I wandered around my parents
were not worried and let me go wherever I wantedA happy
time I rode around everywhere on my biek alone or with my
classmites in the immediate vicinity often
much farther and all aloneIn caramentran I would v otanize Along the
roads   not yet pav ed the roads that went down along
the left bank of the Bleone I pedated or got off and walked
an encounter wi h a flock moving to mountain pastures going
toward the Alps the dogs The shouts of the shepherds the dust
I squeeze myself afainst the emrankment to let the wave pass by
FreedomFreedomI went out without getting dressed up without a hat a bold xx
thing to do in those days in a simple smock with
little checks

The sky
The sky over Digne Aside from the torrential rains in the fall
and spring there were ALWAYS stars And
what starsThe big dipper and the little dipper were
outlined so clearly that the north star itself

was always visibleand the winter nights especially if it froze
solid which often happened   it sparkles and swarmsNever
again have I seen such skies like Boaz asleep

The snow
I will not even try to describe my first snow I had never
seen any in Marseille
the garden
the garden was a splendor

196 On April 19 of this year (1992)

On April 19 of this year (1992) my mother will celebrate her eighty-fifth birthday (though "celebrate" may be too strong a word). The trip to visit her, spanning two consecutive Fridays, will take me from Paris to Carcassonne by train,
then from Carcassonne to the Tuilerie in a taxi. The taxi will turn between the
cypresses onto the bumpy road a little past the "Bagnoles Crossing," it will stop
just before the small bridge, above the basin/swimming pool, across from the
window of the "*maison des vendangeurs*" (the "grape-pickers' house") which
will be inhabited by swallows. I see them.

It will be in the afternoon. My father will be watching television, or the
television will be turned off and he will be sitting there in his armchair with
a book, my mother will be lying down on the right side of her bed with her
radio-cassettes, between two of her short afternoon walks, which she takes
indoors, around the table in the main room, aided, guided, and supported in
this exercise, which is repeated several times before each evening, an activity
prescribed as a way to fight against the lulling stiffness of immobility.

My father will greet me with a gesture, a quick hello with his hand. I will put
my bag in the bedroom, the "bedroom with the copper bed," which is mine. I
will come back into the main room, then into my parents' bedroom. Speaking
over the sound of the music, or the continuous and unnatural flow of voices
from the radio, I will announce my presence. I will sit down on a chair, by the
head of the bed. I will kiss my mother on the forehead; she will take my hand
in hers. And so, there you have it.

And so, I describe this scene from the future, which will happen only after these lines, as yet immaterial, have been set down on paper. At the moment, composing them (in the first days of March), still immaterially, at <u>this</u> instant, the future, verbal time-frame in which I've set the above scene gives it a sort of permanence, a simulacrum of stability, as though its task were to ensure the normality, the indefinite normality of its repetition.

It's true that it won't be the first time I've arrived in this way. I travel there and am greeted this way from time to time. We go there in this way from time to time, all three of us, my sister, my brother, and I—the no longer very young survivors of our generation. This time, I will go there with these pages, so that I can read them to her, if she wants me to, which I hope she does.

And if things do happen this way, I know that confronting the part of this book which is a reconstitution of my childhood memories (even if it's not only that, even if it's not that above all), particularly when it comes to events my mother (and my father) witnessed as adults—I know that this will expose me, inevitably, to accusations of imprecision, even of flagrant errors. I will not correct them. It is not for this purpose that I will be there.

Then why? Because through the simple effect of these images that have been put into words, I will perhaps have access then to a different view of the circumstances surrounding my images, a view that exceeds my own and that falls outside the perspective of the world that used to be mine, but that was nonetheless quite close to the circumstances being described, and far from indifferent to them. I will hear that this was not there, or not thus, that there was also this other thing here, and that this happened after that, which I did not know, or have forgotten, or never knew. And from all this I will perhaps draw a lesson to reflect upon for the remainder of my undertaking—the construction of its paths, its entanglements. For that reason, then.

But also, and no less, for this other reason: because, beyond any necessity for justification, this will be a way to speak and to listen, a kind of exchange, a kind of dialogue.

I will open the rather heavy folder (it contains many pages) on the cover of which I will have written: GFL II, THE LOOP. I will take out the first chapter, INVERSE FLOWER, I will place it on my knees. I will take the first sheet of paper, I will lean over a bit so that my voice will be close enough, clear enough, and I will begin to read the passage with which I began this book, this first **memory-image** from a long time ago, the first, for me, among all the others: I will read

this: "During the night, the mist on the window had turned to ice. **I see that it was still night, six-thirty, seven o'clock; wintertime then, and dark outside; no details, only darkness; the windowpane covered with the patterns of the frozen mist; on the lowest pane, on the left-hand side of the window, at eye level, in the light; this light from an electric bulb, yellow against the intense darkness outside, opaque and wintry, clouded by the mist; not a uniform mist, as when it rains, but an almost transparent frost, forming patterns; a web of translucent patterns, with a certain thickness, the slight thickness of frost, but with variations in this thickness, and, because of these miniscule variations, forming patterns on the glass, like a vegetal network, an entire system of veins, a surface vegetation, a cluster of flat ferns; or a flower.**"

Descriptive Table of Contents

STORY

Chapter 6: *Hôtel Lutetia*

50 One, two, three, or four times a year I set my suitcase down   **190**
closing time – semi-circle of night – Russian campaign – snow – yellow, blood – tall pine – May 1st – Buchenwald – seeing.

INSERTIONS

interpolations

(*from chapter 1*)

51 a vegetal network, an entire system of veins, a surface vegetation, a cluster of flat ferns . . . The map of my hand, the sensitive network of its lines, left no imprint.   **199**
The Great Fire of London, branch, project – insertion, interpolation, bifurcation – reversible insertion – additions, minimal additions – notes – branches.

52 I'm repulsed by phrases like, "I thought that . . ." or "I believed that . . ." when they are presented as immediate certainties   **201**
child, fiction – memoirs – thought – historical novel – language – anachronism.

53 when an adult . . . plays a joke by pretending to put on the child's coat by mistake, instead of his own   **203**
"me" – inside, outside – borders – body – "myyourplace" – coincidence.

54 the objects that are part of my body . . . like the coat, like my totemic stuffed "double"   **205**
stand-in-for-myself – Theory of the Nyanya – Lusson family – telephone – experience of non-thought – NyaNya, nyanya.

55 I will give the generic name of "nyanya"   **207**
generic name – Keture – current of identity, conjunction – eros – protection – hominization.

64 The prescriptions from the arts of memory invented in the Middle Ages and in the Renaissance   221
petty twilight commerce – rigorous knowledge from the cold – Grail of memory – stations, visual images – *bouffettes* from Mens – chaise longue that won't tip over.

65 The inverse route of the train through Castelnaudary   223
shell-boats – threshing – food – philosophy – philosophy professors – tribute.

66 The narration of a memory would be in constant need of the resources provided by Hermogenian rhetoric (speed being a central concept in the Hellenistic treatise on oratory written by this author)   225
idea of speed – brief life – river – *Lente, Lente* – trochaic dipodia – "now".

67 something like Olbers's paradox   227
infinite light – observatory – cosmological principle – Sky – Hubble – forgetting.

(from chapter 2)

68 I also see mulberry trees, with their red fruit lying exploded on the ground around them, like wine, or blood   231
"bold" – descriptions, images, deductive recomposition, childhood – moment, double, elucidation, project, assertions, images, interweaving – pictions – intrication at a distance, juxtaposition – branches, memory-images.

69 I wrote them all at the same time as I wrote the chain of fictive deductions that "began" my Project: in the fall of 1980, nine years ago.   233
maxims, suture points – double – clarity, distinctness – description – photography – oblivion.

77 A caravan of freight barges stretched along the quay, all loaded to the top with coal: brown lignite.   247
also – anthracite – seeing – snow, coal – flakes, lumps – black bucket.

78 the sight of those semi-ruins in East Berlin restored to me all the violence of my initial vision of the war   248
Papritzerstrasse – Dresden – familiar-forgotten – snow – snowbeer – ironical chirping.

79 mastering the sequence of childhood images that I had already set out to elucidate (still following my initial vision of an enormous single "page" being darkened line by line with prose)   250
moving piction – great white mural – mental sheet – first Inter-branch – connecting – moments of prose.

80 my father was never anyone's "disciple"   251
Raymond Queneau – *sorpasso* – Project – counter-mastery – armies – disciples.

81 absences enumerated, like so many tombstones, by names   253
tomb – intermittent afterlife – singular dead – visibility – fig tree, tiles – loop, inverse flower.

(*from chapter 3*)

82 a path through memory, but a labyrinthine path   255
hesitation – image, metaphor, memory, motor, story, allegory, project – elucidate, melancholic eros, dream, rhetorical fiction – dream, destruction, law of the butter croissant – melancholic seeker, go-creeping – Cantorian page, *Tristram Shandy*.

83 I open the doors to each room, one by one, I enter: I was there.   256
story, bifurcation, great sheet of memory – formal future – amplifications – *Never again* – torpor.

91 I believe that I could easily have been converted to the idea of aligning the movement of the needles with that of a vector turning in the direction considered mathematically "positive"   273
Ptolemaic clocks – elliptical dials – naive astonishment – 12? – noon at the washbasin – two-dimensional time.

92 I can almost follow with my (inner) eye the ripening of a tomato on the vine   274
placing – *pois gourmand, mange-tout* – beans – strings – topinamburs, rutabagas – *févettes*, weevils.

93 The garden was planted with the greatest possible variety of edible vegetable species compatible with the climate.   276
deficiencies – vitamin chart – scurvy – cod-liver oil – lemons: pink – hissing.

94 The water immediately absorbed by the avid ground beneath the tomato plants   278
solar truth, apricot tree – solitude – snails – stars – fennel – voluptuousness, rain.

95 The hutches, little dwellings for our peaceful and sympathetic rabbits   280
Night of the Monster Rabbits – *Watership Down* – *lapin Cassegrain* – anthropomorphism – Pooh, the King of the Dogs – "wild rabbits".

96 Brigitte Bardot, that ex-sex symbol of the cinema for the males of my generation, who became a senile soft-hearted protector of baby seals   281
objective chance – int.3b – telegraphically – *MPIRIZIT MPARDO* – chap.3a – gesture of discouragement.

97 A skinny young pig secretly took up residence in the lean-to   283
El Dorado of ham – "piglets" – champions – The Empress of Blandings – *non-doing pig* – one seed of a pippin.

Bifurcation C: *On Clouds*

birch-bark songs – song of the clouds – out-of-time, out-of-space, here-now – permanence of change – memory – generality of the sky – formal indirection – clouds – boats, inscape.

Bifurcation D: *Montée de la Boucle*

garden – trees – idea – orangery – association – PPPCAFV – German – snails
– *Gräber*.

180 I see in the garden, at the heart of its luxurious immensity   468
garden, images, pictions – next door – grand-matriarchy – painting –
immersion – photographic statues – collie – hat, mulberry trees – knit jacket
with buttons.

**181 Immersing myself in the garden, turning from the mulberry trees
toward the house   470**
mulberry trees – silk – ripe mulberries – Pont de la Boucle – property owner
– renter – convictions – apartment blocks – garden.

Bifurcation E: *Childhood of Prose*

182 Throughout the writing of this <u>branch</u> and up until today   473
branch, bifurcation, moment, memory-images, assertions, fictive deduction,
axioms, dream, Project, novel – correspondences – eccentricity – image-
memories – loops – fore-project, infancy of prose, memory – dimensions –
Arts of Memory – seeing – language – mnemonic space – garden.

Bifurcation F: *Truphème Boulevard*

183 Saint-Félix Eighteen December
The right side of the house is reserved for lanmlordMadame   477
lanmlord – suspension – blue flame – bedroom – late afternoon study –
gaslamps – chestnut flour – swimming in the sea – Corniche.

184 Not long before she definitively gave up her typewriter   479
first memory – loops of memory – descriptions – roller – reconstitution –
typescript conjunction – typos – signs – blind.

Index of Terms Appearing in the Descriptive Table of Contents

Afterword

Of Crystals and Clouds: Roubaud's Memory Loops

§   What is *The Loop*? Because it is so difficult to answer this question with
the usual notions and categories (fiction, novel, essay, memoir, autobiography
. . .), I would like to offer a few indications that may be of some use to any
reader of this book, whether a potential reader, a post-reader, a pre-reader, or
a re-reader. *The Loop*, in its length, richness, and complexity certainly lends
itself to multiple, and multiplicitous, readings, and taken in itself, it is (as its
title indicates) eminently re-readable. But it is also part of a larger work whose
configurations and parameters bear some explaining. In doing this, I will also
offer some remarks on the elusive substance that the work attempts to set into
image and language, and on the impetus behind a writing project that has
been developing now for almost half a century.

§   To begin with, some bibliographical information: *The Loop* is the second
installment in a multi-volume series of autobiographical prose works begun by
Roubaud in the mid 1980s and collectively entitled "the great fire of London"
(I will explain the lack of capitals in a moment; Roubaud also refers to the
series simply as "the project"). The first installment was published in English
translation by Dalkey Archive in 1991 under the same title, and with a subtitle:
The Great Fire of London: a story with interpolations and bifurcations; but that
first volume has its own individual title as well: "Branch One: Destruction."
Roubaud's use of the term "branch" for the various volumes of the series is
meant to underscore the non-linear, bifurcating, ramifying, and digressive
structure of the whole and, within the whole, of its distinct parts. With
"Branch Two," *The Loop*, this expansive geometry becomes even more twisting
and complicated in its multiple curves, divergences, and interrelations. In the
twenty years since the first branch was published in French (1989), Roubaud
has completed four more, for a total of five so far.[1] A sixth and final branch

1   To lay out the prose landscape in which *The Loop* finds its place, I here give the titles
and dates of the existing French volumes (all published in Paris by Editions du Seuil):
Branch 1: *Le grand incendie de Londres: Récit avec incises et bifurcations* (1989). Branch

has been projected and is currently in preparation. With the appearance of the sixth branch, the "project"—an entity whose eventual material existence Roubaud often calls into doubt in the early volumes—will be complete. It will be finished; it will exist. The "project" will have been realized.

§   (A side note: There is no reason why one could not first read Branch Two, *The Loop*, before Branch One. And while I draw on the first and subsequent branches in these remarks, they are intended for readers unfamiliar with Roubaud's "project." A synthetic overview of the project's complex structure and chronology will no doubt be useful even for readers familiar with the translation of the first volume. This commentary is offered as an addendum, an afterword (or even, in its more idiosyncratic tendencies, as an independent essay), and not as a foreword or preface to precede or condition the reading: but I write beginning at 0.)

§   It is important to stress the point regarding the actual existence of these books, because the (lower case) project itself is, in part, the account of a grand, unified **Project** (capitalized, and more recently in **bold**) that never came to be. The project, as it exists, supplants the abandoned **Project**, turns back toward it, and shadows it; it tells of the **Project**'s conception and development, its partial realization, and its ultimate failure, ruination, and renunciation. That **Project** was to have included three major components: a poetry project, a mathematics project (Roubaud was a mathematics professor until his retirement some years ago), and a novel, whose title, deduced in the early 1960s from a revelatory dream, would have been: "The Great Fire of London." But as Roubaud explains in the "Preface" to the (actually existing) first branch, it didn't turn out that way. The real written beginning of the existing "project," he says, constituted a "mortal, definitive blow" to the **Project** and, especially, to its unwritten novelistic component, henceforth shattered into the fragmentary

---

2: *La Boucle* (1993). Branch 3: *Mathématique: (récit)* (1997); this is only the first half of branch 3 (see below). Branch 4: *Poésie: (récit)* (2000). Branch 5: *La Bibliothèque de Warburg: Version mixte* (2002). Having been unable to continue with branch 3, Roubaud published it nonetheless in the avowedly truncated version whose title is given above. He recently made good on his promise to provide the second half with *Impératif catégorique*, which appeared in January 2008.

and serial structure in which it now exists. It was thus demoted to "the great fire of London," a title now missing its capitals, for a work with more piecemeal ambitions. (In a further twist, it is of course necessary to write the title of the published version of Branch One in its capitalized form, identical to that of the abandoned Novel (it is in *The Loop* that Roubaud begins to add **bold** to both the upper- and lowercase titles). For the sake of clarity, I will continue to refer to the existing first volume as "Branch One.")

§ Branch One, then, focuses on the failure of this capitalized Project-Novel; it traces the "deductive" elaboration that arose from the dream, and initiates the project as a writing practice to be carried out beneath a title, "the great fire of London," shorn of its capitals and dispersed into the retrospective fragments, which, among many other things, describe the arc followed by the **Project**'s virtual existence. This arc can now be precisely dated: December 5, 1961–October 24, 1978. Like the inscription on a tombstone, these dates bracket the lifespan of the **Project**, and it is to this period that "the great fire of London" turns, for the most part (the major exception being the present book, *The Loop*, which takes a step back to Roubaud's childhood and beyond). This arc or span of time also marks out an experience of loss and mourning, and in its account of the failed **Project**, Branch One points directly to the pain of a recent loss as the source from which the writing in its present time draws a fundamental impetus, though certainly not the only one.

§ The first of the dates mentioned above marks both a birth and a death: December 5, 1961, was Roubaud's birthday, the first day of his thirtieth year. It was during the night preceding this day that Roubaud had the revelatory dream from which the would-be Novel, "The Great Fire of London," was deduced. But it is also a date that falls only a short time after the death by suicide of his younger brother, Jean-René. Roubaud suggests that the shock of this death played an essential role in the conception of the **Project** as such, impelling its initial formulation and elaboration. It set off a movement of great striving, idealizing and grandiose in its ambitions and projections, no doubt (and compensatory? it seems fair to ask . . .), but also to a concrete, disciplined, and highly committed practice. To put it bluntly, it got Roubaud writing. Writing poetry, above all. This pursuit intensified over the next few years—Roubaud traces this development in Branch Four, *Poésie: (récit)*—culminating with the approval and support from Raymond Queneau for a manuscript subsequently published with the strange title ∈ (usually referred to as "the book whose title is the sign for belonging to a set"). During the same period, Roubaud completed a thesis in mathematics (recounted in Branch Three: *Mathématique: (récit)*), which secured his employment as a mathematics professor. So far so good: this much, at least, was underway. But as Roubaud relates in Branch One, the third element, the Novel, proved to be extremely recalcitrant. In the end, it was on the rocks of this hyper-charged task (charged with mourning, with the task of memorialization, with the imperative to respond to his brother's pessimism ("What's the point?"), with a privileged position as a pinnacle or "roof" of the whole (as described in the "Preface" to Branch One)) that the **Project** foundered; a realization that came to Roubaud in 1978, in a scene related at the very end of Branch Five (*La Bibliothèque de Warburg*), in which he literally rips the **Project** (an outline of its projected Totality, including the still-germinating Novel) to shreds and throws it in the garbage. The End: Renunciation (or so it seems . . .). The **Project** thus went from *Everything* to nothing. And was, as it were, decapitalized. The **Project** became, or at least had entered the first phase of becoming, the project as it now (almost) exists.

§   A few years passed before this lowercase project began to take the shape that it has been taking for more than twenty years now. A few years, and another death. On January 28, 1983, Roubaud's young wife, the photographer Alix Cléo Roubaud, died in the early morning hours from a pulmonary embolism. (This information is given on the back cover of Alix Roubaud's personal journals, edited by Roubaud and published almost exactly one year after her death.[2]) The title of Roubaud's first major publication after this event evokes the dominant shade, and the indefinite haze, of the period that followed: *Some Thing Black*. The book is a series of poems that deals unflinchingly, and with disarming directness, with the experience of Alix Roubaud's death, the ongoing loss it opened. It also plays on the silence that

---

2   Alix Cléo Roubaud, *Journal: 1979–1983* (Paris: Seuil, 1984).

ensued, a silence broken by these poems themselves, and then, around the same time, by the prose activity that had become vitally necessary: the pursuit of "the great fire of London" in its real, uncapitalized form (begun, Roubaud tells us in its first lines, on June 11, 1985). Whatever remained of the **Project** at that point, following its internal collapse, was (if one can put it this way) jolted and shattered into life by the violence of this death. Put another way: the **Project**, initially embarked upon (in 1961) as "an alternative to a self-willed disappearance" (Branch One, "Preface"), now enters the phase of its own potentially endless afterlife, its active realization as a project, in the wake of a second devastating loss and following the "mortal blow" of its first inscribed lines. A death on both sides: if it didn't risk sounding too simple, one could say that the **Project** was opened on one side with the parenthesis of one death, and closed on the other, and definitively, by another. Roubaud himself refers more indefinitely to this between-time, speaking simply of "*deux 'bords' de mort*," two edges or margins of death between which he remains caught (*Some Thing Black*, p. 128). Within these edges, a **Project** was crystallized; beyond them, its shorn fragments came to constitute a meandering and cumulative reality, but only by leaving behind a possible world. In this sense "the great fire of London" is (in a phrase used by Roubaud) a "work of mourning," but also (thereby) a relinquishment of sorrow, an active response to its persistent question (again: "What's the point?"[3]), an escape from silence, and a work of affirmation—multiplicitous, energetic, humorous, richly woven.

§   Throughout the existing branches of "the great fire of London," Roubaud refers in some detail to the concrete situation in which he writes, and he lays out the formal parameters of this writing practice. In the opening pages of Branch One, he sets the scene: every morning (or almost), he wakes well before dawn, turns on a lamp, and writes in an otherwise dark room. Roubaud says that he needs these tomb-like conditions of semi-darkness and enclosure, surrounded by the sleeping city in the early morning hours, in order to continue with the daily task of prose. Whatever the setting was to have been for the Grand

---

3   In *Poésie:*, Roubaud relates that this is the question continually posed by his brother before his death; his own response became, "il faut que . . .": I have to, it is necessary . . . It was from this imperative that the project was born *in reality*.

(or Great) Novel, it is now reduced, in its central reference point, to a small circumscribed space lit only by a "cone of light" from a single small desk-lamp (and, subsequently, by a computer screen), bounded by certain hours of the day, and located *at every moment in the present*—a textual present that exists only in and through the act of writing. An everyday practice, then: a persistent repetition, a commitment and a *habitus*. And together with these conditions, a set of imposed formal constraints. A longtime member of Oulipo,[4] Roubaud explicitly lays out some of the formal constraints, closely bound up with the material conditions of writing, that govern his composition activity; these constraints are maintained and reiterated in *The Loop*. (I have already invoked some of them in this description. For clarity and reference, I list them here:

—To write every morning (or with only minimal interruptions, when necessary), in the pre-dawn hours of darkness, at the end of the night.

—To write, during each morning session, one "moment" of prose (as Roubaud calls each consecutively numbered section), and to place these in the text in the order in which they were composed.

—To speak (therefore) from the point of view of the present and to unfold the story as the storytelling itself proceeds.

—Never to go back to correct or revise.

—Always to say only what he believes to be true (even if these beliefs change over time, over the years); that is, to tell the truth as he sees it in the present.

—Not to have a fixed, preestablished plan for what has not yet been written.)

§   This pre-dawn scene of writing, says Roubaud, is "perhaps . . . an allegory of my enterprise as a whole . . ." It provides a matrix (in French, this word (*matrice*) means "womb") for the productive mainspring of the work, and it sets the parameters—temporal, spatial, and linguistic—within which Roubaud the writer attempts to respond to a vital imperative, a "constraint" that can be

---

4   Oulipo: *Ouvroir de Littérature Potentielle* (or Workshop of Potential Literature). A group founded in 1960 by Raymond Queneau and François Le Lionnais, Oulipo is known for devising formal linguistic or mathematical constraints according to which new literary works can be composed. Roubaud joined the group in 1966.

thought of quite simply as the conditions for survival. And for a paradoxical self-portrait. In the semi-darkness of a shuttered room in the pre-morning hours, the writing writer cannot see out. If he looks "out" the window he will in fact be looking *at* the window, and he will see on the darkened panes, lit from within, only a reflection of his writing self. The presiding color, the saturated tinge, of this writing (of the project) is "black itself"—but a luminous black in which the figure of the writer is dimly outlined at every moment. Self-Portrait in a Claude Mirror?[5]

§ *The Loop* takes up this enclosed "self-reflective" image in its opening passage, which evokes in vivid detail a childhood bedroom with an opaque, frosty windowpane as seen in the pre-morning winter darkness. As Roubaud himself suggests, we might think of this as a homomorphic prefiguration, retrospectively cast, of the present scene of writing (already we find ourselves caught up in several loops . . .). The figure of this icy surface is projected as a very precise image for the self-reflection and self-portraiture elaborated by Roubaud in *The Loop* (and throughout "the great fire of London"). He sees in it, in this memory image, the veiny network of an "inverse flower," wintry and frozen and far from the songstruck charms of spring (Roubaud's reference here is to a *canso* by the troubadour Raimbaut d'Orange, and, by extension, to the rigors of poetic form in general); and he thus invokes a branching and brittle geometric pattern, an unstable crystalline structure, as a precise emblem for childhood memory—and for its reconstitution in language.

§ "The great fire of London" tells of the ruination of a Novel. Is it a novel itself? Roubaud often refers to it as one, but he also calls it "my pseudo-novel." It is "pseudo," as a novel, precisely because one of its constitutive constraints is to tell the truth (in the case of the present volume, the truth of childhood memories). And yet, to use a form of logic that Roubaud elaborates in *The Loop* (having borrowed it from Nicolas of Cusa (§58))—in a double negation that leaves not *nothing* but rather a strange residue hovering around the nullity of negated

---

5   I'm referring to those convex black mirrors or polished stones that travelers used to carry around the English countryside in search of picturesque landscapes to "compose" as reflections.

things—we could say that it is also not *not* a novel. It sets out, from the very beginning, to tell a story. At the same time, its truthfulness (as Roubaud points out) is asserted rhetorically above all, and is largely unverifiable. And indeed the voice of the text moves continually within an atmosphere of the fictive, the factitious, the fabricated; even the truth, in Roubaud, is constructed (and from what?), precisely because this truth is one that is *told*, set into language and form (at a certain moment, in a certain language, by a writer speaking in certain conditions). And one of the features of this work that would seem to distinguish it from fiction—the highly reflective and analytical style that it takes on at times, its theoretical incursions and digressions, its Wittgensteinian ethos of (fragmentary, aphoristic) investigation, and its attempts to think through impossible questions of time, logic, and representation—serves in fact to assert its fictive nature more radically than ever. For in these modes Roubaud claims an inalienable right to the fiction writer's irresponsibility, presenting his reasoning as "theoretical fictions" and "pseudo-deductions"— as in the "fictive deduction" that plays such an important role in Branch One (and is echoed in *The Loop* in a section on the theory of "pictions" attributed to a "pseudo-Wittgenstein" (§70) whom one could easily mistake for "the real thing"). Roubaud's erudition (which is vast), his philosophical acumen, and his analytical and theoretical boldness are all mobilized in the discursive mode of a strange "as if." And it is clear that he tends to see academic debates as earnestly staged clown shows, or as schoolboys' quarrels worthy of Lewis Carroll (and starring Tweedledum and Tweedledee), driven by the lure of grasping the firm and final truth at last. For Roubaud, long steeped in the tradition of philosophical skepticism, real seriousness is elsewhere.

§   As a work that includes reflection and analysis (albeit fictive), but that above all tells a singular story in the first person, and tells it (claims to tell it) truthfully—is "the great fire of London" an autobiography? Despite the richness of anecdote, personal reference, and self-presentation, Roubaud often denies it, stating flatly at one point (in *Mathématique:*): "I am not writing an autobiography." In an interview from 1996, he says that he began his prose enterprise with the intention of telling a story, but one that would be "autobiographical only indirectly, obliquely."[6] In *The Loop*, he says that the work is obviously neither a novel, nor a tale, nor an essay, but he admits that it is more difficult to set aside the hypothesis that it aspires to the genre (and therefore to the long tradition, especially in France) of autobiography (§86). Here, too, perhaps it is best, for the sake of a roundabout shortcut (so to speak), to say that whatever it is, it is not *not* an autobiography. The back cover of the French edition (very possibly written by Roubaud) refers to *The Loop* as "a sort of unbelievable autobiography," in which Roubaud the philosophical skeptic does in fact ask his readers to believe what he says, but knows that this can only happen by suspending the disbelief from which all reading begins and following him into the pathways of memory, labyrinthine and notoriously unreliable. In this sense, "the great fire of London" is, after all, a memoir, but one driven by its own skepticism into a reflective and distrustful relation to its own givens: the memory images of the past.

§   "The great fire of London," writes Roubaud, is "a treatise on memory," written "in imitation of a novel" (Branch One, §32), and this is the characterization he continually returns to. In Branch Four (*Poésie:*), he reiterates: ". . . this is still the literary genre that I claim for these pages: the treatise, or treatment, of a reflective experience of memory" (§33). It is a meditation on memory, as refracted through a singular experience. And as such, it continually wavers between general considerations and the grain of the particular—or between deduction and induction. While it is difficult to say which of these two procedures has priority overall, there is no question as to which one dominates in *The Loop*, woven as it is from the texture of individual memories (Roubaud says this himself, placing *The Loop* on the side of induction, in parallel with Branch One's "deductions" (§68)). In Branch One Roubaud writes, ". . . it may so happen . . . that I stand facing the as-yet-unpenetrated forest of things in memory, awaiting me." In *The Loop*, he enters this forest, at the point of its densest and most luminous undergrowth, and follows its multi-directional paths.

---

6   "Entretien avec Jacques Roubaud," in an issue of the journal *La Licorne* (no. 40, 1997) devoted to Roubaud.

§   *The Loop*, then, is a book of memory. A book of memories.[7] Childhood memories especially. As mentioned above, *The Loop* moves back beyond the lifespan of the **Project** (and therefore far beyond the first of the deaths that bracket it) and into what Roubaud calls its "fore-life" (and even farther than that, into his family history). One of the book's primary tasks is to transcribe discreet memory-images of childhood, in all their vivid intensity, in their unique and saturated memory-presence, which Roubaud marks off with **bold type** (in passages sometimes several paragraphs long), as though attempting to saturate, in turn, the very surface of the text. I have raised the question of mourning here as a way to frame the project of "the great fire of London"; and I think one cannot fail to sense the strong undercurrent of loss that impels this work, often emerging (stylistically, emotionally) as a kind of *basso continuo* (in my opinion, it is the very foundation of the project; as I suggested above, the dark predawn space of writing is itself a kind of tomb, or a cenotaph). At the same time, it is equally clear that what we find written *within* that frame of mourning (as it were) is hardly limited to the register of mournfulness or the gloomy tones of melancholy. *The Loop* is held together by a series of images as singular as they are evocative: nodes of memory that, although isolated (on the page, at least), are part of a dense weave of recollection and narrative. Roubaud's "story" is anything but linear; indeed it works against the linear simplifications of autobiography in favor of the interconnected, ramifying structures of real memories. Both a filigree network and an impossibly distant constellation (at least as distant as childhood itself), the story lays out its images in a projected topography of intensities.

---

7   The distinction between *mémoire* and *souvenir*, both translated as "memory," is an important one for Roubaud, particularly in *The Loop*. Roughly, the latter indicates the act of remembering and/or the particular memory images or moments remembered, whereas the former refers to memory as a capacity or faculty or, in some contexts, as the repository of memories taken as a whole (and so as a kind of "place" in which memories can be sought, encountered). In response to a query, Roubaud stressed the importance of this distinction for him, specifying that "*la mémoire* plays a central role in the construction of a story about the past, and *le souvenir* intervenes through images that do not belong to the narration itself." I have tried to mark this distinction, within the limits of English, by rendering *souvenir* in ways that indicate particular instances of memory ("a memory," "this memory," in the plural as "memories," sometimes as "recollection," or else in a verbal form, with "remembering," etc.); *mémoire*, as used here, has been translated with the singular and is rarely preceded by any article other than the possessive ("my memory"), a usage that parallels terms for other faculties, like "sight" or "smell."

§   Certainly, *The Loop* is marked by death and loss—if only the loss of childhood (and what written childhood is not by definition lost?)—but what Roubaud emphasizes in his images saturated in **bold**, in the memories he "empictions" (if I can put it that way), is their vivid intensity in the present, and the intense experience of writing them down. Their intensity is, in fact, *the point*: it is the sharp force that pierces the present, it is their mode of insistence and the reason for their inclusion here (selected from all possible memories), their minute insertion into language (here with the afterglow of a piquant childhood sensuality). Within a framework of mourning, then, the inscribed memory-image vivifies, even punctures the present, here a textual present that flourishes on the ground of its disappearance (for Roubaud repeatedly insists that writing down these intense moments dulls them, reduces their luster). To say it even more simply: Born from death, language revivifies. Invoking the intensity and sensuality of his images, Roubaud often uses the word *vif*, meaning lively, vivid, charged with energy. The word evokes life (*vie*), liveliness, and an enlivened perception. It is in this sense, perhaps, that *The Loop* can be considered "life writing" (the images are indeed much like "still lifes," which the French call, in a complication I find very appropriate here, *natures mortes*). In a study of the Troubadours entitled *La fleur inverse: Essai sur l'art formel des troubadours* (The Inverse Flower: Essay on the Formal Art of the Troubadours), Roubaud seeks to show how the troubadours interlaced and interfused the song of poetry with the very experience of thought and love, and he concludes with this pronouncement: "*La poésie est une forme de vie.*" Poetry is a form of life. I think we can see this Wittgensteinian formulation as a way to link the elusiveness of the image, the profane unfolding of love, and the vivifying force of memory with the language game that Roubaud has so persistently pursued morning after morning—this time in prose—for so many years.

§   As a book of memory, *The Loop* is also, perhaps more than anything else (if only in terms of sheer volume), an archive. This, too—the impulse to draw out a testimony on the basis of a store of material retracing the past—is the very stuff of the "story." It is clear that if Roubaud wants to bear witness to "a form of life," this means describing a very singular view of a certain small portion of one: the childhood experiences of Jacques Roubaud between the ages of about six and twelve, mostly in the town of Carcassonne, and during the German

Occupation (and especially of certain locales whose names figure in the chapter titles: Rue d'Assas, Wild Park, Davila Square, Montée de la Boucle). But this in turn means describing the life of the Roubaud family in southern France (and partly in Paris) between about 1932 and 1945, with a few excursions further back into the family's history. Over the course of the book, we are given fairly vivid character portraits of Roubaud's parents and, especially, of his maternal grandparents. And we see countless details of life under the Occupation, some familiar, some less so (hunger, secrecy, the lies of Vichy, the prestige of "London," but also the scuttled French fleet in Toulon harbor, the clandestine raising of animals for food, the relative obliviousness of children). Finally, we learn that several of Roubaud's family members took the risk of getting involved in the Resistance, especially his grandparents and his father, whose clandestine activities were obvious, if largely incomprehensible, to his eldest son Jacques. It seems undeniable that, beyond the "treatise on memory" and its inductively reached principles, beyond the chain of memories themselves, beyond even the piecemeal reconstitution of childhood in its freedom and sunlight (*The Loop* is not without its touches of nostalgia), it was also the need to trace the shape of a family, embedded in their times, that drove the writing of this book. This too is perhaps a question of mourning, but it is also the soberly sentimental need to inscribe a record and to articulate a singular memory within the history of a family and even, to some small extent, within History itself. Roubaud's staunch defense of memory—and that is also what *The Loop* is—moves in this direction here, as it touches on the historic times in which it is "set." The singular archive, both "internal" and "external" (both remembered and preserved in documents and photos) is thus presented as a testimony, bearing witness not only to evanescent visions but also to a life that was and to human beings who are no more.

§   In one sense, a loop (like *The Loop*) has an open structure. The loop of memory-seeing turns back toward the images of the past in a way that cannot possibly be exhausted; memory, the past, is an open field that cannot be sealed. And yet a loop is also something that closes and fastens (an alternate translation for *boucle* is "buckle"). It is a structure in which an end meets an end and forms a closed circle: ends that do not end, because they conjoin and continue to turn, return, repeat . . . In memory, the turn takes the form of a return, in a two-dimensional and bi-directional movement ("I" go back to a past moment that has become intensely, vividly present; that is: a *memory* surges forth *now*)—a movement that becomes three-dimensional at the extended point where I "see" and see myself seeing: a space of writing, a "volume" of prose, a book, which for better or worse is bounded on all sides, but "opens" endlessly.

§   In Branch Four of "the great fire of London," *Poésie: (récit)* (§169), Roubaud remarks on the self-enclosing structure of the sonnet in terms that cannot fail to evoke the present work. "Every sonnet is like a sphere, a mathematical sphere. Every sonnet is closed. Its end loops back onto its beginning. Its surface curves back, enclosing meaning within it. A sphere, a spheroid, then. Mathematics had taught me that beneath the mask of a Parmenidian perfection, smooth in appearance, the mathematical sphere harbors a veritable swarm of heterogeneous structures, unclear, antagonistic, strange, and at first glance invisible." The circularity of *The Loop* shares many of the structural paradoxes indicated here; beneath its expansive surface is an endless network of knotty entanglements, deliberately tied and tightened, which emerge in profusion under close scrutiny. These are both formal and figural, material and symbolic: entwined and interwoven strands of complex spaces, twists of time, shifting positions, resonating words and names . . . While rewarding analysis, they do not lend themselves to analytic resolution (they tend rather to multiply the unknowns). As for Roubaud, writer and portraitee, he in no way aspires to complete transparency or self-consistency. He knows that, like the clouds, he changes, and that ultimately there is no accounting it. If *The Loop* attempts to come "full circle" (a tempting possibility for the title), it is only in order to provide a fitting shape for the elusive movement of memory and writing. One could say that this is the role of form in Roubaud's prose: to bind together what is too impossibly complex to be unified, to provide a clearly delineated schema, an enclosed and encompassing space (like the walls of the garden on the Rue d'Assas) for something that opens endlessly into its own "swarming" and multiple entwining convolutions.

§ (The word *convoluted* means literally: rolled together in a complex manner. It comes from the Latin verb *convolvere*, for which one dictionary gives "intertwine," a notion of some importance in the figural weave of the work at hand. It also refers, in the adjective *convolute*, to a leaf curving around itself in the bud (which brings to mind the "*grande feuille*," the great cylindrical "sheet" or "leaf" on which Roubaud imagines writing "the great fire of London"). In this sense, *The Loop* and its companion volumes are by design, and magnificently, convoluted.)

§ There is one complex type of form that, in its distant, shadowy, and mobile luminosity, provides *The Loop* with a dense and heavily charged figure-image: the floating and formless forms of clouds.[8] Roubaud is fond of tracking them with a meditative eye, but they tend to appear in a mist of melancholy. An air of sadness blows them about the text. Associated with moments of despondency, the cloud-bound meditations described in *The Loop* (and in Branch One) are closely associated with mourning, and particularly, it seems, with the absence of Alix Roubaud. They are first described in Branch One in connection with the bed beneath the window by the wall covered in shards of mirror (placed there by Alix), fragments of reflection in which the clouds pass into the room where they had lived together (and where Roubaud began work on the project); in *The Loop* these contemplations take on an equally poetic and elegiac tone. They open a space for the only lyricism Roubaud allows himself, a sober acknowledgment of suffering—and of *its* passing, too.

§ Roubaud's attraction to clouds led him to the work of John Constable, the English painter whose "sky studies" attempt to fix these mobile shifting forms. In a beautiful short book that alternates reproductions of Constable's paintings with the pages of a fictional narrative featuring Roubaud's alter ego, a fellow named Goodman, the form/lessness of clouds is linked directly to the most perfectly formal of all material forms: crystals. Goodman, who has lost his mother in a round-up during the war, later becomes a professor of mathematical crystallography at the University of St. Andrews in Scotland.

---

8 I am indebted to the excellent discussion by Ann Smock of the more cloudy features in Roubaud's work in "Cloudy Roubaud," *Representations* 86 (Spring 2004), 141–174.

Roubaud writes that "these mineral objects . . . are the most perfect and most permanent, also the most suitable to abstract reflection . . . [the thought devoted to] crystals has always been a privileged chapter in the thinking about forms and about the history of forms. After the alchemists, the question that haunted men of science since the Renaissance was the following: if the forms of crystals are one of the most striking examples of pure form, how are they born? are they alive? what separates them from other mineral forms, from vegetables, from animals, from human forms? and above all, how to think the formless?"[9]

§   How to think the cloud as a rigorous (crystalline) structure? Clouds are made up of crystals, of course—but how to seek the impossible mathematics of clouds! (I express astonishment, but this mathematics exists.) One could ask similar questions about the prose practiced by Roubaud in "the great fire of London." If we place together a disparate set of interconnected items invoked by Roubaud—the icy panes of glass, the fragments of cloud-reflecting mirror on the wall of the Roubauds' apartment, the photographs taken by Alix Roubaud, the cloud photographs of Stieglitz, the couple's shared interest in Wittgenstein (and in the question of discreet images and sequential writing), the fragmentary or one might say "momentary" form of Roubaud's project, and the fleeting "nowness" of his shifting self-portrait—then a fascinating suggestion emerges. What if we thought of the "moments" of Roubaud's prose as akin to those clouds in which the observer searches for a most intimate and rigorous structure? What if each one is itself like an image, a photograph, a "piction" of time, a cloudy fragment, made up of the minute crystals of language, a frost of letters forming an impossible, always changing, always incomplete self-portrait? One would need to add to all this Constable's cloud pictures and Roubaud's own thoughts on the time units of passing clouds ("cloud-hours")—and we cannot help but see these prose moments as cloud-moments, as the passing formations of Roubaud's formally contained self-

---

9   Roubaud, *Ciel et terre et ciel et terre, et ciel* (Flohic Editions, 1997), pp. 51 and 53. The passage shifts, almost without transition, to a discussion of clouds—and in particular to Goodman's discovery of Luke Howard's *Essay on the Modification of Clouds*, first published in 1803—as though these were the very same topic.

portrait. Seen in this light, these moments are the circumscribed precipitate of language and time, past and still passing. They are the ephemeral shapes of a speaking (writing) self misting the window of language. They are language's elusive memory of itself. They are the ghosts of poems that have lost the sharp contours of verse. They are the impalpable remnants of love (and the invisible luminosity of childhood). They are the meandering but impelled traces of an "I" reckoning with what, in time, cannot be counted.

§   Contemporary with Constable's "sky studies" is a remarkable poem by Shelley entitled "The Cloud" (1820) (both were inspired by Luke Howard's groundbreaking (skybreaking?) work on the classificatory nomenclature of clouds). Its final stanza cannot fail to resonate here:

> I am the daughter of earth and water
>   And the nursling of the sky;
> I pass through the pores of the ocean and shores;
>   I change, but I cannot die.
> For after the rain when with never a stain,
>   The pavilion of heaven is bare,
> And the winds and sunbeams with their convex gleams,
>   Build up the blue dome of air,
> I silently laugh at my own cenotaph,
>   And out of the caverns of rain,
> Like a child from the womb, like a ghost from the tomb,
>   I arise and unbuild it again.

§   I leave it to the reader to listen for the striking echoes sounding here ("by anticipation"?), and will point only to this strange first-person cloud that arises, a seeping speaking structure, again and again, to "unbuild" the empty tomb of blue air: a form undying, or undead, circling through the vast structures of the sky.

* * *

§   Finally, I'd like to relate an anecdote which, I think, reflects something essential about this book and about translating (and memory) in general: In the fall of 2007 I participated in a residency program at the Camargo Foundation in Cassis, France, in order to work on this translation. Cassis is not very close to Carcassonne (much less to Paris), but I contacted Roubaud, who informed me that he would be giving a reading at the Abbaye de Fontfroide, which is close to Carcassonne (and which features briefly in the present book (Chapter 4)). I went to the reading, and Roubaud and I made a plan to meet the following day in Carcassonne (he graciously agreed to answer some questions for me). But the next morning it turned out that he couldn't make it. So of course I went for a walk, in Carcassonne—but in search of what, exactly? At the very least, I wanted to find Davila Square and Rue d'Assas. I found them. I found Roubaud's childhood home. I knew it was his house because of the tall umbrella pine in the middle of the large walled-in garden (Chapter 3), though now it seemed rather scraggly and thin. I earnestly observed and contemplated this place. I saw that the garden itself had grown into a dense impenetrable thicket. (It occurred to me that if I wrote a text for the translation, it could be called "Thicket of Images"—an excellent metaphor for the work of memory in *The Loop*, its entanglements and intertwinings, and for the passage of time . . .) Then I went on my way.

§   Later, back in the U.S., I realized from various clues that this could not have been the right house. How did I make such a mistake? First, the tree had tricked me. It was a tall conifer, but probably not the kind I thought (hopelessly ignorant and distracted in these matters, I wouldn't know an umbrella pine from a hall tree) (though I have since learned (by the way) that there are two kinds of umbrella pine, each corresponding to what I would call an "open" or a "closed" umbrella; this one was neither). Second, the address (a question of numbers): Let's just say that, in France, 7s and 1s often look alike . . . In any case, there I was, burdened with an image that did not correspond. Is that what I get for trying to follow the traces of another man's memories?

§   What I had found, then, was not Roubaud's "garden on the Rue d'Assas," symbolically gone to seed, but a nearby neighbor's overgrown yard. (I might be forgiven for subscribing to Aby Warburg's theory of the "good neighbor," applied in this case not to the book you're *really* seeking in a library (always somewhere next to the one you set out for), but to an actual neighbor—of a textual house that will never be real.) Regardless of how it happened, the result can be summarized thus: my "memory" of Roubaud's childhood home, the image of this house that I saw and that stayed with me for many weeks as I pictured the place described in this book, was in fact no less imaginary than that of any other reader of the book. Except that, for me, it was worse: a "false" but "real" image had powerfully displaced what would otherwise (without the missed visit) be a completely imaginary fabrication, nudging the latter aside and asserting itself instead, in all its vivid clarity. Even when I tried to revert mentally to the entirely imagined house I had conjured before the visit, the center of gravity had shifted. I had imagined Roubaud's book into this real place, as it were, and then could not extricate it—could not *retract* it from what I would call, only half-jokingly, an idio-vision (in reference to my own idiocy, certainly, but also to the "idiomatic" force of my particular memories). And with this you can see, perhaps, that what I had found was also a striking figuration not only of any writer's textual memory work, but of the very idea of translation. (Novalis thought that the idea of poetry is prose; in a similar vein one might say that the idea of translation is "nobody's home.")

—Jeff Fort

Acknowledgments

I would like to thank Jacques Roubaud for his generous and helpful responses to my numerous queries. I would also like to thank Lucinda Karter at the French Publisher's Agency for putting me in contact with Dalkey Archive Press. I could not have completed this project without the support of the Camargo Foundation in Cassis, France, where a three-month residency in fall 2007 allowed me to make substantial progress; I would like to thank the director, Jean-Pierre Dautricourt, along with the inspiring group of fellows I met there; I will never forget them. Finally, infinite and always returning gratitude to Susette Min, for her patience and perseverance.

SELECTED DALKEY ARCHIVE PAPERBACKS

FOR A FULL LIST OF PUBLICATIONS, VISIT:

www.dalkeyarchive.com

SELECTED DALKEY ARCHIVE PAPERBACKS

FOR A FULL LIST OF PUBLICATIONS, VISIT:

www.dalkeyarchive.com